DREAMS
OF THE
DYING

Enderal Book I

NICOLAS LIETZAU

Copyright © 2020 by Nicolas Lietzau-Schreiber

ISBN: 982216744 (Paperback)

Cover Art by Dominik Derow
Cover Layout and Cover Design by Johanna Krünes

In loving memory of Max Henning Ischreyt
There would be no Enderal without you

For Pale
Tae ite nū'iwilo, tae hūnā 'o

„Ich stell' dieselbe Frage, immer wieder
Sie sagen, lebe, liebe, dichte Lieder
Mich sucht dieselbe Leere, Tag für Tag
Ein Punkt im Raum, mein Schlafgemach."

—Katharina Liebenberger, Ein Heer aus sieben Chören

FOREWORD

First of all, thank you for picking up my novel. Life is the number of minutes we have, and you're (at least considering) spending some of those on this book. I hope they'll be worth it. If you're new to the Vyn universe, feel free to skip this section. If you have played one or more of the games, however, please bear with me.

Briefly put, I decided to open up a new canon for the books. It's a drastic step, but there are three good reasons for this.

The first: inconsistency. The Vyn games were created over seventeen years, the earliest one being *Myar Aranath* in 2003. Fascinating as this may be, it also means that the Vyn universe's lore was created by many different authors (the most recent being me; I joined the team in 2011). As a result, the lore of Vyn has always felt a little disjointed and inconsistent. I initially took these inconsistencies as challenges to conquer, but the longer I wrote, the more I realized how much they bothered me and how hard they made it to write the story and the universe I envisioned.

The second is realism. *Enderal* is and always has been on the low-fantasy end of the spectrum—meaning fewer supernatural and fantastical elements—but due to its nature as a video game, realism was often left on the roadside. Examples of this are the nonsensical climate zones of the continent—you could get from snowy mountains to a scorching desert in a few minutes—the complete disregard for geological processes—ruins that are supposedly tens of thousands of years old but are still in perfect shape—or, perhaps a little less obvious, the long lifespans of Aetäerna (prev. "Aeterna"). If you live to be a thousand, your quasi-immortality would be a defining element of your character, and I never felt as though we properly addressed that in the games.

The third and last reason is a trickier one, and his name is Jespar. This character has been in my mind for close to ten years now, and I love him with all my heart; still, the more I immersed myself in the story of *Dreams*, the more I grew aware of how incredibly constraining it is to write a story with a prewritten ending. Because this is a prequel and Jespar is alive in 1234 A.L. (prev. 8234 a. St.), you all know he will never be in any lethal danger. Again, there is undoubtedly an intriguing draw to writing such a "safe" story, but similar to the lore, I increasingly felt like I was writing with one arm tied behind my back.

So, what does all this mean for the story of *Dreams*? It means that the world you will explore in the novels may differ from the Vyn you know and that anything can happen.

I sat down with a professional cartographer and redesigned the map of Vyn to make it geographically realistic. I had a long phone call with an archaeologist to adjust the different eras' time frames and adjusted how Pyrayan (prev. "Pyrean") ruins look. I collaborated with a medieval sword fighting school to make the combat scenes historically accurate. And I worked with a linguist to create a fully functional language for the Makehu, the natives of the Kilayan Archipelago (okay, strictly speaking, *he* created it and I wrote emails.) I retconned the designs and history of the Light-Born, who they are, and when and how they disappeared, I adjusted the structure, history, and politics of the Illumined World (prev. "Civilized"), and I revised the magic system. Minor changes include dates, the spelling of names and locations, and tweaks to the ranks of the Order of Light (prev. "Holy Order"). As for Jespar, I modified elements of his backstory, but his essence remains the same.

It's a drastic step for sure, but, believe me, I'm aware of the love you guys have for this world, and I did my absolute best to do it justice. If it's any solace, I can promise you that the new canon is ironclad; I'm obsessive about consistency and cohesive worldbuilding by nature, but without a solid framework, that was simply a recipe for disaster. Maybe see it as a different but nearby eventuality: details and fates may differ, but the soul of the world remains the same.

Enjoy the novel!
Nicolas

THE KILAVAN ARCHIPELAGO

CHARTED BY THE BLUE ISLAND COALITION

LEHOWAI
(LEHŌ Z AHE)

HAITEMA
(MAHI Z EM)

UUNILI
(ONT Z IL)

MAITEMI
(MAI E TĒMI)

MAITEPO
(MAI E TĒPO)

UUNUMA
(MAI E ŪNUMA)

PAIOLU
(PĀIO E LU)

0   25   50 MI

111°0'W

112°0'W

113°0'W

21°0'N

20°0'N

Help her.
Say something.
"You wanna know a secret?"
Her sobs fade, and her eyes meet his. Slowly they move, fragile little windows turning on rusted hinges.
"It'll get better. It always does."
He sticks out his pinkie.
"I promise."

CHAPTER ?
BUT MY JUDGMENT IS

Day Seven
1ST MOON OF RAINY SEASON, 1226 A.L.

he mind is a malleable thing. Soil, if you're feeling poetic. Depending on the seed, anything will grow in it, from graceful gardens to idyllic meadows, from weedy forests to foggy swamps. Harmonious or chaotic, peaceful or perilous, healthy or ill—it's all a matter of seeds.

That's why Jespar's mind reacted the way it did—quite frankly, in a manner no one would consider sane—when the Corpse found him in the museum of taxidermic animals. Jespar felt nothing. Not when the Corpse came limping out of that dark aisle with his burning hands drawing flickering shadows across the animal exhibits around him. Not when he eased down on the pedestal of the one across Jespar—a giant centipede, its legs unfurling behind the Corpse like a halo of thorns. Not when his lips split in a smile.

No fear, no horror, no panic.

The mind is a malleable thing.

The Corpse clasped his hands between his knees and leaned in. Even now, three years after they first met in Jespar's nightmares, his smile looked so different from that of the dead man he represented. Once, it had been cold and ashamed, the kind reserved for a prodigal son. Now, it was warm and mournful, that of a man sitting at an old friend's deathbed.

"Did you truly think he could keep you safe?"

"You're not here," Jespar said. "You're not real."

The corner of the Corpse's lips lifted ever so slightly. "You are right, boy, I am not. But when did that ever matter? Our minds shape reality … that is why superstitious peasants burn witches, jealous lovers murder their beloved, and lonely veterans put nooses around their necks. Now, tell me, did you really believe it? That the boy could keep us away forever?"

Jespar groped for his brandy flask and took a deep swallow. It stung, but he barely felt it. "Not real."

"So you did. Hm. I thought you knew better." The Corpse closed his eyes and sighed, circling a burning thumb over the bloody lotus flower carved into his forehead. Flames licked at his greasy hair but didn't spread. "It is such a tragedy, you know? None of this would have ever happened had you not refused to see. Sixteen years, boy, sixteen years, and here you are, still choosing to be blind. Then again, I suppose it is only human, isn't it? To prefer ignorance over uncomfortable truths?"

Jespar felt the Pull coming now, that cold pulse beating its way up from the depths of his mind. He killed the rest of his brandy, his head spinning from the packed punch of booze, fear, and utter exhaustion.

"Fine, ignore me if you must. I only want you to know that I never wished for things to end like this. You had your chance to stop it, your chance to see, but you squandered it. Now live with the consequences."

The Corpse stood. The Pull was almost there now, each beat sending chills into his bones as a blue veil closed over the world.

"You're not real," Jespar whispered.

"Maybe not," the Corpse replied. "But my judgment is."

PART ONE

DROUGHT

CHAPTER ONE
GOLDEN SOIL

DAY ONE
6TH MOON OF DRY SEASON, 1226 A.L.

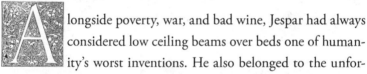 longside poverty, war, and bad wine, Jespar had always considered low ceiling beams over beds one of humanity's worst inventions. He also belonged to the unfortunate few whose subconscious didn't remind them of the danger looming above, which was why reality greeted him with a head-on slam into thirty pounds of solid house support as he jerked awake.

He cried out and dropped back into bed, hands pressed against his forehead, stars shooting across his lids. They blasted on for a bit, then gave way to Jespar's second-least favorite part of waking: the afterglow of yet another crippling nightmare.

"Bloody hell," he muttered. "Bloody hell."

With sixteen years of insomnia and nightmares to his credit, the words "restful" and "sleep" had long become two estranged lovers, but ever since Jespar had accepted that ominous invitation, they seemed to have parted ways for good. Before, two nightmares a week were an exception. In the past seven days, he'd had four.

He lay still for a couple breaths, then forced himself up. As always, the memories of his dreams were a hazy blur, images and sensations connected only by a pervasive sense of dread and recurring motifs, the most dominant one the Corpse with the burning hands.

As always, they left him feeling like utter shit.

"I'm awake," he said. "I'm awake."

When the echoes of the nightmare finally faded, Jespar grew aware of something else: he had no clue where he was.

The room around him had all the allure of a mangy horse forced into a gaudy harness: red upholstery and curvy armrests en masse, but poor-quality wood. The scent was that of patchouli and roses, but with a dash of ammonia. Golden picture frames and garish ornamentation adorned the walls, but it was the sort sold by the jolly peddler who also brews "love potions." Lamentably, Jespar's bed was no exception: while the snake design of the bedposts tried hard for an exotic flair, the peeling paint, a foul-smelling mattress, and dried stains of dubious origin on the bedding dispelled all illusions.

Where the hell ...?

The door burst open. A mountain of fat and muscle stood under the lintel, staring at Jespar from a blocky, hard face that would have looked intimidating even without the scowl and the greasy, long black hair framing it.

"That the freeloader?" he asked someone behind him.

Muttered agreement followed.

Jespar barely made it out of bed before a ringed fist flew toward him. Instinctively, he dodged, but a headache thwarted his plan by flaring up at that very moment; the fist sank into his stomach and hurled him back onto the mattress.

Wheezing, Jespar shielded himself, anticipating the next blow. When it didn't come, he peeked past his fingers and saw the man looming over him, his tree-trunk arms crossed over his lurid green shirt.

"That's for scarin' the girls with yer bloody screamin'. Now, pay the fuck up." His working-class vernacular combined with his accent— *pey awb*—made for a mix that Jespar almost mistook for another language.

"What do you mea—"

"Ye paid for three hours, not a sleepover, that's fifteen sêr extra. Now, pay up and get yer coinless ass outta here 'fore I toss it out the *weenduw.*" *Window?* Most likely. But what-

Jespar glanced at the rumpled clothes on the floor. At the stains on the bedding. At the corset over a nearby chair's backrest.

Things fell into place.

"Sure," he managed. "Sure, I'll pay." He rummaged his pockets for coins and counted them. Eleven sêr and fifty dara. "Here. That's all I've g—"

The man grabbed him, yanked open the shutters, and tossed him out into the predawn night. Two things went through half-naked Jespar's mind before he, wearing breeches only, landed hard in the mud of some alley: first, good thing the room had been on ground level; second, bouncers took their threats quite literally.

A wadded-up ball of cloth splashed into a puddle beside him, sloshing him with brown water.

"Next time, ye'll pay with yer fuckin' teeth!"

The window slammed shut.

A minute ticked by as Jespar lay there and reflected on his life choices. With a groan and as much dignity as he could muster, he got up, dressed, and girdled his swordbelt. A middle-aged woman peered at him from the alley's mouth, and a fat cat from another puddle a few steps over. When Jespar stared back, the woman moved on, but the cat did not.

"What are you looking at?" Jespar asked.

It wagged its tail in what might have been the feline approximation of a shrug. Then it wobbled away.

"Right," Jespar said. He shouldered his haversack, growing aware of an itch on his back. "Right."

Judging by the dark blue of the sky, sunrise was still an hour or two away. Since he wouldn't be meeting his employer until afternoon, that gave him plenty of time to fix himself up and explore this wondrous and exotic country around him. Pulling his scarf a little looser, Jespar oriented himself. Even from here, a dozen miles from the capital, he could see its colossal white walls rising along the slope of the massive mountain in the west.

Uunili.

The Alabaster City, the heart of the Kilayan Archipelago, the wealthiest metropolis in the Illumined World.

A new beginning.

In the half-light of dawn, Jespar made for the marina.

The ship that Jespar had arrived on—the *Morning Dew*—was bound for the capital, but when an overcrowded harbor thwarted that plan, it anchored at Southport instead. The captain encouraged the vexed travelers to look on the bright side: Southport, a colonial harbor town on the eastern cape of the bay bifurcating the southern tip of Uunili, was merely a "nice mornin's walk" from Uunili City, and the "refreshin' sea breeze" was the perfect way to become accustomed to the searing hot, muggy beast that was the Archipelago's dry season.

"Start with the rice wine, then tackle the absinthe," the captain advised. Jespar wasn't thrilled about that walk but shelved the idiom for future usage.

After half an hour of passing through alleys formed by brightly colored houses, Jespar reached its eponymous harbor. He strolled along the marina for a bit, then sat on a solitary crate to appease his post-inebrious headache and appreciate the view of the vast inlet between the two capes. The sun was just rising, tinting the fog over the water a pale orange; tiny boats dotted the horizon, fisherfolk working the seas for their morning haul.

Pretty.

It was only Jespar's second day in Kilay, and he had yet to see the Alabaster City from inside, but he already understood why so many poems mentioned this glittering country.

First, there was the landscape: white beaches with palm trees stretching on for miles. The ocean, turquoise and blue. The green mountain panorama.

Second was Uunili, the colossal city nestled in the junction of the two capes and extending far up the bay-side slope of the mountain that ran along the entire western cape, Mount Ilakato. The tall city walls occluded most of the lower districts from sight, but what Jespar saw of the upper ones could have been taken from a painting: blocky white pyramids with dashes of azure and gold rose within a composition of parks and gleaming streets. The structures grew more imposing the farther up the mountain they were and culminated in several colossal pyramids clustered around the peak.

The magnates' ziggurats.

Jespar could only see three from where he was sitting, but he knew there were seven in total. Especially since the Silence, Kilay's magnates were often likened—and even likened themselves—to gods, and seeing their abodes made it easy to understand why. Egomaniacally inclined or not, awaking in a mountaintop palace basked in a golden sunrise did little to dampen illusions of grandeur.

Jespar scratched his back, then took a sip from his flask and swished the water around his mouth. Down the harbor promenade, three kids were playing with an alapu, a clumsy but energetic animal native to the Archipelago. With their potbellies, bushy tails, and moon-eyed, ursine faces, they seemed a crossbreed between a bear cub, a piglet, and a raccoon. The kids were kicking a tiny round sack to each other, laughing as the alapu chased it, squeaking and tumbling over its paws.

Bit by bit, Jespar's memories of the previous night returned. There had been drinks with the sailors of the *Morning Dew*, which explained the headache. There had been some Kilayan betting game and a bar fight, which explained his empty purse and the bruises that weren't the bouncer's doing. There had been two whores—a woman with heavy makeup and a young man with thinning hair—who had most likely looked prettier when Jespar had been high and hammered.

He sighed. Wasn't this supposed to be a turn of the page? If that mysterious invitation didn't turn out to be a sham—and the advance pay covering the passage to Kilay strongly suggested it wasn't—the job would be enough for him to start fresh anywhere he wanted. No more drifting, no more day jobs, no more sleeping out in the cold.

A new beginning.

Inspiring intentions, no doubt. With sobering success, Jespar tried to imagine an epic tale of redemption that started with the hero getting shitfaced with two strumpets.

He rummaged his hidden boot pouch for money—thanking chance he'd put the Starfall Era coin his Nehrimese contact had given him there and not into his purse—and came up with twenty-one sêr, just enough for breakfast, a pipe, and a bath. Remembering the stains on the brothel's bedsheets, he decided to start with the bath.

As he sauntered down the pier searching for a bathing house, Jespar allowed his impressions of the city to settle in. He had arrived in Kilay with a bagful of preconceptions, finding some of them confirmed and others disproved. The contrast between the "haves" and "have-nots" *was* as stark they said it was: while frescoes and statues adorned the fancier buildings, such as the Blue Islands Coalition's offices, only makeshift posts and scaffolding kept some of the back-alley houses from falling apart. Like he had also expected, no one paid him much attention, despite his skin and hair color making him stick out like a pigeon among blackbirds. People of all races crossed his path, from Kilayan to Qyranian to Nehrimese to the Nomad Folk, the Aetäerna and the Starlings. Jespar was just another traveler.

As far as misapprehensions were concerned, one struck Jespar as particularly curious: a country putting the pursuit of wealth, status, and freedom above all else, Kilay enjoyed a reputation for being as pious as a whore was chaste, yet Jespar spotted a surprising number of people wearing prayer rings around their upper arms—three on the right, four on the left—the symbols of the seven Light-Born. He even came across several priestesses, one of them performing rites before the sculpture of an elegant, bejeweled woman at a town square. The stone woman's hair going down to her feet and a cobra snaking around her skywards-raised arms, Jespar immediately recognized her as Moraia, the Light-Born of fertility, cunning, and sunrises and patron goddess of Kilay.

Jespar knew the nations of the Illumined World differed in devotion to the Light-Born, those supposed deities who had ended the long dark age after Starfall and ruled the world ever since. The Silence— the term used to describe the now two-hundred-year absence of the Light-Born—was the subject of many heated discussions in the more secular corners of Vyn, such as Qyra, Kilay, or Northern Nehrim.

Jespar had often imagined how those scholarly debates in Al-Rashim's universities must have looked like.

"Debased, ungrateful infidels," exclaims the outcast theist professor. *"The Gods are still with us, they merely decided to withdraw as a punishment for our succumbing to Corruption! Every minute of every day, they still watch us from high up in Inodân, watching sadly as humanity debases further, heading toward another dark age! Only if we atone will they return and bring peace to our world once more. Trust in the guidance of the Order of Light!"*

"Ha! You bug-brained fool!" the atheist professor barks back, daredevil in his outspokenness. *"Every lucid mind can see there were no Gods in the first place. They were just a lie promulgated by the Order to legitimize its power! It is time for the corrupt clergy to be trialed for their deception so that a new era of rationality can reign!"*

An incensed post-theist jumps from his seat. *"You ignorant children of a meager camel! Yes, the Gods are no more, but how can you deny the historical records of their great deeds? How can you fail to see the simple truth, that they existed in all their magnificence but have perished? The Order must not step down but simply acknowledge the facts, so that we may find new lodestars together!"*

"My treasured and despised friends," the nontheist states coolly. *"You are all wrong. The Gods both existed and didn't."*

Wild laughter explodes in the hall. *"Listen to this fool! The desert sun has clearly fried all sense from her mind! She is contradicting herself!"*

"I am not," retorts the nontheist calmly. *"Tell me, do the illusions of a street magician not seem divine to a little child? The 'Gods' existed, yes, but they were never true deities—only skilled dimensionists whose powers tricked the Starfall Era commoners into believing they were divine. And, by the excretions of the sacred donkey, the Order is still doing it! Why else would they forbid speaking about dimensionism to the Uninitiated? Why else do they force scholars and Sighted to take the*

Oath of the Arcane lest they be outcast?" She leaps up from her seat and thrusts a triumphant finger at the theist. *"Because there is nothing an oppressor fears more than the cleansing light of knowledge!"*

Indignation, insults, and flying eggs ensue.

While Jespar didn't feel strongly about the matter, he recalled once voicing his own explanation for the Silence to his tutor: perhaps, he had mused, the Gods had withdrawn willfully, as the Order contended. Not out of indignation over the world's Corruption, but because they simply had wearied of humankind's perpetual stupidity and turned toward the more pleasant aspects of life—probably those involving wine, food, and naked skin.

His theory had earned him a stern look.

The priestess placed a bowlful of herbs on the sculpture's plinth and lit them. Then she rose to her feet and successively touched her forehead, mouth, and chest.

Odd, Jespar thought as he watched her go about her way. With all their talk of self-determination and the Great Dream, it really didn't make much sense for Kilayans to be more than lip-service believers or post-theists, at least to Jespar. Yet here they were: prayer rings, priestesses, statues. Probably, he surmised, it was that age-old classic of "making sure." You didn't really believe in the Gods but said your sunrise prayers anyway, just in case Hell and Beyond existed after all.

I confess, now pass me the wine.

Grinning, he went on. By the time Jespar found a bathing house near Southport's market square, the sky's last hues of red had turned into azure. Everything about the place promised refreshment: the blue-golden paint of the three tapering stone blocks it was built from, the sound of splashing water wafting through the unglazed windows, the name painted onto the square recess over the entrance—"Lake of the Gods."

A clerk wearing a thigh-length purple silk coat with golden buttons and loose white silk trousers greeted Jespar inside.

"May you prosper, ma'sao," he chirped. "Have you come to indulge in the divine waters of our humble establishment?"

Jespar, picturing himself in a sprawling pool full of mermaids, confirmed this was the case.

"We have different options, ma'sao."

A minute later, Jespar was back on the street. Divine waters or not, fifty sêr an hour was more than he could afford or would have been willing to spend even if he could have. *A river it is*, he thought and went to a vegetable vendor to ask for directions. The woman told him about a natural pool just two miles out of town. When Jespar offered her fifteen dara in return, she declined. "Nah. Ye'll need it."

"What do you mean?"

A hollow smile on her lips, the woman retied the leather band woven into her hair, sea conches and wood rings strung along its length. "Ye'll see, ma'sao. Ye'll see."

Following her directions, Jespar found his way to Southport's northern outskirts. Cobblestone paving gave way to gravel, varicolored mud-brick houses to adobe huts, and well-dressed officials to farmers and workers in simple linen. Not much later, Jespar was making his way down a path along the eastern coast, a fresh breeze ruffling his hair. A banana plantation spread to his left, a patch of jungle sloped toward the beach to his right, the countless palms sharing the soil with exotic trees and bushes. Jespar couldn't name most of them, but he recognized a few: there were tamukas, thin trees whose branchless trunks culminated in a crown of foliage shaped like a mushroom cap; lightrose bushes with their burgundy and violet blossoms; and, of course, the prismatic tokiflowers that grew in shady spots and were the Kilayans' primary source of dye for their garments. Save for the occasional withered frond and sun-parched meadow—the signs of a long dry season—the landscape was a celebration of life and fertility.

It must have been half an hour until the path forked, one branch continuing down the shoreline, the other turning into the jungle. Recalling the merchant's instructions, Jespar took the latter, working his way through the undergrowth while shooing away the katakos, a species of bloodsucking insects with vibrant butterfly wings. Heat and sweat did their best to worsen the itch on his back, so when Jespar finally heard the sounds of a waterfall in the distance, it was like a horn call proclaiming the end of a battle. His relief waned when he realized voices mixed into the swooshing. There were people down by the pond, and they were talking.

Not talking—arguing. And quite aggressively so.

A hand on the pommel of his longsword, Jespar went on. A few turns and katako bites later, the path sloped down a hill, leading to a natural pool nestled in a rock formation. Bushes and trees adorned the terraces, two rivers cast curtains of water into the basin. The shouting came from four figures on the shingle, all obscured by the thicket.

Warily, Jespar began the descent. The figures became discernible: two men—one tall and one bulky—a woman, and a child. The tall man and the woman wore the indigo shirts and leather cuirasses of the Blue Guard; the man and the girl had on a skirt down to the knees, topless and barefoot. Jespar got a little closer, then crouched behind a bush to observe.

With their dark skin, broad faces, and eyes like willow-leaves, the bulky man and the girl were clearly Makehu; as was custom among the Archipelago natives, the man had umako around his eyes, permanent paint etched under the skin with a hot needle. For the first time in moons, Jespar thought of Naka, his former Makehu comrade. Downing drinks in some rancid inn, Jespar had once asked him what his umako depicted, wild bursts of black framing even darker irises.

What do you think, Etōkoka?

An explosion of birdshit?

Laughing, Naka had given him the finger.

Realizing he was smiling, a cold knot formed in his stomach. He killed the memory and turned his attention back to the argument in progress.

"... i'okatū swimmed them waters 'fore ye wakemō even came here! It's me right to be here, me bloody right!" *Wlaati raitu.* A strong Makehu accent tinged the man's Inâl, exchanging sounds foreign to his mother tongue with familiar ones and adding vowels to words that ended on consonants.

"Yes," the guardswoman replied. "And nobody is denying you that right, as long as you pay. Now beat it."

Fists clenched, the Makehu addressed the male guard. "Kalaia e i'okatū lai," he said—or something along those lines. Three years had passed since the incident in the Village, and Jespar hadn't spoken or heard Makehu since.

The guardswoman frowned. "What did he say?"

Her comrade looked sideways. He shared the man's willow-leaf eyes, but his head was slimmer and his cheeks stubbled. "Doesn't matter."

"I told him he oughta be ashamed of hisself," the Makehu said. "Chummin' up with wakemō, who ain't never done nothin' but hound us. Ye really think yer one of them, huh? Just 'cause ye speak all fancy and suck their golden cocks now?"

The guardswoman put a hand on her scimitar. "You should be very careful now, friend."

"Look," the guardsman said. "This has nothing to do with our blood. Makehu, Kilayan, outlander, the rules are the same for every-body. By the Golden Soil Decree, these waters now belong to Third

Magnate Vel'Nyx, and if you want to use them, you have to pay. I'm sorry."

The girl tugged at her father's skirt and muttered something, but his fists remained balled.

The guardsman tacked on a smile. "Okay, tēmī, tell you what, I'll make it four for you. I—"

The Makehu shoved him. For a tick, the guardsman flailed his arms almost comically as he struggled for balance. Then he crashed down on the shingle, his surprised cry in unison with that of the girl.

"*Fuck off!* Ūkonō, I work for the Coalition when ye two was still shittin' in yer mothers' laps, so don't ye fuckin' dare speak down to me! *Not me!*"

Steel flashed in the sunlight. The guardswoman had drawn her scimitar. "All right, you have-not, that does it. You're going to jail."

The Makehu stepped toward her. "Make me."

Jespar was at least ten strides away, yet something about the Makehu's voice and the look that came with it made his stomach eely. *Hatred.* What he saw there was a pure, seething hatred that went far beyond the words traded in this dispute; this man was a soil sucked dry by years of drought, just waiting for the spark to ignite.

Jespar knew the look. He'd seen it hundreds of times during his years with the Wayfarers.

Just when he decided to intervene, the girl began to cry. The Makehu froze. He looked at his daughter, then to the guardswoman, then to his daughter again, his fists balling and relaxing as though he were battling a cramp.

The fury left him. "Ye ain't gettin' away with this, 'ma'sae,' mark me words." He glanced at the downed guard. "And don't ye ever dare call me 'tēmī' again, miwāmalā. Yer a disgrace."

Miwāmalā. "Mixed waters"—a Makehu slur for biracials that Naka had worn with pride.

The Makehu took his daughter's hand, and they left, stalking right past the bush where Jespar was hiding. He waited for them to pass, then let out a breath and turned his attention back to the guards. The man was scrambling to his feet, his comrade frowning. "'I'll make it four for you, tēmī?' That coinless asshole barks at us for doing our job, and you're giving him a bloody discount?"

"That 'coinless asshole' just wanted a bath and a canteen of water for his family. If you like the idea of that girl crying herself to sleep with a sore throat, fine. I know I don't."

The guardswoman curled her lip. She slammed her weapon back into its sheath. "Well, as you say, Ma'sao Holier-Than-Thou. I gotta piss."

After she had disappeared into the bushes, her comrade sat on a rock by the shingle and gazed into the water. Jespar seized the chance and slipped out of his cover.

Noticing him, the guard rose with a sigh. "I'm sorry, ma'sao, but–"

"Li nekē," Jespar said. "Nekē li. Kaia 'atete āpa." *It costs. I know.*

The guard raised a brow. "You ... speak Makehu?"

"Kōpū." Jespar nodded at the pool. "Did I hear that right? This pond is private property?"

The guard, probably still trying to reconcile Jespar's appearance with his Makehu, didn't answer right away. He rubbed his neck. "Yeah, has been for a moon. Magnate Vel'Nyx bought almost the entire jungle from here to the Mandibles, and apparently that fellow hadn't heard the news yet."

"How do you buy an entire jungle?"

"Courtesy of the Golden Soil Decree. You haven't been here long, huh?"

"Since yesterday. What's the deal with that decree?"

"Well, basically, it puts the entire Archipelago up for sale." The Makehu wiped the sweat from his forehead. *No umako*, Jespar noted.

"Every forest, every beach, and every pebble that doesn't already belong to someone can now be bought."

"Like this pool."

"Yes. And because Vel'Nyx decided she's not rich enough yet, using it now costs." He patted the crest embroidered onto his cuirass, a cobra over two crossed scimitars. "So that's our glorious duty these days: telling folk who barely have enough to feed their kids to get their water elsewhere. Guess you saw what happened?"

"I did."

"Well, I don't blame the man, you know? Kilay has always been run by the folk with the most coin, but, I mean, charging someone for *water*?" He exhaled. "This won't end well, ma'sao. It won't end well."

The guardswoman reappeared from the bushes. The man cast her a tired look. "Anyway, for just six sêr, you can drink and splash about the pool all you like. What do you say?"

After Jespar had paid, the guards went on patrol. He undressed and stashed his clothes, swordbelt, and haversack under a little precipice, then walked waist-deep into the pool and splashed water into his face. A smile claimed his lips.

Funny.

It was as mundane as you could get, but it had always been things like this that made Jespar feel most at peace. Mulled wine following a day out in the cold. Sun on his eyelids. A dry blanket after rain.

You're right, father. I never was a good Dal'Varek.

Sixteen years it had been, yet the memories were still there, Damean Dal'Varek's endless lectures on morality and justice, his tirades on simpletons who wasted their days playing dice, and, of course, the many glowers for Jespar whenever he had once again proved to be a disappointment.

And even so, for all his father's holiness, Jespar couldn't remember having ever seen him content—not when he had eaten the countless delicacies their private chefs had prepared each night, not when he stood before the giant library window and watched the snow dance from the sky, not even when Rorik and Alvric had spent all their savings on buying him a Starling water clock for his birthday. Apparently, virtue only came with a steel rod shoved all the way up your ass.

And what about you, dear Jespar?

No, he surely wasn't the epitome of happiness—after all the shit that had happened, who would be? Still, barring the occasional nightmare and spell of melancholia, he was content.

Life was all right.

The ripples calmed, and a tired face stared back from the reflection.

Ma'sao Dal'Varek, you look like shit.

Jespar's stubble, scarce on the cheeks but dense around the mouth, had grown shaggy, too short to pass as a proper beard, too long to fly as the trademark of the rugged maverick—not that his unrelentingly boyish features had much potential for the manly kind of ruggedness women apparently swooned over to begin with. Bags clung to his eyes, and his hair was an unkempt shock of ash-blond bristles, slightly receding at the temples.

He raked his hands through his hair, ending up with a couple of strands, some blond, some gray. It was getting grayer; he couldn't tell from the reflection, but he remembered how the strumpet from last night had teased him when he had told her he had only just turned twenty-eight.

"I like it," her male companion had mused, trailing his fingers up Jespar's thigh. "I bet he's got experience."

To his inebriated mind, that comment had been the pinnacle of erotic banter. Now he cringed at the memory.

"Jespar Dal'Varek," he muttered, "where's your dignity?"

Wondering if it had ever existed in the first place, Jespar plunged headfirst into the pool.

When Jespar left the basin, his drowsiness had washed off along with the mud and sweat, and the itch between his shoulders felt better. It was a rash, as it turned out; he could feel the bumps. Using one of his throwing knives, he gave himself a rudimentary shave, relying on the reflection in the water to guide him, then changed into his second set of clothes—foregoing the protection of his leather cuirass in exchange for ventilation—and returned to Southport. Three of his remaining fifteen sêr went to a washerwoman to clean his clothes, four to an innkeeper for a classic Kilayan breakfast—rice, beans, fried plantains, and a tangy black herbal infusion called 'tea' that left Jespar feeling pleasantly awake—and, lastly, two sêr initially intended for a cobbler to fix his soles to a hungry urchin.

Judging by the sun, it was about two hours before noon when he embarked on his journey to the capital to meet his contact. There was no need to ask for directions this time. He took a ferry to the other side of the inlet—thanks to the overcrowded harbor, the ones straight to Uunili were laughably expensive—then followed along the great road meandering up the coast, trotting side by side with the stream of travelers, peasants, and fortune seekers. Listening to them chat about work, dreams, worries, and the latest news, Jespar learned that the Golden Soil Decree was on everyone's lips and that the Makehu from the pool was not alone in his outrage. There was also talk of a new underground movement claiming to fight injustice in the country, a trade embargo by Arazeal that threatened many jobs, and some nobleman who had mysteriously disappeared from the public eye.

One and a half hours of "nice mornin' walk" later, he reached the first houses and farms of Uunili's sprawling outskirts, also known as the Stone District. Another two hours, and a blistering lobster sunburn on his neck later, and he had reached the colossal gate of the city's titanic walls that sealed off the inner part of the city. A long queue preceded it, leading up to a pocket of guards who either waved the travelers through or sent them back. Bidding his last hopes at a sweat-free, well-groomed appearance goodbye, Jespar joined the line and waited.

And waited.

And waited.

And waited.

By the time a pockmarked man waved him over, his feet were sore and his throat dry as sand.

The guard thrust out a hand palm up. "Papers, outlander."

Bracing himself for a volley of questions, Jespar handed him the sealed letter of passage that had come with the invitation. He'd been longing to read it for the entire sea journey, but the instructions he'd been given along with the money for the passage had made it clear that doing so or showing it to anyone but a Blue Guard would "end his mission before it started," a delightfully ambiguous statement.

The guard tore off the seal, then read the letter a total of three times, his countenance changing with each run—from annoyance to surprise, from surprise to bewilderment, from bewilderment to a peculiar, intimidated distrust.

"Where did you get this?"

Jespar opened his mouth but caught himself in time. There'd been another instruction: total secrecy.

"Can't say. I'm sorry."

The guard eyed him the way you'd look at someone who was either a mass murderer or the child of a Light-Born. At last, he settled on a nervous smile and returned the parchment. "Of course, ma'sao, thank you. Forgive me for keeping you."

"No sweat."

From "outlander" to "ma'sao" in five minutes, Jespar thought as he crossed the gate. *And all it took was one letter.*

This was getting interesting.

A popular Kilayan sea shanty claimed that among trade, cunning, and fertility, Moraia also counted beauty among her areas of divine expertise. It also contended that the Alabaster City was her favorite mistress and was no less than the goddess's kisses that granted her fabled beauty.

If that were the case, Jespar concluded as Uunili's inner city unfolded before him, Moraia had clearly preferred some body parts over others. While lots of passion and tongue had been involved in the upslope districts with their alabaster villas and green parks, the ones along the foothills had received a mere kiss on the cheek, the architecture shifting focus from beauty to function. Platonic feelings must have prevailed in the slum areas just outside the walls, where colorful but crumbly brick houses shared the ground with adobe huts, all crammed together for, seemingly, the sole purpose of fitting as many structures into as little space as possible.

The shanty sung of the Seven Ziggurats but left out the ramshackle dwellings, praised the bosoms of Kilayan women but skipped the emaciated beggars on the roadside, rhapsodized over the city's unique aroma of spices, perfume, and the sea's breeze but failed to mention the dashes of sweat, piss, and shit. People were everywhere, an endless stream of all colors, shapes, and sizes, drifting through the many streets, alleys, and plazas, melting and flowing like an ever-changing kaleidoscope. Chatter, laughs, and shouts filled the air and mixed with the sounds of feet on gravel, clanging anvils, barking dogs, and braying donkeys. And as Jespar maneuvered his way through the endless crowd, he had a realization: if Uunili were a lover, she was a volatile one.

One day, she'd be your wings, the next, the riptide that drowned you; her promise was tempting but her hunger voracious; her lips invited, but her teeth bit hard. This city gorged on motion and got high on flux, and the boundless energy she exuded in return was as invigorating as it was intoxicating, as mesmerizing as it was deadly.

But there was also something else, an element Jespar imagined hadn't always been there but which now pervaded the city like a pernicious undercurrent. It hid in the details: how the haggling at the market stalls was just a little *too* heated. How there were just a little *too* many patrols. How there just a little *too* many frowns among passersby for them to be the result of a bad day.

Tension.

Uunili was a fabric stretched to the breaking point.

For what must have been two hours, Jespar fought his way through the outer rings of the inner city—also known as the Steel District—dodging dirty wash water sloshed from windows above, traversing narrow alleys, dusty roads, and open plazas. The sun blazing down and the high walls keeping out the wind, Jespar's itch and the sweat had gotten to a point where only the fear of an arrest for public indecency stopped him from tearing off his shirt and going on barechested. And yet, when his destination finally appeared around the corner of yet another busy street, he paused in awe.

The Great Bazaar.

A colossal stone pavilion rose before him, sunlight falling through square openings in the roof and illuminating a carpet of stalls and tents. A flood of smells both exotic and mundane wafted from inside, riding atop the sounds of chatter, shouting, footfalls, and music.

For a while, Jespar just watched. The war had ended a long time ago, yet it was until recently that every trip into a crowd had carried the risk of a panic attack. To his surprise, there had been none of that in Uunili. Yes, he had clutched the pommel of his sword since crossing the city gate; yes, there had been the feeling of someone staring at the back of his neck; yes, a part of him couldn't stop wondering how *anyone* could saunter about so carefree in a crowd where any passersby could theoretically shove a dagger into your side and leave before anyone else noticed. Still, the panic hadn't come. Worse nightmares or not, it seemed like time did some healing after all.

Jespar took a deep breath and entered the pavilion. He had somewhere to be.

As he had expected, the bazaar's assortment was endless. Farmers proffered food, blacksmiths tools and weapons, tailors clothes. A woman with her hair woven into snakelike braids sat at a table full of gems and pendants and offered to read his fortune; a man with a striking mustache promised Jespar a concoction that would grow his manhood to inconceivable dimensions; a fire eater spouted flaming cones before an awed audience. Jespar was almost at his destination when a voice cut over the din.

"Make way! Make way for Third Magnate Vel'Nyx!" The impossible happened when the crowd obliged at once, parting to clear a lane in the middle. An armed escort appeared from toward where Jespar was headed, a dozen guards forming a phalanx around a blue-and-gold litter.

"Make way for Third Magnate Vel'Nyx!" the front guard repeated, banging the hilt of his scimitar against his shield. "Make way!"

Like most people, Jespar stood on his toes and craned his neck as the litter passed him by, but a curtain sealed off the interior, and all Jespar could make out were the lower halves of two women sitting across from each other. Only their hands were visible beneath the rim of the drape, one pair young and smooth with painted fingernails, the other slender and dotted with age spots. When the escort had passed, the lane closed as fast as it had formed, and people resumed their business. Jespar watched the litter fade into the bustle, then followed suit and went about his way.

The meeting point was a *napaawo* in a secluded corner of the bazaar. An abbreviation of the Makehu term *"napāwo e kuluhika,"* which, if Jespar recalled correctly, meant "tent of dreams," a *napaawo* was an establishment where customers could consume various drogae; with the meeting still a few hours away, Jespar was itching to try out some of Kilay's fabled nightflower.

Rug-covered screens dulled the noise and light from the market, blue and violet paper lanterns immersing the place in a dreamy gloom. Jespar ordered a pipe of "Purple Myrad" from Uunuma, First Flush, then made himself comfortable on a secluded chaise. There were only four other guests: a woman whose matronly features and conservative burgundy dress made her look out of place in the establishment, a teenage couple kissing vigorously in the corner, and a man whose glassy stare gave him the air of someone smoking to forget.

The attendant brought Jespar's pipe, proffering it bowl first; guessing the protocol, Jespar smelled the petals and nodded. When the attendant was gone, Jespar leaned into the cushions and took a deep drag. Several breaths went by, then the droga kicked in, warmth forming in his chest, his sight going blurry. When his vision refocused again, the colors were softer, melting into each other like a still-wet painting dipped into water.

Smiling, Jespar fished a book from his haversack—a short story collection he'd bought in Erothin—made himself comfortable, and began to read.

Life was all right.

He had almost reached the other cover by the time the tent flap opened, revealing a tall, bald Qyranian and two guards. The effects of the nightflower had eased off and left Jespar with blissful drowsiness, so he barely paid the newcomers any attention until they advanced toward him. The guards wore chainmail, helmet, and greaves fashioned from scales that glowed a subtle turquoise. Jespar recognized it as nuvium, an ore as durable as steel and as light as leather—a single nugget cost more than what a farmer made in a moon. The Qyranian's long sapphire robe broke with the Kilayan upper class's fashion conventions, but his abundance of jewelry and the blue kohl around his eyes did not, all contrasting strikingly with his sable skin. His gait was slightly jerky, as though he had some kind of impediment.

"Ma'sao Dal'Varek?" Zero accent, neither Kilayan nor Qyranian.

Jespar put down the book and held out his hand. "Yes. Are you—"

"Show me the proof," the Qyranian replied, ignoring his outstretched hand.

Aren't you lovely? Jespar produced the Starfall Era coin from his boot pouch and offered it to the Qyranian. The man studied it briefly, then handed it back to Jespar. "Very well. I'm Zagash Enkshi, counselor of your employer." He glanced at Jespar's pipe. "If I recall correctly, you were instructed to wait, not to indulge."

Jespar smiled apologetically. "I have a habit of missing that part."

Not even a snort. "Follow me."

After hours in the shade, the afternoon sun hit Jespar like a slap with a hot, wet towel. At a brisk pace, Enkshi navigated them through the bustling city maze to the backyard of a grand building adorned with Coalition banners; a blue-and-gold litter much like the one Jespar had seen in the bazaar stood in the shadow of palms, surrounded by about a dozen people, all of whom sprang to their feet the second Enkshi came into sight. Jespar counted seven guards and four bare-chested, muscular men, presumably carriers. Not paying them further heed, Enkshi went straight to a guardswoman whose broad shoulders and cropped hair—unusual for both men and women in the Archipelago—contrasted with her feminine face. Six blue gems adorned the cobra emblem of her uniform. A sergeant, Jespar guessed.

"Ready?" Enkshi asked.

"Yes, Counselor," the sergeant replied. "Is that—"

"Our guest, yes."

The sergeant gave Jespar a once-over, then offered her gloved hand. "Pleased to meet you, ma'sao. I'm Sergeant Maadira." She had no accent, but something about how she spoke sounded stilted.

They shook. "Dal'Varek. Jespar Dal'Varek."

Maadira glanced at his swordbelt. "I will have to ask you to hand that over."

Jespar did as told, the nervous veteran voice in his head deaf to the argument that there were easier ways to murder someone than shipping him halfway across the Illumined World and tricking him into a golden litter.

"Thank you." Maadira took the belt and casually tossed it to one of the guards, a handsome young man, who caught it with unfazed dexterity and passed it on to a pockmarked colleague. Then Maadira signaled to the carriers, who at once took up position between the front and rear carrying poles of the litter. A guard stepped beside the entrance and lifted the heavy curtain, gesturing into the empty box. Enkshi ducked in with all the casual swagger of a jaded king.

Expectant looks fell on Jespar.

Quite unroyally, he hit his head against the doorjamb as he followed the counselor's example.

The mood in the litter turned out as fun as Jespar had expected— Enkshi met his attempts to strike up a conversation with terse answers, and when Jespar carefully inquired whether he'd done anything to vex him, it earned him a scoff. Diagnosing the man with an incurable case of prickhood, Jespar turned his attention to the city passing by beyond the small glass-paned window instead.

Fortune Road.

According to the Kilayan scholar Jespar had often talked to on the three-week ship journey, this was the name of the thoroughfare that meandered up Mount Ilakato in sweeping switchbacks and connected the different districts. "Look at your feet, and you'll know where you are," the woman had explained. "Fortune Road is more than a road. It is a symbol."

Jespar understood now: with every step his journey had taken him up the mountain, the ground under his feet had improved. Dirt and dust for the Stone District where commoners lived, cobblestone for the Steel District that housed the low-class merchants and craftsmen. Now that the litter had crossed a guarded gate about a quarter up the mountain, the carriers treaded on flagstone.

The Jade District. As a person who had grown up in a manor with a thousand square-stride property and who had seen Castle Erothin up close, Jespar hadn't pictured himself marveling at the Alabaster City's fabled upper-class district; yet here he was, spellbound by the beauty passing by the window. It wasn't just the lavishness of the villas, with their multiple stories, expansive gardens, and intricate frescoes; it wasn't the parks waiting around every corner; it wasn't the effortlessly elegant silk-and-leather garments of the denizens who passed them by. It was the coherence of it all. Certainly, everything had its unique touches, but the key aesthetics were the same and gave the place an almost unreal quality, like some fantastical utopia where poverty and ugliness didn't exist, allowing society to focus on the pursuit of beauty alone.

The poor at the bottom, the rich at the top, and a road leading from one to the other.

Not the most imaginative concept, granted, but there was an almost disarming frankness about it. On the Blue Islands, "working one's way to the top" wasn't just a figure of speech. It was reality.

Many miles of luxury later, laughter and music became audible in the distance. Jespar, drowsy from the rough night, the petals, and the sway of the litter, peeked outside, but the westering sun made it hard to see anything.

"A festivity," Enkshi said. "Vel'Tuul is celebrating his name day."

Look at that. He speaks. "Should I know him?"

"The Fifth Magnate."

"Oh. Okay."

"No one worth your attention, though. He's one of those simpletons who inherited a boatload of money from his parents and has nothing better to do than squander it on concubines and lavish orgies. If the nobility didn't enjoy getting shitfaced so much, I doubt Vel'Tuul would still be in the Coalition."

Jespar ventured a smile. "I think I know the type."

"Every country has its share."

Silence followed. Just when Jespar was ready to resume window staring, Enkshi continued.

"Jespar Mitumial Dal'Varek, born in Enderal, 1198 After Light. Your brothers and your father perished in a tragic incident sixteen years ago, effectively making you the last male heir of the family."

Jespar said nothing.

"Seven years following said accident, you left your homeland for Nehrim, where you spent the past nine years, first as a day laborer, then as a mercenary." He leaned in, elbows on knees. "Here's my first question: the Dal'Varek name is still highly respected in your homeland, and you inherited a considerable fortune. Why in the world would a man throw that away for a life as a..." His nostrils twitched. "Vagrant?"

A lump had formed in Jespar's throat. "You're well informed."

"Yes, that's my job. Now answer my question: why leave Enderal and everything you had there behind?"

Because staying there would have smothered me. "Because I wanted to turn the page. You know, be my own man."

"Be your own man," Enkshi echoed. "Why, isn't that a noble sentiment. And that was reason enough for you to leave your own si—"

"Counselor, do you mind telling me what my reasons for going abroad have to do with this mission?"

Enkshi's face clouded at the interruption, but Jespar held his gaze. Finally, the counselor made the smallest of nods, an emperor granting pardon to a traitor. "Well, I suppose you're right, that part isn't relevant. The next one is, though. During those nine years you spent in Nehrim, you first worked as a day laborer, but eventually took to mercenary work, together with another vagrant, who, interestingly enough, was an Archipelago native. It was mostly grunt work at first, but, in the end, you joined the 'Wayfarers', some kind of ... humanitarian mercenary corps?"

Humanitarian, all right. "Yeah, I guess you could call them that." It came out just how he wanted it: flat, neutral, indifferent. Not a hint of the lump in his throat that had grown bigger with each of Enkshi's words. Another sensation had joined it, one Jespar knew all too well and that he had come to call the "phantom noose," a faint pressure around his neck that tightened in certain situations.

"Mm-hm. And do I understand correctly that these 'Wayfarers' fought for the Middle Realm in their war against the South? Against the 'Loons?'"

"Just indirectly," Jespar said. "We only ever did defensive missions, like protecting villages and farmers or helping out refugees. Do-gooder stuff, as you said, but I have a hunch you know all of that already."

The corners of Enkshi's mouth lifted. "You're right, I do. I'm actually more interested in why you left the Wayfarers in 1223 and then essentially vanished from the map for three full years. You didn't even take your Makehu friend with you or collect your outstanding pay."

The noose pulled tighter; the lump grew. "Your sources couldn't tell you anything about that part?"

"Is there anything to tell?"

Yes. A lot. "No. I left the Wayfarers because I was sick of the war and wanted to turn the page."

"Seems like you're quite the page-turner."

Jespar gave a strained sigh. "Look, ma'sao, what's the point of this? I'm a veteran who happens to come from a noble family, that's it. No friends in high places, no undiscovered Sights, just someone trying to get by."

Enkshi studied him. Then he exhaled softly and shook his head. "I don't understand what makes you so special."

"I never said I was."

"Yes, and I believe you. That's the problem. I just can't fathom why the hell we would hire a coinless scrounger instead of a professional."

"You tell me."

"And there's the rub, Dal'Varek: I can't. My master insisted it had to be you and no one else, and when I asked why, all I got were evasive answers. I've been racking my brain over this for the past four weeks, and it simply doesn't make any sense." He regarded his hands, his golden rings reflecting the sunlight falling through the litter window. "Especially not considering what's at stake here."

Before Jespar could answer, someone outside screamed.

INTERLUDE
THE MAN

FORTY-ONE YEARS BEFORE
2ND MOON OF RAINY SEASON, 1185 A.L.

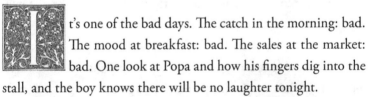

It's one of the bad days. The catch in the morning: bad. The mood at breakfast: bad. The sales at the market: bad. One look at Popa and how his fingers dig into the stall, and the boy knows there will be no laughter tonight.

Around midday, a woman approaches them, not a real upper but wearing quality clothes. She asks if they sell lobsters. Popa lowers his head and tells her they don't.

"Moraia curse me," the woman says. "Ten stinking fish merchants and not one has lobsters? No wonder you're coinless."

Popa stares after her as she stalks off, with that look of his that the boy has come to detest: anger and defeat in the same expression.

Three hours and few sales later, they are dismantling the stall. A man hurries toward them, hair windblown. Do they sell lobsters? The price doesn't matter.

Popa's smile doesn't reach his eyes. "Sorry, ma'sao. We don't."

It's on the way back home that the boy finally asks Popa the question that's bothered him the whole afternoon: why *aren't* they selling lobsters? He remembers they used to.

Popa scoffs. "'Cause the fat cats ain't done nothin' but eat 'em for years, and now they're all gone."

"You mean all the lobsters?" the boy asks. "In the entire Archipelago?"

Popa's lower lip twitches. The boy shouldn't have said it like this, the way an upper would have. "Well, folks say there's some swarms left near Paiolu, but the Coalition ain't lettin' us fish 'em 'cause then they'd go *ixint*." He spits. "Free country, me arse."

"Colonies", not swarms, the boy thinks. *"Extinct", not "ixint".*

The evening passes as expected. Mamah makes dinner, but it's just a scoop of rice and half a plantain each like it has been the whole week. They have leftover dried fish from the market, but Popa wants to keep it for tomorrow. It's stupid, thinks the boy. Who the hell buys old fish when there's fresh ones at the next stall?

The second Popa has finished his plate, he stands and leaves without a word. Mamah gazes after him and sighs. The boy helps her clean up, then asks for her permission to go out and play. Mamah raises an eyebrow and tells him it's late.

"The neighbor's sons asked me over to play Akati with them," the boy replies, knowing it'll sway her. Usually, he chooses to keep to himself, and Mamah wishes he didn't. It works. He can go but must be back by nightfall.

As expected, the boy finds Popa sitting on a tree stump up by what the slit-eyes call "Spirit Hill", a place where they put offerings to their bird god into an iron bowl at the foot of a tall, spiky stone—"obelisk" is the proper word for it. Popa goes there often—not to pray to the bird god, he says, but because the view is beautiful. The boy knows it's a double lie: he's seen Popa drop coins into the bowl and then put one hand to his chest the way the slit-eyes do, and while it's true that Popa always ends up sitting at the hill's lip and looking into the distance, he never does so without a bottle of rice wine beside him. Or two.

The place *is* beautiful, though. Long rainy season showers have restored the jungle's verdant green, and the sun hangs purple and orange just over the horizon. Pink and red tokiflowers grow all around the obelisk, and rainwater fills the offering bowl, mirroring the sunset.

Popa sits at his usual spot, drinking.

"Popa?"

His father whirls around. First, he looks ashamed, but then the shame turns into anger. "Bloody hell. What're ye doin' here, lad? Ye should be in bed!"

The boy lowers his head. "I know, but it's about the lo—" He catches himself and switches to the accent and the vernacular he trains so hard to get rid of. "It's about 'em lobsters."

"What d'ye mean?"

"I think I know a way we can still sell 'em."

"Didn't ye listen, or what? I told ye they's gone."

"Yes, I know, Popa, but what if there's a way even so?"

"Ye ain't makin' sense, lad. Go home."

Sensing Popa's anger rising, it takes the boy all his courage to go on. "Please just hear me out, Popa. When ye cut off the shell, lobster meat is white with a tinge of red, and it tastes mild and a little sweet, don't it? Almost like emperor shrimps."

"Yer point?"

"My point is, with a bit of red salt for the color and some cane sugar juice for the taste, who'd know the difference?"

"Wait a bloody minute. Are ye sayin' we should sell shrimps as lobsters?"

"Why not?"

Popa scoffs. "Don't be daft. The people want the whole thing, not chunks of meat."

"Better odd-lookin' chunks of meat than nothin', right?" the boy says. "And when they ask why we don't sell 'em whole, we just say we had to pickle 'em so they don't go foul. Popa, they *wanna* believe it's lobster meat, so they're gonna buy it."

Popa looks at the boy, squinting. "What if the Coalition finds out?" he asks slowly. "They're gonna whip our backs bloody."

"I don't think they will," the boy says, dropping the vernacular as his excitement grows. "You know the saying, 'If you sign the deal, don't whine if they steal'—it's the customer's responsibility not to get swindled. We wouldn't be committing a crime, Popa, we'd just be playing the game the way the winners do."

The bloody, golden sun bathing Popa in a feverish light, a dragon-fly lands on his shoulder—the spirit animal of Irländah, goddess of freedom, journeys, and dreams. If that wasn't a sign, then what was?

Probably feeling the same, Popa's lips curl upward. It's the faintest of smiles, but still enough to make the boy the proudest child on Kilay. "Come here, lad," Popa says, patting his thigh.

The boy does as his father asked. Popa smells of rice drink, but right now, the boy doesn't mind. He has made him proud, and that's all that matters.

Popa starts to massage the boy's right shoulder, the way he does whenever the boy has done well. How long has it been? "Bright lad," Popa says. "Such a bright lad. Ye always were, y'know? All 'em nice ideas ye got and that fancy way ye talk, 'ma'sao, may I help you' here, 'ma'sao, let me kiss your feet' there. I wonder who ye got it from, really do ... Can't have been Mamah and can't have been me, right?" He kneads harder, his thumb digging into the boy's shoulder. "I mean, we're just two simple, coinless have-nots too daft to understand the way the 'winners' think."

The boy freezes. "Popa—"

"Ye know what I think, son? I think ye need a lesson." Popa stands, yanks the boy up by his neck, and drags him over to the offering bowl at the foot of the obelisk. The boy is so surprised he doesn't even struggle.

"Wait, I—"

Before the boy can finish the sentence, Popa has already thrust his head into the bowl, and the world goes dark. He screams instinctively, and water rushes into his mouth, he coughs, spits, sucks in more.

He can't. He can't.

Harsh words, yes. Slaps, yes. Strikes with a cane, that one time the boy broke the fishing rod, yes. But this?

It's a lesson, he thinks, somehow managing to rise above the panic. *It's a lesson, and he'll pull me up, he has to!*

He doesn't.

His mouth fills with water, his lungs start to burn. *He has to!*

He doesn't.

The boy flails his arms and kicks, feeling his muscles weaken and his sight going dark, *Gods, he has to, he has to, he-*

Air.

His face hovers over the bowl now, his lungs ablaze, his heart hammering into his ribs. He gasps for air, sucks more water into his windpipe, coughs it out, wheezes, coughs more.

Popa squats beside him, his hand hard in the boy's neck. "Are ye listenin', lad?"

Never, the boy thinks. *He'd never do this.*

Never.

Popa shoves him back toward the water. A finger-length over the surface, the boy manages a croak.

"What was that?"

"Yeah," the boy coughs. "Yeah, Popa, I'm ... I'm listenin'."

Yanking him back up, Popa pulls him close so that their faces are level. "Lemme ask ye a question, lad. If Moraia favors the cunnin', why are we here?"

"I—"

"Why do we eat the same shit every night, why does everyone have more than us, *why are we here?*" Spittle sprays into the boy's eyes, and Popa's rice-wine breath makes him nauseous. "Bloody hell, d'ye really think I haven't tried to give ye and Mamah the life ye deserve, d'ye really think I didn't work until me fingers bled and me back broke? For fuck's sake, lad, I did! I tried, over and over and over, but it just ain't workin'! And d'ye know why?"

Not realizing Popa actually wants an answer, the boy just stares into his eyes. Amber in the evening light, the boy doesn't recognize them.

Keeping one hand on the boy's collar, Popa slaps him. Stars explode, blood wells up in the boy's mouth. He has bitten his tongue.

"Answer the *godsdamned* question!"

"No!" the boy blurts out. "Gods, no, Popa, I don't!"

"'Cause we ain't got the same tools! 'Cause this cunt of a goddess did *not* make us all equal, 'cause some folk is born smart, some dumb, some rich, some poor, and if yer born at the bottom, that's where ye fuckin' *stay*! Life's a battlefield and it's eat or get eaten, and us folk, we've never had the weapons to win! Bloody hell, lad, I tried, I *fuckin'* tried!"

He lets go.

The boy drops to the ground like a wet cloth. Moaning, he crawls to the obelisk and presses himself against the stone, hands raised to shield himself from the man he doesn't know anymore.

And then, just like that, Popa is back.

He stares at his hands, water dripping from his callused fingers. Swallows. Opens his mouth. He will tell the boy he's sorry, hug him and invite him to head back home so they can play a round of Akati with Mamah and pretend this never happened.

But Popa doesn't.

Instead, he speaks the words the boy will always remember. "There's a place for folk like us, lad. Sometimes, ye've just gotta make do with the hand ye've been dealt."

And he leaves.

That night, the boy hears Mamah and Popa fight as he lies on his hay bed. They often argue ever since the boy's brother was born dead and Mamah turned barren, but usually, the quarrels are short and end with her falling into line. This time, it goes on and on. Until something shatters, and the door slams shut.

For a time, the house is silent except for Mamah's sobs behind the bamboo screen. Then she stops and appears by his bedroll.

"Pack yer things," she says and thrusts a haversack into his hands. Her right eye is swollen, and there's a gash on her lip.

The boy doesn't argue. He takes his second set of clothes, his carving knife, and his burlap alapu toy. He also takes the Akati cards Popa gave him for his eighth birthday.

They leave.

Only when they're past the village does he dare to speak. "What about Popa?" he says.

The silence that follows is so long the boy is surprised when Mamah does answer after all.

"We're better off without him."

CHAPTER TWO
SCYTHE

The litter crashed to the ground. Jespar managed to steady himself, but the counselor toppled over and slammed headfirst onto the edge of the opposite bench. There was a second scream outside, then hectic voices and boots shuffling on stone.

An ambush, Jespar thought as his mind caught up with the events. Shit.

He staggered to the curtain, tore it open. They were on a small town square, all palms and flowers, the sunset a fierce blaze over the villas' rooftop gardens.

Their escort was in pandemonium. Gathered around the litter in aimless formation, the guards had their shields raised and swords drawn but seemed unsure of what to do. Two litter carriers seemed to have taken off; the other two cowered behind a fountain in the town square center, backs pressed against its basin.

"Outlander!"

Sergeant Maadira. A guardswoman lay motionless at her feet, a bolt sticking out from the slit of her visor; another soldier was on the ground a few steps over, wheezing and clutching a twig buried in his throat. It was the pockmarked man who had taken Jespar's belt; it lay beside him like a discarded stage prop.

Wood exploded.

A bolt had hit the litter just a finger-length from Jespar's right cheek, the fletching quivering from impact.

Instinct took over.

Jespar sprang out of the box, rushed to the dying guardsman and scooped up his belt, then leaped behind the fountain, beside the two carriers. One of them gave Jespar a desperate, pleading look; the other just stared ahead, pressing himself against the stone as though he could become part of it if only he tried hard enough.

"Tortoise!" Maadira's voice rang over the courtyard. "Now!"

The confusion broke. Within seconds, the guards formed a crescent around the litter, crouching with their shields raised above their heads like protective awnings. The next bolt came flying, aimed at the handsome young guard who still had his visor all the way up, but it struck a finger-length over the slit, ricocheting off the steel with such force it sent him staggering backward.

They're good.

Another bolt hit a guardswoman in the unprotected fold between arm and breast. She cried out and almost dropped the shield, but her adjacent comrade steadied her before she could collapse.

Bloody good.

Five bolts, and three of them had struck home with needlepoint precision; that Jespar had survived the one meant for him had been nothing but a fluke. He inhaled deeply, cursing himself for having chosen comfort over his cuirass back at the pool. Not that it would have done much good against crossbow bolts capable of punching dents into nuvium shields anyway.

Hand on his sword, he peeked over the basin. The name of the formation the guards had assumed was depressingly fitting: holed up behind their shields, they were well-protected but equally helpless, a tortoise flipped onto its back.

"Dal'Varek!"

Maadira sought eye contact, her sword hand gesturing at a villa on the square's northern side. At first, Jespar couldn't see anyone, then he spotted a man hidden behind a curtain of hanging wisteria on a third-story balcony. *No, a woman.* She had a crossbow half her size tucked between her knees and was turning the crank mounted to its bridge.

An arbalest.

Another bolt whirred past Jespar's ears, exploded off the pavement. He dropped back behind the basin, the blood pounding in his temples.

Close. Too fucking *close.*

He gave his heart a few seconds to calm, then forced himself to peer again, trying to trace the trajectory of the second bolt. Nothing. There were just too many windows, too many shadows, too many-

A sneeze.

Jespar's eyes darted across the square, stopping on the highest window of a villa to his left. *Gotcha.* The shadows made it impossible to see inside, but there it was, the tip of an arbalest poking out over the sill.

Two marksmen, one north, one west. Now what?

Perhaps the wisest course of action was to just try and hold out until a patrol noticed the ruckus. Then again, the ambush had been going for several minutes now, and no one had appeared on the square since, neither guard nor civilian. Why was that?

The birthday feast.

"Of course," Jespar muttered. What better time for an assassination attempt than while the majority of guards were busy chaperoning nobles getting hammered to loud music? No, they couldn't count on help, at least not anytime soon, and as much as patience was a virtue, its effectiveness against crossbow bolts was debatable.

A counterattack.

That was their only option. They had to take out the marksmen, then deal with the other hitmen who were undoubtedly waiting in some house to swoop in and finish the job once the arbalests had done the legwork.

Maadira must have also noticed the marksman in the western villa and had switched her scimitar for a pistol crossbow, her left hand still holding the shield. She seemed to be the only one in possession of a ranged weapon; the other guards still clutched their scimitars.

Perhaps having noticed her crossbow, the marksman to the left loosed a shot at the sergeant, but her shield caught it. She winced and tossed Jespar a glance, a silent question in her eyes. *Can you help?* He drew his throwing knives—one from a sheath sewn to his boot, the other from one beside his dagger—and cocked his head at the markswoman in the northern building, the one behind the wisteria. Maadira answered with a slight nod.

Jespar calmed his breathing.

A window.

All he needed was a window.

It came with the third exhale. Just as the markswoman had finished winding up her arbalest, a woman appeared in the opening of the alley across her, hair jewels glittering in the setting sun. Seeing the chaos, she stopped dead.

The markswoman, seemingly unaware of the new arrival, aimed her weapon at the litter. Enkshi had regained consciousness and stood groggily in the box's door, a fairground target.

The noble screamed.

The markswoman's hesitated only a single moment, but it was all that Jespar needed. Sending a quick prayer to chance that the other hitman hadn't yet finished reloading, he leaped to his feet, aimed, and hurled his knife. It cut through the air, made a full spin, and hit the markswoman clean in the heart.

Hilt first.

Fuck.

The markswoman appeared petrified. Then she swiveled her cross-bow to Jespar and pulled the trigger.

Or at least that's what she tried to do—before she could loosen the bolt, something struck her at breakneck speed, sending a jolt through her body. Dazed, the woman touched the side of her neck. A tiny dart stuck out from her flesh. Her head turned to Maadira, who stood covered by her comrades' shields, pistol crossbow raised. The markswoman collapsed.

For one hypnotic heartbeat, a hush fell over the courtyard.

Then—as if to compensate for the surreal pause—things snow-balled: the noblewoman let out another scream and bolted back the way she'd come; Enkshi threw himself flat onto the ground between the guards; a cry rang through the courtyard—the other marks-man—and a bolt flew at Maadira that sunk into her shoulder and sent her reeling into the guard beside her. Gripped by an impulse, Jespar spun quarter circle and blindly flung his second knife at the western villa's window.

Jespar was bad at many things, good at some, and a master of few. Considering that knife throwing undoubtedly belonged in the second category, and given the angle, distance, and the rules of probability, his throw should have missed by miles. Since Jespar also believed omnipotent deities had better things to do than correct the course of sloppily aimed throwing knives, the only explanation for why this one *did* hit was simple: he had a shitload of luck.

The knife sliced the air just above the arbalest, then vanished into the shadows of the room. First, Jespar thought he had missed—*of course you did, what did you think, you idiot?*—but then a black silhouette he only now noticed dropped to the ground. The arbalest tumbled over the windowsill and crashed onto the paving.

Jespar was petrified.

Slowly, he turned his head. The guards were staring at him, Maadira among them, her free hand pressed against her wounded shoulder. He had barely come to terms with the fact that that throw had *really* just happened when he noticed something about the handsome young guard with the opened visor.

What the...?

Changing—the guard was changing. Like some pastry bulging and shrinking in the heat of an oven, the man's limbs were morphing under his uniform, transforming. He seemed to be oblivious to it until one of his comrades said something, and he raised a gloved hand to his face. Even from a distance, Jespar could see the man's bones moving under the leather.

The guard screamed and dropped his scimitar. He threw himself onto the ground and tossed about, as though his clothes had caught fire and he was trying to douse them. Like the other soldiers, Jespar watched helplessly until it struck him what was really happening to the man: he was aging. His hair blanched and fell out in tufts; his skin thinned, stretching tighter and tighter over a skull that grew pointier with every passing second.

Necromancy. Holy shit. This is necromancy.

A second later, the idea was confirmed when a shimmer became visible around the guard, like the heat haze over a fire. Somewhere nearby, a dimensionist was shifting on him, using their Sight to drain the life out of this man in front of everyone's eyes. The morbid spectacle went on for what couldn't have been longer than ten seconds, yet felt like minutes; when the guard, now an old man, finally slumped into stillness, it felt like mercy. A short silence hung over the town square—then Jespar grew conscious of a dozen figures in the mouth of the eastern alley, some ten strides from the litter. They were dressed in civilian clothes, but their drawn weapons left no doubt about their intentions; two of them stood out, an Aetäerna man and a woman, skin white as bone, long black hair, and towering two heads over the others. Their physique and weapons were as contrasting as it got—the woman was lithe and held a simple quarterstaff, the man was built like a woodcutter and wielded a heavy saber—yet their features had the unmistakable similarity of siblings or even twins.

The woman slammed her staff into the ground hilt first and locked her gaze on the formation; her brother glanced at his henchmen and raised his saber.

He thrust it forward, and the assassins charged.

There is a myth that soldiers aren't afraid when they charge into battle. It's a lie: the fear is always there, worming through the pits of their stomachs and crawling over their shaking hands. Life or death depends on their ability to kill this fear and let that other beast take over, the one that fought, the one that maimed, the one that turned green boys into killers.

The one that survived.

Two attackers were headed for Jespar, a bull-like man with a two-handed scimitar, and a lanky boy with a curved spear. The kid was ahead of his comrade, probably eager to impress with the kill; going with the sprint, he thrust his weapon at Jespar's unarmored chest.

The beast took over.

In a single motion, Jespar drew his longsword and yanked it up, deflecting the thrust; the momentum sent the Kid staggering forward, but he caught himself, spun his spear back around in an overhead strike; Jespar lunged forward, warded off the attack by raising his sword, then sidestepped and swung at his opponent's neck. The blade cut into his flesh like a hot knife through butter. The boy wheezed once, then collapsed. Jespar was still pulling his weapon from the Kid's corpse when steel flashed in his periphery; he spun around and jerked up his sword, catching a massive strike from the bull-like man a finger-length from his nose. Shock jolted through his arms, pulsed into his legs; he staggered back, muscles burning and knees buckling; the Bull kept pushing into the parry, trying to break it with brute force. *Too strong. Too fucking strong.* The Bull growled, took one hand off his saber's hilt, and slammed its heel into Jespar's chin. Stars exploded. The next moment, Jespar was on the ground, the Bull on top, choking him. Jespar grunted and struggled and kicked, but it was pointless; the man was just too heavy.

"Fucking leech," the Bull hissed. "Fucking *leech!*"

Dagger, Jespar managed to think through the panic. *Dagger!* Stifling his survival instinct to force the Bull's hands from his neck, Jespar let go and reached for the sheath at his own belt, but the Bull saw through his plan and pinned Jespar's wrist with his knee; Jespar croaked, his sight going darker and darker as the air went from his lungs.

Air.

The Bull's grip had slackened.

Jespar didn't think. Gasping, he struggled free and shoved the man off to the side, drew his dagger, and blindly stabbed it at his opponent's head. It sank deep into his temple. Jespar twisted the blade, pushed in deeper, yanked it back out and shoved it in again. Then he sprang to his feet, throat burning, ready for the next enemy.

Only when Jespar realized none were coming did he grow aware of the spear that stuck out from the Bull's back. A man stood a stride off, bloody hands locked around the pole—one of the carriers. Their eyes locked for a long and strange second, then the man dropped the spear and dashed for the nearest alley. Jespar hastily sheathed his dagger, scooped up his blood-splattered longsword, and oriented himself.

The attackers were pummeling the formation with blows, swords clashing into shields; the guards were holding their ground, but it was clear it wouldn't be for much longer.

The dimensionist.

His gaze darted across the square. The Aetäerna woman was still in the mouth of the alley, focused on Maadira. The air had already begun to wrap around the sergeant. Not much longer, and the shift would strike, and Maadira would suffer the same fate as her comrade.

Jespar glanced at the alley down which the carrier had fled. The path was clear, just a stone's throw between Jespar and safety. A tickle traveled up his ankles, cold spread around his neck. Maadira's movements were slowing, and she teetered, like a drunk struggling to keep balance.

Godsfuckingdammit.

Sword raised, Jespar sprinted at the dimensionist. It wasn't until he had almost reached her that he realized she'd been aware of him all along.

She tossed him a sideways glance.

And something hit him.

It was as though someone had gripped his lungs and squeezed them shut; tears shot into his eyes, he struggled for breath, but air wouldn't come. A croak escaped his throat, and he dropped to his knees, the sword clattering off the flagstone.

The world went dark.

———✥———

Jespar awoke to the face of a woman. She was pretty—dainty features with red lips and a button nose, curly, black hair flowing from beneath a violet headcloth that matched the color of her robe. One hand rested on Jespar's forehead, the other on his collarbone. If this was the Beyond, he thought, he was a happy man.

The woman slapped him hard. He jolted up with an unmanly shriek.

"Oh," she said, her gaze sliding to meet his. "You're awake."

Jespar's first attempt at an answer came out as a croak; his throat felt like he'd swallowed fire. "Yeah," he managed. "I am."

"That's odd, the spell should have knocked you out for at least a day. How are you feeling?"

Spell, Jespar thought—the Order-approved term for shifts, a word that often came in the company of others like "witchcraft", "magic", and "wizardry", and that people initiated into the workings of dimensionism were supposed to fall back on when talking to the common folk, the Uninitiated. It made sense for the physician to use it: she had no way of knowing that Jespar, as the heir of a noble Endralean family, had received a formal education. Either that, or she was a low-level physician, who often had no in-depth knowledge of dimensionism themselves.

Opting to take the safe route, Jespar played along. "Woozy. Did you just say I got struck by a spell? As in magic?"

"Necromancy, yes." The woman rose to her feet, offering Jespar a hand up. He took it. "That Aetäerna tried to rot your lungs, but she didn't get far. You got lucky, outlander. Luckier than most."

Muttering some answer, Jespar peered over her shoulder.

People crowded the square. Most of them were Blue Guards, but there were also civilians and a handful of people dressed in the same violet headcloth and robes of the woman who'd woken him—physicians, Jespar guessed. Corpses lay scattered around the litter; the pavement was covered with blood. Mounted torches soaked the scene in amber light and drew warping shadows on the flagstone.

The chill in his stomach was already there, but it was a glance at the dead assassin kid behind him that set off the flashback. How he lay there on the bloody stone, one hand limply on his half-severed neck, his glassy eyes wide open as if staring at some alien horror descending from the sky.

The man with the breadbasket had looked similar.

Calm down. It's not your fault.

Calm down!

Pointless. The phantom noose was already inching tighter, his guts curling into a ball, and there it was, the tang of burnt timber and charred flesh, and the screams, and the Girl, Gods, the Girl, her father, Na—

Something flashed in his periphery, a Loon, coming for him; whirling around, Jespar reached for his sword, ready to slice that fucker open and-

"Ma'sao?"

There was no Loon. It was the physician who'd woken him, and the shiny thing in her hand wasn't a knife but a magnifying glass reflecting the torchlight. "Ma'sao, are you okay?"

Jespar stared.

Calm down. Not your fault. This isn't Nehrim.

Calm down.

The sensations faded and his pulse slowed back to normal.

"Yeah. Yeah, I'm all right, it's just ... sorry. I'm a little rattled."

The physician gave him a skeptical look. Then she shrugged. "That's understandable. You should go see Ma'sao Enkshi, though, he'll want to talk to you. Can you walk?"

"Yeah, I'll go find him."

"Good. May you prosper."

"You too."

The woman brought her index and middle finger to her chest, the Kilayan nod. Then she joined another physician who was treating a guard a little way over.

Massaging his temples, Jespar looked across the plaza once more. The noose and the fear didn't return, and neither did the smell. Instead, a dull melancholy settled inside him, mixed with a peculiar sense of exhilaration. He knew the feeling—it always came after a fight, one part of his brain celebrating the victory while the other struggled to come to terms with the fact that he'd ended another life. When he had discussed this emotion with Naka what felt like a lifetime ago, Naka had assured him he'd harden in time. Jespar never had.

Naka.

There they were again, his name and his face, floating across Jespar's mind. Why? All these years, he had rarely ever thought of him, the occasional nightmare excluded.

Just like you didn't think about her.

Jespar smothered the thought and went on. He found the counselor sitting on a bench at the backside of a villa; his robes were stained with dust and blood, and there was a cut on his forehead. He was talking to Sergeant Maadira and another officer who looked like the theater version of a Kilayan military man: slicked-back silver hair and a ring-adorned beard with a sweeping handlebar mustache, spotless white trousers, decorated indigo coat, and shin-high boots of the same color.

His lip curled when Jespar approached. "No onlookers this close to the scene, ma'sao. Please leave."

"He isn't an onlooker," Enkshi said. "How are you, Dal'Varek? The physician said you were struck by a shift?"

Seeing Jespar hesitate, Enkshi snorted. "Don't worry, we're all Initiated, and I know you are too. How are you?"

Thinking of the aged guard and how closely he had probably escaped a similar fate, Jespar's throat tightened. "Fine, I guess. The shift didn't get through."

"Good," Enkshi said. He sounded relieved, but not necessarily empathetic—more like a craftsman who'd just been reassured his new tool hadn't given up yet. "This is Arik Daato, Major General of the Blue Guard. Daato, this is Jespar Dal'Varek, the mercenary I told you about."

"Oh, I see." Daato offered his hand. "Pleased to meet you, in that case."

Arik, Jespar thought as they shook. As far as first names went, it didn't get more Endralean than that. "Are you...?"

"From Enderal? I'm afraid not, but my maternal grandfather was. They say you're quite the hero, Ma'sao Dal'Varek."

"News to me. I was out for most of the fight."

"Don't sell yourself short, Dal'Varek," Maadira said. "If you hadn't dealt with that other marksman, we wouldn't have held out half as long. Incredible throw, by the way."

"Thanks. What happened? How did we win?"

"A patrol," Enkshi replied. "They got here at the last minute. The twins made a run for it, though, together with some of the others."

"Twins," Jespar echoed. "So, you know those guys?"

General Daato snorted. "You bet we do. They are insurgents, 'Scythes', as they call themselves."

"Let's just call them what they are," Enkshi said. "Terrorists. Those two Aetäerna who coordinated the attack are their leaders. Cara and Vyrias Zaevathal, the Pale Twins."

"They know how to fight, that's for sure."

"Naturally," Daato said. "Vyrias Zaevathal is one of the best swordsmen the Archipelago has ever seen, and his sister is the equivalent in necromancy. They used to serve in the Jade Snakes."

Jade Snakes. The name rang a bell. "That's the elite unit of the Blue Guard, isn't it?"

Daato nodded. Jespar considered asking how a necromancer dimensionist in the army meshed with the Order's laws against the Profane Sights, then decided against it. No point in ruffling sharp feathers.

"The two were their poster children, actually," Daato went on. "At least until the man, Vyrias, decided to bludgeon two comrades to death when they told him during a drinking night that his 'witch sister' creeped them out."

"Surely that convinced them of the opposite," Jespar said.

Daato smiled wanly. "Surely. That whole incident took place about six years ago, and both of them deserted and took to mercenary work overseas afterward. Last Rain, they decided to return to the Archipelago and began to rile up the commoners with their nonsense ideas."

"Which are?"

"The usual have-not garbage, of course," Enkshi said. "'I'm coinless and the world is to blame,' 'the Coalition is greedy and evil,' and 'the working man should run the country.' The Archipelago has had its fair share of them over the centuries, always the same rubbish, but with a different flavor. We'll deal with them."

And just who exactly, are "we"? He had pondered over this a lot during his long journey on the ship, but with little to go on, all Jespar had been able to conjecture was that his employer was wealthy and influential. Hardly ace detective work.

Enkshi touched a ring on his finger, the simple copper loop that stood out against its glittering neighbors. "Either way, we've lost too much time already. Let's be on our way." He turned to Daato. "See that the wounded guards get the best physicians, and the fallen ones a worthy burial. The bereaved each get three years of their loved one's pay."

Daato raised an eyebrow. "Three years?"

"My master will cover the expenses. Also, search the bodies of the attackers and see if you can track down their relatives and close friends. When you do, lock them up."

"And question them?"

"Yes. If we find out where the Scythes recruits their footmen, that might eventually lead us to their nests. Oh, and General?"

"Counselor?"

"Gut their corpses and hang them from the city walls. I want everyone to know what happens to enemies of the Coalition."

Horses replaced the litter, a pair of new throwing knives Jespar's lost ones, and a new unit the fallen soldiers. Not much later, the escort resumed their journey under a star-speckled sky. Maadira and Enkshi were silent, and Jespar didn't mind. He welcomed the break to think.

Quit, a voice urged. *Whatever the offer, this is way above your pay-grade.*

And wind up coinless in the most expensive country in the Illumined World? Great idea, idiot.

Better coinless than dead. Quit.

Frowning, Jespar scratched his rash. His cautious half was right, of course. He was a drifting veteran whose biggest skill was walking a straight line after downing five mugs of ale; he had zero business being here, as Enkshi hadn't tired of pointing out. Not to mention his odd mental state: the nightmares that kept getting worse, his thoughts returning to Naka, and that flashback a few hours ago. It was almost as if something deep down in his mind had been set into motion, a current swirling up sand at the bottom of a river.

Why, though?

Jespar had done plenty of soul-searching during his drifting years; he had asked himself questions, found answers, and drawn conclusions, and he had no interest whatsoever in opening that can of worms again. Yet here he was, unwilling to leave.

The current kept pushing him forward.

The further up the mountain they rode, the more the city's noises gave way to those of nocturnal animals and insects. Patches of jungle broke up the manors, growing wider and wider until the Jade District was a sequence of sequestered villas in the rainforest, white islands in an ocean of green, Fortune Road their isthmus. Only on the rare occasions when the canopy thinned out, allowing Jespar a glance down the mountain, did he remember that he was still in the same city that housed the dirty, overcrowded streets he had slogged through that very morning. The same city that had already almost killed him.

The moon was up high when they passed the lowest of the seven ziggurats, proving a hunch Jespar had had for a while: his employer was one of the magnates. The Seventh Ziggurat was even more impressive up close, a vast palace enthroned on a precipice jutting out the mountain; three adjacent square pyramids made up the main buildings, the middle one at least seven tiers high, about the height of two towers. Enkshi rode past the cobblestone road leading up to the gate without a second glance. It went on like this: every time they went past the next ziggurat, Jespar expected Maadira or Enkshi to give a signal, and every time, they didn't. On and on they rode, following Fortune Road's never-ending twists and turns, the sounds of the jungle and the clopping of their horses' hooves their only company. After the escort had passed the Second Ziggurat, they came to a clearing that revealed a stunning view of Mount Ilakato's final slope. A palace so colossal it was like a city unto itself sat enthroned upon the peak, perfect white against a pool of dark blue night.

The First Ziggurat.

"Ma'sao Dal'Varek?" Maadira asked.

"Yeah. Yeah, I'm coming."

They reached the top of the mountain half an hour later. A sweeping meadow lay before them, backdropped by walls so high they obscured most of the palace they shielded; the final stretch of Fortune Road cut straight through the swaying grass, ending in a colossal gate embossed with the snake-and-scimitars symbol of the Coalition.

Reaching the portcullis, Maadira cupped her hands around her mouth. "Open!"

A man appeared atop the zigzag parapet and examined the arrivals. He shouted something over his shoulder. Feet shuffled, cranks groaned, chains rattled. The portcullis rose, and the embossed cobra's head split in two as the double-wing door parted.

From the smallest villas of the Jade District to the ziggurats, every structure, every road, and every garden had been a contender in a race for extravagance—even the size and splendor of the lowest of the ziggurats were so detached from the reality Jespar knew that all he could do was absorb his surroundings with the numbed awe of a beggar traversing the halls of Inodân. By the time they had reached the walls of the First Ziggurat, he had thought he had seen it all.

He should have known better.

A titanic pyramid rose at the end of a palm-lined avenue, like a small man-made mountain. Colonnades and gardens framed its dozen tapering tiers, strips of lapis lazuli and gold tiles accentuating the white stone; the statue of a bearded, long-haired man with a horned crown graced its apex, arms raised like a god basking in prayer.

"Welcome to the home of His Excellency Jaaros Ismirael Oonai," Enkshi said. "First Magnate of the Blue Islands Coalition, and your employer."

CHAPTER THREE
UUNILI'S SLUMBER

ilence reigned in the atrium. It was of a strange sort: not comfortable like that between two friends, not dreamy like that in an opium den, not eerie like the hush on a graveyard. This silence was so complete that it felt both sacral and unnerving, as if Jespar was in the domain of a god and awaited his judgment.

It must have been a little over an hour since Enkshi had left him here with the statuesque ziggurat guards, and having finished his short story collection, Jespar had run out of things to do. For the tenth time, he took stock of his surroundings, studying the massive columns, the blue and gold carpet bisecting it, and the sculpture of Moraia that towered over the high dais at the hall's end. It was almost as tall as the one of Oonai's on the ziggurat apex, that testament to humility.

Sighing, Jespar scratched his rash. Even the bath the ziggurat servants had poured and the fresh linen clothes they had given him to make him "presentable" made no difference—if anything, the itch had gotten worse. He'd have to see an apothecary about this. *No more brothels*, he resolved, with all the conviction of a drunk declaring his final, "this-time-for-real!" goodbye to the bottle.

Just when Jespar had decided to go for another round of pacing, Counselor Enkshi emerged from a hallway near the statue, his dirty robe swapped for a fresh, crimson one that matched the new kohl he had put on. As he approached Jespar, the atrium doors opened, and a bearded older man stepped in. He was a curious sight: slicked-back white hair and a pressed gray coat with matching trousers contrasted with weather-beaten skin and the patch over his scarred right eye. Despite these striking features, his face had something oddly forgettable about it—like a name so foreign it slips from your mind the moment it's mentioned.

They met at the portal, where the old man bowed to the counselor. "Ma'sao Enkshi. May you prosper."

"Same to you, Agaam," Enkshi replied with a smile. "How have you been?"

"As well as can be expected under the circumstances, ma'sao, thank you." He turned to Jespar. "Ma'sao Dal'Varek, I presume?"

"Yes."

He bowed again. "Then I'm honored to meet you. I am Ma'sao Agaam, personal servant of Ma'sao and Ma'saa Oonai."

For want of a better response, Jespar nodded.

"Is the Ma'saa ready to see us?" Enkshi asked.

"Yes. She's currently in the orchard cottage with the Stone District physician."

"Alone? With a stranger?"

"She insisted."

Enkshi sighed. "Delightful. Well, off we go then."

They went back outside, to the monumental stairs connecting the ziggurat's base to its summit—the atrium hall was on the fourth tier—and began the climb. With every level they crested, Jespar grew more aware of how vast the ziggurat truly was. Even the higher, receded tiers spanned as wide and broad as small arenas, and Jespar could only guess at the number of rooms and hallways within the belly of this massive pyramid. Judging by the moon, it was about two hours to midnight, yet dozens of guards still patrolled the many colonnades, stairs, and battlements. The staff's weekly wages alone must have been more than what Jespar had earned in his year with the Wayfarers. A lot more.

On the eighth tier, Enkshi turned right onto an arcade that ran along its edge and provided a spectacular view of the island. Halfway down its length, they crossed through an archway and entered a garden. If Moraia was still alive, and gardening was one of her pastimes, Jespar imagined it would look like this one: an idyllic grove of palms and hollies splashed with the color of myriad flowers and bushes, nestled in the hooting of owls and the singsong of katydids. A path lit by wayside torches snaked through the grass and ended in a small white pyramid; made from only three tapering blocks and barely ornamented, it lacked the grandeur of its surroundings, but in a pleasant way, like a glass of sweetened water after a hearty feast. Light glowed through the cracks of the curtained window slits.

Agaam reached for the door, but Enkshi held up his hand. "One moment."

The old servant stepped back.

"Two more things before you go in, Dal'Varek," Enkshi said in a low voice. "First, Ma'saa Oonai, whom you're about to meet, doesn't know about the incident that occurred on the journey here, and I'd prefer to keep it that way. It ... wouldn't be beneficial to her current state of mind, if you understand."

Ignorance is bliss. "I think I do, yeah."

"Good. Second, you've convinced me you can carry your weight in a fight, but I still believe there would have been far better candidates for this mission. As I said, though, the Ma'saa insisted it had to be you, which is why I'd like you to ..." He exhaled and ran a hand over his shaved head. "Well, I don't know. Just to try and not be another disappointment, I suppose. Can you promise me that?"

The phantom noose grazed Jespar's neck.

"Dal'Varek? Are you listening?"

"Yes," Jespar said from a dry throat. "I'll do my best."

Small and modestly furnished, the orchard house's interior mirrored the outside. Bookshelves fronted the smooth walls, and brass sconces flickered in the alcoves between them. Only half of them were lit, limning the room in a soothing amber gloom.

A woman sat at the cluttered table that took up most of the space, stroking a chubby alapu on the adjacent chair with one hand while holding a letter with the other. When Agaam, Jespar, and Enkshi ducked their heads under the garland of comet orchids—spirit plants of Tyr and symbols to ward off evil and Corruption—she lifted her gaze.

Jespar's first impression of the Ma'saa was that she reminded him of the old elegiac paintings that framed his mother's memorial shrine: beautiful, melancholic, ever so distant. The Ma'saa wore a sleeveless, wine-purple dress, prayer rings contrasting her dark complexion around her upper arms; loose black hair adorned with delicate gold chains framed a face that probably looked aristocratic on good days but right now struck Jespar as gaunt. He placed her somewhere north of forty.

Not until Agaam had shut the door behind them did Jespar notice there was another woman in the room, standing in a shadowy corner. Trailing her fingers along a bookshelf row, she too glanced at the men, but the twilight obscured her features.

They stood still, Enkshi looking at the Ma'saa as if he expected her to say something. When she only continued to stare at Jespar, he cleared his throat.

"Your Excellency, I bring you Ma'sao Jespar Mitumial Dal'Varek, as requested." He turned to Jespar. "Ma'sao Dal'Varek, this is Her Excellency Ma'saa Nayima Camea Vel'Anelys Oonai, First Dame of Kilay and wife to His Excellency Ma'sao Jaaros Ismirael Oonai, First Magnate of—"

Ma'saa Oonai stood, silencing Enkshi. She crossed to Jespar.

"You're really him," she said. "You're Jespar Dal'Varek."

A statement, not a question. As if she'd encountered an old child-hood friend after a lifetime apart.

"Um ... Yes, Your Excellency."

Ma'saa Oonai closed her eyes and let out a small breath. Then she took Jespar's hands. "Gods be praised, you're here. Gods be praised."

Another pause, infinitely more awkward than the last.

"You are ... acquainted?" ventured Enkshi.

The Ma'saa smiled. "Suffice it to say that I've seen him before."

You have?

"But he only just arrived in Kilay, Ma'saa," Enkshi said. "It's his first time in the Archipelago."

"I'm aware." She let go of Jespar's hands and returned to her chair. A cat darted out from underneath it and took shelter beneath an armoire. "What I mean is that I saw him in a dream."

Jespar had always found the word "flabbergasted" comically hyper-bolic in a real-life context, but Enkshi's expression fit like a glove. Jespar couldn't have looked much different.

Ma'saa Oonai gestured at the woman at the vacant chairs around the table. "Please. Sit."

Enkshi did as she asked. With a wary eye on the woman by the bookshelf, Jespar chose a chair that backed up to a wall.

"Some tea, perhaps?" Ma'saa Oonai asked him, nodding at a ceramic pot between them.

"Um, yes, Your Excellency," Jespar said. "Thank you."

"Please, just Nayima will do. It was the Gods who have brought us together tonight, so there is no need for titles." She reached for the pot and poured Jespar, Enkshi, and herself a cup, a process the counselor observed with a deep frown. Even in a cosmopolitan country, Jespar figured, the First Dame of Kilay offering first-name basis to a vagrant and then serving him tea was probably as close to protocol sacrilege as it got.

Ma'saa Oonai addressed the woman by the bookshelf. "What about you, Ma'saa Varroy? Zarah?"

"I'm fine." The woman's voice was smooth but husky, like fine leather coarsened by long wear. "Thanks."

"Very well. Jespar, this is Ma'saa Zarah Varroy, a healer who is here for the same reason as you."

Healer? Jespar nodded at the woman. "Jespar Dal'Varek. Pleasure to meet you."

"Likewise," Varroy said.

The Ma'saa indicated at Jespar's cut. "Please. Try."

Hesitating, Jespar drank. The tea was a symphony of flavor: hot, bitter, sharp, and lemony at the same time. A world away from the brew he'd had in Southport this morning, and most likely a lot more expensive.

"I could have our chefs prepare a proper meal if you'd like," the Ma'saa said with a maternal smile. "We had a wonderful dinner tonight—swordfish and steamed clams with a lovely mango-lemon relish. I'm sure they can make another portion."

"I'm quite full, ma'saa, but thank you very much." He wasn't, but the still-fresh memory of the fight dampened his appetite, and something about eating in front of this elegant woman made him feel strangely ashamed. It had been almost a decade since he'd last dined in a formal setting, and he barely remembered the etiquette.

"Ah, I see. Well, perhaps another time."

Enkshi cleared his throat. "Your Excellency, you were about to explain what you meant by 'I saw him in a dream.'"

"I told you, Zagash, no titles tonight. But you're right, I've been stalling." She lifted the alapu onto her lap and stroked him behind his floppy ears. He grunted and momentarily opened his eyes, then fell back into his slumber.

"Three moons ago, before all this chaos, I fell asleep during my evening prayers," Ma'saa Oonai said. "This has never happened to me before, and it hasn't happened since. What's even stranger, it all happened in the blink of an eye, no dozing off, nothing. One moment, I was there in the chapel, on my knees praying. The next, I was gone."

"And ... then you dreamed of Ma'sao Dal'Varek?" Enkshi asked. He spoke like an emissary afraid to offend but could not keep the confusion out of his voice.

"I had a dream, yes, but it wasn't a normal one. Do you know those where you suddenly become aware that you are dreaming and can control what happens? It was like that."

"A lucid dream," Jespar said. He'd had that experience several times, that sudden clarity, though unfortunately never during a nightmare.

"That's what the scholars call them, yes. It's really hard to describe to someone who has never felt it, but it was incredible. I *knew* I was dreaming and that my body was asleep in the chapel, and it all felt so incredibly vivid, to the point where I wondered if I had somehow ended up in a different world." Her gaze dropped to her alapu, and she stopped petting him. Using her other hand, she gently parted the fur of his chubby neck fold and plucked something from the crease, a withered orchid leaf. She carefully placed it on the table. "Anyway. The dream started with me lying in bed in our sleeping chamber, but I was alone. And someone was screaming in the distance."

"Jaaros?" Enkshi asked.

"I believe it was him, yes, but something about his voice sounded very odd. It was ... muffled like it was coming from the bottom of a lake. I know it's a strange comparison, but that's exactly what I thought at that moment, I still remember. And I also knew something terrible was happening to him, and that I had to help him, so I got up and tried to find him. It was pointless, though. The entire ziggurat was deserted, and no matter where I went, the screams got neither louder nor softer. It was driving me crazy ... I felt as though I was watching someone who means the world to me walk toward an abyss, but I was completely and utterly powerless to stop him."

Jespar, who knew the feeling all too well from the nightmares involving his sister, felt his fingers dig into the armrest. He forced his hands to relax. "Why didn't you wake yourself up? In the lucid dreams that I've had, I could do that whenever I wanted."

"Yes, the scholars I talked to afterward said you're supposed to have that ability, but I tried, and it didn't work. That was horrifying, as you can imagine. There I was, running through these deserted hallways chasing after my husband's voice, but I could neither find him nor wake up." She let out a small sigh. The alapu grunted as though sympathizing. "It went on for what felt like an eternity. And then, just when I thought I was losing my mind, something happened: I was going down another corridor, and a figure appeared at the end."

The woman at the bookshelf stepped into the light. She was pretty, around Jespar's age, with ponytailed, chestnut hair and a tanned but naturally light complexion that marked her as an outlander. A root-shaped scar ran down her left cheek and vanished behind the collar of a brown cotton jacket. "And that figure was Ma'sao Dal'Varek?"

"It was wearing a mourning mask that covered all but the eyes, so I couldn't tell, but for some reason, it did feel extremely familiar."

"What did it do?" Enkshi asked.

"Nothing. It just stood there and looked at me, and when I finally mustered the courage to call out to it, the dream collapsed, and I was back in the chapel. Now, don't get me wrong, my initial reaction was to brush this whole experience off as just some odd nightmare, but then the incident with Jaaros happened, and for some reason, my mind kept returning to that dream, and I started noticing all these odd coincidences. Like that underlying sense of *significance* I'd had throughout it all, how it had happened to me during prayer, and, of course, the parallels between what I'd seen in the dream and Jaaros' condition." Her gaze lifted to Jespar. "Then, one day, it struck me: the reason that figure had seemed so familiar was the eyes. I had seen those eyes before, in the man who once saved my life."

What? "Are you ... talking about me, Ma'saa?"

"No. About your father."

Jespar was dumbstruck.

"Your father, Damean Dal'Varek, once saved my life. Zagash, you remember what happened the year before I met Jaaros, don't you?"

"Of course I do," Enkshi said. "The marriage."

"What marriage?" the young woman—*Varroy, that's her name*—asked.

"One that thankfully never took place," the Ma'saa replied. "You see, thirty-two years ago, there were some deep tensions between Kilay and Enderal, mostly related to how the Coalition had increasingly emancipated itself from the Order of Light after the Silence. I come from a highly respected Kilayan family, so the magnates decided to marry me off to an Endralean nobleman, to calm the waves."

Varroy cocked a brow. "They can do that?"

"My parents agreed, so, yes, unfortunately, they could. And remember, those were different times. Dal'Bonu, that was the man's name ... Tyr forgive me for passing judgment, but he was a cruel and corrupted soul, and when I saw him at the bride show, I felt sick to my stomach." She fished a green fruit with a rind like reptile scales from the platter and turned it in her fingers. "But to make a long story short, a moon before the marriage, your father, one of Ark's seven high justices, appealed to the Order of Light to cancel it. He investigated Dal'Bonu and discovered that he had bludgeoned his previous wife to death and argued that the political consequences would be disastrous if something like that were to happen to me. Instead, he proposed the United Seas Trade Agreement, as a symbol of reconciliation between our countries."

Enkshi gave Jespar a surprised look. "Wait. That was *your* father? The judge who saved the Ma'saa?"

"... I suppose."

"It was," Ma'saa Oonai said. "Damean Esthal Dal'Varek, High Justice of Ark. As you can guess, the Order accepted his proposition, and I was allowed to sail back home, where I met Jaaros just a few weeks later. I owe your father a lot, Jespar, if not everything, and I was devastated when I learned what happened to him and your brothers. I sent your foster family a letter with my condolences, but you must have been quite young back then, so I doubt you'd remember. Let me say it again, in person: I am terribly sorry for what happened. And I hope the monsters responsible for it were brought to justice."

His head still wrestling with the unexpected turn this conversation had taken, Jespar only managed a grunt.

Enkshi licked his lips. "So, just to be clear: you had a dream where you saw a masked figure whose eyes resembled those of Damean Dal'Varek, and that made you, what, surmise that that figure was his surviving son?"

"Yes."

"How do you know it wasn't Damean Dal'Varek himself?"

"I just did. Trust me, I know how bizarre all this sounds, and, frankly, I wasn't certain until I saw you, Jespar, in person. But I am now. Those were your eyes back in that dream, yours and no one else's."

What the hell?

What. The. Hell?

Enkshi worked his mouth, but no words came out. He started over. "I'm sorry, Nayima, but that … I'm not even sure what to say."

The Ma'saa smiled ever so slightly. "*The Apotheosis* 7, Verse 107. Do you remember it?"

"Why?"

"Do you remember it?"

Enkshi settled back in his chair, fingers laced across his stomach. "Not verbatim, no."

Ma'saa Oonai touched her prayer rings with her left hand. "'And verily they spake unto us: blessed are ye who are kind and humble, for yours shall be our love and shelter.' Now look around you, Zagash. Would you call this humility?"

"I'd call it the fruits of hard labor."

"And it is," Ma'saa Oonai said. "Jaaros earned this through sweat and diligence, the way Moraia earned her apotheosis. But all the money and all the power … it made him forget that it was the Gods' benevolence and generosity that made our fortune possible in the first place."

"Is that so?"

"You may disagree, but, yes, it is. Jespar's father's intervention in my marriage, you and Jaaros meeting at just the right time, the golden harvest right after he bought the plantation ... The list goes on. Now, I know what you're about to say: it's all a matter of seizing chances and playing it right, and I'm not arguing that there is truth in that. Jaaros did play well, and he deserves the prize he's won, but only a fool would deny that he, just like us, has been dealt excellent hands. Think about it: just one misfortune, and everything could have been different. Gods, if that beggar had only been a little bit faster, I wouldn't be alive anymore."

A line etched between Enkshi's brows.

"Jaaros has forgotten this," Ma'saa Oonai went on. "His ambition and constant fear of someone taking away his livelihood, they've made him forget his place in the world. And that's exactly what the Corruption is, isn't it? The voices in our head that constantly try to lead us away from virtue." She trailed her fingers along the rim of her golden goblet as if memorizing the texture. "Jaaros has allowed the Corruption into his heart, Zagash ... it's time to finally admit that. He has lost his way, and that is why the Gods have let all this happen. It's a trial to remind us that, for all our riches and all our power, we are still human."

Enkshi's answer took a long time coming. "And Jespar Mitumial Dal'Varek, a drifting mercenary, is our deliverance. Is that what you're saying?"

Ma'saa Oonai put down the goblet. "Not our deliverance, but our beacon that will guide us toward it. And this dream was a vision Moraia sent me to tell us so."

All was silent except for the crackling of the torches in their sconces.

"I understand," Enkshi said at last.

The Ma'saa's smile was wan. "No, Zagash, you don't. But try to see it this way: even if I were wrong about everything I just said, Jespar and Zarah would still be good candidates for our plan, so it makes no difference. I just told you because you deserved to know." She looked first at Varroy, then at Jespar. "Either way, it's about time I tell you why you're here: five weeks ago, my husband fell into an inexplicable coma. And he will not wake up."

The wind carried a chill through the unglazed windows of the vestibule. They were on the second-highest tier of the ziggurat, and the Oonais' sleeping chambers lay before them, cloaked in darkness.

"Light," the Ma'saa said.

Ma'sao Agaam disappeared into the room. A torch lit up.

The place had no warmth.

It wasn't for lack of beauty: oil paintings adorned the walls, gold lined the cornices, and a frieze depicting a man on a black myrad embellished the stone wainscoting. Windows framed a canopy bed at the other end of the room, the shutters closed, and elegant but nondescript furniture filled the spaces between. And yet, the beauty had an anonymous touch to it, as if placed there to impress visitors, rather than make the owner feel at home.

Beckoning them to follow, the Ma'saa entered. Not until they had crossed half the room did Jespar notice the man that lay in the sea of blankets on the bed.

"His Excellency Jaaros Ismirael Oonai," Enkshi said quietly as they came to a halt beside him. "First Magnate of Kilay."

Jespar knew power and influence didn't necessarily show in a person's appearance, but for this man, they did. Jaaros Oonai's face was clear-cut, with a broad forehead, a pronounced nose, and two vaguely almond-shaped eyes, his hair a black mane down to his shoulders paired with a ring-plaited, magnificent beard. Upright, he must have stood well over three strides, a head taller even than Jespar. *Jaaros Ismirael Oonai.* Jespar didn't know the man, yet he immediately imagined him on some podium, wearing the seven-horned crown that rested on his nightstand, giving a speech that inspired his admirers, intimidated his enemies, and swayed the undecided.

Had Jespar not already known something was wrong with Oonai, he would have noticed it now. While he had seemed merely asleep from a distance, unsettling details became evident up close: how still he lay, corpselike if not for the shallow rise and fall of his chest. How gaunt he was, his pale skin stretching tight over his skull. How the air smelled of herbs, sweat, and sickness.

Ma'saa Oonai eased down on the edge of the bed, took her husband's hand, and kissed it. When she looked up at Jespar and Varroy, she seemed to have aged. "The coma started around Drought Five," she said. "But we believe the affliction that caused it developed far earlier, around the end of Drought Three and the start of Drought Four."

Jespar scratched his beard. "Illumined Calendar?"

"Moneth Seven or Nine, so eleven weeks ago," Varroy said, thumb tracing her scar. Like her voice, her hands were a contrast—slender and graceful but deeply tanned and dotted with nicks and little scabs, the nails neat and short. "This affliction, how did it show?"

"He changed," the Ma'saa said. "You see, Jaaros was always famed for his presence. When he laughed, people couldn't help but laugh with him, when he was angry, no one dared to speak, and when he gave speeches, everyone listened as though he'd struck some spell on them. There was just so much ... life in him, a raw vitality that stopped at nothing. Three moons ago, all that energy drained out of him. At first, he only became a little distant and wanted more time to himself, but eventually, he shut himself off entirely and would spend hours just lying in bed. Whenever we'd ask him what was wrong, he'd get angry and brush us off."

An image formed in Jespar's mind: young Jespar in a sun-soaked hallway, standing in front of a locked door. *Knock, knock, knock.* No answer.

He shook off the thought. "Sounds an awful lot like melancholia to me."

"I was about to say the same thing," Varroy said.

"Yes, that was our first thought too," Enkshi said. "But there's a lot more to the story. Hear the Ma'saa out first."

Varroy propped a boot up against the frieze. "Sure."

The Ma'saa nodded. "Over the next few weeks, Jaaros' state of mind continued to get worse. He became moodier and more withdrawn, until, about three weeks into Drought Four, things escalated completely when he called in an emergency conference at the Coalition: he wanted to revoke the Golden Soil Decree."

Recalling his chat with the guard at the jungle pool, Jespar arched his brows. *Interesting.*

"Wait a minute," Varroy said. "Jaaros Oonai wanted to revoke the Golden Soil Decree? Wasn't the decree *his* idea?"

"You're correct, he had fought to get it ratified for the better part of a year," Ma'saa Oonai said. "Which is exactly why it made so little sense."

Varroy snorted. "Perhaps your husband grew a conscience after all."

"Careful," Enkshi said, a vein pulsing at his temple.

"Or else?"

The Ma'saa raised her hands. "Please. I know the decree must be an emotional topic for you, Zarah, but can we put politics aside for tonight?

Varroy dueled with Enkshi's glare for another second. Then she shrugged. "Of course."

"Thank you. As you can imagine, his appeal was turned down unanimously. I won't lie, the entire thing was a disgrace, and that's putting it mildly. Jaaros just barged into the conclave hall unwashed and unprepared and began shouting like a madman. He was like a different person." The Ma'saa regarded her husband as though pondering her words. "After that, it all went downhill fast. Jaaros locked himself into his room for days and barely ate or drank, to the point where we all feared for his life. The one time we tried to enter by force, he threatened to have the man who broke the lock executed. It was as if ... I don't know. As if the soul of the man I had married had disappeared and some mad spirit had replaced him. I still don't—" The Ma'saa sighed deeply. Tears pooled on her lower lids, turning black from her kohl. She brushed them off and sat up once again. "Oh, my, I believe we could do with a refreshment, couldn't we?" She gave Jespar and Varroy an effortful smile. "Water or wine?"

"Water," said Varroy.

"Wine," said Jespar.

When Ma'saa Oonai gestured at the door, Jespar was briefly confused. Then he remembered that the old servant, Ma'sao Agaam, was still standing in the shadow beside the doorway. Jespar had utterly forgotten about him. Agaam nodded and left.

"Zagash," the Ma'saa said. "Would you mind telling the rest?"

"Of course. Ten days after that conference, Jaaros—Master Oonai, I mean—fell into a coma. What's truly strange is that he actually seemed to be getting better the day before it happened. He even took the Ma'saa for a walk in the orchard and told her of his plans for the coming weeks. Then he went to bed and didn't wake up the next morning."

A chill crawled up Jespar's arms. "Just like that?"

"Just like that, and he's been this way ever since. By now, just about every reputable physician or dimensionist in the Archipelago has taken a look at him, and none of them have an explanation for what's causing this."

"Not even a theory?" Varroy asked.

"None that can hold its ground, no. There are two known brain diseases that can induce personality changes or even comas, but just like melancholia, they don't manifest that abruptly. As for dimensionism—don't worry, Ma'saa, Dal'Varek is Initiated—there are reports of psychomantic shifts that target a victim's sanity or can put them to sleep, but they are incredibly rare and ineffective because they are channelings."

Jespar dusted off the memories of his childhood shifting lessons. "Shifts that are maintained over a long time, right?"

"Yes," Varroy said. "But keeping a psychomantic shift channeled over moons would cause drain enough to kill a myrad. That's practically impossible."

"Exactly. Still, we've had his aura examined just to be sure, and there aren't any signs of an ongoing shift whatsoever. So, unless there's a psychomancer out there who can permanently alter someone's brain structure with a single shift, we can rule out dimensionism."

"In other words, it must be an unknown disease or a Sight that no one has ever heard of," Varroy said.

"Precisely," Ma'saa Oonai said, rejoining the conversation with renewed strength. "Now, there are two more things, but they only make this more perplexing. One, considering we couldn't feed him anything more than sugared water since the coma, his body should show signs of starvation by now, but he doesn't. He has lost a few pounds, but that's it."

Varroy blinked. "Okay, that's odd."

"Not even half as odd as the other thing." Gingerly, the Ma'saa opened the lids of Oonai's right eye with thumb and forefinger. "Look."

The hell?

Milky-blue slime covered Oonai's eye, translucent swirls of vapor dancing on from his iris.

"Feel his forehead," Ma'saa Oonai told Varroy.

Varroy did. "Stars burn me."

"What is it?" Jespar asked.

"He's cold as ice."

The Ma'saa withdrew her hand. "We noticed this slime and the drop in his body temperature about the same time we realized he wasn't losing weight. First, it was just a little chill, but it grew steadily cooler. The physicians are worried his organs will stop functioning if it keeps going like that."

"Huh." Varroy placed index and middle finger on the First Magnate's neck, just below his jaw. Her frown deepened. "He barely has a pulse too. Bloody hell, this ... this doesn't make any sense."

Jespar scratched his back. "In summary, this illness, or whatever it is, is keeping him alive *and* killing him at the same time?"

"It seems to be." The Ma'saa brushed a strand of hair from her husband's forehead. "I've told you I believe this is a trial that we can overcome, and I *do*, but there are moments where I wonder if this isn't just wishful thinking, if, maybe, Jaaros' trial was long ago, and this affliction is his punishment for failing it. A supernatural curse cast upon him by the Gods themselves."

"There is no 'supernatural'," Varroy said. "Only 'preternatural', things we haven't understood yet. Whatever has happened to your husband, there's a scientific explanation for it."

Ma'saa Oonai smiled wanly. "I disagree with the first part, but in this case, I pray that you're right. Either way, we are running out of time—the physicians think he has about one more week until his body stops functioning, two if we're lucky. And we still know absolutely nothing."

They were quiet for a minute, the shadows from the flickering torches ebbing and flowing around them like tired waves. Jespar was about to say something simply to break the silence, but then Agaam returned with a tray of goblets and delivered the drinks. As though the interlude had broken a spell, Varroy began to ask Enkshi and the Ma'saa medical questions; Jespar hardly listened, just as he hardly tasted the wine.

What are you doing here?

Prescient dreams, divine trials, inexplicable comas—the way he had survived three years of vagrancy in a war-torn country was by staying out of trouble, and this job was to trouble what oil was to fire. But, as much as a part of him wanted to walk out of this room right now, another kept him right here, itching to get to the bottom of this, as though the gaunt man lying in that bed was more than just a stranger.

The current kept pulling him forward.

Glancing up, he noticed Varroy had finished her questioning and was now studying him; she leaned against the windowsill left of the bed, holding her goblet in both hands. When their eyes met, the corner of her mouth tugged upward. Jespar smiled back. *Very* pretty, Jespar corrected his earlier assessment. And oddly intriguing at that.

Zarah Varroy. Who are you?

Varroy downed her water and put the goblet on the windowsill. "Fair enough, let me summarize: three moons ago, your husband's personality inexplicably began to change. His mental state continued to decline until, last moon, he fell into a coma that simultaneously keeps him alive and turns his organs into ice. Sound about right?"

"Yes," Ma'saa Oonai said.

"Okay, then what's our role in this?" Varroy nodded at Jespar. "I don't know about him, but I'm pretty sure I can't tell you anything your upper-echelon physicians and dimensionists haven't already. So, if you're counting on us to heal him..."

"They aren't expecting us to heal him," Jespar said. "At least not by conventional means. You have some kind of plan, and we're supposed to carry it out, right?"

Ma'saa Oonai sipped her wine. "You're right. In short, we think the only way to understand this condition and heal my husband is to find out who did this to him."

"You believe it's an assassination attempt then," Jespar said.

"Well, it *could* be coincidence or a divine punishment as I've said but considering jealous rivals have plotted to kill my husband for decades, an assassination attempt is the most realistic scenario, yes. And it better be, because otherwise, we're powerless." Her fingers clenched around her goblet. "Politically or personally motivated, someone out there wants my husband to die slowly and painfully. You're here because we want you to find out who that someone is, what it is they did to him, and how to reverse it."

Varroy squinted. "Why just the two of us, though? You want Dal'Varek because of that dream, I get that, but why not bring in the Blue Guard as well? I mean, your husband practically owns them, doesn't he?"

The Ma'saa and Enkshi traded glances, Enkshi's wary, the Ma'saa's questioning.

"Because they have to keep Oonai's condition a secret," Jespar said. "Am I right?"

Enkshi's mouth twitched, but then he exhaled. "Congratulations, you are a true detective. Yes, Ma'sao Oonai owns the lion's share of the Guard, but it's teeming with moles ... and, ironic as it may be, to investigate a matter of this importance and delicate nature, two out-siders with no ties to Kilayan politics are actually the safest choice."

"But I'm a physician and a biomancer," Varroy said. "Not some kind of, I don't know, private investigator."

Enkshi cast a sideways glance at the Ma'saa, one that somehow managed to be questioning, accusatory, and respectful at the same time. "Quite correct."

Ma'saa Oonai studied her wine, swirling it in slow circles. "You're a priestess of the White Leaf. And the people say you perform mir-acles in that clinic of yours."

"I'm a *former* priestess," Varroy replied. "Trust me, there's nothing holy about me. And as for the miracles, people expecting to die from harmless cuts because there's no money for an antiseptic are quite liberal with that word. I mean, don't get me wrong, if you wanna throw your money at me, I won't object. I just want you to know who you're hiring."

The Ma'saa snorted softly. "Your honesty is a breath of fresh air. I know perfectly well who I'm hiring, and my offer still stands. All I'm asking of you is your medical advice and that you do your best at the other tasks we give you. Can you promise me that?"

There was the slightest of pauses before Varroy answered. "I can do that."

"Thank you. And you, Jespar?"

A creature of habit, Jespar prepared to haggle. Then he noticed the silent plea behind the Ma'saa Oonai's dignified veneer and remem-bered the last time someone had looked at him this way.

"I'm in."

They spent the next half hour going through the formalities. Jespar had expected the pay to be generous, but he had to reread the figure at the bottom of the contract twice. Sixty thousand sêr—the price of a middle-class house in Enderal. They had just finished signing when a chubby man with the wobbliest jowls Jespar had ever seen entered the room. He introduced himself as Ma'sao Ulanees, Oonai's physician, and said he'd come to check on his master's health. The Ma'saa sent Varroy, Enkshi, and Jespar back to the orchard house and told them she'd join them shortly. Wine and fruit waited for them inside, the table had been tidied up, and the candles were replaced.

"Two things before we move on to the details," Enkshi said after they had each taken a seat. "One, as stated in the contract, you are to stay completely silent about the matter toward anyone, unless explicitly instructed otherwise. Are we clear on that, or do you need me to detail the consequences of a breach?"

"Clear," said Varroy.

Jespar nodded.

"Good. Two, I know you, Dal'Varek, are in this for the money, and I know you, Varroy, don't care much about the upper class, but I still want you to understand that this is about more than just my master's health. It's been over a moon since he disappeared from the public, and people are already shooting their mouths off, especially after his unfortunate appearance at the conference. If they were to find out about his condition, or worse, if he were to die—"

"He'd leave a power vacuum," Varroy said.

"Exactly. Take that and toss in a bunch of conceited terrorists and the political unrest over the decree, and you have a recipe for disaster. Now, I think I've made it clear that I'd rather be dealing with specialized operatives instead of you two, but if the Ma'saa thinks it's Moraia's will, then, well, my hands are tied. Still, I need you to remember what's at stake."

Jespar sipped from his wine. "Permission to speak freely?"

"This isn't the military," Enkshi said.

"Why don't you revoke that decree? Wouldn't that appease the populace and these terrorists a little? The, um, Scythe?"

Enkshi scoffed. "The Scythe couldn't care less about the decree—they are just using it as a draft horse for their propaganda. Even if we were to revoke it tomorrow morning, they'd still be out there killing nobles and burning down trading posts."

"Yeah, but it might knock *some* wind out of their sails, right?" Jespar said.

"And stop people from killing themselves," Varroy added. "There have been dozens of suicides in the past two weeks alone."

"A person's choice to end their life is always their own," Enkshi said. "But even if the decree were connected to these suicides, there's no chance the Coalition is going to negotiate with terrorists. We won't sabotage our own country just because a bunch of have-nots are too simpleminded to understand the enormous potential of this legislation."

"Stars burn me," Varroy said. "You're unbelievable."

Enkshi froze. "I beg your pardon?"

"You heard me. I get that your sort doesn't give a shit if people hang themselves because they can't afford a canteen of water anymore, but, man, at least grow a pair and own up to it. 'Enormous potential', my arse. The only ones who benefit from these policies are you, the rich."

Jespar—who thought anything starting with "your sort" rarely spoke of a healthy worldview but agreed with Varroy's overall assessment—tensed. Whatever her strengths were, subtlety wasn't among them.

"You have quite the mouth on you," Enkshi said.

Varroy held Enkshi's gaze, but Jespar noticed that her back was pressing against the chair. "Must be the altitude."

Jespar expected a biting remark or even a tantrum, but Enkshi surprised him by smiling. "Do you know the difference between a master and a pawn?"

"How many rings they can fit on their fingers?" Varroy asked.

"Pawns let themselves be done to, masters do. You can have all the riches in the world and still be a pawn, or you can be a fisherman and be a master. It's all a question of the right mindset. Let's take the Golden Soil Decree as an example: the pawn whines and screams 'woe is me,' blaming the oh-so-evil uppers for his misery. The master scrapes together his last savings, then buys himself a tiny mountain pond outside the city, where he sells his gallons at ten dara less than the competitors. Give it a few moons, and, ta-da, you have a Great Dreamer. You can't blame the jungle if the jaguar's too slow to pounce at the peccary."

"Lovely metaphor," Varroy said. "Except that it's horseshite. Not everybody *has* savings, and sometimes, people just get plain unlucky."

"Ah, yes, misfortune, the eternal excuse of the pawn. Every situation is also a chance, Varroy, no matter how dire. You only have to find a loophole and use it."

"Big words coming from someone who grew up in the Steel District as the son of a wealthy cloth trader and a Coalition official."

Enkshi's smile died. "Well, well. Someone did their homework."

"You're not the only one with sources."

"Apparently not. I wonder, did those sources of yours also tell you my 'wealthy', cloth-trading father barely made enough to make ends meet or that my mother died from consumption when I was twelve? Or perhaps that our 'Steel District house' was a hovel right beside the sewers, which we could barely afford? No, I guess not. Just as they didn't tell you about all those countless have-not brats who took every chance to ridicule and humiliate me."

"I'm sure your lovely personality had nothing to do with it."

Enkshi snorted. Then he pushed back his chair and struck his fist against his right thigh.

A metallic sound rang out.

"If I recall correctly, my being born legless was what they picked on most, so I assume personality was secondary. 'Coal nugget', that was their favorite moniker, inspired by the way I had to drag myself back home that one time my crutches broke on the street. And, you see, I can't even blame them. I *was* pathetic back then, always crying myself to sleep and thinking about when I'd finally drum up the courage to end it. But you know why I didn't? Because one day, it struck me that that would have only proven those bastards right. Instead, I read all the engineering books I could find, convinced a desperate moneylender to give me a loan, and turned to an unsuccessful Yalam-Rashâi tinkerer. Two years later, I had legs and stood taller than them all. Ten years later, the tinkerer and I owned Compass Empire, the largest manufactory of Starling prostheses and siege weaponry in all of Kilay."

Varroy's frown remained. "I'm sorry for what happened to you. That still doesn't give you the right to spit on people who didn't make it."

"At the risk of shaking up your black-and-white morality, it's possible to be successful *and* do good. My company gives away free protheses to veterans and disabled workers every Miwa-e-Kēku, and Ma'sao and Ma'saa Oonai have been running a weekly food bank for the past eighteen years."

"One good deed doesn't automatically outweigh a bad one."

Enkshi seemed about to reply but instead sighed and shook his head. "As much as I'd love to spend the evening discussing politics, I doubt this is getting us anywhere. Unless, of course, Dal'Varek has something to share on the topic?"

Jespar, who questioned the wisdom of insulting megalomaniacs within their own palace walls, raised his goblet. "The wine's good."

Varroy snorted.

"Wise words," Enkshi said, smiling.

A few minutes of forced small talk later, the Ma'saa joined them. She had cleaned up her face and removed the tear-melted kohl, and a firm resolve had replaced her fatigue.

"Your Excellency," Enkshi said.

He made to bow, but Ma'saa Oonai waved her hand and sat.

"Let's waste no more time," she said, looking Jespar square in the eye. "Have you ever heard of the term 'dreamwalker'?"

The island was an ocean of dark green beyond the ramparts, and the city a reef of light arching around Uunili Bay. Jespar tried to remember what it had been like to bustle through the crowded streets this morning, but he couldn't. It was as if, by entering the ziggurat, he had stepped into a different world and left all his memories outside.

Stifling a yawn, he rested his back against the parapet and let his eyes wander up the pyramid: colonnade after colonnade, arch after arch, statue after statue. In the moonlight, the First Ziggurat more than ever seemed like the abode of a god.

Dreamwalker, he thought.

It was funny: Jespar believed Moraia, if existent and still alive, had better things to do than to send clairvoyant dreams to the First Dame of Kilay, yet after that bizarre mission briefing, he wondered if perhaps he wasn't such a lousy candidate after all. For all his shortcomings, he certainly was an expert in matters of dreams and nightmares.

A beacon to guide us toward deliverance, he remembered the Ma'saa's words. The phantom noose tightened, and a familiar anxiety settled in his gut.

"It's gonna be okay," he muttered into his scarf. An odd job, for sure, a bit like jumping into a lake not knowing how deep it was,

DREAMS OF THE DYING

but the pay was just too damn good to pass on, and what the Ma'saa and Enkshi expected of him wasn't that bad or dangerous after all.

"Isn't it a bit warm for that thing?"

He started. Varroy stood on the landing of the battlement stairs, backdropped by the panorama.

"I'm sorry, what?"

Varroy pointed at her neck. "The scarf."

"Oh. No, it's—" *A memento*, he almost said before catching himself. "The cloth is really light. How did it go?"

Varroy had insisted on giving Oonai a thorough medical examination, despite knowing it would probably bring no new findings. She joined Jespar at the parapet and rested her elbows on the balustrade. "Sobering. Crazy as it sounds, finding that 'dreamwalker' might actually be our best shot."

"Huh. Then you don't think she's a fraud? She can actually travel into someone else's dreams?"

"I think it's possible, the rest remains to be seen. I mean, sure, it sounds bonkers, but I read a book about forgotten or extinct Sights a while back, and I think dream manipulation was listed as one of them."

"So it's a form of dimensionism."

Varroy undid her ponytail and shook out her hair, a cascade of dark waves that went down to her shoulders. "Unless you believe in demon possession, magic, and witchcraft, then, yeah, it's gotta be." She slipped the hairband over her fingers and tied her hair up in a loose bun. "I'm thinking some rare and previously unknown sub-Sight of psychomancy, one that allows the dimensionist to project themselves into somebody else's thoughts. Like a shared hallucination of sorts."

"Sounds pretty wild."

"Not half as wild as some of the other Sights scholars speculate about, like the one that allows you to control time or even jump into parallel realities. If you ask me, we've only scratched the surface when it comes to dimensionism. If some people can see and manipulate thermal energy, space, thought waves, or life force, why shouldn't there be dozens of other Sights we simply don't know about, or that were lost in the Starfall Era?"

"Like that Nehrimese beggar who one day showed up at a university and was able to control minds."

"The first psychomancer, yeah." She flicked Jespar a curious glance. "How come you know so much about dimensionism? Enkshi said you aren't Sighted."

"I'm not." *Much to my father's disappointment.* "I just had an upper-class education, basic knowledge of dimensionism and the Oath of the Arcane are part of that. I'm sure I know nowhere near as much as you."

"But you do have a pretty good grip on the basics." She ended with an upward inflection as if inviting him to elaborate.

"I know that there are several dimensions besides the ones everyone can perceive and that Sighted people can sense and manipulate them."

"And how does this manipulation work?"

"By altering the alignment of an element on a particular dimension. When a thermomancer, for example, lights a candle, he does it by changing the wick's alignment on the thermal dimension, which determines whether elements are hot or cold. It's more or less the same thing I do when I change the candle's alignment on the spatial dimension by picking it up or dropping it, except that everybody can perceive and interact with the spatial dimension, but only thermomancers can perceive and interact with the thermal dimension. Is this an exam, Ma'saa Varroy?"

"No, I'm just curious. There'll be dimensionism on this mission, so it's good to know I don't need to tutor you. I'm guessing you're familiar with shifting drain too?"

"Yes, every time a dimensionist manipulates their Sighted dimension, this 'shift' puts pressure on the brain—the bigger the shift, the stronger the pressure. That's why stuff such as resurrecting the dead, conjuring a blizzard, or wizarding yourself from one place to another only works in fairy tales. As far as I know, dimensionists can improve their capacity of drain, but for the most part, their resilience is written into their blood, like the nature of their Sight." Surprised with how much from his old lessons had stuck, Jespar smirked. "So? How did I do?"

"Well, considering that thanks to the Oath, most people still think we're either divine sorcerers or baby-eating witches, I'd say exemplary."

"Hold on, the baby-eating is a lie?"

Varroy chuckled. "I sometimes do it, but only to help with hangovers. But, yeah, good to know you're not superstitious. That'll make things a lot easier."

"Hold on, you're coming too? I thought the Ma'saa wanted you to look after Oonai."

"Which would pretty much amount to sitting on my hands and staring off into space, no, thank you. If I'm getting paid that much money, I'm gonna work for it. Also, I've been meaning to get to Hapana for a while now. There's something I need to look into."

"Huh. Well, I'm happy for the company." To his surprise, it wasn't a lie as usual; ever since the Village, he didn't care much for companionship, even if that companion was as pretty as Varroy. His occasional escapades in taverns and brothels worked for two reasons: one, they were entertainingly shallow, pure pleasure. Two, he could escape them any time he wanted. The next two days with Varroy would not be like that at all, but he found himself looking forward to them. "Where are you from, by the way? I can't place your accent."

Varroy gave him a lop-sided grin. "Guess."

"Um ... Nehrim?"

"Uh-uh."

"Arazeal."

"Far off."

"Hmm. You don't look Qyranian either."

"Well observed. I'll release you from your misery: I'm from Mâlei."

"Really? Well, that explains it. I've never met a Mâleian before."

"And I never an Endralean, so let's call it even." She sized him up mockingly. "Though I've gotta say, you're not what I expected."

"What did you expect?"

"Hard to say. A crusty old priest of Malphas smacking infidels with an incense burner?"

Jespar laughed. "We're not *all* that religious."

"I know, I'm just pulling your leg," Varroy said, grinning.

"Consider it—"

"Ma'sae?"

They turned. Agaam stood on the battlement walkway, hands clasped behind his back. His previously slicked-back, white hair hung down to his chin, and he had exchanged his eye patch for a glass eye, probably for camouflage. "I'm sorry to disturb you, but the horses are ready, and it's a long ride down to the harbor. The winds are unusually strong tonight, so we should leave as soon as possible."

"All right," Varroy said. "We'll be down in a second."

Agaam nodded and descended the stairs.

"Meet you at the stables?" Varroy asked. "I forgot something in the Ma'saa's study."

"Sure thing. One more question, though."

"Shoot."

Jespar offered his hand. "Our introduction earlier was a bit rushed, so how about we try again? I'm Jespar, pleasure to meet you. The Ma'saa was pretty adamant about the first-name thing, so mind if I call you Zarah?"

An untrained observer might have interpreted Varroy's reluctance as exhaustion. Jespar recognized it as the wariness of someone who didn't trust freely.

Smiling, she shook. "Actually, Zarah's my middle name. I'm Lysia."

CHAPTER FOUR
UNDERSTANDING THE OCEAN

DAY TWO
6TH MOON OF DRY SEASON, 1226 A.L.

espar's first brushes with insomnia began a moon after what Enkshi had called "the tragic incident."

"It will get better," his foster father, Meyser Dal'Tarbak, had promised.

When several moons had passed, and it hadn't, Jespar stopped trying to fall asleep and found other uses for those long and restless nights. Some of them, he spent reading in the library of the cavernous house that was supposed to be their new home now, everything from the fairy tale *The Moon Kobold* to *Lethonia*, an explorer's treatise on an undiscovered continent far north of Arazeal, to the two-thousand–page tome that was *The Apotheosis of the Light-Born*. On others, he'd go for long walks through the labyrinthine alleys of Ark's Larxes District. There was something unique about the silence that reigned those nights—a mixture of peace and the haunting but strangely beguiling notion that he was all alone during those nocturnal strolls as if some quiet, otherworldly occurrence had caused everyone but him to peacefully vanish, leaving behind a skeleton world where Jespar was the only person still alive. A boy sleepwalking on the bottom of the ocean.

Had Jespar been born in Uunili, that idea would never have occurred to him. Even though it was nearing midnight, the city still bustled with life as Agaam, Lysia, and Jespar made their way down to the harbor: people chattered and laughed, gathering around fire bowls in the streets; some vendors still had their stalls up, and children zipped through the alleys, giggling and shrieking. Jespar welcomed the distraction. Lysia had been quiet since their lovely conversation on the battlements, and Jespar's attempt at striking up a chat with Ma'sao Agaam had been fruitless, so his mind had done what it did best: go on another round of restless brooding, some on the bizarre task that lay ahead of them, some on the memories the Ma'saa's story about her arranged marriage had stirred up. *That was your father? The judge who saved the Ma'saa?* Back then, Jespar had been too stunned for a proper answer. Now, he wished he would have told Enkshi something else: that whatever heroic deed Damean Dal'Varek had done, he had not done it out of empathy but to prove a fucking point.

"There," Lysia said, pulling him out of his ruminations. She was pointing at an alley branching off Fortune Road. "That one."

"Very well," Agaam said, guiding his horse toward the opening. "Let's be quick."

Lysia wanted to get some things and check on her patients before setting out to Hapana, so Agaam had agreed to take a detour over to her clinic. Even though she had warned them it was on the very border of the Steel District, the word "clinic" had conjured a different image in Jespar's mind than the slim ramshackle building they stopped at. A poppy red house in the shadow of the city walls, all that set it apart from its rundown neighbors was the hanging sign jutting out beside the entrance. A crudely painted milk thistle adorned it, the symbol of physicians across the Illumined World.

An old Kilayan sat on the adjacent house's doorstep, smoking nightflower and eyeing the three of them warily as they approached on their horses. Recognizing Lysia, his wizened visage brightened, and he raised his pipe in greeting. She nodded back, then swung herself from the saddle and knocked on the clinic's door. A young man opened, no older than twenty, his sable hair contrasting with a pair of striking blue eyes. Like the old man, he greeted Lysia with a beaming smile, and they hugged. Jespar and Agaam got a hesitant wave of the hand and a mumbled greeting.

"I'll be fifteen minutes at most," Lysia said. "Wanna come in for a cup of tea?"

Agaam declined politely. Jespar accepted.

The clinic was like a vase broken and glued back together many times over, each round with a fresh coat of paint to conceal the cracks. The bright colors of the walls distracted from the flaky plaster, just as the tapestries distracted from the holes. Scented candles cloaked the smell of herbs and the unmistakable aroma of disease. While Lysia saw to her two patients, her assistant showed Jespar into the kitchen and brewed the tea. Cramped, windowless, and with rows of jars looming on the shelves, the place could have easily felt oppressive had it not been for the child-like chalk drawings on the walls. One stood out, a stick figure with a brown ponytail and a zigzag line running up her right cheek, a friendly-faced sun hovering above her.

Jespar smiled. "Is that Lysia?"

The young man didn't react. His back facing Jespar, he stood by the counter and quietly crumbled the black tea leaves into the simmering kettle.

"It really does me justice, don't you think?"

Lysia stood in the door, grinning. She wore a haversack and a belt attached with pouches and sheathes and had traded her light jacket for a thicker crimson one, somehow managing to make this simple travel attire look stylish.

"It's masterful," Jespar said. "Who's the artist?"

"A boy from down the street. He and his friends drew these after I helped his mother, as a thank-you."

Suddenly reminded of the pencil portraits that his sister had often drawn of him as thanks—clumsy before the incident, impressive after, when art had become her refuge-Jespar struggled to keep up his smile. "That's sweet."

"It is." Lysia studied the drawing, looking tired but content. "Anyhoo, before we have tea, how about you show me that rash of yours? Shouldn't take long."

"My—how did you know?"

"People usually don't scratch themselves for the sheer joy of it, and you've been doing little else the whole evening."

Embarrassed, Jespar turned back to the wall paintings. "Oh. Well, it's nothing, really. Just a heat rash, I guess."

"Jespar, just lemme look at it. You're not the first shirtless man I've been alone in a room with."

Realizing any further protests were probably as pointless as they were stupid, he sighed. "Okay."

Lysia led him into a windowless room with a crude wood recliner and indicated for him to sit. "Take the shirt and the scarf off."

He did as asked, suddenly deeply grateful for the bath he had taken in the ziggurat. Lysia circled him. "All right. I have a hunch, but—" She broke off. "Well. Fuck."

"It's not that bad," Jespar said without conviction. "Really, I think it's getting better."

"And the Yalam-Rashâi think their ancestors arrived on Vyn on the Starfall meteorites. That still doesn't make it true." She went to a cabinet and rummaged through the top drawer.

Suddenly feeling queasy, Jespar's fingers wandered to his scarf. Realizing he had just taken it off, he dropped his hand. "What are you doing?"

"Bear with me." She returned with a pincer and some kind of spatula. "All right ... let's give those little buggers a taste of biomancy, shall we?"

"... 'Buggers'?"

"Yeah, Kilayan itch mites." Lysia traced the rash with her spatula. It went all the way from his left shoulder blade to the nape of his neck. "They get under your skin, dig tunnels there, and then breed like there's no tomorrow. If you do nothing, they'll keep at it until your skin looks like mushroom gills."

"Holy shit."

"Don't worry, it's an easy cure with a good shift. But do you know why Kilayans also call those mites the 'sailor's itch'?"

"Why?"

"Because Kilayans and Makehu have become immune to it over the centuries, so it's mostly sailors and outlanders who catch them. Usually in sleazy harbor brothels."

"I—" Jespar broke off. "I was drunk."

"And that's why you couldn't say 'no' when she climbed on top of you, huh?"

She and he. "I'm a simple man," he managed lamely.

Lysia laughed. "Hey, I'm not judging. Here's the deal: I'll get rid of the buggers for you, but I want something in return for the shifting drain that'll give me."

"What?"

"I don't know yet. A favor."

Jespar sighed. "Fine, you wicked wench. You win."

"Good boy. Now, close your eyes. This will sting a little."

A shameless euphemism.

As Lysia hovered her hand over the rash, there was indeed just a tickle at first. Then what felt like liquid lightning shot through his skin. Jespar screamed and doubled over, but Lysia held him in place with surprising strength; on and on the lightning arced, zig-zagging up and down his back and into his limbs, scorching all skin in its path.

By the time Lysia let go, and he dropped back into the recliner, his sight had gone blurry, his heart was a frenzied hammer, and his ears rang. Lysia went back to the cabinet and reappeared with a canteen and a piece of cloth.

"Yes, I lied. It hurts like a bitch." She handed him the canteen. He drank. "The only way to kill all the mites *and* their eggs is to reset the biomantic energy of the entire top layer of your skin. The resulting contraction of the new tissue crushes the buggers like grapes in a fist."

Only mildly appreciative of the image forming in his head, Jespar returned the canteen. "So, what, I've got insect goo in my skin now?"

"Not goo, just tiny particles that will grow out as your skin renews. You might feel mild discomfort for a couple of days, but other than that, you're as good as—" She winced, then slumped. "Ugh, and here comes the drain."

Jespar steadied her, a bizarrely misplaced thought coming to his mind as he helped her sit on the lounger: how nice her hand felt, warm, strong, smooth. "Will you be all right?"

"Yeah, don't worry, it'll be over in a second." Lips pressed tight, she soaked the cloth with water from the canteen and held it against her forehead. "Come on, feel it. Your skin."

Jespar did as asked. His back was smooth as a baby's. "It's gone."

"Told you," Lysia said. "Easy cure."

Realizing he still—now somewhat awkwardly—had his hand on her shoulder, he let go. "Thank you. Seriously, Lysia, thank you. I owe you."

Lysia smirked. "I'll get back to you about that. Now, come, let's have that tea. We shouldn't keep Ma'sao Stone-Face waiting any longer."

Agaam, the ma'sao in question, was waiting exactly where they'd left him, leaning against a nearby wall and as still as a column. Lysia's assistant watched wordlessly as they mounted their horses, his arms folded and bouncing on his heels.

Lysia threw him an encouraging smile from her saddle. "Hot compresses for Ma'saa Iwelys, licorice and comfrey infusion twice a day for the girl. You got this."

The young man's lips lifted a fraction, and he raised his fingers to his chest. Then he mumbled a goodbye and went back inside.

"Ready?" Agaam asked.

"Mm-hm."

Lysia waved the old Kilayan goodbye, and they steered their horses back to Fortune Road.

"He doesn't speak much, does he?" Jespar asked.

Lysia turned to him, a distracted look about her. "Sorry, what?"

"The boy, your assistant. He's a quiet type."

"Ah. Well, that comes with being deaf and mute."

"Deaf? But he ...?"

"He taught himself to lip-read and imitate speech, yes. Quite impressive, especially considering he's a street kid and had no education whatsoever before I took him in."

Jespar clicked his tongue. "Definitely." Leaving the alley, they returned to Fortune Road and followed Agaam downhill, where the ocean stretched out dark and wide beyond the harbors' lights. "So, your clinic," Jespar said. "It's free for everyone?"

"Everyone who couldn't afford it otherwise, yeah. Which are most people in this country."

"How do you sustain yourself, though? If the question isn't too personal?"

A brief hesitation. "It's fine. Most of it is donations, the rest the occasional paid job I do. It's not much, but enough to get by."

"Huh. That's noble of you."

Lysia faced him. "You know, whenever someone says that, I wonder what kind of person *wouldn't* help someone in need if it was within their power."

"Ask the Gods, I guess. Not helping is their favorite pastime."

Lysia's chuckle left him with a warm tickle in his belly. "Fair point. Fair point."

Except for a scene at the switchbacks down to the coastal district—two guards restrained a shouting drunk commoner—the journey was uneventful. The harbor was an impressive sight to behold, with the pier arching along Uunili Bay as far as the eye could see, count-less ships of all sizes and flags filling the docks. A cool breeze carried the smells of salt, spices, and fish, and, just like in the inner city, people still milled about the dockside, light and laughter pouring from the many inns and taverns. Agaam followed the marina down the coast to a tiny pier, the big ships and crowded inns far behind them. A cutter swayed in the waves.

"One moment, ma'sae," Agaam said. He dismounted and set about unmooring the ship. When Jespar turned to say something to Lysia, she was gazing toward a dark alley across them, one hand on a sheath at her belt.

"You okay?"

"Yeah. I just—I thought I saw someone. Over there."

Jespar followed her indication. "The alley? I don't see anything."

"... Never mind. Stars burn me, I really need to get some shut-eye."

"Ma'sae?" Agaam called from the boat. "We're ready."

Not much later, the cutter glided through the moonlit waters of Uunili Bay. They were bound for the island of Hapana to find the last Makehu dreamwalker.

If the opulence of the First Ziggurat was a statement, then the cutter was its rebuttal. The lower deck consisted of only a single cramped cabin, the ceiling so low that Jespar's hair brushed against it. Two burlap cots stood at the sides, a wall shelf over each bed and a waist-high cabinet by the entrance the only other furniture.

Agaam placed his lantern on the cabinet. "I'll handle the sailing. You two should rest."

Jespar protested out of politeness but was glad when the old servant insisted.

"Finally," Lysia sighed as Agaam closed the door behind him. She lay slumped upon the left cot. "Odd fellow, huh?"

Jespar headed over to the other bed and unbuckled his sword-belt. "Agaam?"

"No, the Moon Kobold. Why do you think he's here? We could have done this on our own."

"True." As casually as it was possible, Jespar slid his dagger under the pillow, a habit he hadn't been able to shake since the war. "I think he's here to keep an eye on us, like a minder."

"Hm. Makes sense, I guess." She yawned and pulled off her boots and jacket. "Anyhoo, let's call it a night, okay? I'm bloody tired."

Jespar was, too, yet he wouldn't have minded speaking a little longer; that warm tickle Lysia's chuckle had sparked in him hadn't left his belly ever since. Then again, they probably *did* need all the sleep they could get, and going by his impression of Lysia thus far, a heart to heart with a prematurely graying drifter who had just caught itch mites from a brothel was the last thing on her mind right now.

"Sounds good."

"Lovely." Briefly, she looked pensive, trailing her thumb over her scar. Then she shook her head and curled up on the bed, facing the wall. "Night, Jespar."

"Night," Jespar mumbled into his scarf. He undressed to his breeches and undershirt, put down his belt by the bedside, and then studied the door. Sleep would be a long time coming with it unlocked, but since Agaam hadn't left a key, the only way to block it would be by moving the cabinet, which would make him seem anything from eccentric to outright strange. Stifling a yawn, he trod over to the lantern.

"Wait."

Lysia was looking at him over her shoulder.

"Can you ... is it okay if we leave it on?"

"Um, sure, no problem."

"Thanks." She sunk back into her pillow. "Night."

Jespar regarded her for a moment—it was sweet, the way she lay there, curled up and hair tousled—then realized it was weird to watch someone sleep, lumbered back to his cot, and lay down. As expected, it wasn't long before anxiety settled in, a blend of the typical unease he always felt in closed spaces with other people, as well as the uncertainty of what would follow: insomnia or nightmares.

He closed his eyes.

Images.

The attack on the litter. The arbalest bolt hitting the wood a finger-length from his temple. The croaking sound the Scythe boy had made when Jespar had cut off his head. The handsome guard, wailing and tossing on the flawless flagstone as he turned into a living corpse.

Grunting softly, Jespar rolled over on his side. Rain was settling in outside, pattering against the hull, first soft, then louder.

More images.

The ziggurat and its countless tiers, rising into a moonlit sky. Jaaros Oonai's gaunt face, the milky, steaming slime on his iris. The horned Magnate's Crown on his nightstand, golden, polished, and cold, like a grave good.

And verily they spake unto us, blessed are ye who are kind and humble.
It's a trial, Zagash.
Not our deliverance, but our beacon that will guide us toward it.

The wheel of thought kept turning, his anxiety swelling with every cycle. After the umpteenth round, Jespar sighed and sat up, his mouth dry and sour. As quietly as he could, he fished his belt flask from the bedside—brandy—and took a gulp, then another. It stung like a bitch, but he already felt himself relax. He had just stoppered the flask and put it back when a nearby voice spoke up.

"Can't sleep?"

Blood rushing to his cheeks—*relax, she probably thinks it's water*—Jespar froze. "Did I wake you? Sorry, I'm just ..." *Restless. As bloody always.*

"No, don't worry." Lysia lay facing him. "I don't think I'm gonna get much sleep tonight anyway. My mind's a whirlwind."

"Yeah, mine too."

"Wanna chat for a bit? There's something I've been meaning to ask you anyway."

Talking was usually the last thing Jespar felt like doing during a bout of insomnia, but once again, his mind surprised him by finding comfort in the idea. "What is it?"

Lysia rested her head on her propped-up hand. "All that stuff the Ma'saa said, about you being a divine messenger. Do you believe it?"

Jespar snorted. "I'm as much a divine messenger as Oonai is an ascetic. Honestly, I have even less business being here than you do."

"Okay, but then what do you make of that dream she had? The vision, if you can call it that?"

"Good question. My theory is that she *did* have that dream in the chapel and saw some guy with a mask in it, but that part about him having my father's eyes was something her mind added in retrospect."

"As in, it adjusted the memory?"

"Yeah, because she was desperate for a ray of hope. If you ask me, that applies to that trial story. 'This is a test from the Gods, but Moraia sent a beacon to guide us' sounds a lot more comforting than 'we're out of our fucking depths,' because that's what they are." He gave it some thought. "Come to think of it, that would also explain why she went with you and not some fancy biomancer from the military."

"How so?"

Jespar sat up and leaned against the wall. Probably a combination of the brandy and the distraction, his anxiety kept easing off. "Well, she thinks the Gods are punishing them for their lack of humility, right? It only makes sense she'd want to work with someone morally pure."

"Morally pure. Right, that's me."

"Well, you *do* run a slum clinic. And as I said, this isn't about logic or reason, it's about subconscious mechanisms. The Ma'saa feels like she has tried all conventional means, so now she's putting her hopes in faith and the supernatural."

"Then she should have hired a priest or a keeper to do the job."

"She should have, yeah. But she chose us."

"Hm."

They were silent for a bit, the rain pattering on the hull. Then Lysia sat up too and rested her back against the wall, the flickering lantern accentuating the scar on her left cheek. Or was it even a scar? The lines were only the slightest bit raised, and there was an almost purposeful symmetry to the pattern. "So," Lysia said, "if you're not a divine messenger, what's your story? How did you end up as a merc?"

Jespar snorted. "Right into the deep stuff, huh?"

"It's past midnight, we're on a boat, and it's pouring buckets. When if not now?"

"Okay, fair point. But I'm afraid I'm not half as exciting as you think. I'm really just an average guy trying to mind his own business."

"An average guy who abandons his noble heritage, joins a peace corps, then drops off the map and lives in the Nehrimese wilderness for years?"

"... You know about that?"

"The Ma'saa told me while we waited. So? Unless you don't wanna talk about it, that is."

Jespar realized he did. He had never been one to wear his heart on his sleeve, but he liked Lysia, wanted her to like him back, and he knew every friendship started with a good conversation. Where was the harm in opening up, at least a bit? Gods knew it had been a long, long time since he'd last done it.

But he couldn't.

The second he decided to speak, he clammed up, a big, fat lump sealing his throat. The phantom noose didn't constrict, but the skin of his neck tingled, like a warning.

"You okay?" Lysia asked.

"Yeah," Jespar said. "Yeah, sure. But as I said, it's not that exciting. I really just wanted to turn the page."

"Ah. Okay, then." It was apparent she didn't believe him, but, thankfully, she didn't push it. The lump gave way slightly.

"Well, all right," he said. "Maybe there was the odd demon in my past. Thing is, I'm just too good of an exorcist."

Lysia smirked. "Really? Share your method, then, I could use some help."

Jespar fished the brandy flask from his belt and raised it. "Always does the trick."

They laughed. It felt good and genuine, the laugh of two people who don't know each other well but want to. His tension eased more; outside, the rain had joined forces with a gusting wind that gently rocked the cutter.

"A toast?" Jespar asked.

Still grinning, Lysia shook her head. "No, thanks. Booze only makes me mellow."

"How about a pipe, then? Helps with the sleep."

"You got petals?"

Jespar untethered his pipe and petal pouch from his belt and held them up. "A master exorcist never journeys without his gear. Purple Myrad from Uunuma, First Flush."

Lysia hesitated, but only for a second. "Ah, to hell with it. Just don't make it too strong, okay? It's been a while."

"Sure thing."

Lysia got up and joined him on his cot. A pleasant shiver ran up Jespar's arms as she plunked down just a finger-length from him, casually, as though they weren't a half-naked man and woman huddled up in a dimly lit cabin. *Maybe she's a same-lover*, Jespar found himself thinking. *Maybe she doesn't care for men.*

Or maybe she does, just not for you.

Internally groaning at his acting like a green boy, he stopped the thought and focused on stuffing the pipe, blending the crumpled, purple leaves of the nightflower with peppermint for taste. He reached for the firetwig in his belt pouch, but realizing it was his last, opted for the lantern candle instead. Sitting back down, he offered the lit pipe to Lysia. "Ladies first."

Lysia took the pipe, pulled deeply, and exhaled. Violet swirls rose from her lips, the cool scent of the mint mingling with the sweet aroma of nightflower.

"This is good." Lysia reclined against the wall. "This is really good."

She passed him the pipe, the stem still warm from her fingertips. He took a hit. It *was* good indeed, even better than the strain he'd smoked in the napaawo. He'd bought it at the Great Bazaar.

"So, since we're on the deep stuff, why does a Mâleian priestess leave her homeland to start a charity clinic in Kilay?"

"Does 'the Mâleian winter is a bitch' count as an answer?"

Handing her the pipe, Jespar returned the "come on" look she'd given him earlier.

"Okay, fine." Smoke framed Lysia's face as she exhaled. "First, you gotta know I never *chose* to join the Convent of the White Leaf. The Sisters found me at the monastery's doorstep as a toddler and brought me up ... I have no idea who my parents are or why they abandoned me."

"Oh. I'm sorry."

The rain was relentless, harrying the wood with needle-strike blows.

"Ah, don't be. You can't miss what you don't know, and the Sisters raised me as one of their own." She pulled up her knees and watched the smoke curl toward the ceiling. "They're good people, you know? Priestesses of Esara, devoting their lives to curing the world of all ailments, and they actually live by their ideals. Which is one hell of a rare thing these days."

"And yet you left." The nightflower was in full effect now, the colors softening and a pleasant tingle dancing over his lips.

"Yes, for two reasons. First, the Silence."

"What's your take on it?" Jespar asked carefully. "Why do you think the Gods have turned away from mankind?"

Lysia made an amused sound. She gave him the pipe. "No need to tread so lightly, I'm nontheist to the bone. In fact, it amazes me how so many people still manage to believe."

Her answer came as a surprise. Considering she was a *former* priestess, Jespar had assumed she wasn't the epitome of piety, but he had placed her in the post-theist or indifference camp at most—certainly not an atheist or a nontheist, radical beliefs that could get you into a lot of trouble in the more religious countries. "So, you think the Light-Born were frauds, then?"

"Just that they weren't the almighty deities the Order says they were. No, I don't believe all the historical records are fake, and I believe the Light-Born were stellar dimensionists and politicians, but Tyr's face certainly wasn't made of pure light, and they didn't live in a city in the clouds or have the power to send someone into a 'Hell' or 'Beyond'. I mean, think about it: *The Apotheosis* claims they became omnipotent, immortal gods through their dimensionism, but to this day, no biomancer can even *slow down* aging, and no thermomancer can stop a blizzard. How does that make sense?"

Jespar recognized the argument. It was a staple in nontheist reasoning. "You're saying, had the Light-Born really known such shifting techniques, they would have passed them on to humanity."

"At least to some extent and at least to the Order, their direct servants. I mean, imagine how much more powerful a handful of godlike dimensionists would have made the Order as a political entity. There'd be zero need for elaborate theological explanations about the Silence and zero need to keep knowledge about dimensionism restricted—the Order's godlike powers alone would be proof for the Light-Born's divinity." She sighed, brushing a strand of hair back behind her ear. "Anyway, we're not here to discuss the Gods. What matters is that I didn't see the point in spending three hours of my day worshipping a woman who I believe is dead." She gestured for the pipe. "Can I?"

Jespar passed it. Lysia took a deep drag and blew out a smoke ring that vanished as it floated toward the ceiling.

"The second reason had something to do with the philosophy of the Sisters. You see, part of their doctrine is that the outside world is full of noise, vice, and Corruption and that you can't cure a disease if you allow yourself to get infected. Hence, they stay within the monastery walls as much as possible, and patients have to come to them to get treated. I always thought that was nonsense. You can't cure something if you don't get up close to see it."

"'How can I understand the ocean if you won't let me swim?'"

Lysia favored him with a lop-sided smile. "You have a way with words, ma'sao."

"Not mine, I'm afraid. That's from *The Apotheosis,* the *Speech of Saldrin.*"

"Well, it fits like a glove. To keep with the metaphor, all the Sisters ever did was stand on the shore and study the waves, at least that's what it felt like to me. I sort of ignored that for a while, but when I realized it meant I'd never see anything more than maybe Mâlas if I were to stay a priestess, it just drove me bonkers. Dammit, how was I supposed to *heal* a world I didn't even know? I wanted to see what was out there, with all the good and bad that comes with it."

She took another hit, the chamber now half-filled with ash. The tickle in Jespar's stomach now stretched all the way to Jespar's lips.

"I know, I know," Lysia said, returning the pipe. "Sounds a little theatrical, doesn't it?"

No. It sounds fascinating. "Not at all. It makes perfect sense to me."

"Well, glad to hear that. To be fair, though, it wasn't all ideal-ism—a part of me also just wanted to *live*. Call me selfish, but the idea of spending my life toiling away in some cloister and watch my lady parts grow rusty with neglect never had much appeal to me. I mean, who knows, maybe tomorrow another meteorite will come crashing down and smash us to pulp the way Starfall wiped out the Pyrayans. And when that happens, I at least wanna be able to say, 'Well, too bad it's over. But at least I lived.'" She was silent for a bit, gaze fixed on her fingers. "Anyway. There you have it, The True Reasons Why Lysia Varroy Became A Runaway. The day I turned eighteen, I snuck out of the monastery, hopped on the first ship I could find and left without looking back."

How awfully familiar. "Hm," Jespar said, passing her the almost empty pipe. "Quite the story."

"I guess."

Jespar watched as she took the last drag.

Damn, he *really* liked her. It wasn't just physical attraction, he realized now. Sure, there was something about her intense gaze, the contrast between her soft features and that curious scar, and, less sophisticated, her butt, that appealed to the primordial parts of his brain—but that was only one piece of the puzzle. He felt drawn to her free spirit, appreciated her wit, and admired her raw idealism, even though—or perhaps because—some of it felt a little too naïve and simplistic to him. Most of all, though, it was that warm feeling he got looking at her, a sense of recognition and comfortable famil-iarity, like seeing a painting's motif from the hallways of your child-hood home.

"Anyhoo," Lysia said. "About that favor."

Realizing he had been staring, Jespar pretended to study the floor-boards. "It's time already?"

Lysia gave him her trademark grin. "Afraid so. Word of warning, you might consider it brazen, though. Too ... direct."

A silly excitement growing in his belly, he tensed. Bloody hell, why was he acting like this was his first time alone with a woman? "Yeah?"

"Can we blaze another one?" she asked, holding up the pipe. "That stuff was bloody fantastic."

The excitement went up in smoke. "Oh. Okay. Yeah, sure."

Feeling like a complete idiot, he prepared and lit a second pipe. Lysia took the first hit, eyes closed and smiling.

Exhaling, she kissed him.

Her lips were soft and warm and chipped from the sun, her tongue sweet from the nightflower. Violet tendrils rose between their faces when they parted.

Damn, you like her, he thought again. *You really do.*

And, just like that, his tension vanished. He kissed back, hard and demanding, pulling her onto his lap, her scent of leather, smoke, and herbs fueling the fire. When Lysia drew back, her lids were still half-closed, and a grin flickered across her lips. The rain had stopped, leaving only the sounds of creaking wood and waves breaking against the hull of the ship.

"I've been meaning to do that for a while now," she said.

"Yeah?"

"Mm-hm. Ten minutes, at least."

"Well. Hope I didn't disappoint."

"Let's just say it was better than I expected."

Lysia laughed; his expression must have spoken volumes. "Don't worry, you're a good kisser. It's just, you're not the type of man I usually fall for. Gray hair or not, you look a bit boyish, and I'm not sure what that weedy stuff on your chin's supposed to be. Plus," she flicked a finger against Jespar's bicep, "from a mercenary, I would have expected more muscle."

"... You sure know how to make a girl feel special."

Another laugh. "Sorry, I'm not very good at this, am I?" She pushed him down on his back and kissed the side of his neck. "I *am* enjoying it, Jespar. Otherwise, would I be sitting on top of you?"

"Ma'saa, you make an excellent point," Jespar said.

He pulled her in for a kiss, but she resisted. "One more thing before we move ahead. What do you expect from this?"

"Expect?"

"Yes. We're gonna be working together, so we should probably, you know, map the road before we go any farther. What are you hoping to get from this little adventure?"

Jespar hesitated. "I'm not sure. You?"

"Just fun."

"... Really?"

"Yeah, just a good time. And there's no need to worry about babies—I took some bitterleaf a few days ago, so we're all safe."

"You took—for who?"

Her grin widened. "Considering I cured you of a whorehouse itch a couple of hours ago, don't you think you should go easy on the indignation? So, what do you say, are we good? Just some fun, no strings attached?"

His disappointment surprised him. What had he hoped for, soppy romance after eight hours of acquaintance? Not that that was what he wanted, anyway. His last serious courtship was ten years ago, back when he was still a green boy on Enderal and before his world had turned upside down for the second time. He didn't count the three short-lived dalliances during his Wayfarer years, all of which ended once the other halves—two women and a man—finally realized how much baggage this tall, blonde Endralean really came with. Every time, Jespar accepted the decision with what must have seemed like stoic sadness; every time, he felt a leaden weight drop off his shoulders because the other person had finally gotten around to what he'd meant to do for weeks but hadn't because he didn't want to be a hurtful asshole. Discussing his failed quest for romance with Naka, his friend told Jespar he probably just loved his freedom too much, something Naka could relate to all too well. Jespar had grunted in agreement but thought to himself that perhaps he was just plain incapable of intimacy.

An assertion he still held on to—even if it didn't feel like that now.

"Sure. No strings attached." He snorted. "Some priestess you are, Lysia Varroy."

"I'm full of surprises," she said as she ran her fingertips down to his bellybutton. "Now, how about you, Jespar Dal'Varek? Do *you* like it?"

He did.

He liked it when she stripped off her shirt, exposing that strange, marring, beautiful scar that reached down to her breast. He liked the way she sighed as he ran his tongue along her thighs. He liked it when she sat on top of him, her hair grazing his cheeks, their bodies naked on the coarse fabric of the cot.

She eased him in and started to move, up and down, up and down, her lips parted, his hips joining her rhythm; a shivering heat unfolded in Jespar's stomach as Lysia broke into a soft moan, he rolled her onto her back and her legs locked around his waist, he kissed her, and their breaths grew shorter and shorter as the heat grew and grew and grew and- exploded.

When they were done, they lay side by side, Jespar's face buried in Lysia's neck, her hands locked around him as she panted.

At last, she spoke up. "Let's finish that pipe."

They did, talking and laughing as time went by, all worries forgotten. After the pipe, they had sex again. By the time Jespar finally slipped off to sleep, the sky must have already been dawning.

THE SWAMP
SEE

SOMEDAY

SOMETIME

A swamp.

The air was both sweet and fresh and earthy and rotten, a marriage of life and decay. Jespar knelt in front of a crude judge's dais, spectator benches all around him, corpses filling the seats.

Jespar knew them all. The villagers and the man with the breadbasket. The Girl and her father. His sister, whom he tried so hard to forget.

"See, boy," the Corpse said. He was in the judge's seat, his burning hands holding a gavel. "See, or you leave us no choice."

Jespar opened his mouth, but he couldn't speak.

"See."

CHAPTER FIVE
HAPANA

Day Two
6th Moon of Dry Season, 1226 A.L.

Jespar woke alone. Swallowing down the sour taste in his mouth, he rolled to the other side and oriented himself. As so often in the mornings, his muscles were stiff and sore, as if he'd spent the night cramped up inside a coffin.

Lysia was on her bed, back resting against the wall and reading a book. Jespar decided it was a sight he wouldn't mind waking up to more often.

Idiot. This is a fling, if at all. Nothing more.

"Hey," Jespar said. "Morning."

She glanced up. "Oh, morning. Slept well?"

See, the Corpse's words from that strange and vivid dream echoed inside him. *See.* "Yeah, fine. You?"

"Better than I have in weeks. I should smoke that stuff more often. How's the rash?"

Sitting up, Jespar felt for his back. "Still gone."

"Good. Sometimes, the shift misses a mite, and then you have to do it all over again. But it seems like we got them all."

"Great."

They were silent for a bit, Jespar tugging at the fabric of his cot, Lysia studying her feet.

"Are you fine about last night?" Jespar asked.

To his surprise, Lysia broke into a grin. "I was about to ask the same thing. Yeah, totally. You?"

"Me too."

They were quiet once more, but this time it didn't feel awkward. Jespar swung his legs over the side of his bed. "Well, all right, then. Let's see where we are, shall we?"

Sunrise reflected in the rain puddles on deck. Agaam was doing repairs on the sail, his rolled-up sleeves exposing arms that were as athletic as those of a bull wrestler. In daylight, his hair and beard seemed even whiter than they had last night, reminding Jespar of an Endralean fairy tale about a boy who became lost in the Whisperwood and suffered such fear that his hair was chalk white when his parents found him.

Agaam made a slight bow. "Ah, ma'sae, good morning. I trust you had a good night?"

"Very good, thank you," Jespar said. "Did you get through the downpour all right? We wanted to come up to help, but we ..." He broke off, realizing "were busy" wasn't the best answer.

"That's fine, thank you. Would you like some breakfast?"

Not much later, Jespar, Agaam, and Lysia sat cross-legged around a crate repurposed into a table, chatting over a pot of tea and a plate of cold rice, fruit, and dried plantains. The conversation flowed well, and there was no hint of tension between Lysia and him, neither of the pleasant nor the unpleasant kind. "No strings attached"— seemed like she'd meant it.

If only Jespar could tell how he felt about it.

Hapana was the easternmost island of the Archipelago—about eight hours' sea voyage from Uunili—so the sun was bearing down from high over their heads by the time they reached it. At last night's briefing, Enkshi had called Hapana a "haven for the lawless and the destitute." Jespar had considered the description a touch dramatic, but what he saw when Agaam steered the cutter into the port of Hapana's capital Kekotoki couldn't have been more fitting.

Built in a barren island's craggy bay rose a monstrous dead turtle made of rusted metal, sun-bleached brick, and weathered wood. A wild web of bridges and ramps connected the platform towers built along the hills and slopes, the crowds filling the plankway and stages so dense they seemed to melt into a giant living ooze that had made the turtle's carcass its lair. The only green Jespar could spot was the mist that enfolded the entire city, culminating in a pillar in the north. No palms, no tokiflowers, no tamuka trees. Just brown shrubbery.

If the Alabaster City was Moraia's lover, Hapana was the misshapen child locked away in the attic.

As no one bothered to ask their name or check their flag, they docked in a vacant berth at the edge of the harbor. On the pier, Agaam set about mooring the cutter; he politely waved off Jespar's and Lysia's offer to help, so both took to studying the city, shielding their eyes from the glaring sun.

"Stars burn me," Lysia muttered. "It's really as bad as everyone says. What a shitehole."

An accurate assessment, as far as Jespar was concerned. "What's that fog?"

"Nuvium dust," Agaam said. He'd finished the starboard ropes and moved on to the stern. "It's a byproduct of smelting the ore."

"It smells ..." *Like shit.* "Like wastewater."

"And it's poison for the lungs, especially when you're exposed to it over a long time," Lysia said. "If only the mining kingpins cared about that part."

Agaam either didn't hear or ignored the comment. He tugged at the ropes and stood. "I suggest you start looking for that woman right away—ideally, we sail back to Uunili this afternoon. I have an errand to run, so let's meet at the ship at dusk." He glanced at Lysia. "Are you still certain you want to go with him, Ma'saa Varroy? Hapana is a dangerous place, especially Kekotoki."

"Thank you, but as I said, I got some business to take care of, too."

"As you wish, ma'saa. Just be careful."

"I will."

"What if it turns out this dreamwalker woman is a charlatan?" Jespar asked. "Or what if we can't find her?"

"Let's cross that bridge when we get to it." Agaam nodded at the harbor. People bustled on the pier, no one sparing them as much as a second glance. "Just make sure to stay on the busy roads as much as possible—the few guards here who aren't corrupt or sympathize with the Scythe have a habit of arriving five minutes late when someone calls for help."

Jespar nodded, turning his attention back to the looming city. They weren't even inside yet, but Jespar already felt the sweat pouring down his sides. A breeze washed over the dock, carrying what smelled like the perfume of a thousand sewers.

"All right. We're going to find that woman and meet you here at sunset."

It didn't sound as firm or assertive as he'd wanted it to. That the prospect of a day in this hellhole enthused him as much as a week of diarrhea might have played a role.

It didn't take them long to find a tavern, but by the time they had, Jespar's lungs were already burning from the nuvium fog, and the heat made him want to tear his cuirass off. Remembering the attack in the Jade District, he didn't.

The faded lettering above the shabby establishment's entrance read "Kreken's Arms," arching over the illustration of an octopus tearing a cobra in two, a political message that wasn't going to be winning any awards for subtlety. Inside, the place was small but meticulously decorated, stuffed fish and harpoons mounted on the walls and nets hanging from the ceiling. It was empty but for a group of sailors playing dice. A round of drinks and small talk with the scrawny innkeeper later, Jespar asked him whether he knew of a Makehu woman whose last name was Nakāni—the only clues they had been given.

It earned Jespar a snort. "Yer gonna have to gimme more than that. Every second Makehu's called Nakāni 'round here."

"She's said to have … abilities," Lysia offered. "Like a, um, seer."

The innkeeper's face shadowed. "Wait, ye ain't talkin' 'bout that crazy woman up the coast, are ye?"

"Maybe," Jespar said. "Who is she?"

"Ah, just some odd woman livin' up north … I ain't never seen her, but folk say she consorts with dead people or somethin'. What d'ye want from her?"

"We're still trying to figure that out," Lysia said.

The innkeeper pursed his lips and shrugged. "Well, none o' me business. I can tell ye what I know, but it's gonna cost ye."

A haggle later, Jespar's purse was forty sêr lighter, and they were on their way to the largest nuvium mine on the island where Nakāni was said to live.

They called it "The Pit."

———— ❧ ————

Time melted into a hot blur as Jespar and Lysia jostled their way through the crowded maze of Kekotoki, always following the dense pillar of fog that rose in the north. Jespar had hoped for a thoroughfare like Fortune Road that would allow them to cut straight through the city, but there was none, forcing them to take the countless rat runs, side roads, and rickety plankways of the platform towers instead. Once more, his composure while navigating these masses surprised him—some unease, and the familiar feeling of being watched, but no panic attacks.

In the outer districts, the roads were less populated and the platform towers smaller, but the overall destitution was worse: gaunt figures wallowed in the shadows wherever Jespar looked, and the buildings were ramshackle to the point of defying physics. At one point—the fog pillar was still a long way off—Lysia stopped in her tracks.

"Mind if we pay that place a visit?"

A house on the roadside had drawn her attention. It was nondescript except for a sign showing a thistle flower. A clinic.

"Is this about the 'business' you mentioned?" Jespar asked.

"Yeah, that's a pesthouse. I wanna take a look at a patient with lung rot."

"Lung rot is what you get from the fog?"

"That's right. One in two Hapanans gets it by the time they're thirty, and it necrotizes your lung tissue and forms these pus blisters that eventually make it impossible to breathe. I've been working on a biomantic shift, and I want to try it out to see if it helps."

Remembering Agaam's advice to stay on the beaten path, Jespar looked about. There were maybe two dozen people in their immediate vicinity, and Jespar even spotted two guards standing in the shade a little way off. Probably as safe as a place like Kekotoki got. "Okay, but let's be quick."

They headed to the pesthouse, and Lysia knocked. Some moments went by, then the grated slit in the door opened and revealed a wrinkled, wary face. "What?"

Lysia told the man she was a physician from Uunili and explained her intentions.

The pesthouse keeper studied her. "Fifty."

"Beg your pardon?"

"Fifty sêr and ye can gawk at our patients as long as ye like. Two of 'em with the rot died last week, but one's still breathin', a lad who came in a few days ago."

"I think you misunderstood," Lysia said. "I'm here to help them. I'm a physician and a bio—" She caught herself. "A mage."

The eyes on the other side of the slit narrowed. "Yer a witch?"

"Call it that if you will. I run a clinic in Uunili, and—"

"Well, this ain't Uunili. Pay or get lost."

Lysia's lips parted as if to protest, then became a hard line. She turned to leave.

"Twenty," Jespar said.

Lysia stopped in her tracks. The pesthouse keeper peered at him as if noticing him for the first time. "What was that?"

"Twenty sêr and you let her look at the patient. It's easy money, and she only wants to help."

Lysia gave Jespar a look as if she couldn't decide whether to be grateful or annoyed about his intervention. The pesthouse keeper frowned, then muttered something and slammed the slit shut. A key turned, and the door swung open. Before them stood a haggard man with thin hair and black mutton chops so bushy and big that they might have fit a bird's nest. Mutton Chops' lips hardened when he spotted the weapon sheaths on Jespar's belt, but then he thrust out his hand. Lysia dropped the twenty sêr, and Mutton Chops waved them inside with a grunt.

The pesthouse was as charming as the name suggested, a set of narrow corridors and dark spaces, the reek of the fog mixing with the leathery smell of sickness. Subdued moans and coughs came from the rooms in the back.

"Show me the boy," Lysia said.

The pesthouse keeper gestured to them to follow and led them to a door down the hallway. It opened to a low-ceilinged, twilit room; the red curtains gave the sunlight filtering through a yellow tint. Perhaps a dozen cots lined the walls, half of them occupied. Most patients appeared to be asleep; two were writhing in their beds to a chorus of coughs and gasps.

Mutton Chops pointed at a cot beside the entrance.

"There."

Had it not been for the boy's soft wheezing, Jespar would have thought he was looking at a corpse. Scabs clustered on the lad's skin, his sheet-draped body was skeletal, and his greasy hair far too thin and patchy for a child. Jespar's stomach tightened when he realized the boy could have been no older than ten. Even after living through a war, Jespar would never get used to this: there was just something so inherently wrong about the brain using the words "children" and "death" in the same observation, something that should have been a paradox but wasn't.

Lysia sank to her haunches beside the cot. She was silent for a moment before she began to examine him, first feeling her way around his throat, then holding a wooden tube against his breast and listening to him breathe.

When she was done, she sat back on her heels and regarded him, her hands laced before her mouth. "I'd like to try a spell on him."

Mutton Chops' brows drew together. "What kind of spell?"

"One that will help him. Stars burn me, when will you believe me that I'm here to help?"

Mutton Chops gave it some thought, then shrugged. "Do what ye want."

Ignoring the remark, Lysia placed her palms on the boy's chest. A faraway look came over her face, the telltale expression of a dimensionist glancing into the millions of possibilities their Sight allowed them to perceive.

The air around her distorted—and the boy jolted with a scream.

Jespar helped her pin him down; he tossed and cried and kicked, but the air kept warping, and Lysia's hands remained firm, veins pulsing at her temples and neck. It went on like this for a bit longer, then Lysia snatched back her hands as if from a hot stove. The boy slumped back into bed, cheeks wet, mouth agape. He stared at Lysia—scared, confused, accusatory—but then his eyes shut again, and he slipped back into a restless slumber.

Aside from one of the patients, who watched them with a dazed expression, all was back to normal. Mutton Chops still stood in the doorway, not moving a muscle.

Jespar hunkered down beside Lysia. "You okay?"

Sweat beaded on her forehead and her eyelids twitched. Shifting drain. "I can't do it. I can't heal him."

"So the shift didn't work?"

"It did, but it wasn't nearly strong enough. I give him a week, maybe two."

A picture rose to Jespar's mind.

The boy, coughing and convulsing on the cot, blood bubbling from his mouth. Jespar, a stride over, helpless. The boy's eyes meet his, wide open. Jespar knows that look.

The tang of burnt timber in his nostrils. The noose, pulling tighter. The—

Gritting his teeth, he killed the image, and gave Lysia's shoulder a light squeeze. She gave him a grateful look, then wiped her hands on her thighs, unclipped a pouch from her belt, and handed it to Mutton Chops. "Etheryme. Give him a pellet a day as soon as the rot reaches the final stages. It won't heal him, but—"

"Numbs the pain, I know. Was that all?"

"Yeah. Yeah, it was. You coming, Jespar?"

Jespar gave the boy a last glance. "Yes."

They were about to exit the building when Mutton Chops caught up to them. "Wait. You dropped this." He was holding Jespar's coin purse. "Earlier, when yer friend was witchin'."

"Dropped". More likely, the man had snatched it from his belt.

Unsure whether to be angry or grateful, Jespar muttered his thanks.

"No sweat," Mutton Chops said, tapping his fingers against his chest. "May ye prosper."

Not quite friendly. But not hostile either.

<hr />

An hour after leaving the pesthouse, they got lost.

Jespar had no explanation for how it had happened. They had stuck to the broad road upon reaching the outskirts, always following the fog pillar as the innkeeper had instructed them to, but at some point, they found themselves in a deserted courtyard. A square of shrubby, sunburnt soil framed by derelict shacks, and with no soul to be seen, it resembled a ghost town; the fly-riddled carcass of an emaciated alapu in the center completed the picture.

A dead end.

"Bloody hell. Where are we?" It was the first thing Lysia had said since their stop by the pesthouse. Jespar's attempts at brightening the mood had borne little success.

Jespar pulled down his scarf, which he had repurposed into a mouth covering. The air still stunk, but compared to the city center, it smelled like fresh grass. "I have no idea. Desolation Plaza in Misery District?"

He had hoped for a snort, but it was as if Lysia hadn't even heard. She sighed. "Mind if we take a break? The drain and the heat are killing me."

Jespar hesitated. They had strayed too far from the crowded areas for his liking, but his legs—still sore from the long rides yesterday—ached too, and the sunburn he'd gotten on his journey from Southport to Uunili stung like a bitch. "Yeah, okay. Good idea."

Lysia muttered something and slumped in the shadow of the nearest shack. When Jespar joined her, she pulled out a jar from her haversack. "Here, for the sunburn."

"Oh. Thanks."

The jar contained a sticky white salve that smelled as pleasant as it felt. Already, he could feel his skin relax. "Thanks," he said, handing it back to Lysia. "You're a lifesaver."

"Don't mention it." She shoved it back into her haversack. "Though I've gotta wonder why Moraia doesn't tell her messengers that the sun over the Bygone Sea is a bitch?"

"Not sure. Maybe she wants us all tanned and musky when we give our reports in her bedchamber."

This time, it got him the chuckle he'd wanted. "You're an idiot," Lysia said.

Jespar grinned. "At your service."

They sat in silence for a while, sipping from their canteens and nibbling on dates and coconut flakes.

"You wanna know the sad part?" Lysia said. "About the boy in the pesthouse?"

Jespar didn't know and didn't want to know, didn't want that image to come back. Hoping to talk about it would lift Lysia's spirits, he let her go on.

"His lungs weren't completely gone yet. A better biomancer than me, or at least a few of them together, could have restored them. Yeah, it would have been one hell of a shift, but still, they could have fixed him." She spat out a date kernel. "In other words, had that boy been born in the Jade District, he would live. He'd find out what it's like to be in love, get his heart broken, or even have kids—but, no, because he had the indecency to be born in the gutter and 'chose to be a pawn,' as that arsehole Enkshi put it, choking to death on his own blood and vomit is what it's gonna be."

"Lysia—"

"It's all just so unnecessary, Jespar. There are plenty of uninhabited islands around Hapana, and it would be perfectly possible to move the residential areas of the city there so the miners would only be exposed to the fog during certain times. But, no, then they'd have to sail to Hapana every single day and couldn't work as many hours, and who wants to pay for that? Let's just make these have-nots die in agony instead, even the godsdamned kids." She looked at him sideways. "Do you know who owns most of the mines here, by the way? Including the Pit?"

"Oonai?" he guessed.

"Exactly, Jaaros Godsdamned Oonai. Not that it would be any different if it were another 'Great Dreamer' running the show, of course. They're all the same: selfish arseholes who don't give a shite about anyone but themselves. I wonder if it's all those riches that made them so numb or if they were just pricks to start with." She took a deep swallow from her canteen, as if to cool her anger. A lizard scuttled past their feet.

"You know, I think—" Jespar broke off. "Ah, never mind."

"What?"

"Never mind. It's a bad time for philosophical discussions."

"Tell me."

"Well ... you asked whether it's the money that makes so many rich people indifferent, or if they were just born this way, right? I think it's neither. It's a matter of perspective."

"As in they choose to ignore the suffering they cause?"

"No, 'choose' is the wrong word. I'm pretty sure those guys *do* know how bad some people have it because of them, and they probably also know that stuff like this new decree will make things a lot worse for the poor. The problem is all this," he gestured around them, "is so detached from their upper-class reality that it's become a sort of abstract concept to them. Take the nomad killings in Arazeal last year. Do you know about them?"

"The heralds tried to sweep them under the rug, but, yeah, I heard about it. This racist underground group was murdering Itzika nomads, and the government indirectly condoned the killings by doing nothing to stop them."

"Right. So, at that time, both of us knew that shit was happening, and we probably felt bad about it. But, if we're perfectly honest with ourselves, did it affect us the same way it would have had we personally known a victim? No, it didn't, because it was all just too abstract and far away from us to *emotionally* care. And, no, that doesn't mean we're bad people—it's just how the mind works: even if you try to feel compassion for things outside the reality of your own life, you'll never care as much as you would if you were directly affected. It's healthy, even, because if you did, your mind would break under the pressure."

"The difference being that Arazeal is thousands of miles away, and the slums of Uunili are a three-hour walk from the Jade District. That comparison doesn't work."

Seeing her frown, Jespar regretted bringing it up. *Well, too late now.* He hadn't known her long, but something told him she'd be even more annoyed now if he rowed back now just to appease her. "You're taking 'far away' too literally. The bad things could be happening next door, and it would still be far enough for us to ignore it. Just think of someone who knows their neighbor is beating up his wife. Of course, they think it's terrible, but do they intervene? Probably not. None of their business, too 'far away.'"

"Okay, I see what you're getting at, but it still doesn't work, Jespar. The magnates *are* the abusers—*they* are beating up the neighbor's wife, to stick with the metaphor."

"True, but I wasn't done yet. Emotional distance is just one part of perspective." Jespar took out one of the scaly green fruits from his provision pouch and peeled it—snakefruits, as they were called. "The other is rationalization. Our minds create these 'lenses' through which we perceive the world, and their job is to always make us look like the good guys, no matter what we do. Those racists behind the nomad killings, for example, surely told themselves the Itzika were a threat to Arazalean society and saw themselves as the guys making the hard calls no one else would. Enkshi's lens, on the other hand, believes that we're all the architects of our own fortune, and failure is therefore always a choice."

"You say that as though believing these kinds of things isn't a choice."

"Well, is it? I mean, ask yourself: had you grown up as the crippled child of a struggling family and managed to fight your way up despite having been bullied to the brink of suicide, wouldn't you believe that if you made it big, everyone else can? I think there's a high probability that you would, just as Enkshi would be sitting here in your place had he lived through your experiences. Nobody *chooses* to do or believe the wrong thing, Lysia. We're all just products of our past and our circumstances."

Lysia pulled up her knees, squinting at the fog pillar that rose in the distance. "Okay, maybe that does play into it a little, but it's still a choice to go on being selfish. If not for that coma business, Oonai could decide to save thousands of lives tomorrow by moving the Hapanan miners to another island, but he doesn't, and the only reason for that is money."

Jespar studied his peeled snakefruit. He tossed it into his mouth. "How much did you pay for those boots?"

"Sorry, what?"

"Your boots," he said, chewing. "Those look like good craftsmanship to me. How much were they? Two hundred sêr, three hundred?"

"I don't remember. What are you on about?"

"Well, I'm just wondering why you don't give them away. I'm sure some beggar could sell them for enough to feed himself for a moon."

Lysia scoffed. "What, I'm like Enkshi and Oonai 'cause I don't give away my only pair of boots? Are you serious?"

"I am, actually." Jespar swallowed. "On a theoretical level, what makes your keeping the boots any less egotistical than Oonai keeping his riches?"

"Let me think: Oonai has a thousand pairs of boots, and I have just one?"

"One that you could easily trade for a cheaper pair and use the money to save a beggar from starving. I mean, it's not as if a few blisters would kill you, would they?" When Lysia narrowed her brows, Jespar raised a hand. "Look, you're probably the least selfish person I've ever met—it's just a thought experiment. My point is that we all draw a line between the good we could do and the good we actually do. Not that I'm any different, mind you. From the coin I spend on petals each week, I could probably feed an urchin child for a moon, but do I do it? No, my mind conveniently ignores that possibility and spins some story of why *my* egotism is perfectly acceptable. It's exactly the same mental mechanism the Great Dreamers have, Lysia."

"But on a completely different scale! Not giving away your last pair of boots isn't the same as letting miners choke to death on this bloody fog!"

"You're right, it's not, but where is the line, and who gets to draw it? If a middle-class merchant buys his wife some overpriced silk dress he has been saving toward rather than saving a beggar from starvation, why is that any less 'evil' than what the Great Dreamers do? Is it about the body count? If you go that route, people like Oonai or Enkshi have probably saved as many people with their food banks as they've killed." A fly landed on the sticky snakefruit hull in his fingers. He shooed it off. "As I've said: we could all do a lot more good than we actually do, and the only reason folk like to blame the rich for that impassiveness is because they are better off. Yeah, sure, some people are more selfish than others, but unless you live at the bare minimum and invest all your money into philanthropy, you still in some way or another choose your own comfort over someone else's life. All the time." The fly returned with reinforcements. Jespar flicked the hull toward the alapu corpse, making the insects turn around. "It's not even a choice to start with. Life makes us who we are, and our minds tell us we're all right. That's just how it works."

A long pause followed.

"And?" Lysia asked.

"And what?"

"And what's your solution? I mean, this is all very profound and philosophical, but let's assume you're right. Then what can we do to make people like Oonai change their perspective? Do we just sit around, drink wine, and talk about how wicked the world is?"

Wine sounds like a good place to start, Jespar thought. He really shouldn't have gone on this stupid lecture—it was probably the last thing Lysia needed to hear. Then again, he had always been like this—big on theorizing on the human soul, unable to talk about his own feelings. "You want an honest answer to that?" he asked.

"No, please lie."

"I don't think there's much we can do. People have believed whatever they felt like believing ever since humans first existed, and, in most cases, asking someone 'have you tried not being evil, you asshole?' achieves the complete opposite because it only antagonizes them further. It's sad, and I wish it were different, but I believe the world as a whole would be a whole lot better off if we all just minded our own godsdamned business and tried to do as little harm on the way as possible."

Lysia was silent for a time, studying the alapu carcass. Its ribcage showed through its patchy fur, a mockery of the overfed, clumsy specimen the Ma'saa kept.

"No, Jespar," Lysia said. "That's just lazy. What you're describing is resignation, and that's exactly why the oppressors have it so easy. If we—"

She broke off. Four figures had emerged from the alleyway and were coming toward them: three men and a woman, all armed.

Trouble.

Jespar's eyes flitted across the square, looking for an escape route, but the alley was the only way in and out. Giving Lysia a sideways glance, he got to his feet. With a worried expression, she followed his example.

The Hapanans stopped a few steps from them. The woman seemed to be the leader, a middle-aged Makehu with wild broad-stroked umako that contrasted her otherwise delicate appearance.

"So you're the wakemō healers," she said in perfect Inâl. "Hm. I expected something else."

Lysia blinked and worked her mouth. Jespar understood. "That pesthouse keeper sent you after us?"

The Makehu said nothing.

Jespar felt an odd ripple of guilt at the hurt in Lysia's face—as if that mutton-chopped asshole sending his thug friends after them had somehow been Jespar's fault. "Look, we really don't want any trouble. Just take what you want and let us go."

The Makehu scoffed. "You think that's what we are? Thugs?"

You surely aren't kind wayfarers, Jespar thought. "Who are you then? And what do you want?"

A haggard man with bad pockmarks joined in. "We're here 'cause Zuulan says ye work for the leeches."

Leeches. A memory stirred somewhere in Jespar.

"You're with the Scythe," Lysia said.

"And you're with the Master Leech," the Makehu replied. "Jaaros Ismirael Oonai."

Jespar's hand inched toward his longsword, but he stopped when he noticed something in the Makehu woman's expression. Doubt.

Of course.

Had they been sure about this, they wouldn't have bothered revealing themselves. Jespar and Lysia had eaten lunch out in the open like complete fools: two crossbow bolts to their neck, and the problem would have been solved.

Jespar forced himself to raise his hands, away from the sword, away from what might be their only chance at survival. "Wait a minute, this is a misunderstanding. We *don't* work for any magnate."

"That so?" another one of the men said, small and with hair wiry as steel wool, almost like a Starling's. "Then what is two outsiders doin' on Hapana?"

Jespar dithered as he struggled to come up with a good answer. Lysia came to his aid. "I'm a physician, and I'm here for research.

Didn't your pesthouse man tell you that?" Her right hand was by her hip, something shiny flashing in her palm. Probably a dagger. "This guy here, he's my bodyguard."

Jespar held back a sigh of relief. *Good one.*

"What kind of research?" the Makehu asked.

"On the lung rot. Come on, your man must have told you that. I examined one of the patients there and treated him, a little boy."

The Makehu didn't reply at once, but the hand on the pommel of her weapon relaxed the slightest bit. "Then what about that coin your bodyguard is carrying around?"

"Coin?"

The Makehu jutted her chin at Jespar's belt. "Zuulan said your friend had some Pyrayan coins in his purse. Everyone knows the Master Leech collects 'em."

The Starfall copper from the invitation. *Shit.*

"I was a merc on Nehrim," Jespar said, his heart picking up the pace. "We found a couple of those in a ruin."

Wiry Hair scoffed. "Sure."

The Makehu studied Jespar from beneath narrowed brows, then flicked a hand at the man to her right. "Vaal, search him."

"For what?"

"Moraia's knickers, of course. Anything to prove they work for the Leeches."

Trying his best to seem unfazed, Jespar's mind raced through his belongings. His shirt and trousers were from the ziggurat, but unless Jespar misremembered, they had no revealing embroidery. There was the skystone Enkshi had given them as payment for the dreamwalker, but he had hidden that one in his secret boot pouch, and even if they found it, he could probably bullshit his way out of—

Fuck.

Oonai's letter of passage. It was still in the inside pocket of his cuirass.

Vaal approached Jespar, gaze locked on Jespar's sword. "Yer belt. Now."

Four against two. Bad odds, even if Lysia knew how to fight.

"Ye deaf, outlander? Yer *belt.*"

"No," Jespar said quickly. "Sorry." He did as asked, palms coated in sweat as he handed the man the girdle. Vaal inspected Jespar's longsword, then set about searching his belt pouches, starting with the purse. Jespar swallowed into a dry throat. Had he really put the letter in the inside pocket? Or had he stashed it in one of the belt pouches? With all that had happened, he couldn't tell for sure.

It was the inside pocket. For su-

"There's somethin'," Vaal said, his hands lost in a pouch.

Shit.

Shit, shit, shit, shit, shit!

"What is it?" the Makehu asked.

Vaal drew a folded piece of paper from the pouch. "Looks like some kind of letter."

"Read it."

"I can't re—"

She tore the paper from his hands and skimmed through it, Jespar's pulse rising with every movement of her eyes. *Four against two,* he thought again. He and Naka had beaten those odds, more than once, but Naka was a Makehu giant with a two-handed war hammer. Whatever Jespar did, he needed to do it now, or-

The Makehu snorted.

"What is it, boss?" Wiry Hair asked.

She flipped the paper. A jumble of writing and symbols filled it top to bottom, stylized moons, suns, stars, and comets. "This is a guide to Akati."

Akati?

When his racing thoughts caught on, Jespar let out an inaudible breath. On his voyage from Nehrim, one of the first things the Kilayan scholar had taught him was a Kilayan card and gambling game—Akati. He had kept her instructional notes for reference.

"Right," Jespar said. "A friend of mine taught me. Haven't gotten around to playing much, though."

The Makehu eyed him, unblinking. "Are you with the leeches or not?"

"We're not."

Breaths came and went.

The woman's features relaxed. She flicked Vaal the note. "All right, you can go. Be more careful next time, though—we aren't thugs, but this area's crawling with 'em. It's a miracle you haven't been mugged already."

"Must be my stalwart physique," Jespar said, forcing a smile.

The Makehu surprised him with a snort. "Come on, lads. Let's go."

But Vaal didn't move. "Lemme search the rest of him, boss. And the woman too."

"Why?"

"Due protocol and all. Ye know leeches lie for a livin'."

Jespar looked at the Makehu, doing his best to seem indifferent. "Whatever you want."

Say no.

Just say no and leave, please.

The Makehu sighed. "Fine, but be quick ab—"

Jespar drew the throwing knife from his boot and slashed it across Vaal's throat. He croaked and grabbed for Jespar's wrists; Jespar rammed his knee into the man's groin and sent him to the ground. In a single motion, he scooped up his belt and drew his sword.

One down, three to go.

The others awoke from their stasis.

The fight was quick and brutal, a blur of steel and blood in the scorching green heat. When it was over, Wiry Hair lay dead at Jespar's feet, and the Makehu curled up beside the alapu's corpse. She clutched a growing red patch at her thigh, blood bubbling at her lips.

Screaming, behind him.

Lysia.

He whirled. The bald Scythe had pinned Lysia against a wall, his dagger at her neck; she was gripping his wrist with both hands, trying to keep him off, but the blade was inching closer.

Jespar lunged at the man, bringing down his sword in an overhead strike; the Scythe spun and hurled Lysia at Jespar, into the arc of his attack. Reflex or fluke, Lysia stumbled and fell, Jespar's sword missing her by a hair's breadth, the force of his swing sending him staggering forward. He was still struggling for footing when the pockmarked man shoved his dagger at Jespar's throat. Jespar sidestepped but was too slow, and the blade sunk deep into his right shoulder. The world went red. The Scythe yanked out the blade and stabbed him in the belly.

The cuirass caught it.

There was an instant of confusion on both sides, then the man grunted and thrust at Jespar's neck again; this time, Jespar caught his hand. They struggled back and forth, Jespar trying hard to fight off vertigo and the pain flooding him.

The Scythe went limp.

Lips parted, his eyes rolled up. Then he dropped his dagger and collapsed.

Numbly, Jespar stared at the corpse, his ears ringing, and his mind trying to make sense of what had happened. Only after two heartbeats, he grew aware of Lysia, who stood a stride behind the dead man.

"You're bleeding." Her voice shook, but her intonation was monotone.

Lifeless, Jespar thought. He unclenched his fist, still in mid-air where the Scythe's dagger had been seconds ago. "I'm okay. What did you- what did you do? How—"

"You're not okay," Lysia said. "Your shoulder's a mess."

She was right. Pain pulsed down his right arm, blood soaking his shirt.

"Lemme take a look at it."

Too dazed to press her about what had happened to the man, Jespar let Lysia lead him back to the shaded spot; the pain worsening with every step as the battle fervor ebbed away. She helped him sit, then knelt beside him, and pulled down Jespar's shirt. The wound bled profusely, making it hard to see just how deep it was.

Hands trembling, Lysia pulled a vial with a clear liquid from her belt. She soaked a piece of cloth in it and cleaned out the red mess on Jespar's arm.

"You got lucky," she said, still speaking in that monotone. "A little to the side, and he'd have hit the artery. Still, the cut's pretty deep, so you'll need stitches."

She gave Jespar a pellet of etheryme for the pain, then set about treating the wound. Even though she carried out all the steps—disinfecting, applying the tourniquet, making the stitches—with the routine and precision of a shoeshiner polishing his thousandth pair of boots, her lips trembled throughout the procedure.

When she was done, she sat back on her heels and stared at the stitched wound as if it bore the answer to an unasked question.

"Are you all right?"

No reaction.

"Lysia? Is everything okay?"

"You saved my life." There was no weight to her statement, no gravitas. She said it as if reading from a book.

"And you mine."

"Mm." Slowly, she raised her chin, fixing on the pillar of nuvium fog in the distance. "I rotted his heart."

"What?"

She weakly flicked her chin at the pockmarked man in the dust. "That man, you asked what I did to him. I rotted his heart."

"... A shift."

"Necromancy, yes. I just *felt* for where his heart was and putrefied it. It was so easy, Jespar, like ... like ..." Her eyes cracked and she buried her head in her hands. "Gods, I didn't mean to kill him! I'm a physician, I'm a healer, not a fucking murderer! *Fuck!*"

Jespar struggled for words. "Lysia ... that was self-defense. These guys, they would've killed—" He broke off when he realized how familiar her expression was. He'd seen it a hundred times during the war, most often on young recruits returning from their first battle; he, too, had probably looked like that once, that day a bunch of thieves had turned what should have been a simple warehouse guard job into a bloody nightmare. "Wait. That was your first time?"

Lysia nodded, tears trailing down her cheeks. "I mean, I've lost patients, dozens of them, but this? Never." She gulped in air and exhaled sharply. "Gods, how can you take it? This is messed up, this is so fucking *messed up.*"

Jespar looked at the corpses in the backyard. Unlike at the ambush in the Jade District, there was no flashback this time, no tang of charred timber, no phantom noose, no sobs from the Girl. Only that hollow sense of victory.

"It was them or us," Jespar said. "You just have to leave it at that."

Lysia was silent for a little longer. Then she reached for Jespar's wound again, cupping her palms over the wound. "Hold still."

"What are you doing?"

"Just hold still."

Warmth poured into his flesh, first burning, then soothing. It went on for some five seconds, then withdrew her hands, wincing. Sweat ran down her temples and some color had drained from her cheeks.

"Are you okay?" Jespar asked. "What'd you do?"

"Just a little shift to speed up the healing." She dressed the wound and pulled the bandage tight. "I could heal the whole thing, but with three shifts in the past twenty-four hours, that would put me to bed for a day."

"... You didn't have to do that."

An empty smile curved on her lips. "This mission has been going on for less than a day, and it already got bloody. You gotta be able to fight."

For want of a better answer, Jespar grunted and squeezed her hand. With Lysia's treatment and the shift, the wound hurt more like a bruise than the stab from a knife. Lysia held on to his hand for a second, then gently removed it and picked up her weapon from where she'd struggled with the Scythe—it wasn't a dagger but a clawblade, a curved knife with a thumb loop at the hilt. She gestured at the Makehu woman, who still lay curled up beside the alapu cadaver, clutching her bleeding thigh. Her quiet moans mixed with her ragged breaths. "She's still alive."

"Not for much longer. I think I hit her artery."

"I have to at least look at her," she said. "We can't let her bleed out in the dust like that."

Jespar sighed but didn't argue. He checked the square for any unwanted company—none but the corpses—then went over to the woman with Lysia. Jespar had figured the Makehu was unconscious by now, but when they squatted down next to her, her eyes opened, and she weakly raised her head.

"Fucking leeches," she muttered. "Rot ... rot in ..." She dropped back into the dirt.

"Maybe it's not too late," Lysia said. "We can still save her."

"And then what? Bring her back to her pesthouse friend and tell him we did this? She's lost gallons of blood, Lysia, even if you shift the wound shut. What are you gonna do about that?"

"I ..."

"Lysia," Jespar said softly. "It's over. All we can do is give her a quick death."

Lysia's lips parted as if about to argue. They fell shut. "Okay. Can you do it?"

"Yeah." Jespar drew his dagger and put it at the Makehu's throat. He gestured for Lysia to look away. She shook her head.

He cut.

For a time, silence filled the abandoned courtyard. When Lysia stood at last, her tears had dried, and a dullness had taken over her face. "We gotta do something about the bodies."

After a brief discussion, they hauled them into one of the deserted shacks; Jespar did his best to ignore the image of children stumbling upon them while playing. Then they washed their hands and faces with what little water they had left, shouldered their haversacks, and went back the way they'd come. Looking back one last time, Jespar saw that the flies had let off the alapu's carcass.

They scented new food.

CHAPTER SIX
TAKANA

DAY TWO
6TH MOON OF DRY SEASON, 1226 A.L.

The fog grew denser as they closed in on the Pit. By the time they reached the mining districts at the city's eastern edge, it had turned the sun into a hazy silhouette behind the green shroud, obscuring the passage of time. As the terrain had become more level, the hillside platform towers and the cramped shacks had given way to workshops and warehouses, and the rat runs and plankway to broad roads and symmetrical alleys. Workers swarmed in and out of the buildings, hauling crates and pulling handcarts of turquoise ore that glowed faintly through the fog like luminescent coral in a murky reef—nuvium. Jespar had gotten used to the stink of the air by now, but somehow that only made it worse—like breathing in invisible parasite eggs one didn't notice until they hatched.

After the umpteenth turn on yet another bleak road, Lysia put a hand on Jespar's shoulder. "Look."

A massive pit sunk into the ground ahead. Cranes swiveled, mine-carts rolled, and countless figures scurried along its edge, all shrouded in a din of shouting, clanking, and creaking. Behind it all rose the colossal fog pillar, spawned from the huge chimneys of a cluster of buildings. The smelteries.

"Seems like this is it," Lysia said. They hadn't spoken much since the incident, and Jespar was relieved to hear some life in her words.

He grunted. "Let's ask around."

"The Pit" worked as a name, but Jespar found that "The Crater" or "The Abyss" would have been more fitting: wide enough to fit a castle, the mine's eponymous trench was so deep that fog completely occluded the bottom. Circular tiers ringed it, tapering downward, all crowded by hundreds of miners that worked the turquoise patches on the ground and the walls. Scaffolding rose from bottom to top, holding a network of plankways, rails, and pulleys. With one nuvium nugget priced at several hundred sêr, Jespar tried to imagine the amount of money this mine produced daily. A mind-dazzling number, no doubt. Not much of it stayed here in Hapana.

They approached one of the overseers, a man with a long black mane luxurious enough to put any fairy-tale princess to shame, and asked him about Nakāni.

"The crazy one? What in the world d'ye want with *her*?"

"What's so crazy about her?" Jespar asked, evading the question.

Black Mane scratched his beard. "Well, folks say she makes 'em feel, y'know, twitchy. There's that one flotsam scavenger who lives out by the shore, and he always says he gets a queer feelin' when he's close to her house and bad dreams the night after. If ye believe him, it's 'cause the wench's possessed."

Bad dreams. He traded a glance with Lysia.

"I see," she said. "Could you tell us where she lives?"

"Um, sure." Black Mane flicked a thumb over his shoulder. "Just go past the longhouses and cross the plains to the cliffs. She lives in a shack by the precipice, it's easy to find. Ye—"

"Kaawan!" a woman shouted. "Ye ain't gettin' paid to chat!"

"All right, all right!" he called back, raising his hands in mock surrender. "Sorry, friends, ye heard the boss. May ye prosper."

Jespar watched him leave. "Nightmares whenever he gets near the house? Are you thinking the same thing as I am?"

Lysia nodded. "We're onto something."

The longhouses turned out to be a block of brick buildings extending past the smelteries on the barren plain. While their poor condition had the same air of impending catastrophe the Kekotokian platform towers emitted, their brightly painted façades contrasted with the bleakness of their surroundings: men and women of all ages chatted on chairs and benches on the forecourts; children zipped through the streets playing catch; a woman danced to an elderly man's lively drumbeat while bystanders clapped in rhythm. The scene reminded Jespar of the refugee camps he'd visited during the Nehrimese war. Even under the dreariest circumstances, people made their islands of levity.

The sun was well down west by the time Jespar and Lysia reached the cliff that covered the eastern coast. Fatigue filled his muscles, his shoulder wound throbbed, and his throat hurt from the noxious air. Already, the memory of the courtyard fight had a muddy feel to it. It was a familiar experience: once the visceral reality of the killing faded, the mind forgot. It had to.

Reaching the lip of the cliff, Lysia stopped dead.

Jespar caught up. "What is it—"

The ocean was tainted.

Beyond the gravel beach at the foot of the cliff, a mat of black molasses with a turquoise sheen stretched out into the sea, at least fifty strides before it faded to blue. Silver sticks were scattered on the shingle, glittering in the evening sun—dead fish.

"Worship the land as ye worship the Gods," a verse of *The Apotheosis* went. The magnates clearly begged to differ.

"What the hell is that stuff?" Jespar asked. "Does that come from the mines?"

"It does," Lysia replied, pulling her scarf higher over her mouth. "When you melt down a nugget, it separates into the inner and the outer layer, the essence and the mud. Only the essence is good for smithing, so ..."

"They dump the mud into the ocean."

"Yeah." Lysia turned away. "Let's find that woman."

Nakāni's home was a hut on a lichenous promontory jutting out over the shore. It was lovingly decorated, as though protesting its dreary surroundings: the walls were painted bright azure, bird figurines stood at the base of the front wall, and seashell chimes hung from the porch eave, tinkling in the wind.

They climbed the bluff and stopped at the porch steps. "Hello?" Jespar called.

No reaction.

He cupped his hands around his mouth. *"Hello?"*

Nothing.

Lysia went to the front door and raised her fist to knock.

And the world vanished.

Jespar stood on a frozen ocean.

It stretched as far as the eye could see, an endless expanse of ice under blue-gray clouds. There was no sun, not even a silhouette, yet a pale twilight immersed the landscape.

What the fuck?

Jespar looked down at him. A black depth stretched out under the clear ice, and something was floating up toward him, something small, something round.

No.

No, this isn't happening.

But it was. Up from the abyss floated the Corpse's severed head, strands of muscle and flaps of skin trailing from his neck, a cloud of black blood following him like octopus ink.

The world flickered.

Jespar was back on Hapana. Warm air surrounded him, the stench of the polluted ocean in his nostrils. No ice under his feet, just the weather-beaten planks of the porch.

Lysia's fist was frozen midair. "Did you-did you just ...?"

"Yeah," Jespar managed.

"What in the seven holy *fucks* was that?"

"I have no bloody idea. One moment, I was here, the next—"

"You were on an ice lake?"

"Yes."

Lysia looked at him as if hoping he had an explanation. He looked right back.

Pressing out a breath, Lysia shook her head. "Well, I'm sure Ma'saa Nakāni will be eager to explain."

She knocked again. This time, nothing happened—no ice lake, no Corpse, no hallucination.

Also: no answer.

Lysia tried again, knocking harder. Same result.

"Let's just wait," Jespar said. "She'll come back event—"

A shrill scream from inside cut him off.

They traded an alarmed look. Lysia rattled the doorknob, but it didn't budge.

Jespar joined her. "Lemme take a look." He sank to his knees and examined the door. The wood was cheap, probably weak enough to kick in, but as far as friendly negotiations were concerned, barging in like a burglar wasn't a good way to start. "There's probably some kind of lock bar on the other side. I could pick it."

Lysia didn't seem enthused about the prospect, but she didn't protest either. Muttering something under her breath, she stepped aside to let him do the work. A minute later, they slid into the hut and quietly closed the door behind them.

The green-yellow rays of the westering sun fell through the slits in the bamboo walls and illuminated the otherwise dark house. The interior was as nicely decorated as the outside: drawings covered the wooden screen that divided the hut in two, and the round stone table in the center of the front section was covered with an artfully embroidered green runner.

A moan.

Jespar's eyes shot across the room. A woman sat in a wicker chair beside the room divider. Obscured by the half-dark and still as a sculpture, she blended so well with her surroundings that she could have passed as a piece of furniture. His palm on the hilt of his longsword, Jespar gave Lysia a questioning glance.

"Hello?" Lysia ventured.

The woman moaned again.

"Are you okay?" Jespar tried his luck. "I'm sorry we came in, but we heard screams and wanted to make sure everything's all right."

Nothing.

"I don't think she can hear us," Lysia said.

"No. You think that's her? Nakāni?"

"Could be. I have no idea."

Slowly, they crossed the room.

For some reason, Jespar had imagined Ma'saa Nakāni as a kind, eccentric crone sharing a roof with her son or daughter and their kids. The woman in the wicker chair was nothing like that—no older than forty, long black hair framed a beautiful face, youthful except for the deep frown lines along the forehead; her umako, black brushstrokes pointing outward from her eyes like compass needles, reminded Jespar of Naka's; the eyes it framed were lost on the opposite wall as if it were a window to a different world.

"Ma'saa Nakāni?" Jespar said. "Can you—"

Flicker.

The ocean.

Jespar was back on the ocean, but this time the ice broke under his boots. Cold swallowed him, he screamed, clung to a floe seeking purchase, but then something *bumped* into his hip and floated up beside him, the Corpse's severed head, and he opened his mouth and—

Flicker.

Nakāni writhed and tossed in her chair. Barely having recovered his senses, Jespar reached for her, but before his hands had touched her shoulders, the convulsions stopped. With a gasp, she sank back into her chair and her head lolled to the side.

Gods. By the fucking Gods, what's happening?

Dazed, Jespar turned to Lysia. She was pale as bleached bone, and her hand clutched the hilt of her clawblade. Her lips opened, as though she were about to say something—but then Ma'saa Nakāni spoke.

"Peiu ū?"

Son.

The door swung open. Jespar whirled around, sword readied in beware stance.

Four silhouettes filled the doorframe, outlined by the setting sun: a girl, a boy, and two men, the younger one supporting the older with an arm around the shoulder.

Her family. This had to be her family.

Spotting the intruders, the girl shrieked and darted behind the young man. He let go of his father, hissed something in Makehu, and drew a knife.

For one, two, three heartbeats, no one moved.

Lysia raised her hands. "This is a misunderstanding."

The sun behind the family made it impossible to see their faces, but all of them stayed in place, the young man's knife pointed toward them. Not until Lysia shot Jespar a hard look did he remember that he still had his sword drawn. He sheathed it, then followed Lysia's example and put up his hands.

"We're not burglars," Lysia said. "Please, let us explain."

"Ye's breakin' into me house," the older man said, his Makehu accent blurring the words into one another. "Can't misunderstand that."

Bit by bit, Jespar's composure returned.

"Loku lo kīti lonu leie," he said. "Kapaka moio o'ipa e ite ... um ... lite mio 'atete kīti lonu nele nō." *Your wife was screaming. We just wanted to make sure she's safe.*

Lysia gave him a surprised look—a perfect mirror of the Makehu's expression.

"I Makēhu ite 'ōi 'ia?" the old man asked slowly.

"Toli, kōpū to." Jespar switched back to Inâl. "It's the truth, I swear it. We heard her screaming and just wanted to make sure she was okay."

The old man opened his mouth, but his wife beat him to an answer. "M-Mato? Is that ... is that ye?" She spoke quietly, her gaze still focused on that spot in the middle distance. "I'm sorry, everythin's ... so blurry today."

The tension dissolved.

"Takana?" the old man asked. "Ete ite 'ī?"

Ma'saa Nakāni stuck to Inâl. "Just a bit blurry. We have visitors today, Mato. They're people of good, troubled but good." Turning to Jespar, her lips twitched. "Very troubled, this one. Don't get lost in the swamp, pi'a. Don't."

Jespar's heart skipped a beat. "I'm sorry?"

It was as if she hadn't heard. She blinked once, then resumed staring into the wall. "The ocean's endless. Ain't nothin' but water, just dark water 'til the horizon ... and yer alone, always alone, and it's eatin' ye. But ye know why I hold on? 'Cause I know that one day, Īmīte come from its nest in the sky and help us sleep. It make us dream, dream like everyone else do, and when we wake, we are finally happy." Tears forming on her lids, she looked at Lysia. "Did Īmīte send ye, watōko? Are ye Īmīte's nestling?"

"I-I'm sorry, I don't—"

"Ye got to help us, me and him. Just one night in silence, y'know? Hīo mē'a ... mē'a e ... kuno ..." Here, her voice trailed off into an unintelligible mutter.

Grunting, the old Makehu pushed past his son and went to his wife—Takana. There was a limp in his gait and he winced at every step, yet he walked fast and passed Jespar and Lysia without a second glance. He hunkered down by Takana's side, took her hand, and spoke to her in low tones.

The mumbling went on for a little longer, but eventually, she fell quiet, sunk back into the chair, and stared at the ceiling.

Her husband rose to his feet. A solid umako framed his dark brown eyes, like a thief's mask from a theater play.

"Kawu," he told his son. "Make tea. The wakemō have some explainin' to do."

As the Ma'saa and Enkshi had instructed them to, Jespar and Lysia kept their story vague: an Uunilian merchant plagued by nightmares had heard about a mysterious Makehu woman capable of entering other people's dreams and wished for her to visit his own to find out what was causing them. The "dreamwalker" would be generously rewarded for her help—once upon signing the contract, and again should her aid contribute to curing him.

When they were finished, the father, who had introduced himself as Maiato Nakāni, took a long sip from his tea. Jespar, Lysia, Maiato, and the son, Kawu, sat on wooden stumps around the stone table, and Ma'saa Nakāni was asleep in the back of the hut; the two younger children had been sent out to play. The skystone Enkshi had given Jespar for Nakāni's initial payment lay between them, scintillating in the glow of a candle. With seven colors, it must have been worth well over a hundred thousand sêr.

"I understand," Maiato said at last. "But I'm afraid me wife can't help ye. Maybe ten years ago, she can. Not anymore."

There was a brief silence.

"She's ill, isn't she?" Lysia asked softly.

Maiato grunted in agreement.

"What does she have? I might be able to help her. I've treated mental afflictions before."

A knot appeared between Maiato's brows.

Jespar pointed at his temple. "E'ēka ... e'ēka e ..."

"E'ēka e tau?"

"Toli."

"Ah. I see."

Lysia nodded. "As I said, maybe I can help. There are draughts, herbs—"

"Thank ye, but that will not work. It ain't a 'mental affliction', and it can't be cured 'cause it's her gift that's doin' it. The gift *is* the illness."

"What do you mean?" Jespar asked.

Maiato sighed and told his son Kawu something in Makehu, too low for Jespar to catch. The young man's demeanor had changed since the hostility had evaporated; he had followed the conversation quietly, gaze glued to the table as if too shy to look up. Age difference aside—the boy could have been no older than twenty, maybe twenty-two—he was a mirror image of his father, the same soft, handsome features, the same beardless cheeks, the same straight black hair, cut to a finger-length. Only his skin and his eyes took after his mother: light brown and hazel, respectively. He had no umako.

"Kaia auli 'ī?" Kawu asked, sounding surprised. *Are you sure?*

"Toli," Maiato said. "Excuse me, ma'sae. I will go get some air." With that, he limped out of the room.

When the door had fallen shut behind him, Jespar turned to Kawu. "Wei'o lo apa nō 'ī?" *Did we offend him?*

Kawu made a little snort. "It's *wai'o*, not *wei'o*. 'Wai' is 'to offend', 'wei' is 'to cook over a fire.'"

Lysia snorted.

"Right," Jespar said. "Sorry."

"No problem at all. Your Makehu is very good for a watōko, ma'sao. Where did you learn it, if you don't mind me asking?" Unlike his father, Kawu spoke flawless High Inâl. Not even a trace of an accent, Kilayan or Makehu.

"A friend taught me," Jespar said. "Why did your father leave?"

"As he said, he just needed some air." Kawu was turning his cup on the spot, eyes following its movements. "He also asked me to tell you about my mother's gift."

"Thank you," Lysia said. "We appreciate that."

"It's fine—it's better for us to tell you than have the islanders smear her name with their talk of witchcraft and demons. Perhaps it's best if you start, though. What have you heard about her?"

"That she can enter other people's minds," Lysia said.

"And cure people from or give them nightmares," Jespar added, remembering the hallucinations. They hadn't mentioned them yet.

"I see. Well, she can do all these things, but they are just ... byproducts of her gift, you might say. The core of it is that my mother's mind works differently from that of a normal person." He sipped from his tea, then resumed turning his mug. "You see, most people believe thoughts and dreams are private and only exist in our heads, but that's a misconception. There's actually something that connects us all."

"Are you talking about the psychic dimension?" Lysia asked.

Kawu looked up, surprised. "You are ...?"

"Initiated, yes. I'm a biomancer."

Kawu stopped turning his mug, gripping it tightly. *No wonder.* Though Jespar suspected Kilay was far more lenient than Enderal in that regard, talking openly about dimensionism certainly still passed for a crime, or at the very least, a punishable misdemeanor.

"Don't worry," Jespar said. "We're not gonna get you in trouble. Lysia spoke about it first."

"Exactly," Lysia agreed. "The question is, rather, how come *you* know about this? You're not a scholar or a dimensionist, are you?"

Kawu's fingers relaxed. "No," he said. "No, I'm not. But I work as a servant for a scholar, and he has taught me some things. As for your question, you're right: dimensionists refer to this realm of thought as 'the psychic dimension,' the space where our thoughts manifest as mental energy."

Knowing little about the workings of psychomancy—it was a Profane Sight and had therefore not been a part of his dimensionism curriculum—Jespar struggled with the concept. "When you say thoughts 'manifest' in that dimension, what do you mean? Do they become, like, physical? Tangible?"

Lysia helped Kawu out. "Just imagine it as sound: when you speak, you cause vibrations to travel through the air, which, in turn, cause your own eardrums to vibrate, which your brain interprets as sound. Thoughts aren't that different: whenever someone thinks of, say, a panther, that panther temporarily materializes in the psychic dimension the way the person imagines it. But whereas most of us can hear sound because we have functioning eardrums, these 'thought waves' are imperceptible to people, except psychomancers—and even they have to deafen themselves to it, so they don't go mad."

"That's a good comparison," Kawu said. "We lack the 'psychic eardrums,' so to speak."

Jespar's head swam. "So it's like a ... collective consciousness that no one's aware of? A world that contains everyone's thoughts?"

"In short, yes. As your friend said, it's like sound waves."

For a strange moment, Jespar saw himself from a bird's eye view, pictures and letters floating from his mind like dandelion seeds. *You live and learn.* "Okay, I think I get it. Then I assume your mother is a psychomancer?"

"In a way. My mother has 'psychic eardrums,' but they're different from the ones a cusping psychomancer has, in that they only work while she is dreaming. In waking life, she is as deaf to the psychic dimension as we are."

Lysia looked spellbound. "So it *is* a sub-Sight of psychomancy, just as I thought. How exactly does that work, then? Perceiving the psychic dimension while you're asleep? Does your mother become some sort of, I don't know, thought specter when she dreams?"

"I suppose you could call it that. We all become thought specters when we sleep."

"... Now you lost me," Lysia said. Jespar sympathized.

"It's complicated." He resumed turning the mug, eyes fixed on the clay. It was painted a sky blue—probably a color not often seen on Hapana. "To understand, you first need to know that our consciousness goes through three stages when falling asleep: first, it shuts itself off from the waking world and completely submerges itself into the psychic dimension, the *Imūma*, as we call it. We *become* thought, in other words. Then, our consciousness takes on the form of an imaginary body and uses it to traverse the Imūma until it reaches its *kuluhika*, one's personal dream realm inside the psychic dimension. Finally, it enters this kuluhika and dreams until waking up propels it back into reality. Are you still with me?"

"I think so," Lysia said. "But I'm not sure I understand why our minds would need to go to some 'personal dream realm' in the psychic dimension to dream. I mean, aren't dreams just a firework of thoughts inside our own heads?"

"It makes sense to assume that, but, no, according to my mother, they aren't. Dreams unfold in a separate plane, on a deep level of the psychic dimension."

"Why?" Jespar asked. His brain felt like it was rodeoing on a ball of lightning.

"Well, my mother believes it's because the mind needs to be on this deep level to recuperate properly, but that's just a theory—the truth is, we don't know." He stopped moving the mug. "Now, as you can probably guess considering how no one knows about all this, us normal people are completely oblivious to this process, even psychomancers. We just fall asleep and then wake up, and all our brains remember are bits and pieces from what we experienced in our kuluhikas, nothing of what happened in between." He lifted his gaze from the mug. "And that's where dreamwalkers are different: they are aware of the entire experience."

Jespar tugged at his scarf. "The whole thing?"

"The whole thing. Everything from falling asleep, to their consciousness traversing the Imūma in search of their kuluhika, to the dreams that unfold inside it—they perceive it just like we perceive reality right now. For a dreamwalker, falling asleep is like slipping into another world."

Lysia blinked. "That's ... fascinating."

Jespar, for whom the idea of consciously living through a night's worth of nightmares was not at all appealing, said nothing.

"I can see why you'd feel this way," Kawu replied. He seemed about to say more, but then he let out a breath and shook his head instead. "Would you care for some more tea, ma'sae?"

They concurred. While Lysia remained seated and studied her hands with a pensive expression, Jespar stood and stretched his legs, watching Kawu as he heated another kettle on the crude kitchen stove. In the yellow-green sunset that poured through the slats, Jespar now saw that the young Makehu's eyes weren't hazel as he had thought, but an unusual dark green, like some plant that only grew at the bottom of the ocean. *Unusual like him*, Jespar thought. He prided himself on being good at reading people, but Kawu gave him a hard time; there was something odd, something contradictory about him that Jespar couldn't quite figure out.

"All right," Jespar said after Kawu had made them tea and served the three of them. "So that ability to stay aware while sleeping also allows your mother to enter other people's dreams?"

"If they are also asleep, yes."

"And how does that work?" Lysia asked. "Can she just enter their dream spaces, their 'cooloo-heekas'?"

"That's complicated," Kawu replied. "And it doesn't really matter. But when my father said that my mother's 'gift' is also her illness, he meant that her Sight takes a toll on her." His eyes wandered to the curtain door in the room divider, toward the back room where his mother slept. "This constant awareness my mother has, it also means that her mind never gets to rest. Whereas a normal person blacks out at night and wakes up refreshed in the mornings, life to a dreamwalker is just one continuous experience, from reality to dream and back to reality, until the day they die. And the human mind simply isn't made for that, I don't know, that barrage of impressions. That's why most dreamwalkers eventually break under the pressure."

"Is that what happened to your mother?" Lysia asked softly.

"It is." Kawu studied the skystone on the table between them. His expression was perfectly neutral, as though studying a nondescript piece of furniture. "That pressure can affect the brain in all kinds of ways, but for my mother, it made her lose the ability to tell the difference between the psychic dimension and reality—she either sees them both at the same time or flickers between the two. Until last year, she had a few clear days every week, but now, a couple of hours each day are a blessing from Īmīte. It's been—" He broke off. "Ah, well, you didn't come here to listen to my self-pity. It is what it is."

A pause.

"I'm sorry," Jespar said.

Kawu looked up, then immediately back to the table.

"I'm sorry too," Lysia said. "If I may ask, does your mother's condition also have to do with these hallucinations we've had?"

"Hallucinations?"

"Yeah, I don't know what else to call them. One moment, we were here, the next we were on some kind of ... frozen ocean? It happened twice."

Kawu sighed deeply. "Oh, Īmīte. I apologize."

"So you know what it was?" Jespar asked.

"Yes, one of my mother's seizures—she has them from time to time, but they've gotten worse lately. Whenever they happen, she accidentally strikes a shift on everyone in her vicinity and pulls their minds into the Imūma alongside her."

Jespar chewed on that for a moment. "Wait. Are you saying that that ocean we saw is the psychic dimension?"

"It is. The shifts are harmless and only last a few seconds, but still, I imagine it must have been terrifying. I'm deeply sorry this happened to you ... maybe you understand now why we live so far from other people."

"Actually, I've been wondering about that," Lysia said. "How come your mother never went to a university? Scholars from all over the world would fight over a chance to study an undiscovered Sight like this. She would have been a sensation."

Kawu's smile was hollow. "And just how would she make the passage to Uunili? Imagine her having a seizure in the middle of a crowd. Even if the drain of a collective shift like that wouldn't kill her, the people probably would afterward. Yes, to the scholars, my mother might be a sensation, but to these superstitious folk, she'll always be a witch or a demon caller." Kawu shook his head. "And even if we made the journey somehow—we won't let scholars use us as experimental rats for the rest of our lives. We won't."

As if those words were his cue, the door opened, and Maiato returned. He limped to the table, but instead of sitting down, he stood with crossed arms. "Did me son answer yer questions?"

"He did," Lysia said. "We were just discussing—"

"Good, then ye know me wife can't help. Now leave, me son will take ye back to the city."

Kawu seemed as baffled by his father's sudden brusqueness as Jespar did. "Father, we—"

"Kunō 'ō, pi'a u." *Quiet, son.* He glared at Jespar and Lysia. "Please leave. Getting late."

Jespar fumbled for words. "I'm sorry, can't we at least—"

"*Leave.*"

Jespar looked from Maiato to Kawu, then at the skystone on the table. *A hundred thousand sêr at your fingertips, and you don't even bother looking for solutions?* How in the world did that make sense? Then again, if Takana Nakāni's condition really was as bad as her son had said, Maiato was probably right: this woman couldn't help them, dreamwalker or not. Hell, the mere fact that she wasn't able to speak for herself proved it.

Jespar made to get up and thank them for their time. Then something clicked.

"You're a dreamwalker."

The attention shifted to Jespar.

His gaze was on Kawu. "You have the Sight too, don't you? You're a dreamwalker."

The inkling of doubt he'd still had disappeared at Kawu's hesitation.

Bull's-eye.

Kawu's fingers went back to clutching his mug. "I don't know what you're talking about, ma'sao."

"Yes, you do. Earlier on, your mother said, 'You have to help us, me and him,' and just a minute ago, you said, 'We won't let the scholars use us as experimental rats.' Even if your mother can't help us, you could."

Kawu's eyes sought his father's.

Maiato's mien shifted from grim to hostile. "All right, the wakemō's very smart. Still, the answer's no."

"But why? Sorry, but that doesn't make any sense. This gem is worth a fortune, and it's yours even if it turns out you *can't* help our employer. Why not at least give it a shot?"

"Peie to hawaka huwe lai!" Maiato burst out. *Because it's dangerous!* "Dreamwalking ain't no 'gift', dreamwalking is a rotten curse that poison everything, and me son won't risk his life so some greedy fat cat from Uunili get richer! Now, one last time, *leave!*"

There was an uncomfortable silence. Jespar gave Lysia a sideways glance, seeking aid. There was a way to convince them; he was sure of it. They only had to find it.

Lysia let out a sigh. "Okay, all right. Can you give us one more second, though? There's one thing you should know before you make that decision. If you still want us gone after that, fine."

Maiato scowled but flicked his hand in agreement.

"Thank you." She rested her elbows on the table. "We're actually not supposed to tell you this, but considering what's at stake, I think you have to know before you make that decision: we're not working for just any merchant, but for the First Magnate, Jaaros Ismirael Oonai."

Jespar gave her an alarmed glance. She ignored it.

Maiato shifted his weight from one foot to the other. "And?"

"And he isn't just suffering from nightmares. He's dying."

While Kawu's face blanched at this, his father's remained stony. "Dying," Maiato echoed. "From what, a disease?"

"That's the thing, no one knows. He has fallen into this odd coma, and all the physicians and dimensionists in Kilay are clueless. And that's why we're here—because First Dame Nayima Oonai was hoping your wife can enter the First Magnate's dreams and find out what happened to him." She looked at Kawu. "Now, I don't care much for the magnates myself, but the fact is, if the First Magnate dies or word of his condition gets out, that'll have nasty consequences. I'm sure you're familiar with the Scythe?"

Maiato tentatively raised his middle fingers to his sternum.

"Good, then you also know how powerful they've become. Now, what do you think is gonna happen if the Scythe learns that the head of this country is on the verge of death? That's right, they will pounce at the opportunity, and before you know it, you'll have a terrible civil war raging across the entire archipelago, all the while the remaining magnates will vie to fill the power void." She leaned back. "Now, perhaps you think that this would finally put an end to the injustices in this country, but trust me, war always hits the innocent the hardest. This isn't the way. We need to cure Oonai as fast as we can, and, as it stands, your son is the only hope he's got."

Maiato studied Lysia. "Do ye know the story of our island?"

"Not the details," Lysia said.

"Pi'a?" he asked Kawu. "Tell them."

"Of course, father." Kawu finally let go of his mug. "You see, ma'sae, Hapana wasn't always like this. It was never the greenest island in the Archipelago, but things looked very different fifteen years ago. Have you ever heard of the Onelyses?"

Jespar and Lysia shook their heads.

"They were the family who owned most of the mines back then. Great Dreamers, for certain, but they never stopped caring about the people who worked for them—so much, in fact, that they would continue to pay their miners when they became too old to work or got into a workplace accident." He studied his hands. Unlike his father's, they were lithe and uncalloused, not those of a laborer. "And that was their demise. Word about how good the miners of Hapana were off spread, and eventually, people from across the Archipelago rose up and demanded the same rights."

"Which didn't sit well with the magnates?" Jespar asked.

"Not at all. Just when those protests were at their peak, there was a terrible 'accident' in the Pit, a rockslide that buried well over four hundred people under it. The damage ruined the Onelyses, and the Coalition pressured them into selling their mines to Magnates Oonai and Vel'Ravan, who immediately ended the pensions and accident pays, and instead opened up even more veins on the island." Kawu looked up, face blank. "You see what it led to."

Ma'saa Nakāni moaned in the back of the hut, then broke into a whisper. The muddy sunset light was fading, darkness trickling into the room. Maiato sank to his knees by the table and pushed the sky-stone back to Jespar. "Maybe you understand now. We don't want Oonai to die, no, but we ain't gonna cry if he does. Now go, we're done here." He gestured to Kawu. "Maheio 'ō nō lonu nele hupe, peiu ū." *Show them out, son.*

Kawu nodded and rose, collecting the teacups from the table and carrying them to the kitchen counter. Maiato jutted his chin at the door.

"... Fair enough," Lysia said. "Fair enough."

Jespar was just about to pick up the skystone and slip it back into his pouch when a memory crossed his mind. Enkshi and Lysia, arguing.

Every situation is also a chance, Varroy, no matter how dire. You only have to find a loophole and use it.

"You're wasting a chance," he said.

All eyes turned on him.

DREAMS OF THE DYING

"What did ye say?" Maiato said.

"I said that you're wasting a chance. Look, you don't care if Oonai lives or dies, I get it. But do you really think your personal feelings should be the deciding factor here?" Jespar glanced around the house. "That skystone alone will probably bring you about a hundred thousand sêr on the market, and that's just the first part of your payment. Are you aware of what you could buy with that amount of money?"

Maiato's brows narrowed. With his thick umako, it looked like the mouth of a cave closing. "We don't need yer blood money."

Like hell you don't, Jespar thought. Maiato was a cripple, the two children were too young to work, and, with her condition, his wife was practically bedridden. In all likelihood, Kawu was the breadwinner of the family, and no amount of charming decoration could hide that the coin he brought home was barely enough to get by.

"That may be true for you," Jespar said, "but what about your children and your future grandchildren? That money would not only be enough to ensure a good life for your generation but also for the ones after you, if you invest it right. Would you really make that decision for them?"

"Atete ite ka'o lai." Maiato spoke quietly, but the hurt shone clear through his words. *You know nothing.* Jespar felt a pang of guilt for putting the man on the spot, but he also knew he had no choice if he wanted his argument to work. After all, it wasn't the old Makehu Jespar was trying to convince.

"Maybe not. But I know that you're not the only one who's going to be affected by your decision, and I'm not just talking about your family. Think about your people, the Makehu."

"What do you mean?" Kawu asked from the kitchen counter, the empty cups in his hand. It earned him a hard look from his father, but he kept his gaze steady.

"Well, how many of the magnates are Makehu? Zero?"

"There is the Band of Elders."

"Okay, the Elders. But how much influence do they *really* have? Judging from what I heard, the Coalition only asks their opinion when they know it doesn't go against their own interests."

All Jespar really knew about the Elders were things he'd picked up from his conversations with the scholar on the ship to Kilay, yet Kawu and Maiato's reactions showed he'd hit the nail on the head.

"What I'm getting at," Jespar went on, now looking at Kawu, "is that the Makehu need more voices in the upper class who represent them, and even the best minds sometimes need a leg up. Which is exactly what this could be for you. The money from this job would not only give you and your family the life you deserve but would allow you to start your own business and work your way to the top."

"You say this as though it were simple," Kawu said quietly.

"It isn't, and maybe you'd fail. But you'll never find out if you throw this chance a—"

"Out." Maiato's fists were shaking at his sides. "Now."

Jespar remained a second longer, eyes trained on Kawu with what he hoped parsed as a silent plea. Then he shrugged. "All right. I tried."

He went to the door. His hand was on the knob when Kawu spoke up.

"Wait."

Jespar turned around.

"I'll help you," Kawu said, putting the cups onto the counter. "I'll do it."

A pause.

"To leikū, pi'a." Maiato's words were like a blade. "Wilō ite." *Wrong, boy. You will stay.*

Kawu flinched as if he'd been struck, but his expression remained firm. "Stay and do what? Keep serving meals to that sad old man for the rest of my life? Īmīte, you know why he wants me to stay so late sometimes, don't you?"

Maiato scowled and gave a sharp reply that was too fast for Jespar to catch; whatever Kawu answered only added to his father's anger. The argument went back and forth until Maiato unmistakably gestured for Jespar and Lysia to leave.

They did.

"That was manipulative," Lysia said as they sat on the lip of the cliff, the setting sun soaking the dreary landscape with sickly yellow light. The two Nakāni children were collecting some kind of plant a little way over, walking so dangerously close along to the edge Jespar feared a gust would blow them over the precipice.

"But true. I mean, you saw how they live, right? They need that money as much as this island needs trees."

"And what if the mission goes south? What do you think is gonna happen to this family if the boy doesn't come back?"

"Lysia, we're not hiring him to take down the Scythe with his bare hands. We'll be back in the ziggurat tomorrow, he'll do his dream-walking thing, and then he'll go home with enough money to buy a house. Easy."

"So far, nothing about this mission has been easy."

Fair point. "Would you rather I did nothing, and we just walked away?"

Lysia stared out to sea, rubbing the scar on her cheek. "No. No, I wouldn't. I'm sorry, I'm just ... tired, I guess. This whole thing hasn't been what I expected it to be."

"I'll drink to that."

They were silent for a time, watching as the last sliver of the sun sank into the tainted ocean.

It was dark by the time the door of the hut swung open. Kawu approached them, a bag over his shoulder, wearing a black-brown barkcloth shirt, a matching skirt, and sandals. He stopped some steps before them, looking at the ground. Apparently, his new-found resolve hadn't changed his inability to make eye contact with strangers. "I promised I'd be gone for no more than a week. If Ma'sao Oonai isn't cured by then, I'll return, second payment or not."

Lysia gave Kawu an odd look Jespar had trouble placing. Scrutinizing? Nervous? "That's fine," she said. "It should only take a couple of days."

"Very well." Kawu tugged at the collar of his shirt. "There is one more thing, though: I'm not nearly as good as my mother used to be. I *have* dreamwalked into another person's mind before, but that was years ago, and I don't know if I can do still do it."

Jespar swallowed the snakefruit he'd been munching on. "No way to know until you try."

"Yes. I suppose so." Kawu's lips parted as though he meant to say more, but then he closed them and looked down the edge of the cliff. "I'll go say goodbye to my siblings then we can leave. Is that all right with you?"

"Of course."

Kawu went to his siblings and hugged them both. A weight settled on Jespar's shoulders when the younger boy started to cry.

Thanks to Kawu's knowledge of the city, it took them less than two hours to get back to the harbor. Agaam was waiting for them at the pier, his forehead wrinkling when he noticed Kawu. Introductions were made, explanations given.

"Fine," Agaam said. "Welcome aboard, Ma'sao Nakāni."

Soon after, the cutter was on its way back to the Alabaster City, and Jespar was leaning against the mast, a pipe of nightflower between his lips. After a bath in the seawater and with a meal in his stomach, he almost felt like a human being again.

Jespar finished his pipe and walked over to Kawu, who stood at the starboard railing, watching Hapana's jagged silhouette shrink into the horizon. Shrouded in the glowing fog, it looked like skeletal teeth poking into the night.

"Hey."

Kawu glanced up, then immediately back to the ink-black water. "Oh. Hello."

"I, um, just wanted to thank you for helping us. Must have been hard crossing your father like this." It wasn't just an empty phrase. Back when his own father was still alive, Jespar had never dared to do.

"It's fine," Kawu said. "Your friend was right. If there would be a civil war, and I could have prevented it, I'd share part of the blame." He rubbed the back of his neck. "Not to mention that we *do* need the money, regardless of what my father says. He's proud and afraid of losing me, but he doesn't understand that he might lose all four of us if it keeps going on like this." His hand went back to the railing. "So, yes, Ma'sao Dal'Varek, there really is no need to thank me. If anything, I should be thanking you and Ma'saa Varroy for reminding me not to be another one of those people who talk big but only care about themselves when it matters."

Something about the way he said it gave Jespar pause. He understood now what it was about Kawu that he found so intriguing: he somehow seemed old and young at the same time. His appearance, constant nervousness, and timid demeanor made Jespar place him at no more than twenty-two winters, but there was a weary melancholy to him that seemed more befitting a much older man.

"I'm afraid that's the majority," Jespar said, elegantly omitting that he had proven time and again that he was part of it. "Listen, we only have two cots, but you can have mine if you want. I'm used to sleeping outdoors."

"Thank you, ma'sao, but that won't be necessary. I don't sleep the way you do."

"Right. Your gift."

"Mm-hm."

When Kawu said nothing else, Jespar nodded. "Well, I better leave you to it, then. Oh, and by the way, call me Jespar. I never liked formalities."

Kawu offered him a pale smile. "Very well. And you can call me Kawu."

Jespar made his way down to his cabin, nodding at Agaam in passing, who sat by the stern with a hand resting on the tiller. He returned the gesture.

Lysia sat on the edge of her cot, reading like she had been this morning.

"Rejoiceth," she said, closing the book and tossing it on the night-stand. "At last, yon noble adventurer hath come to proffer unto this humble wench some company."

Grinning, Jespar dropped onto the cot beside her. "What a day—"

She kissed him.

It blanked out all the rest: the sting of his shoulder wound, the fatigue in his bones, the lurking images of the blood he had spilled, and the lives he had taken.

When she drew back, Jespar chuckled. "Now that came out of nowhere."

"Yeah, well, I needed a change from all that gloom." That lop-sided smirk was back on her lips, but something about it seemed off. She trailed her hand up Jespar's thigh. "How about you?"

There was a tickle in Jespar's stomach, but it died quickly. He took her hand and kissed it. "You're beautiful, you know that?"

Lysia's smirk faded. "I sense a 'but' coming."

"Well ... I don't know." He rested his back against the wall. "I guess I'm still a bit shaken."

Sighing, Lysia slid up beside him. "Yeah, me too, and that was my attempt at distracting myself. I just can't stop thinking about it."

"You mean the fight? Lysia, I told you, it was self-defense. Those guys chose their own—"

"Let's not talk about it. Please."

"Okay, sure. Whatever you need."

Her smile resurfaced—weaker, but more authentic. "Appreciate it. Now, I *do* have to ask you to take your shirt off, though, I gotta check your wound. Can you handle that much nudity?"

"I'll do my best."

Jespar stripped off his shirt and removed the bandage. Lysia cleaned the wound, applied some salve, and replaced the dressing. "Can I ask you something?" she asked.

"Sure."

"That lad. What's your take on him?"

"Kawu?"

"You're on a first-name basis now?"

"Yeah, we spoke earlier."

"Okay, so what do you make of him?"

"Hm. He's hard to read."

"I see." Lysia fastened the bandage and tucked the loose ends together with a pin. "Doesn't he make you feel ... I don't know, jittery?"

"What do you mean?"

"Well, like, uneasy. Something about him gives me the willies, and I was wondering if you feel it too." She nodded at the bandage. "All good, by the way."

"Thanks." He put his shirt back on and buttoned up the collar. "You're right. There *is* something different about him. I wouldn't say it makes me uneasy, though." *Quite the opposite.* The intrigue he'd felt since their conversation was still there whenever he thought of Kawu, stronger than before.

Lysia wiped her hands with a cloth and yawned heartily. "Maybe it's just me then."

"Maybe. Hey, can I ask you something, too? It's been on my mind for a bit."

She looked up, surprised. "Yeah?"

"If you hate the magnates and the Coalition so much," Jespar said, "then why did you accept the mission?"

Lysia hesitated.

"I mean, if you don't wanna talk about it, that's—"

"No, it's fine. I'm in debt. Up to my eyeballs."

"Oh."

"Yeah, oh. Remember when you asked me if the donations are enough to run the clinic? They aren't. I bought the place five years ago, and I took out a big loan to afford it."

"And the donations weren't enough to cover the installments?"

"No. I mean, yes, they would have been with the paid work I did on the side, but—" She sighed, rubbed her temples. "Oh, Stars burn me, what am I beating around the bush for? I used to gamble. A lot."

It wasn't what Jespar had expected, but it made sense. Her impulsiveness, her vigor, her verve—it reminded him a lot of Naka, who had been a lifelong gambler. *It's not about winning or losing*, he'd told him once. *It's about that moment of reveal. When the way the dice fall is all that matters.*

"Dice?"

"No, Akati," Lysia said. "I haven't touched a card in years now, though. Anyway, I got behind on my payments, interest kept piling up, and ... well, you know the story."

"Hm. How much is it, if I may ask?"

She studied the mattress. "Nearly forty thousand."

"Holy shit."

"That's one way to put it. If I don't make ends meet by Second Rain, I'll have to put Juusew back onto the street, and the bank will impound my clinic and put me into servitude."

"Servi- you mean they're gonna enslave you?"

"They don't call it that, but yeah, that's the law over here. The Coalition clears your debt, and in return, you work for them for a starvation wage until your debt's cleared. 'Reparations' is what they call it."

"Wow. Well, I guess working for a magnate beats that."

"By miles. All the debt, poof, gone, and enough money left over to give the place a makeover and Juusew a raise and buy some new equipment on top of that. A fresh start." She tied back her hair, twisting it into a bun. "Also, as much as I think this country's system is broken, I wasn't lying earlier when I said the Scythe isn't the way. There have to be other ways to bring about change than a civil war."

"Hm." Jespar gave her hand a gentle squeeze. "We'll make this work, Lysia. I promise."

Lysia snorted. "Look at that. You got some White Knight in you after all."

Jespar searched for a witty reply, but he was too tired, so he left it at a grunt. "Should we call it a night? Something tells me we have a long day ahead of us tomorrow."

"Words of wisdom," Lysia said. "Would you like to ...?" she gestured at her cot.

Her offer made the weight of the day just a little lighter. "I'd love to."

They undressed and curled up on her bed, the lantern on the cupboard glowing in what would otherwise be perfect darkness. Lysia lay with her back cozied up to him, his arm over her shoulder. She had long been asleep when Jespar's restless mind finally drifted off too.

THE SWAMP
No One Should Go There On

Someday
Sometime

espar stared at the foot of the judge's dais, but he could feel the corpses' eyes upon him. The villagers, the man with the breadbasket. The Girl and her father. His sister, whom he tried so hard to forget.

It was a dark and terrible place, this swamp. No one in their right mind would go there. No one ever should.

"You worry us," the Corpse said. His burning hand stroked his beard, the bloody lotus flower on his forehead the only shade of red in the gray desolation. "We asked you to see, but you do not even seem to try. On the contrary, it almost feels to me as if you were provoking the fire."

Jespar's lips were frozen, the mere thought of speaking making his guts curl. There were many people out there who deserved to be heard, and he wasn't one of them.

The Corpse leaned in. "This is our last warning, boy. *See.* See, or you will regret it."

INTERLUDE
THE MAN

"You could hire someone to look for him," his friend says. "You have the means now."

The sunlight reflects on the marble floor, the golden goblets, and the mahogany desk between them. *All yours.* As so many times in these miraculous past moons, a part of him struggles to accept this thought as the truth. The part that walked his feet sore because there was no money for shoes. The part that watched his mother nearly work herself to death just so they could afford that stinking hovel beside the tavern privy. The part that still believes that "sometimes, ye've just got to make do with the hand life's dealt ye."

"I won't," the young man says.

"But ... he's your father."

"He's a useless drunk whose biggest accomplishment was squirting his seed into my mother's belly. Let the fishes have him, I couldn't care less." How true it was. And yet, how wrong. The young man downs the rest of his wine. "Did you do the other thing I asked?"

His friend regards him. Then he shrugs, pulls a stack of papers from his bag, and rifles through them. Watching him, the young man is once again surprised at the strength of the trust he feels toward him. Probably it's because they're both outsiders—even if his friend's otherness, with his dark skin, metal legs, and taste in lovers, is much more apparent than his own. Outwardly, the young man fits the role like a glove: height above average, a face that's masculine but not crude, dark eyes that can be astute, piercing, or amiable, whichever fits the occasion. Inwardly, however, he couldn't be more different than the people he keeps company with these days, his friend excluded. Why? Because he *is* what they pretend to be, a Great Dreamer. Their fathers gave them money and property; his gave him bruises. They have affluent friends to cushion their fall when push comes to shove; he and Mamah fell back to the streets when she ruined her back and had to quit the spinnery.

They were given success. He fought for it.

Of course, that's not how they see it, and the young man knows better than to point it out. So he plays along, laughs at their jokes, felicitates their achievements, and fakes camaraderie, pretending these spoiled, stuck-up fools know the first fucking thing about hardship.

"Here you go," his friend says, sliding a parchment across the mahogany desk. The young man picks it up and studies it.

"He's ruined," he says.

His friend only nods.

"So that mysterious nuvium mine on that mysterious island was made up?"

"No, but it's been exhausted for years. The plantation was his only source of income."

The young man shakes his head and puts down the paper. "A coinless fraud. Just what he always called me."

His friend cocks his head. "What's that look?"

"What do you mean?"

"You look as if you feel guilty."

"I don't."

His friend sighs in that way people often mistake for condescension. "Look, that fool brought this on himself. Come on, 'miracle fertilizer' for two harvests a season? What dimwit believes that kind of thing and then soaks his entire plantation with it before even testing it out?"

"Someone desperate to make money and seduce that beautiful 'miracle merchantress' we sent him for the sales pitch?"

"... I don't know what you're talking about."

"Oh, come on," the young man says, laughing. "This is my home, no one's listening."

His friend regards him silently. Then he gestures at the parchment. "Would you mind?"

As the young man slides the paper across the table, his friend leans in and grabs his wrist. "Never. Assume." He speaks quietly and evenly, but his vulpine eyes are narrowed to slits. "Do you really think you're safe now that you live among them? That coinless fraud, he would have ruined you if you hadn't outplayed him. Sure, people suspect you had a hand in it, but that's good because it shows them you bite when you bark. The instant you give them the slightest opening, though, even if it's just some bloody eavesdropping servant, they'll use it against you." He lets go and sits back in his chair. "Don't ever think cunning makes you invincible. Life is an arena, and even if you're the champion, one second of weakness is all it takes for the lions to pounce. *Always* remember that."

Silence.

At last, the young man refills his goblet and takes a swallow, swishing the wine around his mouth while he studies his friend like someone searching a piece of cloth for moth holes.

His friend shifts in his chair. "Look, I'm sorry if that came out harsh. I just—"

"That's a quote, isn't it?"

"... What?"

The young man grins. "That line, 'Life is an arena,' 'all it takes is one second of weakness,' and so on. That's from a book, isn't it? No way you just came up with that on the spot."

The tension is gone.

"Guilty as charged," his friend says, returning the grin. "Ibram Sha'Yus, *The Wandering Scepter*."

"Worth reading?"

"Hell, yes."

"I'll get myself a copy, then. Regarding that fool, just see to it that his wife doesn't end up on the streets—it's not her fault she married an imposter. Their divorce still isn't through, is it?"

"No."

"Then find a way to speed it up before the bank forces her into reparations, too. He—"

Someone knocks on the door.

"Enter."

It's the old servant who came with the place. His azure long sleeve and trousers combination is low-quality and outdated, a look that was fashionable a decade ago. *You really must get them new outfits*, the young man thinks. He'll take care of it tomorrow. Crimson coats with gold embroidery and belt, white loose-cut trousers, and tall cuffed boots dyed to match the top. Fashionable, but not gaudy, dignified, but not snobbish. For the materials, probably Qyranian antelope leather for the boots, and either Itzika silk or lightweight cavana wool from Mâlei for the textiles. Expensive, yes, but a servant reflects his master.

"Ma'sao, the carriage is here."

A smile tugs at the young man's lips. His heartbeat rises. "And you did as I asked?"

"Yes, ma'sao. The driver kept the windows closed and told her to stay inside."

"Good. I'll be down in a minute."

"Yes, ma'sao," the servant says and leaves.

His friend's mouth stands ajar. "She still doesn't know? Are you serious?"

"I am. I told her I went bankrupt and that we're moving back to the Stone District today."

His friend's exaggerated groan cannot hide his boyish grin. "You're one of a kind, my friend. You're one of a kind."

Outside, a breeze sways the junipers and palms that frame flag-stone street, the westering sun washing the scene in a blast of gold—a picture of calm, quite contrary to the way the young man's heart races. He eyeroll-smiles at his own childish glee, ushers the carriage driver aside, and opens the door.

"Mamah? You can come out now."

An uncertain voice comes from inside. "That ye, son? They closed 'em shutters, I can't see a thing."

'You', not 'ye', the young man thinks. *'The', not 'em'*. He doesn't say it, not today. Now that they live here, she'll pick it up.

"Yes, Mamah, it's me. You can come out now."

Mamah mutters something, then clothes rustle, and the door slides open. "Son, what by Moraia's goin' o—"

The words die in her mouth.

Moments tick by.

Heartbeat after heartbeat.

Breath after breath.

"Welcome," the young man says, "to our new home."

Mamah doesn't react. She just stares at the manor. With its alabaster archway and the sculptures of Moraia and Malphas worked into the stone, the goddess of prosperity and the god of protection. With its rooftop garden, curtains of ivy, wisteria, and lightroses trickling down the façade in a vibrant cascade. With the six servants who line the garden path like statues, heads bowed as if receiving a queen.

She wakes from her awe. "I ... I don't understand."

Gently, the young man takes her hand and guides her out of the carriage. "I told you," he says, trying his best to sound casual when all he wants to do is laugh and cry and hug her for that look on her face, that look that made all those crushing years worth it. "It's our new home."

"But ... ye said I gotta go back to the wheel and ..."

"Well, I might have stretched the truth a little. You know that big nightflower plantation up north, by Bluefort?"

"'Course I do. The Makehu used to work there."

"The Makehu": Mamah's nickname for the old man who runs a homeless shelter in the city outskirts, the one who took them in after Mamah ruined her back. The young man made an anonymous fifty-thousand sêr donation to the shelter just yesterday. He would tell Mamah about that another time.

"Well, turns out the plantation owner suffered a misfortune last dry season, and his whole property went barren. I bought it for a steal, reconditioned the soil, and the money from the first harvest has just come in. Let's just say it was a bit more than I expected." He hooks his elbow under hers and leads her to the doorway, where his friend is waiting, his grin no smaller than his own must be. They stop at the portico stairs.

"Do you understand, Mamah? This is our new home. From here on out, you'll eat the best foods, wear the best clothes, and never have to work the wheel again, ever."

But Mamah doesn't seem to hear. She just keeps looking, like a woman seeing colors she never knew existed. A few well-dressed district residents have gathered up the street, watching him, murmuring. Ten years ago, they wouldn't have given him a second glance. Now, they all know him.

The Have-Not.

The Prole.

The Fish Boy.

He doesn't mind their staring. In fact, he relishes it, and if they were closer and Mamah weren't here, he'd tell them he's come to stay. That he *will* become the champion of the arena, no matter the price.

A toothless smile tugs at his lips as he imagines they're Popa.

Bring in those lions, Fate.

I'll kill 'em all.

CHAPTER SEVEN
DREAMS OF THE DYING

DAY THREE
6TH MOON OF DRY SEASON, 1226 A.L.

The harbor bay was a sweep of ships and colorful buildings backdropped by an overcast sunrise. Agaam reefed the sail and brought the cutter down to a crawl, then told them to get their things. When Jespar stepped from the hatch a little later, he noticed Kawu leaning against the mast, watching him. As always, the young Makehu looked away when their eyes met.

Finding himself smile, Jespar approached him. "Everything okay?"

"No," Kawu said hastily. "I mean, yes, I'm—" He broke off. "Actually, I was wondering if I could speak to you."

"Sure." Jespar leaned against a nearby barrel. "What is it?"

Kawu hugged his arms tighter. "Well, I ... I was wondering whether you feel it. My presence."

"I can see that you're here if that's what you mean."

"No, that's not ..." He sighed. "You seem to know a bit about dimensionism. Are you aware that Sighted people have different auras from Unsighted ones? And that they can cause a kind of—how to put it?—reaction in people?"

Jespar recalled his dimensionism lessons. "Like how standing next to a choromancer can make you feel like you're falling?"

"Yes, that—it's called an 'auric resonance', or just 'resonance'. Those seizures my mother has, they are a product of hers."

"Oh. Do you ...?"

"Get them too? No, my resonance is different. I ..." He trailed off and looked out over the bow. Fishing boats glided through the waters, a galleon flying the Arazalean colors approached from the east. "Well, there's no good way to say it: I make people feel uneasy. Some more than others, but I've never met anyone who doesn't feel it to some degree."

Jespar remembered Lysia's words. *Something about him just gives me the willies.* "You're asking if you make me feel nervous too?"

"Nervous, uncomfortable. You know."

Quite the opposite, Jespar thought. "No, Kawu, I don't. Not at all."

A peculiar look appeared on Kawu's features, one that might have been sadness, gratitude, or distrust. Or perhaps all three. "I see."

Jespar was going to say more, but then the hatch opened, and Lysia swung herself up the ladder. Blushing, Kawu bowed. "Excuse me."

Kawu's face was a canvas of wonder as they made their way down the pier of Uunili Bay, his attention seesawing between the anthill bustle of the crowds and the Jade District villas and ziggurats up the slope of Mount Ilakato. It was a busy day even by Uunili standards—as Lysia explained, this was due to the upcoming *Miwa-e-*

Kēko, a Makehu-Kilayan festival celebrating the start of the rainy season. Set to begin a fortnight from now, Miwa-e-Kēko would bring thousands of people to the capital to marvel at the Starling tinkerers' latest creations, gaze at the midnight fireworks, or simply celebrate. Lysia explained that this year, probably in an attempt to mollify the commoners, the festival would be more lavish than ever before, and the city expected tens of thousands of visitors.

The sky was full blue when they reached the harbor switchbacks that led up to the Stone District. They made it as far as the third ramp when a crowd blocked the way. A unit of Blue Guards had cordoned off the top of the ramp, the throng booing and hurling insults. Instructing them to wait, Agaam disappeared into the crowd, somehow managing to slip through with ease. Jespar, Lysia, and Kawu jostled their way to the sidelines, where Jespar approached a woman on the roadside. With her plump, motherly face, and a conservative long-sleeved shirt and white skirt, she looked out of place amidst the commotion.

"Excuse me, ma'saa, do you know what's going on here?"

At first, it seemed the woman didn't understand the question. Then she blinked. "What d'ye care, outlander?"

"We're just curious. Is this some kind of protest?"

A tall man joined them before the woman had a chance to answer. He had the willow-leaf eyes of the Makehu but lacked their dark skin and broad features; his copper hair was braided into long, matted strands. Half-Arazalean, half-Makehu.

"Ye bet it is," he said. "Someone washed up from the sewers again, the third one this week. This time, 'twas a young lass, and she was carryin'."

Lysia approached them. The woman made a quick nod and disappeared into the crowd.

"Was she murdered?" Lysia asked.

The Arazalean creased his forehead. "Wait a minute, ain't ye that miracle healer-witch? Vurroy?"

"Have we met?"

The Arazalean flashed her a row of crooked teeth, purple from chewing nightflower. "Nah, but ye helped me cousin last moon when he broke his leg workin' the plantations. He and his folk would be livin' with us now if it wasn't for ye, so Moraia bless ye for that." His grin faded as fast as it had come. "But, no, that lass wasn't murdered. She ended it herself."

Memories resurfaced. Jespar pushed them back. "She killed herself, you mean?"

"Killed herself, ended it, went for a swim with the okepi, call it what ye will. Her mother said she'd left her a letter, but they never found the corpse, so the poor woman held on to the hope the lass just ran away with her lover or somethin'."

"But she didn't," Lysia said quietly.

"No. And I'm telling ye, just like me neighbor and the ten dozen others, she did it 'cause of that fuckin' decree."

Jeers erupted from up the ramp as if to approve his statement. Two guards in the front row were restraining a man who was cursing wildly. The Arazalean glanced at the scene, his jaw clenched.

Jespar loosened his scarf. "Ten *dozen* people have killed themselves over the Golden Soil Decree?"

"That hard to believe, outlander?"

"No, I ... I just had no idea it was that many. I mean, the decree hasn't been in effect for that long, has it?"

The Arazalean gave him a tired look. "Imagine ye got three kids and a wife at home, and yer job barely pays enough to make ends meet. Then, one day, ye wake up, and some bloody guard tells ye the drinkin' water now costs. And, oh, by the way, them fruits ye pluck from the jungle at night for some extra coin? Sorry, ye can't do that no more either. Now, ye know ye can pull through this week and maybe the next, but after that, it's either watch yer kids starve or move to the streets 'cause ye *just can't afford it.* So what d'ye do?"

More memories. Jespar wanted the man to stop talking, regretting having asked. "I hear you."

The Arazalean grunted. "Now, ye may call folk like me neighbor Gavaan a coward for givin' up, but Gods, I get why he did. I mean, keep fightin' when ye know tomorrow's gonna be even harder, and it's just gonna go on and on and on like that 'til ye kick the bucket? If ye ask me, them fuckin' officials might as well have cut his throat themselves." He took one of his braids, harshly twisting it around his finger. "As for that lass, I didn't know her, but ye bet I wouldn't wanna be a young girl with a kid in the makin' these days. Might as well spare the poor thing the misery."

The clamor at the ramp had died down a little; the cursing man was gone. Agaam emerged from the crowd. For the first time, he looked tired and worn out, as if whatever he had seen up the ramp had aged him several years. "Ma'sao," he said to the Arazalean when he reached them. "Would you kindly give us a moment in private?"

The man gave Agaam a once-over, frowning as he reached the spotless gray coat that screamed upper class. Then—oddly enough—his lips curled into a placid smile. "O'course, ma'sao," he said, and padded away.

Agaam beckoned to Kawu, who stood with his back pressed against a building, arms hugged tightly around himself.

"I've spoken to the guards and they will let us through," Agaam said. Come on."

Once more, the people miraculously stepped out of the old servant's way as he cut through the crowd. Beyond the cordon, two physicians with turtle shell-shaped masks depicting Esara's wizened visage hoisted the corpse of a woman in a murky yellow dress onto a cart. Jespar's heart stung when he saw her bulging belly.

A comatose magnate, insurgent terrorists, furious commoners.

Enkshi was right: this country was a wildfire waiting to happen.

They obtained horses from a Coalition office in the Steel District and continued their journey in the saddle; like with his flawless Inâl, Kawu surprised Jespar when he revealed he could ride. Partly because Lysia had been relatively quiet since the sewer incident and partly out of curiosity, Jespar spent most of the ride talking to Kawu. What started as an awkward stop-and-go eventually turned into Kawu asking Jespar all sorts of questions about his travels through Nehrim. It was a curious but pleasant experience: though Kawu didn't share much about himself, he seemed genuinely interested in Jespar's story, and the few words Jespar *did* get out of him were always a charming contrast between a deep understanding of the world, and an unblemished, at times naïve, idealism. For example, Kawu knew all about the Nehrimese War but did not understand how Jakal, the prophet and founder of the Creator's Temple, had gone from benevolent healer to mass murderer. Lysia believed people chose to be bad because they were selfish; Jespar believed that bad was highly subjective, and the subconscious did the choosing for them; Kawu simply could not wrap his head around how someone could not see their actions were despicable and therefore choose not to do them. When they reached the First Ziggurat around noon, Jespar's intrigue at the young dreamwalker had only grown.

The place was even more breathtaking in daylight than it had been last night: the moon had given it a sacral air, whereas the sun pronounced its grandeur, chasing away the memories of the platform towers in Hapana, which already seemed like distant delusions. After a stable girl had seen to their horses, Agaam and Lysia made for the ziggurat stairs. Jespar was about to follow when he noticed Kawu standing rooted to the spot behind him, staring at the massive palace.

"Impressive, huh?" Jespar asked.

Kawu blinked and faced him. "I always thought the stories were exaggerations."

"Me too."

They met Enkshi in the atrium, where he was talking to a lanky young woman whose short stature, curly red-and-blonde hair, and amber eyes marked her as a Starling. As soon as she noticed the groups' approach, she bowed and left.

Enkshi looked them over, his blue kohl unable to hide the shadows of exhaustion under his lids. "Where's the dreamwalker?"

When they were done explaining, Enkshi sized up Kawu with a scowl. Jespar recalled their conversation this morning. *People always feel like there's something wrong with me.*

"So you can actually travel into people's dreams?"

"It is difficult, but yes, I can."

"How is that possible?"

Kawu opened his mouth, but Lysia beat him to the answer. "Maybe we can discuss the details with the Ma'saa? I can attest that the lad is Sighted, and not in any way I'm familiar with. I'm pretty sure he's not a fraud."

Running a hand over his shaved head, Enkshi grunted. "Fine. Seems like this is the age of unconventional measures. Come, Ma'sao Nakāni, you're expected."

The Ma'saa awaited them at her desk in her orchard cottage, reading *The Apotheosis*, a chubby alapu and a cat toying around at her feet.

She beamed when they entered. "Thank Moraia, you're back. Did you bring her?"

"No," Enkshi replied. "But we brought someone else."

After Jespar and Lysia had told their story for a second time, a contemplative silence unfolded.

"I'm sorry those misguided souls attacked you," Ma'saa Oonai said at last. They sat around the desk, except for Agaam. "I had no idea the Scythe had become so brazen."

Thinking of the attack on the litter two days ago, Jespar struggled to make sense of her words. Then he realized Enkshi probably still hadn't told her.

"I'll make sure General Daato learns of this," Enkshi said. "Perhaps it's time to send a unit of Snakes to Hapana and smoke out their hideouts."

Ma'saa Oonai shook her head. "We can't spare any, not with that conference in Port Iwelo going on and Miwa-e-Kēku coming up. Is there any word from the Order of Light yet?"

Enkshi glanced at Jespar and Lysia.

"It's all right, Zagash, I trust them. Any news?"

"Well, yes," Enkshi said slowly. "I meant to tell you about it later. We received a letter from Hierophant Dal'Veram this morning, and she's going to send a division in time for the festival."

"How many keepers?"

"One-hundred fifty, give or take."

"That's not many."

"I know, but the Hierophant says it's all she can spare."

Ma'saa Oonai sighed. "Well then, it is what it is. Malphas guides their swords, so hopefully, they will be able to restore order." She regarded Kawu, a mixture of motherly affection and that same look of involuntary unease Enkshi and Lysia showed whenever they were near Kawu. "So, your name is Nakāni? Kawu Nakāni?"

"Yes." Kawu's eyes were lowered.

"How old are you, Kawu? You don't mind if I call you that, do you?"

"No, Ma'saa. And I'm twenty-three."

"My, so young." There was a sad twist to her smile. "And you can actually do it? Travel into my husband's dreams? Gods, it sounds so ridiculous ... I feel silly just asking you."

"As I said, it's been a long time since I last dreamwalked, so I can't make any promises. And even if I succeed, there's no guarantee the dream will give you the information you want, let alone a cure for your husband's condition."

The Ma'saa's smile waned. "Is that what you think?"

"Yes. Dreams are enigmatic at best and absurd at worst, so there's a good chance all you'll get are cryptic images and motifs." He hesitated. "You might also see things you never wanted to see."

The Ma'saa drank from her wine, emptying it. "'And only if thou venture boldly, treasure thou shalt find.' *The Apotheosis* 6, Verse 15. What do you need to do it? Maybe another psychomancer to help with the shift? It *is* psychomancy that you're doing, isn't it?"

"A sub-Sight of it, as Ma'saa Varroy said—at least that's what I believe. Dreamwalking has never been studied academically. As for your other question, unless it's another dreamwalker, they can't help me. What *would* help, however, is if someone came into the dream with me."

"You can do that?" Jespar asked, intrigued and uneasy in equal measure.

"With a bit of preparation, yes."

"Interesting." Ma'saa Oonai refilled her glass. Her third since the start of the conversation. "Why do you need help?"

Kawu rubbed his neck. "Well, there are two reasons, actually: first, if something happens to a dreamer's body during a dreamwalk, that can have dire consequences in the real world."

Jespar lifted a brow. "But it's only a dream."

"True, but engaging in a dreamwalk changes how the brain processes things. I can explain how this works later, but the fact is, it's helpful to have protection."

Enkshi made a strange sinus sound that should have probably been a snort. "Are you saying you need a bodyguard for a dream?"

"I'm afraid I do, Ma'sao Enkshi."

"Regarding these 'dire consequences'," Lysia said, "just how dire are we talking?"

"According to my mother, anything from phantom pain to brain death."

Silence.

"It's that dangerous?" the Ma'saa asked. "You can die during a dreamwalk?"

"I'm afraid so, ma'saa. It should be safe, but it's better to take precautions."

"Should be safe." The famous last words of every adventurer.

"What's the second reason?" Jespar asked.

"That one is less troubling. The shift I'll strike to take us into the dream realm is a channeling. Depending on how long it'll take us to find Ma'sao Oonai's kuluhika ..."

"It can cause a boatload of shifting drain?" Lysia suggested.

"Yes. I might be quite exhausted by the time we actually enter the dream, so it will help to have a second pair of eyes."

"That makes sense," the Ma'saa said. "Well, I suppose that leaves us with the question of who will go."

Enkshi glanced Agaam's way—Jespar had once again forgotten Agaam was even there, standing in the corner of the room—but the

Ma'saa shook her head. Kawu was fidgeting with his collar again, his mouth tight.

Afraid, Jespar thought. *Kawu was afraid.*

The words were out of his mouth before he could stop them. "I'll go."

All the attention fell on Jespar.

"That would work," Kawu said hesitantly. Was that gratitude in his voice? "But as I said, it'll be dangerous."

"I can handle it," Jespar said, trying to make it sound as if his words hadn't been pure impulse. "I mean, this is what I was hired for, isn't it? Besides, if you send anyone else, you'd need to do a lot of explaining first, which will only cost us more time. I'll go—unless the Ma'saa has any objections, that is."

Ma'saa Oonai studied him. Then she nodded. "I don't. Moraia told me our fates are linked, so I can see no harm in you being as involved as possible. Still, if there's anything we can do to make this safer or easier for both of you, please tell me."

Kawu gave it some thought. "Perhaps Ma'saa Varroy could watch over our health during the shift just in case anything goes wrong. And neki, neki will help too."

"I'll do what I can," Lysia said. "What's neki, though?"

"A droga," Kawu replied. "A spiky herb that only grows at the foot of Mount Tatana, on Lehowai. I'd need at least three ounces, whole, not powdered if that could be arranged."

"Agaam?" Ma'saa Oonai asked.

"I know that herb," Agaam said. "It'll be hard to come by this time of the year, but I should be able to get some by nightfall."

"Then please do so at once. We cannot afford to lose any more time than necessary."

"Of course, ma'saa."

When Agaam had left, Ma'saa Oonai turned back to Kawu. "Very well. Now tell us: how does one dreamwalk?"

———— ⟡ ————

Light rain fell from the dusking sky as Jespar reached the vestibule of the Oonais' sleeping chamber. The door stood ajar, and faint voices sounded from inside. Jespar stopped in front of it and felt for his longsword, the pommel's steel cold and comforting in his palm.

As he had spent the afternoon in a guestroom waiting for the ritual to commence, Jespar had gone over Kawu's explanations and instructions over and over. The result was always the same: at some point, his mind simply knotted up. It was like the stargazing sessions he'd done with his sister a long time ago, when they had imagined those heretic scholars were right, and each star really was a world like their own. You could try to comprehend the concept, but you'd never truly *know* until you set foot on one of those stars or at least looked through the giant telescope of Il-Quan Xagasha University.

Jespar stepped in.

Only a cluster of candles by the First Magnate's bed broke the darkness that shrouded the room. Kawu knelt at the head end, Enkshi and the Ma'saa behind him. Like Jespar, he wore nuvium boots, greaves, and chainmail, which looked at odds with a chunky bone necklace that went down to his belly. Enkshi acknowledged Jespar with a nod, the Ma'saa with a smile.

"Well, aren't you looking dapper?" Lysia was leaning against the wall beside the door. A rosy scent clung to her, probably from that bath she said she'd take, and that Jespar wouldn't have minded joining. He looked down at his armor, the candle glow reflecting in the turquoise scales.

"Dapper enough to becharm a nightmare?" he said.

"Maybe if you try real hard."

Jespar's smile felt fake. The more Kawu had expounded on the dangers of dreamwalking, the more Jespar had regretted his well-intentioned offer to volunteer: the reason a regular dreamer was safe in their kuluhika—their personal dream bubble at the deepest layer of the psychic dimension—was that their subconscious knew the events of the dream weren't real, even if their conscious mind believed so. Therefore, any harm that befell the simulacrum during a nightmare might *feel* real to the mind but never had consequences for the body. The reverse was true for a dreamwalker: they knew they were dreaming, but the instant they projected their simulacrum into another person's kuluhika, it effectively became a part of that other person's psyche, thereby subjecting itself to its mercy. Kawu had likened it to entering the fantasy of an alien god. The moment you were inside, it didn't matter if *you* believed that lance in your chest wasn't real. The god did, so your subconscious followed suit.

What this meant in practice was that the brain interpreted any harm inflicted on a simulacrum in a foreign kuluhika as real harm, albeit with different results. A punch into the face translated into local phantom pain upon waking that faded after a few minutes; a stab through the heart or a fatal fall meant brain death.

Aside from religiously following the rules that Kawu had laid out, and being as careful as possible, the best means of protecting oneself was as simple as coming prepared. A simulacrum wore whatever the dreamer wore at the time of falling asleep, so something as simple as good armor and weapons could make a world of difference.

About to enter a dying man's dream, wearing a fortune's worth of nuvium armor and a sword to ward off the dangers. He'd had droga trips less fantastical.

Other concerns had come as Jespar had waited, such as how his own nightmares or his—how to put it?—*fickle* state of mind lately would play into the dreamwalk, but he had forced himself not to think about them too much. He had manipulated Kawu into joining. He'd make sure he got through it unscathed.

Jespar sat on a nearby chair, jutting his chin at Kawu, Enkshi, and the Ma'saa. "What are they doing?"

"The lad's 'memorizing Oonai's psychic signature,' whatever that means. And we're still—"

The door opened, and Agaam stepped in, carrying with him a breeze from the outside. Ma'saa Oonai face brightened. "Do you have it?"

"Yes, but I could only get two ounces, and the leaves are dried. I requested to have fresh neki shipped from Port Lehowai, but that'll take two days."

"We don't have that time," Enkshi said. "Nakāni, can you make this work?"

"I will try."

⁓⟶⟵⁓

Jespar sat at the foot of the bed, Kawu across him. The others all stood a stride off, keeping quiet and out of the way.

"My shift will keep you aware," Kawu said. "It'll feel just like reality. Are you ready?"

No. "Yes."

Using a pair of food-sticks, Kawu fished a glistening little ball from the bowl beside him, the dried neki soaked in coconut oil. "Please chew thoroughly. The herb will enter your blood through the mucosae in your mouth."

Ignoring his rising unease, Jespar did as Kawu asked. The herb tasted surprisingly good, sweet and bitter. He couldn't have been chewing for much longer than a few seconds when he felt it kick in,

190

a warm prickle climbing from his throat to his head, like nightflower but with double the punch. Leaden fatigue seeped into his mind.

Kawu placed the food-sticks beside him. His mien was the picture of calm, but trembling hands gave him away. It was oddly comforting. Jespar was in over his head, but at least he wasn't alone in it.

"Ma'saa," Kawu said, "the marriage beads, please."

Ma'saa Oonai wavered, then took a big necklace from a casket on the nightstand, dozens of marble gems strung along it. *The Compass*, Jespar remembered from Kawu's explanations. Since the psychic dimension was endless, finding Oonai's kuluhika without any sort of guidance would have been akin to looking for the single blue grain of sand in all the beaches of the Archipelago. As an item of great personal significance, the marriage beads would act as a divining rod.

The Ma'saa handed Kawu the necklace. "Be careful, please." Her words sounded blurred and distant now as if she spoke to them from another room.

"I will be." Cupping his hands around the pearls, Kawu's expression turned absent. "Your husband really loves you, ma'saa."

The Ma'saa's lips curved ever so slightly. "I know."

Kawu drew a long breath. "Are you ready, Ma'sao Dal'Varek? Remember, when you're under, do *not* move until I find you. Not a single stride."

"... Yes." Struggling to stay awake now, Jespar had to force the words out. "Don't ... move."

"Good."

Slipping the beads over his right wrist, Kawu placed both hands on Jespar's temples and splayed his fingers. Two thoughts passed through Jespar's droga-lulled mind when Kawu touched him.

First, among all the strange things he had done in his life, this was the strangest.

"Sleep," Kawu whispered.

Second, it was the first time he and Kawu had touched.

He dropped into darkness.

Water.

Jespar was floating in an ocean.

It was silent and cool, dark all around except for pale shafts of light that fell through the iced surface far above him.

The psychic dimension.

I'm dreaming.

As Jespar had told the Ma'saa, he knew how it was to be awake within a dream; still, when he had first come across the term "lucid dream" to describe this phenomenon, he had found it misleading. Yes, he knew he was dreaming whenever it occurred, and, yes, it gave him the ability to influence the events, but everything still felt hazy, jarred, mercurial—not "lucid" at all.

This was different.

His mind was as clear as a bright winter's day, every thought forming with a crystalline clarity. He was Jespar Dal'Varek, and this was the Imūma, the psychic dimension, the invisible space of thoughts, ideas, and dreams. He was Jespar Dal'Varek, and his real body was sleeping at the foot of the bed of Jaaros Ismirael Oonai, whom they were here to save.

I'm Jespar Dal'Varek, and I'm dreaming.

Gingerly, he tried to wave his hand. It moved. He kicked his legs. They obeyed. He breathed, air pouring into his lungs even though he was underwater.

It was fascinating.

He knew it was the neki that kept him so calm. Even as a non-dreamwalker, it was possible to walk without it, Kawu had explained, but chances were the absurdity of the experience would cause the inexperienced mind to panic, which could have unforeseen effects and result in lasting damage to their psyche. The neki dulled the part of the brain responsible for reactions such as fear, anxiety, or panic and made a smooth passage into the target kuluhika possible.

It worked.

Smiling, Jespar spread his arms and gazed up, watching the play of the sunrays filtering through the ice. The water gently rocked him from side to side, like a cool river in summer.

Why had he been so nervous?

Why was he *always* so nervous, so uneasy, so restless?

The Corpse wasn't real, and the nightmares weren't either.

Someone touched his shoulder.

Kawu hovered before him, Oonai's marriage beads in his hands, and the bone necklace floating around his neck like porcelain splinters. Jespar tried to speak, but only bubbles came out. Kawu put a finger to his lips and took him by the wrist.

Together, they sunk into the darkness.

Besides sedating the consumer, neki also blurred the passage of time. It was helpful for the dreamwalk—not only had Kawu warned that it could take "many, many hours" to find Oonai's kuluhika even with a Compass, time in the psychic dimension also passed at a far slower rate than in waking life, one hour in dream time amounting to approximately five minutes in reality. When Kawu finally came to a stop, Jespar couldn't say how long they had been sinking—minutes, hours, or days. Neither could he make sense of the sudden look on Kawu's face. Surprise? Awe?

No.

Shock.

A current gripped Jespar and tore him away.

His droga-induced serenity lasted another second; then panic broke through. Jespar struggled and swam, but the current caught him like debris in a riptide, pulling him away and down, a figure swept past him and clutched his ankle, the hand burning despite the water, it was the Corpse, Jespar screamed and kicked, but the current was just too strong, and, Gods, he was racing toward a giant bubble now, inside was a swamp, *his* swamp, *his* dream, and—

The current stopped.

For a flicker, he hung suspended in the water, the Corpse beneath him.

Then the pull changed direction and ripped Jespar away.

He only had a second to be relieved before the current spun and flung him through the dark ocean again, only that this time, it carried him to a different bubble, a ziggurat, ruined, black, dead.

Jespar crashed through the membrane.

The current let go the instant he was inside, but now that there was no more water but air, Jespar was falling; faster and faster he fell, toward the ziggurat ceiling, the wind whipping at his face, panic tearing at his mind as he realized that the stone would crush him, that death in a dream was death in reality, that-

He passed through the ceiling into a dark room.

Briefly, he hung suspended in midair, like a ghost hovering over its victim's bed.

What the—

He slammed to the ground.

Shallow breath followed shallow breath as he lay there, battle fervor pumping through his veins as his mind struggled to catch up with what in the *fucking world* had just happened. Very, very slowly, he moved first his fingers, then his arms, then his toes and finally his legs. He propped himself on his elbow, expecting a headache to send him right back down onto the stone, but nothing came. Except for a mild throb in his temples, he felt perfectly fine, his skin and clothes dry as a summer's day even though he had just spent hours underwater.

Imaginary water.

"Bloody hell," he muttered. "Bloody hell."

Rubbing his forehead, he tried to make sense of the events. His thoughts still had that syrupy feel of the neki, but it was wearing off now that he was inside a kuluhika, just as Kawu had promised.

He got to his feet.

And froze.

Dead fish filled the room. As large as pigs and decapitated, they hung suspended from their fins, a salty rotten smell mingling with the aroma of spice and something foul. It was dark except for a cone of light falling through the half-open door on the other end of the room.

Jespar's hand wandered to his longsword. Was this Oonai's dream? It had to be. Dropping from the sky in screaming panic, he hadn't exactly taken the time to appreciate the scenery, but from the outside, the place had certainly *looked* like the First Ziggurat, albeit ruined.

What now?

Wake up.

That was the sensible thing to do. He'd wake up, they'd discuss what had gone wrong, then try again. Sure, perhaps this place was harmless, but it wasn't too much of a stretch to say a room full of giant dead fish didn't bode well. How *could* he wake up, though? Kawu had explained that a shift-induced dreamwalk usually lasted until the dreamwalker ended it with another shift, meaning no amount of shaking or pinching Jespar's simulacrum body could get his mind out of here.

Someone screamed beyond the door. *Screamed?* No, that had sounded like a cry, like something animal. Or both?

Jespar gripped his sword tighter.

Think. Use your fucking head, Jespar.

The immersion.

Of course.

It was the most mind-bending of all the rules Kawu had explained to them: once inside someone's kuluhika, the walker had to do everything in their power to keep the dream's internal logic, its "immersion", intact. Logic, in this case, was not to be confused with realism. As anyone who had ever had a vivid dream knew, the sleeping mind could accept anything from flying dogs to a family of corpses visiting for dinner as logical. Problems only arose when something made the mind *aware* of that absurdity, such as another dream character pointing out that canines don't have wings and therefore had no business in the sky or one of those friendly corpses explaining that the dead usually had reduced interest in social activities. If it was the dreamer's mind bringing up this paradox, the dream simply ended. If it was a walker, they were kicked right back into reality. "Play your role," Kawu had said. "Whatever you see, act as if it's perfectly logical."

That was it, then. All he had to do was signal the dream that he was an outsider, and it would reject and propel him back into reality.

"I'm dreaming," Jespar said.

Nothing happened.

"I'm in a dream, and I want to wake up."

Futile. He tried other things, such as envisioning himself bolting awake, reciting an awkward soliloquy about who he was and why he was here, or even pinching himself, but nothing changed.

Another howl from the hallway. Sweat beaded on Jespar's temples.

Oonai.

Maybe that was it. Maybe, for a walker to break the immersion, the host dreamer's simulacrum needed to be nearby to notice the breach. Which, in turn, meant his two ways out of here were to either find Kawu or Oonai. And if he managed neither?

Then, dear Jespar, you're well and truly fucked.

"Okay," he muttered. "You got this."

He had survived the war in Nehrim, a blizzard in the Cahbaet Mountains, hundreds of fights. He'd manage this too.

Jespar inhaled deeply and made for the door. His muscles bunched as he reached the fish carcasses, but he went on, clutching his longsword's pommel as though trying to break it.

Nothing happened.

Another step.

Another.

The door was inching closer.

See? It's all ri—

A shriek.

Jespar whirled, drew his sword. A fish in the back was swaying from side to side, blood trickling from its severed neck.

What the hell?

It went still.

Sword pointed at the dead fish, Jespar backed off toward the door.

Just a dream. Just a bloody dream.

He'd only taken three steps when another shriek sounded, this one twice as loud. He jerked around; a nearby carcass was moving, swinging back and forth like a grotesque pendulum, a red jet of blood gushing from its neck. Jespar waited for it to stop, but instead, it shrieked again and swung faster and higher. Hands shaking, Jespar backed off to the door, one step, another, toward the light, toward safety. At the next shriek, his blood iced over. It came from inside a cadaver to his right.

And it was human.

Four fish started swinging at once, so hard they smashed into the ceiling, their necks squirting fountains of blood all over the room; screams came from inside their stretching, bulging bodies.

Jespar bolted for the exit. More and more carcasses set in motion around him, morphing and shrieking, swinging and bleeding; he was almost by the door when one fish *tore open* beside him, spilling guts and something else onto the ground, a creeping, screeching little thing, one tiny hand stretched out to him; he leaped through the door and whirled around intending to fling it shut, but then he caught a glimpse of the creature and stopped dead.

A human embryo with a fish's head.

Jespar slammed the door, and the wailing ceased.

For the better part of a minute, Jespar just stood there, staring at the handle. At last, his breathing calmed.

Just a dream. Just a bloody dream.

Wiping the sweat from his forehead, he turned around.

The hallway before him erased his last doubts regarding his whereabouts. The walls were gray and webbed with cracks, but spots of untarnished alabaster remained; the violet moonlight falling through the windows gave the carpet a bruised hue, but the golden fringes and the embroidered cobras were unmistakable. This was the First Ziggurat—or rather, a ruined surreal version of it.

Jespar didn't move, gazing at the purple reflections in the marble. Then he gave a chuckle that would have fit right in at a madhouse.

The good news: he'd made it into Oonai's dream.

The bad news: it was a messed-up nightmare, he was on his own, and he couldn't wake up.

———— ❧ ————

Unsurprisingly, the fish-head embryos weren't the only horrors that the dream offered. Following the hallway, Jespar came into a section lined with portraits that probably depicted Jaaros and Nayima Oonai's ancestry—at least in the waking world. Here, the proportions of the depicted figures were skewed, their necks as long as arms, their arms as thin as fingers, and their eyeballs too far apart.

They moved.

In a bizarre, lethargic pantomime, their hands pressed against the insides of the paintings—had there been such a thing—as if begging Jespar to release them from their prison, their mouths working in soundless screams. Jespar hurried past them.

When he found his way to the outside stairs, Jespar paused at the sight.

The island was dead.

Gray mountains unfolded around him, the ocean a black desolation spanning beneath a moon that was as purple as frostbitten limbs. No plants or trees were to be seen, save for fleshy red creepers that climbed half the ziggurat's length.

"Kawu!" Jespar called.

Nothing.

Again, from the top of his lungs. *"Kawu!"*

His voice echoed through the desolation.

He swallowed hard and went on. Lacking a plan or strategy, he went to the Ma'saa's little orchard pyramid first, but it was as derelict as the land surrounding it. A woman in a dirty dress squatted before a bed of withered flowers along the cottage's side wall; she was digging a hole with her bare hands, the corpses of cats spread around her. Jespar backed off, but the woman noticed him and turned around. Her face was blank, smooth as a pearl except for a pointy nose and a thin mouth. What looked like soot or charcoal smeared dark smudges across it, clustering where there should have been eyes. Jespar drew his sword and pointed it at her, but she made no advances. Instead, she wrapped her arms around her belly and began shifting her weight from one foot to the other, slowly swaying her upper body left and right.

He tried the sleeping chambers next, but all he found were two corpses dining at the table by the entrance, scraping their food-sticks over empty plates. One of them wore prayer rings around her upper arms and had a decayed alapu on her lap; the other had rusted metal legs and a chunky gold amulet. Bile shooting into Jespar's throat, he couldn't hold back a gasp. The corpses turned their heads and looked at him, their lips moving but no sounds coming out.

Slowly, Jespar backed out of the room.

"Just a dream," he said when he was back on the main stairs, sinking down on the steps. "Just a dream."

So far, none of the creatures had shown signs of hostility. Even if they had, so far, they were nothing his sword, dagger, and throwing knives couldn't handle. He'd faced worse.

Really?

Fear had many shades: there was the blazing kind you felt when an enemy charged at you; the chilly kind you felt traversing a dark alley; the harrowing kind when you were trapped in a cave during a blizzard, hoping someone heard your screams. To Jespar, however, the worst had always been the pernicious and silent kind, like when you suddenly realized your little sister hadn't left her room all day and how eerily quiet the house was.

Surely, she is just taking a nap, you'd tell yourself. *Surely, she's at her desk drawing and has simply lost track of time the way she does so often. Surely, everything was going to be all right.*

Except that, sometimes, nothing was all right. Sometimes, there really was a monster in the closet.

A whimper pulled him from his thoughts. Jespar's eyes flicked up. There it was again, and it came from the colonnade to his right. He wavered. Part of him was afraid to go, the same part that hadn't wanted to open the door to his sister's room that day—as if ignoring something long enough could make it go away.

He had no choice.

Jespar stood and followed the whimpers.

He passed door after door as he moved down the colonnade, the whimpering growing louder with every step. A breeze had picked up and whistled through the cracks and crevices, mixing into the moans. Jespar had almost reached the corner of the pyramid when he drew to a sudden halt in front of a metal door. He leaned in and listened. No doubt. This was where the sounds came from.

Jespar looked down the walkway one more time, a part of him hoping to see Kawu hurrying toward him and telling him to stop, telling him he'd handle this, telling him he knew what to do.

The colonnade was deserted.

Breath bated, Jespar opened the door.

A heartbeat went by as his brain translated what he saw into meaning.

On a chair at the opposite side of a gloomy room sat Jaaros Ismirael Oonai. His face cadaverous and his clothes in tatters, the Magnate's Crown rested upon his head, two of the seven spikes broken. A man in purple physicians' robes knelt before him, his hands sunk in a gaping hole in Oonai's stomach.

Gods.

Seven bloody Gods.

Slowly, the physician pulled a gooey clump out of Oonai's belly and lifted it onto a table beside him, right next to a bloody mound of meat.

Organs.

Jespar whirled and retched.

When it was all out, he kept staring at the flagstone, his heart pounding in his throat. It took five breaths for him to muster the courage to look again.

The physician had just finished pulling another piece of flesh from Oonai's insides; Oonai should have been screaming, but all he did was make that moan Jespar had heard before, his glassy eyes fixed at the ceiling. Jespar stood rooted to the spot, fighting down the impulse to bolt out of there and slam the door shut.

Think, Jespar.

Just think.

This was horrifying, this was fucked up, but panicking and fleeing wouldn't solve anything. He had to analyze, assess, improvise. It's what a calm man would have done, a man in control, a man who was *sane.*

Break the immersion.

Of course. That's what he had set out to do, before these fucking phantasms, or whatever you wanted to call them, had decided to give his sanity the beating of a lifetime.

He unsheathed his sword and crossed the room, his pulse hammering into his wrists. Shelves lined the walls, stacked with books, vials, herbs, and other medical paraphernalia; a simple chandelier was the only source of light. He was a few steps from the two men when he noticed a fist-sized tumor on Oonai's head.

Tumor?

"Bloody hell," Jespar whispered.

It was an insect. Roughly a finger long, it grew from a hole just above the First Magnate's right ear. It resembled a giant centipede, its legs as long as a spider's and its segments fat and round, expanding and contracting in a hypnotic rhythm like a waterskin filling and emptying at regular intervals. At the protruding end, a bulb swayed left and right in unison, five black-dot eyes and three long feelers marking it as the creature's head.

Vomit soured Jespar's throat, but he kept it down. If Oonai or the physician had noticed him, they chose to ignore him.

Break the immersion.

"I'm in a dream," he said.

Nothing happened.

"You're in a dream, Jaaros Oonai. Your wife sent me here to figure out what's wrong with you."

No reaction. The physician extracted another chunk of flesh and put it onto the table. Entrails.

"Wake me the fuck up!"

Screaming at a rock would have yielded the same result. His breath short and ragged, Jespar backed off until his back pressed against the metal. Either Kawu had been wrong about the immersion, which was plausible considering how inexperienced he was by his own admission, or something was stopping Oonai from hearing Jespar.

Trapped, he thought. *You're trapped.*

You're trapped and you'll never get out of here again until they come back and find you, and five minutes in reality is an hour in a dream, and-

"Stop it," he told himself. "Calm the fuck down."

His spiral of panic slowed as his mind sluggishly obeyed. Fine, apparently breaking the immersion was off the table. Unless he was missing something, that left him with two options: wait for Kawu or improvise and find another way out. Considering the time distortion between dream and reality and the toll his brief stay in this lovely place had already taken on his sanity, the choice was an easy one.

But how? How could he get out of another person's nightmare?

It struck him.

Of course.

It was obvious. Why the hell hadn't he thought of it sooner?

With calm determination, Jespar sheathed his longsword and drew his dagger. He crossed to the physician with a single step, yanked his head up by his hair, and slit his throat. There was no struggle, no resistance, no sound. The physician went limp and sank to the floor, purple blood spurting from his severed artery. Jespar wasn't surprised to find his face blank except for mouth and nose, just like the girl in the garden; he shoved the body to the side and studied Oonai. His gaze was still locked into middle distance, but he had fallen silent, and the insect had stopped its pulsing.

Jespar touched Oonai's knee with the tip of his boot. No reaction.

He turned his attention to the insect.

It's you. Aren't you? You're the trouble.

It had to be. Whatever that thing, that creature was, it had to be responsible for Oonai's coma.

Jespar inhaled deeply. Then he gripped Oonai's greasy hair and cocked his head to the side, exposing the insect's slimy fat body. It was even uglier up close—as if some mad scientist had taken a tick, a cockroach, and a centipede and combined their most alien features into a single, messed-up creation.

For a single moment, Jespar wished he believed in a higher power.

Please. Please, please, please work.

He slammed his dagger into the creature.

Back in the war, Jespar had once assisted a physician after a skirmish. A comrade had been trapped under the wheels of a battering ram, and Jespar had pinned him down while the physician cut off his leg with a bone saw.

The scream Jaaros Oonai gave when the blade sunk into the insect was the same.

A mistake, was the last thing Jespar thought as a piercing cold raced up his arm, the side of his neck, and buried its fangs deep into his skull.

The world went blue.

Memories.

A burning house. Dead bodies, tied to the gate, father's dirty-snow eyes, a lotus flower carved into his forehead.

A light-soaked room. Blood on the sheets, Sparkhooves turned away from the bed. It'll get better, it always does.

The village, screams, smoke, charred flesh. A girl sobs, a man grunts.

More memories, but not his own.

A house between mountains, a magnificent sunset.

He and a woman, walking along walls of green.

Anger, shame, you can't stop me.

Every sin leaves a mark.

I'll clear my name.

I'll fix this.

INTERLUDE
THE MAN

3RD MOON OF DRY SEASON, 1212 A.L.

"That's him," the warden says.

A dark corridor. All the cells are empty, except for this one. A figure cowers in the corner, hugging its knees.

"Thank you," the man replies. "You may leave."

"What? Ma'sao, he's dangerous!"

"You think he's gonna chew his way through these bars?"

"No, but the commander said—"

"The commander is on my payroll. Leave."

The warden tugs at his frayed uniform while his gaze darts along the ground like he's chasing invisible rats. Like many people these days, he's afraid to look the man in the eye. Finally, he settles for a weak salute and pads back down the corridor.

The man takes a torch from a nearby sconce and walks up to the cell. Light pours through the bars. The prisoner is awake, but he sits with his chin on his chest, shadows obscuring his countenance.

"We will strike a trade," the man says.

No answer.

"A merciful death in exchange for the truth. That's my offer."

The prisoner's lips twitch, but no response comes out.

Anger rises, but the man keeps it in check. Something Popa never managed to do. "Well, I trust you've thought this over. 'Death by honey' might sound like dessert, but let me assure you, it truly isn't." He trails his free hand across the bars, his rings clinking on the steel. "On the day of your execution, you will be shipped to a pond in the Lehoomake swamp on Uunuma. There, the hangman will make a hundred shallow cuts into your skin, cover them with a thick layer of honey, and string you up between two posts. Care to guess what happens then?"

The prisoner remains silent.

"The insects come," the man says. "Every kind, katakos, bloodflies, mosquitoes, ants, roaches ... They'll crawl up your skin, suck up the honey, and lay eggs in your wounds." His stomach curls as he says this; he never cherished violence, much less senseless cruelty, even though he knows that sometimes it's necessary. Then he remembers what this creature has done, and a cold resolve replaces his unease. "The hangman will check in on you every day to give you food and water, so it can take up to a week for you to die. Isn't that incredible? One week strung up over a pond in the searing sun, watching yourself turn into a living ant colony. You'll get all kinds of diseases before the infections kill you—fever, diarrhea, gangrene ... the list goes on. I saw a prisoner once who lasted almost ten days. He barely looked human anymore with all the pus oozing from his body." The last bit is a lie for effect. He has never witnessed an execution like this, and he hopes he never has to.

The prisoner continues to stare at the ground.

Bastard.

His heart beats faster, his fists clench.

Pathetic have-not, how dare you ignore me after what you've done, how-

No.

Calm.

Control.

The man exhales slowly, touching one of his golden beard rings. He doesn't want to say what he's about to, but he must. That his wife survived the attack was pure luck, and as much as she thinks prayers and blessings will shield them from future harm, the poison or blade that gives a fuck about divine authority has yet to be concocted.

"I heard the best tailors in the Archipelago are in Cale's Folly, on Paiolu."

The prisoner's eyes flick up. They're bright blue, the kind that hints at outlandish blood and that superstitious grandmothers teach their grandkids never to trust. There's something canine about his features, but without the dangerous element from the taxidermic wolves the man has shipped over from Enderal for his collection.

A dog.

Speak, you fool. Please. Don't force me to do this.

Silence.

So be it.

"In fact," the man goes on. "I know this one great tailor from up there. Started from nothing, and now he owns the biggest spinnery on the island ... a true Great Dreamer, that one is." He studies the ceiling. "Come to think of it, last time I talked to him, he told me he got this apprentice a couple of years back, a girl from Uunili.

Truly bright, truly tenacious, a promising future ahead of her. He also told me that most people underestimate how dangerous this job can be, with all the lye they use for bleaching. Now, I was thinking, wouldn't it be tragic if that promising young girl slipped and fell into a basin? Just imagine what it would do to her face. If—"

"I don't know her."

The prisoner is finally looking at him, lips parted in half a scowl and half a plea. He really *does* look like a dog, an ugly gutter cur with ugly blue eyes. Picturing this animal pouncing at his wife, the man's guts ball up.

"I beg your pardon?"

The dog draws a rattling breath. "That girl," he says, trying hard to sound indifferent. "She's me brother's, and I ain't seen her since he died. There really ain't no point in bringin' her into this. I barely know her."

"Oh? You don't care what happens to her then?"

The dog shrugs in a bluff so obvious it would make a monkey playing Akati a master of deception.

"Fantastic," the man says. "Because I've already arranged for everything."

"W-What?"

"I believe I spoke clearly. There's a storm coming tomorrow morning, and the rain will turn the floors slippery. The girl has the first shift, so—"

The dog leaps to his feet. "*No!*"

"Excuse me?"

"Please, ma'sao," the dog whimpers, "I'll talk, I'll say whatever ye want, but please leave the girl alone, please!"

It's the man's turn to play the silent one. Then he steps up to the bars. "What I want is the truth. Tell me who set you up to do this and your niece will live—and you might just get a merciful death."

"But I told 'em already!" the dog whines. "I ain't workin' for nobody, I was just tryin' to mug her!"

Dryindomugge. His have-not accent makes him sound as pathetic as he looks.

"Yes, so I've heard. The problem is, I don't buy it. Even a drunken beggar as daft as you knows better than to mug the future First Dame in broad daylight."

"I was drunk, ma'sao! I didn't thi—"

"It's one of the magnates, isn't it? Oh, they'd just *love* to see Fish Boy go back to the mud, wouldn't they?" The man scoffs. "That crusty old hag is my guess. She's scared out of her bones that I'll snatch the crown from her at the Voting, so she figured she'd send me a message. I mean, I get why she'd pick you, I really do—you're a nobody with no wife, no kids, and no home. You're practically invisible."

The dog opens and closes his muzzle like the idiot he is. *Pretending he doesn't know what I'm talking about.* Anger burns in the man's throat, verging on fury. "Or perhaps you're just some sick pervert who likes to hurt women, is that it? She just happened to be the first pretty thing you spotted, so you jumped her. You—"

"*No!* No, I'm not like that, please! I told ye, I was drunk, and I wasn't thinkin' straight!"

Lies. Lies, lies, *lies!* If it weren't for the bars, the man would shove the torch right into the dog's snout, smell his skin singe, and hear him scream the way his wife must have screamed when she thought she was about to die—*his wife*, the woman who is a better soul than he'd ever be, the woman who couldn't hurt a fly.

That animal wants to play games? Fine.

"That storm will come," the man says. "If the girl is lucky, she'll be disfigured for the rest of her life. If not ... well. Suffice it to say that it'll be a long and painful death." Even now, a part of him revolts at his words, but his fury is bigger. He likes how it feels. "This is on you."

And he walks away.

"*I was angry!*"

The man stops dead. Turns. The dog is at the lattice now, clutching the bars and pressing his muzzle against the steel.

"I was just so *fuckin'* angry." He's crying now, snot dangling from his nose.

When the man finally recovers his composure, his words come out thin and flat. "You were angry. At my wife."

"No, I—" The dog sobs. "At everythin'. I was so angry at everyone, the world, the uppers, meself, everythin'."

The man feels his teeth grit. "No," he said. "Someone put you up to this, and they did something to keep you from speaking."

"No, that ain't true, I swear it! I just ... Gods, I don't even know what I was thinkin'! I'd had some rough days beggin', and then that man came and gave me twenty sêr, a bloody fortune, and I was gonna buy me some rice and stash the rest, but then ... then ..."

"You spent it on booze."

The dog's lips press together, tears pooling on his lids. "Yeah. Fuckin' wasted it on rice wine, to the last dara. I must've been drunk for two days straight, or three, I don't bloody know anymore, only that when I woke up that day, me gut was on fire 'cause I was starvin', and me skin was singed from the sun 'cause I'd passed out right on the street."

The dog gawks at the man as if expecting him to say something. *Does he expect pity?* No, even an animal like him knows he doesn't deserve it.

"I just ... snapped. I got so angry all of a sudden and told meself how bloody unfair it all was, how *everyone* got more than me, even them slit-eyes. I mean, I tried, right? I never wanted to end up like this, never. I wanted to be a Dreamer, like me brother and like *ye*, but it didn't matter what I fuckin' tried. I always made the wrong fuckin' calls and disappointed everyone." He sobs. "Gods, I even stole from me woman, can you believe it? The only one who saw me as more than the useless pile of shit that I am, I stole from her 'cause we were outta coin, and I wanted a drink and—"

"So you realized what a failure you were," the man says. "And decided to add 'murderer' to your credentials. Is that what you're telling me?"

The dog blinks like an idiot. Of course. He doesn't know what "credentials" means.

"Why her?" the man asks, unable to keep the tremble out of his voice. "Why my wife? Why not someone who deserves it?"

When all he gets is more blinking, the man realizes it's pointless. Whatever potential this creature once had, he snuffed it when he chose the wine bottle over hard work, laziness over discipline, surrender over ambition. He took the easy way, and now he's just a mangy cur waiting to be put out of his misery.

The man is about to leave for good when the dog surprises him and speaks.

"No reason."

It's all gone. The pain, the pleading, the yearning for pity. The two words are devoid of emotion.

The man speaks like a diplomat repeating a declaration of war. "No. Reason."

"Yeah. I was angry and wanted to hurt somethin', and then she came along wearin' that nice dress. I just ... I just snapped."

For a few breaths, the man can't speak.

Then he says, "Do you know the food bank? The weekly one at the temple?"

The dog nods.

"My wife runs it. She thinks it's the responsibility of us Great Dreamers to care for the meek because it was the Gods' benevolence and generosity that made our fortune possible. I mean, I should know, shouldn't I? I grew up in the gutter, just like you, wore the same tattered clothes, just like you, and ate the same bland rice, just like you, because who in the world can afford spices? If you think about it, we're really not that different."

The dog blinks, lips half parted.

"Or are we?"

More silence.

"Answer my question."

"No," the dog mutters. "No, we ain't."

"Then how, my friend, is it that, tomorrow evening, I'll be enjoying a lovely dinner with my lovely wife in my lovely villa, while you'll be strung up over a pond and get eaten by insects?"

A bit of fear creeps back into the dog's eyes. He opens his mouth and closes it. "I'll tell you," the man says. "It's because you're a pawn. Yes, it's true, some people do get luckier than others, yes, some people do get privilege, and those things aren't choices. But do you know what *is* a choice?" The man steps up to the lattice, so close he can smell the dog's stink, a mix of sweat, piss, and failure. "Being a coward. Failures like you, the have-nots, you all have one thing in common: you'd rather wallow in your own misery for the rest of your lives than get up and do something for a change … And with every single day, that misery grows until you can't help but turn it into anger. Because that's so much easier, ain't it? It's so much *easier* to be angry instead of admitting there were chances, and you squandered them, it's much *easier* to beat up yer wife and yer kid than to smack yerself for not gettin' yer ass up when it mattered, it's so much easier to kill an innocent woman that would never hurt a soul than to put the knife at yer own throat where *it fuckin' belongs!*"

The dog cries out, stumbles and falls, then curls himself up and starts to cry, stupid, yapping wheezes fitting the animal that he is. The man from a moon ago would have felt pity for him, but this one doesn't.

"I'm done with your sort," he says. "I cared, I helped, I tried to be fair, but your lot just doesn't deserve it."

Footfalls from down the hallway. Probably the warden.

"Please," the dog whimpers. "Don't harm her, ma'sao. *Please!*"

The man's smile is skeletal. He hasn't, he won't, and he was never going to, but he doesn't want the dog to know that. He wants him to fear for his niece like the man feared for his wife when he learned a beggar had stabbed her in the belly four times while she was on her way to the animal shelter.

"We'll see," he says. "Best hope I don't snap."

CHAPTER EIGHT
LEECH

DAY THREE
6TH MOON OF DRY SEASON, 1226 A.L.

old. Every bone, every sinew, every muscle. Jespar couldn't move, couldn't speak, couldn't think.

A voice.

Someone was talking to him, but the words were muffled as if he lay buried under a layer of ice.

"... arek!"

Cold.

Too ... cold.

He slipped away.

The first thought he had was about the sky. How strange it looked. Dark, purple, not how a sky should look at all.

The next: Oonai.

The nightmare.

He jolted upright.

The nightmare, Oonai, Kawu, the fish, the insect, Kawu, Kawu-

"Ma'sao!" A face hovered over him, a familiar face with dark green eyes, two hands grabbing him by the shoulders. "Ma'sao Dal'Varek, please, calm down!"

Jespar's panic lasted a few more ragged breaths, then ebbed off. He tried to speak, but his tongue failed him. When he succeeded at last, his voice sounded hoarse and alien, like that of a stranger. "K-Kawu?"

"Yes. Yes, it's me." He placed his splayed fingers on Jespar's forehead. "Please, hold still." The air between them turned wavy, a wince flickering over Kawu's mouth. The chill in Jespar's head vanished.

"There. Do you feel better?"

Jespar touched his temple. "... Yeah. What did you do?"

"There was some kind of hypnotic shift on your simulacrum, and I lifted it. Come, I'll help you up." He slid his arm under Jespar's and pulled him to his feet. Vertigo assailed Jespar, and he teetered, but Kawu held him steady. They were out on the colonnade in front of the physician's room; Oonai sat inertly on his chair and stared at the floor. The pile of organs was still on the table, but the hole in his stomach was gone, and the insect had wrapped itself around his neck like one of those tamed snakes Aetäerna minstrels sometimes use in their shows.

What the hell happened?

He retraced his memories, everything from entering the room to trying to kill the insect in Oonai's head, but everything from the second that he stabbed the creature was oblivion.

"Can you stand on your own?"

"Yeah," Jespar said. "Thanks. When did you get here? There was this current, and it pulled me away."

"I know." Kawu let go of him. "I think I came here not long after you, but I just couldn't find you, and when I did, you had passed out. What happened, Ma'sao Dal'Varek? That creature, did it ... attack you?"

Growing aware of how foolish and reckless he had acted, Jespar felt the urge to lie, but he dismissed the idea right away.

He took a deep breath and told Kawu about what happened.

They were leaning against the banister, looking out over the deadland. A drizzle had set in, the drops tinted violet by the moon.

"A dreameater," Kawu said. "It has to be."

Jespar looked up, surprised. "You know what that thing is?"

"'Know' is the wrong word. I'm merely guessing. But how it looks, Oonai's condition, the stories ... it just fits. The current that separated us in the Imūma, it must have been a shift it struck to keep us out. A defense mechanism, so to speak."

"Wait. You're saying that thing can use dimensionism?"

"The Makehu stories call it 'hexing', but yes, in scholarly terms, it would be a shift." Kawu exhaled heavily, his fingers digging into the balustrade. "I should have never agreed to this, ma'sao. I haven't dreamwalked in years, and the last time was into my baby brother's dream to help him with a harmless nightmare. This is my fault, ma'sao, and I take full responsibility."

Jespar. Just Jespar.

"Come on, now you're too hard on yourself. We're all out of our depths here, and you did all you could."

"Yes, I did. And it wasn't enough."

"That's life for you, the cynic would say."

Kawu smiled faintly, but his jaw remained tight.

"So, this 'dreameater'," Jespar said, changing the subject. "What exactly is it? Some kind of ... brain parasite?"

"I suppose you could call it that." Kawu pushed himself away from the railing. "But we should discuss this with the others. There's no reason for us to stay here any longer."

Jespar glanced over his shoulder at the closed door. He had shut it while telling Kawu his story. "What about Oonai, though? Do we just leave him here?"

"We have to," Kawu said. "If I'm right about this, then there's nothing else we can do."

There was no need for Jespar to remain lucid for his ascent back through the Imūma, so Kawu broke the shift he'd struck on him and made him return to reality the way normal people do—unaware.

Kawu placed his fingers on Jespar's forehead, and everything slowly melted, the ceiling blurring with the purple sky, the floor with his feet, like paint dissolving in water. A prickle crept into Jespar's limbs, and his lids grew heavy.

"I'll guide you up, ma'sao. Just close your eyes."

Jespar did as Kawu asked. When he opened them again, he was back in the world of the waking.

"A brain parasite that feeds on suffering and fear," Enkshi said flatly.

They sat around a table in the sleeping chamber. The sconces were back on and the shutters wide open, revealing a star-speckled sky. A chubby white cat lounged on Jespar's lap, and Jespar petted it absently, trying hard to banish the image of the two corpses who had sat at the very same table in the nightmare version of this room.

"As I said, it's a theory." Kawu cradled a cup of gruntroot infusion for the shifting drain, the brew's woody, pungent smell strong even across the table. "But that creature just fits the descriptions from the stories too well. Everything from how it looked to Ma'sao Oonai's symptoms."

"If there were stories about this creature," Enkshi asked, "then why the hell didn't you tell us sooner?"

Kawu winced as if struck. "Because I didn't think of it, ma'sao. I told you, up until now, I thought they were just a legend, a scare story you tell your children."

Enkshi scoffed. "I'm not buying it, none of this. That's just absurd."

"Is it, though?" Lysia asked. She sat next to Jespar, her hair still damp from the bath she'd taken before the ritual. While Jespar and Kawu had spent half a day in the psychic dimension, barely an hour had passed in reality. "Because if you ask me, a brain parasite that traps its hosts in a hallucination is the most grounded thing I've heard in the past three days."

"A *monster* from a Makehu myth that traps people in an everlasting nightmare and gorges on their suffering," Enkshi said. "All the while *magically* preventing the host from starving and turning him into an ice block." He passed the Ma'saa an apologetic glance at this, though she seemed unaffected, or maybe she hadn't been listening. The more Kawu and Jespar had recounted—they had left out the part about her husband getting disemboweled—the more withdrawn Ma'saa Oonai had grown.

Lysia shrugged. "All possible. Dreamwalking for the hallucination and the coma, biomancy and thermomancy to retard the starvation of the host."

"Last I checked, Sights were exclusive to humans, and it was impossible to have two at the same time, let alone three," Enkshi said.

"Those are paradigms and not facts. Theories exist to be challenged, that's the whole point of science."

"Didn't the dimensionists who examined the Ma'sao say there were no signs of an ongoing shift, though?" Jespar asked.

"The insect's shifts could have a different energy pattern than the ones we know how to test for, or maybe that thing knows how to disguise itself," Lysia said. "I mean, it had a defense mechanism to try and keep you out of Oonai's dream, so the idea that it also knows how to conceal its shifts isn't that far off."

Enkshi sighed and leaned back in his chair. "All right, then please explain how something can 'feed off emotions' to stay alive."

Lysia looked off, tapping her finger against her lower lip. Then she nodded. "Essences."

"I beg your pardon?"

"Essences. One of the sisters in my monastery had devoted her life to studying the brain, and she found that the brains of all animals emit certain substances when they feel emotions—'essences', that's how she calls them. It's how dogs smell fear."

The cat on Jespar's lap purred as if in agreement.

"And the dreameater could feed off of them," Jespar said. "Makes sense."

Enkshi furrowed his brows but had no immediate reply. He turned back to Kawu. "If I recall correctly, you said that in the late Resurgence Era, some evil Makehu tribe bred and used these 'dreameaters' as weapons? Until a good tribe came along and wiped the bad tribe out, bugs included?"

Kawu blinked. "I'm not sure you can call the I'Okokepe tribe 'evil', they were just deeply misguided. Their chieftain, Katōia, worshipped Īmīte's jealous sibling, Okokepe the Ocean-Spawn, because her husband had died in a terrible famine. She was hoping Okokepe would give her the power to—"

"Yes, yes, all right. My question is, even if we assume the good tribe had sneakily kept a handful of those bugs alive, how in the world could this have been kept a secret for nearly two thousand years, particularly after the Colonization? We're talking about a potential superweapon here."

"I don't know. Maybe some of the Elders kept them hidden, and—"

"How does one get infected? Through the skin, through the orifices?"

"I don't know, I—"

"How do dreameaters procreate, what's their lifespan, how—"

"*I don't know!*"

"Exactly, you don't know! All you have is fragments of a bedtime story that roughly fits our predicament, and now you expect us to swallow it and send you back to Hapana with a fortune in your pocket. I've dealt with frauds my entire life, Nakāni, and you're one of them."

Enkshi's attack on Kawu had come so fast and sudden that Jespar only now found the time to react. He thought he knew where the counselor's sudden hostility was coming from—faced with unpleasant explanations, people often resorted to defensiveness, especially when a lot was at stake. He also thought that didn't justify being a godsdamned asshole to the person who least deserved it. "May I make a suggestion, ma'sao?" he asked.

Enkshi tossed him a frown.

"How about you contribute something helpful for once?"

Lysia snorted. Enkshi blinked. Kawu stared into his cup as if hoping he could jump in there and disappear.

The Ma'saa leaned in. She wore no jewelry except for the seven prayer rings. "You're right, Zagash, Kawu's theory is bizarre, and he doesn't have all the answers. But what would you have us do? What's your alternative?"

"... I don't have one."

"And yet you'd rather ignore what Kawu and Jespar saw and go back to helplessly watching Jaaros die?"

"You know that's the last thing I want."

"I do—which is why I don't understand your skepticism. Yes, I won't lie, this entire parasite business is disturbing, to say the least, but, to me, it looks as though it's all we have. We'd be well-advised to at least consider it."

Enkshi sighed. "You're right, Nayima. Forgive me, I was ... I don't know."

"You're under a lot of pressure, and you want Jaaros to get well. Don't worry, no one understands that better than I do. Still, at this stage, we must take what we can get." She faced Kawu. "Let's just assume you're correct, and my husband does have one of those dreameaters: could the coma perhaps be the last stage of infection? If other symptoms precede it, that would explain Jaaros' strange personality change before he fell asleep."

Kawu had returned to studying his gruntroot infusion. "I suppose it's possible."

"What do you think, Zarah? You're the physician."

Lysia tapped her finger on the table. "Hard to say. But brain damage is known to cause personality changes, and symptoms from parasitic infections usually exacerbate over time, so it's plausible."

"That's what I thought." Ma'saa Oonai took a little breath and laced her fingers. "Now, the important question: how would you go about curing something like this?"

Lysia hesitated. "Well, the first step would definitely be to verify. Whatever we do, we can't act on assumption."

The Ma'saa nodded. "But how can we do that? Perhaps a psychomancer could search Jaaros for this creature's thought patterns?"

Lysia trailed her thumb up and down her scar. "If those upper-echelon dimensionists you had look at him didn't find anything last week, I doubt they would now, especially if that thing knows how to mask its aura. The only thing I can think of is surgery, but that's a big risk to take without knowing where that creature is located."

Enkshi rejoined the conversation, looking slightly guilty. "Do we have a choice, though, if dimensionism is off the table? The upside of a surgery would be that we could take that bug right out, if it's actually there."

"That is true," Lysia said. "But you should get an expert for that. I've done surgeries like this, but there are better physicians who specialize in that kind of thing."

"I agree, and we will find one. Nayima, let me consult with Ma'sao Ulanees about this. He—"

"You can't."

Kawu had spoken softly, but Enkshi broke off at once.

"I'm sorry?" asked the Ma'saa.

"The dreameater. If it really is one, then you can't just cut it out like that." His gaze was riveted to the table, and he was turning his mug on the spot, just like he had on Hapana. "I was going to tell you this, but the reason dreameaters are so dangerous is that there is no way to remove them from a host once they've nested."

"Why?" Lysia asked. "Medicine has come a long way. I've seen surgeries like this done."

"It's not about the surgery," Kawu said. "If a dreameater is forcefully removed from a brain or even senses someone is about to do that, it releases a poison that kills both itself and the host immediately. I don't know for sure, but even just opening Ma'sao Oonai's skull to look inside might be perceived as an attack."

They were quiet.

"There must be a way," Ma'saa Oonai said. "Please, Kawu. There must be a way."

Kawu closed his eyes.

"There *must* be."

Another moment came and went. Then Kawu stopped moving the mug and he looked up. "The imprinter. Maybe through the imprinter."

"Who?" Lysia asked.

Kawu emptied his infusion. "If I recall correctly, the legend mentions two ways of becoming infected," he said. "The first is through a wild dreameater, which essentially means you were in the wrong place at the wrong time—in this case, the infection was practically a death sentence. The other way was through an imprinted dreameater, one that someone else was controlling."

Jespar pulled his scarf looser. "You mean like a tamer?"

"No, it's more than that. If I recall correctly, the I'Okokepe tribe subdued the dreameaters through a mental link that allowed the human to command the dreameater like a bloodhound. And because dreameaters are supposed to be extinct, chances are extremely slim that it was a wild one."

"What you're saying is, someone put that thing into Ma'sao Oonai's head?" Jespar asked.

"Yes—the imprinter. And it's possible that they can still call the dreameater back."

For the first time since the start of their conversation, a glimmer of hope found its way into the Ma'saa's expression. "You mean, they could undo the infection?"

"As I said, it's possible. Please, ma'saa, you need to keep in mind that this is all based on Makehu folklore that I barely even remember. Ma'sao Enkshi is completely right about that. I wish I could give you more certainty, but for now, this is the best I can do."

Enkshi adjusted his ring. "Nothing to be sorry about. If this is true, this means we have a potential solution—we just need to find whoever did this and force them to remove the parasite."

The Ma'saa nodded. "I agree. Kawu, you said this imprinting is done through a mental link of sorts. Does that mean that the imprinter has to be a dreamwalker or a psychomancer?"

Kawu gave it some thought. "I don't think so, no."

"What makes you so sure?"

"Well, I tried to tell you this earlier, but the reason the I'Okokepe's chieftain, Katōia, started the War of Oblivion was that her husband died in a dry season famine and hoped Okokepe would grant her the gift of dreamwalking so she could live with him in her kuluhika. At the same time, she was said to have controlled a colony of a thousand dreameaters."

"So she was imprinted but not Sighted," the Ma'saa said.

"Yes. And she started a terrible war because of it."

"Okay," Lysia said. "But psychomancy *must* have been involved one way or the other. You don't create a mental link between an insect and a human by asking it nicely."

Jespar reentered the conversation. "Maybe it takes a dreamwalker or a psychomancer to do the imprinting, but they aren't necessarily also the imprinter? That would at least mean our assassin consulted with one at some point. Plus, he or she must have been well funded and well connected—I can't imagine it's easy to get one's hands on an extinct parasite."

"That's still a lot of potential suspects," Enkshi said, "but you're right, that narrows it down." He turned to Ma'saa Oonai. "We'll compile a list of all known psychomancers in the Archipelago, then send some operatives to question them, starting with the Elders. They must know something about this."

"The list is fine, but no questioning," Ma'saa Oonai said. "Not only would that draw more attention to us, but if the assassin is in any way connected to the Elders, they will know we're on their trail and might decide to speed up the course of Jaaros' disease."

"Well, I'm sure we can do *something* to keep them silent. We could—"

"No. No blackmail, no coercion, no dirty tricks. Succumbing to Corruption is what got Jaaros here, and it's *not* what will help us pass this trial. There is another way, and Moraia will guide us to it."

Enkshi was the picture of frustration. "Then she better start guiding. This is a political assassination attempt we're talking about, Nayima, and you don't kill okepi by sending in guppies."

"There *is* another way," the Ma'saa repeated. "We only need to think."

A minute of table-staring slouched by. It broke when a grunt sounded from the entrance, and Ma'saa Oonai's alapu clumsily slid through the crack. The cat jumped from Jespar's lap and rushed to greet him.

Ma'saa Oonai sighed and passed an apologetic smile. It felt forced. "Silly me, I completely forgot to feed the pets. Would you excuse me? I believe we could all use a little recess."

No one argued.

She left the room, the cat and the alapu at her heels.

"Well," Enkshi said, after the door had fallen shut. "I suppose she's right, we could do with a break. Agaam, bring them some food. I'll go for a walk."

Some fifteen minutes later, Jespar, Kawu, and Lysia sat over richly set plates and ate a venison stew with a hearty, Endralean-style gravy.

Jespar had just brought his fourth spoonful to his lips when suddenly, the lost memories from his blackout in the nightmare returned with the force of a sledgehammer.

A burning house. Dead bodies, tied to the gate, father's dirty-snow eyes, a lotus flower carved into his forehead.

Jespar stared down at the chunk of meat on his spoon.

He dropped the spoon, turned sideways, and retched. The first heave was barely out before the second influx of thoughts assailed him; Lysia leaped to his side, hands on his shoulders and saying something, but he didn't listen—all he could think of were those pictures, those terrible, vivid memories, some his own, some foreign to him.

A light-soaked room, blood on the sheets, Sparkhooves turned away from the bed, it'll get better, it always does, the village, screams, smoke, charred flesh, a girl sobs, a man grunts, a house between mountains, a magnificent sunset, he and a woman, walking along walls of green, anger, shame, you can't stop me, every sin leaves a mark.

I'll clear my name.

I'll fix this.

When the onslaught finally ceased, Jespar looked up to the concerned faces of Kawu, Lysia, and Agaam, all squatting beside him.

"What's wrong?" Lysia asked. "Stars burn me, Jespar, what happened?"

Catching sight of the puddle of vomit and stew between his knees, he gagged again but managed to keep it in. He took a long breath, then another. When he scrambled to his feet, the gap between Oonai's bonesaw scream and waking up on the colonnade had closed.

"I think you should get the others," he said. "They'll want to hear this."

Jespar had expected at least Enkshi to react with skepticism or ridicule, but the previous discussion seemed to have drained his reserves for either—he sat still like the others and studied Jespar with mild confusion. A servant had cleared the stain on the carpet and the table, and a bowl of fresh fruit stood between them, untouched.

Ma'saa Oonai broke the hush. "I'm not sure I understand. How can these memories be my husband's?"

"I wish I could tell you," Jespar said. "All I know is that they felt like somebody else's. I don't know how else to put it."

"Hm. What do you make of this, Kawu?"

"I suppose it's possible." Kawu was sitting on his hands, gazing at the candles on the table. "We were in your husband's kuluhika, so technically speaking, we were a part of his mind for the duration of the dreamwalk. If I had to guess, I'd say that the dreameater had struck a link between Ma'sao Dal'Varek and Ma'sao Oonai, its host."

"A mental bridge between the simulacrums," Lysia said.

"Yes."

"I understand." Ma'saa Oonai swirled the wine in her goblet. "And, Jespar, you said you saw a house?"

"Yes."

"Can you describe it?"

"Um, it was white, like the ziggurat, but smaller. And there were mountains all around, lots of them."

The Ma'saa drew a soft breath. "Kaiawaika Manor."

"One of your properties?" Lysia asked.

"Yes, up north, in the Kaiawaika Massif ... very secluded and very quiet. Jaaros goes there every other moon to take a break from the stress of city life. What else do you remember, Jespar?"

"Well, uh ... there was a woman, and she and your husband were walking through some kind of hedge maze, I think it was."

The Ma'saa's lips pressed together. "What else?"

Jespar gave it some thought. "I think that's it—some parts are still blurry, like what happened right before I passed out. But I felt a lot of emotions with those images, I remember that."

"What emotions?" Enkshi asked.

"... Anger, mostly. Incredible anger."

"That makes sense," Kawu said. "The dreameater feeds on the suffering of the host, so those memories must have been something that causes Oonai a lot of pain."

Remembering the share of pictures during the attack that had been his own, the phantom noose inched a little tighter. *It saw.* All those corpses that still haunted Jespar's nightmares, the dreameater had seen them.

Oonai too?

"... look like?"

Jespar broke out of his thoughts. "I'm sorry?"

"The woman Jaaros was with," Ma'saa Oonai said. "Did you see her face?"

"No, I'm afraid not. Just her silhouette."

Ma'saa Oonai sipped from her wine. "Probably a business partner. He often invited people up there to discuss business."

The kind sometimes conducted in bed, I'd wager. Judging by the exaggerated indifference in the Ma'saa's voice, she feared the same thing. Jespar felt sorry for her.

"Probably," Enkshi said. "But that's a big step forward. If these are Jaaros' actual memories, they might be the most valuable lead we have."

Lysia squinted in his direction. "How so?"

"Well, if Jaaros' brain connects these images to such strong emotions, they might have played a role in what brought about this assassination attempt, right? Obviously, it's not a guarantee, but it's a lot more promising than tracking down and questioning every psycho-mancer in the Archipelago. What do you think, Nayima?"

"I agree," Ma'saa Oonai said, still seeming elsewhere with her thoughts.

"Well, all right then." Enkshi turned to Agaam. "Have Sergeant Maadira send a squad of Snakes to the manor. I want them to search it for clues as to the woman's identity and question every one of the serv—"

"No," Ma'saa Oonai said.

Enkshi turned to face her.

"No military, no Coalition contractors. Zarah Varroy and Jespar Dal'Varek will look into it, and Agaam can take them there."

"With all due respect, Nayima," Enkshi said, "that would be taking it too far. I understand your desire for moral purity, but this is the best lead we've had since all of this started, so we *need* profes-sionals, not amateurs."

"These 'amateurs' and my 'irrational plan', as you called it back then, have yielded better results than your professionals did in two moons, so forgive me for being stubborn. Also, two outlanders will attract far less attention than a squad of elite soldiers galloping across the island, don't you think?"

"But—"

She slammed her hand on the table. "I'm not asking for your per-mission! I told you, this is a trial, and Moraia sent us these two to help, so *we will obey!*"

Probably as surprised by the outbreak as Jespar, Enkshi worked his mouth, his expression swaying between disbelief and anger. Then an eyeless smile creased his lips. "Of course, Your Excellency. If that is your wish."

"It is. And if you so much as think about crossing my orders, you'll never set foot into this palace again. Am I clear?"

"Quite clear, Your Excellency. Thank you."

"Good."

Jespar studied the Ma'saa. *It's not just the trial, is it?* Yes, the Ma'saa was a theist if there ever were one, and Jespar no longer doubted that she believed Moraia had sent her a vision with him in it. Still, there was more to this, and Jespar thought he knew what it was: as much as Ma'saa Oonai feared Moraia's judgment, she also feared that those Snakes Enkshi had wanted to send to the manor would find that her husband had secrets—secrets that might not have any bearing on the coma, but which she did not want anyone, including herself, to know.

Her mien softening, she turned to Agaam. "Agaam, I want you to leave come daybreak and escort Jespar and Zarah to Kaiawaika Manor on horseback. Can you do that?"

"Certainly, ma'saa. Why not take a myrad, if I may ask?"

"Because Jaaros' myrad is currently on Maitemi, and if we use one from the Coalition, we might as well invite all the curious officials to tag along and tell the imprinter we're on their trail. It's a day and a half's ride, and we should be able to spare that much time. Or rather, we must."

Agaam nodded.

"What do you want us to look for?" Lysia asked. "Anything in particular?"

"Clues concerning what my husband was doing there and whether it's connected to the assassination attempt. We are following Moraia's path, and the truth will reveal itself to you, I can feel it. In the meantime, Zagash and I will gather more knowledge on this dreameater creature and will track down and *humanely* question the psychomancers of the Archipelago, registered or underground. As for you, Kawu, I suggest you stay here until the matter is settled—we might need your services again."

Kawu lowered his head. "Ma'saa, if it's possible, I'd like to go with them."

"Why? It might be dangerous."

"I ... I just think it would be wise. Please."

Ma'saa Oonai pursed her lips in thought, then nodded. "Very well, you may join them. You're a good soul too, Kawu, and this endeavor needs all the good souls it can get. Now, if you'll excuse me, I'm quite tired." She rose and went to the door, pausing before she made an exit. "Jaaros is a good man. Whatever the truth behind this is, there is an explanation. I know there is."

She left without another word.

The moon was almost at its zenith when Agaam guided them to their sleeping quarters. No wind blew, and even the insects were quiet, weaving an oppressive silence.

"Here we are," Agaam said, stopping in the mouth of yet another hallway. If it hadn't been for a row of nondescriptive landscape paintings on the wall, Jespar wouldn't have recognized it; it was the same a servant had led him and Lysia to as they had waited for the dream-walk to commence. "Would you like something more to eat?"

Jespar—hungry once again now that his memory-induced nausea had subsided—said he did. Lysia and Kawu declined.

"Very well, I'll send for it. Unless there's anything else, I advise you get some rest. We have a long ride ahead of us tomorrow."

There was nothing, so Agaam bowed and left. Before he was even around the corner, Kawu wished them a hasty "good night", and fled into his room. The key turned in the lock.

Lysia scratched her scar. "What's the matter with him?"

"No idea." Jespar was surprised at his disappointment—he had been hoping for a chat with Kawu, to discuss the events in Oonai's nightmare. *Nonsense,* a voice in him said. *You don't want to "discuss the events," you just want to spend time with him because you like him, more than you should.* Somewhat reluctantly, Jespar told himself that the truth was somewhere in the middle. "He's probably just tired. That shift must have been intense."

"True that," Lysia said. "Anyway, you wanna share a room? I could use some company."

Remembering last night—Lysia snuggled up against him, her warmth, the comfort—he smiled. "I was gonna ask the same thing."

"Lovely. Shall we say in an hour, though? It's been a whirlwind, and I need some time to unwind."

"Yeah, sure. I'll take a bath in the meantime."

"Sounds promising." She squeezed his hand. "Knock when you're done, okay?"

"Okay."

Lysia went to her chambers, Jespar to his. The rooms were as luxurious as one would have expected: spotless white walls with a row of windows revealing the starry tropical sky. A bed big enough for three occupied one half of the room, a stylish set of mahogany furniture in the other; a bathroom branched off at the entrance.

Jespar kicked off his boots and dropped onto the bed. He had felt strangely lightheaded ever since the memories had surged back as if he'd spent the whole day solving puzzles. After studying the bas relief in the ceiling for a bit—skillfully made yet somehow bland, it showed what must have been a historical scene from the Archipelago—he sat up again and stuffed himself a pipe, finishing just when his late-night snack arrived. Delicious as it was—a fancy pudding garnished with dates, coconut shavings, and an explosion of exotic spices—he only managed a few forkfuls before his appetite ceased again.

"Sorry," he told the servant girl when she returned for his tray. "It was really good, though."

Her smile was perfunctory, and Jespar couldn't blame her. The price for that dessert alone could have probably bought her family food for a week. "Anything else, ma'sao?" she asked.

"Actually, yes. Would it be possible to run me a bath? I'd do it myself, I just don't know where you heat the pails."

"I will take care of it, ma'sao. No problem."

Half an hour later, Jespar lay floating in the bath's colossal marble basin, rose-scented steam rising from the hot water. His wooziness had improved with the pipe, but now a headache coupled with lingering anxiety had replaced it, making him wonder if getting high had been a smart idea after all.

"Ma'sao Dal'Varek," he muttered, "your cunning is unrivaled."

He closed his eyes and slid under the water.

Images came.

Lysia and that lopsided grin of hers.

Kawu and how warm his fingers had felt on his temples.

The pregnant, dead girl in the harbor, the burning manor, bloodstained sheets.

Jespar jerked up and gasped for air.

On the edge of the basin sat the Corpse.

Time stood still.

Jespar cried out and recoiled, smashing his elbow into the wall behind him; the world exploded in a blast of pain, his vision blacked out. When it returned, the Corpse still sat there, a glass of wine in a burning hand.

"See, boy," he said. "See, or you will reap the storm."

He raised the red liquid to his lips and drank.

CHAPTER NINE
THE DEAD SISTERS

Day Four
6th Moon of Dry Season, 1226 A.L.

"That's mean, it's *my* turn!" His sister stood in the door, little fists thrust into her sides like an adorable, angry garden gnome. "You've been in there forever!"

Jespar flopped his heels on the rim of the tub with exaggerated pleasure. "That's high purbolee, you know?"

"What?"

"'High purbolee'," Jespar said with a wise grin. "It's when you say 'forever', even though it was actually just fifteen minutes. Didn't you pay attention to Meyser Gunnar's lessons?"

Her lips moved as she looked for an answer, the way she so often did when he dished out a quip and she struggled to find a follow-up. At last, his sister settled for a glare. "Jes, you're *so mean*!"

"Mean as a bean," Jespar muttered, leaning back into the foam.

Why was he acting like this? She was the last person he should be picking on. Probably it was because a part of him enjoyed the feeling of power; the same part that had hurt so badly when Father had given him that disappointed look twice today, once after Jespar had lost the sparring match against the Dal'Kaban boy Diethmar, then again when he had found Jespar crying in the stables. The worst part was that the twins had been with him. Both younger. Both better Dal'Vareks than he would ever be.

His sister went on complaining about how the water would get cold, but Jespar barely listened anymore. He stayed right where he was, nestled in that warm sea of bubbles, that stupid bully grin tacked solidly to his mouth. It only faded when he realized his sister was right: the water *was* getting cold. It was barely lukewarm, and that pleasant pine smell was gone too.

Also, when had his feet and legs and hands gotten so long?

When had the tub turned to stone?

Jespar woke with a gasp.

This wasn't the Dal'Varek manor. He wasn't eleven, and he hadn't lost the sparring match against Diethmar today.

He was in the First Ziggurat and had fallen asleep in the tub.

His heart picked up and his stomach clenched as the memories returned. *The Corpse.* He had sat right here, regarding him with that sorrowful smile and drinking, the bulge in his throat moving up and down as the wine had dripped from his mouth and formed red puddles in the water.

Jespar exhaled, pressing his hands against his temples.

"Just a dream," he muttered. "Just a bloody dream."

His neck ached, and his skin was wrinkly from the eternity he must have spent in the tub—the water was cold. He heaved himself out of the basin and dried himself with a rose-scented towel, scrubbing harshly, as if to cleanse the nightmare's memory from his skin. Dry, he sighed and leaned against the wall, his skin feeling clammy on the tiles.

Company. He craved company.

Not until he looked into the mirror across—an admittedly pitiable, tired, unshaven face gazing back—did he remember Lysia.

Fuck.

He hurried into his room and glanced at the water clock on the wall shelf above the bed. Almost two hours past midnight. Cursing, he threw on his clothes and hastened to Lysia's room, hair still damp and the floor cold under his feet. She answered on the fifth knock.

"What?" a drowsy voice came from behind the door. "Who is it?"

"Me," Jespar said. "Can I come in?"

"... I thought you were asleep. You didn't answer the door when I came over."

"Yeah, I dozed off. I'm sorry."

A pause, then the sound of rustling sheets and footfalls. A key turned, and the door swung open. Relief flooded Jespar at the sight of her.

"You know, it's really late," she said. "We don't have to—"

We do. I do. "Please, Lysia. Can I come in?"

Something about how he said it must have gotten to her; Lysia fell quiet and let him in. Jespar went straight to a wingback chair between two windows and dropped into it with a sigh. Lysia closed the door behind him, then turned and studied him curiously. She looked pretty, hair loose and disheveled, wearing a nightgown down to her knees—provocative in Enderal, common in Kilay, prudish in

Qyra. A candelabrum near the bed splashed an orange glow across her unscarred cheek.

Gods, how glad he was to see her.

"Are you okay?" Lysia said. "You look—"

"Like shit?"

"Kind of. What happened?"

Jespar opened his mouth, meaning to tell her about the nightmare. He couldn't.

Just like on the cutter to Hapana, a lump blocked his throat, stopped him from speaking.

"Are ... you okay?"

Jespar felt for his scarf, then dropped his hand when he realized he wasn't wearing it. "Yeah, sure. I just ... I had a pipe too many and fell asleep in the tub. I'm sorry."

Lysia cocked her head. "That's it?"

No, it's not. You saw a creature from your own bloody nightmares. Tell her, godsdammit.

Pointless. "Yeah. Strong stuff."

Lysia sighed. "You know what, I've just decided I'd rather be alone tonight. Would you mind?"

"What? I thought you wanted company?"

"Uh-huh, and, come to think of it, I still do."

"That doesn't make any sense."

"Yeah, right? It's almost like I feel one thing but say the other."

Jespar had no reply. Lysia's voice softened. "Look, Jespar, I get it, you don't like talking about feelings or whatever, but trust me, it can help. Gods know you've been through enough shit today to deserve an open ear."

He did, and he wanted it. *Just tell her, you idiot. What's wrong with you?*

The self-chastising didn't help. Not only did the lump persist, but the phantom noose had joined it. Maybe he *should* just drop it and leave. Lysia was right; it was late, they had a long day ahead of them tomorrow, and-

No. No, wherever this came from all of a sudden, he wouldn't let his mind mess this up.

It took him all the strength he had to force down the lump.

"Something really fucked-up happened."

A quarter-hour later, Lysia sat on a chair across Jespar, the backrest facing him, her arms resting on the top rail. They had opened the shutters, letting in the katydids' song and the fresh mountain air.

"And that Corpse was the same as in those recurring dreams you've been having?"

After finishing his account of that hallucination in the bathroom, he had confessed to her that he'd been struggling with nightmares for a long time; he had kept their contents vague and hadn't talked about where they came from. Not just because the mere thought of going there made the lump and the noose lurch with a force he simply didn't have the strength to defy, but also because he simply didn't want to speak of it. What was the point? Lysia had her own things to worry about, and if a session of "woe-is-me" and mutual shoulder-patting were all it took to cure the soul, the Gods would have long run out of supplicants.

"The nightmares aren't really recurring," Jespar said. "Only the Corpse. He shows up in almost every dream I have."

Worried Lysia would pry about what or who he thought the Corpse represented, Jespar dug his fingernails into his palms. She didn't.

"Okay. This is gonna sound silly, but you know all that didn't really happen, right? That Corpse wasn't really there, that was just a trick your mind played on you."

"I'm not crazy, Lysia. It's just that ... I don't know. It felt so bloody real."

"Yes, about that. Hold still, will you?" She leaned in and felt his forehead. "Mm-hm. Just as I thought."

"What?"

"You're running a fever. Not much, just a tad above average, but it explains that wooziness you described."

"Really?"

"Feel for yourself." She guided his palm to his forehead. It was true, his skin was hot. Strangely enough, though, it only felt this way on his palm. To him, his forehead felt chilly.

"I'm guessing that's drain from the dreamwalk," Lysia said. "You didn't strike the shift yourself, but the lad made you part of it, so you got a taste of what it feels like. Drain by proxy, so to speak."

"And that can cause hallucinations?"

"It's not unheard of. Everyone reacts differently."

Shifting drain. Of course—why hadn't he thought of this sooner? His anxiety lifted a little. "Huh. I see."

Lysia went to her belt, which lay spread out on a nearby dresser, and returned with a vial of green pellets. She handed him one. "Catroot and a bit of etheryme. If the drain hasn't eased off come morning, I'll give you another."

"Thanks. You're a lifesaver." He ate it dry, wincing as a bitter, mealy taste spread in his mouth, like crumbly old cabbage.

Lysia watched him, grinning. "Tastes like horseshit, I know. It's a Kilayan folk remedy, Juusew gave me the recipe."

"Your assistant."

"Yeah, he's a prodigy when it comes to herbs and concoctions ... it's crazy." She poured them two glasses from a pitcher on the bedside and took a long gulp from hers. "Anyhow, back to the dream thing. Mind if I tell you a story?"

"I've been talking your ear off, so be my guest."

"All right. Did you ever wonder how I got my scar?"

"I did, actually. I just wasn't sure if it's okay to ask."

"I was hit by lightning."

Not what Jespar had expected. "Really?"

"Uh-huh. When I was thirteen."

"How did it happen?"

"Just plain bad luck. You know Mâlei is mostly tundra and snow, right?"

"Yeah."

"Well, the monastery of the White Leaf is in the middle of a tundra in the north, so it's just earth and shrubs as far as the eye can see. I was out gathering herbs with another Sister, and around early afternoon, a storm came up. We have a word for these sudden storms in Mâlei, 'white vein tempests,' because the sky looks like a web of flashing blue-white veins when the lightning crashes down on the horizon. It's a chilling sight, really."

"I can imagine."

Lysia took another sip. "Anyway, the monastery was still an hour away, so we ran like hell looking for cover, but there was nothing, just shrubs over shrubs. The wind picked up like crazy, and it started pouring buckets, and before we knew it, lightning was shooting down in the distance, again and again and again, as though the storm was trying to crack the godsdamned ground." Her face was as flat as her voice, but a twitch had crept into her right eye. "The rest is a blur. I remember my Sister screaming at me to get down, then I realized I had wet my pants, and that, bloody hell, the sky really did look like veins. After that," she popped her lips, "the memory ends. Just a gaping black nothing."

"The lightning struck you."

"Uh-huh. I was in a coma for three weeks, practically brain-dead. Later, the Sisters told me that no one expected me to wake up again."

"But you did."

"Yes. Overnight, even."

"I guess that's unusual?"

"Very. Normally, people take moons or years to come out of a coma. And that's not all: the lightning had also triggered the cusping of my Sight. Late, I know—the Sisters think I might never have cusped if not for the trauma, and the idea fascinated them, so they ran all kinds of tests on me in the next weeks.

"It was a shite time, I'll tell you that ... I was high on etheryme and nightflower most of the day to quell the cusping flickers, but whenever the drogae wore off, I felt like I was trapped in a nightmare." Her eyes were dull as they met Jespar's. "You know what they're like for a biomancer? The flickers?"

"I read about it, I think. Your mind simulates potential shifts in your environment, so you start hallucinating. For a biomancer, it's stuff like wilted flowers or dead rabbits coming back to life."

Lysia snorted. "Oh, yes, the flower and the bunny ... that's the Order-approved version of it. What it ignores is that there is no such thing as a purely biomantic Sight. Biomancy is *always* just one side of a medal."

Remembering what Lysia had done to Scythe on Hapana, a chill prickled up his scalp. *I rotted his heart.* "Because every biomancer is also a necromancer."

"Exactly. But since the Order has deemed necromancy Profane, biomancers are forbidden to use the death aspect of their Sight, and scholars everywhere except for Qyra are forced to pretend it doesn't exist. It's ridiculous, really, especially considering that every army in the world secretly makes use of the Profane Sights because they're so damn useful."

"Preach water, drink wine."

"A classic. But, yeah, back to the flickers. Yes, you do hallucinate those flowers coming back to life, but you also get the opposite, things decaying and dying. And I'm not just talking about bunnies here. Just like thermomancers can feel their bedsheets burst into flames, choromancers see someone's organs move from one place to another, and psychomancers hear voices in their heads, we see people rotting and putting themselves back together right in front of our faces."

"Holy shit."

"One way to put it." Her lips pressed into a line, she studied the lemongrass bowl on the windowsill for a while, put there to keep insects out. A katako with scintillating violet wings buzzed about in front of it, but drew back whenever it got close. "Yeah, so that was an unpleasant time in my life. The flickers ceased eventually, and the Sisters stopped their experiments when they realized the lightning hadn't turned me into some dimensionist wonder child, and things pretty much got back to normal. Except I was now the proud owner of a mediocre biomantic Sight and," she flourished her finger down along the scar, "this lovely piece of art marking the path where the lightning traveled down my body." Her gaze sought Jespar's but then immediately flicked away—much like Kawu's often did.

She's ashamed.

"Believe it or not," Jespar said, "it actually looks pretty good."

Lysia's smile looked weary. "We already shagged, Jespar. No need to butter me up."

"No, seriously." He meant it. "It looks ... daredevil."

She rolled her eyes, but her smile seemed just a little more real. "Well, thanks, I guess. But back to the story. In the years after the strike, I kept having this messed-up nightmare."

"I had a hunch that's what you were getting at. About the storm?"

"No, about the night I got out of my coma. The Sister on duty in the infirmary had gone out for a walk, so I was all alone when I woke up. Pretty damn scary, as you can imagine. Little Lysia, all by herself on one of those stone slabs where the Sisters have taught her to dissect corpses, her last memory that terrible tempest, and the flash of light. She was so scared she probably wouldn't have moved all night if it hadn't been so *bloody* cold."

Lysia reached for her scar. For a second, her fingers hovered over the thin, red-brown lines. Then she dropped them into her lap, and something about her expression and intonation changed, became distant and flat, like a physician recounting the details of a surgery. "Now, in reality, Little Lysia ran through the monastery bawling like a baby, until one of the Sisters found her, tucked her into a warm blanket, and woke the others. That's not what happens in the nightmare, though."

Jespar's mouth felt dry. He drank. "No one finds her?"

"Close. In the nightmare, Little Lysia also runs and bawls, but the monastery is deserted, and no matter where she goes, she's alone. It goes on and on until she finds herself at the stairs to the morgue and pulls to a stop. She doesn't know why, she just does. For a few heartbeats, nothing happens. But then ... sounds. There are noises coming from downstairs, like feet dragging over tiles and wheezing and rasping moans. Little Lysia is horrified; she can barely breathe, but something keeps her rooted to the spot, gawking down the corridor like a fool. Even when those white faces show up in the darkness ... she just doesn't move."

"Living corpses?"

Lysia nods. Her eyes were glassy but slightly widened, as though a time window had opened inside her goblet and she was gazing into the past. "For some reason, it's the embalming liquid Little Lysia notices first. Not how some of these moving cadavers don't have skin, not how some of them are missing limbs, not how entrails ooze from their bellies. It's the godsdamned embalming liquid that leaks from their ears, mouths, and eyes like blood." The twitch in her right eye grew stronger as if rebelling against the monotony of her voice. "Step by step, the corpses drag themselves up the stairs. Until they come to a stop, not even a stride from her, and one of them, Old Sister Teimarah, speaks. Do you know what she says?"

"No."

"'Welcome home.'"

The katako found its way past the lemongrass bowl and circled over Lysia's head, as if waiting for an opening to attack. Lysia didn't react.

"And that's when Little Lysia suddenly notices something she should have noticed long before. The stink that comes from her own skin, how cold her breath feels on her lips. That odd, twisted angle of her hand. *Gods, how ugly it looks*, she thinks. *I'm a cripple now.* But Teimarah doesn't think so. As though Little Lysia had actually said this, Teimarah gently takes that ugly hand and whispers, 'You're perfect.' And then she and the other cadavers guide her back down to the morgue, lead her to a coffin, and lift her inside."

"Bloody hell. That's dark." As if summoned by Lysia's story, pictures from his own nightmares had risen in his mind, clotting like little spheres of blood. Most prominent among them was the quiet one from last night and the night before: Jespar, kneeling in the swamp court.

Lysia didn't seem to hear. "And then, just as the corpses close the lid, something bizarre happens. The fear vanishes. Just like that, Little Lysia isn't scared anymore, and this immeasurable relief washes over her like a giant wave. Why? Because she finally realizes that this is where she belongs. That she *should* be in that coffin because there's no way someone could have survived a lightning strike, that she *should* be in that coffin because her waking up is just some messed-up fantasy her mind spun to convince herself she's still alive."

The second the last word was out, the katako darted for Lysia's neck. She swatted it without looking. Slowly, she looked at Jespar, as if just remembering he was there.

He cleared his throat. "I'm not sure what to say. That sounds pretty horrifying."

Lysia held his gaze for a very long moment. Then she let out a small breath, and her lid stopped twitching. "It was," she said. "But I didn't tell you this for sympathy. My point is that dream was as uncomfortable as it was important. It was my mind's way of showing me something I had to confront."

Jespar crossed his legs. "That you're a walking corpse?"

"No," Lysia said, smiling grimly. "That life is fleeting and that I didn't want to spend it growing old and lonely behind those monastery walls. If that nightmare hadn't been so bloody tenacious and hadn't pushed me to the limit, I might never have left." She flicked the dead katako from her shoulder. "So, yes, that lightning almost killed me. But, in a way, it also showed me how to live."

"A very philosophical lightning," Jespar replied with the hint of a grin.

Snorting, Lysia mock-slapped Jespar. "You're an idiot. Look, what I'm getting at is, while some nightmares are random nonsense, others come for a reason. And maybe, if you find out what that Corpse in your dreams represents and fix the underlying issue, it will stop coming. The dead sisters did."

Clicking his tongue, Jespar gazed out the window. There was nothing new about her words. Not only because he already knew who the Corpse was and what he was connected to, but because he'd had similar thoughts during his drifting years, read similar things, and reached similar conclusions. Had that changed anything? No.

The nightmares were still there, as was the noose, and the occasional day of melancholia—and until he'd come here, it had been all right that way. Some scars came to stay.

"*Did* you fix it, though?"

Lysia curved her brows. "What, the dream?"

"No, that 'underlying issue'. That feeling that you should be dead."

"Well, I left the monastery, didn't I? I chose to live."

"Yeah, but—" He broke off. Why say this? Lysia had obviously only meant to comfort him; hell, to some extent, she'd even succeeded. This wasn't the time to strike up some stupid discussion again, the way he had on Hapana. "Ah, never mind."

She frowned. "Tell me. I insist."

Great, Jespar. Well done. Jespar shifted in his chair. "Well, I haven't known you that long, but there is a certain pattern to what you do, right? Working in the slums and subjecting yourself to a wagon-load of diseases, joining Agaam and me for Hapana even though you knew it would be dangerous. I mean, maybe you *are* still trying to prove something, you know? Constantly confronting death and danger has a way of making you feel alive. I mean, I was a soldier, I know how that is."

"Being a killer and being a healer are two different things."

It was only a few words, yet they struck home like the cut of a scalpel. Images pushed in—the Village in flames, the cottage, the Girl standing in the shards of the shattered vases. Naka.

The noose constricted.

Jespar's hurt must have shown. Lysia's expression softened at once. "Sorry, that was a shite thing to say. Fuck, I'm sorry."

Jespar's answer took some time coming. "It's all right—it's late, and we're both tired." He forced the corners of his mouth upward. "And as to what you said about dreams, I'll think about it. Maybe you have a point."

"Yeah, maybe you do too. To be honest, I've had the same thought a couple of times. Probably that's why I got so prickly."

The noose let go. "Well, aren't we civil? I always thought you're not lovers if your quarrels don't end in heartbreak and shattered vases."

It came out sounding a lot less casual than intended, but, contrary to his fears—*no strings attached*—Lysia only smiled and said nothing. It was a good silence. Familiar. Connected.

A painting from the hallways of your childhood home.

"About that," she said. "I've been meaning to ask you something."

Jespar raised his hands in mock surrender. "'Just fun', I know. All fine by me."

"No, that's not it. I was wondering—" She broke off, raked hair from her forehead. "Stars burn me, now I feel stupid."

"No need to. What is it?"

"Okay, fine. I was wondering what you feel for the lad. Kawu."

It was the last question Jespar had expected. Then again, maybe he should have. "What do you mean, 'feel for him?' I barely know him."

"Maybe, but you fancy him, don't you? As he fancies you, I might add."

Though Jespar said nothing, his expression seemed to be all the answer she needed.

"Right," she sighed. "I had a hunch you swim both sides of the river. Can I be open, Jespar?"

"... Sure."

"I like you. More than I expected."

Jespar was once again silent. Not because her admission bothered him—the opposite was the case. He just didn't know what to say.

Lysia gave him a tense smile that managed to be both defiant and vulnerable. "Yeah, I know, it's stupid considering what I said on the boat and how long we've known each other. I mean, Stars burn me, how long has it been? Three days?"

"Four, if you count today."

"There you have it. The thing is, I can giggle at how silly this is all I want, but it doesn't change my feelings. So, here's the deal: if you wanna pursue this thing with me, whatever it is, I'd like you to promise me that we'll keep it exclusive. This job is bonkers enough as it is, and I have zero interest in adding a love triangle to my list of worries." She opened her palms. "So, what do you say? Rest assured, no hard feelings if the answer is 'no'."

Jespar wrestled for an answer. "Are all Mâleian women so—"

"Open about their feelings?"

"Yeah."

"No, but having been fucked over and ditched in the worst way imaginable makes you cautious. If people just *talked* about what's going on in their heads before acting like arseholes, this world wouldn't be the messy pile of shite it is." She had probably meant to sound dry and blasé, but the way it came out gave Jespar pause.

Hurt?

She looked away, thumb brushing her scar.

Yes, hurt. And a damn lot of it. He'd be damned if he were going to add more to the pile.

"Okay," he said.

"Okay what?"

"Okay, let's be honest with each other, and, okay, let's make it exclusive."

"Listen, I really don't wanna force you. Only say it when you *really* mean it, I—" She sighed. "I know it's stupid, but this is important to me. That's all I'm saying."

"Yes, and it is to me too." Jespar took her hand. "I promise, okay? Let's ... Let's just figure out where it takes us."

He meant it. Yes, he fancied Kawu, as she had so aptly put it. Yes, he would like to get to know him better. But not enough to sacrifice the bond he had with Lysia, fresh and unexplored as it was.

It felt real.

She met his gaze and held it, oddly defensive as if she were searching his face for signs of dishonesty. Then the corner of her mouth curled upward, and she nodded. "All right, it's a deal then. My, aren't we romantic?"

Jespar let go of her hand and eased back in the chair. "I'll take it. Now, how about we call it a night? Something tells me we need all the sleep we can get for tomorrow."

"Yeah. We probably do."

They didn't get much.

Sex had been the last thing on Jespar's mind when he had knocked on her door an hour ago, but when they slipped under the blankets, and Lysia's lips sought his, one thing led to another.

She's right, he thought as she lay cozied up to him after, head on his chest, her breath ebbing and flowing in the equilibrium of sleep. This thing between them *was* strange. As strange as the past week that had so quickly turned his quiet and lonely life upside down. Here he was, the drifter Jespar Dal'Varek, in a luxurious bed in the palace of the richest man in the Illumined World. Next to a woman he was falling in love with.

Irrational.

Rushed.

Daunting.

But right.

THE SWAMP
WE ONLY MEAN WELL FOR YOU

SOMEDAY
SOMETIME

"I am disappointed, boy. We scream and scream and scream, and here you are, sowing the wind. Can you not understand that we only mean well for you?"

The lump was a fist of ice, crammed into Jespar's throat, blocking all words. And maybe it belonged there. After all, what right did *he* have to a confession? What had he done to deserve a listening ear when there were millions of suffering souls out there who longed for catharsis too, good souls who hadn't sinned, good souls who bore no black mark like he did, good souls who didn't poison everything they touched.

So Jespar remained silent.

"Well, so be it, boy," the Corpse said. "You leave us no choice."

A noose appeared around Jespar's neck, black and slimy like a rotten tentacle. Something *moved* inside his guts, crawled up his esophagus.

"Forgive me."

INTERLUDE
THE MAN

FOUR WEEKS BEFORE
3RD MOON OF DRY SEASON, 1226 A.L.

"Home," the man says. It feels like a lie—and perhaps it is. After all, only his memories make the house in the moonlit palm grove more than just an abandoned shack. Only his memories make it the place where he spent the first nine years of his life.

"Home."

Nothing. No warmth, no comfort, no nostalgia. Not even anger.

Absently, the man adjusts his cheap linen cowl and pulls it back over his mouth.

What did he expect?

It's his first return here since that evening on Spirit Hill, and the life the man leads now could not be more different from that of the boy who had left with Mamah that night. He imagines walking to the market at dawn, the way he had so many times with Popa. Back then, no one had given him a second glance. Today, he would inspire anything from knee-falls to assassination attempts—in light of what he has done, probably more of the latter.

Yes. Because you're a monster.

"Nonsense," he mutters. This isn't him having these thoughts— it's the fog, that godsdamned black fog that has been clouding his mind for a week now and just won't go away.

This isn't him.

The man pads around the rickety hut, the grass rustling under his myrad leather boots. The once bright yellow walls have faded, and vines and purple lightroses cover them all, like beautiful tumors. He reaches the door and places his palm on the handle.

Home.

Even on the bad days, the house had always radiated a sense of comfort to the boy. It was why life with Popa had never been all bad, like Mamah later insisted it was. It's also why the man still lies awake at night sometimes, wondering how Popa must have felt when he had found the house empty the morning after they had left. The way the man imagines it, he had probably just gone on to the market and expected them to come back a few days later, the boy's back bloody from the deserved whippings he'd gotten for stealing, and Mamah's cunt sore from the geezers she had to fuck to afford the food.

How wrong he'd been.

Mamah never sold her body, and the boy never stole. No, he challenged fate instead, and after every battle he lost, he got back to his feet and tried again, until the victories finally starting coming, and he ended up climbing Fortune Road at a pace that was now the stuff of legends.

Even so, the comfort never returned.

Not after the man made his first million, not after he bought that villa in the Jade District, not after he met the love of his life and they moved into the ziggurat at the top of the mountain. Mamah never understood, not until the womb fleshrot took her. To her, leaving Popa was the best choice she'd ever made.

The man opens the door.

It's all still there, buried under a coat of dust: the stone table in the center of the room. The shabby palmwood chairs and shelves. The threadbare carpet. It's all still there, except for the comfort.

Because the room is a carcass.

A thought forms, cold and crisp and clear, as if it were more than just an assumption. As if it were a known truth.

Popa never came back.

That night, after he hit Mamah, he went to the beach and drank himself to death.

The man wants to scream and slam his fist into the wall, but the black fog smothers his despair and leaves him hollow. With a croaking sound, he lets himself slide down the door jamb and buries his head in his hands.

What's wrong with you? Why are you doing this, why are you here? Why are you being *this way?*

"Fool," he whispers. "You bloody old fool."

CHAPTER TEN
THE GREAT DREAM

DAY FOUR
6TH MOON OF DRY SEASON, 1226 A.L.

hey broke their fast with sweet rice balls, fruits, and fried plantains. Pallid dawn light filtered into the dining chamber, and cool air washed through the open windows, much to the disdain of a chubby cat napping in the corner. Kawu, Jespar, and Lysia all wore feather-light nuvium chainmail and greaves, concealed with a layer of clothing to avoid unwanted attention—Jespar with a Kilayan coat, Lysia with her cotton jacket, Kawu with a green poncho. Kawu spoke little during breakfast, and when he had finished up, he immediately excused himself into his chamber.

Lysia relaxed visibly as the door fell shut behind him. "You really don't feel it? That weird ... vibe?"

"I don't. But it's related to his aura; he told me about it."

"His auric resonance, you mean?"

"Yeah. Apparently, he makes people uneasy."

"Huh, I hadn't thought of that." She forked up her remaining rice ball. "Poor boy."

Jespar rubbed his eyes. He hadn't slept again after waking from the swamp nightmare, partly because of an aimless anxiety, partly because the phantom noose hadn't loosened all day. "Do biomancers have a resonance too?"

"Only extraordinarily strong ones—they can make people tired or energetic just by being close, depending on how they are feeling themselves. I'm too mediocre for that, though."

After breakfast, they met Kawu and Agaam at the stables, four saddled horses beside them. A crimson spot around the muzzle of one of them drew Jespar's attention: Arazalean steppe-runners, the fastest and most enduring horses in the Illumined World. The telltale red streaks in this particular breed appeared to have been either bred out or dyed for camouflage purposes.

They were about to mount when a figure came hurrying toward them. Enkshi. Clad in simple white robes and wearing no jewelry except for his copper ring, he looked like a shadow of himself.

Agaam dropped the reins and bowed. "Ma'sao Enkshi."

Enkshi gave a tired nod. "Ma'sae, there's something we should talk about. Wait here, Agaam."

He led them into a spacious, light-soaked study, all bookshelves and chests. A black desk packed with neatly stacked scrolls occupied the center, backdropped by the giant painting of a smiling Starling man. Enkshi sat in the wingback behind the desk and gestured Jespar, Lysia, and Kawu to take a seat across from him.

"A drink?"

All three declined.

"Very well." He steepled his fingers. "There are two things I believe you should know before you set out. First, we received a report from General Daato last night. It seems like the Scythe have not only doubled in number, they are also spreading rumors that Ma'sao Oonai is dead."

"You think they know?" Jespar asked.

"Either that or they are gauging our reaction. If we quell the rumors too harshly, they might interpret it as confirmation, but if we don't refute them at all, then that's also an answer. And that's not all: The Coalition is getting nervous. We just learned that Third Magnate Vel'Nyx sailed to Arazeal under the pretense of some business matter a week ago, and Second Magnate Vel'Ravan has requested an audience with Ma'sao Oonai 'as soon as possible.'"

"What do you plan to do?" Lysia asked.

"I'm not sure there is much we can do except getting this bug—if that *is* what's making him sick—out of Jaaros' brain as soon as possible. He needs to make a public appearance, preferably before Miwā-e-Kēku. If there's no word from him by then, I bet my left hand these terrorists will use the chance for a grand-scale attack, or even a coup."

"So, why are you telling us this?" Jespar asked.

Enkshi poured himself a glass of water and downed it in a single swallow. "To remind you what's at stake, I suppose. I know you didn't ask for this responsibility, but it seems the fate of this country has ended up on your shoulders, at least to a certain extent. I still think it's foolish to send you and not a specialized squad, but you saw how adamant the Ma'saa was. Just do what you can, I guess that's what I'm trying to say."

"We will," Lysia said.

"Good. That's good." He poured himself another glass. "The second matter is something you should know about the Ma'sao, about Jaaros. He ... how to say this? He wasn't faithful to his wife."

Shock of shocks, Jespar thought. "You mean he had a mistress."

"No, not in the classic sense of the word. Jaaros' love for Nayima is enough to move mountains, that's one thing I'm absolutely certain of. Those women whom he took to Kaiawaika Manor from time to time, they were just dalliances, diversions."

"Whom the Ma'saa knows nothing about," Lysia said.

"This is between him and her," Enkshi said. "It's not my place to judge."

Kawu spoke up—the first time this morning. "You think that woman Ma'sao Dal'Varek saw in those memories was one of his dalliances."

"It's a possibility, yes. I'm just letting you know so that you have the whole picture. And before you ask, no, I don't know that much about his affairs. He kept that part of his life very private."

Jespar scratched his beard. "Wouldn't those women all be potential suspects? Especially if they ... parted with Jaaros on bad terms?"

"In theory, yes. In practice, it's unlikely any of them would have the means or connections to get their hands on a dreameater. From what little I know, most of them were young Coalition hopefuls looking to speed up their careers."

A vein pulsed at Lysia's temple, but her voice remained calm. "They could have had help, though. Or maybe they got their hands on it some other way."

"*And* found a psychomancer or dreamwalker to do the imprinting for them? I mean, you're right, we can't rule out the possibility, all I'm saying is that it's unlikely. Finding out whether I'm right or wrong is your job. I suppose I don't have to tell you that the Ma'saa must not learn of this matter? No point adding to her grief."

Jespar briefly considered telling her out of an odd sense of loyalty, but then he realized solving the Oonai's marriage problems *really* wasn't part of the job. Judging by her shrug, Lysia seemed to have come to the same conclusion. Kawu's face betrayed no emotion at all.

"All right then," Jespar said. "Is there anything else?"

Enkshi's lips began to move, as if about to form a 'yes'. Then he began to stack a sheaf of papers that didn't look like it needed stacking. "Actually, there's one more thing. I believe I owe you an apology."

Jespar thought he had misheard.

"For what?" Lysia asked.

"For my behavior, of course. I'm afraid I haven't shown myself in the best light." He went on sorting, arranging the papers so that their edges matched up perfectly. "The truth is, I'm as devastated by this whole situation as the Ma'saa is. I know you probably see Jaaros as some greedy, ruthless tyrant, but please trust me, the Ma'saa was right when she said he is a good man. Yes, he believes people should have to work for their success like he had to, but once you earn his trust, you'd be hard-pressed to find a more loyal and generous friend. I've known him for almost thirty years now, and he ..." He stopped sorting, sighed, and looked out the window. "He has helped me through some dark times, let's just leave it at that. And the thought of him trapped in that dream, and being tortured by this creature, it ... well. It breaks my heart."

A bluebird landed on the window ledge, cautiously peeked inside, then fluttered away. Enkshi laced his fingers, finally meeting their eyes. His expression was a mix of his trademark low-key disdain and a pleading vulnerability that looked out of place on him. "So, here it is—my apology. Do with it what you will, but it had to be said."

Kawu was the first to answer. "Thank you."

"Yeah," Jespar said. "Thanks."

Lysia's reply took a little longer, but there wasn't a hint of scorn in her voice when she answered. "Apology accepted. Actually, I've been meaning to ask you a favor, so maybe now's a good time."

"I'm listening?"

Lysia adjusted the collar of her jacket. "I'd like an advance. Not much, just five thousand sêr. I've had some unforeseen expenses, and this undertaking is requiring more time than I'd expected."

"Unforeseen expenses," Enkshi echoed. "I take it you're referring to your debt at Tuujan and Associates?"

Lysia's hands froze, blood rising to her cheeks. "What do you mean?"

Enkshi snorted, but there was no mockery in it. "I do my research, Varroy, just as you did yours. But, yes, you'll get your advance. I will arrange for it to be sent to your assistant, Juusew, directly after this conversation. Now, enough time wasted—good luck out there."

They left the ziggurat via a path along Mount Ilakato's bayside slope, the Alabaster City, a glowing white vision beneath them. What the mountain breeze made a refreshing experience at first turned into an ordeal when the cliff path descended into the central jungle that covered most of Uunili's south. Long before noon, Jespar's shirt was soaked with sweat and the nuvium scales chafed against his armpits, his hands and neck marred with mosquito bites despite the lemongrass extract he'd rubbed onto his skin. He was ready to sacrifice all safety and decency by tearing off his clothes and continuing the ride stark naked when the jungle thinned out at last, and the strait separating the northern and the southern half of the island became visible. To keep a low profile, they forewent the well-traveled bridge in the center and instead crossed to the northern island via the Mandibles, a lagoon-dotted isthmus on the eastern coast that owed its name to its curved shape.

The contrast between northern and southern Uunili was as stark as that between the Stone and the Jade District. While the city, the rainforest, and scattered plantations marked the former, the latter was a hilly expanse of sun-parched grass, most of the jungle cleared for the many rice terraces and plantations built around the Owa e Īkomo delta, the lifeblood of the northern island. An imposing mountain range rose in the northwest—the Kaiawaika Massif, their destination.

Even though Lysia had told Jespar that last night's promise in no way meant he wasn't allowed to talk to Kawu anymore—in fact, she hated possessiveness—Jespar had been worried that his ensuing conversations with Kawu might become awkward. It was a non-problem: Kawu spent most of the journey in the rear, and speaking little, if at all. Well past noon, they made their first stop of the day at a tavern near Bluefort, a colonial town at the delta. A cloud of smells met them upon entering; rice, fat, and sweat, a thick blanket of nightflower smoke hanging just under the beamed ceiling. The place was packed, and most of the guests were commoners, except for a couple at the far end whose bodyguards and silk clothes screamed money. Despite the laughter and chatter, the same tension Jespar had witnessed in Kekotoki and Uunili permeated the tavern.

Agaam led them to a corner table where they signaled for the tavern maid. Clad in a tightly fitted dress, the woman had dense black hair that framed her pretty face—classic good looks made more interesting by a sharp nose. When it was Agaam's turn to order, he regarded her wordlessly, a hollow look in his good eye that made it appear oddly similar to the glass one.

"Um, ma'sao?"

Agaam snapped out of his trance. "I beg your pardon, ma'saa, what did you say?"

"I asked, d'ye wanna eat somethin'?"

"Oh, yes. Yes, I would, thank you."

The waitress took his order.

"Are you okay?" Jespar asked when she had left.

"I am, ma'sao," Agaam said after a small pause. "Please forgive me, it's been a long and strange week."

Jespar considered it an excellent line for a toast.

Because Agaam and Kawu were about as loquacious as rocks, Jespar and Lysia shouldered most of the luncheon conversation, speaking of the gods and the world while expertly avoiding the topic of their mission. When they'd finished eating, they ordered another round of coconut water, and Jespar went out to relieve himself. Lost in thought, he found a solitary palm tree a few steps past the backyard, and-

Cold.

His hand shot to his forehead. An icy spot pulsed just over his right brow, sending a dull pain into his scalp and into his temple. Except for the cold, it was the same lightheadedness he'd felt after yesterday's pipe.

What the-

The spot disappeared.

Jespar did not move.

"The drain," he said. It was that damned shifting drain again. It had to be. Resolving to ask Lysia for more pellets, he finished his business and went back to the tavern.

He noticed something was wrong when he reached the doors. It had been noisy before, but there was an angry quality to the din coming from inside now, the kind Jespar had learned to avoid during his vagrant years. For a second, he considered making a run for it. Then he remembered his companions were still in there and entered the tavern.

Four men stood around the table of the wealthy couple, all clad in dark uniforms. One of them, a mountain of a man with long black hair who struck Jespar as familiar, held the nobleman by his neck while the woman was in tears. The couples' bodyguards were nowhere to be seen.

"Gods, someone help us!" the woman sobbed. *"Anyone!"*

The crowd was still.

"Well, well. Seems like yer on yer own." The tall man let go of the noble; his head flopped into the bowl, spilling stew across the table. "Tell me, friends, why is that?"

Not until the mountain faced the crowd and revealed his chalk-white complexion did Jespar recognize him.

The Pale Brother. The leader of the Scythes.

"Why?" the Aetäerna repeated.

The guests were quiet. Jespar shot a glance at his group: Kawu was as still as a sculpture; Lysia's lips were pressed into a white line. Agaam was as calm as a man watching the peaceful sea, one hand slid inside his coat.

"That's right," the Pale Brother said, turning back to the noble-woman. "They ain't helpin' 'cause they don't give a shit. Ugly feelin', ain't it? To be on the other end of the whip for a change?"

"Please," the woman sobbed, "we'll give you anything you want, just let us go."

The Pale Brother frowned. "Right, I forgot: yer sort's used to gettin' yer will if only ye say the right thing. Words, words, words ... they're yer weapons, ain't they? The clay ye use to shape the lies us fools suck up like a toddler drinking milk from its mother's teats."

He addressed the crowd. "The Great Dream. That's their favorite story. 'We're the architects of our own fortune,' 'chances, not obsta-cles,' the fairy tale that we all can one day live with the uppers if only we work hard enough." He heaved a sigh, inspecting the smoke at the ceiling. "Ah, the Great Dream ... It's a nice story, I'll give ye that. Too bad it's a fuckin' lie."

Slowly, the Pale Brother let his almond-shaped, purple eyes wander over the crowd as if memorizing each of their faces. Save for the noblewoman's sobs and some dish sizzling in the kitchen, it was utterly silent now.

"Think of a farmer. Like most of us, he dreams of movin' up the Road, and with the little patch of land his folks left him, he's even got a chance. He's a decent fellow, and his soil grows good fruit, so he easily makes enough to feed hisself and his family." He held up his index finger. "But then somethin' happens: the people like his fruit so much his market stalls are empty by midday. What's he to do? Right, he buys more land and hires a helper so he can grow and pluck twice as much fruit. It all goes well till the farmer realizes that, with the helper's wage, every basketful he sells only earns him a bit more than it costs to produce. Sure, he still takes some coin back home, but at that pace, it ain't never gonna be enough for a bigger farm, let alone a nice house in the Jade District, and if he raises his prices too much, people ain't gonna buy from him no more.

"But then he gets an idea: why don't he just pay his helper a little less? True, the lad might quit, but there's hundreds of coinless buggers out there who's desperate for work, and he'd surely find someone new. So, it's decided: he breaks the bad news to his helper, and the lad grins and bears it. In fact, he takes it so well that the farmer also tells him to work for an hour longer each day ... and while we're at it, why not buy that cheap nuvium-tainted bit of soil by the shore? If he just lets the fruit grow long enough, the sugar's gonna cover up the bitter taste." Opening his hands, the Pale Brother stepped toward the crowd. "Five years later, our farmer owns a full planta-tion and has eight helpers doin' all the work for him. Just a couple more good years, and he'll finally have what he always dreamed of: a house beyond the pretty white arch." A smirk played on the Pale Brother's lips. "Don't sound so bad, does it? The man played the game, and he played it right."

Mutters of agreement.

"Well, well. Too bad there's one problem." His smirk iced over. "Ye all think yer the farmer. I mean, it's true, ain't it? Surely, *yer* not gonna be the helper in that story. Yer the one who finds their fortune!" He raised his voice. "And *that's* the lie the leeches don't want us to see, brothers and sisters! Godsdammit, just think for a bloody moment. If we were all farmers, who's gonna pluck the fuckin' fruit?"

Angry approval.

"The dream is a lie! It's a candle the leeches keep lit in the midst of fog so we stay nice and docile, so we keep hopin' and don't see the truth they try so hard to hide! That this country, brothers and sisters, is rotten to the *fuckin' core!*"

Shouts and stomps. "Damn right!" a man roared, slamming his mug on the table.

"And, boy, ain't the leeches havin' fun!" the Pale Brother said. "Sittin' in their pretty manors while *we* don't make enough to keep our kids fed, watchin' from the mountaintop as we break our backs in the mines! Godsdammit, d'ye really think we're people to them? Bullshit, we're material! We're tools to be ditched when they get rusty or break, and when we tell 'em we're strugglin' and beg 'em for help, they laugh and say it's all *our* fault 'cause we're lazy!

"But I ask ye, brothers and sisters, are we really? Is all this our fault? What of the petal picker who's gotta spend all his coin on his sick mother? What of the fisher who lost her boat in a storm and can't afford a new one? What of the miner who lost his legs, what of the feebleminded and the cripples, what of the ones Fortune just pissed on 'cause she don't give a shit who lives and who dies? 'Coinless', the leech says, 'lazy', 'just another have-not not worthy of a life of fuckin' dignity!'"

Riotous roars, boots stomping the ground, palms slamming the tables.

The Pale Brother glared at the sobbing noblewoman. "Ain't that right, 'ma'saa'? That's what ye think when ye sit in that house ye built on our backs, what ye think when ye drink the wine ye tapped from our veins, what ye think when ye eat the fat ye sucked from the fuckin' marrow of our bones. That this is what *we deserve*."

"Ma'sao, please, have—"

He smashed his fist into the table. "Answer the godsdamned question!"

The noblewoman shrieked and jerked back, her back pressing against the chair. The crowd booed.

"Cut her fuckin' hands off!" a woman screamed. "Teach that bitch a lesson!"

The noblewoman made a sound that could only be described as a whimper. "Please, ma'sao," she sobbed. "We always tried to do the right thing, we ... if only you knew us, you'd—"

"Vaalos," the Pale Brother said. "Remind me."

Another Scythe spoke up. "Dijaam and Katos Vel'Doraan. They own the biggest armory in the Archipelago."

A grin split the Pale Brother's lips. "Why, would ye look at that? Looks like I *do* know ye."

"Ma'sao, please! We *never* did any harm, we *never* exploited anybody, we always—"

"Ye know what me sister did to the last leech she got her hands on? She cut off his eyelids so he couldn't choose to look away anymore whenever it bloody suits him. I gotta say, I like the idea. Brutal, but ... how would yer sort put it? Poetic."

The Pale Brother drew his saber, sparking cheers from the crowd; the woman wailed, burying her head in her hands.

Do something, Jespar told himself. *You have to do something!*

Are you mad? They'll fucking butcher you!

Even if Agaam and Lysia chose to help, it was three versus four, and Jespar doubted General Daato had called that three-and-a-half stride tall Aetäerna "the best swordsman in the Archipelago" for no reason. None of that was taking the crowd into consideration, most of whom seemed perfectly at ease with the idea of mutilating a defenseless woman right in front of everyone.

The Pale Brother pointed his saber's tip at the noble, so close it almost drew blood. He raised it.

"Do it!" the woman from before shouted. "Just do it!"

The Pale Brother slammed his saber back into the sheath.

"Well, guess today's yer lucky day," he said. "It's true, ye and yer husband ain't the worst out there, so we're gonna let ye go, long as you promise to pass on a message. Could ye do that for me?"

The noblewoman stuttered a reply, nodding weakly.

"Good. Then go home and tell yer leech friends that the have-nots have finally woken up. Tell 'em to run as far as their fat legs can take 'em, 'cause once we come for 'em, there'll be no mercy." He leaned in and brought his lips to her ear. "Tell 'em we're gonna start a fire."

A hush fell.

Then the Pale Brother tore the woman's purse from her belt and shoved her. The chair toppled, and she fell over, crashing to the ground with a shriek. The Scythes laughed, some guests joined in.

The Pale Brother regarded her with a bleak smile, then tore off her husband's purse too, and turned to the innkeeper. "Keep their cargo and their horses but give 'em mules in return, brother. They gotta get to the city somehow without ruinin' them nice clothes of theirs."

The innkeeper tapped his chest with a trembling hand. "As ye say, ma'sao."

"I ain't no ma'sao. None of us are." The Pale Brother turned back to the noblewoman, who lay curled on the floor, cradling her stomach like a child crying for her mother. "Now get the fuck outta here, leech. And take yer fat husband with ye."

Sobbing, she scrambled to her feet, heaved up her husband, and dragged him out of the tavern. Struggling under his weight, she had to stop several times, even dropping him once, which sparked a burst of laughter from the onlookers; even though Jespar spotted some pity among their faces, no one came to the woman's help until, halfway to the door, the pretty waitress with the pointy nose muttered something and helped her out of the tavern.

The laughter went on for a bit, then the attention returned to the Pale Brother, who had watched the scene with a wolfish grin. He tossed one of the purses to the innkeeper and then hurled the other against the ceiling, sending a shower of coins clattering down upon the room. Gasps went up as the money bounced and rolled over the floorboards, but no one moved.

"Split it fairly, or yer no better than them," he said. "Meals and drinks are on me."

The Scythes left.

The hush that followed after the door fell shut behind them went on for a good minute—as if the Aetäerna's presence had left an echo that had to fade before normalcy could return. Then a man cheered and slammed his mug onto the table. Someone else joined in, then another and another and another, until the entire tavern was roaring with laughter and cheers.

Like pebbles forming a rockslide.

CHAPTER ELEVEN
STORIES

"It's just horseshite," Lysia said. "You don't fight fire with fire."

They were riding along the western coast. Waves crashed against sunbaked cliffs to their left, meadows spread inland to their right, flowing into the wavy ridges of the Kaiawaika Massif rising ahead. Lysia and Jespar rode at the core of the file, while Agaam was up front and Kawu at the rear.

"'Fire with fire' is the mantra of just about every revolution that's ever happened," Jespar said. "I mean, how do you think the Light-Born united the warring factions of the Qyranian and the Nehrimese empires?"

"That's over a thousand years ago! We should be better than that by now."

"Okay, then what do you suggest the commoners do instead? Protest peacefully and hope the uppers hear them while they sip wine in their villas?"

"It would be a bloody start. In Arazeal, the working people vote representatives into the court of the Empress, and those representatives fight for their interests."

"Yeah, most of whom are pawns to some political faction, if I'm not mistaken. Be realistic, Lysia, the only time a running system ever changes is in response to a crisis. As long as life is all right for the majority, nothing's gonna happen."

Jespar pulled the little jar Lysia had given him from his belt pouch and, with one hand on the reins, took another catroot-etheryme pellet. When he had told her about his drain flare-up at the tavern, Lysia had upped his dose to three a day. "And when things *do* go south, people will always resort to violence. It's just human nature."

"Ah, yes, good old human nature. Did it ever cross your mind that maybe this kind of complacency *is* exactly why things never change? That the only way we can be better is if we actually try it?"

Jespar tucked the jar back into his pouch. "Yeah, and if we all came to war armed with flower bouquets, every battlefield would be a gardener's dream."

"Now you're just being cynical."

"No, just realistic. Even if ninety-nine out of a hundred soldiers bring flowers, one idiot will always show up with a sword, and you bet he's gonna use it. That's just a fact, as much as I wish it weren't."

Lysia seemed about to reply, but then she leaned forward in her saddle instead. "Agaam?"

He turned his head. "Yes, ma'saa?"

"I've been wondering. How do you feel about what that Aetäerna said? You know, the leeches, the helpers, the dreamers?"

"Why do you ask, ma'saa?"

"I'm just curious. You work for Oonai, so do you think all the Scythe say is nonsense?"

Agaam looked out over the ocean, a perfect blue under the cloudless sky. "I believe it's a story."

Jespar, who had expected an evasive or vague answer, fell into a trot beside them. "What do you mean by that?"

"I mean that both the Coalition and the Scythe only use parts of the truth and fashion them into a narrative that serves their purpose. Believe me, every single upper knows parts of the system are unjust. They simply turn a blind eye to it." Agaam shooed away a red katako buzzing around his horse's neck. For some reason, insects seemed to avoid him. "The Scythe are no different in that regard. Yes, they are absolutely correct that the Great Dream only has room for a few big farmers, but then they ignore that there *are* wealthy people out there whose success isn't based on exploitation and who actually try to make the world a better place. Not to mention that the idea of absolute equality has always been a pipe dream."

"Is that so," Lysia said.

He gave her a sideways glance, his glass eye locked forward. "For as long as humans have existed, it's been in our nature to compete. A part of our brains simply wants hierarchy, and even if we were to overcome it, we will never all be equal. Think about it: if the Scythe came to power, who would make the decisions? There would still be big farmers and helpers, only that some other distinguishing feature would decide who is who. Take Qyra, for example. Power and influence there are all about prestige and spiritual virtue. Just other currencies, you could say."

"Well, we're not gonna find out until we try," Lysia said.

"That may be so. But the Scythe isn't the way, and they know it. Even if their revolution were to succeed, the Illumined World would *never* accept their reign. Which means war."

"What makes you so sure?" Jespar asked. "The Order has enough problems as it is, so maybe they would strike a treaty."

"And thereby encourage terrorists to follow the Scythe's example, in a time when scholars question the very legitimacy of the Gods themselves? That's out of the question, trust me on that. This revolution is doomed to fail, the only question is how much havoc it will wreak in the process. And, believe me, the Pale Twins must know this as well as we do."

"But they either don't admit it to themselves or don't tell their followers because it doesn't fit their story," Jespar said. "The narrative."

"Precisely. Even if they did, their lambs likely wouldn't believe them because they don't want to. Once the mind commits to a story, the facts become secondary. Truth bows to bias."

A few silent moments passed by. They crossed a small bridge over a river from the mountains, the westering sun casting diamond-like reflections on the water.

"If both ideas are unjust," Lysia said, "then what's the answer?"

Once more, Agaam looked toward the sea, the sun revealing his every wrinkle. "I don't know. But the Scythe seeks to answer violence with more violence, and even if, against all odds, their revolution were to succeed, it would all just come back around. If you fight injustice with injustice, no matter how deserved it may feel, you'll always end up as just another turn of the wheel."

Jespar, intrigued by Agaam's words, but too tired for further debate, was ready to let the topic rest, but then Kawu spoke up behind them. "Whatever that Aetäerna said, he didn't mean it."

All three of them glanced at him.

"How do you know?" Jespar asked.

"Because that man, the Pale Brother ... he's a lie. He says all the right things, and uses the right words, but in the end, it's a charade.

He doesn't care the first thing about these people he claims to fight for."

"I'm not sure I follow," Lysia said.

"It's difficult to explain, ma'saa. We have a word for people like him in Makehu, *tawahe,* which I suppose you could translate as 'soul-dead'. Someone who is tawahe doesn't feel emotions the way we do."

"Are you talking about crystal minds?" Lysia asked.

"I'm not sure what that means, ma'saa."

"It's a term the scholars use for people who have difficulty understanding other people's emotions. Their brains work differently than ours."

"Ah. No, tawahe do feel and understand emotion—what sets them apart is their complete lack of compassion. They are just ... inhumane, that's probably the best way to put it. Even their kuluhikas look different from ours, all black, like a sky without stars and the moon."

An elderly man on a horse-drawn cart came toward them. It was the first traveler they'd met in hours.

"You didn't see the Pale Brother's dreams, though, right?" Jespar asked. "So how can you be sure?"

Kawu hesitated. Then he sighed. "My uncle Onāko was tawahe. And that look in the Aetǎerna's eyes, the way he moved and talked, it was him all over again."

The old man was almost within earshot. They guided their horses to the side of the road, allowing him to pass. He nodded at them in greeting when he realized they meant no harm.

"So," Agaam said, steering his horse back onto the road. For the first time, the old servant sounded intrigued. "You're suggesting the Pale Twins are impostors?"

"At least the Brother, yes," Kawu replied. "He doesn't care in the least about equality and brotherhood."

Tawahe, Jespar thought. He didn't know about black dream worlds, but he too had noticed something disquieting in the Pale Brother's speech, mesmerizing and passionate as it may have been. He tugged his scarf a little looser. "Then what does he care about? What do you think is it that the Pale Brother wants?"

Kawu's answer was a long time coming. "Probably the only thing that gives a tawahe a sense of fulfillment. Violence."

———

Another hour of steady trot along the coast later, the path branched off into a jungle that marked the first slopes of the Kaiawaika Massif. The road got wilder the farther they ventured, storm-felled trees and virulently growing ferns obstructing the way. The old man with the cart was the last traveler they met.

It was already dusk when Agaam finally decided to make camp in a clearing near the road. They bathed the sweat off in a nearby river, then dined on nuts, cold rice, and fruit. As Agaam excused himself to hold watch by the clearing's entrance and Kawu ventured into the jungle to 'sort his thoughts', Lysia and Jespar were soon left alone by the campfire, where she redressed his shoulder wound. They talked for a bit, discussing this afternoon's discussion, but it wasn't long before the fatigue from a full day in the saddle got the better of them. Jespar took another herbal pellet, then they spread out their blankets by the fireside, curled up next to each other, and slept.

At least Lysia did.

Jespar was restless. His thoughts spiraled on and on, passing from the memories of the dreamwalk to his night with Lysia, to the swamp nightmare, on and on and deeper and deeper until they reached the quicksand that was his past.

Bad shit happens wherever we go.

Just animals waiting to go rabid.
You said it'll get better, Jes.
It always does.
Always does.
Always.
See.

Sighing, he opened his eyes and sat up. Agaam was still at the mouth of the clearing, motionless as the rock he was sitting on. Jespar watched him for a few breaths, unsure of what to do. He needed to sleep, otherwise tomorrow would be an ordeal.

Oh, screw it.

He fished for his belt and unclasped a flask of banana brandy that he had purloined from his room in the ziggurat. It was disgustingly sweet, but after a few swigs, the alcohol took effect, and his unease lifted a little. He stoppered the flask and went back to his bedroll.

"So last time was not enough. You truly want us to hurt you."

Sorrow tinged the Corpse's eyes, and those of the ghouls on the seats mirrored it. The villagers, the man with the breadbasket. The Girl and her father. His sister, whom he tried so hard to forget.

"Gods, I simply do not understand. Why now? We were friends for so long, and now here you are, acting all rebellious. Can you not see where this will lead? Are you truly this ... this *blind*?"

The lump was bigger than ever, but somehow Jespar forced his lips to move.

"I ... I ..." Every sound was torture. Like moving a dead limb.

"Yes, boy?"

The way the Corpse said it—hopeful, curious—gave Jespar strength. Even after all this time, after all the times Jespar had failed him, the Corpse still believed in him.

"I ... see."

The Corpse was silent, weighing the truth in Jespar's words. Then blankness closed over his melancholic gaze. "No. You do not."

The noose was back around his neck, cold and black and slimy. His stomach stirred, and once again, he felt as if something was moving up his esophagus.

"We truly did not want to do this, but your foolish actions leave us no choice. We will not let you summon another storm."

The *things* inside Jespar had almost reached his throat now, tightly sealed by the noose. Unable to breathe, the swamp around him turned black.

"We will not."

The noose let go, and a swarm of locusts burst from Jespar's mouth.

CHAPTER TWELVE
IT ALWAYS GETS BETTER

DAY FOUR
6TH MOON OF DRY SEASON, 1226 A.L.

He jerked awake.

Sweat soaked his skin, his neck hurt, his heart hammered against his ribs. There was a metallic taste in his mouth; he must have bitten his tongue.

"I'm awake," he whispered. "I'm awa—"

Cold exploded in his forehead. He cried out and slumped back into the sheets, a palm pressed to his right temple where the pain clustered. *The drain*, he managed to think. *That* fucking *drain*. This time, however, the cold didn't let up; it just raged on, radiating up his scalp and into his temples and then down into his jaw. Only after what seemed an eternity, it faded into a slight prickle.

Jespar slumped back on the blanket, panting.

Something's wrong. Something's—

"Jespar?"

It was Lysia. She lay propped up on her elbow, regarding him with concerned and tired eyes. "Everything okay?"

No, he wanted to say. *Nothing's okay, and I'm* fucking *terrified.*

He couldn't. The lump was back, as stifling as in the nightmare, and he didn't have the power to fight it.

"Sorry, I didn't mean to wake you. It's just ... the drain spiked up again."

"Huh. Lemme feel." She sat up and placed her palm on his forehead. "Well, damn, your head's on fire. How long has it been like that?"

"Just now. But it's not that bad." *No. No, that's not what you want to say.* Pointless. As soon as he did as much as think about mentioning the nightmare or how terrified he was, his lips either locked up or moved on their own.

"Still, that's very odd." She drew back her hand. "The shift was more than twenty-four hours ago, so the drain should be gone by now. Maybe it's got something to do with the dreamwalk after all."

An image: the dreameater, growing from Oonai's head, five onyx eyes set on Jespar. He felt the pulse at his neck. "Like what?"

"No idea, maybe some kind of dreamwalk-induced migraine. We should ask Kawu in the morning." She fished her belt from the bedside, went through the pockets, and handed him two brown pellets. "Here, those should help, at least for the time being. We should look into this tomorrow."

Jespar muttered thanks and tossed the pellets into his mouth. Unlike the other ones, they were crunchy and moist and had a bitter, slimy taste that made him grimace.

"Be honest, Lysia. Should I be worried?"

She gave it some thought. Then she shook her head. "No, I don't think so—it's probably just a stubborn case of drain. Just don't obsess over it, Jes. It always gets better."

His heart skipped a beat. "What?"

"What do you mean, 'what'?"

"Why did you just say, 'It always gets better?' And why the hell did you call me 'Jes', you've never done that before."

Lysia arched her eyebrows. "What are you on about? I didn't say anything."

"You just said—"

She sobbed.

Jespar broke off. Stared.

"Hello?" Lysia asked. "Someone in there?"

"I ... why did you—" The word died in his mouth. "Why did you just sob?"

She did it again; or at least *something* had sobbed from her direction because her lips had been closed. This time, Lysia seemed to have heard it too. "The hell?"

Another sob.

Another.

Jespar made a croaking sound and reached for his swordbelt. Halfway there, he froze.

Something tickled in his mouth. Moved. Crawled.

He gagged and spat out the pellets. A second ticked by, as his brain refused to make sense of what it saw: two locusts lay on the blanket, or at least what was left of them. Crushed green-black pulps coated in saliva, tiny their legs clawing at the air, twitching and thrashing in concert with what must have been their wings.

Jespar vomited.

His mouth on fire and his stomach revolting, he spat out clumps of vomit and food and pieces of the bugs, more bile shooting up his throat at the sight. When it was all out, he stared at the spew, blood pounding in his temples.

Gods. Bloody fucking *Gods, what the* fuck *is going on here?*

A touch on the shoulder.

"Jes?"

Sob.

"Jes, I think something's wrong."

Slowly, he turned. Lysia's head was melting. It sagged down her skull like hot wax, distorting her widened eyes and gaping mouth into a grimace. Another sob from within her, another and another, each louder than the previous one. Stuttering incoherently, Jespar scrambled away from her, but then the campfire erupted in a volcanic blast; the lava missed Jespar, but it left pools of fire wherever it hit the earth, which in turn spawned lines of flames creeping toward Jespar like fiery tentacles, growing higher and higher with every finger-length they crawled.

"*Liar!*" Lysia threw herself at Jespar, grabbing his shoulders with melting hands. Her face had turned into a mess of fat and muscle, blood spraying out of her nostrils and eyes and ears and wrists, her hair falling off in strands; something was moving inside her belly, her shirt bulging with every sob. "*You lied!* You said it gets better, you said it gets better but it doesn't, it hurts so much, so much, so much, I'm drowning, I can't breathe, I just want it to end, I—"

Screaming, Jespar kicked at her, tried to back off, but the flames had surrounded them now, a cage of fire. Lysia threw back her head and let out an animal howl, and her stomach *ripped* open, and something clawed its way out of her body, the Girl, *Gods,* the Girl from Nehrim and she was crying and holding a bloody porcelain shard and she reached for Jespar and-

Was gone.

Jespar lay on his back, his arms flung around his chest, the fingers digging so hard into his biceps that it hurt.

For a few seconds, he lay still as a corpse. Then his hands slowly, slowly relaxed as his gaze wandered to the left. Lysia lay with her back turned toward him, her breathing calm and even. The fire was down to glimmering embers.

No cage of fire.

No melting Lysia.

No girl from Nehrim.

Jespar heaved a long breath and turned on his side. Only when he slipped his arms back around Lysia and gently pulled her close did he notice something was off.

Her body. It didn't feel right. Too big.

And why were her hands burning?

This time, he did not scream. A paralyzing calm took hold of him.

No, some part in his brain decided. No, this didn't make any sense. The Corpse wasn't here because he *couldn't.* He wasn't here because he only existed in his imagination. Jespar was still dreaming. That was the only explanation.

"I'm awake," he whispered. "I'm awake."

But nothing changed. The Corpse just lay there, his body soft and boneless like rotten fruit.

For a second, the horror was so overwhelming Jespar that wanted a hole to open beneath him and swallow him. Then he withdrew his arm from the Corpse and slowly slid back, off the blanket and onto the grass, his gaze locked on that creature that had sat on the edge of the bathtub last night because it hadn't been a dream, it had been real, and deep down, he'd always known. Some five strides from the blankets, he clambered to his feet and ran for the jungle.

Not until he had reached the edge of the clearing did a calm voice in his head stop him and told him this was madness, told him to *look* and convince himself that everything was all right.

He turned around.

The Corpse was still there.

Jespar ran for his life.

CHAPTER THIRTEEN
WHEN ALL THIS IS OVER

DAY FIVE
6TH MOON OF DRY SEASON, 1226 A.L.

ripping over a root, Jespar snapped out of his panic. He struggled for balance, found purchase on a nearby branch, and caught himself. For a few shallow breaths, he didn't move, just stared at the undergrowth beneath him.

Dizziness.

Idiot. You bloody idiot.

What was more likely to kill him? A hallucination that had somehow bled over from a nightmare, or a tropical rain forest teeming with poisonous plants and animals? What had he been thinking, bolting off into the jungle like a godsdamned imbecile?

Sighing deeply, he palmed the sweat off his forehead. His lungs burned from exhaustion and his feet from the countless nicks and cuts he must have gotten from running into thorny bushes or vines and only now grew aware of. What little he could make out of his surroundings all looked the same, and he couldn't pinpoint where he'd come from. Judging by the moon, sunrise was still a long way off.

The river.

His best chance of getting back was the river they'd bathed in before dinner. There had been a rock jutting out over the water, shaped like a finger, so all he had to do was follow the river upstream until he reached it, then find his way back to camp from there.

He listened.

There it was, faint and distant. Rushing water.

"He wasn't there," Jespar said. "He wasn't there."

A dozen more nicks on his soles later, he had found the river. He went to the bank and cleaned out the wounds on his feet, then drank deeply, washing away the phantom aftertaste of locusts the dream had left in his mouth. Then he followed the stream. When the finger-shaped rock became visible through the vegetation, poking over the stream like a tiny precipice, a weight lifted off Jespar's shoulders. He had barely reached it when someone spoke in the darkness.

"Ma'sao Dal'Varek?"

His head jerked up. Someone was sitting atop the rock, looking at him.

"Kawu?"

"What ... are you doing out here, ma'sao?"

Two feelings came at once. First, a silly disappointment Kawu still wasn't calling him by his first name. Second, an immeasurable relief at seeing him. Familiar. Comforting.

Grounding.

He opened his mouth, then caught himself. What was he supposed to say? That he had hallucinated Lysia turning into a corpse and had darted off into the jungle like a madman?

"I couldn't sleep," he said. "What about you? I thought you were coming back to the camp."

"Oh, I was planning to." He wore a sleeveless shirt and rolled-up trousers only. The nuvium mail, his poncho, and his boots lay in a heap beside him. "I just wound up here and decided to make it my meditation spot for the night. I like the sound of the water; it's always so calming."

"Ah. Yeah, I know what you mean." Pretending to study the environment, Jespar wondered what to do. The smart thing was to head back to camp, make sure Lysia hadn't woken up and wasn't getting worried, but the mere thought of it turned his stomach, the Corpse's phantom stench still in his nostrils. Also, in the few nights they'd spend together, he'd found her to be a sound sleeper. Chances were she wouldn't wake until sunrise.

He cleared his throat. "Listen, um, do you mind if I sit with you for a bit? I could use some company."

Kawu looked confused, as though he didn't understand the notion. *Makes sense.* Thanks to his auric resonance, people probably didn't ask him often.

"Yes," he said. "Of course."

"Great." Jespar climbed the rock and sat beside Kawu, dangling his legs from the ledge. He had unintentionally sat a bit closer to him than he would've with someone else, but Kawu didn't seem to mind.

Jespar felt his hands relax; his fingernails had been digging into his palms. "This is nice. Really nice."

Kawu didn't meet his gaze, but his lips curved upward. "It is."

A pause.

Jespar cleared his throat. "Hey, can I ask you something?"

It was Kawu's turn to tense. "What is it?"

"You've been so silent lately. Did I do or say anything to offend you?"

"What? No, not at all, I'm sorry if I made you feel that way. It's just—" He broke off. "I always need some time to myself when I'm around people for too long. That's all."

Something told Jespar Kawu had meant to say something else, but it didn't feel like a lie either. "I can relate," Jespar said. "I get that too, sometimes."

"Really? You always seem so ... talkative."

"Well, yeah, I can be, but only for a while. At some point, I need to withdraw, just like you. Refill my social reservoir, so to speak."

"I see."

Another pause followed, but it wasn't uncomfortable; probably because Jespar felt Kawu wanted him to stay. Or did he?

Say something. Keep the conversation going.

"Speaking of withdrawing," Jespar said. "There's something I've been wondering about. You said dreamwalkers are always aware when they sleep, right? From when their consciousness crosses over into the psychic dimension until they wake up?"

"That's true."

"So every single dream you have is lucid."

Kawu nodded.

"Wow. How does that feel? Like in Oonai's nightmare? I mean, it was so incredibly real, like, I don't know, a parallel world rather than a dream. Is it the same in your kuluhika?"

"For the most part." Kawu drew up a leg, lacing his fingers around his knee. There was a cut on the back of his hand. Jespar wondered where he'd gotten it. "The only difference is that I control what's happening."

What Jespar would give for that ability. "Then you probably never get nightmares?"

"No, unless I want them. My dreams are quite different from what you know." Kawu looked at him, his eyes a dark green in the scant light. "Just imagine a world that feels as real as this one, but you're its god: you can give it any shape you want, create landscapes, animals, and people, all with as little as a thought. The world *is* you, and you *are* the world, so the only limit is your imagination."

"That sounds fascinating."

The corners of Kawu's mouth lifted, but the rest of his face remained a mask. "I used to feel the same way when I was a child."

"A child? I thought Sights don't cusp until puberty?"

"Normally they don't, that's true, but mine did at six. By the time I was nine, I had created this entire world, with mountains that grow upside down from the sky, and huge cities with hundreds of thousands of creatures living inside them, humans, talking animals, and entirely different species altogether." His smile brightened ever so slightly. "Imīte, I even had these creatures that were just huge glowing blobs of slime and made these silly squelching noises when they moved. Don't ask what I was thinking, I have no idea."

Taken in by Kawu's smile—how rare it was—and the idea of his fantasy world—Jespar's anxiety from the nightmare faded further. "Kids come up with all kinds of things. You don't want to see the things I drew back when I was little."

"Oh, you can draw? I always wanted to learn. My father said Inâl is the gate to the world, though, and recommended I spend my time reading and practicing instead."

Jespar's father had said something similar, but there had been less recommending involved. At least he'd been able to pass on the basics to his sister. "Past tense," he said. "I'm proud if I manage a stick figure these days. Honestly, though, what you just described sounds incredible. I wish my dreams were like that."

Kawu's lips froze. "As I said. I felt the same way."

"Did you get bored of it?"

"In a way, I suppose I did. But that's not the core of it." Kawu studied the river rushing by beneath their feet. "I realized it was all fiction."

"Wait, you didn't know?"

"Well, I did, and I didn't. You know many things as a child, such as that your parents won't be around forever, but you don't really *grasp* them, do you know what I mean? What opened my eyes was this one night when I spoke to a boy in my kuluhika who was my best friend, or at least that's what I saw him as. We talked like we always did until it suddenly struck me that he only ever said what I wanted him to and that he was really just a reflection of myself, like everything in that dream world. And that realization, it just ... I don't know. Crushed me, I suppose. I had his entire world, and I was its god, yes, but, in the end, it was all just more of myself. It was like–" He sighed. "Ímíte, I probably sound so silly, don't I? So theatrical."

"Actually, no. That makes a lot of sense."

Kawu grunted pensively. An animal had hopped up to the river-bank—a wild alapu, judging by the silhouette.

"So, what happened to the cities?" Jespar asked. "What did you do?"

"I made them disappear," Kawu said. "The only reason I visit my kuluhika these days is because the human mind needs a couple of hours of dreaming each night to stay sane. The world is just an ocean I can walk on now, just water as far as the eye can see."

"Like the Imūma?"

"Well, the water isn't frozen, it's sunset, and there's nothing beneath, but yes. Like the Imūma."

"Sounds beautiful." *And lonely.* A strong impulse—craving, almost—to put his arm around Kawu overcame him, to pull him close and comfort him, but he fought it down. Besides the fact that it would have been incredibly awkward, he'd given Lysia his word; a former mercenary, people were quick to assume he gave his word lightly, but there were few things Jespar loathed more than someone who went back on their promises. How majestically he had fucked up on the two occasions people had put their trust in him probably played a role in that.

It wasn't your fault. Gods, Jespar, you've been there. It wasn't *your fault.*

Watching the alapu shuffle along the bank, Jespar guided his thoughts to Lysia, looking for comfort in her memory. Nothing. Not only did the idea of heading back to the campsite still make him nauseous, but the mere thought of her also made the phantom noose inch tighter. Why? It had been a dream, a bloody dream.

"... something too."

Jespar snapped out of his reflections. "Sorry, what?"

"Um ... I was wondering if I could ask you a question too."

"Ah. Yeah, sure."

"How come you speak Makehu so well? There aren't many watōko who do, and you're not even from the Archipelago."

"Watōko? I thought it's wakemō?"

Kawu chuckled. "Īmīte, no. Watōko is the official term, it means 'bringers of gifts.' Wakemō is 'bringers of black,' and it's considered an insult."

"Bringers of black? Where does that come from?"

"It refers to the disease an Arazalean traveler inadvertently brought to the Archipelago when they colonized the Archipelago, the Black Fever. It killed about three-quarters of the native population in the 860s, that's why there are so few Makehu these days."

"Holy shit. I didn't know."

"Most history books don't mention it."

"... Huh. I see." It wasn't a good answer, but the best Jespar could think of. "As for your question, I traveled with a Makehu back in Nehrim, and we ended up serving in the war together. He taught me some of his language."

"Then you must have traveled for quite some time, because your Makehu is really good. What was his name?"

The lump returned, but it was weak. Jespar forced it down. "Naka."

"Naka," Kawu echoed. "'Turtle'. He was from Uunuma then? The Lonu Ni'e tribe?"

"Might have. He never liked talking about his past."

"I understand. So, how did you end up traveling together?"

"That's a funny story, actually. We got into a fight over a game of dice because he thought I'd cheated." Jespar plucked a tuft of grass from between the rocks and squeezed it between his fingers. "When he realized I hadn't, he bought me a round, and we ended up talking into the morning hours. Bloody hell, that guy could talk, you have no idea. I mean, I can be a rambler, but if Naka was drunk, he wouldn't stop until everyone else had passed out from exhaustion. Anyway, that was back in Erothin, and when we found out we were both headed for Cahbaet in the north, we decided to travel together. Things just kind of went their own way from there."

"Sounds like you were fond of him."

Jespar snorted faintly. Yes, he had been fond of him. "Brother" was a word soldiers often used when speaking of their close comrades, but to Jespar, that didn't quite capture it. It was a bond civilians simply couldn't relate to, the kind that comes from facing death with a comrade, from feeling the blood seep through a makeshift tourniquet you made to keep him alive, from depending on him to cover your back when you take a shit in a forest swarming with enemies.

"Yeah," Jespar said. "I guess I was."

The inevitable question—"what happened?"—was written across Kawu's face. The lump swelled, Jespar tensed.

"I see," Kawu said.

Jespar felt the lump soften, then disappear. He relaxed. Kawu stretched his legs over the ledge, the moon limning his delicate face and the dark hair that hung loosely onto his forehead; they must have moved closer during their conversation because their elbows were touching, but Kawu didn't seem to mind, and Jespar didn't either.

"I admire that, you know?" Kawu asked.

"What exactly?"

"Your travels. I mean, you must have seen so much ... all *I* know is our hut on Hapana and the way to Ma'sao Tuuni's house. It's the same thing every day: get up before dawn, walk two hours across the island, get back after nightfall, and take care of my mother and my siblings before I go to sleep myself." He winced. "Can I tell you something, ma'sao?"

"Of course."

"Being here, I enjoy it. And I'm ashamed of how much."

"Ashamed? Why?"

Kawu began to smooth the wrinkles of his trousers. "Do you remember that conversation we had on the ship? When I told you I came with you because it was my moral responsibility?"

"Yeah."

"Well, if I'm honest, that was only part of the reason. The other is that I wanted to get away from it all. No more waking up in the middle of the night because my mother is screaming, no more comforting Ikē and Nawi because they had to go to bed hungry, no more carrying my father up to our house because he tried to go to town all by himself again." His voice was quiet and even, yet every word seemed like a cut into his own skin. "It's just so ... tiring. It doesn't matter how much I give, how hard I work, or how much I sacrifice, it'll never be enough to make a difference, and I know that. My mother will never be her old self again, and my father will never go back to the life he had before the accident. There are times when I feel so completely and utterly useless, you have no idea ... and now, now I'm here, and all I can think of is how glad I am to be gone." His eyes were glistening. "*That's* why I'm ashamed, ma'sao. I mean, what kind of person would feel this way? What kind of person would leave their family behind and be *happy* about it?"

The thought came like a voice from the grave: *You're looking at him.*

Before Jespar even had a chance to answer, Kawu blushed and looked away, harshly wiping his tears. "Īmīte, I'm sorry. I really shouldn't be burdening you with this. You have enough on your mind as it is."

Jespar was quiet as he wrestled for words.

"You know what I'll never understand?" he asked.

Kawu shook his head.

"How some people have such skewed perceptions of themselves. You're one of the most selfless people I've ever met, Kawu."

Kawu wiped his cheeks again. "You don't need to say that, ma'sao."

"I'll say it because it's true. If you were so selfish, would you be sitting here and feel bad about what you just told me?"

"Self-pity and selflessness are two different things."

Jespar sighed. "Look, my point is, even if part of the reason you took that job was that you wanted a break, so what? In the end, all that matters is that you'll return to your family a rich man, whether we end up healing Oonai or not. Your siblings will never go to bed hungry again, you and your family can move into a big house on another island, and, who knows, maybe you will even find some fancy physician who can fix your father's leg. Who do you think will give a damn about *why* you did what you did?"

"Īmīte sees everything," Kawu said. "It's always watching from its nest in the sky."

"Well, then here's hoping it was busy watching someone take a leak when you left and didn't notice."

Kawu chuckled, but immediately stopped himself, color shooting to his cheeks again. "One shouldn't jest about Īmīte, ma'sao."

Jespar grinned. "Lētō e āpa, I'm sorry. But seriously, cut yourself some slack, will you? You've spent your entire youth taking care of your family, so who can blame you for wanting a break from that kind of responsibility? Results matter, not intentions."

Kawu's lips tightened, as though he were about to protest. Then the frown dissolved. "Well," he said, "I suppose you have a point. Thank you for saying this, ma'sao."

"At your service. Can I ask one thing in return, though?"

"What?"

"Will you start calling me Jespar?"

Kawu looked at him, perplexed. Then he gave that chuckle again, small and quiet, something Jespar would have loved to hear more often. "All right. Jespar." He said the name slowly, as if working out the pronunciation. "Jespar."

"That's me."

Kawu averted his eyes again, but the last bit of awkwardness between them was gone. The sides of their hands were now touching, but neither moved them away.

"You know," Jespar said, "as weird as this entire job has been, I'm glad we—"

The cold struck like a hammer.

Crying out, Jespar buckled over; a blue veil raged over his vision, frozen nails punching into his skull. He screamed, gripped his head, but the pain kept coming, on and on, burying the world under a layer of ice. When the attack finally subsided, vomit filled Jespar's mouth and his sight was blurry from the tears. Kawu was moving his mouth, his hands on Jespar's shoulders, but Jespar couldn't hear.

"I'm ... I'm okay." At least that's what he thought he said; his voice sounded muffled and alien, as though he were speaking underwater. "It's the drain from the dreamwalk, it—"

Kawu shook his head vehemently. His lips moved again, and this time, Jespar could make out something, but it wasn't enough. He shut his eyes once more and covered his ears, taking slow and even breaths. In and out, in and out. When the droning let off at last, and he looked again, Kawu had fallen quiet and was regarding him intently.

"I'm okay," Jespar muttered. "I'm okay."

Kawu let go of his shoulders and sat back on his heels. The bashfulness and affection were gone from his expression, and a shadow had taken their place.

"What happened tonight?" he asked. "Why did you really come out here?"

The lump, hard and cold. "What do you mean?"

"Jespar, please. Tell me."

It was the slow and deliberate way Kawu said his name that somehow broke through Jespar's barriers. Clenching his fists, Jespar forced back the lump. Then he told Kawu what had happened: about the lingering unease and light-headedness he had been experiencing since the dreamwalk. About the hallucination in the bathtub. About the flash of cold in the tavern, about the horrible nightmare, about how Lysia had turned into the Corpse.

When he was done, the shadow on Kawu's face had darkened. "I knew it. Oh, Imīte, I'm such a fool, I *knew* it."

Oddly enough, part of Jespar knew what would come next; it had known since his blackout in Oonai's nightmare. "What did you know?"

"That the dreameater infected you."

It took Jespar several breaths to recover his words. "How?"

"I'm not sure, Jespar. It must have happened when you tried to kill it."

Jespar was about to argue that this was madness, that the bug hadn't even *touched* him, but then the last blanks from the blackout filled in—the part before the dreameater had joined his and Oonai's mind.

Jespar's dagger, sinking deep into the creature's carapace. Oonai's bonesaw scream.

The insect's feelers, wrapping around Jespar's wrist.

A ripple of illness, cold and alive, shooting up to his brain.

Infected.

Jespar shut his eyes, forced himself to breathe.

Infected.

"No," he said. "No, that doesn't make any sense. How the hell can something from the psychic dimension physically infect me?"

Infect. There it was again. That fucking word.

Exhaling, Kawu rubbed his temples. "Do you remember what I told you about the I'Okokepe? The tribe who commanded dreameaters?"

"... I think so, yes. Why?"

"Well, I've spent all of last night dreamwalking through my mind trying to piece the story together, and I realized there's one detail I had completely forgotten. The reason the I'Okokepe were beaten is that their chieftain, Katōia, went mad."

"What does that have to do with me?"

"I'll explain. The way the story goes, Katōia grew distant and irritable about a year into the I'Okokepe's conquests. She'd snap at her closest advisers for no reason and even had some of them executed when they 'disappointed her'. Then, one day, she fell into an 'eternal sleep'."

"A coma."

"Yes. The tribe's dreamwalker immediately suspected a dreameater and counted Katōia's colony to see if one was missing, but all eight hundred eighty-two were still there … so he traveled into her kuluhika instead to find out what had happened."

Kawu clasped his hands tightly in his lap. "According to the legend, he found her in a ruined city at the bottom of the ocean, trapped in the tentacles of some colossal sea monster, and a dreameater was growing out of her skull. The monster was ripping Katōia apart limb from limb, but they regrew, and she was laughing between each of her wails and screamed that she'd finally made the sacrifice that would win Okokepe's favor once and for all."

The fool part of Jespar's mind, the one that often quipped in the worst possible situations, wanted to thank Kawu for giving him something to look forward to. He didn't. He was too terrified to speak at all.

"The dreamwalker panicked and fled to reality, but when she woke up,

she realized all of Katōia's dreameaters were missing. And that the entire tribe had fallen asleep."

"She had infected her own people," Jespar said hoarsely.

"Yes. Now, when the other tribes seized the defenseless village, their Elders questioned Katōia's dreamwalker, and she insisted that her chieftain's infection must have happened in someone else's mind. Sometimes, when a prisoner was about to be sacrificed to Okokepe, Katōia infected them beforehand and had her dreamwalker take her into the prisoner's kuluhika to convince herself that their suffering would be enough to please Okokepe. One time, one of them died during the dreamwalk, and his parasite jumped right out of his head and into Katōia's face. That was shortly before her madness started."

Time ticked by.

Everything felt too intense, too harsh, too vivid; the humid air was a coat of animal saliva on Jespar's skin, the rushing of the river a swarm of droning hornets, the jungle a hungry green maze waiting to swallow up foolish travelers. Jespar pictured an egg nesting inside his brain, gray-blue and slimy and translucent, the silhouette of an insect writhing within it.

"Look, Jespar, maybe I'm wrong, I—"

"You're not."

Kawu fell quiet.

"Unless shifting drain can cause hallucinations and the feeling of something living *inside* your brain, then you're probably right." He made a strange laughing sound, like an inverse wheeze. "I mean, I'm fucking dying of curiosity to hear some scholar explain to me how the fuck you can get infected by *a thought,* but hey, everything about this job has been a trip through a madhouse so far, so I'm guessing sky's the limit." His tone had a shrill edge to it; he took a second to collect himself. Yes, this was messed up, but if the war and three years of drifting had taught him anything, it was that panic led nowhere, even when there was a parasite in your brain that could trap you in a nightmare and torture you for an eternity, because five minutes in reality were an hour in a dream and-

Stop!

Stop.

Calm.

Exhaling, he straightened his back and laid his hands flat on his thighs, an almost satirically cool-headed pose, as though he were frantically trying to convince himself he had everything under control. "The question is: how do we get rid of the thing?"

Kawu looked almost desperate to answer, but then he looked away. "I don't know, Jespar. I really don't know."

Another breath, slow and steady. "Maybe we can dreamwalk into my kuluhika and kill it there?"

"I told you what happens if a dreameater dies during the infection."

The poison. Of course.

"Okay, but it's only been a day, and I'm still awake, so it can't have hatched yet, right?"

"Maybe not, but that doesn't mean it hasn't developed the toxin yet. We can't take that risk, Jespar, we *can't*."

Something about Kawu's agitation—*care, fear, concern*—gave Jespar an idea. "What about its broodmother?"

Kawu gave him a quizzical look.

"I mean, they've got to be linked somehow, right? Maybe if we manage to get Oonai's dreameater out, mine would leave too. Maybe she is its ..."

"Imprinter."

"Yeah."

A short silence. Then Kawu raked his hands through his hair and laced them behind his neck. "Yes. Yes, you're right. It's a stretch, but it might work."

"I'll take 'might' over 'won't' any day," Jespar said, willing an optimism into his words that he didn't feel.

"Of course. The only question is—" Kawu broke off.

"What?"

"Look at me. Look at me and hold still."

He put his thumbs on Jespar's forehead, and the other fingers on his temples. His eyes sought Jespar, then turned glassy.

A shift.

Warmth flooded Jespar's head, an exhale of summer sweeping through a cave of ice. The echo of the headache ceased, his wooziness disappeared; the world snapped back into focus. When the sensation ceased and Kawu withdrew his hands, he was looking at Jespar with a mixture of worry and hope. "How do you feel?"

"... Better. Great, actually."

"Really?"

"Yeah. What did you do?"

Kawu's hands relaxed. "I struck a shift on you. It's a simple one I often use on my siblings and my father to protect them from my mother's auric resonance."

"From her seizures?"

"Yes." A katako with black-purple wings landed on the side of Kawu's neck. He waved it away. "You could say that the shift anchors your consciousness to the real world—as long as it lasts, your simulacrum couldn't descend into your kuluhika, even if you were to fall asleep. I had no idea if it would work on you, but I'm glad it did."

Jespar grunted and felt his forehead. The cold spot was gone. "So these hallucinations are ... what, shifts from the dreameater?"

"I suppose so. I might be wrong about this, but I'm guessing that it takes over its host by gradually pulling their consciousness away from reality and into the deeper layers of the psychic dimension. The things you saw must have been thoughts the dreameater injected into your mind and that your brain mistook for elements of the real world because it was starting to submerge. You shouldn't get any more now that you're anchored."

"Will it last?"

"I'm afraid not, no. The shift will wear off over time, so I'll have to keep redoing it until we get that thing out. I'm sorry, but it's the best I can do for now."

Panic stirred up once more, but with the clarity from the anchoring, it was a shadow of the dread from before. It was as if Kawu's shift had locked it away in a chest and buried it under the earth, allowing Jespar to hold on to his sanity. At least for the time being.

"Thank you," he said. "Really, Kawu. Thank you."

"Of course."

Their gazes met and lingered. Surprisingly, it was Jespar who broke eye contact, looking off into the jungle. It was still dark, but the katydids had quieted down. An odd calm settled inside him, a blend of acceptance and cautious optimism. He recognized it as the feeling he'd come to know before battle: the cards were dealt, the rules explained, the stakes made clear. Nothing left to do but play and hope for the best.

He picked up a pebble and tossed it into the river.

And now what?

With every minute he spent here, the chance that Lysia or Agaam would note his absence grew—if that hadn't happened already. Since Kawu's anchoring, the horror at the idea of returning had also dwindled, even though thinking of Lysia still gave him no comfort. On the contrary: the image of her and the bond they had shared last night felt strange now, almost foreign. Remembering their first evening together, a thought crossed his mind. He snorted mirthlessly.

"Is something funny?" A slight nervousness tinged Kawu's voice, as if he were expecting himself to be the reason.

"Ah, just a random thought." Jespar picked up another stone and turned it in his fingers. "I just realized that I seem to have a habit of relying on other people to save my ass. Lysia helped me get rid of a nasty traveler's disease a few days ago, and now you're here, saving me from that bug. Kind of makes me wonder."

"About what?"

Jespar flicked up the stone and caught it. "What I've ever done to deserve this, I guess. It probably sounds stupid, but sometimes I feel like ... I don't know. Like I'm not good for people around me."

Bullshit. That's bullshit, and you know it. Why did you say that?

"I don't believe that," Kawu said. "You've been very kind to me."

The words were barely out and Kawu had already averted his gaze again. He opened his mouth, but then closed it again and started tugging at a tuft of grass. Jespar couldn't help but look at him: at his algae-green eyes that seemed to care too much for his own good.

At his slender fingers, made for turning pages. At his lips, which smiled too rarely.

He felt like he finally understood the essence of Kawu's contrasting personality: ever since his Sight had cusped at age six, Kawu had lived two parallel lives, one in reality, and another in his dreams, both of which he spent fully aware. Considering the time distortion in the psychic dimension, how many years had Kawu lived both lives combined? Forty? Seventy? A hundred? Yes, he was younger than Jespar—but only if you counted age in the number of years weighing on your bones, and not the hours your mind spent conscious. Questions zipped through Jespar's head like wayward fireflies. What was it like to live this long, mostly alone inside one's own mind? Had Kawu ever taken someone with him onto the sunset sea that was his kuluhika? Had he ever been in love?

And: why did Jespar like him so damn much?

On a surface level, they couldn't possibly have had less in common: Kawu, who grew up in a palmwood hut. Jespar, who grew up in a manor. Kawu, who was a dimensionist wonder child. Jespar, who was a talentless disappointment. Kawu, who cared about his family and felt miserable for leaving. Jespar, who had left the last of his kin behind and never looked back.

Maybe, he thought, it was Kawu's untarnished idealism and benevolence he felt drawn to, qualities Jespar liked to believe he used to have but had lost. Maybe it was the fact that Jespar knew all too well how it felt to be an outsider. Or maybe it was that familiar, underlying frailty he sensed under Kawu's stoic façade that made Jespar desperately want to protect him after he had so gloriously failed to protect everyone else.

"You should probably go back now," Kawu said. "Ma'sao Agaam and—"

Jespar kissed him.

DREAMS OF THE DYING

Kawu resisted. Gave in. Jespar cupped his face and drew him closer, found Kawu's tongue, Gods, how good it felt, how *right*, how—

Kawu shoved him.

Jespar teetered, getting dangerously close to the edge, but caught himself. Kawu stared at him, shaking hands raised as if to shield himself from a blow.

Guilt hit.

Idiot. You fucking *idiot.* What had he been thinking? He hadn't just broken his promise to Lysia; he had forced himself on Kawu like some drunken, randy fool.

Kawu lowered his hands. "Īmīte, I'm ... I'm sorry."

"No," Jespar said. "*I'm* sorry. I shouldn't have done that. That was stupid."

"It's fine, I just—" He exhaled, clasped his hands behind his neck. "Īmīte ū, āpa 'ōi hē? What am I *doing*?"

Jespar slowly sat up. "Aren't you interested in men that way?"

"No. I mean, yes, I think I am, but—oh, ūkonō, I don't know what to think or feel anymore."

"Then let's just pretend this didn't happen, all right? As I said, I shouldn't have done that, Lysia and I, we're ..."

"Lovers?" Kawu asked quietly.

Lovers. How right the word had felt last night, how wrong it felt now. All he saw when he thought of Lysia was the image of the Corpse by the campfire.

He sighed. "It's more complicated than that. Still, I shouldn't have done that, and I'm sorry. I don't know what I was thinking." Hadn't he, though? Had he not wanted to do this the whole evening, hell, ever since the first evening on the boat?

Kawu's expression was cryptic. Disappointment? Anger? Jespar's stomach was a hard ball, sweat beading at his temples. Finally, Kawu let out a breath and studied his lap. "It's fine. We were both tired and confused."

"Yeah. Yeah, we were." He paused. "Is it all right with you if I tell her? I owe it to her."

"What would you say?"

"Just that I messed up, and we kissed and that it wasn't your fault. If that's okay for you, of course."

Jespar expected Kawu to protest. He didn't. "Do you think she'll be hurt?"

She will be. Because she told me how important it was, and I promised. He tried to imagine how Lysia would react, but couldn't. Neither a tantrum nor a pat on the shoulder seemed like her. Probably, he decided, she'd just end this thing they'd had going, whatever it was. And putting guilt and pride aside, wouldn't it be for the better? Who was he, in the end? A penniless, cynical drifter with nothing to offer but an endless supply of nightflower, bad jokes, and problems. *Yes,* he thought. Maybe Lysia would be angry for a few days, but ultimately, she'd see that she was better off without him.

"I don't know," he said. "I think she'll be fine, though. I'm sorry again, I'm an idiot."

"It's all right."

Silence stretched out between them. Was Jespar imagining it, or was there something pleading in the way Kawu looked at him?

"Anyway," Jespar said. "I'm gonna head back to camp."

"You should. The others might have noticed you're gone."

"Yeah. They might have."

Neither of them moved.

Jespar loosened his scarf. "Then again, another hour or so probably won't make a difference. There are no signs of a fight or something, so they'll probably just assume I'm with you." A nonsense argument and Jespar knew it. Still: he really didn't want to leave.

"That's true," Kawu said, a little too quickly. "So you will ...?"

"I can stay a bit longer if you want me to, yeah."

"I'd like that. What, um, do you want to do?"

"Good question." Jespar looked skyward. "How about we appreciate the view for a start?"

"That would be nice," Kawu said.

They reclined, fingers laced behind their heads. Dark and blue, the sky was a magnificent sight—like an upturned ocean, the stars like thousands of luminous creatures too alien to fathom. And as he lay there and watched, Jespar couldn't help but ponder what a strange turn his life had taken.

Three years it had been since that terrible day in the Village, three years since he had left the Wayfarers and become a drifter. Three years alone. Sure, there had been sex, sometimes free and sometimes paid, seldom sober and never intimate. Friendship was no different: many jests and many laughs shared with strangers whenever he had stopped in a village, but, at dawn, he always left the tavern alone. Had life really been all right, as he kept telling himself? And was this riptide current that kept pushing him ever since he'd set foot on Kilayan soil really all bad?

Sure, things were looking everything but rosy: he was in over his head on a job he had no business being in, wrestling a bizarre recurring nightmare, and infected with a brain parasite. And yet there it was, a strange exhilaration filling him from head to toe, daunting and liberating at the same time.

Alive.

That was how he felt. He felt alive, with all the good and bad that came with it. As if he had spent the past three years locked up in a coffin, and this journey had finally cracked open the lid.

"Jespar?"

"Hm?"

Kawu was looking at the sky. "Is it true that in countries like Enderal, the trees turn the color of a sunset at the end of the year?"

"You mean ... autumn?"

"I think that's how it's called."

Of course. How would he know? "Yeah, they do. It's quite the sight, actually. The leaves go all red and gold for a time before they fall."

"And then they start growing again, a few moons later, right? And that's called spring?"

"'Spring', yeah. After winter."

Kawu turned to look at him. "When all this is over, and you go back to Enderal, do you think I could come with you? I'd love to see what that looks like. Autumn."

A cozy warmth spread in his belly. "Come with me?"

"As a companion," Kawu said quickly. "Like your friend, Naka. But never mind, it's probably a silly idea. I'm sorry, I—"

"No, it's not silly at all. Just ... what about your family?"

"Well, we could go for only a while, couldn't we? You've said it yourself, I'll be rich after all this, so I could hire someone to look after them while I'm gone. But, truly, if you don't want to, that's fine. You barely know me."

But I'd like to. "You're more than welcome to join," Jespar said. "I'm not sure yet whether I'll go to Enderal or someplace else, but we can make it somewhere with four seasons. Who knows, maybe even somewhere in the Great Uncharted.

The way Kawu's face brightened at his words made those past mad days worth it. "When all this is over, then? Kito nū'i kei kuio e li?"

Smiling, Jespar closed his eyes. "Yeah. When all this is over."

Chapter Fourteen
Kaiawaika Manor

N *o nightmare.*

This was Jespar's first thought when he woke to a lightening sky. For the first time in almost a week, he'd had no nightmares—neither the one in the swamp court nor the disjointed, hazy visions he was used to.

He lay still as a log, his breathing flat and deep, afraid to move. This had to be a false awakening, like his dream with Lysia at the campfire. This wasn't real.

It was.

Birds circled through the lightening sky, treetops swayed in the breeze, frogs croaked by the river. How long had he slept? It couldn't have been more than four hours, yet he felt fresh and rested. Gingerly, Jespar sat up and groped for his water flask. After the first swallow, a memory cut through his thoughts like a scalpel.

Infected.

You're infected.

No panic. No dread. Both were there, prickling in the pit of Jespar's stomach, but the peculiar serenity from that peaceful night—he had forgotten how that felt, "peaceful"—quelled it. *The anchoring.* Whatever it had done to suppress the parasite's shifts must have also suppressed his nightmares.

"Good morning," a voice said beside him. "How are you feeling?"

Kawu lay on his side behind him, cheek resting on his arm. Except for a tuft of disheveled hair at the back of his head, he didn't look the least bit sleepy.

"Better than I probably look," Jespar said. "I slept like a baby."

"That's good, isn't it?"

Jespar snorted. "A miracle's more like it. I haven't slept like that in weeks, maybe even moons. That shift you struck on me, it's incredible."

"What about your head, any signs of a Pull? You know, from the dreameater?"

"No, nothing. How long does this anchoring normally last?"

"At least a couple of days." Kawu sat up and shook out his legs. "But I'll do it again tomorrow morning, just to be safe."

"That would be great. Will you be okay, though? You know, drain and all that?"

"Don't worry, it's an easy shift. As long as we ensure you're anchored whenever the dreameater tries to pull you under, everything will be fine. Still, we need to get this thing out of you as fast as possible."

"Shame, I was planning to ask it out for drinks."

Kawu had no comeback as Lysia might have given, but his smile was all the reward he needed.

"Speaking of," Jespar said. "Do you mind if we keep my, uh, new condition between you and me for now?"

"Why?"

"Well, I'm sure Agaam and Lysia have enough on their minds already. No point adding more to the pile." It wasn't a lie, but not the truth, either. All Jespar knew was that the idea of telling anyone made him anxious to the point of nausea. And really, what reason was there to tell them right away? "And we should be fine as long as you keep anchoring me, right?"

"... I suppose."

"Good. Then we tell them only in case it gets worse."

Kawu chewed on his lower lip. He nodded. "All right. Should we go back now?"

They probably should have, but Jespar didn't want to just yet. He squinted at the horizon and gauged the hour. "Dawn's still a little off. Mind if we stay a little longer?"

"Not at all," Kawu said. "What would you like to do?"

Jespar considered. He broke into a grin. "You know what, I have an idea."

Without waiting for a reply, Jespar got to his feet, stripped off his shirt, and dashed for the ledge. He was already in mid-air when it occurred to him that he had no idea how deep the river was and might therefore very well be on his way to the most ungracious death in the history of adventuring.

Cool blue enfolded him.

They stayed in the river for what must have been an hour, swimming, chatting, and lounging on the bank. There was no talk of parasites or Oonai, no mention of dreamwalking or nightmares, the Scythe, or an upcoming civil war. When Kawu climbed out and redressed, Jespar dived under one last time and let himself sink all the way to the riverbed. And, sitting there between the algae and watching shoals of fish zip by, he couldn't help but grin at the absurdity of it all. Here he was, splashing about a river like a carefree boy, while the next few days would decide his fate and that of an entire country.

A strange turn indeed.

The sun had just begun to climb the horizon when they returned to the camp. Halfway there, they ran into Lysia. She stopped abruptly. "Stars burn me, where were you? I've been looking for you all around the clearing."

Until this point, some part of Jespar hoped—or at least expected—his feelings for her would return once they saw each other. It didn't. The nightmare and the Corpse had killed it.

Jespar tugged at his scarf. "Actually, it's a long story. Mind if we talk for a minute?"

Kawu went ahead to the camp while Jespar and Lysia headed to the foot of a nearby tree. He told her he'd had nightmares and had gone for a walk through the jungle to calm himself. There, he had run into Kawu and, after a long conversation, had kissed him on the spur of the moment. Surprisingly, the lump stayed away for the entire course of his account; Lysia listened silently, repeatedly poking a fat yellow mushroom with the tip of her boot. Sunrays broke through the thicket, reflecting in the dewdrops on the ferns and flowers.

"So?" she asked. "What now?"

"That depends on you, I guess. The question is whether you're willing to look past this."

Lysia kept prodding the mushroom. "Do you want me to?"

It wasn't the answer Jespar had expected. "What do you mean?"

"I think you know. How do *you* want this conversation to end? Do you want me to say, 'I forgive you, let's keep going?' Or would you rather have me give you the finger and end our little fling so that you are free to chase after the lad?"

At Jespar's hesitation, Lysia's eyes cracked. Beneath it lay the same deep hurt that had shown through two nights ago, when she had asked for his promise.

Are all Mâleian women so open about their feelings?

No, but having been fucked over and ditched in the worst way imaginable makes you cautious.

The fracture disappeared as fast as it had come.

"Yeah," Lysia said. "That's what I thought. Seriously, Jespar, shite happens, and I'm the last one who'd put this job at risk because her sellsword sweetheart made a blunder. But do you know what else I'm not? A fool who chases after someone who simply doesn't want her. I've done that before, and it's always a waste of time."

Jespar bunched up. "Lysia, I told you, this has nothing to do with you. It's just ... that nightmare, it ... oh, I don't bloody understand it myself." He tried a conciliatory smile that probably looked as pathetic as it felt. "I mean, you've said it yourself, right? 'Demons to wrestle.'"

Lysia's lips drew into a line. She sighed. "Well, it's probably for the best. Just make sure all that demon wrestling doesn't get between the lad and you, too, okay? Kawu, he's ... fragile."

"I don't even know if there'll be a 'me and him' anyway."

"No, of course not. Anything else, or can we get going?"

"... No. Nothing."

"Good."

She was already some strides away when Jespar spoke up once more.

"Hey. Lysia."

Tell her.

She stopped.

Tell her about that hallucination. Tell her about the infection. Tell her you meant that promise and didn't want *this connection between you to die.* "I just want you to know that I ... you know ..."

Pointless. He just couldn't bring himself to say the words.

"... that I'm sorry," he said. "I'm sorry if I hurt you."

It was genuine, yet it came out in the condescending tone of someone on the winning side of a break-up.

Lysia's expression was blank. "It's fine."

She went back to camp. Jespar looked at the yellow mushroom for a good minute. The stalk had broken.

He followed.

Kawu was saddling his horse when Jespar told him about the conversation.

"It's my fault," Kawu said, roughly adjusting the saddle. "I shouldn't have come between you."

"What are you talking about? *I* kissed *you.*"

"And I wanted you to!"

Blood shot into his cheeks. He dropped his gaze. Then he sighed. "Forgive me. It's just ... I never wanted anyone to get hurt because of me. Also, I don't even know if I can live up to your expectations. As I said, I'm no good at these things, and ..." Another sigh. "Oh, it doesn't matter. We should go."

I wanted you to, Jespar thought. So Kawu did return his feelings. Sure, with the way he'd acted last night, one might say it wasn't much of a surprise; and yet hearing him admit it so directly felt almost as good as that kiss had last night. "There are no expectations," Jespar said, doing his best to hold back an idiotic grin. "Especially not with

all that's going on. Why don't we just keep going and see where we
stand when all this is over? Kito nū'i kei kuio e li?"

For a while, Kawu looked at his horse. Then he gave the smallest
of nods. "All right. Kito nū'i kei kuio e li."

"It's a deal then. I gotta saddle up too, meet you with the others?"

"Yes. And ... Jespar?"

"Hm?"

"I'm glad we met. I truly am."

Honoring Jaaros Oonai's penchant for rather obvious symbolism,
Kaiawaika Manor was built upon the massif's eponymous mountain, a green colossus taller than Uunili's Mount Ilakato, it rose
behind the coastal town Tamakaha, which they skirted. Jespar spent
most of the ten-hour jungle slog talking to Kawu, and even though
Kawu still preferred to be the listening part of the conversation, the
bits of personality that shined through his answers only strengthened Jespar's affection. They spoke about many things, personal and
worldly: after some carefully phrased questions, Jespar learned that,
unlike he had somehow assumed, Makehu culture was not opposed
to same-love. As long as one kept their proclivities private and still
started a family with a "true partner" to fulfill their obligations to
the community, they were accepted. It was not so unlike Jespar's
own experience in Enderal's upper class: while a second or a third-
born child could pursue whomever they pleased, firstborns like him
were expected to perform their duty to the dynasty.

Another interesting conversation revolved around the role of the
Makehu in Kilayan society. The Colonization had started out as a
peaceful coexistence in 790, when the reigning hierophant at the
time symbolically passed the Lambent Scepter to the high-chief-

tain of the Six Great Tribes and he the Bone Crown to her; the two nations traded openly and welcomed cultural exchange, yet each had their own territories and cities. Despite the Order and the Coalition's claims now, however, it wasn't all rainbows and roses: the colonizers' technological superiority established an imbalance of power, so tensions would always lurk just beneath the surface. The Black Fever Kawu had told Jespar about last night marked the first turning point: catalyzed by the lively trade routes between the islands, the plague wiped out three-quarters of the native population, leading the Coalition to integrate the decimated Makehu into Kilayan society. The Six Great Tribes were no more, and no amount of good intentions and symbolic legislation could stop the natives from being pushed further into the margins. The second turning point was the Silence: to limit the damage across the Illumined World, the Order's new hardline hierophant enforced an array of radical decrees to restore the Light-Born's authority in the already secular-leaning Kilay, one of them banishing the practice of the "heathen" Makehu religion into private spaces and forcing all natives to officially adopt the Faith. The decree was not only ineffective—most Makehu simply paid lip service to the Light-Born—but it also deepened racial tensions; and even though the Coalition repealed the resolution in the 1100s and made some attempts to coalesce Kilayan and Makehu culture, such as officializing Makehu festivals and holidays like Miwa-e-Kēku, the scars of the Early Silence Era remained.

"What's your view on the Silence then?" Jespar asked. "What do you think happened to the Light-Born?"

Kawu thought about this for a long time. "I don't know. Perhaps they grew weary from caring."

Reminded of the conversation Jespar had once had with his tutor—the Gods had given up the world in favor of a laid-back time—he smirked. "You mean they couldn't be bothered to put up with humans being incorrigible idiots anymore?"

Kawu glanced at him, brow raised. "No, I mean that they grew weary from seeing all this pain. Imagine you have all this power and all this responsibility, and while everybody is looking for you to save them, you know you can never save them all. I don't know about a god, but I don't think I could take that."

Deciding Kawu was clearly a better person than him, Jespar left it at a "Hm."

Around noon, they stopped at a creek to wait out the worst of the sun; Jespar took a nap in the bower of a natuka tree. Kawu's anchoring kept away the nightmares, yet he had an odd, disjointed dream about Lysia that left him with a deep sense of guilt when he woke. Blinking away the sleep, he looked across the clearing until he found her; she sat at the creek, munching on a rice ball, feet dipped into the water. Noticing his gaze, she half-heartedly raised the ball in greeting but then turned her attention back to the water. Sighing, Jespar looked for Kawu. He was by his horse, stroking its mane as it drank.

Jespar smiled.

It was sunset by the time the rain forest thinned out and revealed a view of the island-facing slope of Mount Kaiawaika, a steep sea of brilliant green. The manor nested upon a plateau about halfway up its length.

At the word "manor", Jespar had pictured a Kilayan version of the estate he'd grown up in: the roof flat and greened instead of slated, the windows square and unglazed instead of arched, the avenue from portal to gatehouse lined by palms rather than poplars.

He should have known better.

Enthroned upon the plateau stood another ziggurat made up of six tapering tiers of white stone. A couple of houses and an orchard with a hedge maze surrounded it, shielded by walls almost as tall as Uunili's. Amidst the untouched wilderness and cloaked in the evening sunlight, it had a surreal quality to it, like a mirage spawned by the imagination of a famished traveler.

"I guess that's it?" Jespar asked.

"Yes," Agaam replied, sounding strangely wistful. "That's Kaiawaika Manor."

It took them another two hours to reach the place, and when the gate came into sight, at last, a drizzle had set in. The sunset gave the drops the faintest red tinge, like ichor dripping from a fresh wound.

Agaam jerked up a hand. "Wait."

"What's wrong?" Lysia asked.

The old servant jutted his chin at the gate, golden wrought iron in an overgrown arch. "It shouldn't be open."

He reached into his coat and drew a nuvium blade from a sheath hidden there. It was too long for a dagger, too short for a sword. Ignoring the group's puzzled expressions, he swung himself off his horse and gestured for them to do the same. "Dismount. We're going to take a look at this."

No more "please", no more "ma'sae". An order.

They got off their horses and tied them to a nearby tree. Jespar drew his sword. "They should stay," he told Agaam, indicating Kawu and Lysia. "It's too dangerous."

"Not any more so than out here all by themselves. Come."

It didn't take them long to find the first corpses: a short, balding man, and a chubby woman, both sunk headfirst against the basin of a fountain in the garden. Agaam dropped to his haunches beside the man and lifted his chin with the hilt of his knife. Kawu covered his mouth. Lysia inhaled sharply.

On his journey from Southport to Uunili, Jespar had seen a fisherman kill a squid by smashing its head repeatedly against a rock. The servant's face reminded Jespar of what the squid had looked like afterward.

"Ejkaan," Agaam said.

"You—" Lysia started over. "You knew him?"

"Yes, he was the head servant of the manor. I believe the girl is his daughter. It's been years since I last saw them." Agaam eased the man onto his back and stood. "The blood still hasn't dried, so the murderers might still be on the premises. We need to be wary."

They made their way to the orchard, sticking to the lengthening shadows of the trees. There were four more corpses: two guards lying in the shadow of a pergola, and a woman and a child, both propped against a fig tree by the wayside. The boy's head rested against his mother's shoulder, the top half of his white shirt dyed red with the blood from his slashed throat; the woman's neck had been snapped so hard her head was almost facing backward. Surrounded by the garden and soaked in sunset and rain, they looked like the motif of some morbid painting. A sound between a croak and a wheeze drew him away from the sight. Kawu was throwing up. Jespar hurried to his side and put a hand on his back, but he couldn't think of anything to say. "*They're okay*"? "*It's all right*"? They weren't, and it wasn't.

When Kawu was done retching, Jespar offered him his canteen. He took it and drank, then spit the water right back out. Lysia joined them, the color drained from her cheeks. "You think the Scythe did this? Or bandits?"

"I don't know," Agaam said. "But it was someone who doesn't want to leave any witnesses."

Reaching the manor's entrance—it stood ajar—Agaam snuck up to the archway and peered through the crack. Then he slid inside, and they followed.

The lobby was a slaughterhouse.

A decapitated guard at the foot of the stairs across the entrance. Two young servants in a puddle of blood on the blue-and-gold mosaic in the center. An elderly man slumped over the mezzanine railing. Many, many more.

Kawu seemed about to throw up again but kept it in. Lysia muttered something that sounded like a prayer. Agaam was impassive except for a twitch of his lower lip. Jespar began to speak, but Agaam put his forefinger to his mouth, nodded at the staircase, then pointed at his ear.

Voices.

Someone was talking somewhere on the second floor. Agaam's fingers tightened around his knife; Jespar put his hand on the pommel of his sword. They snuck up the stairs and found the mezzanine deserted. Busts and vases on plinths lined the walls, which were adorned by paintings, a series of pretty and forgettable landscapes. Glancing into the lobby, Jespar realized the bloodied mosaic showed a stylized version of a young Nayima Oonai, her floating bejeweled hair framing the face like the crown of a sea goddess.

Agaam gestured for their attention. He stood at a doorway leading into a lit corridor; the voices originated from inside it. As silently as possible, they went in, the voices growing louder with every step they took. They were three in total, two women and a man: one of the women was crying while the other spoke in calm tones, and the man interjected on occasion. Jespar couldn't make out a word. They followed the hallway until it ended in a double-wing door, a pair of corpses fronting it. The crying woman's pleas grew louder, frantic, the other replied tonelessly. All Jespar caught was the word "document".

Agaam slid up to the door and peeked through the crack; Jespar edged up beside him. A woman knelt before a monstrous desk surrounded by bookshelves. Her captors loomed over her, both facing the doorway. Jespar's first thought was how utterly ordinary they looked: average height, innocuous clothes, forgettable faces. Had it not been for their haggard, bony bodies and their weapons, they might have been two ordinary peasants from a nearby village. The woman wore two shortswords, gladiuses but with cross guards, one on each side of her belt. The man held a sickle in one gloved hand and had a buckler mounted to the back of the other.

"... nothin'!" the kneeling woman sobbed. Her hair hung in front of her face, concealing her features. "Gods, what d'ye want me to do, what—"

Using his bucklered hand, Sickle Man slapped her so hard she fell over. Jespar gave Agaam a sideways glance, but he didn't seem to notice: a vein pulsed at his neck, and his good eye fixated on the two intruders.

Two Swords squatted down and lifted the servant's head by the hair, bringing their eyes level. "Look, I get it, you're scared of what your master will do to you if you spill the beans." She spoke with no discernible accent. "Thing is, it'll be nothing compared to what my partner is capable of. I mean, you saw what he did to your friends, right?"

The servant sobbed a reply, too garbled to catch.

"Yes, I thought you did," Two Swords said. "And that's just the beginning, you know? Last time someone didn't talk, my friend pulled out the fool's fingernails, one by one, and when even that didn't convince him, he peeled the skin off his hands. Honestly, you'd be surprised how much pain people can take before they go unconscious. By the end—"

The servant croaked something.

"What was that?"

"I'll talk," the woman said. "By the Gods, I'll talk!"

Two Swords nodded, like a teacher proud of a student's answer. "Good girl. How about we start at—"

A sob behind Jespar.

He whirled. Kawu was staring at him, covering his mouth.

Hell broke loose.

Two Swords let go of the servant and drew her blades, her partner raised sickle and buckler; Agaam sprang to his feet, barged in, and lunged at Sickle Man, his nuvium blade gleaming in the torchlight. He was as fast as a viper, but the man parried the attack with ease. Jespar had just enough time to see Sickle riposte, then Two Swords came dashing at him with a crisscrossed strike of her blades. He jerked up his longsword and parried, but rather than drawing away, the woman shoved her gladiuses forward at Jespar's throat. He staggered back and avoided the stab by a hair's breadth, and she went in, locking Jespar's sword between the crossguards of hers. They struggled, but after mere seconds, she wrenched the blade from his hands, flung it away, and sent him reeling with a kick to the stomach. Winding, he fought for balance, tripped over something—*a corpse*—and crashed to the ground, falling right onto his wounded shoulder. By the time he recovered his senses, Two Swords was looming over him, blades raised.

This is it. It's over.

It wasn't. Lysia lunged at Two Swords' back, her clawblade stabbing at the woman's neck. She spun around, slammed her elbow into Lysia's nose; the clawblade missed its mark and sunk into Two Swords' shoulder. Jespar reached for his dagger and clambered to his feet, but before he could stand, Two Swords was back at him and smashed her knee into his face.

Blackness.

When his sight returned, Two Swords was looming over him. Devoid of expression, she tore the clawblade from her shoulder and tossed it away. Two thoughts went through Jespar's mind as she drove her gladiuses toward his heart.

First: he'd never stood a chance against her.

Second: Two Swords' wound didn't bleed.

Chapter Fifteen
Overgrowth

The thrust stopped halfway.

Her gladiuses hovering finger-lengths from Jespar's chest, Two Swords was frozen, mouth agape. There was a wet, *slicing* sound from the study. A scream. A croak. A clatter.

The woman's face blanked. Then she dropped her left gladius, flipped the other one around, and drove it into her throat. It passed through her skin smoothly, in one end and out the other. She stood still for a single wheeze, eyes wide as if trying to comprehend what by the Gods she had just done; then she collapsed.

Jespar didn't move.

What the hell?

What the bloody hell?

Slowly, he picked himself up, staring at Two Swords, still expecting her to spring back to her feet. Only when someone moaned nearby did he manage to tear his gaze away. Lysia sat slumped in the corner, her hair in tangles and one hand pressed to her temple. Her expression was as aghast as Jespar imagined his own.

"Are you wounded?"

It was Agaam. He stood in the doorway, blood spattered across his beard and arm.

"No," Jespar said. "No, I'm not. What just ... I mean, how ...?"

"He's a psychomancer," Lysia said, getting to her feet. "That was mind control."

She sounded wary, and Jespar couldn't blame her. It was one thing to talk about it, that rare Profane Sight that allowed a dimensionist to plant thoughts into someone else's mind. It was another to see a woman coerced into ramming a sword up her own throat.

Psychomancer.

In retrospect, the writing had been on the wall all along. How hard it was to remember Agaam's face. How you just kept forgetting he was there. How effortlessly he stole through crowds, as if people stepped out of his way without even noticing they did. Jespar just hadn't made the connection.

"You're right, ma'saa," Agaam said. "I tried to strike the shift sooner, but they must have had some mental training to protect themselves. I've never seen anything like it." He crossed to Two Swords and rolled her onto her back with his boot. She was still alive, twitching and wheezing, the gladius buried in her throat. Agaam squatted beside her, lifted her head, and drove his nuvium blade into her temple. She went limp. Agaam kept the blade in for another moment, then pulled it back out and used it to cut her shirt open down the collar; it was thickly padded—more fitting for a wintry climate than the tropics. When the tear was down to her belt, Agaam turned over the flaps and exposed her body.

Lysia drew in a sharp breath. Jespar stayed quiet, but a chill had settled in his stomach. Usually, the word "skeletal" was used hyperbolically, but it was accurate in Two Swords' case. Her torso was all edges and angles, just a thin layer of pale skin stretched over bones. Her bosoms were almost flat, and the muscles one would have expected from a swordswoman like her were nowhere to be seen. Jespar's heart skipped a beat when he grew aware of the small symbol branded onto the center of her collarbone.

A red lotus blossom.

"Revenants," he said.

Agaam turned the flaps of the shirt back over. "So it seems."

"What do you mean 'revenants'?" Lysia asked. "You're saying these guys are ... undead?"

Jespar picked up his sword and sheathed it. His hands were shaking. "No, that's just what they call themselves. They're an order of assassins, the best that money can buy."

Lysia looked from Two Swords to her comrade's corpse in the study, her mouth opening and closing. "Why the hell do they look like that?" she asked hoarsely. "With that level of starvation, they shouldn't even be—"

"*Zaqua.* It's a plant found on an island somewhere in the Great Uncharted. Their order gives it to the urchins they recruit, and it drastically alters the way the bodily humors work." Agaam turned out Two Swords' pockets. Some coins, but nothing else. "The zaqua kills seven out of ten, and the other three have a near-death experience. When they wake up, they have extraordinary strength and endurance but a drastically shortened lifespan."

"Hence the name," Jespar said. "The lotus flower represents rebirth." He did his best to sound calm, even though his mind was a whirlwind: the mix of his brush with death mere minutes ago and an onslaught of old memories. No, he had never *seen* a Revenant before. What he had seen was their symbol, carved into the foreheads of his dead father and brothers.

"You're well informed, Ma'sao Dal'Varek." There was something odd about the way Agaam said it, as though he knew exactly where Jespar's knowledge on the subject came from. Chances were, he did.

"I read about them," Jespar said. "Where's the servant? Is she all right?"

"She panicked, so I struck a sleeping shift on her. It'll take her a bit to come out of it, so I suggest you go look for Ma'sao Nakāni in the meantime."

The name struck like lightning.

Kawu.

With the battle fervor and all that had happened, Jespar had completely forgotten he had been there just minutes ago. He turned, finding the corridor was empty.

"Where did he go?" he asked from a dry throat.

"Ran off during the fight," Lysia said wearily. "Can't say I blame him."

Agaam wiped his blade on the Revenant's pants, slid it back into his coat sheath, and stood. "He can't be far, though. Like I said, ma'sao, I suggest you go look for him while we take care of the servant. We'll question her when you come back." *Suggest. Ma'sao.* With the danger gone, Agaam had returned to his polite self.

"What if there are more of them?" Lysia asked.

"There aren't. I've sensed the area for human thought patterns, and the five of us are the only ones left alive."

There was a lot to be said or asked about this sentence, but Jespar was too dazed and worried for Kawu to do so.

"Okay," he said simply. "I'll find him."

He went back to the lobby mezzanine, his fresh bruises throbbing with every step. There was something haunting about the hush now, as though the many dead had left echoes of awareness that now floated through the corridors and watched him as he passed them by.

Following a trail of subtle footprints in the carpets and a toppled vase, Jespar found Kawu on the balcony of a sleeping chamber a few floors up. He sat crouched against the railing, knees drawn up and his head buried in his hands. The hedge maze spread out beneath him, tinted a pale gray by the gibbous moon that poked out between the clouds.

"Hey."

Kawu's head jerked up. Recognizing Jespar, his mouth parted. "Oh, Īmīte. You're alive?"

Courtesy of a psychomancer, Jespar thought, sinking to his haunches in front of Kawu. "Hanging in there, but yeah. Are you all right?"

"Ūkonō," Kawu said, rubbing tears from his cheeks. "I'm so sorry I ran. I panicked, and I—"

Jespar hugged him.

"You're okay," he said. "You're okay."

Thoughts buzzed through his head, bright and disjointed how the Revenants would have killed Kawu too if Agaam's shift hadn't worked, how it was Jespar's fault Kawu was here in the first place, how bad Jespar must have smelled after a day in the saddle and a fight for his life. How good it felt to hold him.

When he let go, Kawu's breathing had calmed.

"We're safe now," Jespar said. "Agaam dealt with those guys."

Kawu, looking equally uncomfortable and relieved, made a vague noise and peered past Jespar into the building. "What about Ma'saa Varroy and the woman they were holding captive? Are they all right?"

"Yeah, they're fine." Jespar stood and offered Kawu a hand up. He took it. "We're gonna talk to the servant once we're back downstairs. Hopefully, she can tell us what happened here."

"Good. That's good. Is anyone else—I mean, are there more survivors?"

Jespar shook his head.

"... I see." Kawu turned back to the balcony. Under different circumstances, Jespar would have found the view stunning: three verdant giants in the untamed wilderness, reaching high into a starry sky.

"This world is so rotten," Kawu said quietly. "It's so terribly rotten."

"Yeah. It can be."

They were silent for a while. Then Jespar took Kawu's hand and squeezed it lightly. "Let's get back downstairs? The others are probably getting—"

He felt the Pull a second before it hit.

It was strong, stronger than before and faster, a freezing phantom claw reaching through his forehead and trying to yank his mind out of his skull and *down*. The world went blue and Jespar gasped, clutched the railing, tried to resist, but he couldn't, the claw pulled harder and harder and harder until—

The ice shattered.

Jespar didn't move, his pulse hammering against his wrists. Kawu was holding him, hands pressed to Jespar's temples.

"Īmīte, are you all right?"

Jespar felt for his forehead. His skin prickled, but the cold had withdrawn. "Yeah. Yeah, I think so. The bug, it ..." He didn't finish the sentence.

"I figured." Kawu drew back his hands. The bags under his eyes had grown darker and sweat beaded on his temples. "I don't understand, Jespar, this doesn't make any sense. The anchoring should have lasted until tomorrow evening at the very least."

"Maybe something went wrong with your shift last night?"

"No, it didn't. Maybe—" Kawu blanched.

"What?"

"I-I'm not sure, maybe ..."

"Please, tell me."

Kawu sighed deeply. "Maybe the reason the dreameater's Pulls are getting stronger is that it's getting closer to hatching. Because it's ..." He forced out the word. "Because it's growing."

There it was again: the image of the gray-blue egg, a silhouette squirming behind the translucent membrane.

Growing.

Jespar was very quiet when he spoke. "Are you sure?"

Kawu's looked up, tears on his lids. "No, Jespar, I'm *not* sure. I wish I was, I wish I knew what to do, I wish I wouldn't be so bloody useless, but I am, and I'm *sorry.*"

Taken aback by Kawu's outburst, Jespar wanted to comfort him, but he couldn't; everything felt too heavy and too bright again. He craved a smoke, a drink, a fight, *anything* to quell the dread stirring and scratching at the lid of that chest Kawu's anchoring had buried it in just one night ago.

Calm yourself. Calm the fuck down and say *something.*

"Okay." Deep breath. "Okay, let's think this through. When did we do the anchoring this morning, like four, five hours before dawn?"

Kawu turned back to the panorama. "Something like that."

"And now it's about four hours to midnight, meaning it lasted roughly twenty hours—that's still plenty of time. If you just anchor me more often, I should be fine, right? You said it's a simple shift."

There was a long pause before Kawu answered. "It is. You're right."

"Well, then it could be worse, couldn't it? All we need to do is keep me anchored until we find the imprinter. How about you do it every two hours or so just to be safe?"

"I don't think we can do that. It's too risky."

"For you?"

"No, for you. Even if it's a benevolent shift, it's still a shift on your mind, and there will be side effects if we overdo it. Once or twice a day is fine, but any more and we're entering dangerous territory."

"What kind of side effects are we talking?"

"That's impossible to predict, but it could be anything from personality changes to brain ruptures."

"... Shit. So what do you suggest?"

Kawu gave it some thought. "We just need to be smart about it. I suggest we start with one anchoring every fifteen hours and take it from there. Does that sound all right for you?"

Wondering what other choice he had, Jespar nodded.

"All right. I will do all I can, Jespar, I promise you that. All I can. Now, shall we go downstairs?"

"Okay. And Kawu?"

"Hm?"

"Thank you. For everything."

The servant looked a mess. A woman in her forties, her plump face was swollen with bruises and her dress spattered with blood. She sat on a chair behind the desk, backdropped by a row of windows. Lysia, Kawu, and Jespar stood a little ways off. Thanks to Agaam's shift, she was still asleep, her chin resting on her chest.

Agaam took her wrists in his hands. "Very well. I'm going to break the remainder of the shift now."

He focused on the woman and went still. A moment floated by.

She gasped softly, and her lids parted. First, there was only confusion. Then she tensed. "Wh-where am I?"

There was something odd about how she said it—the fear was real, but she lacked the panic and disorientation Jespar had expected.

DREAMS OF THE DYING

"Safe," Agaam said. "We neutralized the hitmen."

The woman worked her mouth, her gaze traveling through the group and the room, and back to Agaam. "Who are ye?"

"Friends. What's your name?"

"Are you sure there aren't more? What if–"

"Ma'saa, you are safe. Now please, your name."

The woman let out a little breath. "Uula. Me name's Uula."

"I see. Uula, I know this must be hard for you after everything that's happened, but I need you to answer some questions for us. Is that all right with you?"

Uula muttered agreement.

"Good. Am I right to assume you're a servant here?"

"Uh-huh."

"What's your position?"

Uula fidgeted with her hands. "I'm just a cleaner. Dustin' shelves, moppin' floors, y'know the drill."

"Mm-hm."

"Ma'sao, are ye really sure ye got all of 'em? I saw just the two, but there might be more—"

"You're from Paiolu, aren't you, ma'saa?"

She broke off. "Beg yer pardon?"

"'Uula' is a Paioluan name, isn't it? You're from Paiolu."

She blinked. "True, from Mumalaia. Why ye askin'?"

Agaam gave her an empty smile. "Because I had a hunch you're putting on an act. Now I know for sure."

"... What on the earth are ye on about? Look, whoever ye are, ye should get back to the village and tell the Guard about this, they've gotta—"

"Ma'saa, please ... just stop. You're way too composed for someone whose friends were just brutally murdered by two assassins, and who barely got away with her own life. Yes, you are afraid, but you *have* been in situations like this before."

"Yer crazy. Yer completely nuts." Uula turned to Lysia, pleading. "Please, yer friend ain't thinkin' straight, ye've gotta—"

"Also," Agaam went on, "Uula isn't a Paioluan name. If anything, it's telltale for Maitepo or Maitemi. Were you really from Paiolu, you would have pointed that out."

"Uula" stared at Agaam, a picture of confusion. Then her expression cracked.

It was then that Jespar realized he had seen her before. He made to speak, but Lysia was quicker. "Hold on. I know you."

The woman remained silent.

"She was at the protest," Lysia told Agaam. "You know, when the guards found that girl in the sewers. We talked to her!"

Still no reaction from the woman. She had turned her attention to a nearby candelabrum, as if it were some kind of secret door that could take her out of this mess if only she looked at it hard enough.

"You were also in the napaawo, weren't you?" Jespar asked her. "Back when I met with Counselor Enkshi five days ago?"

"All right, you got me," the woman said. Her tone was an odd mix of defiance, scorn, and fear. "So, what now? Will I become yet another corpse in the graveyard you dig for your master, Ma'sao Agaam?"

"Tell us who you are and why you're here," Agaam answered.

"You know very well why I'm here."

"We do not."

She scoffed. "Of course."

That accent. Jespar knew that accent. "You're from Enderal," he said.

Her eyes met his, hard and dark like sunbaked clay. How innocuous she would have looked if not for them: just an honest, hardworking woman with four ruddy-cheeked kids and a husband waiting at home for her. "As are you, Jespar Dal'Varek. I must admit, out of all the things I've expected to encounter on this mission, High Justice Damean Dal'Varek's prodigal son wasn't one of them."

Jespar found himself short of words.

"Please, ma'saa," Agaam said. "Answer my question. Who are you and why are you here?"

"I've said all I will say. Now, if you're going to kill me, go ahead and do it."

Agaam studied her, his mien inscrutable. At last, he sighed deeply, massaging the bridge of his nose. "I trust you're Initiated?"

No answer.

"Of course you are. Then you also know that cusping psycho-mancers can read minds. Quite frankly, I've always found the phrase to be a little misleading—'hear thoughts' would be a little more accurate. A cusping psychomancer hears every single thought of every single person around them. What decides whether they end up as stable dimensionists or screaming lunatics in a madhouse is whether they learn to block these thoughts out permanently to preserve their sanity. 'Sever the cord,' as we call it."

"How elucidating. Your point?"

"My point is that, as a functioning psychomancer, my inability to read your thoughts puts me in a quandary. I can't even coerce you into telling us the truth because any shift more delicate than 'don't notice me,' 'get out of my way,' or 'kill yourself' might affect your sanity and therefore make your information unreliable." Using thumb and forefinger, Agaam gingerly turned her head left, as though inspecting her cheek. A scar trailed down its length; blood clotted the clay powder she'd used to conceal it. "Which sadly leaves me two options: one, you believe us when we tell you that we're on the same side in this, and you cooperate willingly; two, I make you cut the skin off your face flap by flap until you break and confess." He stood. "I'd be truly sorry if it came to the latter. But we're running out of time and thousands of lives depend on us, so I'll do what I must."

There was something momentous about the hush that followed. Like that between two diplomats whose words would decide the fate of a country.

When the woman answered, a deep weariness had replaced her defiance. "You're telling the truth, aren't you?"

"I am."

She glanced at the open doorway. The emaciated corpses of the Revenants sat propped against the corridor wall, beside the two murdered servants.

"Izabela Esme Dealatis," she said. "That's my name. Can we speak elsewhere?"

The observatory was a hexagonal room atop the pyramid manor. A massive telescope graced its center, mounted onto a circular platform, and pointing toward an oculus in the roof. Metal bookshelves and measuring devices filled the rest of the space, all limned by the milky moonlight that fell through the many windows. They were gathered at a desk that curved around the pedestal.

"Let me get this straight," Lysia told the woman. "You're an agent of the Order of Light."

"An inquisitor, yes."

Agaam stood in front of a shelf, studying a copper sphere he'd taken from one of the drawers. "I always thought the Inquisition was just a rumor."

"That's the purpose of a clandestine organization," Dealatis replied, running a hand through her hair. A trace of red showed along her hairline, probably her natural color. "We were founded a few years after the Silence to keep the Illumined World together. If it weren't for us, it would have probably broken apart many, many times already."

"So you're, what, spies?" Jespar asked. Even as an Endralean noble, he'd never heard of this organization. He wondered if his father had known.

"Well, I guess that's one word for it. We have undercover operatives in almost every government or relevant political faction in the Illumined World. To keep a finger on the pulse, so to speak." She scoffed, shook her head. "Blazes, I can't believe I'm telling you this. They'll suspend me the day I get back."

Agaam the sphere back on the shelf. "So, normally, your job is to shadow the Coalition, but you started investigating Ma'sao Oonai after his attempt at revoking the Golden Soil Decree."

"'Screaming session at the gathered officials' seems a better way to describe it, but yes." Dealatis studied her hands. "With those ex-Snakes and their merry little terrorist band out and about, Kilay has been a hotbed of political instability for a while now, so, naturally, Hierophant Dal'Veram got nervous when she heard about that tantrum and hired me to figure out what had gotten into Oonai. Suffice it to say that what I found wasn't what I expected. Now, I'm quite sure my first conclusion won't shock you: I believe Ma'sao Oonai is either gravely ill or dead." She gave Agaam a questioning look as if inviting him to elaborate.

He didn't. "How much do you know?"

Dealatis' mouth curled upward, but the rest of her features didn't move. "No details, rest assured. And, frankly, considering my second conclusion, I couldn't care less about whether Oonai is alive, dead, or flew off on the Lost Children's airship." She stood and crossed to the window. "The truth is, I *wanted* to be wrong about this, up to the last moment. But with what the head servant here told me, and those hitmen showing up, I'd be delusional to deny it any longer."

Resting her hands on the window stool, she looked out over the landscape. The clouds had now fully cleared, and an earthy smell clung to the air—the aftermath of the rain.

"What is your second conclusion?" Jespar asked.

Dealatis sighed again, eyes closed. "I know your son and your wife passed away, Ma'sao Agaam. But you're close to your granddaughter, aren't you? What was her name again?"

Agaam's mouth twitched, but he said nothing.

"Fine, stay silent," Dealatis said, "It was a rhetorical question anyway. The reason I'm asking is, if there's *any* way at all you can use what I'm about to tell you to fix this mess, I want you to swear that you'll try. Call me foolish and sentimental, but I need to hear it. I want you to swear it on your granddaughter's life."

"I swear."

The complete absence of hesitation in Agaam's words seemed to be the last push Dealatis had needed.

She nodded slowly and began to speak. "Jaaros Oonai and Third Magnate Makiima Vel'Nyx are plotting a coup. They want to murder the five other magnates and half of the Blue Islands Coalition officials to become the sole rulers of the Archipelago." Dealatis paused. "They call it the 'Overgrowth Plan'."

INTERLUDE
THE MAN

he candle bowls float in the temple pool like iridescent water lilies.

What are you doing here?

It's not just that he's risking everything they have worked for; it's that this is the last place he ever imagined himself to be in a situation like the one he's in. A theist only to the public and his wife, the man stopped caring for the Gods a long time ago when he realized how drastically his understanding of believing differed from the average soul. Even back in his more pious days, the essence of Silent Era Faith was never in the question of whether the Light-Born were alive, dead, imposters, or nonexistent. The essence was the tale of the Apotheosis. Yes, maybe the Light-Born had just been exceptionally gifted dimensionists, or they were fictional all along, or they were dead. None of it made the message of the tale that was the foundation of the Illumined World less powerful: that anything is possible if you set your mind to it, even godhood. Sadly, this was not how most people saw it; to them, the Faith was all about asking favors from celestial beings who lounged about in a city in the clouds. One candle to Irländah for unrequited love, one to Moraia for a good harvest. One to Esara against a wart on the ass. How easy life must be for the fool who lays off responsibility.

The man stares into the pool.

Stop this idiocy. Get a hold of yourself and go home.

But he can't. The mere thought suffocates him.

"Ma'sao?"

The man turns around. A priest stands in the entrance, the sunset drawing a dreamlike outline around him. Shadows cloak his features but judging by his stiff posture and tense tone, he's trying to determine whether that towering, shrouded figure standing in his temple is a threat.

Think. What would a have-not do?

The man bows. "Father, may ye prosper. Please, forgive me imposin'."

The accent is supposed to be part of his disguise—a magnate passing as a worker—but just how naturally it comes makes the man wonder if perhaps the disguise wasn't always the other way around. Either way, his words do the trick.

"Nothing to forgive, son," the priest says.

Son. The man tries to feel amused, but instead, he feels angry. He *calls me "son"*.

The priest crosses the aisle. His long face reminds the man of an armadillo, and he's so skinny his prayer rings clink against each other as he walks. There's a moth hole in his cheap linen robe, just below the collar.

Stopping uncomfortably close to the man, he nods at the scarf the man has pulled over his mouth. "Please unveil yourself, son. The Gods are watching."

He calls me "son" and he gives me orders.

The man looks away in what he hopes passes as shame. "I'm ... I'm disfigured."

"Oh. I understand." He comes even closer. A rosy smell clings to him, the kind of perfume you'd expect on a whore. "But, trust me, there is no reason to be ashamed. We're all the same before the Gods."

The man barely suppresses a laugh. "Forgive me, Father. I should go," he says. He makes for the door. As expected, the priest reaches for his shoulder.

"Wait. Wait, son, I didn't mean to upset you. You may remain shrouded if you wish."

"Thank ye, Father. That is very kind of ye." *Superstitious fool.*

He lets the priest lead him to a pew. They sit.

"Well then. Why are you here?"

The man glances at the mural on the opposite wall. It shows the seven Gods gathered in Inodân, Tyr with his scepter and his face of light towering above them all. It feels like their stone eyes are watching him.

Madman. You're risking everything. Madman!

"I'm lost," the man says. "And I need guidance."

He tells the story he has prepared. The words come slowly at first, but soon they pour from his mouth, and although his tale drastically differs from the truth to conceal his identity, he manages to maintain its essence. By the time he is done, he feels hollowed out, the way he has felt so often since that day. As if something vital has been ripped from his soul, and cold fog has filled the empty space it left behind.

Why?

It doesn't make any sense. Yes, to outsiders, his actions in these cursed past moons might seem heartless. What they don't understand is that reality had left him no choice. The higher he'd climbed up Fortune Road, the more lions had shown up in the arena, doubters becoming sycophants becoming traitors, snide nicknames becoming libel and attacks on his life. "Dry season fires" burning down his plantations, "pirates" looting his ships, "bandits" attacking his caravans. Only by being smarter, stronger, and harder than the rest had he managed to stay on top, to protect the livelihood he had worked so hard to attain.

The world is hard, a voice in his mind says. *You need to be harder. Monsters exist*, another replies. *And you're one of them.*

The black fog grows again, so dense and overpowering that the man wants to scream. He grits his teeth, balls up his fists, and waits for the priest to say something. But the priest doesn't. He just studies him with those armadillo eyes, as if preparing his judgment.

Speak, you bloody have-not. Fucking say something!

"You must make amends."

A pause.

"Amends?"

"Yes. It means to make up for what you've—"

"I know what it means," the man cuts him off. "I just don't see what I should make amends for. I told ye, I had no choice."

"You had a choice, and you made it. And even if your intentions were as pure as you say, it's the results that matter." The priest meets the man's eyes, and, bizarrely, the man averts his own. As if that have-not clown had *any* sort of authority over him. "But something tells me you know that already, don't you? You're here because you know you made a mistake, and your guilt is consuming you."

The man snorts. "Ye know nothin' about me."

"No, maybe I don't." The priest puts a hand on his shoulder. "But I know a good man gone astray when I see him."

A good man.

Somehow, it is those three words that tear down the walls.

It's your fault.

Yes. With the denial gone, he is baffled at his delusion, at the ridiculous lengths he went to rationalize his actions.

Your fault.

Monsters exist, and you're one of them.

The fog spreads mercilessly, and a swarm of horrible thoughts hides inside it, thoughts that are the logical conclusions to spring from this realization, thoughts that pierce his mind like hornets, again and again, until all he wants to do is claw out his eyes and scream and get away from this stranger, away from this world, lock himself into the hold of a shipwreck at the bottom of the ocean where no one will ever find him.

But then, just when he's sure he will jump up and flee, a resolve he didn't even know he still had inside him pierces through the fog and delivers a single thought.

This isn't you.

It's true. This isn't him. Self-pity? Despair? Giving up? Hadn't it always been his iron will and his tenacity that had set him apart from the lion fodder and the whiners? All right, maybe he did make a mistake; maybe he had let his paranoia get the better of him and allowed a lapse in his judgment.

So what?

He'll fix it. He'll make up for what he's done, turn defeat into victory, he'll atone and become a better man—then the black fog, which must be the voice of his guilt, will vanish. Action and consequence. Cause and effect.

"Yer right, father," the man says. "I made a mistake."

"I'm glad y—"

"And I'll make amends, as ye say. I'll fix this, and I'll clear me name."

The priest sighs. "You still don't understand, son. There is no 'fixing this'."

"Everythin' can be fixed if ye try hard enough."

"Not this. Gods, can you even hear yourself? You talk as if all you did was steal one of your neighbor's sheep! Let me say it again: someone *died* because of you!" He shakes his head, sending a perfume cloud in the man's direction. "Amends aren't about washing away your guilt and clearing your name. They are about the people you've hurt and about saving your soul."

Anger. How dares this fool lecture him? What has he *ever* accomplished, other than jamming those brass rings on his arms and acting all pious?

Calm. Control. "I'm not sure I understand, Father."

With a condescending shake of the head, the priest adjusts the collar of his robe. He doesn't even seem to be aware of the ugly, gaping moth hole at the shoulder; it drives the man crazy. "Every time we sin, it leaves a mark on our souls," the priest says. "And that mark, it stays with us for the rest of our lives, to remind us of our transgressions. That's what I mean by 'there is no fixing this.' There *is* no going back to the way things were, not now, not ever again, so the best you can hope for is forgiveness."

"From whom?" The man snorts. "The Gods?"

"No," the priest says calmly. "From yourself. If we ignore the marks for too long, they start to fester, and that's precisely what has happened to you. At this point, the best you can hope for is to stop them from getting worse."

The man stares. *Nonsense.* If he truly is to blame for what has happened, he would also be to blame for a list of thousands of other transgressions for which he never atoned, thousands of marks he has allowed to fester.

Nonsense! This is religious bullshit, the kind the clergy use to keep their lambs nice and docile.

But the rationalization doesn't work. If what the priest said was nonsense, then why does the man feel the fog? Why does he feel that pain, why does he feel that guilt, why does he just want to lock himself in a room and shut out the world? One mark of thousands. Thousands that have festered. What must his soul look like now? A putrid growth. *A tumor.*

The fog grows, floods his mind, his heart, his lungs. Shaking, he raises his eyes to the priest.

It's the moth hole that makes the man snap.

No.

This have-not doesn't get to judge him. Not him.

"Fuck your forgiveness."

"... Son?"

"You heard me. Yes, fine, I've made mistakes, but how dare you tell me I'm beyond absolution? *One* word from me and this place will be razed to the ground, *one* word and your wife and your kids will be on the streets, *one* word and your coinless corpse will be danglin' from the city walls, *one* word!"

"Ma'sao, I—"

"I *will* clear my name, just wait and watch. For every coin of blood money I've made, I'll buy an orphan boots, for every house someone lost to my empire, I'll build him a new one, for every life I ruined, I'll save another, and by the time I'm done, people will pray to me instead of yer useless Gods, cause unlike them *I'm here to listen!*"

Quiet unfolds. The man's finger is on the priest's chest, trembling. The priest's mouth stands ajar, a comical gesture befitting the clown that he is.

Fear.

That's more like it. That he can work with. What was he thinking, asking this have-not for guidance? How did he become so pathetic?

"Just wait and watch, 'Father'. I will fix this."

With that, the man stands and leaves. His skin burns and his heart hammers into his ribcage, yet he walks slowly and with his back upright.

Gods don't run.

Chapter Sixteen
Wildfire

Day Five
6th Moon of Dry Season, 1226 A.L.

gaam's next words summed up Jespar's feelings. "That's absurd."

"You almost sound like me," Dealatis replied.

The old servant looked at her as if expecting a punchline. Then he closed his eyes and leaned against the telescope pedestal, brushing the lid over his glass eye with his thumb. When he looked again, the disbelief was gone, and utter fatigue not unlike Dealatis' had taken its place. "Please tell us what you know."

There was a flash of satisfaction in Dealatis' features, but it faded as fast as it had arrived. She sighed. "The irony is, my finding out about this was a coincidence, not outstanding detective work. I was investigating an affair Oonai had up here, with a servant girl."

"He had many affairs, didn't he?" Jespar asked.

"Yes, but that particular one went on a lot longer than the others, so I figured there might have been a connection to Oonai's strange personality change. The whole thing turned out to be a dead end, but when I dug into the comings and goings in the manor, I discovered Oonai had been holding regular meetings with someone else up here, ever since last Drought. Magnate Vel'Nyx." She gave Agaam a probing glance.

"I knew nothing about these meetings," he said. "And neither did the Ma'saa or Enkshi. Ma'sao Oonai and Ma'saa Vel'Nyx must have gone to great lengths to keep them private."

"You're right, they did. Vel'Nyx always took a ship to Tamakaha and then rode from there instead of just going by myrad, and Oonai had the staff sign contracts that bound them to total secrecy. Just a single word to the wrong person would have been akin to financial suicide."

"And yet they told you everything the second you showed up here?" Agaam asked. "That doesn't make any sense."

"They told me everything after I showed them my Mandate, yes."

Agaam seemed surprised. "You have a Divine Mandate?"

"Signed and sealed by Hierophant Dal'Veram herself. I received it two days ago. In fact, that's why I could finally stop tailing you and come here."

"What's a Divine Mandate?" Kawu asked. He sat on the spiral staircase to the telescope, the epitome of exhaustion. Jespar wanted to join him, do something to make him feel better, but he couldn't think of anything that wouldn't feel misplaced for the occasion.

"A decree from the Order of Light," Lysia said. "It's the equivalent of a command from the Light-Born themselves, and it trumps any authority of the individual governments of the Illumined World."

Agaam nodded. "So you used the Mandate to pressure the servants into breaching their agreement?"

343

"Believe it or not, there actually wasn't any pressuring involved," Dealatis replied. "The second they realized the Mandate protected them from repercussions, they couldn't wait to talk." She blinked and frowned, as though remembering something. "I never asked: the Revenants, did they get Head Servant Ejkaan and his daughter too? They meant to go to Tamakaha this morning, to organize an escort for me. Did they ...?"

"They didn't make it," Agaam said.

Dealatis looked sideways and mumbled something. When her gaze found its way back to the group, her expression was hollow. "I've been doing this job for decades, but that's the one part I'll never get used to. You try to do the right thing, and suddenly, a dozen people are dead because of you."

All too familiar with the scenario, Jespar tried to steer the conversation back. "So, you think the hitmen were here for you?"

"I was the only one they didn't kill right away, and they kept on asking who I worked for and what I had found out. Whoever sent them after me probably thought I was some private eye who'd been hired to dig up dirt on Oonai and found a whole rotten swamp instead. Which is disturbingly close to the truth."

"So they decided to silence you," Lysia said. She sounded composed enough, but her thumb was running up and down her scar, as so often when she was agitated. *"Agitated" is probably putting mildly.*

"Me and any potential whistleblowers, yes."

Agaam studied the tiling for a bit, as if dissecting and scrutinizing her words. "Tell us about that scheme. The Overgrowth Plan."

"I will. But I need a drink first. Anyone offering?"

Jespar unclasped his brandy flask and passed it to her. She mumbled her thanks. Watching her drink, a trail of cold wormed its way up Jespar's back.

The Overgrowth Plan. The Revenants. The parasite.

Everything was connected. It was a spider's web of lies and schemes and secrets that had ensnared not just Oonai and the people of Kilay but also Jespar, whose life was now tied to the magnate's. Whatever this woman would say next could be the knife to cut them out of their traps—or the sound of the spider returning to its lair.

"All right," Dealatis said, wiping her mouth. "Let's start with the outline, shall we? Oonai and Vel'Nyx believe the Coalition has, I'm quoting, 'degenerated into a stinking swamp of regulations, bureaucracy, and corrupt, fat aristocrats that hinder any real progress.' They want to burn down that 'overgrowth' so Kilay can become the dominating force in the Illumined World it deserves to be."

Kawu's face looked pallid in the moonlight. "By 'burn down', you mean murder?"

"I'm talking about mass murder, lad. Oonai and Vel'Nyx want to get rid of the part of the Coalition they deem useless and restructure it to their own liking. With the two of them as the sole rulers."

"I don't understand," Lysia said. She either wasn't trying to or couldn't hide her upset anymore, her mien a marriage of outrage and disbelief. "If Oonai wants to make the Coalition more efficient, why doesn't he just alter the laws? Bloody hell, he's the First Magnate!"

"That doesn't mean he can do whatever he wants," Agaam said. "He may be the most powerful of the seven, but he still needs at least three other magnates, or a majority among the officials to support his decisions."

"Exactly," Dealatis said. "But I have a strong hunch that all that talk about efficiency is just a charade anyway, so they don't have to admit it's really just power they're after."

Lysia worked her lips as if preparing a retort, but then she just scoffed, her fingers returning to her scar. Jespar could relate to her incredulity all too well—he had reacted similarly back on Nehrim, upon learning Chancellor Acarno could have ended the war in the first year when scouts located Prophet Jakal's hideout; Acarno decided not to strike as he wanted the North to completely conquer the South first before putting an end to the fighting. As cliché as it sounded, it had taught Jespar that in politics, human life was all too often an expendable resource, a stock of pawns to sacrifice on the chessboard. And yet, even so, his throat felt dry at the implications of Dealatis' words. It was one thing to *know* such machinations took place. It was another to be a firsthand witness as they were happening.

"And how are they planning to do that?" Jespar asked. "Kill five magnates and hundreds of officials?"

Dealatis' lips creased in a smile Jespar could only describe as defiant, the sort you'd see on an empress at the funeral of an old friend. Grief under a carapace of resilience. Weakness clad in an armor of strength. "See, that's where it gets real interesting. Did you ever wonder how the Scythe rose to power so quickly?"

"The long Drought and the Golden Soil Decree played a big role," Agaam said. "Why?"

"Because, sometimes, a pile of shit stinks so bad that no one ever stops to wonder whose ass it dropped from." She emptied the whisky and slammed the flask on the windowsill. "The Scythe aren't real revolutionaries. They're a tool. Oonai and Vel'Nyx built them up."

Agaam's face flickered between astonishment and confusion, mirroring Jespar's emotions. "That's absurd."

"Really? If you were a magnate scheming the mass murder of half the Coalition and your biggest rivals, how would you go about it, hm? Send hitmen after every single one of them and make them suffer an 'accident'? Or maybe you'd go with a blatant coup?" She picked the flask back up and circled her thumb over its neck. "Even if you found a way to make that work, no way you'd still have the support of the populace after that, not to mention the Order of Light. A bit of skullduggery here, a dash of blackmail and intimidation there, some nepotism for good measure ... Everybody can look past that because it's just how the world works. But the mass murder of an entire political class? No way they'd get away with that." With a dexterity that was at odds with her appearance, Dealatis stoppered the flask and tossed it back to Jespar. He caught it. "What you need is someone who can be hangman and scapegoat at the same time. Someone who seems so *utterly* unrelated to you and your ambitions that the idea of connecting them to you is completely ludicrous."

A ripple of cold went down Jespar's spine when he understood. "The Scythe," he said softly. "Bloody hell."

"Bloody indeed."

Agaam crossed his arms. "What are you basing your theory on? Do you have any evidence?"

"Are you asking me if I have the testimonies from the servants who overheard Vel'Nyx and Oonai's conversations? I'm sorry, they were all butchered, and I forgot to bring a transcriber. I have proof of Vel'Nyx's ties to the Kekotokian mercenary underworld and reports on the inexplicable gaps in Oonai's real and reported expenditures, but, unfortunately, they are all in my office in Uunili. If you'd like, we could take a leisurely walk back to the city, and I can show them to you, Ma'sao Agaam. Alternatively, you could ask yourself what in the world I, an inquisitor of the Order of Light, would gain from lying to you. Especially at this point."

Agaam held her glare. Then he ran a hand through his beard and leaned against a nearby pillar. "So, the Scythe are mercenaries. That's what you're saying."

"At least the Pale Twins and the core are, yes. I'm sure the footmen the Brother is drawing in with his speeches genuinely believe they're fighting for a better world."

Jespar tugged at his scarf. "Which doesn't matter as long as Oonai and Vel'Nyx control the leadership."

"Correct. The oppressed fight for the oppressor without even knowing it. I mean, you have to appreciate the irony."

"But why?" Lysia asked hoarsely. "Why would they need the—"

Jespar connected the dots. "Because they're gonna start a riot."

Dealatis put on her funeral smile. "Young man, you win the prize."

"Only that it's not an actual riot," Jespar went on, head swimming, "but a smokescreen for the murders. Once the riot is going, the mercenary part of the Scythe is going to systematically murder the five other magnates and the 'overgrowth' officials."

"That's one possibility, yes. The more I think about it, though, the more I believe they may just let the mob do the work for them. A frenzied horde, seething with hatred for the Great Dreamers, all at Oonai and Vel'Nyx's fingertips ... what else do they have to do but toss them some weapons, send the Blue Guard elsewhere, then have the Twins guide the mob through the Jade District? They're going to raze through those streets like a force of nature."

Kawu blinked. "But ... what about the civilians?"

Dealatis' smile cracked. She looked off, lower thumb pressed to her lip.

"No," Lysia said, a pleading tone to her voice now. "No, that's horseshite. If they just send the mob on a rampage, how would they make sure it only hits the 'overgrowth'?"

Agaam beat Dealatis to an answer. "The conference on Maitepo. It's taking place over the next three weeks, and only select Coalition officials were invited."

Dealatis scoffed. "Look at that, I completely forgot about the conference. There's your answer, Ma'saa Varroy."

"Stars burn me." Lysia sank down on the edge of the table. "That's insane. That's *fucking* insane."

"No argument there. Though I haven't even gotten to the juiciest part yet." Dealatis stood up and strolled to a nearby contraption, a sphere consisting of intertwining rings, and gave it a gentle spin. "I take it you know about the recent suicide epidemic sparked by the Golden Soil Decree?"

Nods all around.

"Well, if you believe the servants, it's part of the plan too. The Golden Soil Decree was never about money, it was about depriving the poorest of what little they had and wreaking havoc on their lives."

Jespar's heart sank at the look on Kawu's face. "You mean they *wanted* those people to kill themselves?" Kawu asked.

"Frankly, I don't think they care a thing about what those people did, as long as it would rile up the population."

"So people would flock to the Scythe and bolster their ranks," Jespar said. It came out flat, like a coroner reading out the death toll of a plague. Jespar knew the tone—it was a defense mechanism he'd witnessed often in the war, on himself and others. When things happened that were too monstrous to grasp, the mind had no choice but to detach itself emotionally. "Dry out the soil, strike a spark, and let the wildfire burn down the forest."

"Funny you'd say that," Dealatis said. "According to the servants, Vel'Nyx and Oonai actually referred to it as 'controlled burning'."

"Hold on," Agaam said. "This doesn't add up. Let's assume all this is true, and the mob goes on a rampage and eliminates all the targets. What's to stop them from taking down the Coalition entirely? Even if the Twins manage to guide the mob to the 'overgrowth' like you said, there's no way the rebels are just gonna lay down their weapons and go home because the Pale Twins tell them to."

Dealatis spun the sphere again, faster. "That's the part I haven't figured out yet. I am, however, sure they have something prepared. It's safe to assume at the very least one high-ranking military official is in on the scheme, and if Oonai and Vel'Nyx control the leadership of both factions, putting a stop to the riot is child's play."

"How?" Lysia asked.

"I'm not an oracle, young lady, but there are dozens of options. For example, the Scythe's inside men could split up the mob once the killings are done and lead them into an ambush by the Blue Guard, so they can swoop in and save the day."

"Staged battles," Jespar said.

"Exactly. If it works and Oonai reveals himself as the mastermind behind this 'strategy' in the end, it would make it even easier for him and Vel'Nyx to seize power afterward. But, as I said, this is just an educated guess. I'm sure they've figured out a way."

"And when do you think all this is going to happen?" Agaam asked.

"Anytime between now and the end of the conference." Dealatis stopped the sphere. "Though my guess is during Miwa-e-Kēko. With the festivities going on, it would be easy to gather a large group of people without anyone noticing."

Agaam grunted and went back to study the tiles. For a time, no one spoke, Jespar's thoughts zipping back and forth like moths buzzing around a bonfire.

"So?" Agaam asked Dealatis. "What will you do?"

She cast him a long, appraising look. "I think it's your turn now. I've told you a lot, and you still haven't given me anything in return. Yes, you saved my life and I owe you for that, but I still have no idea what in the world brought Oonai's dreaded psychomancer-shadow plus eccentric entourage here, just in time to save me from those hitmen."

"I would tell you if I thought it was relevant."

Dealatis' chuckle was bitter. "Would you now?"

"Yes. Believe it or not, this is the first time I've heard any of this, and I'm as shocked as you are. All I can safely disclose is that you're right: something did happen to Jaaros Oonai, and that's why we're here. Because we're trying to get to the bottom of it."

"Then let me help you," Dealatis said. "Even if I were to tell the Coalition right away, they might not believe me, and even if they did, with the Scythe being as strong as they are, I'm not sure there's anything they could do to stop the riot. If you know of *any* way we can still fix this mess, you *need* to let me know. You promised you would."

"I promised that *we* will do all can, not that you'd be a part of it. I'm sorry, Ma'saa Dealatis."

Frowning, Dealatis looked Agaam straight in the eye. He matched her gaze. Lysia's attention shifted from Agaam to Dealatis and back, her lips half-open like she wanted to say something but didn't dare; Kawu looked at the ground. Jespar's head was still swimming.

Dealatis ended the staring. "Fine. You'll have to live with that decision, not me." She sounded like a soldier too tired to march on. "Will you at least let me go now that you got what you wanted? Or are you going to dispose of me like you disposed of those miners on Hapana?"

Something flashed across Agaam's features at the mention of the island. *Hurt? Anger?* Jespar couldn't tell. "Is that how the story goes?"

"Oh, come on, we both know—" Dealatis never finished the sentence. Her eyes went wide, like a prophetess foreseeing some unknown horror. Then they rolled back, and she collapsed. Agaam caught her.

It was Lysia who spoke first. "What. The. Hell."

"Just a sleeping shift," Agaam said, gently easing Dealatis to the ground. "She'll wake up in four days."

"She's a godsdamned agent of the Order! She could've helped us!"

"No, ma'saa, she couldn't have. You heard her, there's nothing she could have done here on Kilay, and even a black myrad needs three weeks to get from here to Enderal—in other words, she has no immediate access to the Order's resources." He stood and smoothed out his coat. "Also, regardless of what she said, she wouldn't have just let us go about our way, no questions asked. Worst-case scenario, she would have activated her fellow inquisitors and meddled in our mission, and we cannot afford that risk."

Lysia stared at Agaam, lips parted. Then she scoffed and went to the door.

Jespar jumped to his feet. "Hey! Hey, where are you going?"

Lysia turned on her heel. "What do you think? I'm bloody done with this shite! No way I'm putting my life on the line for some genocidal maniac! And honestly, if you have any decency left, you'll leave too!"

It was Jespar's turn to stare. *I'm sick,* he wanted to say. *I'm sick, and if Oonai dies, I'll die too.* Of course, he couldn't—that fucking lump was back and blocking his throat again, turning him into a broken ventriloquist puppet. Bloody hell, what was wrong with him? How hard could it be to *fucking* ask for help?

"Please. We- we need you." It was all he managed.

Lysia seemed to waver. Then her features hardened. "Remember what you told me on Hapana? All that stuff about lenses, perspective, and stories, how we have way less control over our choices than we believe?"

"I—"

"It's horseshite, Jespar. Some people just *choose* to be arseholes, and that's really all there is to it. You know why those pricks always end up at the top? 'Cause that's how we've designed the fucking game. To become a winner, you just *have* to take without consideration, you *have* to play foul, you *have* to kill your conscience and blind yourself to the destruction you leave behind because if you pause for *one bloody moment,* you'd realize what a hull you've become." She shot a finger at the window, her hands shaking. "This man we work for, he doesn't deserve to be saved, it's that simple. I don't care about his stupid wife, I don't care about politics, I don't care about my bloody debt—if we help Oonai, we condone *everything* this fucking bastard has done!"

I don't give a shit about Oonai, I'm sick! I need help! "Godsdammit, Lysia, not everything is symbolic! If what this woman said is true, then Oonai might be the only one who can still stop that plan!"

Lysia scoffed. "Stars burn me, he *designed* the bloody plan, Jespar! Why in the world would he stop it now? You think if we ask him nicely, he'll, what, see the error of his ways? Face it, the second we wake this arsehole up, he'll just weasel his way out and pick up right where he left off! And, besides, what can *I* do anyway? I'm not a dreamwalker, or some secret agent, or a fucking psychomancer-assassin. I'm just a bloody physician who some crazy rich woman thinks is her ticket to divine absolution. No, Jespar ... this is it. I'd rather spend a lifetime in Coalition servitude than help this greedy excuse of a human being and betray everything I believe in." She gave Agaam a bitter look. "Provided that Ma'sao Agaam doesn't just decide to 'neutralize' me, of course."

The ghost of an emotion flickered across Agaam's wrinkled face again, the same from when Dealatis had mentioned Hapana. Gone too fast. "It'd be a shame to lose you, Ma'saa Varroy. But as long as you abide by your agreement to silence, it's your choice."

"How very fucking generous."

She opened the door and stepped into the hallway.

"Jespar is dying."

Lysia turned around. Kawu stood on the telescope pedestal stairs, both hands gripping the railing.

"What in the world are you talking about?" she asked.

Kawu's eyes sought Jespar's. "I think he should answer that question himself."

No.

No, he couldn't, and he wouldn't. That godsdamned lump was too strong, and he was too weak, and even if it weren't, he didn't deserve to be heard or be helped, not him, not-

"Jespar?" Lysia asked. "Talk to me. What does Kawu mean?"

Jespar forced his lips open.

Every word was like moving a mountain.

CHAPTER SEVENTEEN
CROWN

DAY SIX
6TH MOON OF DRY SEASON, 1226 A.L.

"Are you all right, Lysia?"

Had Jespar asked himself the same thing, he couldn't have said. Since he had come clean about his infection, the dread in the buried chest had changed. Until now, it had been like a ghost, a pernicious entity you knew was there but could still ignore. Not any longer. He could hear it breathing now, its skeletal fingers scratching on the inside of the lid.

Waiting.

It seemed an effort for Lysia to turn away from the window. The moon lit the scarred half of her face while shadow cloaked the other. "I'm just trying to understand why you didn't tell us sooner."

"We didn't find out about it until last night. And I didn't want to ..." He struggled for words. "I don't know. Be a bother."

"Hm." Lysia looked at Kawu, who had sat back down on the telescope stairs, huddled up between the railings like an animal seeking shelter. "And you really think killing Oonai's dreameater is going to kill Jespar's too? It sounds so bloody bizarre."

What about this fucking mess doesn't?

"We really don't know," Kawu said. "It's just our best guess. Oonai's dreameater created Jespar's, so it's possible it's also its imprinter."

Lysia gave it some thought, then half-snorted and shook her head. "A kingdom for a tittle of certainty. All right, I'll stay and do what I can."

A weight fell from Jespar's shoulders. "Thanks, Lysia. I—"

"For you *and* for the money. I wasn't thinking straight before— if Tuujan and Associates impound my clinic and force me into reparations, Juusew will end up on the streets again, and the people in the district wouldn't have a physician anymore. I could never forgive myself for that." She said it defiantly and looked at Dealatis while she spoke, as though she were trying to justify her decision toward the unconscious inquisitor. They had moved Dealatis to a nearby column, back propped against the stone.

Lysia turned to Kawu. "How long do you think you'll be able to keep that thing at bay with your shifts?"

"I don't know," Kawu said. "It depends on how fast it gets stronger."

"Guess, then."

He glanced up at the ceiling. "A couple of days. Perhaps a week."

"That's not long. Maybe you could help him, Agaam? You can access the psychic dimension too."

"Yes, ma'saa, but our Sights are completely different. I'll think about it, but I strongly doubt there's anything I can do."

"In other words," she said, "if we don't find Oonai's imprinter within a week, Jespar will fall into a coma just like Oonai?"

Silence was the answer.

Inhaling deeply, Lysia looked back out the window. "We're fucked."

"It's not all that bad," Jespar said with forced optimism. "I mean, at least we have something to go on now. This whole conspiracy and the dreameater, they must be connected."

"That's a false equivalence," Lysia said. "Just because both things happened around the same time doesn't mean they have anything to do with each other. The dreameater could still be from one of Oonai's business rivals or someone else with a personal vendetta against him."

"In theory, sure, but what are the odds?" Jespar asked. "Also, remember, in that vision I had, I saw Oonai talking to a woman in a hedge maze. That could have been Vel'Nyx, right?"

"Did you see her face?"

Jespar went through his memories. "No."

"Then she might as well have been one of Oonai's affairs or someone else."

"You're right, ma'saa," Agaam said, "but I agree with Ma'sao Dal'Varek nonetheless. This 'Overgrowth Plan' is our best lead, so we'd be fools not to pursue it. What we should do is ask ourselves who in this plot might have benefitted from Oonai's illness, then scrutinize our theory."

"Okay, how about Vel'Nyx?" Jespar asked. "Maybe she decided she wanted the throne all for herself, so she used Oonai as a draft horse until everything was set up, then infected him with the dreameater and sent the hitmen to take care of any potential whistleblowers."

Lysia didn't look convinced. "I don't know about that. Unless Dealatis got something seriously wrong, then Oonai is a vital element of the plan. Remember, he owns the Blue Guard, so it all stands and falls with him."

"Agreed," Agaam said. "Also, Third Magnate Vel'Nyx is known for being a pragmatist who only takes very calculated risks. This whole scheme is mad enough as it is, and unless there's an extremely good reason we don't know about, I cannot see her risking even more by planning a coup within a coup. It's possible, of course, but not likely."

Jespar looked for flaws in their arguments but found none. The dread stirred in the chest, fingernails scraping on wood. "Okay, then what about those other possible conspirators Dealatis mentioned? The ones in the military?"

"Same shite, different smell," Lysia said. "Whoever they are, they'd also be taking a huge risk pulling off a scheme inside a scheme. Not to mention we have no idea who they are."

"Then the Scythe. Maybe they turned on the plan and now want a real revolution after all."

Agaam stroked his beard. "If they did, and they managed to get close enough to Oonai to infect him, they might as well have killed him. They'd gain absolutely nothing from prolonging his death."

"Don't they?" Kawu asked. "What if they wanted to buy themselves time to prepare the coup undisturbed?"

"Could be, but that's still guesswork. Not to mention it's far from certain we could get a hold on the Twins, even if we tried—they have avoided capture for almost a year." He looked at Jespar. "What we need is something solid."

"Then we'll find it!" Hearing how hysterical he sounded, the dread grew louder—slow, jerky thuds against the chest's lid. He leaned against a nearby wall and rubbed his brows, trying to calm. "Look, this place *is* the key to what happened to Oonai, I can *feel* that, as stupid as it sounds. The answer is here somewhere, we just need to look in the right places."

It was a lie. The only thing he felt was exhaustion, the result of four days that had been an avalanche of emotions, brushes with death, and experiences so bizarre that Jespar couldn't help but wonder if it all wasn't part of some fucked up, endless nightmare. *Infected,*

infected, infected. All he wanted was to forget, to lie down and let sleep drown out the world.

But he couldn't.

He had to fight, had to keep going, the same way he had in those first moons after fleeing the Village, when the melancholia had been so overpowering he had wondered if maybe the cynics weren't right after all when they said hope was just fashionable self-delusion.

He had to fight.

He had to keep going.

He had to fix this.

Jespar iced over.

Lysia was saying something about searching the manor.

Fix this.

The words echoed in his mind, buzzed from one end to the other like puzzled fireflies.

You can't stop me. Every sin leaves a mark. I'll clear my name. I'll fix this.

"Bloody hell."

All eyes fell on him.

"Oonai," he muttered. "He backed out of the plan."

Lysia's squinted. "I'm not sure I follow."

"I'm sorry, it's just that ... I remembered something. Oonai, he—" He started over. "The things I saw in that vision, Oonai's memories. Remember how I told you they came with these powerful emotions? Kawu, you said I felt them because they are what the dreameater feeds off the most, right?"

Kawu nodded. "You said you felt anger."

"Yes, I did, but there was also something else." He paused, trying to remember, trying to *feel.* "Shame. It was anger, yes, but most of that anger was directed at Oonai himself. He felt terrible shame and regret for something he had done."

The room grew quiet.

"You think he felt guilty about the conspiracy?" Lysia asked.

"I do." He studied the ground, trailing the delicate lines and streaks in the marble. Chaotic as they seemed when observed separately, they formed a beautiful, wild symmetry when seen as a whole. "This shame, it was the strongest in the memory where he was talking to the woman in the hedge maze. He felt deep regret and wanted to 'clear his name.' That's what I heard over and over: 'I can clear my name' and 'I will fix this.'"

Excitement grew inside him; the dread was losing power, its punches against the wood growing weaker. "It adds up, doesn't it? Late in Drought Three, Oonai starts acting strangely. Drought Four, weeks after the Coalition approves the decree, he calls in a conference and tries to revoke it, which, naturally, makes zero sense to everyone else since he was the one who pushed for it, and because the devastating ripple effects like the suicide epidemic aren't apparent yet. They have no idea Oonai and Vel'Nyx are well aware of them already."

"Because causing suffering among the commoners was the whole point of the decree to start with," Lysia said. "So, what, you believe Oonai grew a conscience, realized how fucked-up all of this was, and tried to backpedal?"

"Believe" is a strong word, Jespar thought. *"Desperately hope" is more like it.* "It would explain a lot."

Agaam crossed his arms. "That would maybe explain the 'why', but not the 'how'. Had Ma'sao Oonai really wanted to revoke the decree, he wouldn't have just barged into the Jade Hall and screamed at officials. He would have done it smartly."

"The sane Jaaros Oonai, maybe, but not this one," Jespar said. "The pain he felt in the memory, that was more than just a nagging conscience—it was full-fledged desperation, and desperate people do desperate things." Jespar picked up a bronze disc from the table and turned it around in his hand. "Think about it: Oonai knew damn well that backing out of the plan at this stage was pure madness, especially since Vel'Nyx probably didn't share his sudden scruples. He must have agonized over this decision for weeks, all the while the death toll from the suicides kept climbing, and he knew *he* was responsible for them. Calling in that conference must have been an act of pure desperation, because he probably couldn't bear to look at himself in the mirror anymore."

Lysia pinched her lip. "Honestly, that sounds pretty far-fetched to me. I mean, Oonai calmly plans to drive people into suicide to radicalize the commoners, and then he goes remorseful all of a sudden? I don't buy it. Also, I'm not sure betting all our money on that one 'vision' you had is a good idea."

As if cued in by the word, Kawu looked up from his lap. "I'm sorry, but I disagree with the last part, ma'saa. Jespar *was* Oonai during that vision, so, in a way, it's the most valuable evidence we have. Whatever he saw and felt during those memories is taken right out of Oonai's mind."

Lysia raised her brows but said nothing else. When Jespar turned his attention away from her, he realized Agaam was studying him, a strange, assessing look in his good eye. The moment their gazes met, Agaam's brows narrowed and his jawline hardened, as though he were gritting his teeth. The expression was subtle and gone as fast as it had come, but something about it was unsettling—like a small current draft concealing a violent undertow.

"I think I understand where you're headed," Agaam said. "You believe that Vel'Nyx got wind of Oonai's doubts and had to stop him. Correct?"

Jespar's fingers cramped around the disc he'd been tossing between his hands. "She and the other conspirators, if there are any, yes.

Oonai was putting everything at risk, so they had to find a way to take him off the playing field."

"The dreameater."

"Yes. Think about it, until now, we thought the only advantage of infecting Oonai instead of just killing him is to see him suffer, but this changes things. The conspirators would have known killing Oonai at this stage of the plan would spark massive political unrest and an investigation. A coma, on the other hand ... it's the perfect solution."

Lysia rubbed her scar. "Hm. If you say it like that, it actually makes a lot of sense."

Encouraged, Jespar went on. "Personally, I think Vel'Nyx is our best bet. You were right, Agaam, backstabbing Oonai just to gain more power would have been too risky, but if he was planning to jeopardize everything, he gave her no choice. Not to mention that a woman with her means could get a hold of a dreameater and a psychomancer to imprint it upon her without a problem." He snorted. "I mean, you have to hand it to her, it's smart: she calls in a private meeting with Oonai and infects him, he falls into a coma, and the Ma'saa and the ziggurat staff are forced to keep it under wraps in order to prevent a power vacuum. Vel'Nyx gets exactly what she wanted. Time to finish the coup."

"But then what about Oonai's 'descent into madness?'" Kawu asked. "Does that mean ...?"

Jespar tossed the disc back onto the desk. "It probably never had anything to do with the parasite, no. That was just crippling guilt at work."

And you'd know all about that, wouldn't you?

A pause followed.

"If your theory is true," Agaam said, "then we have a problem. Vel'Nyx isn't on Kilay anymore."

Jespar went still. "What?"

"He's right," Lysia said. "Enkshi told us, remember? Vel'Nyx left for Arazeal because she was nervous about the Scythe."

Agaam nodded. "At least that's what she told everyone. If we're right about all this, she probably just fled the city because the riot is about to happen."

Jespar wrestled for words. The dread in the buried chest came back to life, its strikes now even stronger than before. "Then we need to catch up to her."

Lysia scoffed. "If she left a week ago? Forget it, she'll be far out on the Bygone Sea by now. Also, there's more than just one route to Arazeal, right?"

"Three," Agaam said.

Clang, clang, clang, went the lid. Tendrils of mist were crawling through the cracks now. "So we go by myrad," Jespar said. "A black one is five times faster than a ship."

Agaam shook his head. "We'd need to either buy or borrow one from the Coalition to do that, and it would take us at least a few days, including the journey back to Uunili. Not to mention it's next to impossible and incredibly dangerous to ride a myrad without training, especially at such a high speed and for days straight."

"Then bring in the Guard! We can just tell the Coalition about the coup!"

"Yes, and then what? Think this through, ma'sao. Even if the officials were to miraculously believe us with no questions asked, it would take them days to decide on a plan of action. And do you really think they'd go after a fugitive conspirator first? No, they wouldn't. They would focus on neutralizing the immediate danger, which means stopping the riot and the Scythe, and finding the inside men in the Guard. As far as Vel'Nyx is concerned, they'll simply order the embassy in Xarmon-Amar to have her arrested the day she sails into the harbor."

"But Oonai—"

"—is not their priority, *especially* if they believe he's involved in this. On the contrary, they'll be content to let him simmer in his own poison for just a little longer. And as far as your health is concerned, ma'sao, you're not important enough for them to care. Ma'saa Oonai can insist you're a divine emissary all she wants, but to the Coalition, you're just a pawn who got in over his head. I'm sorry, but that's how it is."

Jespar glared at Agaam for another heartbeat. Then his gaze dropped to the ground, his fingers digging into his trousers. The chest was shaking under the dread's punches now, the lid about to burst. He couldn't let it end like this. He couldn't, he wouldn't, he had to-

Kawu muttered something.

All faces turned toward him.

"Kawu?" Jespar asked hoarsely. "Did you say something?"

"I said, maybe there is another way." His words were slow and even. "We could confront Vel'Nyx in her kuluhika."

Agaam creased his forehead. "I thought you need to be close to the dreamer's body for the shift to work?"

"That's just the least straining way to do it. In theory, a dreamwalker can access any kuluhika from anywhere—locating it is the hard part. For example, if I tried to walk into the dream of someone on the Skarrag Isles, it would take me years in dreamtime to find it because our physical bodies are so far apart."

Jespar's mouth was dry as he answered; the dread kept punching on, but the strikes had grown weaker. "But someone on the Bygone Sea could work?"

"Maybe. It could take me weeks in the Imūma to find her, but it's possible."

Lysia sighed, massaging a temple with the ball of her thumb. "Just to be clear: you want to confront Vel'Nyx in her *own dream* and convince her to release the parasite?"

"Her simulacrum, yes," Kawu said. "In fact, that might even work to our advantage, because the human mind is extremely susceptible to manipulation while it's dreaming. If we do it right and don't break her immersion, she'll perceive us as part of her kuluhika, as part of herself, so to speak."

"And we could plant all sorts of ideas in her head," Jespar said. "That's good. That's really good."

Kawu nodded. Resolve was replacing the weariness in his features; the sight gave Jespar hope. "All we need is a Compass to guide me to her kuluhika."

"Like Ma'saa Oonai's marriage beads?" Agaam asked.

"Yes."

Jespar wiped the sweat from his brows. "Could we break into her ziggurat somehow?"

"Too heavily guarded," Agaam said. "Especially if she's expecting a riot. But maybe ... hm."

"What?" Lysia asked.

"The Magnate's Crown."

Jespar remembered: cold gold, seven prongs, on Oonai's nightstand. "Oonai's crown?"

"Well, technically speaking, it still belongs to the Coalition— the First Magnate only gets the privilege of wearing it. You probably don't know this, but when First Magnate Vel'Tani resigned and the officials elected his successor, Ma'saa Vel'Nyx lost the vote to Ma'sao Oonai by only five votes, despite being considered the presumptive nominee for decades."

Lysia plopped her lips. "You think she's still bitter about it."

"I do. Officially, she congratulated him and the two became allies, but I always thought that was only because she knew there was nothing to be gained from antagonizing the most powerful man in the country. If you ask me, she never stopped resenting Oonai for getting that crown."

Jespar scratched his beard. "And yet she planned a coup with him?"

"As I said earlier, she's the definition of a pragmatist—petty vengeance just isn't her style. What do you think, Ma'sao Nakāni? Could this work?"

A beat of silence. "We have to try."

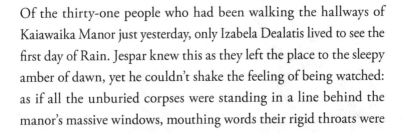

Of the thirty-one people who had been walking the hallways of Kaiawaika Manor just yesterday, only Izabela Dealatis lived to see the first day of Rain. Jespar knew this as they left the place to the sleepy amber of dawn, yet he couldn't shake the feeling of being watched: as if all the unburied corpses were standing in a line behind the manor's massive windows, mouthing words their rigid throats were unable to form. Jespar imagined they were warnings.

Warnings that the bloodshed had just begun.

PART TWO

RAIN

CHAPTER EIGHTEEN
FISH FLOOD

Day Six
1st Moon of Rainy Season, 1226 A.L.

At the tavern near Bluefort, Agaam untethered the unconscious Dealatis from his horse's back and carried her inside. It was early afternoon and clouds covered the sky.

"Will she be all right?" Kawu asked when Agaam returned alone.

"I gave the innkeeper a thousand sêr to see to her until she wakes up, and I promised him another thousand next week. She'll be fine."

Riding as fast as their horses allowed, they made it to the Mandibles by nightfall, where a violent downpour and strong winds forced them to a stop. They camped under a precipice, where they dined on cold rice, dried fish, and nuts, the rain lashing down around them. There was conversation, but Jespar only listened with one ear. The dread had gone silent since they'd settled on their plan, but he could still feel it lurking inside the chest.

After dinner, Kawu and Jespar went to the foot of the precipice, where Kawu anchored him. A tingle spread all the way from Jespar's head to his belly, some from the shift, some from Kawu's touch.

He's your lifeline.

When Kawu withdrew his hands, he looked exhausted: bloodless skin, a film of sweat on his forehead, shaking fingers.

"Are you okay?" Jespar asked.

"Yes," he said. "It's just been a little much. How are you feeling?"

Jespar turned inward. He felt as put together and rested as after ten hours of good sleep. "I'm great. Thanks, Kawu."

"Of course."

They were silent. Agaam was by the fire, prodding the logs with a stick, jaw tense and lips pressed together. Lysia sat at the shelter's edge and watched the rainfall.

"Jespar?"

"Mm?"

Kawu studied the ground. "Can we talk?"

Jespar smiled. "We are, aren't we?"

"No, I mean ... naiātē."

"Naiātē". Roughly translating as "alone between us," it was a phrase normally reserved for family, lovers, and close friends. Naka had sometimes used the word with Jespar.

"Um, sure." He squinted into the darkness. The rain made it hard to see far. "Where, though?"

Kawu gestured into the near distance. "There was another rock overhang a bit farther back. Just a stone's throw."

Jespar was tired to the bone but didn't hesitate a second. "Lead the way."

They told the others where they were going—prompting a nod from Agaam and a shrug from Lysia—and jogged out into the rain. It didn't take them long to find the shelter Kawu had described, an alcove under a small overhang that sunk into the rock like the cutout of a cockleshell. Soaked to the skin, they huddled inside it and watched the rain for a few moments, catching their breath.

"So?" Jespar asked. "What did you wanna talk about?"

"I ... It's probably silly."

"Color me intrigued."

Kawu absently took the rim of his poncho in hand and twisted the fabric around a finger. Raindrops beaded on the back of his hand. "My resonance. Do you ... I mean, do you really not feel it *at all*? I don't make you uncomfortable in the slightest?"

Kawu's resonance. After all that had happened, Jespar had almost forgotten about it. "No, Kawu. Not in the slightest."

"But ... I don't understand. Ever since my Cusping, I haven't met a single person who doesn't."

Jespar understood neither but couldn't have cared less. "Guess there's a first time for everything."

Kawu looked up to him, almost defensively, as if scrutinizing his expression for signs of a lie. At last, he exhaled and resumed ground-staring. "You know, there's this Makehu saying—'kaia 'ō kā teteie e māu kū.' Do you know it?"

"'Look out for ... the emotional fish.'"

Kawu snorted. "Not quite. I suppose the closest you could get in Inâl is 'beware of fish flood feelings.' It means to be wary of sudden strong emotions because they are often like fish floods."

"What is that? A 'fish flood'?"

"Right, how would you know. It's a rare weather event here in the Archipelago. The ocean suddenly withdraws and then swoops back in, like a rapid change of the tides. In our faith, fish floods happen when Īmīte and Okokepe fight out in the sea—if Īmīte wins, the flood doesn't go far inland and often leaves piles of fresh fish along the shores that the villages can feast on for weeks. If Okokepe wins ..."

"The flood wreaks havoc on the islands?"

"Yes. What the saying teaches is that unexpected, strong emotions are often just like that ... they come fast and leave either a treasure or a trail of devastation."

Beware of sudden emotions. Shelving the line as a suitable epitaph for his tombstone, Jespar couldn't help a grin. "I'm guessing this is a reference to the two of us?"

Kawu blushed and looked away. He twisted the poncho tighter around his finger.

"Sorry, I didn't mean to—"

"No ... No, it's fine. I actually admire how openly you talk about things. I was never good at that."

Jespar suppressed a snort. *If only you knew.*

"Personally, I've always wondered how you can tell if a fish flood will bring treasure or havoc," Kawu went on. "I mean, if you feel something, how can you tell whether it's real and lasting, or fleeting and destructive?"

"Hm." Jespar looked off into the rain. It had strengthened, as though determined to drown all of Uunili. "Do you want an honest answer to that?"

"Please."

"I don't think you can split it up like that, 'real and lasting' or 'fleeting and destructive.' Sometimes, something that lasts isn't real and is destructive, and sometimes, something is real but doesn't last. I mean, there are cases where everything works out just the way you imagined it, but they're very rare. The way I see it, the only thing you can tell right from the start is whether something feels right to you or not. If you want to find out the rest, you just have to take the plunge and risk failure."

"And that thought doesn't scare you at all? I mean, to know that even if something feels right and real in the moment, there's absolutely no telling what will happen if you give in to it?"

It did scare him. The intensity of his emotions. Not knowing where this would lead. The fear of hurting Kawu the way he'd hurt so many.

"Maybe," Jespar said. "But at some point, you have to stop agonizing over the what-ifs. Nothing in life is certain."

"Hm." Kawu let go of the poncho and exhaled softly. "Oh, Ĭmīte, I'm doing this all wrong, aren't I? Here I am, overthinking and talking everything to death instead of just saying what I ..." He broke off and looked at Jespar, his eyes a deep green pool of curiosity, hope, longing, and fear.

Jespar put his arm around Kawu and drew him close. This time, Kawu didn't tense. He just eased into the embrace and rested his head on Jespar's shoulder as if it were the most natural thing in the world.

"You don't have to say anything."

Kawu muttered something and edged closer. Warmth filled Jespar, putting a smile on his lips he would have had considered impossible only hours ago. The parasite, the dread, the fear—they were all still there. But Kawu allowed him to look elsewhere.

"Stay," Kawu whispered. "Please, Jespar. Stay."

"Yeah," Jespar said. "I will."

There were a hundred things they could have spoken about as they sat there, huddled in the cockleshell alcove while the rain roared down around them: things Jespar wanted to ask, like where Kawu had gotten that little scar on his chin Jespar had only just discovered, or what his mother had been like back when she had still been healthy. Things Jespar wanted to tell him, jokes to make him laugh, travel anecdotes to kindle his imagination, stories to make him ponder. He also wanted to tell him about all the dark mud the current had whirled up inside him since his journey to Kilay, that mud Jespar had tried so hard to convince he had washed away years ago.

Soon, Jespar thought as he closed his eyes.

Soon he would tell Kawu everything, but not now; right now, there was nothing to be done and nothing to be said, because Kawu had asked Jespar to stay, and that was all that mattered. Jespar felt sleep approach, but he wasn't afraid. There would be no nightmares, no swamp court, and no Corpse, because Kawu kept them away.

Kito nū'i kei kuio e li.

He'd tell him everything. When all this was over.

INTERLUDE
THE MAN

SIXTEEN DAYS BEFORE
4TH MOON OF DRY SEASON, 1226 A.L.

As the man lays out his plan to revoke the decree, it's likely only his stature that stops the officials from bursting into laughter. He grows irritated at first, then angry, until he ends his speech screaming. He knows it's a mistake even as he does it—emotion is a powerful rhetorical tool, but only when used judiciously. Calculated anger can be terrifying. Tantrums and hysteria are pathetic.

A ballot is called. The clerk reads the results aloud.

Of the five hundred officials, only forty-two support his proposition.

The man leaves the conference hall and flees into his private office on the top floor of the Council of Commerce. Shaking all over, he sinks into the wingback chair behind his five thousand sêr mahogany desk.

The man stares at the floor for minutes, the ivory tiles reflecting the majestic sunset.

A knock on the door.

"Enter," the man forces himself to say.

It's the Second Magnate. His excessive jewelry and his choice of navy-blue kohl remind the man of his friend. His friend: he wishes he were here but knows he couldn't look him in the eye if he were. Despite his advanced age, the Second Magnate's outfit—poison-green popped-collar coat with a white cravat and neatly cut pants of the same color—is the latest fashion, making the man painfully aware of his own jumbled attire. What had he been thinking?

The Second Magnate gently closes the door, then saunters over, casually eyeing the room as if admiring the architecture.

"You look tired, old friend," he says.

"Say what you want and get the hell out of here."

Fool. You *never* start a conversation with insults. It makes you seem rash and the other person reasonable.

The magnate studies the man with an infuriating mixture of curiosity and pity. Then he smooths the cuffs of his coat. "I shall be brief, then. If something like this ever happens again, you'll resign."

The man stares.

The magnate smiles.

"You're threatening me." Whether it is surprise or the sheer absurdity of the situation, it comes out calm and even, a touch of the man's old self—before the black fog turned him into a screaming maniac.

The Second Magnate hesitates, but merely a second. He pulls a scroll from his coat. "Here, read this." A pause. "If you will."

Five minutes later, the man's disbelief and anger are gone.

"If a member ever acts against the interests of the Coalition, it may issue a vote of no confidence," the magnate says. He stands with his back resting against one of the windows, the sky a bloody contusion over the gleaming white city behind him. "And I daresay revoking a decree you initiated and paying a fortune of 'reparations' to a bunch of angry have-nots qualifies. Wouldn't you agree?"

The man says nothing. He knows this. Of course he does, because it was he who pushed for this legislation in the first place, to prevent the conservative wing from "halting progress".

How in the world did he forget?

"Let me be clear, old friend: I have nothing but respect and admiration for your achievements, and I mean that. Your recent actions, however ... missing conferences, public tantrums, and now this." He clicks his tongue. "Let's just say they don't seem quite in character. What is it you're trying to do, exactly? Turn our country into a charity house?"

"It was a mistake," the man mutters.

"That fiasco down there? Indeed, it was."

"No, the decree. The decree was a mistake."

"Why? Tell me again, old friend, calmly, then maybe I'll understand."

Another order, the man thinks. He can't let that stand. He opens his mouth, intending to put this man in his place, to regain his authority, but the moment his lips part, the black fog seizes control, and his mouth moves on its own. "Because it's evil."

"'Evil'," the magnate repeats. He says like a parent reacting to his son saying he met the Moon Kobold.

"Yes, evil." A tremble steals into the man's voice. "We deprived the poor of what little they had left, just so we could become even richer. And then, when they decided that no life at all is better than one without dignity or hope, we laughed in their faces and watched them jump." He makes a strange sound at the back of his throat, half a croak, half a scoff. "We *laughed* and *watched them jump*."

The magnate's expression is a blank wall. "You're talking about the suicides."

"You know *damn* well what I'm talking about."

More swearing, more insults. *Stop, stop,* stop!

"If I remember correctly, the words 'to kill oneself' imply volition," the magnate says. "The rules got harder, yes, but it's not our fault those people chose to flip the playing board instead of—"

"*Fuck you!*"

This time, even the Second Magnate seems shocked. Inside the man, something winces, curses, tries to halt him, but it's pointless. The fog has him, prods him, spurs him on.

"For fuck's sake, you're as rotten as the fuckin' rest! Godsdammit, how can ye be so blind, it's *us, we're* the sickness, *we're* the destroyers, and I can't live like this anymore, I just ... I ... I ..." He claws his hands into his temples, the tears burning his lids. "Gods, I just want to stop feelin' this way, *I just want it to fuckin' stop!*"

For a time, the man's sobs fill the room. When the magnate speaks again, he sounds different. Until now, a wary kind of respect lingered behind his challenging tone. Now, it's all flatness and unease, the way one speaks to a battle-shocked soldier who just had a breakdown.

"Clear your mind, old friend. Go home to your wife, say some prayers, see a physician." He steps toward the door. His hand lingers on the handle as he casts the man a final look. "I was your supporter back when they still called you 'Fish Boy'. But if this continues, I'll be the first to toss you back into the gutter. Are we clear?"

Back home, the man writes the Third Magnate a letter and requests a meeting right away. She agrees to tomorrow, alone and on neutral ground.

He locks the door, drops onto his bed, and prays for sleep. It doesn't come.

A pond near the ziggurat. Frogs croak, crickets sing, a breeze makes the high-Drought heat bearable. She awaits him on a stone bench by the shingle, clad in her trademark gray vicuna robes that match her hair, hands buried in the opposite sleeves. *A dagger?* It's not unlikely. She probably thinks he's here to kill her.

"Well?" she asks. Her eyes, a cool brown in their wrinkled sockets, are as cryptic as always.

Remembering his disastrous conversation with the Second Magnate, the man does his best to rein in the fog and summons what little composure it has left him.

No insults. No anger. Control.

He tells her they have to call off the plan. Too much collateral damage, too much bloodshed—it would tear a wound in the Archipelago that could never heal. She listens, her gaze lingering on her lap. When he's done, it wanders off to the pond.

Speak, he thinks. *Just speak.*

She turns back and puts an arm across his shoulder.

For her—a woman who, as the sailors joke, has seen more cunts than a cathouse and fewer cocks than a convent—it's a gesture so unusual the man tenses at first, expecting her to follow up with a stab of that dagger she's undoubtedly hiding. The thought doesn't scare him. Death while trying to atone? There's worse.

No stab comes.

"Not in a million years."

The man opens his mouth. Closes it.

"There was plenty of time for doubt," she says. "But it's too late now. And even if it weren't, how do you intend to stop it now? This isn't a banquet, my friend. We can't just call it off because we feel like it."

"We could muzzle the general and have the Blue Guard deal with those mercenary freaks."

"I assume you're talking about the Twins. We don't know where they are."

"So what, we'll find out. Bloody hell, they're working for us."

She shakes her head with a sad smile, the kind a tutor gives a foolish pupil. "Even if that were to work, what about the foot soldiers? The Scythe has thousands of followers by now, true followers who believe they're fighting for a better world. Do you really think they'll lay down their pitchforks and merrily go about their way just because their leaders have suddenly disappeared? If anything, they'll think the Coalition tracked them down and murdered them, which will only rile them up further."

"Kill the shepherd and the sheep scatter."

"A striking metaphor, but sadly unfitting. If anything, we're dealing with wolves here, and ravenous ones at that. They're radical, have hideouts on every island, and, courtesy of ours truly, an entire cutting-edge arsenal at their disposal. Be realistic, if we remove the leaders, they'll just find themselves new ones who won't let their forces saunter right into the general's trap." She withdraws her arm, her fingers brushing against the nape of the man's neck. "And all that is not even considering the risk that the Twins might decide to spill the beans if they realize we're planning to backstab them. There's a lot of money to be made in revealing a conspiracy—even a failed one, don't you think?"

"We could at least try," the man insists. "For all we know, the Twins might decide to talk even if the plan succeeds, so what's the difference?"

"The difference, my dear friend, is that we'll be in power when the plan succeeds, and where there's no judge, there is no hangman."

The man has no reply.

Her tone softens. "Look, you're clearly not thinking straight. Something has gotten into you, and it has clouded your judgment. I mean, when was the last time you took a look at yourself? You look and smell like you've taken a swim in the sewers."

"... You don't get it," the man says quietly. "You just don't understand."

"No, I truly don't." She slides her hands back into her sleeves. "But what I do understand is that we're in this together. And I will not let you drag me down with you because you've suddenly decided to pursue a career in sainthood."

The man makes that throaty sound again, half croak, half scoff. "A saint? That's what you think this is about?"

"Frankly, I don't know what this is about anymore."

"How about not becoming a monster?"

She looks surprised. Chuckles.

Anger rises. "You think this is funny?"

"You already are."

"What?"

"You heard me: you already *are* a 'monster', as am I." She chuckles again. "See, this is the part of you I was never quite able to wrap my head around. Even back then, when we were sauntering through that lovely hedge maze and calmly discussed sacrificing thousands of people for our little adventure, you always found a way to bend the story so you're still the good guy. 'I'm doing this to protect myself,' 'the world is an arena and we're the champions,' 'they'd do the same,' blah-blah-blah. You know, it took me a while to realize that you were actually serious about this nonsense, and even now, I simply don't see why you bother. Is it about pride? Sometimes, I wonder if that's all men are about." She sighs and brushes a strand of gray hair from her forehead. "Well, I hate to crush your fantasies, my dear friend, but if recklessly prioritizing your life over the lives of others is what makes a monster, then that's what we are."

It is a while until the man recovers his words.

"You admit to it?" he asks hoarsely. "Being a monster?"

She shrugs. "I suppose. I've always found it amusing how desperate we humans are to label and judge. Would you cry for the deer the wolves tear apart? No, there we say it's the natural order of things." She shakes her head. "We humans are no different: the strong eat the weak. There's nothing prideful about it and nothing noble, it's simply the way it is."

Sweat beads on the man's forehead, and his irises burn. *Don't*, he thinks. *Don't cry.* Thoughts race through his mind, elaborate card-house arguments of why she's wrong about him, but the fog topples them before he can put them into words. When he speaks at last, all he manages is, "How? How can you live like this?"

A thin smile. "Frankly? Quite well." She stands and smooths her robes. "If suffering is what you're concerned about, remember that stopping the plan at this stage will only cause more of it. Feel free to be as saintly as you want once the coup is through, but for now, your idealism would only ensure our mutual downfall. If the Coalition finds out about this, they'll string us up over the ponds, pour honey onto our lovely buttocks, and have the insects eat us alive."

The man doesn't lift his eyes. "And if I don't care about that?"

"Then you should keep in mind that your precious little wife and your crippled friend would be strung up right beside us."

She's already a few strides away when the man calls out after her. "I'll find a way. With or without you."

She glances over her shoulder. "And I'll be prepared."

The man stays on the bench for a long time. Only when a ghostly blue stripe on the horizon heralds the onset of dawn does he return to the ziggurat and locks himself into one of its two hundred and fifty-seven rooms, those dead crypt-like places no soul has ever felt at home in. He lies on the ebony bed and stares at the ceiling.

He is the First Magnate.

He is the richest man in the Illumined World. He is a god. How can it be so hard to do *good*?

There is a solution. There must be. And he won't leave this room until he finds it.

CHAPTER NINETEEN
PROTECTOR

The mushy roads made for rough going, so it was early afternoon when they reached the spurs of Mount Ilakato. Several arduous hours of uphill ride followed, then the jungle gave way to shrubs and grass, and they were back on the path along the mountain's ridge they had embarked upon three days ago. After a while of silent trot, Agaam let his horse fall back into step beside Jespar's.

"I believe I owe you an explanation, ma'sae."

Lysia, riding a little ahead of Jespar, glanced up. Kawu's eyes were stuck on the road, glassy and framed by dark circles.

"You do?" asked Jespar.

"Yes. You deserve to know the full picture, especially in light of recent events." He spoke in his trademark calm, but there was a hint of defensiveness in his words, an emotion that seemed out of place for him.

"As you know by now, I'm more than just an ordinary servant—my background is in the military—the Jade Snakes, to be precise. I was their general until a certain incident."

"What incident?" Jespar asked.

"It's irrelevant. All you need to know is that the Coalition axed me and took away my pension in response to said incident and that I would have spent the rest of my days in poverty or as some second-rate sellsword if it hadn't been for Ma'sao Oonai. He hired me to serve as his personal protector."

"Personal protector," Lysia echoed.

"I wasn't his pet assassin if that's what you're thinking. Hard as that may be to believe considering what we just found out, Oonai used to strongly oppose these 'tactics'. My job was to keep him and the Ma'saa safe and give counsel when needed." Agaam squinted toward the jungle that carpeted the slope and the valley, pure green except for the occasional village and the yellow and violet rows of banana and nightflower plantations. "He wasn't always a bad man."

A katako landed on the mane of Jespar's horse. He shooed it away. "And how do you feel about him now?"

Agaam scoffed. "Oh, please, ma'sao, just say it as it is: Jaaros Ismi-rael Oonai has become a terrible man. I'm many things, but I'm not delusional."

"And yet you still work for him," Lysia said.

"I do. It feels wrong to say it after what we just learned, but Oonai isn't as one-dimensional as you may think. Yes, he is merciless toward his enemies, but he is also incredibly loyal and generous toward his trusted ones and employees. If I had to pinpoint when his 'moral flexibility' started going too far, it was probably when a beggar tried to murder his wife, and his mother died from womb fleshrot shortly after." Agaam paused. "Things just spun out of control. Those forces that had always driven him—his relentless quest for power and his fear of losing his livelihood, they became more and more extreme and—"

"I'm sorry," Lysia said. "But are you seriously trying to excuse what your master did? Orchestrating mass murder?"

"He was *never* my master." The anger in Agaam's words came so suddenly Jespar flinched. Lysia stared at her horse's mane.

Agaam sighed. "Please forgive me. I'm ... I'm not quite myself lately. You pose a valid question, of course, and, no, I am not telling you this to excuse anything—trust me, far from it. I suppose what I'm trying to say is that I've always been aware of the dark potential in Ma'sao Oonai. Frankly, that's the true reason I agreed to work for him, to limit the damage. If I hadn't taken the job, one of the thousand yes-men and bootlickers who surrounded him would have, and there would have been no one to rein him in when he was in danger of making a mistake." He scoffed softly. "At least that's what I was trying to do. Considering all this, it's clear that I fa—"

He buckled over.

For a second, Jespar didn't understand. Then he saw the feather-tail stuck in Agaam's chest. A crossbow bolt, right to the heart.

Shit.

A second bolt whirred and sunk into Agaam's horse's flank. It neighed and bolted down the slope.

Lysia's scream pierced the air. "*Go!*"

Jespar snapped out of his stupor.

He yanked his horse around full turn—glimpsing three black-clad riders on a rise to their right—and spurred it. Bolt after bolt whipped past him as Jespar hurtled back the way they'd come, hoof-to-hoof with Lysia's horse; Kawu was up ahead. The next moment, the jungle swallowed them, and they were crashing down an overgrown path, branches whipping him; not before his horse's gait became jerky and it wheezed from the exertion did Jespar slow down enough to glance over his shoulder.

The road was deserted.

Jespar brought his steppe-runner down to a fast trot, blinking to clear the stinging sweat from his eyes. Lysia was still a bit ahead, but he couldn't see Kawu.

"Are they gone?" Lysia, too, had slowed her horse, the steed's massive flanks heaving with its fast breaths.

"... I think so." Jespar took stock of his surroundings. Jungle all around. No Kawu. "Where's Kawu?"

"I'm sure he's fine—he was in front of me, so he can't be far. Let's find him."

They found him further up the jungle path, sitting stiffly on his horse. Hands shaking, he was clutching the reigns so hard the white on his knuckles stood out, and his eyes darted about the thicket like those of a frightened animal. A hollow feeling settled in Jespar's gut.

"Hey," he said as he led his horse up beside Kawu. "Hey, it's all right. They're gone, we're safe."

Kawu turned his head. "They killed Ma'sao Agaam. They killed him."

"We don't know that," Jespar said. "We'll go look for him."

Lysia joined them. "I hate to say it, but that's a bad idea. We'd have to search the entire mountainside, and chances are those hitmen are trying to find him as well. I'm pretty sure they were after him, not us."

"What, so we just let him die? He saved our asses back in the manor, Lysia."

"I'm aware. But he also got a bloody crossbow bolt to the heart and his horse is probably dragging him through the jungle with one foot in the stirrups as we speak. As a physician, I can tell you the odds of surviving that are damn low. Also, we *really* can't afford to lose more time, for your sake."

Realizing she was right, Jespar sighed and rubbed his forehead. "Okay, okay. I don't think those were hitmen, though."

"Why not?"

"Because assassins don't usually wear all black; it only draws attention. Remember the Scythes from the inn at Bluefort? They had the same clothes, didn't they?"

"Fuck. You're right." A red bird zipped through the air above them, disappearing in the treetops. "Why would the Scythe attack Agaam, though? I mean, unless we got everything wrong, they're acting under Oonai's command, aren't they?"

A dark suspicion stirred somewhere in Jespar's thoughts, but it passed too quickly for him to grasp it. "Maybe Vel'Nyx ordered it, or maybe they were acting on their own. Either way, it doesn't matter, we need to get to the ziggurat. I say we go through the ci—"

The Pull struck with the speed of a viper. His mind slipped away, the world blurred, his vision turned blue.

He snapped back.

Jespar hung sideways in the saddle, Lysia's elbows hooked under his armpits. Kawu's hands were on his temples, warmth radiating from the tips of his fingers.

"Jespar? Jespar, ete ite 'ī?"

Nodding feebly, he slowly heaved himself upright, his side aching from the sudden stretch. The pulse of the Pull was abating.

Lysia let go. "That was one of those seizures you were talking about, wasn't it? The 'Pull'?"

"... Yeah."

"I don't understand," she said to Kawu. "I thought you anchored him this morning?"

"I did, yes, less than ten hours ago. I didn't think ... I mean, it shouldn't have—"

"It's growing faster than we thought." How calm Jespar felt saying this; as if the dread had decided to spare him, knowing the dreame-ater's victory was now inevitable.

Lysia stared at him, as if waiting for a "but". When Jespar remained silent, she slowly turned her head to Kawu. "And anchoring him more often will put his brain at risk." It was a statement, not a question.

Kawu nodded feebly. "I will try to increase the frequency to every six hours. But more than that ..." He broke off. "We need to hurry."

Lysia squinted into the distance, up Mount Ilakato. The First Ziggurat was a white, ghostly palace on its peak. "Then we better ride fucking fast."

They reached the main road of Uunili Bay's northern farmlands without further incidents; the dense jungle still occluded most of the city from sight. It was there that Jespar could not deny the hunch he'd had for a while now any longer.

Something is wrong.

The road should have been teeming with travelers. It was deserted. Trading glances, they followed it southward until Jespar spotted a group of people blocking the path.

He pulled his horse to a stop. "Look."

Lysia did, shielding herself from the westering sun. "Looks like commoners to me. But—"

"—what the hell is a group of commoners doing lollygagging in the middle of a road on an ordinary evening?" Jespar finished her sentence.

One of the peasants noticed them. He was leaning on something—a walking staff or a spear?

Spear.

"Fall back," Jespar said. "Slowly."

Turning their horses around as inconspicuously as they could, they backtracked to the last crossing and discussed how to proceed. In the end, they settled for Lysia's suggestion to follow a lesser-known path along the shoreline and enter Uunili via the harbor.

An hour later, smoke began to rise from the rooftops of the Alabaster City.

The riot had begun.

CHAPTER TWENTY
HAY BOY

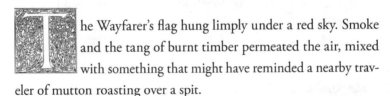he Wayfarer's flag hung limply under a red sky. Smoke and the tang of burnt timber permeated the air, mixed with something that might have reminded a nearby traveler of mutton roasting over a spit.

It's not mutton.

The thought was dull and distant, like a voice muffled by walls.

How had it happened? Only an hour ago, everything had been normal. Now the world had turned upside down and nothing made sense anymore.

They were guardians.

They protected villages from raiders and refugees from highwaymen, they dug wells and rebuilt farms, they brought food to the hungry. That's what the Chancellor had hired them for, to tend to the wounds this long and pointless war kept tearing into the border region between North and South, so that the Northern Army could deal with the Loons and their mad prophet.

A scream.

Jespar numbly turned his head. A comrade he didn't recognize was pressing a woman against a wall, tearing her skirt off. A villager burst out of a burning house, made five steps until an axe cut him down. Its wielder, a wiry woman with wiry black hair tossed Jespar a blank look, then sank to her haunches and went through the man's pockets as he choked on his own blood. *Ewah.* She was in Jespar's unit. They had joked around at the campfire last night.

A foolish impulse to talk to her, to patiently explain why what she was doing was wrong, overcame him. He stood right where he was. Ewah got up and stomped hard on the man's neck. He went still.

Naka, Jespar thought.

He had to find Naka and get out of here. Naka had gone to guard the northern entrance, with Volker, Jorik, and Wilma, the pretty young redhead he had unsuccessfully flirted with last night.

Find Naka. Get out of here.

Jespar sheathed his sword and tightened his blue scarf. He stepped over the man with the breadbasket, whose scowl had started this madness, and went looking for Naka.

The search was a hazy dream. His eyes perceived the fires, but he didn't see. His ears noted the screams, but he didn't listen. His nose smelled the charred flesh, but he ignored what it meant. People rushed past him, but nobody paid him attention, as if his trance had turned him into a ghost.

The northern gate was deserted. Unscathed by the fires, eerily silent, and with the bucolic panorama of wheat fields extending beyond the village border, a surreal air cloaked the place, like a pale blue spot on a painting of hell.

Find Naka. Get out of here.

It was when he turned around that he noticed the sobs. Why they managed to pierce through his apathy while the hundreds of screams and wails didn't, he could not say. Maybe because of how soft they were. Maybe because of the deep grunts that mixed between them.

A heartbeat went by.

Sob, grunt.

Two.

Sob, grunt.

Three.

Find Naka. Get out of here.

Jespar followed the sounds.

The cottage they came from was only a few strides from the gate. With a thatched straw roof, crude but endearing kobold sculptures adorning the porch, and its dark wood walls, it might have looked inviting had it not been for the cacophony from uptown, and the toppled potato basket by the entrance.

Sob, grunt. Sob, grunt. Sob, grunt.

Find Naka. Get out of here.

A pressure formed around Jespar's neck, like a phantom noose. Cold spread in his gut and his ankles prickled. Somewhere deep inside him, a voice begged him to turn around and leave, to just head back to camp and pretend none of this had ever happened. It was the same one that had urged him not to enter his sister's room that day in the summer.

Jespar went in.

The brain works in curious ways: with sunlight drenching the room, the scene should have been clear from the start—yet Jespar noticed the details first.

First, the clay shards and the broken chair on the floor. Then the dead man in the corner and the two figures bent over the table, big and small, a man and a woman.

First, her bright red hair and how many freckles she had. Then that she was far too young to be called a woman, her tears, and how she winced with the man's thrusts.

First, the Wayfarer's crest on the man's cuirass. Then how familiar he looked, with his broad, beardless face and the painted flames around his eye sockets.

Naka glanced up and froze.

There was no shame. No shame, no surprise, no trace of that animal look war apparently brought out in soldiers. It was just Naka.

The girl wrenched free, darted into the adjacent room, and shut the door. Naka didn't move. He just stood there and gawked, his pants down to his knees and his cock going flaccid.

He pulled up his pants. "Wilō—"

Jespar tackled him.

They crashed down on the floor, rolled and struggled; Jespar ended on top. Naka grunted and tried to wrestle him off, but Jespar punched him in the face, he cried out, Jespar punched again, and again, and again.

Pain.

Jespar screamed and buckled over—a shard stuck in his thigh— Naka seized him by the collar and smashed his forehead into Jespar's nose.

The world spun.

Naka loomed over him, his tree-trunk legs pinning Jespar's arms. A blood-smeared fist flew toward him and sunk into his mouth, splitting his lips.

"To ite tēmī!" Naka screamed. Another fist. "To ite ūkonō tēmī!"

Another, another, another. Blood filled Jespar's eyes, trickled into his mouth and made him gag. *This is the end,* he thought; beaten to death by Naka, beaten to death by his friend, his comrade, his brother.

The punches stopped.

Naka was still on top of him, his palms flat on Jespar's chest, tears on his cheeks, and his lips miming as though he wanted to say something but couldn't. Jespar's skull was ablaze, and his ears rang like someone had struck a temple bell right beside him.

"Tēmī—" Naka began.

Jespar swept up a shard of glass from the ground and rammed it into Naka's hip. Naka cried out, toppled over. Ignoring the tempest of pain, Jespar hurled him the rest of the way off, rolled to his side, gripped Naka's shoulders, and slammed his knee into Naka's groin. Then he got on top, tore the glass shard from Naka's hip, and slashed it across his brother's throat.

At least that's what he *tried* to; his hand stopped halfway.

He's Naka.

He's a monster.

He's Naka.

He raped her.

He's Naka!

He killed her father and fucking raped *her in front of his corpse!*

But Jespar's muscles wouldn't oblige.

When Naka's eyes met his, quiet anger seethed beneath his tears. "Come on, Etōkoka, just do it. Get it fucking over with." *Etōkoka.* Short for "pi'a e etōkoka," "the boy with parched-grass hair." Naka's nickname for Jespar.

Crying from behind the door. The girl.

"Why?" Jespar managed. "This isn't right, Naka, this *isn't* fucking right!"

Naka scowled. "They were hiding a Loon. If you hadn't thrown that knife, he would have blown us all to pieces."

"It wasn't tyenite, it was a *breadbasket*! Fuck, Naka, that guy wasn't a Loon, he was a civ!" Images assailed him, a hot, red gust. The man jostling through the crowd, scowling at Jespar, hiding something under his cloak. A rush of panic. A throwing knife in the man's chest, bread tumbling over the hardpan. Hell breaking loose.

Jespar sobbed, clutched the shard. "I just don't get it, I don't fucking get it! Why did everyone go fucking mad?"

Naka's stare didn't waver. "He. Was. A Loon."

"*We don't know!*"

"Okay, and what if?" Naka burst out. "Ūkonō, do you really think those cunts didn't *want* to kill us? They hate us! We came here to help and all these woolheads ever do is fucking sneer! Wake up, Etōkoka, they're all fucking Loons down south, and if it was our corpses out there right now, they would have cut off our cocks and tossed them to their fucking pigs! You already forget what that farmer did to Kristen, huh? These cunts are all the same, they're fucking crazy and they had it coming!"

Jespar stared, chewing on Naka's words. Then he pressed the shard harder against Naka's neck, droplets of blood blossoming on his skin. "That girl too? You think she had it coming, you think she would have 'tossed your cock to the fucking pigs?'"

Naka's grin died.

His eyes fixed on some corner of the ceiling. When they came back, they had changed. Yes, they were still his, with that quicksilver brown that could go from smirk to sadness within seconds, but there was something else in them, something wolfish and cold. Was it new? Or had it always been there, and Jespar simply hadn't seen it?

Naka's voice was as bleak as his gaze. "All right. All right, if you're so fucking holy, then why don't you go on out there and save those poor peasants? Huh? Go on, noble Etōkoka, be a hero and throw your life away for someone who hates you even though all you ever did was try to *bloody* help."

You're dodging the question, Jespar wanted to say. *You're dodging the fucking question!* But the words wouldn't form. Jespar just kept staring, transfixed by this new and alien look in his friend's familiar eyes.

"Yeah, didn't think you would." Naka sat up slowly, leaning back on his elbows. Jespar dug the shard harder into his neck, but Naka didn't stop moving. "It's all bullshit, Etōkoka. Everyone acts like they're so bloody righteous, but when you throw us into the pit, we're all the same. Just fucking animals waiting to go rabid." His lips split in a grin, his teeth tinged purple by years of nightflower addiction and red by blood. "And you know what? That's twice as true for people like us. That dark stain we got on our souls, Etōkoka, it turns us into a plague that causes bad shit to happen wherever we go. And maybe it's time you finally accept that. Some people build and some people destr—"

Jespar's slammed his elbow into Naka's face.

Silence.

Heartbeat after heartbeat went by as Jespar sat there, staring at his former friend. Naka, who had taught him Makehu. Naka, who laughed at every one of Jespar's jokes, no matter how dumb they were. Naka, who never talked about his past and snored like a bloody walrus.

Naka, his brother.

Jespar closed his fist around the shard. It hurt like hell, but he only clutched harder, like a shipwrecked traveler holding fast to a piece of flotsam. When he finally dropped it, blood flooded down his wrist.

He looked at the door across the room. The girl's crying had ceased, but the sobs were still there, jagged and sharp like she was sinking and gasping for air. He'd heard those sobs before. They were the sobs of someone who had died but was still breathing.

You promised, Jes. You promised.

Bad shit happens wherever we go.

Go on, save them.

When had he, Jespar Dal'Varek, ever changed anyone's life for the better?

He stormed out of the cottage and ran for the fields. That night, sleeping alone under a cedar tree, Jespar dreamt of the Corpse for the first time.

Chapter Twenty-One
The Dream Is a Lie

Day Six
1st Moon of Rainy Season, 1226 A.L.

"espar?" a voice said.

The noose was tight, his breathing fast and ragged.

"What's the matter with him?" the voice asked. A woman. "Is it the bug?"

"I don't know," a man replied. "I don't think so."

The woman's answer dissolved in a blur.

"I'm okay," Jespar said in what was almost a whisper. "I'm okay."

"Jespar?"

"I'm okay. Everything's all right."

He meant to sound firm, but it came out shaky. Jespar's mind crept back into the present; the phantom noose let go, feeling returned to his fingers.

You're here.

The war was over, and this wasn't Nehrim.

The year was 1226 After Light, and he was in Kilay.
Jespar tried to remember what had happened.

The harbor gate stood open. Instead of soldiers, a dozen commoners guarded it, some in civilian clothes, some in black uniforms. As
there was no other way into the inner city, Jespar, Lysia, and Kawu
slowed their horses to a walk, doing their best to hide their unease.

"What's yer business?" a uniformed woman asked.

Jespar squinted through the gate. The harbor was as deserted as
the road to the city.

"I asked ye a bloody question."

"The dream is a lie," Jespar said. "We're mercs. We're on your side."

It was improvised, but it seemed to do the trick. The woman's
frown relaxed. Another Scythe joined them. "If yer with us, how
come I ain't never seen ye before?"

Lysia came to Jespar's aid. "We're from Paiolu and were told to
come here, but our ship was held up. If you'd rather we head back to
Southport and have a drink on the pockets of the Twins, sure thing."

The woman mulled it over. "Fine. Go in and follow the Road 'til
ye find the crowd. One of our brothers is gonna tell ye what to do."

They went in.

With the streets deserted, the windows barred, and smoke rising
in the distance, the harbor felt like an omen of the things to come.
When they climbed the harbor switchbacks, the outmost circles of
the Steel District opened before them, and the visceral reality of the
destruction sunk in. A torched house, a woman wailing in front of
the doorstep. A well-dressed man in a puddle of blood, bludgeoned
beyond recognition. A bathhouse, the windows shattered, the word
"LEECH" smeared onto the façade.

They found the first traces of a skirmish at a town square not far from the Great Bazaar, well into the wealthier parts of the Steel District: the wooden gazebo in its center was on fire, corpses cluttered on the cobblestone around it, commoners and guards in puddles of blood.

Jespar froze. His stomach curled, his fingers prickled. A sharp tang filled the air, charred flesh and burnt tinder, too close to his nostrils to be real.

No. No, this isn't Nehrim. This isn't Nehrim. This isn't-

A sob.

The noose pulled tight.

"Hey. Hey, are you listening?"

Jespar snapped out of his trance. "Sorry. What did you say?"

"I said, we've gotta stop by the clinic." Lysia was looking northward, toward the big city gate in whose shadow her clinic was built. Her mouth twitched. "I'm sure everything's all right, but I need to know."

The clinic.

Of course.

"Okay."

Lysia took the lead. Her clinic was in a far poorer district than the burning town square, yet somehow—perhaps because it was farther up the slope—the destruction was worse. Corpses on the road were the rule and not the exception; every other shop or house had been vandalized or torched. People strayed, ran, or limped in and out of the buildings and alleys with shock, horror, confusion, and apathy on their faces. The din in the distance lost its shapeless quality and became a weave of roaring fires, crashing, clanging, and, above all, thundering voices. *The mob.* They were chanting something, but Jespar couldn't make out the words.

Lysia had started out at a leisurely pace, but by the time they reached the little alley that led to her clinic, she'd brought her horse to a canter. At first sight of the poppy red building, Jespar felt relief. No smoke, no fire, no smashed windows. The mob had spared the clinic. *And why wouldn't they?* Lysia had spent the past five years of her life treating them for free, ignoring her growing pile of debts.

Then Jespar saw two men hurrying out the clinic's doorway, carrying a crate each. Spotting Lysia, they froze. She shouted something incomprehensible, then sprang off the saddle, dashed past them, and rushed into the building. The two looters awoke from their stupor and bolted for the alley exit.

"Hey!" Jespar shouted. "*Hey!*"

They didn't stop, running toward Kawu and Jespar's horses. Jespar raised his sword, but as they came into reach, he hesitated; a second later, they were already past him and had disappeared around the corner of the alley. Jespar yanked his steppe-runner around to make chase, but then a scream sounded from inside the clinic.

He halted.

Godsdammit.

Jespar and Kawu swung themselves off their saddles and hurried into the clinic.

The place was ravaged: the shelves were empty, the colorful wall cloths torn down, the chests and barrels cracked open and plundered; even the ingredient jars in the kitchen had been looted and shattered. This could not have been the work of just the two plunderers they'd encountered outside—they had only been the last in line.

"Lysia?" Jespar called.

No answer.

They found her in the sickbay, sunk against the flaking purple wall, and staring at the ceiling. A man lay at her feet, a pool of blood under his head. Kawu paled. Jespar's chest tightened. Even when they stopped right in front of her, Lysia didn't acknowledge their presence. Tears streamed down her cheeks, snot dangled from her nose, and she gasped softly.

It was Juusew. The boy's eyes were shut but his lips parted, his stomach a patchwork of messy stab wounds. Jespar could see it clearly: Juusew, catching a looter red-handed. Panic on both sides. A scuffle with a deadly end.

Jespar tried to think of something to say but came up with nothing. He sheathed his sword, sank to his knees, and hugged her. She was tense as a rock; her chin sank into his shoulder and her moist cheek touched his. After a few seconds, Kawu hunkered down beside her too and put a hand on her back. The distant roar of the riot and Lysia's small sobs were all that filled the silence.

She wept for a long time.

———�писⱁ———

They carried Juusew into his room in the attic, one of the few that hadn't been looted. The walls were honey yellow, and potted plants lined the desk by the small window. Shelves ran along the walls, exhibiting an impressive collection of impossible bottles: most contained miniature ships, but there were also more unusual items, such as a deck of playing cards, a Makehu figurine, and a cockleshell the size of a fist. A wooden statuette of Erodan stood by the bedside, patron Light-Born of Nehrim, god of endurance, endeavors, and homes.

They eased Juusew onto the bed. Lysia covered him with a blanket, then sunk onto a chair by the bedside and regarded him for a while.

"There was this girl." Like her face, her voice lacked all expression. "Juusew had been writing to her."

Jespar didn't respond. It seemed like the right thing to do.

"I taught him how to write a few years back, you know? It's crazy how fast he picked it up. He had so much potential, even—" She broke off. "Anyway, he'd been writing letters to this girl from Maitemi. It was a mystery, that whole thing ... Juusew was cagey about it, never told me how he'd met her or who she was, and whenever he came back with a new letter from the courier's office, he hid it from me like it was some kind of secret weapon." She looked out the tiny window. Flames licked the building across the street; it would only be a matter of time until they spread to the clinic. "I wonder what she'll think when she gets no more letters."

"Perhaps you could tell her what happened when this is over?" Kawu asked.

"I don't know her name or where she lives, and we have no time to search for Juusew's stash. I guess it'll burn with him and the rest of this place."

Jespar reached for her shoulder. "I'm sorry, Lysia."

"We gotta go."

She kissed Juusew's cheek, got up, and left the room.

"Stars burn me. Look."

The Great Bazaar was burning.

Flames licked through the pavilion's roof and along its eaves, the inside a haze of smoke and fire; bodies lay around the entrance and silhouettes hurried through the gloom, fighting, weeping, looting.

"They razed this place," Jespar muttered.

"That's not what I meant." Lysia pointed up the mountain. "There."

Jespar stood in his stirrups and squinted into the distance. At first, he thought she was referring to the fires rising from the villas in the Jade District, which had spawned a black-red blanket of smoke. The walls and the perspective shielded most of the area from sight, but after witnessing the havoc the mob had wreaked upon the lower districts, Jespar shuddered at the idea of what they had unleashed on the homes of the Great Dreamers.

Then he noticed what Lysia really meant.

Holy fucking seven Gods.

"Is that ...?"

"Yeah," Lysia said. "That's the mob."

A crowd filled a visible stretch of Fortune Road which led up a slope dotted by villas. "Filled" was literal—the throng was so massive it seemed like a living organism, a colossal snake slowly slithering forward, its scales a mix of bright colors and black: the civilians' bright toki-dyed clothes, and the monochrome uniforms of the Scythe.

"Īmīte help us," Kawu said. "Those are thousands."

Lysia's jaw was a hard line. "Tens of thousands is more like it. And if they get to the First Ziggurat before us, we're done for."

A man carrying a stack of silver plates came running from the burning bazaar and headed for the alley behind the group. Nearing them, he wavered, but dashed past their horses when they paid him no heed.

"They'll never make it up the mountain," Jespar said with a resolve he didn't feel. "The Blue Guard is gonna stop them before they reach Oonai's ziggurat."

"They might or they might not," Lysia replied, still no emotion in her voice. "Keep in mind, this is just what Dealatis *thinks* is going to happen. It's also possible Oonai and Vel'Nyx will have the mob tear the whole district to the ground, ziggurats included, and let the Blue Guard deal with them afterward. We just don't bloody know."

"That would mean Oonai is putting his wife and entire livelihood at risk. He's a bastard, but he wouldn't go that far."

"Yeah, well, too bad he isn't calling the shots anymore, and Vel'Nyx is safe and sound on her ship to Arazeal. Who knows, maybe she decided to spice things up a little when Oonai bailed out and changed the plan to make it even more believable."

A staccato of images popped up in Jespar's head: the First Ziggurat, burning. The Ma'saa and Enkshi, gutted and strung to the walls. Oonai's emaciated corpse, tossed down the giant stairs, twitching and jerking like a dying fish as it rolls down the steps. If Oonai's parasite died before Vel'Nyx recalled him, what would happen to Jespar's?

Calm, he thought. *Don't give in to fear. Focus on the "what is", not the "what-ifs".*

One of Naka's sayings.

He let out a slow breath and methodically smoothed out the mane of his horse. "It's all gonna work out. Let's just get to the ziggurat as fast as we can."

Lysia knitted her brows together. Then she gave a single nod. "I know a shortcut up to the Jade District. Lemme go see if the path is clear."

"By yourself? Is that safe?"

"I'll be fine."

Before Jespar could reply, Lysia had steered her horse back onto Fortune Road and galloped off into another alley. Jespar sighed and turned around to look at Kawu. Gaze lost in middle distance, he had a vial in one hand and a couple of green pellets in the other; noticing Jespar, he tossed them into his mouth and stuffed the vial back into his belt pouch.

"What's that?" Jespar asked.

"Dried taka leaves against the fatigue—I got them from Ma'sao Agaam. Would you like one?"

Realizing how exhausted Kawu did indeed look, the phantom noose cinched a little tighter. "No, you keep them for yourself. Are you sure you're all right?"

"I'm fine, Jespar." Kawu's smile was a ruin. "At least as fine as anyone could be under the circumstances. If anything, I'm worried about you."

"Maybe it's safer for you to stay down here or, you know, outside the city. We could bring the Magnate's Crown to you."

"That would take far too long. And even if it didn't, who would keep you anchored in the meantime?"

"I—"

Kawu took Jespar's hand and pressed it lightly. "Hio, it's fine. We'll go to the ziggurat, cure you, and then get out of this city. We can do this."

Hio, Jespar thought. Makehu for "treasured thing".

Jespar wanted to reply, but then Lysia returned to the alleyway. "Okay, the path is clear. You coming?"

"Yes," Kawu said. "But I should do another anchoring, just to be sure."

"Go ahead, then."

Jespar felt calmer and clearer when Kawu was done, but the phantom noose was still tight.

With the glowing smoke cloud hanging over the manor roofs and the massive mob marching up Fortune Road, Jespar had formed a mental image about what the destruction in the Jade District would look like.

He had not expected an inferno.

Everything burned. Houses, trees, people. The air was a miasma of smoke and death and heat, cloaking the hundreds of corpses that lay scattered on the flagstone, commoners, guards, and many, many nobles. While the mob's snake-like body had reached the upper edges of the district by now, the tail still slithered through the lower areas, vandalizing, torching, and killing whatever its fangs had missed. Rhythmic chanting rang down the mountain, the same sentence over and over, ten thousand voices shouting in unison.

Jespar understood the words now.

"The dream is a lie."

They slowed their steppe-runners to a trot and trailed the mob for a bit, but after several suspicious glances at their expensive steeds, they sent them off in a side alley and continued the ascent on foot, avoiding Fortune Road whenever they could. The closer they came to the core of the crowd, the louder the chanting became, until it rang out into the sky like an incantation.

"The dream is a lie!"

"The dream is a lie!"

"The dream is a lie!"

Deceived, battered, exploited. Starved, ridiculed, humiliated.

This was the commoners' judgment.

Rioters pinning a man against the wall of a villa, caving his face in with a rock; rioters setting a boy on fire, his silk coat as brightly orange as the flames consuming him; rioters raping a woman on a park bench, her shawl stuffed into her mouth to muffle her screams.

That Jespar had no more flashbacks, let alone symptoms, was a miracle. Perhaps, he thought as they passed a gutted nobleman strung up against a wall, it was the scope of it all. Why would your sadist mind plunge you back into a flashback when reality was worse or as bad as whatever memory you could relive?

Uunili, the Alabaster City, the Jewel of the Archipelago, had become a living hell.

dThey took a short break in a small, unscathed orchard on a hill a little ways off the main road after an hour's walk. Catching his breath, Jespar leaned over the garden's fence and gazed back over the city.

And the horror sunk in.

It wasn't the immensity of the mob. It wasn't the burning, it wasn't the looting, it wasn't the killing. The horror was a feeling as shapeless as grief at a burial, the quiet before the storm, the stare between wolf and prey, a feeling intangible and yet so powerful, so sickening, so visceral that it drowned out everything else.

Hatred.

What Jespar witnessed was a seething, pestilent hatred that had infected thousands of people, the kind that made the peaceful fisher drive his gutting knife into a man's heart, that had turned the Wayfarers from protectors to defilers, that reduced humanity to its basest instincts.

And it had been growing for a long, long time.

In the Makehu worker who had been denied access to the pond. In the Hapanan woman who watched her son cough up blood from his nuvium-stained lungs. In the sewer workers who had found the washed-up corpse of a pregnant young woman, one the haves insisted had just been "too weak to handle the pressure." It was the spawn of centuries of injustice, a virulent growth that had infected and parched the soil of the people's soul and had only waited for the fatal spark to jump.

The Overgrowth Plan had worked.

Lysia touched his shoulder. "We gotta keep going."

"Yes."

They managed to skirt the mob until they reached a steep slope leading to the district's uppermost neighborhood. There were no side streets they could take, only Fortune Road running its length in three switchbacks, and the narrowness of the path forced the mob into a single file. Jespar, Lysia, and Kawu shouldered their way along the sidelines, but at some point, the density of the throng made advance impossible. Jespar was being shoved from all sides, and his ears buzzed from the din; when someone pulled at his arm, he jerked around, almost drawing his dagger. It was Lysia, Kawu beside her. She gestured down the slope, saying something the chanting drowned out; someone elbowed Jespar from behind and sent him staggering forward.

"Move it, man!"

Jespar muttered an apology, then found his way to the sideline. He looked for Lysia and Kawu; sweat broke out on his neck when he couldn't see them. Banishing the picture of Kawu and Lysia getting trampled by an angry horde, he decided to go back down to the foot of the slope. When he finally reached it and stepped out of the crowd, it felt like a steel clamp around his chest sprang open. Lysia and Kawu stood a little way down an adjacent side road, wildly gesturing in his direction.

He let out a sigh of relief and hurried over. "I thought I'd lost you."

"We did too," Lysia said. "Look, this isn't working. If we keep going like that, we'll never make it to the ziggurat before the vanguard of the mob gets there."

"Agreed. Any ideas?"

Lysia gazed up at the switchback, then shook her head.

"I have one," Kawu said.

———⟊⟊⟊———

They found what they were looking for in the garden of a nearby villa. About a dozen corpses lay between the rhododendrons and hyacinths, the silent witnesses of a skirmish. The mansion was aflame, but the fire miraculously hadn't spread to the trees. Six corpses were commoners, five guards, three Scythes. Kawu gave Jespar and Lysia a questioning look. They nodded and got to work disrobing the Scythes. Not much later, they wore their black uniforms over their nuvium cuirasses and returned to the slope.

It worked.

The road was still as congested as before, but when they filed back into the sideline, it was now possible to advance. People stepped out of their way as soon as they noticed their black clothes, and the few who frowned when Jespar jostled past bowed their heads when he shot them his best impression of a righteous scowl.

On they went, past the burning mansions and into the rain forest beyond the edge of the district, all the while the firelit sky sunk deeper and deeper into a shade of blue and crimson as the sun continued its descent. It wasn't until they reached the head of the snaking mob that Jespar truly understood how well the Scythe coordinated the mayhem: whenever the throng passed a villa that, Jespar supposed, was a target, two Scythes would detach from the crowd, instigate a dozen or more rioters to join them, then let their fury do the rest. They had an answer for every obstacle: portable battering rams to tear down the gates, archers to take out guards, fire bowls to ensure the mob's voracious torches were always tended to.

Controlled burning.

The only time Jespar felt something remotely close to hope was when they passed the Seventh Ziggurat. Its imposing battlements manned, Jespar figured that even an army would suffer heavy casualties before breaking through; he hadn't even finished the train of thought when a horn blared, and the crowd parted. A group of

Scythes was pushing a cart stacked with barrels up the road, followed by another group carrying a bronze cylinder on four wheels. *Cannons.* Sinfully expensive, it was the latest masterpiece of Starling siege weaponry, a contraption capable of hurling a fifty-pound metal boulder through its cylinder when the purified tyenite inside it was ignited.

Lysia pressed his shoulder. "Come. Let's push on."

As they advanced up the sidelines at the briskest pace they could manage without drawing attention, a deafening boom cut through the shouting. The crowd fell almost silent. Heads turned, necks craned, whispers traveled. Another bang. Another. The crash of stone collapsed. The mob broke into a roaring cheer—then they resumed their chanting, more powerful than ever before.

The dream is a lie.

The dream is a lie.

The dream is a lie.

CHAPTER TWENTY-TWO
TAWAHE

DAY SIX

1ST MOON OF RAINY SEASON, 1226 A.L.

This time, Jespar felt the Pull coming—it was a cold pulse in the depths of his skull, like chilly waves that grew stronger with each beat. He could only guess as to why he was suddenly able to sense it: maybe the previous attacks had made him sensitive to the signs, maybe it had to do with the dreameater getting closer to hatching. Either way, it was too soon. The last anchoring couldn't have been more than four hours ago.

Cursing, Jespar shouldered his way through the crowd, catching up to Kawu and Lysia, and reached for Kawu's shoulder. "Hey, I'm—"

A stranger faced him, confusion written across his face. Jespar muttered something and fell back, then jostled his way to the sideline. The Pull grew stronger, the waves now blasts of ice that nearly reached his forehead. His eyes darted over the crowd, but Kawu and Lysia were nowhere to be seen. *Fuck.* Fuck!

"Kawu!" He might as well have screamed into a storm. "*Kawu!*" A few quizzical glances, but that was it. The Pull was nearing his temples now, its frosty claws tearing at his mind; the dread was punching against the inside of the chest again, cracking holes into the lid. Jespar arrowed ahead, frantically searching for Kawu, but it was pointless; there were simply too many people.

Behind him, a scream. He whirled.

A few steps over, at the edge of the jungle, three rioters were beating up a nobleman on the ground, harrying him with kicks and cudgels. He screamed and struggled and begged for mercy, but that only seemed to spur them on. He was young, no older than Kawu.

Kawu. You need Kawu.

He turned back the crowd.

"Boy."

Jespar should not have heard it; even a scream would have been hard to make out amidst this ruckus, and the word had barely been more than a whisper. Yet he had.

Don't. Don't do it. Don't look.

He did.

Of the three rioters bludgeoning the young noble, one was staring at him, but the hand holding his cudgel was aflame. The Corpse's blue lips split in a sorrowful smile, casting wrinkles that reached all the way up to the lotus blossom on his forehead.

The Pull hit.

Ice exploded inside his head. His sight went blue, white, black.

He collapsed.

⁂

The psychic dimension, but something was different. Not in how it looked; the lake was the same as always, endless ice under a twilight sky. Not in how it felt; the air still had that amorphous quality, thin and scentless, neither warm nor cold. Not in how it sounded; alien silence all around.

You.

The difference is inside you.

The hallmark of a healthy mind, Jespar now understood, was the ethereal cord that tethered the mind to the body, the psychic to the physical. This link was vital: all body, and a human became a hull, unable to think or dream. All thought, and they lost the ability to walk the soil of reality, became echoes waiting to fade.

The parasite had weakened Jespar's cord. This was how it trapped its victim in the psychic dimension: it corroded their brains' links, so the path back to reality was blocked forever.

The ice beneath Jespar cracked.

Split.

He didn't scream when he slipped through nor when the water enfolded him. He didn't scream when he had sunk so deep that all the light from the surface had faded, and he didn't scream when the Corpse's severed torso and head floated up from the depths, spine and muscles dangling from the hips like tentacles.

He didn't scream because he had accepted that his struggle was pointless; if your own mind was the enemy, where could you run?

Bubbles rose from his lips as he spoke. "Father."

The Corpse reached for him. The sorrow was still there in his dirty-snow eyes, but there was something else inside them now—the pride of a father whose stubborn son had finally learned his lesson.

Jespar took his hand—the fire shrouding it didn't hurt—and they sank together. Toward a nightmare from which there was no waking.

A face. Someone was there, kneeling over Jespar, hands pressed to the sides of his head. Jespar jerked up, a series of impressions punching into his brain. The mob. The din. The red sky.

"Hio? Are you okay?"

Kawu. Gods, Kawu. That was him kneeling there right before Jespar.

Exhaling, Jespar leaned back on his elbows. *Close. Too fucking close.* His head swam as he tried to fathom what would have happened had Kawu appeared just a few moments later; something told him that would have been the end of it.

"Jespar?" Kawu's eyes were wide, a vein showing at his temple. "Jespar, talk to me, please."

"I'm okay," Jespar said. "I'm okay, I was—"

A cough cut him off. Something was stuck at the back of his throat; turning away, he coughed again, wheezed, then again, until a blob of slime popped into his palm.

Jespar stared. A milky blue mucus, swirls of vapor rising from it. The same stuff that had coated Oonai's iris.

"Jespar?" he heard Kawu behind him. "Jespar, what is it?"

A cannon fired in the distance. The mob erupted in cheers.

"Hio!"

Frantically rubbing his hand against the grass, Jespar turned back. "I'm all right, I just ..." He couldn't tell him. "I'm all right."

Kawu's gaze didn't waver. "It had you, didn't it? The dreameater pulled you into the Imūma?"

Jespar grunted.

Exhaling heavily, Kawu rubbed his face. "Īmite, three hours ... It has gotten so strong. I should have never waited this long, that was so *stupid.*"

"You couldn't have known."

"But I should have," Kawu said. "No more risks from now on, Jespar. We'll stay together at all times, and I'll anchor you every single hour, no exceptions."

"What? But the side effects, you said it would damage my brain."

"I said that it might. But you've responded well so far, and it's safer than risking something like this happening again. If that thing had already pulled you into your kuluhika, I wouldn't have been able to bring you back." He gazed up the mountain and nodded to himself once. "You need to hold out a little longer. Once we have the Magnate's Crown and find Vel'Nyx, you'll be all right again."

He said it as though there weren't a million "ifs" surrounding that "all right again," but Jespar was too tired to point it out.

"Okay, let's stay close to each other." He stood and offered Kawu a hand up. Kawu took it. "Where's Lysia?"

"We split up when we realized you were missing," Kawu said, smoothing his uniform back over his nuvium cuirass. "She said we should meet her by the waterfall farther up the mountain."

Jespar rummaged through his memories. Only six days had passed since his first ascent up Mount Ilakato, yet it felt like a different life. "You mean the one by the bridge?"

"Yes, I think so. I don't remember."

"Must be. All right then."

Jespar oriented himself. The mob was as dense as ever, chanting and marching along in their dark procession. The torch glow up the slope suggested the vanguard had reached the upper fifth of the mountain by now, closing in on the Third Ziggurat. If Jespar remembered correctly, the waterfall was two, maybe three miles uphill.

How much longer would the Blue Guard let this go on? When would they finally quash this riot and put an end to this madness?

"We need to move," Jespar said.

They filed back into the crowd and marched on, staying close to each other. Jespar had hoped the upper ziggurats could defy the mob longer, but both the Fifth and the Fourth had fallen by the time they passed it; even the gates of the Third, Vel'Nyx's, were wide open, flames sprouting from the three magnificent pyramids that were the heart of the temple complex. Though they witnessed pockets of combat, it was clear that the big fight was over. *Talk about uncompromising,* Jespar thought. There was something almost impressive about the viciousness of the plan; Vel'Nyx had not just thrown tens of thousands of lives into the gambling pot, but also her own livelihood. Jespar's blood chilled at the possibility that Dealatis had been wrong in her theory about the Guard ending the riot before it reached the First Ziggurat. What if the plan really *was* to raze everything to the ground, and then re-establish order?

No. No, that doesn't make any sense.

Had that been the intention, Oonai would have surely arranged for his wife, for Enkshi, and himself to leave the island under some excuse so they'd be out of the firing line—neither the Ma'saa nor Enkshi had mentioned such a plan.

And what if there was one, but Vel'Nyx changed it after Oonai had attempted to bail?

"Faster," Jespar told Kawu. "We need to go faster."

They pushed on, pausing just once after cresting a hill that allowed an obstructed view of the city. The destruction seemed surreal from up here, those thousand fires raging on the white roofs and tinting the sky a dark amber. The Jade District was the epicenter, but the chaos spanned across the entire city and well into the sprawling periphery. Come daybreak, Uunili and its prosperous bay would be a ruin.

When they reached the waterfall at last, Jespar was surprised; the din had completely blotted out its sound. Last night's tempest had drastically widened the riverbed, and uprooted trees and branches floated and spiraled down the torrent like jetsam. As stealthily as they could, they freed themselves from the mob and hurried into the rain forest. Lysia instantly emerged from behind a tree.

"Stars burn me, I thought I'd lost you. What happened?"

As calmly as his nerves allowed, Jespar told her about the Pull and his brief trip into the Imūma. When he was done, Lysia was leaning against the tree, tightly hugging her elbows. Her expression gave nothing away—the same blankness she'd had since the clinic. "I see."

"We can still make it," Jespar said, speaking half to himself. "We just need to get to the ziggurat. Now that we're up here, we can take a shortcut through the jungle."

"Easier said than done," Lysia replied. "Remember that meadow farther up? Past the Second Ziggurat?"

"The clearing with the fireflies."

"Yeah, that one. I did some eavesdropping while I waited, and it seems like the Scythe are expecting something to happen there. Plus, I saw a couple of Blue Guards sneak through the jungle earlier. They're around here somewhere."

"Do you think ...?"

"It might be the 'trap', yes, or something else. Whatever we do, I don't think we should cross the meadow before the mob does."

More problems. Of course. The image flashed up again, Oonai's corpse tossed out the ziggurat and crashing down the stairs.

What-is. Not what-ifs.

"Okay," he said. "Then we gotta sneak around it."

"I was just gonna suggest that. We follow the crowd up to the clearing, then slip off into the jungle and ditch the uniforms so the ziggurat guards won't fire at us, then we circle the meadow while whatever show the Scythe and the Guard have planned goes down without us."

Jespar thought it over. It was a detour that would cost them time they did not have—then again, what was the alternative? "All right. Let's do it."

Kawu's hands were chilly and damp when he anchored Jespar, yet his touch was like a blanket in the cold. As soon as he was done, the three of them filed back into the mob. Past the bridge, the rebels had already launched their assault on the Second Ziggurat, the one built into the mountain itself. With rows of archers manning the battlements, it was certainly the toughest stronghold to crack, but even so, it was obvious its guards were fighting a losing battle: for every rioter that the arrows felled, three new ones took their place.

As they neared the firefly meadow, the mob fell into a hush. Jespar's headache welcomed it, though it only made the tension worse. The silence felt like that of a predator closing in for the kill.

"Fuckin' poetic, huh?"

A Scythe had fallen into step beside Jespar, boyish looks contrasting scarred and weather-beaten skin.

Beside Jespar, Kawu tensed up.

"... You bet," Jespar improvised.

"Them leeches have no fuckin' idea what they're in for. Bloody hell, I'm gonna enjoy this."

Jespar grunted in what he hoped sounded like agreement. The man flashed him a wolfish grin, then slapped him on the back and upped his pace, joining the head of the snake.

"What in the world do they have planned?" Lysia asked quietly. She was walking behind them.

"No idea," Jespar said. "But something's gonna happen soon."

By the time the meadow opened before them, the clouds had scattered. The full moon tinted the scene dark silver, and a breeze sent ripples through the tall grass. Fortune Road was an arrow cutting straight through the clearing.

The vanguard had come to a stop.

People craned their necks and stood on their toes to see what was going on; Lysia elbowed Jespar in the side and cocked her head in the direction of the jungle. Then she casually entered the thicket. Jespar and Kawu followed; it was only a few strides between the road and the green, but when they dropped into a crouch behind a cluster of shrubs, Jespar's back felt hot, as if the whole mob had been staring at them.

"Ready?" Lysia asked.

"Ready."

Quickly and quietly, they skirted the meadow, staying as close to the border as possible. Mosquitoes and katakos harried them, lured by their sweat and fear; a peculiar scent clung to the jungle, smoky, sweet, and pungent, a marriage of fresh and rotten, of living and decaying. Halfway around the clearing, the three ditched their black coats, tied them around their waists, and moved on. They must have been about three-quarters of the way when Lysia stopped so fast Jespar bumped right into her.

"What's wro—?" He fell silent.

A small opening in the shrubbery allowed for a clear view of the meadow. The mob had advanced halfway into it, but they were no longer alone. An army faced them, filling their side of the field from one end to the other.

"The Blue Guard," Kawu whispered.

Jespar grunted. Dealatis had been right about the trap after all. This was where the Blue Guard would put an end to the false rebellion.

This was the finale.

Though Jespar knew the lion's share of the mob had yet to arrive, the sight of the army gave him hope. The Guard stood thousands strong, side by side in perfect formation, the center unit clad in full nuvium armor. These were real soldiers, weapons that had been forged, beaten, and honed by years of training. The rioters, on the other hand? Barring the Scythe's mercenary core, they were commoners. Violent, furious, and armed to the teeth, for sure, but still commoners who didn't know the first thing about warfare.

And they know it.

The contempt and the lurking aggression were palpable even from here, but a sense of unease crept through the mob, people fidgeting, their attention flicking around.

"Do we keep going?" Lysia asked.

Jespar gave it some thought. "Too risky. I bet the Blue Guard is keeping an eye on the woods, and if we go now, they might take us for rioters."

"So we wait?"

"Yeah, at least until the battle starts. Once it gets going, we should be able to slip past."

Lysia nodded. They took cover behind a bush and started to watch.

A figure each had detached from the two opposing crowds, a female Blue Guard officer in decorated nuvium armor, and a tower of a man with long black hair. The Pale Brother, saber at his hip. They stopped a stride from each other and started talking. Jespar couldn't make out what they were saying, but the longer the conversation went on, the more agitated the Guard officer appeared. In contrast, the Pale Brother remained the epitome of calm. Considering this confrontation was probably staged, it must have meant one of two things: the officer was either a damn good actor or clueless about the plan. Jespar guessed it was the latter. Even with an upper-echelon co-conspirator in the military, there was no way thousands of soldiers would have agreed to betray their country. Most likely, all of them believed the battle was real, that they were the last bastion standing between this riot and the fate of Kilay.

Jespar felt his tension ease. This was good. Once the Blue Guard had won this orchestrated battle, the rest of the mob would most likely scatter. All Jespar, Lysia, and Kawu then had to do was get to the First Ziggurat as fast as possible, take the Magnate's Crown, and-

An explosion tore through the night.

For a few heartbeats, no one moved. The crowd had fallen silent, all heads turned toward the peak of Mount Ilakato.

The peak?

The realization came like the cut of a scalpel—the First Ziggurat. The explosion had come from the First Ziggurat.

"What the hell?" Lysia muttered. "What's—"

Fast as a panther, the Pale Brother unsheathed his saber and hacked it into the officer's armpit. She screamed, keeled over; the Pale Brother jerked out the blade and brought it around in a swing that took the officer's head clean off her shoulders.

A hush.

Then screams erupted from the jungle on the other side of the clearing, and a wave of black figures crashed into the rear of the Blue Guard battalion. Facing the mob, the Pale Brother thrust his saber into the air.

"Kill the leeches!"

He charged at the Guard and the horde followed.

Kawu's lips opened and closed, opened and closed. "That ... that does not look like a charade."

"It has to be," Jespar said. "They're just making it bloody enough so it's plausible." It sounded ridiculous even as he said it. Charades didn't start with actual beheadings.

Lysia stood. "Real or not, we gotta go. That explosion came from up the mountain, which means the mob has already reached the First Ziggurat."

That cursed image, again: Oonai's corpse, a gutted Ma'saa and Enkshi. Despair gripped Jespar. "But that doesn't make any fucking sense! If this is the trap, then the mob *isn't* supposed to conquer the ziggurat!"

"Jespar, who the hell gives a shite? We *need* to—"

"Maima e Īmīte kīe."

Īmīte save us.

Kawu was staring at the jungle across the meadow. Jespar followed his gaze. A colossal creature floated over the treetops, black-feathered wings spread wide. It was as big as a house, its giant tail swinging left and right like a pendulum. Two curled horns grew from its goat-like head, set over two pairs of yellow eyes.

Kawu turned to Jespar, lips trembling. "Is that—"

"A myrad," Jespar replied hoarsely. "A black one."

Someone perched atop its neck, holding reins the size of anchor chains. The rider yanked the reins, and the myrad dived at the battlefield.

CHAPTER TWENTY-THREE
BARGAIN

DAY SIX
1ST MOON OF RAINY SEASON, 1226 A.L.

The myrad dived from the sky like the judgment of a god.

Panic broke out.

The mob scattered, screamed, dashed off in all directions. Halfway down its nosedive, the myrad opened its maw, yellow mist glowing behind rows of dagger-like teeth. *Poison.* Jespar had seen it before, in the war. Just before the myrad would crash into the crowd, the rider would make it sweep over the battlefield and let it spew a carpet of mist over the mobsters. Entering their bodies through their pores, the poison would paralyze their muscles, limbs, lungs, and hearts, leaving behind a graveyard of croaking and twitching figures.

"We should go," Jespar said hoarsely. "If we—"

A screech pierced the night.

The myrad was sweeping over the meadow just like Jespar had anticipated, but instead of spewing poison, it beat its wings erratically, talons clawing at the air as if desperately seeking purchase. The rider—*that's General Daato!*—was tearing at the reins, but the myrad kept wheeling, until, halfway toward Jespar's hiding spot, it jerked up into a steep ascent, throwing Daato back in his saddle. Up and up it soared until it was a jerking, screeching silhouette in front of the moon; Jespar barely had enough time to ask himself what the *hell* was going on before the myrad went still.

And fell.

Head pointed groundward and wings limp, it plummeted from the sky and crashed into the crowd like a boulder squashing an anthill.

Time stood still.

Both the rioters and the guards stayed rooted to the spot, staring at the massive mound of black feathers and fur; screams sounded from the impact site, people trying to claw themselves out from underneath its body.

Lysia's cheeks were bloodless. "What in the world was that?"

"I've no idea," Jespar said. "It looked like it just … died up there."

"The fur." Kawu gestured at the myrad's corpse. The fighting on the meadow slowly resumed. "Can you see it? It's gone gray."

Jespar squinted. Kawu was right: the myrad had not only gone from black to silver, but it was also thinner, its spine drawing a jagged line along the back. *Frail. Old.*

"The Pale Sister," Jespar muttered.

Lysia gave him a puzzled look. Then she blinked. "Necromancy."

"Yeah. She did the same thing to a guard when they ambushed Enkshi and me on the first day, so she must be around here some—"

An explosion cut him off. A fireball shot across the battlefield and hit the Guard's flank, slashed a good fifteen strides into the formation, then went up in a blast of flames so bright that Jespar saw stars.

When they faded, he wished they hadn't: while the projectile had left a line of blood and limbs and bodies in its wake, it had reduced the point of detonation to a charred crater with burning figures screaming and tossing in its periphery.

The noose tightened around his neck.

He tore his attention away from the havoc and traced the path of the projectile. A group of Scythes was at the clearing's northern border, not far from Jespar, Kawu, and Lysia. An Aetäerna woman with ivory skin and black hair stood amidst them, tall despite leaning on her quarterstaff—the Pale Sister.

At first, Jespar thought the fireball had been her doing—some elaborate thermomantic shift, however that was supposed to work— but then he saw the Starling cannon beside the group. Two Scythes were loading it with a glowing rock.

Kawu had noticed them as well. "What in Īmīte's name is that? What are they doing?"

Killing, Jespar thought. *Effectively.* "I have no idea. Must be some kind of special siege weapon."

"It doesn't matter," Lysia said, getting to her feet. "We gotta go, right now. This battle is over."

They were quiet as they skirted the rest of the clearing, staying as far from the border as possible. The din of battle melted away, a muddled blend of dull explosions and clanking metal, shouts, and screams. When they finally reached the other side of the meadow, they stayed within the jungle and began Fortune Road's final, steep ascent to the summit. The darkness and the jungle canopy obscured the peak but seeing no smoke in the sky made Jespar believe the First Ziggurat had not been breached.

Yet.

As they were trekking through a carpet of ferns, Lysia fell into step beside Jespar. "What happened there?"

"I guess the Scythe outsmarted the Guard."

"That's not what I'm talking about." She spoke as flatly as she had at the clinic, but a nervous edge underpinned her words as if she wanted to be upset but couldn't. "I mean, why didn't the Guard destroy the Scythe? I could wrap my head around letting the mob conquer all of Uunili before the Guard puts a stop to it, but *annihilating* the entire Kilayan military? How the hell is Vel'Nyx planning to regain control of the Archipelago without soldiers?"

That's a damn good question. Jespar ducked his head under a cluster of branches. "Honestly, I don't know. Maybe there's another stage to the plan after the riot is over."

"And what would that be? Kindly asking them to put down their weapons?"

Jespar exhaled. "I don't know, Lysia. And, frankly, I don't give a shit anymore. It's not like there's much the three of us can do against a mob of murderous assholes anyway. All I want is to find that fucking crown, deal with that fucking bug, and get as far from this fucking island as possible."

"Maybe the Twins betrayed the plan," Kawu's voice came from behind them. "Maybe the Guard was *supposed* to win this, but the Twins just didn't play along."

"... You mean they tricked Vel'Nyx and Oonai?" Lysia asked. "As in, they want an actual revolution?"

"No, I don't think so. Remember when I told you about them on the way to Kaiawaika Manor?"

"You said that they're both insane," Jespar said.

"They're 'tawahe', yes. They take pleasure in violence."

A picture: the Pale Brother in the tavern at Bluefort, saber hovering over the sobbing noblewoman's neck. Back then, Jespar had been too distracted to notice, but now, a detail stood out like a corpse's arm poking out of a swamp. The look in the Pale Brother's eyes.

Leering.

"Are you saying they did all this just to cause chaos?" Jespar asked.

Kawu's silence was answer enough.

When they reached the plateau of the First Ziggurat, Jespar's heart sank. He had hoped to find a small group of Scythes laying siege to the palace, maybe a few dozen. It was far from it. Hundreds of rioters stood gathered in front of the snake gate, chanting their chorus and punching their weapons into the air, and more were pouring onto the plateau every minute.

And that's just the vanguard. As soon as the battle—or, more accurately, the butchering—in the meadow ended, the rest would follow.

"No way we're getting in through the front door," Lysia said. They were crouching behind a giant fern at the jungle border, some thirty strides diagonally across the gate.

Jespar grunted. Smoke curled in front of the portcullis, probably a failed attempt at blasting it apart; archers and cannons stood on the ziggurat's battlements, but no shots were fired, and no arrows loosened. Jespar considered looking for a back entrance; then he remembered that the pyramid's opposite side butted up to a jagged cliff. *If only Agaam were here.* There had to be some kind of secret tunnel in and out of the palace, there *had* to be, but with no one to show them, they were looking for the needle in the haystack.

Kawu touched his shoulder. "Look. Something's happening."

The Twins and an entourage of Scythes had appeared at the crest of the slope, the cheering crowd clearing a lane as they crossed the plateau. They stopped some twenty strides in front of the gate; the Pale Sister raised a hand. The entourage behind her scattered, revealing a woman kneeling in their midst, arms tied behind her back.

"Imīte, help us," Kawu whispered.

Jespar would not have recognized Nayima Oonai had it not been for the prayer rings around her upper arms. Her black hair hanging in her face, the Ma'saa didn't struggle—she just knelt there, gaze on the ground. Drugged, Jespar guessed, his mouth feeling dry as parchment.

Yes, Jespar. You know.

He knew Nayima Oonai wasn't a devil, knew her only crime had been ignoring her husband's wrongdoings, knew she had wanted to atone. The mob didn't. To them, she was just another selfish, rich bitch feasting on the fat her leech husband had sucked from the marrow of the workers' bones.

The Pale Sister flicked her hand at a Scythe beside her, a bald man with a long gray beard that made him look like a fairy tale character. He nodded and focused on the Ma'saa.

At first, nothing happened. Then her sandaled feet slowly rose off the ground, and she floated into the air, like a marionette lifted by strings. She remained perfectly still, her chin resting on her chest as if she were sleeping.

Kawu stared. "Is that—"

"Choromancy, yes," Lysia said. "He's manipulating space."

The Ma'saa's ascent ceased when she reached parapet height. Silence ensued, the guards and the mob alike seemingly spellbound by the sight. The Pale Brother advanced toward the gate. The ziggurat guards nocked their arrows and took aim, but the Aetäerna kept going until he halted a few strides from the portcullis.

"Oonai!"

Cheers exploded from the crowd. The Pale Brother raised his hand, quieting them.

"Jaaros Ismirael Oonai!"

There was no answer.

"Are ye such a coward?"

Nothing.

"Well, well," the Pale Brother said. "Fine."

He signaled to his sister. She focused on the Ma'saa. The air around them both began to shimmer. Jespar could have guessed what was about to happen, yet his brain didn't—or didn't want to—make the connection until the shift took effect. The guard. The myrad.

Now the Ma'saa.

Nayima Oonai's body twitched once. Then her joints began to twist under her dress, her limbs grew longer while her waist and chest shrunk, her hair faded from black to gray; her droga-induced sleep went on for another heartbeat, then she flung her eyes open and screamed. The awful sound rang across the entire meadow, shrill and prolonged and ululating, more animal than human. She writhed and tossed, but the shackles and the choromancer's shift held her in place like a witch bound to a pyre.

A voice from the battlements cut through her screams. "*Stop!*"

The distortion faded, and the transformation ceased. The Ma'saa kept wailing for another second, then she went limp. Jespar's blood felt cold as he watched tufts of hair float down onto the meadow, all gray. In seconds, she had aged two decades—not yet a crone, but close. A burning impulse to barge in there, sword swinging, overcame him, but he knew it was pointless.

The Pale Sister buckled and held fast to her quarterstaff—two Scythes jumped to her aid, but she waved them off. Above the gate, the guards stepped to the side and revealed Enkshi and Sergeant Maadira.

"We'll string you over a pond for this!" Enkshi shouted. "I swear it, we'll string you up and let the bloodflies eat you, the whole lot of you!" Though the sheer hatred in Enkshi's words was intimidating, the sharp edge to his voice gave it a hysterical note.

"We want the Master Leech," the Pale Brother called back. "Not the fuckin' cockroach!"

A cheer.

Enkshi clawed his hands into the parapet. "Go to hell! You bloody have-nots aren't worth his attention!"

Jeers went up in the mob.

The Pale Brother waited for them to die down. "Well, well," he said. "Let's see what we can do about that."

He faced the crowd. All eyes were on him, longing, like acolytes craving guidance. The Pale Brother was silent as if assessing whether they were worthy.

He thrust up his saber.

The mob went mad. Cheers shook the mountain, boots rocked the earth, weapons and fists and torches pierced the air, again and again, until the shouts turned into the chorus, and a thousand throats screamed it into the night.

"The dream is a lie!"

Someone took Jespar's hand. Kawu, his lips a thin line in his pallid face. Jespar squeezed it back—the most comforting thing he could manage, considering the fear he was feeling himself.

"I really hope Enkshi has a plan," Lysia said. "Because whatever he's trying, it's not working."

The commotion went on for a long minute until the Pale Brother raised his hand, and it died down at once. He turned back, shoving his saber into the ground.

"If this ain't worth his attention," he shouted, "then what is?"

Enkshi said nothing.

"Somethin's happened to the Master Leech, hasn't it? Is he dead?"

"He's alive and well."

"That so? Well, I guess it don't matter. If the cockroach is what we're gettin', we'll make do." He gripped the pommel of his saber and casually leaned into it. "Here's the deal: ye open them gates, and we're gonna spare ye, the First Dame, and yer soldiers a *very* nasty fate. The Master Leech dies, o'course, but ye lot might just get away with yer lives. Keep 'em closed, though, and me sister will make the Ma'saa turn into a corpse right in front of yer eyes, and then we'll take the damned place by force. Yer done for anyway, so ye might as well save yer men the bloodshed."

Maadira whispered something into Enkshi's ear.

"How do I know you'll hold your end of the bargain?" Enkshi called back.

"Ye don't. But it's either take the gamble or lose for sure."

Enkshi's looked from the Ma'saa to the Pale Sister and back. He seemed about to speak, but then Ma'saa Oonai lifted her head. She seemed to say something to Enkshi.

"Cara?" the Pale Brother said. "This is takin' too long."

His sister tapped forefinger and middle finger against her sternum and focused on the Ma'saa.

The scream came at once. Throwing back her head, the Ma'saa struggled and writhed; her wrinkles grew so deep Jespar could see them from afar, her back swelled into a hunch, and white hairs floated onto the meadow like dandelion seeds.

"Enough!" Enkshi screamed.

The Pale Sister kept going.

"*Enough!*"

When the Pale Sister finally ceased her shift, Ma'saa Oonai had fallen silent, her head lolling to the side.

"You win," Enkshi called. "You coinless, fucking monsters. You win."

The Pale Brother's grin was wolfish. "We won hours ago. Open the gate, and we let her down—ye have me word."

"Forget it. You let her down and have one of your men carry her to the portcullis, *then* we'll open."

The Pale Brother exchanged a glance with his sister. She gestured at the choromancer. The man nodded and slowly shifted the Ma'saa back to the ground—the second her feet touched the gravel, the air around her ceased shimmering, and she collapsed. A jolt went through the choromancer's body, and he teetered; a nearby Scythe steadied him.

The Pale Brother said something to one of his men. The Scythe saluted, then roughly hoisted the Ma'saa over his shoulder; a crone now, she looked so frail Jespar feared her body would snap. The man carried her to the portcullis, eased her down, and returned to the mob.

The Pale Brother's eyes were fixed on Enkshi. "Yer turn."

The pause that followed was enough to make the whole world hold its breath.

Enkshi raised his hand. A crank groaned in the near distance. The portcullis gave a yank, then crept up.

"What's he doing?" Lysia said under her breath. "What is he *doing?*"

The grate ground to a halt. A heartbeat went by, then another mechanism sounded.

This is it, Jespar thought numbly as the golden cobra on the ziggurat's gate parted. Out of love for the Ma'saa or an attempt to minimize the damage, Enkshi had sacrificed not only the last bastion of

Kilay but also Jespar's last chance of survival. Whether the Twins stuck to their end of the bargain or not, one thing was sure: in a matter of hours, Oonai would be dead.

This is it.

The coup had been real all along.

The pawn had outwitted the master.

INTERLUDE
THE MAN

NINE DAYS BEFORE
4TH MOON OF DRY SEASON, 1226 A.L.

even days later, the man still stares at the ceiling. He did not find a solution—the Third Magnate was right about everything she said—but he found much more to think about. The bas relief above him, for example: it shows a scene from the Colonization, the Order's hierophant symbolically handing the Makehu high-chieftain the Lambent Scepter while he gives her the Bone Crown of his people. Quite fittingly, too, it now gathers dust in some museum. The bas relief is one of the less expensive works in the ziggurat, yet it cost him a hundred thousand sêr. Or was it eighty? He doesn't remember. Either way, more than Popa would have made in thirty years of work, probably even fifty.

Ugly.

It's ugly, it's showy, it's tasteless, it has no spirit, no soul. It's a shallow display of power and wealth with no purpose but to convey his affluence. *And that was the point, wasn't it?* Power and wealth, the brick and mortar the man's life is built upon, the lodestars of the refurbishments undertaken after his predecessor handed him the keys to the First Ziggurat. The endeavor had taken five years and cost tens of millions of sêr: every room was redone, every sculpture replaced, every tree ripped out and sowed again. If tearing down the whole place and building it anew wouldn't have taken a lifetime, he would have done it.

Why?

Power and wealth.

Someone knocks on the door—made of imported Endralean black oak, which is as expensive as it sounds—and says something. It's his wife again, his hio, his first and true love. She's one of the three people whose smile hides no deceit, contempt, or self-interest. She still loves him, and even through that viscid black fog, he knows he loves her too, always has and always will. The thought brings no joy. Not only because he doesn't deserve her love, not only because he has betrayed her trust countless times, but because he has realized that no good comes from his affection, because beneath all the glitter and allure, the man is as lifeless as this palace: a skeleton with the bones painted gold.

His wife knocks again. Says something about dinner. He fails to answer. Even through the wood, he can sense her waiting, hoping, hurting. Soon enough, her footfalls fade away.

Under the greatest effort, the man turns his head toward the window. It's bright outside, the sky a pallid blue, the sun a gleaming disk of bone. The black fog is worse on clear days. Worse in those afternoons that refuse to end.

He rolls over and hides in the last haven he knows.

Sleep.

CHAPTER TWENTY-FOUR
HAVEN

Day Six
1st Moon of Rainy Season, 1226 A.L.

A grin split Enkshi's lips.

"Now!"

The gate swung open. A colossal golden cannon filled the archway, an orange glow growing in its gaping black mouth.

The Pale Brother whirled. "*Cara!*"

A deluge of fire burst from the machine's maw.

The jet roared through the air just a stride over the unconscious Ma'saa, headed for the crowd; the Pale Brother threw himself to the ground, but his sister and the choromancer were too slow; the flames devoured, then engulfed the mobsters in a lurid blaze.

A horn blared.

The guards raised their bows, nocked, loosed. A hail of arrows rained down on the burning chaos, felling rioters by the dozens, exploding upon impact—tyenite tips. The ziggurat's battlement cannons roared, tore holes in the panicking crowd; soldiers swarmed out of the jungle and clashed into the flank of the mob, their nuvium shields reflecting the fire, their armor adorned with golden cobras arching around the arms—the Jade Snakes.

Jespar watched, hypnotized by the terrifying spectacle.

Then it struck him.

This is it.

This was their chance.

"To the gate! Now!"

He leaped to his feet, yanking Kawu up by the hand, and started running; Kawu joined in. Halfway across the meadow, the heat from the fire jet hit them; he coughed, wheezed, slowed; a cannonball hit just a few strides away, tearing two rioters to pieces. Jespar glanced over his shoulder, noting with relief that Lysia was only a few strides bit behind, sweat pouring down her grimy face.

"Faster!" he shouted.

Ten strides from the gate, the siege machine's fire stream cut off, so abruptly that Jespar stopped in his tracks—and reality sunk in. Clashing blades, whirring arrows. Wails and screams, black mummies in the wake of the blaze, human torches screeching and tossing like madhouse patients.

He heard a sob. The noose pulled tight.

A Loon was coming at him from the side. Jespar dodged the attack, drew his dagger, and put the man in a headlock, blade at the throat; he'd cut that fucker open, he'd show him what it meant to mess with him, he'd—

"Jespar, no!"

The voice yanked him out of the flashback. It wasn't a Loon but Kawu, *his* Kawu, hands clawing at Jespar's arm.

The sobs faded, and the noose lifted.

Killed him.

"Jespar, what ..."

You almost killed him.

"Gods." Jespar let go of Kawu's hand. "Gods, I'm so sorry, I—"

"We're on your side! Bloody hell, we're with the Ma'saa!"

Jespar spun around. Lysia stood by the gate, facing a row of guards who had formed a crescent around the fire-breather, spears poised over their shields. A Starling woman pulled levers atop the siege machine, frantic fear muddling her face; Lysia was gesturing wildly, and while the guards didn't attack her, their frowns made it clear they would if she came any closer.

"Bloody fucking hell, we're on your fucking side!"

Jespar snapped out of his daze. He caught up to Lysia, pulling Kawu along with one hand while frantically waving the other. "She's telling the truth!" he called. "We work for Enkshi and the Ma'saa, we were here just two days ago!"

Two of the guards traded hesitant glances. Another stabbed his spear at Jespar. "Back the fuck off!"

"*We're on your*—" Something whirred past Jespar's head; a cry erupted from the fire-breather. The Starling on top of the siege machine staggered backward, a spear sticking from her chest. She floundered, then collapsed and slipped to the ground.

"You fucking bastards!" a voice screamed behind them.

The Pale Brother stood in the trail of burning grass, a corpse at his feet. *His sister.* At least that's who Jespar thought it was—the fire jet had turned her into a tall black mummy.

"Close the gate!" one of the guards called out to someone in the courtyard. "*Now!*"

Cranks groaned.

No. No, no, no, no, no!

Panic kicked in. Jespar searched the phalanx for an opening, but there was no way through, no weak link, they'd have to—

There.

A guard on the right, staring at the Pale Brother, had lowered his spear. Jespar lunged forward and threw his weight into the man, his shoulder like a battering ram. His wound went up in a red-hot blaze, but he kept pushing until the guard staggered and crashed to the ground. The guardswoman beside him swiveled her spear in Jespar's direction, but he was faster and slammed his boot into her shield, sending her reeling into her comrades.

"*Now!*" Blindly grabbing Kawu's hand and praying Lysia heard it, Jespar leaped over the fallen soldier and dashed into the court-yard, pulling Kawu with him; they barely made five steps before a trio of guards came at them, weapons drawn. Whirling, he looked for another getaway, but soldiers were closing in from all sides.

Steel rattled, crashed.

The portcullis was down, and the gate was closing. For one terri-ble second, Jespar thought Lysia hadn't made it—*you left her there, you abandoned her*—but then he saw her pinned to the ground beside the siege machine.

The ziggurat gate fell shut.

Panting, Jespar raised his hands in surrender.

"We're on your side," he said. "We're with the Ma'saa."

Why it worked this time, he couldn't say. Perhaps it was luck, perhaps it was the utter defeat in his voice. Perhaps, it was the strange feeling that had overcome the courtyard the moment the gate had closed. As if it had sealed off the only pathway into another world, drawing a line between the chaos outside and this beautiful haven that no war, no terror, and no danger could ever blemish. Or so it seemed.

A guard approached him, scimitar drawn. "Who are ye?"

"Jespar Dal'Varek. The Ma'saa hired us."

The guard's grip on his weapon relaxed. "The sellsword."

Yes, you idiot. And you almost killed us. "Yes. We need to talk to Enkshi, we think we know how to—"

Jespar broke off. A figure in blue robes lay on the fire-breather, a spear stuck in his throat. His legs, twisted in a grotesque angle, were made from metal.

CHAPTER TWENTY-FIVE
SNOW

Flames, dancing on logs. What a strange sight it was: a crackling fireplace here in the tropics, where the weather always felt like a wet blanket. That the hearth was the only furniture in the chamber except for a marble table, a chandelier, and some chairs only made it feel more alien. On and on the fire danced, and as Jespar stared into the flames, shapes formed inside them.

Pulsing insects in translucent eggs.

Human torches, waltzing on the burning grass.

The Corpse, floating through an endless ocean.

"I still don't get why you keep wearing this thing."

The shapes disappeared. Lysia was standing beside him, holding two goblets of wine.

"Wear what?"

"The scarf. This place is a bloody oven."

To an unknowing observer, she might have sounded like her old self, but Jespar knew she wasn't. The monotone was gone, but something was missing in her voice, a spark that had been as essential to her as her tree-root scar and her lopsided smile. Jespar knew the feeling. It would be moons or years until that spark returned, if at all.

"Ah," Jespar said. "It protects against the sun." Not a lie, but not the truth either. He wore the scarf because it was one of the few reminders of the place he had once called home. At least that's what he'd told himself all those years. Ever since that current had turned his mind upside down, he didn't know what to believe anymore.

Lysia squinted skeptically but left it at that. She handed him one of the goblets. Jespar took it and downed it in one swallow.

"That was supposed to last longer," she said.

Another good line for his epitaph. "Sorry."

She studied him, her expression wavering between concern and fatigue. Fatigue won. She dropped into a chair by the hearth. "Where's Kawu?"

"He went out while you were gone," Jespar said. "He just anchored me again and said he needed some air."

"Hm." She turned her goblet around in her hand. "He's tough, I gotta hand it to him. So many shifts at such short intervals ... the lad's got a strong Sight, that much is for sure."

"That's true."

They sat in silence, the crackling fire a soothing backdrop.

"I want him to see, you know?" Lysia said. She was staring into her drink, not moving a muscle. "Oonai. I want him to wake up and see the ruins of his life, see what he did to his wife and to Enkshi, and the city. I want him to walk down Fortune Road and see the corpses in the ditches, I want him to breathe the ashes of all the houses he burned down, I want him to look all those orphans in the

eye and explain to them why his lust for power was more important than their parents' lives." Her hand clenched her goblet so hard
that Jespar almost expected it to bend under her pressure. "I want
him to see what he's fucking done."

*He, Vel'Nyx, the Scythe, and the thousands of commoners who happily
joined in the massacre.*

"And then?" Jespar asked.

"Then I'll make sure he pays. One way or another."

Jespar had no reply to this, but Lysia, gaze lost in her goblet,
didn't seem to expect one. Jespar returned his attention to the fire.
It felt bizarre and wrong to sit here waiting for Maadira while the
dreameater grew with every second, but they had no choice. With the
Ma'saa incapacitated and Enkshi presumably dead, just barging into
Oonai's sleeping quarters and taking the Crown was off the table.
They needed Maadira's permission, and her knowing no particulars
except for the fact that Oonai *was* in a coma made it a lot harder;
explanations had to be made, and they had to be smart about it. So
here they sat, sipping wine as the world burned down around them.

After a time, the sergeant and Kawu returned, looking similar
in their exhaustion: dark bags under their eyes, their bristly hair
greasy and disheveled, their clothes soot-stained. Maadira gestured
at the table, empty except for a bust of Jaaros Oonai and the wine
decanter. They took a seat. Maadira exhaled and rubbed her face
with the heels of her palms.

"I'm sorry I let you wait." *Sowry, led.* Her working-class accent
was more pronounced than the last time they'd met. "We had to
organize our defenses."

"Will we be able to keep them out?" Jespar asked.

"For a while, yes," Maadira said. *Yuz.* "We're doing what we can
to keep their cannons out of firing range, but the tinkerer, Moraia
rest her soul, only delivered ours yesterday, and we're already low

on tyenite and boulders. The same for our archers—we weren't pre-pared for a siege, not to mention the mob is in the thousands, and we're about two hundred."

Lysia studied her hands. "How long do you think?"

"Three to four hours is my guess. The night at most." Maadira seemed about to go on, but then she stopped and let out a long sigh. "I still can't believe all this. The city, in flames. The counselor, dead. The Ma'saa ..." She trailed off.

Sharing the sentiment but aching to get to the point, Jespar sup-pressed the impulse to drum his fingers on the table. "How is she?" he asked, partly out of genuine concern, partly to push the conver-sation forward.

"She's stable. But the ziggurat physician says the aging's perma-nent." She turned to Lysia. "Maybe you could—"

"Shift her back to her former condition? That won't work. Nec-romantic damage to tissue is permanent—that's why it's so feared."

"... I understand. Gods, I should've *never* let her go on that walk, never. It was so careless."

Lysia glanced up. "She went on a walk? With all that's going on?"

"Yes. She wanted to visit that pond near the ziggurat, the one she always used to go to with the Ma'sao. I sent guards with her, but obviously, they weren't enough. It's just ... I didn't expect anything to happen before Miwa-e-Kēko." She drew a long breath. "Anyway, tell me what happened on your journey. The guards said you know a way to cure the Ma'sao, is that true?"

"We think we do," Jespar said.

The story Jespar, Lysia, and Kawu presented Maadira was a mar-riage of truth, lies, and omissions. The central falsehood was that Oonai was innocent and that Vel'Nyx and a Blue Guard general had plotted the Overgrowth Plan to establish a dictatorship. Since Oonai controlled the military, Vel'Nyx had infected him with the dreameater to take him off the chessboard until the coup was over. All this, they had learned from Izabela Dealatis, a secret agent of the Order of Light, whom they had saved from Vel'Nyx's hitmen in Kaiawaika Manor. She had gone on to Tamakaha to report her findings to the Order but asked Jespar, Lysia, and Kawu to travel back to the capital and save Oonai so that he could stop the coup before it was too late.

When Jespar first suggested the lie, Kawu seemed indifferent or simply too exhausted to care, while Lysia's disbelief and anger had been her first show of emotions since she'd found Juusew dead in her clinic. Eventually, though, Jespar had swayed her: without Agaam to support the truth, there was no knowing how a devoted leader of the Blue Guard would react to being told her master was responsible for the death of thousands of soldiers. Even if Maadira didn't write them off as lunatics, the scope of Oonai's betrayal might prompt her to kill him before they could wake him up. Jespar had seen similar things happen during the Nehrimese war.

When they were done, Maadira stood by the eastern window, looking out over the untarnished jungle. "And you are certain Ma'sao Agaam is dead?"

"He took an arrow straight to the heart," Jespar said.

"Hm. I see." She was silent for a while. "There's just one thing I don't understand. If that story is true, then why are you here? You risked your lives to get back up here."

Leaving out Jespar's infection had been Lysia's idea: not only was there a chance Maadira would see a terminally ill sellsword as a potential liability to their escape, but it would also undermine the credibility of their motivations.

Lysia's lips curved in a sardonic smile. "My clinic's gone, and if the whole country falls apart, I won't see a bloody dara of my reward. Also, if we can goad Vel'Nyx into releasing the bug, and Oonai confirms Dealatis' theory, that's two more pieces of evidence we can use to make sure Vel'Nyx gets what she deserves."

"Grand Justiciars Nulaka and Vel'Pawos owe their position to Vel'Nyx, so it's likely they will cover for her," Maadira said. "That means if even one of the three other justiciars doesn't believe that secret agent of yours, Vel'Nyx will go free. We need solid evidence."

"Everything except for the trap went down exactly as Dealatis' theory foresaw it," Jespar argued, his pulse picking up the pace. They had lost too much time already. "And now we got a mob at our doorstep itching to shove pitchforks up our asses. That should count as corroboration, shouldn't it?"

"Hm." Maadira turned back to the window.

"Oh, please, come on," Lysia said. "Do you really think we're making this up? We risked our lives to—"

"No, I don't think you're making this up, Ma'saa Varroy. I'm trying to convince myself that you do, but I can't." Maadira sighed. "As much as I hate to put Ma'sao Oonai's life at risk a minute longer, though, I can't let you do this 'dream run', at least not tonight. I'm expecting the preparations for the evacuation to be done within the hour, and we need to leave at once."

Jespar's heart sank.

Evacuation. Focused on the dreameater and the Magnate's Crown, Jespar had utterly forgotten the possibility that he, Kawu, and Lysia wouldn't be the only ones interested in getting off this sinking ship as soon as possible.

Think. Think, think, think, there's got to be a way to convince her. "There's a way out?" he asked, buying himself time.

"Of course, what did you think? There's a tunnel in the ce—" She broke off. "There *is* a way out, let's leave it at that. But we can't risk anything happening to the Ma'sao during the evacuation, so you will have to perform this ritual once we're somewhere safe. We'll probably head to the garrison on Maitepo and hold out there until the Order's reinforcements get to the Archipelago."

His pulse beating faster, Jespar racked his brains for a convincing argument, but he came up short. What was he supposed to say? Even if he came clean about the infection, how could a single sellsword's life justify risking the safety of Kilay's First Magnate, his Dame, and his entourage even one second longer than necessary?

"How much time do you need for the preparations?" Kawu asked. "You said an hour?"

The attention shifted toward him at once. Kawu had remained silent for the entire conversation.

"At most," Maadira replied hesitantly. "Thirty minutes is more likely."

Kawu nodded. "Then it can be done before you leave."

"Didn't Ma'sao Dal'Varek say it could take you days to find Magnate Vel'Nyx's dreamworld? Because she's so far away, and such?"

"Up to a day, and, yes, he said that. But he didn't tell you he was talking about dreamtime."

"'Dreamtime'?"

Dreamtime. Of course. Jespar had completely forgotten about that.

"Time passes at a different speed in the psychic dimension," Kawu said. "Hours in a dream are only minutes in reality."

"What? How is that possible?" Maadira asked.

"Because time is a mental construct," Kawu replied. "Didn't five minutes ever feel like an hour to you, or the other way around? The only reason we perceive time in the psychic dimension at all is our minds are used to it and because we're still tethered to the real world. It is hard to give exact numbers, but a day in a dreamwalk amounts to roughly an hour in reality."

A lie. Before their previous dreamwalk, Kawu had told them one hour in reality was half a day in dreamtime, not a full one.

Jespar could see the thoughts turn over Maadira's face. "So what you're saying is, you can do that shift of yours and be back in no more than an hour. Is that it?"

"Yes."

"And what will you do if Vel'Nyx isn't asleep right now?"

It was a concern Jespar had voiced several times. Kawu gave Maadira the same answer he had given Jespar. "We just have to hope it doesn't come to that."

When Maadira still seemed hesitant, Jespar added, "We have to at least try, sergeant. You've seen the state the Ma'sao is in—for all we know, the dreameater might kill him within the next hours."

Maadira's mouth gave a twitch. Then she raked a hand through her hair. "Fine. Do it."

Jespar released a small breath. "Right away?"

"At once. But let me be clear: if you're not done by the time the evacuation is ready, we'll come and wake you up." She let out a deep sigh and gazed out the window. When she turned back, her frown lines had deepened. "Why are ye still here?"

Bitterness flooded Jespar's mouth as he swallowed the neki. The three of them sat cross-legged at the footboard of Oonai's bed, the Magnate's Crown on Kawu's lap. Oonai looked worse than he had when they had left, white slime oozing down the corners of his eyes, the same Jespar had coughed up hours ago.

"And this stuff wears off once we're in the dream?" Lysia was holding a ball of neki pinched between her fingers, the unease written deep into her features. Kawu had been adamant about his idea to bring her along, arguing that they needed all the help they could get—even if it meant a slightly stronger shifting drain for him.

"Yes," Kawu said.

Lysia regarded the crumpled herbs a second longer, then tossed them into her mouth and swallowed. "And now?"

"Now we wait a few minutes for it to take effect."

Kawu quickly reiterated the most important rule of dreamwalking—they *had* to act as part of the dream lest they'd break the immersion—then they went over the conversation strategy they had come up with to persuade Vel'Nyx's subconscious to release the dreameater.

When they were done, Jespar's lids had grown heavy, and his head bobbed forward. The next thing he knew, Kawu was leaning over him, fingers on his forehead, warm, familiar, trusted.

He looks so tired, Jespar thought as his mind drifted away. How could he not? Kawu's life before the mission had been far from easy, but this past week had probably scarred him for life. And who had coaxed him into coming along?

Protect him, Jespar thought. *You have to protect him.*

"I'm taking you under now."

Protect-

The world turned blue.

There had been a lake in the pine forest surrounding the Dal'Varek manor—navy and white in winter, cobalt and green in summer. Jespar was eleven and his sister eight when they had made it their haven. Twice or thrice a week, they had gone to the lake, where Jespar read to her and taught her how to swim, and she showed him her weavings and drawings. The twins never joined, too busy being the golden sons that father had wanted Jespar to be.

She and Jespar had also been there the night it happened.

His recollections of that day were fractured. He remembered it had been a swelteringly hot summer day, the kind where your skin stays sticky the whole night. He remembered they had tiptoed past the snoring governess. He remembered they had run through the forest, he carrying her piggyback, both of them laughing. He remembered the two of them stargazing on the shingle, Jespar showing her the constellations, Saldrin's Owl, Irländah's Flute, the Lambent Scepter.

Next, his sister noticing a pretty orange glow over the treetops.

Next, a tang of smoke as they went back home.

Next, blood-soaked bodies tied to the gate, Father and Rodrik and Alvric, lotus blossoms carved into their foreheads.

Everything had fallen apart that night, and yet—or perhaps precisely *because* of that—Jespar never forgot how incredibly light he had felt before they'd noticed the glow. How light he had felt laying there with his sister as he showed her the constellations, the stars as timeless as that bond they once shared, the kind only children are capable of before they realize nothing lasts forever.

The world had been easy.

Thanks to the neki, their long journey into Vel'Nyx's dream felt similar. All sorrows forgotten, Jespar floated through that timeless black ocean, Lysia beside him while Kawu guided them deeper and deeper, the Magnate's Crown in his hands like a divining rod.

Warm. Light. Free.

When a colossal bubble came into view in the darkness, Jespar had lost track of time. Hours, days, or years—what did it matter? They passed through the membrane, a shiver crawling over him as cold air enfolded them. For a few seconds, they floated in a sky, looking down upon a gray-white landscape, the word for which Jespar's drogaed mind couldn't remember.

They fell.

Slow at first, then faster, until the white was racing toward them at breakneck speed, the biting wind tearing away Jespar's false serenity and the panic breaking through. Before Jespar could scream, a yank went through his body and drove the air out of his lungs. He hung suspended in midair. And dropped to the ground.

Cold.

Gods, it was cold. Jespar tried to push himself up from the white floor on which he had landed, but it gave in under his hands.

Snow. This is snow.

He tried again, slow and careful, distributing his weight evenly between arms, knees, and feet. It worked. Grunting, Jespar rose, his hands pained from the chill; he stared at the snow under his boots as his brain, the neki lifting, slowly caught up.

Snow. A dream. They were on a dreamwalk, and this was Vel'Nyx's kuluhika.

Jespar lifted his eyes.

He was on a promontory, white mountains surrounding him. A castle stood enthroned at the lip of the precipice, some hundred strides away, all gray stone, pointed roofs, and rounded towers. It was Golden-era architecture from the early 900s, the kind you mostly found in North Nehrim or Enderal. A black, wrought-iron fence stretched around the property, and light glowed behind the arched windows.

"Hey! Over here."

Lysia stood by a nearby rock. She was shivering with her arms wrapped around her nuvium mail, snow speckling her ponytail.

Relieved at the familiar sight, Jespar felt himself relax. "Are you all right? Where's–"

"Jespar!" Kawu's voice rang out over the snow. "Jespar, kena 'ō!"

Kawu was some fifteen strides behind them, partially concealed by a rock, and dangerously close to the promontory's edge; he was on all fours, the Magnate's Crown between his knees, frantically trying to pull himself up. This was his first time seeing snow.

"Kena 'ō! Iepa, lehō lehō!" *Help! I'm sinking!*

Jespar started toward him, but the snow gave in and swallowed his leg to the knee. "Bloody ..."

"Don't move!" Lysia said.

"We have to help him!"

"You're not helping anyone if you sink in and freeze to death." She looked off, her thumb rubbing her lower lip. Then she nodded to herself. "All right, stay here. And Kawu, you don't move either, okay? The cold won't kill you, just *don't move.*"

Kawu nodded. Jespar, out of options, lifted his leg back out of the snow and did the same.

Walking in stork-like steps, Lysia set off toward a nearby cluster of shrubs and returned a few minutes later with a bundle of twigs under her arm.

"What's this?" Jespar asked. He was *really* starting to feel the chill, and Kawu was looking more miserable by the minute. *No wonder.* Jespar's body was accustomed to a four-season climate; Kawu was like a gecko on a frozen lake.

Lysia lowered the bundle to the ground and sank to her knees. "You'll see."

Not much later, Lysia had arranged a third of the branches in two oblong shapes the size of a serving tray. She unbuckled her belt, emptied her pouches, then cut their cloth into even strips, which she tethered around the twigs to fix them in place. Finally, she halved her belt and slung one part each around each oblong like loops. When she slipped her boot into one of them and cinched the noose tight, Jespar understood.

"Snowshoes," he said.

"Mâleian hunter's trick." She slid on the second shoe and took a probing step forward. It held.

"Okay," she said. "Let's get to it."

Lysia fashioned two more pairs of snowshoes and brought Kawu and Jespar one each; a few cautious steps later, they had gotten the hang of it and made for the castle, Kawu wearing Jespar's scarf, which he had given him for warmth. Trudging on as fast as the snow and the bitter cold allowed them, Kawu told them it had taken him even longer than expected to find the Third Magnate's kuluhika. Wherever the real Vel'Nyx was, she was far from the Archipelago.

"How much longer are we talking?" Jespar asked between shallow breaths. "Five hours, six?"

Kawu's answer came after a pause. "I can't know for certain, but I'd say it took us somewhere between seven and ten hours to get here. That means we have between two and five hours left until Ma'saa Maadira will wake us."

... and we're done for, Jespar added in his thoughts.

By the time they stopped before the black gate, the cold had made every movement agony. A queasy feeling settled in Jespar's stomach as he realized they might have never reached the place without freezing to death had they landed even just a little farther away.

Thank chance for small favors.

With shaking hands, Kawu held the Magnate's Crown toward the gate. The courtyard beyond it was deserted: an iced-over fountain rose in the center, the sculpture of a majestic myrad enthroned upon it, maw raised toward the sky. Skeletal shrubs hinted at what must have once been flowerbeds.

"Yes," Kawu said softly. "Vel'Nyx is in there."

Jespar pulled at the gate. It opened without a sound. "Time to end this, then."

The snow crunched softly under their boots as they walked toward the gold-framed entrance. Whatever they would find beyond would decide the fate of the Archipelago—and Jespar's life.

CHAPTER TWENTY-SIX
MIXED WATERS

DAY SIX
1ST MOON OF RAINY SEASON, 1226 A.L.

Blood rushed into Jespar's limbs, leaving trails of burning prickles; his lungs stung as the warm air replaced the frost.

Eerily reminiscent of the old Dal'Varek estate, the lobby stayed faithful to the Golden-era aesthetic of the exterior: wood-paneled hallways branched off to either side, and a vaulted stucco ceiling contrasted with dark floorboards. Curvy furniture, hunting trophies, and suits of armor decorated the room.

Not a soul in sight.

Closing his eyes, Jespar leaned back against the door. *Tired.* Gods, he was so bloody tired. When he looked again, Kawu was sitting with his back against the chunky doorpost, some color back in his cheeks. Lysia was a few steps into the hall, observing the surroundings. Catching Jespar's gaze, she pointed at her ear.

Jespar heard it. A soft string melody floated through the manor.

"Music," Kawu said.

"Uh-huh." Lysia nodded toward a hallway on the left. "And I think it's coming from down there."

———⟿⟾———

A red carpet ran down the corridor like a trail of blood. Portraits of rugged landscapes and elegant women lined the walls, illumined by the torch sconces filling the spaces between. All the rooms they passed were empty, and after a few turns, the hallway ended in a spiral staircase that led to a corridor, identical to its predecessor, except for the lack of windows. They followed it, only to find themselves in yet another corridor indistinguishable from the others. It went on like this for a time, the only difference between the levels Jespar's rising anxiety, until they reached the sixth floor below. Halfway down its length, Jespar stopped dead. A young woman peeked around the turn at the end of the hallway; wet red curls framed her elfin face, and a rakish grin creased her lips.

She giggled and disappeared behind the corner.

"Did you ... see that?" Jespar asked.

Lysia put a hand on the sheath of her clawblade. "Uh-huh. Kawu, a person's simulacrum can look like anything, right? You think that was ...?"

"Vel'Nyx? No, that was just an ordinary dream character—I would have felt it otherwise." Kawu studied the ceiling, shifting his weight from one leg to the other. "Though there is something odd about this place. It's so ... stable."

"'Stable'?"

"Mm-hm. Normally, a dream is in constant flux, as in, the environment changes often, and nonsensical things happen all the time. Oonai's kuluhika was different because the dreameater controlled it, but this one ..." He trailed off.

"Should be a lot more chaotic?" Jespar offered.

"Yes," Kawu said. "Though I believe some drogae, like opium or caratin, can stabilize dreams. Either way, we should see where this dream character went—chances are she might lead us to Vel'Nyx."

There was no sign of the girl in the hallway below, but wet footprints marked the carpet, and a trace of patchouli clung to the air. They were halfway down its length when the girl appeared again, peering with her fingers curled around the corner like a curious kobold. This time, they called out to her, but she just giggled and disappeared; one level below, Jespar sprinted toward her the second she showed up, but he found nothing but more footprints and perfume. The fact that the melody grew steadily louder was the only thing that suggested they weren't moving in circles. It must have been after the dozenth round of this bizarre game of hide-and-seek that something changed at last: reaching yet another corner, the corridor opened into what seemed to be a bathing hall.

Amid a cloud of mist flowing from a spacious inground pool, dozens of women lounged, nude, distinct in appearance but alike in beauty and youth. Candelabras bathed the scene in an orange glow, cushions and blankets had been laid on the marble floor, and a voluptuous woman in a white dress plucked a harp. A second ticked by before it struck Jespar why the sight seemed so surreal: though the women's body language suggested they were talking, the hall was void of conversation. Nothing but the splashing of water and the plucking of the harp.

"Look," Lysia said, pointing at an older woman in a gray dress on a chaise beside the musician. She observed them curiously, one hand holding a goblet, the other trailing through the braided hair of a young Qyranian, who lay with her head resting on the elder's lap.

"Is that her?" Jespar asked Kawu. "Vel'Nyx?"

"Yes," Kawu replied, carefully placing the Magnate's Crown on the ground. "This is her simulacrum."

Lysia's eyes were narrowed to slits. "Let's have a chat, then."

Except for Vel'Nyx and the girl with the red curls—she sat on a pillow by the entrance, flashing them a conspiratorial grin as they passed by—none of the women reacted to the newcomers' presence. Not until Jespar, Lysia, and Kawu stopped in front of her did Vel'Nyx acknowledge them.

Lacking Oonai's air of power and the Ma'saa's saintly majesty, Makiima Vel'Nyx's most prominent characteristic was her inconspicuousness: she was of small stature and had a broad face with delicate features that even old age hadn't hardened. Never would she have drawn Jespar's attention on the street without her expensive gray silk robe, and even that was understated by Kilayan standards. Had it not been for the calculating edge in her dark brown eyes, Jespar would have struggled to believe that she was not only one of the most powerful politicians of the Archipelago but also a mass murderer.

Sweat beaded on his neck. This was the only chance they had; one wrong word and the immersion would break, kicking them out of the dream and toward his doom.

And if she isn't the imprinter after all? a voice in his head said, a familiar one he'd tried hard to keep silent these past two days.

She was. She had a motive, the means, the opportunity.

It had to be.

Bizarre and risky as this whole undertaking was, it had one decisive advantage: convincing Vel'Nyx's conscious self to release the parasite would have been near impossible. Her subconscious was a different story. Entering a person's kuluhika meant becoming a part of their thoughts and subjecting oneself to their perception, but it also meant the ability to communicate beyond all the barriers of reason, logic, and preconceptions the mind normally surrounds itself with. When they had devised their strategy, Kawu had used his "fantasy of an alien god" metaphor to illustrate his point: speak to the god directly, and it will laugh you off. Enter their head, and you have access to a million levers in its mind, some obvious, some cryptic, most invisible. Persuasion was just a matter of finding the right ones. The wisest course, according to Kawu, was to communicate in generalized ideas and raw emotions, and to avoid specifics like names, dates, or places that could conflict with the dreamer's reality and thereby break the immersion.

As though she'd been expecting them, Vel'Nyx sized each of them up. Her eyes crinkled upon reaching Lysia. "Well, well. I haven't seen you before, have I, love?"

Lysia tensed, her fists clenching. Her resolve returned, and the play began.

"I doubt it," she said. "It's a beautiful place, though."

She did it well, speaking as if her being here was the most natural thing in the world.

"Oh, you think so?" Vel'Nyx casually looked around the bathing hall. The women continued their pantomime, paying no heed to their conversation. "I suppose age has made me jaded, then. That's one of its many gifts, you know? Wrinkles, vaginal dryness, and a whole boatload of boredom." She glanced at Kawu. "Your Makehu friend doesn't seem to be feeling too well."

"It was a long journey," Lysia said.

"I can imagine. Where are you from?"

Generals, Jespar thought. *Not specifics.*

"Down south."

"Uh-huh. I see."

The woman sleeping on Vel'Nyx's lap roused and gave a hearty yawn. Vel'Nyx ran her fingers down the woman's neck and toyed with one of her braids. "Say, love, why don't you stay and unwind a little? Take a dip in the pool, warm yourself up ... your friends are welcome to stay, too, of course. I'm sure we can discuss whatever boring and worldly reason brought you here in the morrow."

Jespar joined in. "I'm afraid we don't have time for that. There's news from the capital."

Vel'Nyx flashed him an annoyed look. "One more reason to hold off on it, then. I couldn't care less about that stinking cesspool."

It wasn't the answer Jespar had expected.

Lysia came to his aid. "Let's cut the banter. We know about the plan."

Vel'Nyx's mouth twitched. "What plan?"

"The Overgrowth Plan," Lysia said. "You and Oonai built up the Scythe, and you orchestrated a riot intending to murder the five other magnates and half the Coalition."

Vel'Nyx's smile stayed in place, but the harpist's song took up speed, the woman's head rocking from side to side.

"You're confused, love. I think it's time for you to leave."

Lysia passed Jespar a glance—his cue.

Please, he thought. *Let this work.* "We also know you're behind Oonai's coma. You infected him with the parasite when he got second thoughts."

Her smile cracked, and the music ceased.

Bull's-eye.

"I have no idea what you're talking about, young man."

But it was an act. There was clarity behind Vel'Nyx's blank expression, a sense of knowing, and Jespar felt it as clearly as he had felt something was amiss after that first cursed dreamwalk where he'd gotten himself infected.

"Yes, you do," he said. "You infected Oonai with a dreameater when he tried to back out of the plan, and then you fled the country to wait out the storm. Well, guess what, the Scythe turned against you. They slaughtered the Blue Guard, and now they're laying waste to the ziggurats."

Vel'Nyx stared. Her thin lips quivered at the edges.

Encouraged, Jespar stepped toward her. "Are you aware what that means? It means you messed up. Once the Scythe is done on Uunili, they will move on to the other islands and take everything you own: your properties, your treasures, your livelihood. The whole thing will go on until the Order of Light intervenes, and then the entire country will plunge into a full-on civil war. This great scheme you and Oonai devised, it went up in flames—the Scythe outsmarted you, and soon, the whole Illumined World will know it was your fault."

Vel'Nyx was silent.

Say something.

Say something, you bitch.

The harpist resumed her play, her fingers now conjuring swift and somber arpeggios. Vel'Nyx took a wine glass from a cocktail table beside the chaise and sipped slowly. "No," she said. "This doesn't make any sense."

Lysia's brows narrowed. "So you admit to it."

"The Twins *know* the revolution is a pipe dream," Vel'Nyx said, ignoring her question. "They are perfectly aware the Order of Light would intervene and have them hanged if this phony revolt were to actually succeed. There's absolutely nothing to gain for them."

"Well, it happened," Jespar said. "Believe me, we saw it. The mob butchered the entire Blue Guard on that ambush spot, and now they're laying siege on the First Ziggurat."

Vel'Nyx took another sip. "You have an active imagination, young man. Now go, you've overstayed your welcome."

Lysia tossed a glance at Kawu, who had been listening silently with his arms hugged tightly around himself. He gave a weak nod.

Had Jespar believed in the Gods, this would have been the time for a prayer.

"Here's the thing," Lysia said. "The Order of Light knows what you've done. They investigated you and Oonai, and it all came to light. As soon as you arrive in Arazea–"

A blunder. Vel'Nyx's simulacrum didn't believe herself to be on her way to Arazeal, but in some lonely mountain castle. Lysia had pointed out the discrepancy.

Nothing happened. Vel'Nyx continued to study her drink, her fingers trailing up and down the neck of the woman.

"—you'll be incarcerated and trialed," Lysia finished.

"They'll hang you, if you're lucky," Jespar said. "But in all likelihood, the punishment will be much, much more painful. Either way, the result will be the same: you'll lose everything, be proclaimed a traitor, then die with the masses shouting at you."

Vel'Nyx's mien didn't change, but dissonant notes mixed into the harpist's arpeggios. In his periphery, Jespar noticed the nude women had all gathered in a half-circle behind them.

He suppressed the urge to take a deep breath. *And here we go.* "Unless you cooperate."

"Cooperate," Vel'Nyx echoed. "How?"

It's working. She's taking the bait.

"By releasing Oonai," Lysia said. "Call back the parasite so Oonai can save the island."

Vel'Nyx didn't lift her eyes. She traced her forefinger along the sleeping woman's jaw, then down her neck and across. "Didn't you just say the Scythe burned down all the ziggurats?"

"All except his. And, like it or not, if anyone can still stop the Scythe at this point, it's him."

Vel'Nyx drew a slow line across the woman's throat. "And just how is dear little Fish Boy going to do that?"

"Together with the remaining Blue Guard divisions on the other islands," Jespar lied. He had no idea whether the Guard still had reserves, let alone how large they were. "If Oonai survives, he'll flee the ziggurat, sail there, assume command, and then fight the rebels until the Order of Light arrives and helps him finish them off. If he dies, on the other hand—"

"The soldiers desert, and the country falls into anarchy," Vel'Nyx said. "I get the idea. He's the last pillar of the old order. And you're saying the Order sent you here to tell me they'll judge leniently if I help save what's left, is that it?"

"Yes," Lysia said.

"Mm-hm. Who are you three, exactly, some kind of ... what, holy sellswords? Two outlanders and a Makehu boy?"

"We're your last chance of making it through this alive," Jespar said with a firmness he didn't feel. "That's all you need to know."

Vel'Nyx grunted pensively. Then she returned her attention to her drink, all the while drawing slices across the sleeping woman's neck.

"Well, what should I say? I'm humbled by this unprecedented display of generosity. There's only one problem."

She softly slapped her lover's cheek. She awoke. Vel'Nyx made a dismissive gesture at the pool. The woman rose with a bizarre giggle, then sauntered to the pool and jumped in beside three other girls, who shrieked in delight as water splashed over them.

"I know absolutely nothing about a parasite."

For a second, Jespar felt nothing at all. Then the dread woke in its tomb.

Lysia stepped forward, fists balled. "You're a liar."

Kawu gave Jespar an alarmed look.

"I don't get it," Lysia said. "What's the fucking point? We all know it was you, so why not fucking admit it?"

Vel'Nyx's was a picture of calm. "Because there's nothing to admit, love. I don't have the slightest idea what 'parasite' you're talking about. But, I must say, it was quite entertaining to listen to you. Now, I suggest—"

Lysia lunged forward and grabbed her by the throat. "Liar! You bloody liar!"

Shit.

Jespar reached for Lysia—or tried to, at least. For some reason, his boots were glued to the floor, his muscles refusing to act. *What the hell?*

"Kill it!" Lysia screamed. "Kill that *fucking* bug!"

Vel'Nyx croaked and kicked, but Lysia's grip was ironclad; the harp's arpeggios sped faster, dissonance jarring the notes.

"Release it, or I'll fucking kill you!"

Do something! Bloody hell, do something!

But Jespar's body refused to obey. Lysia kept screaming into Vel'Nyx's reddening face, all the while the harpist played faster and faster until her fingers sped across the strings like a spider's legs and blood trickled down her wrists; with a scream, Lysia let go of Vel'Nyx's throat, drew her clawblade and shoved it deep into the Third Magnate's heart.

A string broke and the music cut off.

Vel'Nyx croaked. Stared at the knife in her chest. And collapsed onto the floor.

A heartbeat went by in stillness.

His mouth open, Jespar stared at the Third Magnate's lifeless body. His thoughts were a hot haze as his brain struggled to make sense of what had just happened. Even the dread had fallen silent again.

Another beat.

Lysia stood over Vel'Nyx's lifeless body. Blood dripped from her blade, mingling with the red pool on the tiles. The girls in the hall shifted about, trading puzzled looks.

Another.

"What did you do?" whispered Jespar. "What the hell did you do?"

Lysia turned. Her face was ashen. "That ... that wasn't me. I didn't-I couldn't move, I couldn't stop, I just—"

Chuckles. The women had stepped back from their semicircle, opening a clear view on the four girls in the basin. They were looking at Jespar, Lysia, and Kawu, mischievous grins tacked onto their mouths.

What the hell? What the fucking hell?

Kawu muttered something. Gripping the hilt of his longsword—Jespar's body once again obeyed his will—Jespar sought his eyes. "Kawu? Kawu, what is this?"

The girls chuckled louder. Some outside the pool joined in.

"She knows," Kawu said. "Īmīte, she knows."

The hall burst into laughter.

Jespar unsheathed his sword and backed off, tip pointed at the women, but none of them advanced toward him; they just stood there and laughed, like children ridiculing another who'd done something incredibly stupid.

"What's going on here?" Jespar shouted. "What the fuck is going on?"

A female voice cut through the din.

"You amuse me." It came from all directions at once, reverberating off the high ceiling. "That's what's going on."

More laughter.

"Enough," the voice said. "Quiet, now."

The women ignored her. The laughter swelled, bordering on the hysterical.

"I said, 'Enough'!"

Silence.

"Out. Now."

The girls looked at each other, their cheeks red and their eyes teary. Then they formed an orderly line and left the hall in single file. His emotional capacities exhausted, Jespar watched numbly as they emptied the room, still standing in beware stance and holding onto his longsword like a child onto a blanket. Even when Vel'Nyx rose to her feet as if she'd lain down on purpose, he failed to feel surprised. Calmly, Vel'Nyx straightened out her dress—her wound and the bloodstain were gone—and sat back down on the chaise, resting one arm on the seatback.

"Toli, pi'a ū," she said in flawless Makehu. "Kaia 'atete leie ite koma'e e kuluhika."

Yes, boy. I know you're a dreamwalker.

All the color drained from Kawu's cheeks.

"You know we're ..." Jespar trailed off when Lysia shot him a pointed look.

"Relax, love," Vel'Nyx said with the hint of a smirk. "You're not going to break the immersion. I know you're visitors."

Jespar's hands felt clammy. "How?"

"Can't you guess?"

"She's a dreamwalker," Kawu said quietly. "She has the Sight too."

"Smart little pi'a. Frankly, I was a little surprised when I saw you saunter in here. I thought the woman from Hapana, that curmudgeon from Lehowai, and I were the only ones left. Unless ..." She clicked her tongue. "Of course, those pretty green eyes. You're Takana Nakāni's son, aren't you?"

When Kawu didn't answer, she snorted. "Well, my condolences. I always found the Makehu word for our abilities rather ironic. 'Koma'e e kuluhika e hapī', the 'gift of walking through dreams.' Always awake, an auric resonance that makes people hate you, and vastly increased chances of ending up in an asylum: I don't know about you, but had I been given a choice between this 'gift' and a lifetime of diarrhea, I'd have built myself a fancy outhouse and stepped up to the challenge." It was when her eyes crinkled that Jespar understood. They lacked the skin fold of the upper lids that Kawu had, but the mild downward slant at the corners left no doubt. How had he not seen it sooner?

"You're Makehu," Jespar said.

"Your cunning is a force of nature, young man. Yes, I'm Makehu ... a half-blood, you could call me, or 'miwāmalā' if you prefer the fancy insult. Makiima is an Inâlized version of my Makehu name Akīma, and I bought the last name and title off a struggling official of noble heritage."

"You knew we weren't part of your dream all along?" Lysia asked hoarsely.

"Of course I did, love. You're pretty, but I'm afraid your acting doesn't quite cut it yet."

Suddenly, the humid air felt oppressive. "But why the charade, then? Why didn't you just ...?"

"Kick you out? Fair question." She stood and walked over to the harp, trailing her fingers over the bloodied strings. "I suppose it comes down to entertainment. As I said before, seventy-one years in waking life plus an eternity in your dreams make you quite jaded. Not to mention it's been decades since I got an actual visitor in this place, so, naturally, I was curious. What in the world brings two outlanders and a Makehu dreamwalker into my dream? Well, now I know."

"And making me stab you?" Lysia asked. All the anger, all the determination she'd had mere minutes ago was gone again. "Was that also part of the entertainment?"

"I suppose. All diversions are welcome." Vel'Nyx plucked a dissonant chord. "So, that old fool got himself infected by a dreameater, hm? I always thought those beasts were extinct."

Jespar groped for words. "You really aren't the imprinter, are you?"

"I'm afraid not, young man, that part wasn't an act. Seems to me you've been chasing phantoms."

No.

The dread stirred again, smoke licking through the cracks. A cold spot pulsed over Jespar's right brow.

"But you're the only one with a motive and the means," Lysia said weakly. "It *has* to be you."

"Repeating a statement doesn't make it any truer, love. Yes, Oonai did try to back out, but I never planned on killing him." She scoffed. "And even if I had, there are much easier ways. As I said, I didn't even know dreameaters still existed."

"But you had to keep him quiet," Jespar insisted.

Vel'Nyx rested her elbow on the harp's neck. "Why?"

"What do you mean, 'why'? He could have come clean to the Coalition and blown up your entire scheme."

"And sentenced his wife and treasured friend to a gruesome death in the process?"

"They had—"

"Nothing to do with it, I know. That's beside the point. Use that thing between your ears for a change, young man: how do you think the Coalition would have reacted to someone as powerful as Oonai confessing to high treason? Correct, they would have turned our punishment into the bloodiest spectacle in the history of the Archipelago—it's called 'setting an example.' The last time a magnate plotted the murder of another, a fire 'broke out' in the traitor's ziggurat and killed his entire family and staff. The fire was so smart it even put him, his wife, and his daughters in shackles before eating them alive, imagine that."

"Oonai doesn't give a rat's ass about his wife," Lysia said. "He cheated on her for years."

"And yet he loved her to death. The world isn't black and white, you're old enough to know that. We actually talked about this one time, back when he was obsessed with that servant girl, Talin or whatever the hell her name was. Those flings, they were just toys to him, and they never in *any way* competed with his emotional loyalty to his sweet, angelic Nayima. Bizarre, I know, but that's Jaaros Oonai for you: the man could convince himself the sky is green if he wanted it bad enough."

"So, what," Jespar said, "you just let him go his merry way when he told you he was backing out? Do you seriously expect us to believe that?"

"Frankly, I couldn't care less what you believe. But, no, it wasn't like that. *He* wasn't a risk, but some other people were, so I took some precautions before I left."

"The servants of Kaiawaika Manor," Kawu said quietly.

Vel'Nyx raised an eyebrow. "You know, then. Did the hitmen get the job done, at least? They better, those folk were dreadfully expensive."

When no one answered, Vel'Nyx shrugged and pushed herself away from the harp. "Well, I suppose it doesn't matter. If the Scythe already did their job, there's no one left to judge."

What? Jespar gripped his sword tighter. "Bloody hell, are you even listening? The Scythe didn't do their job—they ratted out on you and are about to take over the whole fucking country!"

"That *was* the job, young man."

Had Vel'Nyx declared she was a Light-Born, Jespar's reaction would not have been much different. He stood still as a statue, blinking, clenching and unclenching his hands around the hilt of his sword.

Lysia was the first to recover her words. "What are you talking about?"

"You heard me: if what you said is true, then the Scythe did exactly what I paid them for, to a tee. They are burning it all down."

When neither of the three said anything, Vel'Nyx's dour smile resurfaced. "What, you thought I had no idea what I was in for when I hired those two lunatics? I know they're tawahe, I would have known even without my Sight. They wanted chaos, I wanted chaos—a match made in heaven."

Jespar fumbled for words. "So the Twins don't ...?"

"The Twins don't give a shit about the 'struggle of the commoner'—they just want to chop some heads off and later reminisce about the memory over a glass of wine. Exactly what I needed, in other words: Scythes to slash away the overgrowth. Crude ones, I admit, but damn effective."

Vel'Nyx snorted and shook her head, as if contemplating a joke only she understood. "Overgrowth ... the word describes our entire culture. Fortune Road, the Great Dream, it's all nonsense—this country was never about who works the hardest, it's about being born into the right family or fitting the narrative. Take Oonai: do you really think he won the Magnate's Crown because he had the right qualifications or because we all imagined what a great emperor he would be?" Her glare wandered over each of them. "Of course not. He got it because he fit the story."

A thought formed, a piece of driftwood offering itself to a man who was drowning: Vel'Nyx was lying. Like the charade before, this was just some bloody mind game, her way of toying with their desperation.

But Jespar couldn't believe it, no matter how much he wanted to. Not only would this lie have been far too complicated and specific, but there was also an intensity behind Vel'Nyx's soliloquy that simply felt too real to be acted.

"The tall, handsome man with the mighty beard and intense stare, the Fish Boy who worked his way to the top of Fortune Road and married the beautiful, pious daughter of the fabled Vel'Anelys family. What a sweet, sweet tale, fit for the ballads." She pinched a bloody harp string between forefinger and thumb and slowly bent it back and forth. "Me, though? Just an old hag without a husband or heirs who prefers to listen rather than hear herself talk ... Just a miwāmalā who got lucky. How did I even think I stood a chance?

"I have a piece of advice, my fellow Makehu," Vel'Nyx told Kawu. "Don't ever believe them when they tell you you're equal. Yes, we now have the same rights on paper, and, yes, there's the Band of Elders, but that's all just window dressing. People may say they respect you, and they might even mean it, but in the end, your role in the story has been written the moment you were born with those tilted eyes of ours. The day the Order and that stupid Chieftain struck the treaty, the wakemō became the protagonists ... and they always will be." She let go of the string, conjuring a high note that echoed off the domed ceiling. "The sad thing is, in a way, I was no better than Oonai: I ignored the truth and bought into that foolish fairy tale that we can all be who we want, if we only try hard enough. Half my life, I spent in the Coalition, half my rotten life, and then? Out of nowhere comes this green boy with barely thirty years on his back, and just slips past all the obstacles I fought so hard to overcome. But I learned my lesson. I grinned and I bore it, I watched, and I listened, until I finally got the chance to get even."

Kawu's voice was lifeless. "So you did all this for revenge?"

"I did this to burn the overgrowth."

"But what about the rest?" Lysia asked. "The thousands of innocents who died?"

"Collateral damage. I made my point. That's all that matters."

A part somewhere deep inside Jespar rebelled at the monstrosity of the statement, but he was too dazed to pay it any attention. What was it to him? In a few hours, he'd be trapped in a nightmare, getting tortured for eternity.

"If you didn't infect Oonai," he managed, "then who did?" He was surprised at how composed he sounded—all he wanted to do was scream.

Vel'Nyx looked at him blankly, no sign of empathy or hatred. Just a blank canvas.

"Please," Kawu said softly. "You achieved what you set out to do. If you have even the slightest idea, I beg you to tell us. Oonai's dreameater, it infected my friend, and we think that killing it is the only way to kill—"

"I don't know."

Kawu fell quiet.

"I don't know. And even if I did, if saving you means saving that cocky bastard, then I wouldn't tell you. Who knows, maybe rotting away in an endless nightmare will finally teach him some fucking humility."

"Then we'll tell the Order what you did," Lysia said. "We'll tell them everything."

"I'd love to hear that story," Vel'Nyx said. "'We sauntered into Vel'Nyx's dream where she gave us her full confession.' You have nothing on me. Even if you had, who do you think they would believe? The respected magnate who lost everything to the cruel commoners, or three dirty peasants?"

Vel'Nyx stood and smoothed her dress. "Good night, ma'sae. For what it's worth, I'm sorry you got caught up in this—but as I said, some choices aren't ours to make. Such is life."

"Please," Kawu whispered. "Jespar will—"

"May you prosper."

The dream collapsed.

Chapter Twenty-Seven
Hulls

Day Seven

1st Moon of Rainy Season, 1226 A.L.

espar had but a single thought upon waking: *It's over.* They had bet all their money on one horse, and it had been the wrong one.

Where was the dread? Where was the horror? Where was the panic?

Lysia sat up beside him, asked if he was okay. He said yes. It wasn't even a lie. He felt nothing, even though his last hope of a cure had turned out to be a mirage. He felt nothing, even though it meant the dreameater would hatch and drag him into an endless nightmare. He felt nothing, even though the Corpse was sitting on a chair across the room, holding Oonai's severed head in his burning hands. He felt nothing, even though the stone floor beneath him had turned into a frozen ocean.

Kawu pulled him back.

They briefed Maadira in the Ma'saa's study. A black cat eyed their conversation from atop a cupboard, as if wondering where her mistress was and what these curious intruders were doing here. The comet orchid garland across the entry had begun to wither, its browning petals pooling on the floor.

"She will hang for this," Maadira said. "If it's the last thing I do in this world. That harpy will hang for this."

No one answered.

"Well," Maadira sighed, "as much as I wish this undertaking of yours had worked, it changes nothing about the plan. Preparing the evacuation took us longer than expected, but we're almost ready now—once the Ma'sao and the Ma'saa are safe on Maitepo and the keepers have the situation under control, we'll start the investigation. We will find this 'imprinter', you have my word on that. The only question is when."

And the answer is, "too late". "Makes sense," Jespar said hoarsely.

Maadira nodded. "The good news is, the walls are still holding, and the men I sent to scout the tunnel should be back any minute. Provided the path is clear, we'll be off this island come daybreak."

Lysia was absently trailing her finger over the table in front of her, drawing slow circles. "How much longer until we leave?"

Maadira glanced at the water clock. "Half an hour, give or take. We've sent scouts to make sure there are no nasty surprises at the end of the escape tunnel. Everyone else is already waiting in the atrium."

"Everyone?" Jespar asked. "But the battlements are still ..." He faded out when he understood what it meant.

"It's the only option," Maadira said in a tone that was both remorseful and defensive. "Evacuating the entire place would take us three times as long, and without archers and cannoneers to hold the have-nots off, they'd be through the gate in no time. The best we can do is to make sure their sacrifices won't be in vain." She paused,

NICOLAS LIETZAU

as if reflecting on her words. Then she stood. "Atrium, half an hour. If you're not there, we'll leave without you."

When the door had fallen shut behind her, silence ensued. Lysia stared at a candle between them, the wick struggling in the growing pool of wax. Kawu sat still, his eyes two half-closed crescents underlined by deep violet circles. Jespar slumped in his chair, one arm hanging limply over the backrest.

A drink. He needed a drink.

"We can still do it," Lysia said. The wax closed in on the wick. The flame flickered, but then recovered. "There's no way we'll let it end like this. We won't let Vel'Nyx get away, we'll make sure Oonai sees what he's done, and we will fix you."

"Will we?" Jespar asked, surveying the room for a decanter or a bottle.

"Yes, we'll just keep investigating. Think about it, we'll be out of here in a couple of hours, and instead of following the others to Maitepo, we stay behind and continue to look for answers, they can't stop us from doing that. The Jade Hall would be a good place to start, maybe Oonai's or Vel'Nyx's office. We could even go back to Bluefort and find Dealatis so she can show us her evidence and ..."

Her voice faded into the background. No decanter, no bottle, no flask, not on the desk, not on the mantelpiece, not on the table by the entrance. No *bloody* drink, nowhere.

"Lysia," Jespar said.

"... saw that place in your vision, that's gotta mean something, we just have to ..."

The candle died.

"Lysia!"

She fell silent.

"There's no way I will hold out that long. Kawu's shifts are getting less effective, and I think I'm starting to feel the side effects." He took a long breath. "It's over. It's time for me to admit that. No matter what we do, the bug is gonna win."

Cannons fired in the distance, like exclamation marks to Jespar's words. Shouting, loud enough to reach them even here. The mob must have launched another assault on the gate.

"No," Lysia said slowly. "You're not giving up."

"This isn't about giving up. Look, Oonai has been in this coma for more than a moon, and he's still alive, right? That means you'll still have weeks to cure me, even after I ... well. You can continue looking for the imprinter, but without having to worry about me going nuts every other hour." He paused, looking at Kawu. Gods, how tired he seemed. And whose fault was that? If not for Jespar, Kawu would still be on Hapana, safe and sound with his family. *Bad shit happens wherever we go, Etōkoka.* "Not that I'd blame you if you two would rather call it quits. All I've done is bring you trouble, and I can't expect you to risk your lives for me any longer than you already have."

It was as if Lysia hadn't heard. "That's insane, Jespar, you saw what thing is doing to Oonai! It's gonna torture the living shit of out you 'til you die!"

Many thanks for the reminder. "I can take it," Jespar said, doubting he could. "Just find the imprinter as fast as you can."

"You just don't get it, do you? Even if we manage to cure you in, say, a week from now, that still means you'll spend *moons* in—"

Lysia broke off, staring at Kawu. His eyes closed, he had sunk into his chair, chin resting on his chest.

"... Kawu?" Jespar asked.

Like rusty portcullises, Kawu's lids struggled open. The corners of his mouth lifted weakly. "I'm ... I'm fine."

He collapsed.

Bathed in the crimson glow of the fires, the stars looked dull. The mob was a glowing mass on the plateau, growing bigger with every minute and filling the air with their never-ending slogan.

The dream is a lie.

It was clear by now that the guards stood no chance. Enkshi's Jade Snakes had fallen, their corpses hidden in the tall grass, except for the pinpricks of light their nuvium armors and shields reflected. The rebels repeatedly advanced on the gate, small groups pushing cannons and battering rams under the cover of a tortoise-like shield formation—they never went farther than halfway to the portcullis before turning back under a hail of arrows and the occasional cannon-boulder. What may have looked like little victories for the guards, Jespar recognized as a strategy: the purpose of these forays wasn't damage but rather a means of wearing out the defenders and depleting their ammunition. A few hours from now, the mob would launch its final, devastating assault.

Jespar thought about all this as he stood at the railing of the ziggurat's seventh tier and gazed out over landscape, but it made him feel nothing. His heart was with Kawu, filled with a sickening blend of guilt and fear.

"Jespar?"

Lysia stood under the archway into the Ma'saa's orchard. Cloaked in shadow and framed by purple and red rhododendrons, there was something surreal about her appearance.

Jespar hurried over. "How is he? Is he okay?"

"He's alive," Lysia said, stepping out of the shadow. "I think there's something you should know, though."

"What?"

She nodded at a bench a little ways over. They sat.

"Kawu has a severe case of shifting drain," she said. "That's why he collapsed. Had he done any more shifts, it would have killed him."

"Killed". His whole body tensed up at the word, yet it left him feeling strangely empty. As though his brain refused to translate it into emotion. "Because of the dreamwalk?"

"That, too. But a lot of it is from the anchorings."

What? "What are you talking about? He said—"

"—that they were as easy as lighting a candle. Yeah, he told me that too."

"Then why ...?"

Jespar understood. "He ... lied?"

Lysia nodded. "He must have, at least later on. My guess is that the anchorings were easy at first but got harder the closer the dreame-ater got to hatching."

Jespar's words came slowly, as if coated in mud. "No, that doesn't make any sense. I mean, yeah, he looked exhausted, but he didn't show any signs of shifting drain, didn't he? He should have had fever, vertigo, nausea—"

"I know the symptoms. Kawu barely had any because he was high on drain suppressors the whole journey back from the manor."

"Drain suppressors?"

"Herbs that stall the symptoms. Gruntroot, blackroot, etheryme, and those are just a few. My guess is he got them from Agaam after the first dreamwalk."

A memory. Kawu, in the alley by the Great Bazaar, swallowing pellets. *They're for the exhaustion.*

"I also think those potential side effects of the anchorings were made up," Lysia said. "There probably are none."

"But I did feel weird after his last two shifts."

"Weird how? Woozy, detached? I've been feeling like that for days, Jespar, it's called fatigue. You were never at risk, that's just some-thing Kawu told us to explain why he couldn't anchor you more reg-ularly." She exhaled and pressed her right palm against her forehead.

"I mean, if anyone should have seen this coming, it was me. Psycho-mantic shifts aren't a walk in the park, especially for someone with no formal training. But I just—I don't know, I didn't pay attention, I was too absorbed, I—"

Jespar stopped listening. All he could think of were Kawu's words from that night on the finger-shaped rock, about how useless he felt, about how no matter how much he gave, it was never enough to make a difference. He had tried to make one by saving Jespar—and almost killed himself in the process.

But why hadn't he told him what those shifts had cost him? Why lie?

Because he knew you wouldn't have let him do it otherwise.

His emotions finally caught up, a black hole eating its way into his stomach while the phantom noose tightened. A response to the shock? Or to the guilt of knowing that none of this would have happened had Jespar not been stupid enough to get infected, that fucking *none* of this would have fucking happened had Jespar not talked Kawu into joining this suicide mission?

"... a stretcher," Lysia was saying.

Jespar blinked. His eyes stung, but, as always, the tears refused to come. *Heartless bastard.* "Sorry, what did you say?"

"I said, I convinced Maadira that we're never gonna cure Oonai without Kawu's help, so she agreed to have him carried on a stretcher. They're in the atrium, ready to go. The scouts came back and reported that the bay is clear."

"Oh. That's good."

"What about you? How are you holding up?"

It took Jespar a moment to realize she meant his infection and not his emotional state. *Better this way.* "I'm all right, I guess. I feel like that last anchoring was a lot more potent than the ones before."

"Feel" was the relevant word here: he did feel sharper and clearer than after the previous anchorings, but for all he knew, that was just wishful thinking. In the end, it didn't matter—with Kawu on the brink of death, there would be no more anchorings. Sooner or later, the dreameater would eat through the anchor Kawu had created to root Jespar in reality and pull him down into whatever living hell it had prepared.

"Good," Lysia said. "Then let's hope it stays that way until we're in the bay. I'll carry you once the bug ... you know. When it becomes necessary."

Jespar managed a pale smile. "Some White Knight I am."

The Lysia from a week ago might have come back at him with a quip. This one just looked off and touched her scar. "They'll be leaving any minute now. We should go."

⁕

About thirty people were gathered in the atrium. Jespar only recognized Oonai's stout physician and Maadira at the far end of the hall, who stood in the shadow of the statue beside the Oonais' stretchers.

Relief washed over Jespar when they found Kawu on another one behind a column. He still looked ill, but some color had returned to his cheeks, and his chest rose and fell evenly. Jespar sank down beside him and took Kawu's hand.

"I gave him some ambrosia and etheryme, but what he needs most is a week of rest," Lysia said. "No shifts, in other words. Even the simplest one could cause serious brain damage at this point."

When Jespar didn't reply, she squatted next to him and put a hand on his shoulder. "Hey, this isn't your fault, okay? It was his choice not to tell you, and you couldn't have known."

Yes, I could have. Because knowing Jespar Dal'Varek never ends well.

He knew it was a stupid thought, yet it stung like a scab torn off a wound refusing to heal. He wanted to say something meaningful but couldn't think of anything. "So he will be okay?" he asked hoarsely.

"Yes. As long as we make it out of here."

Maadira's voice rang across the hall. "Dal'Varek, Varroy! Over here."

Lysia got up and offered Jespar a hand. "Come on. Duty calls."

Jespar regarded Kawu another moment. Then he took Lysia's hand, and she pulled him up.

Maadira got straight to the point. "Varroy, you'll be up front with Ma'sao Ulanees, by the Ma'sao and the Ma'saa, in case either of them need medical attention." The physician, Ma'sao Ulanees, nodded at Lysia. She nodded back.

"Dal'Varek," Maadira continued, "you'll be in the rear with Private Zuulan and Private Beyma."

Jespar swallowed. "Shouldn't I help carry Ma'sao Nakāni's stretcher? He's our responsibility."

"Anybody can carry a stretcher. You're one of the most skilled fighters here, so I want you to watch our backs. We should be far off the island by the time the have-nots break through the gate, but it's better to be prepared."

Jespar flicked Lysia a concerned glance. She gave a slight nod, as if to say, "It's all right."

"Understood," he said.

"Good." Maadira cocked her head at the stairwell behind her. "The escape tunnel starts in the wine cellar—the entrance is extremely well hidden, but we'll tear it down with tyenite once we're through, just to be safe. I'm telling you this so you won't be surprised when Private Zuulan performs the detonation. Any questions?"

When they had none, Maadira shouted orders, and the crowd began to line up. Lysia checked on Oonai, the Ma'saa, and Kawu one last time then joined Jespar at the end of the line, where he stood with the two privates. The young one, Beyma, had reacted warmly to Jespar's introduction, but the veteran had ignored his hand.

Lysia took Jespar aside. "All right," she said in a low voice, "here's what we're gonna do: the second you feel the Pull, you holler as loud as you can, and I'll come running. I'll blame it on your exhaustion or a consequence of the dreamwalk and ask to have you carried."

"What if Maadira refuses?"

"Even if she were that cold, leaving you behind halfway or even before the escape tunnel would be a risk, so I'm pretty sure she won't do that."

"Fair point." Jespar paused, then snorted. "Kind of makes you wonder."

"About what?"

About what I've ever done to deserve your help. "Never mind. Thanks, Lysia, I really appreciate this. And I'm sorry for ... you know. Breaking my promise."

Lysia's smile didn't reach past her cheeks. "Trust me, Jes, failed love affairs are the least of my worries right now."

Jes. Barring the nightmare, it was the first time she'd called him that. He wished it had been under different circumstances.

"Moving out!" Maadira shouted.

Lysia returned to the vanguard, and the group began their march. It wasn't just the ziggurat and the three hundred soldiers they left to the flames.

It was an old order.

———

The solemn procession followed Maadira into the bowels of the palace, their footfalls in turns echoing and muffled as carpet gave way to marble, and marble to carpet. To avoid thinking about the parasite, Jespar pondered on other things: he pondered on how different the two privates walking before him were, one young and nervous, the other grizzled and stoic. He pondered on how ludicrously vast the ziggurat truly was, offering shelter for hundreds but home to merely two. He pondered on what it would be like when the mob stormed it. What would they feel walking over a carpet worth a lifetime of clothes? What would they feel seeing a pantry with enough food to feed a village? What would they feel staring at Jaaros Oonai's statue on the apex that must have cost twice as much as they'd earn in a lifetime? *Righteousness*, Jespar thought. They would tell themselves that their end was the right one and justified any means—just like Oonai had told himself.

The march came to a halt. Jespar craned his neck—the vanguard had stopped in front of another staircase, but unlike the previous one, this one's archway was fashioned from coarse bricks rather than white stone. The entrance was narrow, so the evacuees entered the corridor one by one. Jespar was the last to descend, and when he emerged in a large, dark hall at the bottom of the winding steps, he stopped in his tracks.

A horde of animals stared at him. It was a bizarre mix of wolves and tigers, lizards and horses, as well as species Jespar couldn't name, including a gigantic, four-legged beast with dark wrinkly hide and a hose-like snout dangling between two tusks. While Jespar's fatigue stopped him from drawing his sword, his shock must have been apparent. Private Beyma, the young guard, gave him a grin.

"Don't worry," he said, "They're dead. *Tacksea-dermee.*"

Jespar's mouth felt dry. "What?"

"Y'know, stuffed animals and all. 'Twas one of Oonai's favorite pastimes, but then he got bored of it and had 'em moved down here. Spooky, ain't it?" There was something exaggerated about his cheerfulness, like a boy lost in a dark forest whistling loudly to convince himself everything was all right.

Jespar felt his nerves settle and looked down the aisle cutting through the menagerie. The escort crossed it at a brisk pace, their scattered torches the only source of light in the otherwise perfect darkness.

"Are you saying those used to be real animals?" he asked, looking at the tusked beast with the hose-like snout. "All of them?"

"Yeah," the soldier said. "The Ma'sao had 'em shipped over from all over the world, some of 'em even from the Great Unchar—"

"Boy! Shut yer trap and come!" Private Zuulan, the grizzled soldier. He was a few steps ahead, two horned creatures coated in golden scales framing him. "Ye too, outlander. I know this is all just a bloody job for ye, but if ye dally and get lost, trust me, we ain't gonna come lookin'."

Beyma muttered something and caught up to his superior. Zuulan shot Jespar a glare, then resumed walking too. Jespar followed.

The old soldier's obvious contempt had taken Jespar aback, but he got it. Hundreds of the man's comrades had stayed behind to die in order to secure the evacuation—knowing nothing about the nature of Jespar's mission, he probably saw him as an overpaid outlander bodyguard who would get through this night alive just because he had friends in high places. The thought left Jespar with a strange melancholy.

Why? Who cares? He was a terminally ill mercenary fleeing from a blood-crazed mob. Nothing, absolutely nothing, in the world mattered *less* right now than some old soldier's misguided hatred.

Except that it did.

Somehow, the veteran's words had punched a crack into that little chest of dread in Jespar's mind, which miraculously had been holding its contents at bay ever since the dreamwalk. And now that crack was growing wider with every step.

It's the animals.

Jespar slowed down. He knew they were dead, knew they were harmless like the mounted bear in father's study had been, yet he couldn't stop a deep horror rising inside him as he looked into their dead, glassy eyes. *Hulls.* That's what they were: corpses stripped of everything that had once made them alive, hearts, lungs, livers, and blood. Dolls made to fool onlookers into believing they were looking at a living being.

In a few hours, Jespar would be no different.

He stopped. His breathing was fast and shallow, and sweat trickled down the nape of his neck. The dread in the chest crawled and stirred, but, despite the cracks in the wood, it didn't break through. It lurked, waiting for Jespar's mind to do the rest.

Walk, godsdammit, walk! You're losing them!

But Jespar didn't. He stood there and watched as the glow of the torch lights moved farther and farther away from him, inching toward the portal on the other side of the menagerie. No one had noticed him falling behind.

It was at that moment the dreameater reached out to him.

There were no words; there was no voice. All the parasite sent Jespar was an image of the world it had prepared for him.

The swamp court.

The Corpse and the corpses are there, limned in moonlight, staring at him with sullen eyes. The villagers, the man with the breadbasket. The Girl and her father. His sister, whom he tries so hard to forget.

Jespar lies in the mud. The noose has snapped his neck and the locusts have torn apart his throat and mouth. A dreameater grows from his head, slithering through the mud. Jespar knows it's only a matter of time before the torture will start again.

And again.

And again.

And again.

The chest shattered and the dread broke free.

Hopeless.

A sob escaped his lips; his knees buckled. He staggered backward as if he'd been struck, gripped an exhibit in a last attempt for balance.

It's hopeless.

That's what it came down to, wasn't it? Even if Lysia carried him, even if they somehow made it off the island, what were the odds? What if Oonai's imprinter had already fled the country? What if Lysia and Kawu never found him?

What if he was dead?

As Enkshi had once said, a man like Oonai had enough enemies to fill a city, and even if someone beat the odds and someday found the culprit and convinced them to release the parasite, it could be years until it happened—years in reality, decades in a nightmare.

None of these thoughts were new, yet Jespar only now truly grasped their meaning. It was like he had been falling with his eyes closed, and the dread had finally forced them open.

Down the aisle, the glow of the torches faded into darkness as the escort passed through the doorway. The privates still hadn't noticed Jespar was missing. Or maybe they had and simply didn't care.

It was hopeless. And worse: every second that he stayed here, clinging on to the illusion there still *was* a chance, he was putting Kawu and Lysia at risk. These two people who'd given so much to a man who brought nothing but misery into their lives.

No more.

Jespar vanished between the exhibits.

CHAPTER TWENTY-EIGHT
SPARKHOOVES

Day Seven
1st Moon of Rainy Season, 1226 A.L.

Jespar strayed through the maze of dead animals. He had no goal, no direction—he walked to walk, walked to get lost. At one point, he stopped, held his breath, and listened. What for? Alarmed voices, maybe. Footfalls. Lysia, shouting his name.

There was nothing.

He waited for another minute, then went to the nearest exhibit, a giant wolf, and dropped onto the plinth. For a time, he gazed into the silhouette-filled darkness.

Then he took a deep swallow from his hip flask, wincing as whatever liquor he'd filled it with this time flooded his mouth. He put the flask on the plinth, stuffed himself a pipe, then rummaged his belt for his tyenite tin and his last firetwig. He studied the latter—two of its three resin pouches had popped, but the one left was big enough for a good flame. He dipped the thumbnail of his other hand into the tyenite and flicked it across the pouch; it popped open, the powder connected with the resin, and lit the twig.

Light poured over his surroundings.

The exhibit of a colossal stuffed centipede was across from him, rearing up on its hind segment.

Jespar snorted. *How bloody fitting.*

He lit his pipe, watched the twig flicker on for a while, then tossed it into the darkness, and took the first hit.

Inhale. Exhale.

Booze and petals.

Not the most poetic way to spend his last minutes in reality—*or life*—but there had been worse.

Inhale. Exhale.

Qyra's Golden Queen in the 900s, for example, who had broken her neck slipping on the way to the throne dais.

Inhale. Exhale.

Or that one hierophant who had died from poison on the latrine seat.

Inhale. Exhale.

There had been worse.

By the time the chamber was empty, Jespar's lungs stung from the smoke, and the darkness around him shifted like boiling tar. He put the pipe next to the flask and drew his dagger. It was a good knife, only mildly rusted despite years on the road; judging by the size of the cuts in his sister's wrists, the one she had used must have been similar. The numbness he had felt the day he'd found her wasn't too different from the one he felt now.

Nine years.

Nine godsdamned years, but the memory was still as fresh as raw meat. The way the curtains had billowed in the summer breeze.

How tidy the room had been, the furniture dusted and polished to a gleam. His sister's stuffed toy horse, Sparkhooves, on the night table, the head turned away from the bed as if she hadn't wanted him to see what she was about to do.

Jespar hadn't screamed or cried. For the first twenty seconds or so, he had merely stood there and gawked like an idiot.

Next came the rationalizations.

The sheets were red because she'd spilled juice. Her eyes were shut because she was sleeping. Her lips were blue because she was ill.

All those years, Jespar had ascribed his lack of emotion to shock. Now, he wondered if maybe there wasn't another explanation. If perhaps the reason he hadn't felt anything, hadn't even fucking cried, was because a part of him knew his abandoning her and his idiotic promises were part of why she'd done it in the first place. Yes, she had been the one to drag that knife across her wrists. But hadn't he put it in her hands?

No. That's fucking bullshit.

You were a boy, and you were hurting too. You couldn't have known.

It's not your fault.

Sure. Just like he couldn't have known he'd manage to hurt Lysia days after their paths had crossed. Just like he couldn't have known his noble quest with the Wayfarers would end with him inciting the massacre of an entire village. Just like he couldn't have known his convincing Kawu to accept the mission would end in a young man almost killing himself, because his misguided infatuation had somehow made him believe Jespar's useless ass was worth saving. Like he couldn't have known that dark stain on his soul caused bad shit to happen wherever he went.

Oh, fucking get off it! You know that's bullshit!

He'd suffered thoughts like these countless times after his sister's suicide attempt and after the massacre of the Village, and he'd dealt with them, decided they weren't true, decided they were just symptoms of guilt, decided he would not let this fucking voice in his head get the better of him. And life had been all right, so what the hell was the matter with him now? Why had this fucking trip to this fucking country brought back all this shit, as if he'd never dealt and come to terms with any of it?

Maybe because you never dealt with it.

Maybe because you never came to terms with it.

Maybe because all you did was bury it.

Like an answer to the thought, a single cold beat pulsed in the depths of his skull. Jespar looked up and found the Corpse standing across him.

He felt nothing.

Not when the Corpse came limping out of that dark aisle with his burning hands drawing flickering shadows across the animal exhibits. Not when he eased down on the pedestal of the one across Jespar, a giant centipede, its legs unfurling behind the Corpse like a halo of thorns. Not when his lips split in a smile.

No fear, no horror, no panic.

The mind is a malleable thing.

CHAPTER TWENTY-NINE
BUT MY JUDGMENT IS

DAY SEVEN
1ST MOON OF RAINY SEASON, 1226 A.L.

The mind is a malleable thing. Soil, if you're feeling poetic. Depending on the seed, anything will grow in it, from graceful gardens to idyllic meadows, from weedy forests to foggy swamps. Harmonious or chaotic, peaceful or perilous or healthy or ill or dead. It is a matter of seeds.

It is a matter of seeds, son, malleable thing. Soil, if you're feeling poetic. Healthy, ill Will grow in it, from weedy forests to foggy swamps. It's all weedy forests to foggy swamps. Harmonious or chaotic, he althy, ill, or dead. It's all about those

Perilous, healthy, ill or dead. It's just a seeds. You a and that is why your mind did react how it did. or dead, it's all about the seeds. Did you had your chance, boy, to just see. are not real, Jespar said. You're not real.

real, Jespar said. No, boy, maybe I are not real. No, he replied. You're right, boy, I'm not. I am not, the Corpse rep I'm not. But my I'm not. Yet my judgment is. judgment is. judgment is my judgment is. lied. And yet my Does it matter? the Corpse said.

No fear, horror, no panic. You are not here. You are right, boy, I am seeds, horror, no panic. You are not here, Jespar said. You know my You are right, boy, I am not. You see that you're not real, Jespar said. No fear, n e could keep you safe? the Corpse said. you think h about those seeds. Jespar felt nothing.

CHAPTER THIRTY
QUICKSAND

espar stared into the darkness as his mind slowly slipped away. Toward the ocean. Toward the swamp court. Toward the nightmare from which he'd never wake.

His eyes dropped to the dagger in his hand. Come to think of it, it wasn't the first time he had looked at the knife this way, longing, fearful, hopeful. There was that cloudy afternoon the day before he decided to leave Enderal. There was that rainy afternoon a week after the Wayfarers had burned the Village to ashes. There was that sunny afternoon when he had locked himself in a room of some shabby tavern. Afternoons. Always the fucking afternoons.

Perhaps life hadn't been so "all right" after all.

What are you waiting for?

It was the right thing to do. Not only because a swift end was better than decades of slowly dying while being tortured in a nightmare, but because not doing it meant putting Kawu and Lysia at risk again. Yes, perhaps Lysia would eventually accept that finding the original imprinter was impossible, but Kawu would never give up the quest to fix him; he would chase after that fata morgana until the quicksand inevitably swallowed him.

The pulse was almost at Jespar's temple now, his sight blurring with each beat. He trailed his thumb along the dagger's edge, drawing a thin red line into his skin. Four incisions—two from each wrist up to the elbow crease, set vertically, not horizontally—that was how you did it. Had his sister known, had she cut the right way, she would probably not have survived. Four cuts. Just four cuts, and it would be over.

Yes, that's right. Now come on, get it over with. Save yourself the suffering and make sure you'll never hurt anyone again.

Four cuts.

Oh, you bloody coward, what are you waiting for? Just do *it!*

Just four cuts.

Fucking do it, you worthless piece of shit!

He sobbed and dropped the dagger.

He couldn't. He just didn't have the fucking courage. His father had been right after all—he was a complete and utter failure, even when it came to something as simple as calling it quits.

The Pull hit, and the world turned blue.

CHAPTER THIRTY-ONE
KOHL AND ROSES

omeone grabbed Jespar's head, and red light exploded. It only lasted a second, yet the headache struck him with the force of a burning sledgehammer. He screamed and collapsed, hitting his forehead on the edge of the plinth.

Darkness.

When Jespar came to, the blaze in his head had given way to a prickle—a bit like Kawu's anchorings, but raw and sharp, the way wounds burn after disinfection. Someone was kneeling beside him.

"Can you hear me?"

You know that voice, Jespar managed to think through the fireworks in his head. He knew that voice. Was this the dream?

"Ma'sao Dal'Varek, can you hear me?"

Jespar lifted his eyes. The centipede. The mammoth. The wolf. He was still in the menagerie.

Still here.

"Ma'sao, talk to me."

Still here. Still in reality.

Jespar fought to get the words out. "Agaam? But you ... we thought you were dead."

Blood stained the old servant's eyepatch and beard, and a bandage covered his shoulder. His hair hung loose in greasy, clotted strands. He lifted the bandage, revealing the scales of a nuvium mail. "It caught the bolt. I got lucky."

Unable to think of something meaningful to say, Jespar grunted and sat up. Vertigo assailed him, and the burning in his head swelled, but both passed after a few seconds. He felt for the spot over his right eyebrow. No pulse, no cold. "Did you ...?"

Agaam stood. "I struck a control shift on what I guessed was the dreameater's mind and forced it to retreat. I had no idea if it would work, but it seems we got lucky."

Still dazed, Jespar dropped his hand. "Will it last?"

"Only until the parasite recovers." Agaam sat on the centipede's plinth. "My estimate is around two hours, maybe m–" He groaned and doubled over.

"Are you all right?"

Taking a sharp breath, Agaam massaged his temples. "Just the drain ... that shift was incredibly hard to strike. Give me a few minutes, and I'll be fine." He sat up and gazed at the ground for a bit. Then something in his expression changed. "I suggest we use the time to talk, ma'sao. I know who infected Oonai. And I know why."

INTERLUDE
THE MAN

FOUR MOONS BEFORE
1ST MOON OF DRY SEASON, 1226 A.L.

On Day One of Drought, the man sees the girl for the first time.

It's early morning, in a hallway of the manor. Dawn light filters through the grated windows, illuminating the specks of dust dancing between the alabaster walls. He finds his way to the library, looking for a book that will help him kill another dull day. Instead, he finds her standing before a shelf and dusting the tomes.

There's nothing special about her. She's young and skinny, her complexion the color of watery mud. Everything about her is pointy: her bones, her nose, her lips, the nipples that poke through her linen shirt, dyed a washed-out yellow from cheap toki dye. Her kohl-lined eyes blankly follow the motions of her menial work.

Nothing special, but she'll do.

The man crosses to her and presses his lips to hers, pushing her against the bookshelf with one arm while groping between her thighs with the other. Her lips are chapped, and she tastes of something bitter, yet a prickle spreads in his belly and shoots into his groin.

Better than you thought.

Then, pain.

Gasping, he breaks from her, feels for his lips. His fingers come back bloody.

She bit you.

That have-not bitch bit him.

Confusion turns into disbelief, and disbelief into anger, but, for some reason, he can't translate it into action or words. He stands there and gawks like a fool, blood trickling into his beard. When he finds his words again, his voice trembles. "How dare you?"

The girl matches his gaze, one arm slung across her breasts, the other with the book extended as if trying to ward him off. "How dare *I*? Gods, what's wrong with you? Who *are* you?"

The question stings like a smack to the ear. "Do you ... are you..."

"Get out of here, or I'll tell the head servant what you did! The Ma'sao arrives tomorrow, and he'll have you whipped to the bone for this."

She doesn't know who you are.

Of course. It makes sense. He arrived a day early, and, with his thin-spun cavana wool shirt that could easily be mistaken for linen and without the gold beard rings, his semblance to the flattering statues isn't that obvious.

"Are you deaf?" the girl says. "Get the hell out of here, you pervert!"

The man hesitates. Then—absurdly, outrageously—he does as asked. Halfway down the corridor, he hears the door slam shut behind him.

Why did he do that?

Why in the world would a god flee from a servant?

The Third Magnate arrives the same afternoon. They spend the evening in the orchard, discussing the plan, but the man isn't really there—like moths drawn to a candle, his thoughts find their way back to the encounter this morning. The girl's pointy nose. Her chapped, warm lips. That raw hatred she had looked at him with, an emotion no one had dared show him in a long, long time. The black kohl and her rose perfume.

A ruckus pulls him from his reverie—muffled voices from the manor lobby, a man and a woman. He gives the Third Magnate a hasty excuse better suited to a servant, then hastens across the courtyard, childish excitement overcoming him.

In the lobby, on his wife's floor mosaic, stand the girl and the head servant. He has her by the wrist, and she tries to struggle free, cursing; she has a haversack over her shoulder and wears shoddy hemp travel clothes that give her an androgynous appearance. When they realize they are no longer alone, both freeze.

The man opens his mouth, but then the girl's eyes again meet his, and he falters. *Hatred.* She hides it, yes, but it's there—pure hatred.

He clears his throat. "What's going on here?"

Fear flickers across the girl's face, but then her features harden. "I have ended my contract."

"You can't!" the head servant clamors. "The contract states—"

"That you won't pay me a single dara for the past two weeks if I quit prematurely, I'm aware. It doesn't change a thing. I *quit.*"

The man can't help but smile. "You really had no idea who I am, did you?"

"... I just want to go." The hatred is still there, but the fear is thicker now. *Of course it is.* Yesterday, she thought he was a pervert servant. Now, she knows he's a pervert king.

He bursts into laughter.

It's liberating, riotous, a kind of laughter his ears aren't used to anymore. The way the head servant and the girl gawk at him only makes it funnier.

When the amusement finally passes, he crosses the hall. The girl tenses. A stride from her—the proper distance between man and woman in formal environments—he takes her hand and bows deeply. "I beg for your forgiveness, ma'saa."

Disbelieving looks.

"I beg for your forgiveness for what I did yesterday. It was wrong, and it cannot be excused, but I would like you to stay. Please."

The head servant's astonished expression couldn't be more comical. He looks first at the girl, then at the man, then settles on his feet.

The girl answers at last. "I want a raise."

And she stays.

It has nothing to do with affection, of course. As the man learns, the girl comes from a middle-class family and plans to study alchemy and herbalism; the university she has chosen, Il-Quan-Xagasha in Al-Rashim, is not only the most prestigious in the Illumined World but also the most expensive. Her mother has put up the lion's share, but about ten thousand sêr are still missing.

She stays because she needs the money.

The man invites her for dinner the following night, but, predictably, she makes an excuse and declines. He tries the next evening and the evenings after that, too, but not until the fifth invitation does she agree.

The man enjoys himself more than he has in a long time.

It isn't because they get along so well. The girl smiles in all the right places and reveals just enough to prevent her reticence from becoming overtly disrespectful, but it's painfully apparent she still hates him. The man believes the reason she accepted the invitation and continues to receive them night after night is as complex as the play of threads in the meshwork of a fine Qyranian carpet.

One thread is obligation: the raise he gave her is outrageous, and no matter how she feels about him, her contract obliges her to abide by her master's wishes.

Thread two: convenience. Each dinner they share is worth a moon's payment for a worker: black lobster on caviar and thinly sliced avocadoes. Grilled Maitemi goat with figs and myradfruit, sprinkled with grated gold. Red wine from the cellars of Erothin, vintage 923. Luxury and extravagance are their own kinds of magic.

The final thread is admiration. He knows she loathes the side he showed her when they met in the library, and she's aware of his reputation, but as a young Great Dreamer, she cannot help but respect his accomplishments. Because a Dreamer she is. Just like him, she has that fire, that verve that can turn a fisherman's son into a king.

Obligation, convenience, and admiration—it's invigorating.

But that's all this is, the man thinks as he watches her from a window, helping the gardener trim the hedges. An adventure, a dalliance, a distraction, like all the other women he has fucked over these past two decades, none of which had ever rivaled his feelings for his wife. He loves her, and he always will, no matter how many pretty servant girls, overconfident seductresses, or lonely noblewomen throw themselves at him, hoping to win a special place in his heart if only they suck his cock well enough.

This girl is just another conquest.

She heaves a sheaf of twigs onto a cart and cracks her knuckles, a strangely masculine gesture the man finds all the more alluring. Her hair hangs loosely around her shoulders, the way it did at dinner yesterday. The man told her it suited her. Does she wear it like this today because she knows he watches her?

"No," he mutters.

All his compliments last night earned him was a raised eyebrow; the girl wears her hair down today because she wants to and because she knows she doesn't have to fear repercussions, even though it's against the dress code. *Brazen*, he thinks but finds himself smiling. Wild, untarnished, free. He is not used to people acting this way around him, and he likes it.

His heart stings at the thought that he may very well never win her affection.

But he does.

It's like unearthing a fossil. He must chisel off every layer with great patience and care, lest he irrevocably damage the shell. He never touches her during their dinners and walks, never makes inappropriate remarks, and, once he realizes his witty soliloquies bore her, he begins to listen. When was the last time he has *truly* listened to anyone?

The girl's story and soul are as complex and intriguing as her free spirit promised. Her mother is a no-name Coalition official, her father a cloth merchant who died of stomach fleshrot two weeks before her birth. She attended a mediocre school in the Steel District, barely covered by the modest inheritance and her mother's salary, and excelled in science and mathematics. All this, she shares reluctantly, but she *does* share, and every dinner reveals a new facet of her life from there on out. Three weeks into Drought, during their eighth dinner, the girl reveals that her mother considers her plans to study in Al-Rashim a pipe dream and won't contribute a single dara toward it. The girl scraped up most of the money herself with a little enterprise she started while still in school.

When she tells him what it is, the man chuckles. "Draughts to stop hair loss?"

"Slow, not stop," the girl says. "You'd be surprised how much men pay to keep their mane."

The man, whose hair is as black and full as when he was a boy, grunts pensively. "And they work, those draughts?"

The ghost of a smirk flickers over the girl's lips. "Of course. Do I look like a fraud?"

"Scams aren't a reliable investment," the man says. "You're smart enough to know that."

"I most certainly am."

She sips from her goblet, the candle's flame reflecting in the polished gold. The man drinks from his own, then slowly traces his thumb along its rim.

"You must think I'm a monster," he says.

The words came out of nowhere. The girl seems less surprised by the question than the man is. "What makes you think that?"

"I'd be worried about your self-respect if you didn't." Again, his tongue moved before he knew it.

The girl wrinkles her forehead. Then she studies her wine, slowly swirling it around in her goblet. "I don't really believe in that, you know. 'Monsters.'"

"Then, you're either extremely idealistic or extremely naïve."

"Or maybe you have a reductionist view of people." A mild slur has stolen into her voice. "What I believe in are monstrous actions.

We are so obsessed with labels as if there were some kind of, I don't know, mystical scale in our souls that tilts one way or the other and makes us either a saint or a monster. Tell me, if a woman murders a man, cuts him into pieces, and then feeds his flesh to her pets, does that make her a monster?"

"... Most people would say so, yes."

"Even if he kept her as a slave and abused and raped her for years?"

"Depends on who you ask, but the majority would exonerate her."

"All right," she said, taking another sip. "Then what if that man she butchered was also a wonderful father to his children, who will now starve to death in the streets?"

"I get your point. The world is messy, and it isn't always black and white."

"It isn't, but that's not what I was getting at. My point is, all these discussions about good and evil, where do they ever lead? A man is dead, and three children were orphaned. No amount of moral judgment and labeling will change that. Instead, we should ask ourselves what factors led to this situation and then work on improving those. Cause and effect, that's all that matters." Her eyes lock with the man's, dark, piercing, beautiful. "And, frankly, ma'sao, you haven't effected much good."

That evening the man falls in love with her.

More dinners and more luncheons fill the coming week, and, finally, the man feels the girl's hatred fade. During the fifth week, he sits down to write his wife. They usually exchange letters once a week, but he has only written a single one during his entire stay, shortly after meeting the girl. He spends twenty minutes sorting the clutter on his desk and adjusting his chair before he carefully places a parchment before him and dips his quill into the inkwell.

He stares at the paper.

Guilt.

For the first time in thirty years of marriage, he feels guilty.

Because it's not just an adventure. Because you're cheating.

He chokes off the thought—*nonsense, this is* nonsense—and writes. How is she? He is genuinely sorry about the delay in correspondence—too much work. Yes, he knows, he's here to unwind, but she knows how he is, always thinking, always running. He lies by omission. Then he hastily signs and seals the letter before the ink is dry, sends it off via myrad courier, and erases it from his memory.

Three days later, he decides to make a move. He can't bear it anymore, her black eyes and how they look at him, her red lips, and the way they move. They meet in the orchard, where she waits beneath an arch of wisteria, her back facing him, wearing a pale-yellow dress exposing her shoulders. The fabric is a cheap Itzika silk imitation, but it looks spectacular on her. They stroll through the hedge maze, then sit on a bench on one of the islands. Amidst the birdsong of the tropical dusk, they talk, the man's throat dry with anticipation.

Do it.

Kiss her.

But he can't. He, the wealthiest and most powerful man in the Illumined World, is too shy to kiss a twenty-one-year-old girl. After an eternity of meaningless conversation, he finally musters the courage to slide his hand over hers.

His heart stings when she withdraws it.

"How?" she asks.

The man swallows, trying to hide his disappointment. "What do you mean?"

"How is this supposed to work? Gods, even if you weren't the most heartless man in the archipelago, I'm almost thirty years younger than you, and you have a wife, and—"

"I don't love her anymore."

Once again, the words are out before he knows it. Guilt follows like a cold bite, but he knows it's the truth. "I don't love her anymore," he repeats softly.

The girl's chuckle is bitter. "What, and you think that's an argument in your favor? Hell, you're so detached from this world. Do you really think I don't know how this works, you and your so-called 'dalliances'? You find a woman, use her until she bores you, then send her back in a sobbing heap, crushed under a million 'agreements to silence.'"

Whatever his expression looks like at that moment, it makes the girl roll her eyes. "Oh, come on, did you honestly expect me to ignore that part? Yes, I do like you, hell knows why, but that doesn't mean I'm gonna ignore your history."

"This is different." It sounds as pathetic it feels. "*You're* different."

"Mm-hm, sure." An empty smile tugs at her mouth. "Remember that conversation we had, about monsters and saints?"

"I—"

"I said that in the end, all that matters is what effects your actions have. And I hate to break it to you, but after decades of breaking women who were foolish enough to let all that money of yours blind them, only an idiot would assume she's the exception. I'd be worried about my self-respect if I did."

To the man's surprise, all he feels in response to her words is a peculiar emptiness. It takes him a heartbeat to understand it's because it resonates with a far more profound thought, a corpse in the closet whose stench he's been masterfully ignoring for over a decade.

That maybe she's right.

That maybe everything he has told himself to justify the things he had done had stopped being reasons and started being excuses a long time ago; excuses so he wouldn't have to confront a far simpler truth.

He has caved to power.

"... I want to be better," he says quietly.

"And you think cheating on your wife with a twenty-one-year-old servant is a good place to start?"

Suddenly, the man's many rings feel tight on his fingers, and his Valozai silk coat weighs heavy on his shoulders. "No. It's terrible."

"But?"

The man exhales. "But I just don't love her anymore. I love you."

Something in the girl's eyes changes, like fog over a lake clearing. The next instant, it's gone. "And for how long? Even if this really is different for you, even if you really want to be better, how do I know that two weeks from now, you're not just gonna change your mind again and toss me away like all the others?"

"Because I'm telling you it won't happen! Bloody hell, I've met hundreds of women, and none were like you, not a *single one.*"

"Hundreds? I'm impressed."

"I told you, they were just—"

"Prove it."

He's silent.

"Prove it," the girl says again. "If you're serious about all this, tell your wife what you just told me."

"But—"

"No 'buts.'" She stands. "I'm not going to be just another one of your conquests, so if what you have said is more than just talk to get me into bed, tell your wife you've moved on. It's the least you can do for her."

And she leaves.

They don't talk the rest of the day, nor the day after. Two restless nights later, the man asks her into his chambers.

"So?" she says, closing the door behind her. She looks incredible, wearing the ethereal cavana wool dress he gave her a week ago, the fabric tinted a dark ruby red achieved only from the expensive dye of crushed aketi larvae. It contrasts with her working-class seashell pendant and the palmwood-ring bands she wears around her wrists and over her right ankle. A rags-to-riches queen who finally found the wealth she deserves but still honors her roots.

"I wrote her a letter," the man says. He sits on the edge of the bed, barefoot and clad in a simple white mulberry silk shirt and trousers.

The girl crosses her arms and looks at him sternly, but the man senses a glint of excitement hiding beneath her countenance. Or is he imagining it? "What did it say?"

"That I met someone and fell in love with her. And that it's over."

She snorts and frowns, but her eyes cling to his. "Aren't you charming?"

The way she says it makes his gut tingle. He stands and steps toward her. "I did what you asked."

Gods, how he wants her. He's a castaway clinging to a piece of flotsam, craving potable water.

She uncrosses her arms and looks sideways. "I don't know. This is a bad idea."

"But what else do you want me to do? I—"

Her lips press on his. It's all he thought it would be, and more.

Entrancing.

Absorbing.

Devouring.

But as the primal part of him goes mad with excitement, another understands something the instant their tongues touch: this won't end well. Yes, he's shipwrecked. Yes, her saliva is the liquid he craves.

But it's saltwater.

He pulls her close and kisses harder, drinks her scent, blood rushes into his chest and groin. Her hands shake as she pulls off his shirt, her breath warm on his cheeks; they stagger to the bed, now naked, and the next moment he's inside her and thrusts, kissing her, biting her neck, drinking her scent and pulling her closer, closer, *closer*, Gods how he wants her how he needs her how-

Moans.

Ecstasy, greed, fulfillment.

Catharsis.

All the strength drains from his arms, and he rolls off her. Silence cloaks them as they lie beside each other, their breathing fast and shallow. Then the man chuckles, and the girl joins in. It's not long until they do it again, then again. After the fourth time, a worry stabs through the hypnotic bubble. He voices it. She grins and fishes an empty flacon from her dress that lies rumpled by the bedside. Bitterleaf.

He is relieved, but there's a tinge of disappointment too. He wonders why. All those years, he'd wanted nothing more than to start a family until he had, at last, come to terms with the idea of remaining childless. Now the wish is back, resurrected by that strange young woman he has known for just over a moon.

He buries the thought.

They lie back down, side by side. He trails his hand through the girl's wonderful hair—not a strand of gray.

You didn't lie, he thinks. He did write the letter.

He just didn't send it.

His remaining three weeks in the manor passed in a feverish dream. He continues his meetings with the Third Magnate, but his thoughts are often elsewhere. In the end, she leaves, telling him they'll pick this up once he has outgrown his second adolescence.

He doesn't care. The plan, his empire, his palace—it all feels like a distant memory fading further into obscurity with every day he spends with the girl.

Sex and intimacy add a new layer to their relationship, but it doesn't become its unique focal point, as is so often the case. They talk, they laugh, they play chess and Akati, and with every day, his affection grows. Her pleasure is his pleasure, her joy is his joy, her dreams are his dreams, and he will do everything to bring them to fruition. Because the girl vehemently refuses his offer to pay for her journey and tuition, he secretly sends a letter to Il-Quan Xagasha's Grand Erudite to improve her chances, which aren't favorable to start with. He also resumes writing to his wife, extensive letters full of questions and irrelevant details. Whenever he receives one from her, he skims through it, gathering just enough to address their main points in his reply, then folds and seals the paper before the ink is dry.

One evening, the man surprises the girl by bringing in a troupe of Aetäerna glee folk, musicians, jugglers, and dancers, who stopped by in the nearby village. The night takes a curious turn as a peculiar sexual tension unfolds with every emptied decanter and ends with the man and the girl inviting one of the dancers into the sleeping chambers. The man doesn't care for the Aetäerna, but the sight of the girl riding him fills him with a twisted, jealous arousal that almost drives him mad with desire.

And yet, when the dancer leaves at dawn, the man is relieved. If this little escapade showed him anything, it's that he wants the girl only for himself.

Wants? Or needs?

The first time he asks himself this is during a round of Akati some days later. Tapping a card against his lower lip, he watches her brood over the next turn.

It's strange.

He still craves and loves her, but there's a hollowness in the pit of his stomach now whenever they meet, and it's strongest after sex.

His thoughts drift back to their first kiss.

Saltwater.

You drink and drink, but it never quenches your thirst. He pushes the thought aside, but it comes back again and again, like a tenacious katako. He can't recall ever having felt this way about his wife, even in the early days of their courting, when their love still had the heat and thrill and mystery that always fades to either trust or boredom. Yes, he had been madly in love, and yes, just a day apart from her had been torture, but this? Two hours away from the girl, and he's like an opium addict craving his pipe; four hours away, and he compulsively masturbates to her image.

Who is he, some kind of dog? A slave to his urges?

The fights begin when she finds out about his letter to the university. She accuses him of disrespecting her wishes; he calls her naïve, tells her Xagasha only accepts thirty students a year, all of whom usually have wealthy patrons. She says she'd rather have her own story end in failure than become a footnote in his. The argument ends in sex, but it's only the beginning. Politics, philosophy, personal matters—somehow, every topic of conversation is enough to set them off.

Saltwater.

The fifth week of his stay, he wakes at night, his arm wrapped tightly around the girl's skinny body, like a drunkard clinging to his last bottle of wine.

It can't last. She's bad for him. They are dancing toward an abyss.

Suddenly, the man longs for his wife. Those warm eyes that couldn't hurt a soul. The way she always leans into their embraces, relying on him to hold her up. That sad and affectionate look she has when tending to her pets.

"I don't love her anymore."

Had he really said that?

Why?

Why the fuck would he *ever* say that?

Yes, maybe their marriage lacks the feverish passion he shares with the girl, but his wife has always been there for him, has always trusted in the good in him that, nowadays, so few people still see. Whenever he fell, she was there to catch him, and his empire wouldn't exist without her counsel.

If he's shipwrecked, she's the flotsam that prevents him from drowning.

Disgust overcomes him: disgust for himself, for this woman in his arms. He slips out of her embrace, gets out of bed, and goes for a walk he doesn't return from until the early morning hours.

It's the beginning of the end.

As he thinks and even speaks about his wife more often, his fights with the girl become more vicious. She realizes she's losing him and clings to him tighter; he pushes her away even harder. On the last day of his seven-week sojourn in the manor, they get together one last time.

By now, everything about this affair sickens him. The entitled look on her face, as if the world owes her something by default, her moodiness, her pointy nose, and her bony ass. How in the world did he ever consider betraying his wife for this naïve twenty-something with nothing to offer but hubris? There's no anger left in him. Only resolve.

He asks her for a walk through the hedge maze. She hesitantly agrees. With his foul mood gone, it's a pleasant experience. They talk and laugh, carefree, almost like they did at the beginning of their romance. In fact, it goes so well he feels a cloud of doubt by the time they sit on the very same bench where he told her he wants to be better.

But isn't that what he's doing?

No more cheating, no more lies. By succumbing to this fever dream, the man has inadvertently realized what truly matters: his wife. *And I'll tell her*, he thinks. He'll let her know about his unfaithfulness, he'll beg for her forgiveness, and if she cannot grant it and leaves, so be it. Either way, this is the first step.

The girl studies him with crinkling hazel eyes, probably thinking this marks the end of their arguments and a return to the old days. *She's beautiful*, the man thinks. *Beautiful, smart, passionate.*

And saltwater.

He makes his case: She's too young, he's too old. The gossip about them would harm her career. She'll forever be the woman who slept her way to the top. Write your own story, don't be a footnote. Of course, he knows nothing he can say will convince her—not just because she told him her love for him has only grown, but because, in the end, all these arguments are a steaming pile of bullshit. He changed his mind. That's all there is to it.

By the time he's done talking, the girl's smile has died. "You said you wanted to be better."

"I do," the man says. "And this is where I start."

"How noble of you."

When she says nothing else, the man reaches for her shoulder. "Hio—"

"Don't call me that."

The man sighs. "Look, this just has no future. I'm married, I have a life, and you have yours ahead of—"

"You're bored of me. That's what this is really about, isn't it? You're bored of me, and now you're dumping me just like I said you would."

The man withdraws his hand. "I'm not bored of you."

"Yes, you are," she says flatly. "You fucked me, and now the novelty has worn off, and you're ditching me like all those other bitches before me. I'm just another cunt in your trophy chamber." She makes a noise that was probably meant to be a chuckle, but it comes out as a sob. Tears pool in her eyes. "Gods, how could I be so stupid? I knew this would happen, and I ran into it with open arms. For fuck's sake, how could I be so *fucking stupid*?"

Perplexed by her uncharacteristic vulgarity, the man fishes for words.

"Just say it. Just admit you're bored of me and be done with it. I can take it."

"I'm *not* bored, I–"

"Say it."

"Come on, hio, this–"

"Fucking say it!"

He snaps. "All right! Bloody hell, you want the truth? You annoy me! You annoy me, you smother me, you make me uneasy. I just don't *like* you!"

She stares at him, mouth twitching as if she had expected him to backpedal. "But you said you loved me."

The man exhales, raking a hand through his hair. "Yes, and I thought I did. But this ... it wasn't love. It was self-destruction. You're destructive, and I can't take it anymore. I'm sorry."

Her stupefied veneer lasts another heartbeat. Then, as if he'd driven a spear into her back, she slumps over, buries her head in her hands, and cries, the kohl trickling down the sides of her cheeks in black rivulets. "I hate you," she sobs. "Gods, I hate you so much."

He awkwardly reaches for her shoulder, but she slaps his hand away and bolts up from the bench. "You know what?" she says, her voice trembling. "I was wrong: monsters do exist. And you're one of them."

And she runs off.

The man stays and studies the gravel. He feels nothing.

INTERLUDE
ONE DAY BEFORE

The man swims through a sunken ziggurat. It's deserted, rotten, the carpets infected by some virulent underwater growth. Dead squids, crabs, and fish float about, their tentacles, carapaces, and fins brushing the man's skin as he swims past.

He's looking for his wife.

He can hear her clearly, shouting his name, feeling so close yet remaining so distant. When he reaches the doors to his sleeping chamber—her shouts come from inside there—he yanks them open. A swarm of dead fish rushes toward him, slimy and skeletal; he chokes and shields his face, but it goes on for an eternity. When they finally pass and reveal the room, the man's blood ices over.

His wife isn't there. Instead, the girl's corpse sits on his bed, skin purple and bloated, limbs askew, her back propped against the headboard. Black liquid seeps from her empty eye sockets, clouds in the water like octopus ink. She's naked except for the rusty Magnate's Crown on her head, all seven spikes broken.

On her lap rests Popa, or what's left of him. Bizarrely tiny lobsters crawl all over his body, swift as crabs, nibbling at his rotten visage, one buried inside his gaping mouth. There's a hole in his torso just above the waist, white bone poking through, and his claw hand clutches a bottle of rice wine.

Popa's eyes snap open.

"Forgive me, son," he says. "Forgive me, for I was wrong."

Shaking and tossing in his bed, only the man's subconscious notices that strange nearby ticking sound. Like a fly throwing its body against glass, over and over.

INTERLUDE
THE MAN

THREE MOONS BEFORE
2ND MOON OF DRY SEASON, 1226 A.L.

Life is good.

His wife is the woman he loves, not some merchant hopeful with a pretty face and nice ass. How did he ever doubt it? Yes, there had been *something* between him and the girl, but it had been a dangerous concoction from the start. Their temperaments were just too similar. Shaking his head at his folly, he lifts the curtain of the carriage window and watches the landscape pass by. The manor and the mountains are far behind him by now, and they'll reach the capital tomorrow at dawn. The thought of embracing his wife while the alapus and cats dart around their feet puts a smile on his lips.

Maybe, he thinks, all this has been a blessing in disguise. Perhaps it sometimes takes an expedition to realize that the green grass on the other side is actually poison ivy.

No more experiments. No more distractions. No more cheating.

He'll come clean to his wife and rekindle their marriage, then sit back and watch as the plan exterminates the scheming jealous lions once and for all. Not that it's just about them—the coup will tear a deep wound into the flesh of this country, but if you spot a tumor, you have to cut it out before it spreads. Not only has the overgrowth part of the Coalition mastered the art of bogging down every step forward with mountains of bureaucratic bullshit, but it also turned it into a swamp of hypocrisy, where race, class, and sex, rather than the scope of your ambition decide your place in the world. Once he's in power, there will be none of this: legislation will be fast and effective, the old money abolished, and the country reshaped into a place where everyone can be a Great Dreamer, no matter who they are born to.

Drastic progress requires drastic measures.

Outside, the sun is a fiery marble hanging over the jungle. Two guards from his escort share a jest and laugh. Lulled in by the rocking of the carriage, the man's thoughts drift off and return to the girl. Is she a liability?

No.

He told her nothing of the plan—thank Gods his lovestruck insanity didn't go *that* far—so all she could do was make their affair public, and she was smart enough to know how pointless such an endeavor would be. Dozens of women had approached the Coalition with similar stories, and all had left the Jade Hall in sobbing heaps upon realizing how little their have-not word weighed against that of a living god.

Monsters exist, her words echo in his mind. *And you're one of them.*

The man's smile falters. Then he pushes the thought back to where it belongs.

The day after his return, he surprises his wife with a candlelight dinner in the garden, accompanied by music from the country's most famous harpist, whose sonatas and serenades she adores.

They end the evening with a long walk to the pond near the ziggurat, talking and laughing like the old days. In bed, they make love for the first time in years.

Yes, she's his flotsam. He sees it now.

Watching her sleep cuddled up against him, he decides to postpone his confession for another day. Whatever beautiful dream she has right now, he doesn't dare disturb it. *Tomorrow,* he thinks before gently planting a kiss on her forehead. Gray has crept into her hair, and the lines around her mouth have grown deeper. People might say she is not the most beautiful woman in the Archipelago anymore, but she is to him.

She's his flotsam.

He doesn't come clean the next morning, nor the days after. A moon later, he decides it's better this way. It's not as if she hadn't known, is it? She knew about his affairs, knew he'd been lying, and she chose to ignore it. Why not spare her the humiliation of forcing her to admit her self-deception? Not to mention that he can't afford to lose her support now that the plan is finally starting to unfold: the decree has been ratified and will be circulated in a few weeks, and those the Aetäerna lunatics the Third Magnate has fished out of the bowels of the underworld are doing an awe-inspiring job at riling up the commoners.

Things are looking up.

But then he gets the letter.

The cramped, precise handwriting tells him who sent it even before seeing the signature—the girl. She wants to see him concerning a matter of "great importance". Probably aware that the man is unlikely to respond to threats, her tone is polite, and ends on a plea rather than a demand. The man tears it up and tosses it into the hearth.

The same night, the thought he first had in the carriage comes back, louder than before.

Monsters exist, and you're one of them.

He ignores it.

A week later, it's so loud he can't focus, and he agrees to meet her in one of his warehouses in a secluded part of the harbor. The high-Drought sun turns the city into a red-hot vision as his guards escort him down the pier. Seagulls mew, sailors bustle, waves toss against the quay. He tells the soldiers to wait outside and enters.

The girl looks striking. She wears a slim-cut pale yellow silk shirt with a white cravat, brown trousers, and white, high-heeled boots—androgynous yet feminine. Her hair is in a loose ponytail, and her kohl extends slightly past the corners of her eyes.

They regard each other for a heartbeat. He stands in the doorway; she sits on a barrel across the room. Dust motes dance in the stuffy air, walls of crates and barrels tower around them, dampening the laborious din from outside. How odd it feels to see her. Alien.

The man closes the door and sits on a nearby crate. "Well?"

"Thank you for coming. I—"

"Get to the point."

She scoffs. Then she closes her eyes and draws a deep breath. "I'm pregnant."

Silence falls.

"Nonsense," the man says hoarsely. "You took bitterleaf."

"Stranger things have happened."

"No. No, that doesn't make sense. You're lying."

"Feel free to stick around and watch my belly grow."

The man fumbles for words, his stomach a cold knot. "End it, then."

"... What?"

"End the pregnancy. I'll find a biomancer, he can have it done in an hour."

The girl's face falls. "You're joking, right?"

"I'm not. There's also an herb you can drink that flushes the thing out and—"

"Stop it!" Her lips tremble. "Gods, how—how can you even say that? That's our *child* we're talking about, not some-oh gods, I don't even know what to say! I'm keeping it, and if you want to stop me, you better have one of your goons make sure I don't make it out of here alive. Do you understand?"

"You're not thinking straight, this—"

"I said, do you understand?"

The man swallows hard. *You can't let her talk to you like that. You're a god. She's a nobody.*

But that's not how he feels. He feels small and pathetic, as though his clothes and skin have gone translucent and are exposing his soul. *The heat,* he thinks. *It's that godsdamned heat and the lack of sleep.*

Or maybe it's that fucking voice that just won't shut up.

Monsters exist, and you're one of them.

Monsters exist, and you're one of them.

Monsters exist, and you're one of them.

He grits his teeth, smothers the thoughts. His composure returns. "All right. What do you want from me?"

The girl's gaze doesn't waver. "What do I want from you?"

"That's what I just said."

She frowns. "What I want is for our child to grow up with a father, but I'm not a fool. Even if, in some wild fairy tale, you'd agree, I couldn't allow it, not with your wife being barren. It would break her, and I don't want that on my conscience."

"Don't you dare smear her name."

"Oh, come on, it's not like it's a secret. What other reason could there possibly be for the First Magnate and his Dame not to have an heir? It had to be either you or her, and this," she points at her belly, "kind of solves the conundrum, don't you think? I mean, I've gotta hand it to you, the fact that you didn't dump her and find yourself a breeding mare is a testament of your character." She smiles, all lips, no eyes. "You must truly love her."

When the man doesn't answer, the girl sighs. "Anyway. Since the three of us are not gonna become a happy family, I'm asking for your support instead."

"My support."

"That's what I just said. I won't go to Qyra if that's what it takes to give that child the life it deserves, but I just can't afford to do it myself."

"Can't your family help you?"

"My lovely mother broke off all contact when I told her I was carrying a bastard. My only other living relative is my grandfather, and I can't tell him about this."

"Why not?"

"Because he spent his entire life working for people like you and always warned me to stay away from them. No way I'll come to him with this." The man starts to reply, but she lifts a finger. "A thousand sêr a moon, that's all I'm asking. Enough to afford it a fair chance in 'the arena'."

Her demand is more than reasonable, yet a childish resistance wells up inside him. "I didn't get a fair—"

"*Shut up!*" She stares at him, her finger shaking. "Gods, just shut your fucking, selfish mouth! This isn't about you, it's about your *child*. Is that so hard to understand? It's about your own godsdamned child, and if your own flesh and blood isn't worth the price of your bloody boots to you, then you better pray the atheists are right that the Gods never existed, because if they do exist, and they weigh your soul, no amount of gold you coat it with is gonna hide that it's fucking *rotten!*"

For a few moments, the whirlwind in the man's head blots everything out: the din outside, the heat, his rising panic.

Monsters exist.

You're one of them.

I'll be better.

His voice is almost a whisper. "Okay."

"What did you say?"

The man forces himself to look up.

"I said, 'Okay'. You'll get your money, and four thousand on top."

"... Are you serious?"

"No, I'm in a particularly humorous mood today. Five thousand sêr, first of each moon. Now, is there anything else? I have business to attend to."

The girl opens her mouth. Closes it. "No. No, I ... that's it."

"Then go. We can't be seen leaving together."

The girl hesitates. Then, her mouth frozen in a joyless grimace, she pats the dust off her trousers and walks to the door. Her hand is resting on the knob when she goes still.

"You know," she says, "when I came here, some foolish part of me actually hoped you *would* change your mind and raise a baby with me. Now I think it's better this way."

A hot, sour taste is in the man's throat. "Do you."

"Yes. Even a life on the streets would be better than growing up with a father like you."

She twists the knob. The sound of chatter, waves, and seagulls come pouring in.

"I'm not like him."

The girl freezes. "What?"

"I said, 'That was a mistake.'"

She turns, hand still on the knob. "Look, I just meant that—"

"You'll get no support." The man stands and slowly approaches her, step after step. "I'll make sure every bank in Kilay refuses you a loan, and I will track down your mother and grandfather, fire them from their jobs, and buy any property your family owns. No business will take you into their service, from the Coalition offices to the stinking whorehouse in the harbor. You won't have a single dara to raise this child with, just as my mother and I didn't, and maybe then, one day, you'll wake up on the streets with a crying brat at your teat and wish the child would have had a 'father like me.' Seven Gods, you'll *fucking* wish."

The girl blanches. Her lips quiver. "You ... you can't do that. You can't do that."

The man steps forward. They're so close that he smells her rose perfume the way he had that day in the library. How fragile she looks, tears running down on her cheeks, all that hubris and entitlement gone.

Just another have-not.

"I do what I want."

INTERLUDE
THE MAN

THE DAY
5TH MOON OF DRY SEASON, 1226 A.L.

unger and thirst yank the man awake. He comes to blearily, the images of a nightmare still oozing through his mind. The girl and his wife, dining on the man's severed head. It rests on a silver platter with jade marbles for eyes, black silk for hair, and a set of golden canines for teeth.

He sits up on the edge of his bed, the stink of his sweat and the bathroom's full chamber pot sharp in his nostrils. The sun sets behind the window, red and purple blending like blood and bruises.

Drink.

He can bear the hunger, but he needs to drink.

The man forces himself to his feet, his muscles stiff from the days in bed, and staggers to a wine decanter sitting on a table across the room. He empties it in one long draw, red liquid spilling over his lips, onto the marble and his bare feet. He puts the decanter back on

the dusty table—he feels like slamming it, but he's just too tired—
and limps back to bed.

Halfway there, he hears a noise. He stops and listens. Muffled,
irregular thumps, like a finger flicking against a glass pane.

They come from his nightstand.

He crosses to it, and the sound gets louder. When he sinks to his
haunches and opens the top drawer, a chill seeps down his throat. A
square object is nestled between folded stacks of garments, covered
by a purple cloth. The man removes the cover with shaking hands.

It's a glass cube, and inside it sits a cockroach.

No, he thinks. *It's something else.*

The creature looks like the spawn of a leech, a centipede, *and* a
cockroach all in one. No longer than half the man's pinkie finger
and a quarter of its breadth, the insect's gray, moist carapace reminds
him of squid skin; dozens of stumpy legs poke out on either flank,
and five black dots and the writhing feelers mark one end as the
head. The chill worms farther down his windpipe as he watches the
thing move through its prison in jerky motions, repeatedly throwing its weight against the panes of the cube.

It's alive.

He's surprised how much the realization shocks him. As though it
wasn't him who bought that egg from the old Makehu on Lehowai.
As if knowing that this creature had been incubating right beside
his bed hadn't been all that kept him going.

It's alive.

The black fog smothers the shock and leaves behind a numb, iron
calm. Taking the glass cube between forefinger and thumb, the man
brings it level with his eyes. The insect stops twitching and faces him.
Only its feelers move, drawing slow circles. As though communicat-
ing with him. As though telling him it knows.

"I'll imprint it on you," the dreamwalker had said after placing the chilly gray egg on the man's palm. Then he'd instructed him to recreate its image in his mind. The man had done as he asked. There'd been the slightest of chills in his skull, coming and vanishing like a graveyard specter. The dreamwalker's visage had creased into a sea of wrinkles. "It's done. You control it now."

The man looks outside. The sun has sunk below the treetops.

Tears trail down his cheeks.

He puts the cube back and covers it. This time, the thumping sounds don't resume. He closes the drawer and sits on the edge of his bed. Then he takes a folded paper from the breast pocket of his shirt.

He reads it.

Rereads it.

Again.

Nothing. No grief, no anger, no pain. Only that iron calm.

When the man made his fortune by ruining and then buying a rival's nightflower plantation, a farmer hung himself from the balcony of the plantation's Great House. He had stolen some of the "miracle fertilizer" the man had tricked his rival into using, and had thus tainted his own fields. The man felt terrible—it wasn't the first time his actions caused suffering, but it *was* the first time the chain of cause and effect was so clear. The man's friend pulled him out of his melancholy with another quote from his favorite book, *The Wandering Scepter*. "The choice to end our lives is always our own," had said. "When we're in the dust, bleeding and the lions coming at us, it's still our decision whether we fight until the end or throw ourselves into the spike pit behind us." The man found solace in his friend's words, made them his creed. Now he knows it's not that simple.

Yes, perhaps you can't blame gladiators or lions for fighting if that's what the games are about. But if you're the man who built the arena and cashes in on the tickets, you may not be the one who pushes the fighters into the pits, but you damn well play a role in their deaths.

It was no different with the girl.

Her decision to jump off that cliff had been hers alone. Dropping from the height of a ziggurat tower onto solid stone. Shattering every bone in her body. Crushing their unborn child.

But hadn't he led her to the cliff?

He remembers the first time he read her letter two moons ago, the last letter she'd ever write. There were no accusations, no insults, no demands. Mechanically, she had laid out her arguments and her conclusion, as well as where and how she'd do it. Like a merchant listing the reasons for closing a shop that just can't maintain itself anymore.

At first, the man didn't believe her—he thought it was just another way to extort money from him, or perhaps a plea for mercy. His denial was short-lived, though. Not even an hour after he received the letter, he sent a guard to the girl's house and another to the cliff by the rice fields to stop her. The first one found nothing. The second one did. Numbly—as if that would undo what had happened—the man ordered them to dump the girl's corpse in the sewers.

And as the guards closed the door behind them, the man broke at last.

He went to his childhood home looking for comfort but found only a carcass and the inexplicable knowledge that Popa *had* died the night they left them. He went to the priest looking for guidance, but only found out that his soul was long rotten. He went to the Jade Hall looking for absolution by becoming a better man, but found only that the very laws he created would forever prevent him from doing just that. There was no stopping the inferno, and tens of thousands of people would die because of him, joining the hundreds of corpses the man's sins already left in their wake.

Monsters exist. You're one of them.

The man lifts his gaze, the magnificent, blood-soaked sunset blurring under his tears. The sun would soon be gone, ushering in that short period of half-light the Makehu call "Spirit Hour", where their two rival sibling gods rest briefly from their eternal struggle, allowing all ghosts and souls to wander freely.

Numbly, the man gets up and walks over to the only sconce in the room that's still burning. He reads the letter one last time, then burns it. The fire devours the paper, smothers the words, erases their meaning. When the flames reach his fingertips, he clings to the paper, endures the pain until it's nothing but ashes. As if the girl never existed.

He tidies up his room, calls a servant, and orders a bath.

Freshly washed and wearing a white cavana wool coat, antelope leather sandals, and dark brown mulberry silk trousers, he finds his wife in the orchard. She's reading a book, one of her alapus is dozing on her lap—Crumb, this one's called. The last patches of blue sky have turned black, and the wayside torches are burning, bathing the scene in warm light. Despite the fatigue he has caused her in the past moon, she's still the most beautiful woman in Kilay. She gasps as she sees him, drops her book, runs toward him, and falls into his arms. Warmth spreads in his chest, the same warmth he felt that day he saw her for the first time, in the Jade Hall corridor beside her harpy of a mother, talking to some sleazy official she was supposed to marry. The same warmth he felt when he put his marriage beads around her neck after she put hers around his. The same warmth he felt that night he had promised her he'd stay no matter what, after the physician told them the beggar's knife attack had destroyed her womb and that she'd never bear children.

The fog kills it.

You're poison.

Arm in arm, they stroll through the garden, talking and laughing like they did in the old days. How bizarre it is. Only two hours ago, the mere idea of leaving his chambers turned his stomach. Now, being here with her almost gives him comfort. Probably because it wasn't until the insect hatched and he burned the letter that he truly made his decision.

He plays his role well, nodding in the right places, even managing a smile or two. He has prepared an excuse explaining his moodiness and reclusion during the past moon, but his wife gently presses his hand and tells him there'll be plenty of time for explanations later. They dine, then the man retires to his chambers. His wife offers to join him, but the lie that he just needs one more night to himself leaves his lips as easily as the order to dump the girl's corpse in the sewers did.

Back in the room, he lifts the insect out of its prison and hides the glass cube in a cupboard where no one will ever find it. He eases down on his freshly made bed and rests his back against the mahogany headboard.

He thought about leaving his wife a letter of confession for closure, but he's too much of a coward to even do that. Perhaps in a last desperate bout of vanity, he doesn't want to destroy the illusory image she still clings on to, the mirage of a man who was sometimes reckless but good at heart.

He studies the insect.

Despite its small size, a terrible chill radiates from its moist carapace, cold like a corpse's kiss. The lack of irises in its five eyes makes it impossible to tell what they're looking at, but the man knows they are locked on his.

Monsters exist, and you're one of them.

The girl had been wrong. He isn't just a monster; he is the father of monsters, the architect of the arena, the god of suffering. The thought he had in the temple had been right after all: there were a million marks on his soul, and they had festered into a cancerous growth. Tears trail down his cheeks. He lets them come, wishing they were acid.

Absolution?

The forgiveness the priest offered was more than he deserved. There is no clearing his name; there is no fixing this. It's like the Third Magnate said: no matter what he does, the inferno will come, because he sowed the flames that others must reap, just as he has done his entire rotten life. He let workers die of minor infections because his slave pay didn't provide enough for antiseptic; he let miners choke to death on the nuvium fog because it was cheaper to have them live near the pits; he drove hundreds of penniless men and women into suicide just so their relatives would join the Scythe and get his mad plan rolling, and all for what? Just so that *he*, Fish Boy, could finally feel safe from the phantom lions, just so that *he* could be even richer in his ugly prison of stone, just so that *he* could keep telling Popa's ghost, who just wouldn't stop haunting him, that you did *not* have to accept the hand life dealt you and to *fucking look how far he'd come.*

He.

Jaaros Ismirael Oonai.

Liar. Tyrant. Murderer.

Killed his own child and lover over the cost of a pair of boots.

As if listening to his thoughts, the insect moves its feelers, its eyes five gems of perfect darkness, black as kohl, black as silence, black as oblivion. No, he can't stop the inferno. No, he can't undo his sins. No, he will never be better, and, no, there will be no absolution.

But at least he can pay for what he's done.

The man nods.

The dreameater shoots up his arm, slithers over his shoulder and onto his chin. For a second, it lingers. Then it vanishes inside his nostril. Cold flares up in his temples. He leans back into his pillows as numbing exhaustion overcomes him, and his mind slips into a blue-black fog.

It's almost peaceful.

CHAPTER THIRTY-TWO
SUNSET TREES

"She was your granddaughter?"

"Yes."

Jespar's thoughts were a hazy mess, struggling to keep up with what he'd just learned. *Don't sit there gawking. Say something.* "I'm sorry. I really am."

Agaam nodded, then looked off into the dark. "It's sad to think that this might have ended differently if only she had told me about the job in Kaiawaika Manor. She must have thought I would have advised against it or something."

"Would you have done that?"

"Probably, yes. But not just because it was Oonai." He felt for his bandage, which had come loose at the edges, and untied it. "The Magnates, the Great Dream, Fortune Road. If there's anything that forty years in the Coalition's service taught me, it's that there's a price for dreaming big. That race, the 'arena' ... it always takes something from you, be it your integrity, your soul, or even your life." He grimaced, then rolled the bandage back around his shoulder and pulled it tight. "Yamin knew I felt this way because I kept reprimanding her for that alchemy scheme she had been running. Now I wonder if, maybe, that was a mistake. If I had been less judgmental, if I hadn't been so self-righteous about my moral superiority, maybe she would have confided in me about what had happened in the manor, and then ... well. Maybe she'd still be here."

They were quiet for a bit.

"You'll never run out of what-ifs," Jespar said. "Trust me on that."

Agaam gave him a cryptic sideways look. Gratitude? Sorrow? When the old servant said nothing else, Jespar broke eye contact, picked up his dagger, and slid it back into its sheath. "And Oonai had no idea she was your granddaughter? None at all?"

Agaam resumed adjusting his bandage. "No," he said. "When I joined the Snakes, I learned to keep my family life secret. Of course, Oonai could have found out had he wanted to, but the idea probably never crossed his mind. And as for why Yamin didn't tell him herself, I'm fairly certain she didn't want him to think I greased palms to get her the job—it was incredibly important to her to be the architect of her own fortune instead of just another upper-class kid who rides on her family's coattails." With the bandage secured, he rested his hands on his thighs and regarded them. "You still haven't asked the question, ma'sao."

He's right. Why haven't you, Jespar?

"If you knew Oonai did it to himself," he said slowly, "why didn't you tell us?"

Agaam nodded. He studied his hands for a little longer. "I suppose there are two reasons. The first is because I wasn't entirely certain. Yes, I found out about Oonai's affair with Yamin, I knew his breakdown happened shortly after he received her letter and she disappeared, and I knew that the infection probably took place in the four weeks after that, but the rest was mostly conjecture. A part of me even refused to believe Yamin was dead until I saw her corpse. Do you remember that protest in the harbor, when we came back from Hapana?"

"The dead girl was Yamin," Jespar said. He had made the connection during Agaam's explanation, but it had felt wrong to point it out.

"Yes."

Jespar sought for a meaningful reply but found none. "You said that was just one reason. What's the other one?"

"That one will have to wait," Agaam said. "The drain is bearable now, so we should catch up to the others. I'm assuming Maadira is evacuating the ziggurat via the escape tunnel?"

"Yes."

"Then we might have a problem. I have reason to believe the Scythe know about the tunnel and have set up an ambush in the bay."

"What? But Maadira had two guards–"

"Scout it, I know, but I think they might be moles. Trust me, I hope I'm wrong about this, but considering how well the Twins undoubtedly have thought this through, I'm almost certain I'm not. I believe Oonai is our only chance of making it through this alive."

"Oonai? Why Oonai?"

"Because he's both the last remaining magnate and the best negotiator in all of the Archipelago—if anyone can bargain a truce with the rioters, it's him. We have to wake him up, Ma'sao Dal'Varek."

"Yes, but how–" He broke off when it dawned on him. "Oonai," he said slowly. "If he infected himself, then ..."

"... odds are he is also the imprinter, yes. I think our best chance is to dreamwalk into his nightmare one last time and persuade him to release the parasite."

A thought, cutting like a scalpel: *Kawu.* Jespar's mouth went dry. "We can't do that."

"Why?"

"Because Kawu had a shifting drain stroke and passed out. The anchorings he did on me, they weren't as easy as he said, and after the dreamwalk into Vel'Nyx's mind, he just collapsed."

"How long ago was that? How many hours?"

"I don't know. Two or three, maybe?"

"Then he might have recovered enough for one final shift."

"What? No, Lysia said that could—"

"I'm aware of the possible consequences, ma'sao, but I also know waking Oonai up is our only chance to make it out of this alive. And if the last shift was several hours ago, then Ma'sao Nakāni could safely do it." He rose, struggling for balance at first, but steadying himself. "I think I'm good to walk now. Come, we have to go."

Dizzily, Jespar rose from the plinth. Then they went down the dark aisle into which, only minutes ago, the Corpse had vanished.

The ziggurat's wine cellar was a sequence of spacious underground hallways, endless rows of giant barrels lining its sides. Halfway down the fourth corridor, a figure came around a corner, shrouded in shadows. Spotting Jespar and Agaam, it froze.

"Easy," Agaam called. "We're with the Guard."

The figure approached them slowly, and Lysia's wary face emerged from the dark. "Ma'sao Agaam?"

Agaam tapped his fingers on his chest as if no more explanation were necessary. "The others are already in the tunnel?"

Lysia was looking at Jespar.

"Ma'saa Varroy, are the others already in the tunnel?" Agaam repeated.

"They weren't when I left, around ten minutes ago. What did you do, Jes? The guards said you disappeared." *Why did you do that?* was the question between the lines: if Lysia hadn't already surmised that Jespar had purposefully fallen behind to die, his guilty look had told her. *Because I didn't want to drag you down,* he wanted to say. *Because I didn't want to be more of a plague to your lives than I've already been.*

The lump kept him quiet.

Agaam ended the staring. "I'm afraid the explanations will have to wait. The sergeant is planning to bury the entrance, isn't she?"

"Yes," Lysia said. "They brought tyenite."

"Then we have to hurry."

Treading down the tunnel as fast as Agaam's injuries and his shifting drain allowed, Agaam gave Lysia a summary of what he'd told Jespar. When the conversation was over, Lysia's eyes still bore their torpid anger, but there was something new to it now: a weary sorrow. Jespar couldn't blame her. All along, the answer had been right there, dangling before their noses.

They walked until Agaam stopped in front of what seemed to be a random barrel. He circled it, and reached behind it; something clicked, and the barrel moved up slightly. He gripped the hoop with both hands. "Please help me, ma'sae."

They gathered around the barrel, then, on Agaam's mark, yanked as hard as they could. At first, it didn't seem to budge, but then there was another click, and the barrel slid forward so fast that Jespar almost lost his footing. There was an opening in the wall behind it, a dark tunnel extending deep into the rock. Agaam held up a hand and stepped to the entrance; his good eye turned glassy, and the air around him shimmered.

He held the shift for a few seconds, then turned back to Jespar and Lysia. "There's still a big cluster of human thought patterns not too far from us, so they might not have made it to the bay yet. Come."

The tunnel was long, low, and narrow, with crude stone paving. Because the floor was slick, and often sloped steeply downward, crossing it became an exercise in frustration; every bit of Jespar wanted to run, but they had to tread with extreme care. After what seemed like forever, voices became audible farther down the tunnel. Agaam raised a hand and stopped.

"What is it?" Jespar asked.

"They aren't moving."

He was right—there were no footsteps, and the distant voices also had a nervous edge to them. Wary, Agaam gestured forward, and they went on. A few turns later, light mixed into the darkness ahead; the evacuees and guards filled the tunnel wall to wall, standing shoulder to shoulder. The two privates were still in the rear, the youngster shuffling about, the veteran leaning with his back against the wall and staring ahead. Noticing Agaam, the young one reached for his scimitar.

"Stay where ye are!"

Agaam continued forward. "Easy. We're on your side."

A voice cut through the tunnel before the boy could reply. "Put down that weapon, now!" Maadira elbowed her way through the file; everyone was looking at the new arrivals. "That's Agaam," she said, halting before them. "That's Ma'sao Agaam."

"Sergeant," Agaam said. "I need to have a word with you and Ma'sao Nakāni."

Maadira cast Lysia and Jespar an uncertain glance. "That might be a problem, ma'sao."

"I know he had a shifting drain stroke. Still, it's important."

"No, that's not it. Ma'sao Nakāni had another stroke again a few minutes after we entered the tunnel, so Ma'sao Ulanees had to give him a sedative."

Jespar's stomach balled up. "Why in the world would he have another drain stroke? He didn't shift, did he?"

"No, he was asleep the whole time. It just happened."

"Could be an echo," Lysia said. "Sometimes drain strokes happen in bouts."

"Well, we'll have to wake him up and see," Agaam said. "Where is he?"

Maadira hesitated, then gestured down the hallway. "Follow me."

They proceeded down the tunnel, the throng parting with perplexed expressions.

"There's something else you need to know," Maadira said. "It concerns the Scythe."

"They are waiting for us in the bay?" Agaam asked.

"You ... know?"

"I suspected. How many are there?"

"At least a hundred, possibly more. Definitely too many for us to take on in a fight." She said it matter-of-factly, but the undertone spoke a different language: *we're screwed.*

Agaam nodded. "One more reason to cure the Ma'sao."

"Wait, what—did you find out who infected him?"

"We did, but now is not the time for lengthy explanations. I need to speak to Ma'sao Nakāni first."

Maadira seemed unhappy but didn't object. They stopped at an alcove, the rock bathed in dim light by two mounted torches. Kawu lay on his litter beside the Oonais, what little color Lysia's medicine had brought back to his cheeks gone. His jaw and cheekbones drew hard lines in his youthful face, and his skin had developed a pale green tint. Legs numb, Jespar sank to his haunches beside Kawu's stretcher and took his hand.

"I don't get it," he said softly. "He was getting better."

Ma'sao Ulanees emerged from a corner. "He was. It must have been an afterglow, an echo."

"That was my thought too," Lysia said, hunkering down across Jespar. She felt Kawu's forehead. "What did you give him, ma'sao?"

"Blackroot to make him sleep and etheryme for the pain."

"Do you think he can survive another shift?" Agaam asked.

The physician's confusion was tangible. "Another shift? In his condition?"

"Yes. What are the chances of it being fatal?"

Fatal. The word bounced back and forth in Jespar's mind, an echo refusing to fade. He felt like he should say something, weigh in, but he couldn't think of anything. Guards had gathered at the mouth of the alcove, craning their necks to see what was going on.

The physician shifted his weight from one foot to the other. "Well, I've seen dimensionists pull through worse drains, but there's no way to be certain. We don't know anything about that Sight of his, nor how draining these 'dreamwalking' shifts are."

"He's right," Lysia said. "The only person who could tell us for sure is Kawu."

"Then we need to wake him up," Agaam said. "Do you have any herbs to counteract the blackroot?"

"No, I'm afraid not," Ma'sao Ulanees said. "At least none that work instantaneously."

"I could try and purge the blackroot from his blood," Lysia said. She gave Jespar a sideways glance as if asking for his permission.

The word "fatal" still floating through his mind, Jespar opened and closed his mouth. What was he supposed to say? Just brushing with the idea of Kawu dying made Jespar's thoughts recoil, like some haunted forbidden manor room that you simply did not enter. Then again, with the Scythe waiting in the bay, didn't not even *trying* the shift amount to sentencing the whole lot of them to death, Kawu included?

"Can't we just … fight?" he asked.

"You heard the sergeant," Agaam said. "They're hundreds, we're not even fifty. And only a dozen or so are fighters."

"But we have you."

"Even if I shifted myself to death, I couldn't take on more than a dozen, at most. We cannot win this fight, ma'sao, not with violence." He said it without any discernible emotion.

Jespar wanted to protest—some silly, nonsense argument—but he stopped himself. Not only was it pointless because he knew Agaam was right. It also wasn't Jespar's choice to make. "Do it, Lysia."

The air over Kawu turned wavy, goosebumps spread up Jespar's arms.

Kawu jerked awake.

The distortion vanished. Lysia gasped lightly and teetered; Maadira steadied her. Only the crackling of torches and the shuffling of feet filled the silence.

Kawu blinked once, twice. Then he looked around, confusion written all over his face.

"Ite litō," he said when his eyes fell on Jespar.

"Toli," Jespar said softly. "I'm here."

"What … what happened? We were in the study, then …" Kawu trailed off.

Agaam turned to the crowd.

"Everyone except Ma'saa Varroy and Ma'sao Dal'Varek leave. Now."

No one moved.

Maadira sighed and repeated Agaam's order. The crowd did as they were told.

When the alcove was clear, Agaam told his story for the third time.

"So you truly believe Ma'sao Oonai can save us?" Kawu asked when Agaam was done. He spoke as if every word took the utmost effort to form. "That he can stop the riot?"

"It won't be easy, but I believe he can, yes," Agaam said.

"But the people loathe him."

Lysia nodded.

"And that's precisely why they'll listen," Agaam replied. "The opposite of admiration isn't contempt, it's indifference. As much as those people out there despise Ma'sao Oonai, he still has a certain power over them, at least emotionally."

Kawu was silent for a time. His gaze wandered up to meet Jespar's as if meaning to ask a question, but then it dropped back to his lap.

"'Ilonūka e untu'," he said. "I believe I understand."

"'Black respect'?" Jespar asked.

"'Dark respect'. It's a term the shamans often use to describe how one feels about Okokepe. You despise him for bringing so many bad things to the world, but he's still a child of I Āneikui, the Shaper of Worlds, so ...'"

"... you respect him," Lysia finished. "But the mob knows they have won, so why would they possibly be intimidated by Oonai?"

"I don't know," Agaam said. "But I am telling you, if anyone can do it, he can. I will strike a shift on them to calm their minds, at least enough for Oonai to have a chance. The rest will be up to him."

A pause stretched out in the alcove. A mad plan, yes. Then again, what was this week but a mockery of sanity?

"Can you do it, Kawu?" Lysia asked. "Can you take one more dreamwalk?"

It seemed as though Kawu hadn't heard. Then he closed his eyes and let out a breath that seemed to hold all the exhaustion of those past seven days. When he opened them, the frailty was gone. "Yes. I can."

A dark feeling settled in Jespar's gut. The door to that forbidden room had inched open, a cold and moldy wind blowing through the crack. "Kawu ..."

"It's only a single shift. I can take it."

Just like you could take the anchorings? Jespar didn't say it out loud, but his expression must have said enough. Kawu's face clouded. Then the corners of his mouth lifted ever so slightly. "Āpa ,atete io pō ānū li e ni'ē ku, hio. Keiete to lai."

He knew Kawu had said it to reassure him, but somehow, his words only pushed the door open wider. *You can't let him do this. You can't.* But it was a fool's errand. Even if this were Jespar's call to make, there was no choice. Once again, Kawu had to shoulder the burden of others.

He can do it.

"What did you say to him?" Agaam asked.

He can do it.

"Only that I feel strong enough for the shift," Kawu lied. "I'll take you into Oonai's kuluhika."

He can do it.

Agaam knelt beside the stretcher and placed his hand on Kawu's bony shoulder. "Thank you, lad. You're very, very brave."

A trace of pride lit up Kawu's face, but it disappeared within a heartbeat. The pain must have driven it away.

"Who goes?" Lysia asked. "You, Agaam?"

Agaam mulled it over. "No. There's no saying how entering the psychic dimension would affect a psychomancer, and I need to save my strength for the negotiations. This isn't the time for experiments."

For the negotiations. As if waking Oonai was already an accomplished fact. "Ma'sao Nakāni, you said whether you take one or two makes no difference in terms of shifting drain?" Agaam asked.

"Hardly."

"Then Dal'Varek and Varroy should both go. Can you do it right away?"

"Yes. There's just one problem: we're out of neki."

"That's the droga, isn't it? Is it essential?"

"No, but a dreamwalk can be extremely stressful for the mind otherwise, especially if you're not used to it. We can go under without it, but it might be ... disturbing."

"'Disturbing' is better than 'dead'," Lysia said. "What about that defense mechanism? You said the bug tried to keep you out of Oonai's dreamworld last time, didn't you?"

"It did, yes, but only because I wasn't expecting it. I should be able to mask our approach now."

"What about the Compass?" Jespar asked. "The marriage beads?"

"I don't think I will need them. I have memorized Oonai's psychic signature."

"Very well," Agaam said. "Then we should waste no more time. I suggest we do it right here."

"Wait a minute," Lysia said. "How are we supposed to persuade Oonai once we find him?"

"I was about to get to that. I have a plan."

Agaam told them his strategy. When all questions were answered, and most doubts put at ease as much as they could be, Agaam called Maadira and Ma'sao Ulanees back into the alcove and told them what they were about to do. Lastly, Agaam anchored Jespar one more time. It hurt even more than back in the menagerie—if Kawu's anchorings were warm summer gusts, Agaam's were branding irons pressed deep into the tissue of Jespar's brain. They moved Kawu's and Oonai's stretcher to the corner of the alcove, so Kawu could sit with his back resting against the stone; Lysia and Jespar knelt between the two. This time, Kawu took Lysia under first. When it was Jespar's turn, something about the way Kawu looked at him put a weight into his heart.

He can do it. He told you he could.

He promised.

Only the last thought brought some reassurance.

"You'll be okay, won't you?" Jespar said, so quiet only Kawu could hear.

The ghost of a smile set on Kawu's lips as his fingers touched Jespar's temples. The air between their faces shimmered.

And sleep came.

Traversing the Imūma with a lucid mind made Jespar understand why so many dreamwalkers went mad. Except for when the dreameater's defense mechanism had separated him from Kawu, Jespar's two journeys through the psychic dimension had been an uncanny, yet fascinating experience. Lulled in by the neki, his mind had simply accepted what was, no matter how bizarre.

Now Jespar felt lost.

Here they were, three specks of dust floating through this infinite black ocean that held the thoughts and dreams of a billion minds. How had Jespar ever believed he mattered? How had he not gone mad looking at the night sky, realizing how unfathomably small and fleeting he was, not even a flicker in the face of time?

You are nothing.

Trying to get a grip on the cold horror spreading inside him, Jespar focused on his breathing, ignoring his brain's wildfire protests that a man underwater shouldn't be breathing at all, ignoring the crushing dark vastness around him, ignoring the look on Kawu's face the second before he had taken him under.

Time passed by in that quicksilver way which made it impossible to tell minutes from hours and hours from seconds, sand swirling through an hourglass full of water. They followed Kawu as he guided them deeper down the Imūma, his emaciated body and sickly pallor giving him the air of a sinking corpse. Whenever Jespar tried to catch up to him, Kawu sank a little faster, always remaining a few strides ahead. Unease joined the horror in Jespar's chest, and it grew with every second, his thoughts going back and forth between the promise Kawu had made and the cryptic expression just an instant before he'd struck the shift. However, it wasn't until the bubble of Oonai's dream appeared beneath them that a realization tore through Jespar's carefully built wall of denial.

Finality.

The look in Kawu's eyes had been that of a man who had accepted his fate. Kawu couldn't take this shift, and he had known. The promise he had made to Jespar in Makehu—that he was going to see the Sunset Trees, no matter what—had been a lie.

Panic hit.

No.

Gods, no, you have to stop him, you have to wake him up, you -
Kawu went limp.

There was no scream, there were no convulsions. Nothing. One moment, Kawu had been sinking, hands raised slightly, and his gaze fixed on the ruined ziggurat inside the bubble. The next, he was still as a puppet discarded into the ocean.

CHAPTER THIRTY-THREE
FALLING

DAY SEVEN

1ST MOON OF RAINY SEASON, 1226 A.L.

e isn't moving.

At first, the thought caused no emotion—just those three words, as flat and silent as the water around them.

He isn't moving.

He isn't moving.

He isn't moving.

When his brain finally assigned meaning to the realization, horror washed over Jespar in a black wave. He spun around and swam to Kawu, large and frantic strokes, all else forgotten. He grabbed him and shook him and shouted, his words coming out as a soundless stream of bubbles. Nothing. —Kawu's eyes were glassy, his body lifeless. Jespar wrapped his arms around him and drew him close, as if that could somehow undo what happened, as if that could somehow fix him and bring him back to life.

"Back to life?" No, no, why would you think that?

Kawu wasn't dead, he couldn't be dead, this was a dream, dammit, this was all in their heads, so how could it have any bearing on the real world?

But it had, and Jespar knew it. The anchorings, the fatigue, and the three dreamwalks had driven Kawu's mind to the precipice. This last one had pushed him off the cliff.

Jespar didn't know how long he floated there, Kawu in his arms, and Oonai's nightmare beneath his feet. All he knew was that, at some point, Lysia appeared before him, pointing down at the bubble. Her mouth moved, but the water kept her silent.

Jespar nodded weakly. Lysia lingered, giving him a pleading look, then sunk toward the sphere and passed through its membrane. She briefly levitated in the air, then fell, until her shape was but a dot on the deadland that fronted Oonai's nightmare ziggurat. Jespar didn't move.

What was the point?

All of these sacrifices, and what had they achieved? Nothing. Seven days, they'd been grasping at straws, and every single one of them had crumbled into ash the moment they touched them. The city, in ruins. The parasite in his brain, about to hatch. Kawu, dead. This mission had been a losing game from the start.

He looked at Lysia's tiny silhouette. She couldn't see him from down here, he knew that, yet he almost felt her gazing at the sky, waiting for him to descend. His thoughts went up to the waking world, to Agaam, to the Ma'saa, to Maadira, to all those people in the tunnel who were waiting for salvation.

You can't give up.

Not now, no matter how weary he was, no matter how pointless it seemed. He couldn't give up because these people relied on him and Lysia to do what had to be done; he couldn't give up because that would mean Kawu had died for nothing.

Jespar crossed the membrane. The instant he passed through, it morphed into the kuluhika's sky, the moon a violet orb poking through dark clouds. He fell toward the ziggurat pathway, the warm and earthy air rushing into his nostrils like the smell of a freshly dug grave. Near the ground, his fall yanked to a stop, and he floated down to the stone path. Lysia was immediately by his side and helped him ease Kawu onto the cracked stone. Jespar sank to the ground, watching numbly as Lysia felt for Kawu's pulse and heart and listened for his breath, her face cracking a little more with each task.

When she closed her eyes and sat back on her heels, fury seized Jespar.

Fury at Oonai and his endless greed and cowardice, fury at Vel'Nyx and her petty quest for vengeance, fury at those lunatic Aetäerna twins and all those murderous idiots who had done nothing but answer injustice with more injustice while feeling like gods passing judgment. But most of the fury he directed toward himself—because wasn't the simple truth of it all that Kawu's drain would have never gotten that bad had Jespar not been so fucking stupid and gotten himself infected? Kawu was dead because Jespar was a useless idiot—that was the long and short of it. A useless idiot with a poison soul that hurt the people close to him, the way it had his entire godsdamned life.

This time, the reasonable voice in his head stayed silent, the one that usually protested and had so firmly convinced him that his sister and the Village were also not his fault. The voice had told him that life was all right when, in reality, nothing had ever been all right or would ever be all right again.

When the fury finally died, something inside Jespar died with it: a young plant that had defied all odds by sprouting on a ruined soil but had now been ripped out with its roots before it could grow.

For a while, they knelt there in silence, the ruined ziggurat rising before them.

"He lied." Jespar's eyes burned, but there were no tears.

Lysia said nothing.

"When I asked him if he really had the strength to take another shift, he promised me he did." *And that he'd go see autumn with you.* "It was a lie, and he knew it."

No reply.

"We should have just fought, dammit. We should have just bloody fought, we could have beaten those fucking assholes, *we could have fucking beaten them!*"

But he knew it wasn't true even as he said it. The Scythes in the bay were hundreds, and they were dozens. Kawu had known that too.

"I don't understand why we're still here," Jespar said.

A strange emptiness had taken hold of him—he felt no more shock, no more fury, not even grief. As if a fog had flooded the barren swamp of his mind and shrouded everything in an amorphous gray haze.

Lysia gazed up from the ground. "You mean why we didn't wake up when he ..."

Died. "Yeah."

"Because it's not a channeling." Just like Jespar's, Lysia's voice lacked emotion. "I don't know how this 'hypnosis shift' works, but it seems to be an instantaneous one. Like a lever, in a way."

"A lever that decides whether the sleeping mind stays lucid?"

"And keeps it asleep, yes. Ours are still flipped to 'dreamwalk-ing', so to speak."

"Doesn't that—"

Jespar broke off. A small creature had shuffled out of a nearby thicket, a haggard alapu, but it had a jawless woman's head. Spotting them, the monster made a gargling sound and retreated into the dead bushes. Jespar's hand was on the pommel of his sword, but he otherwise barely reacted, and neither did Lysia.

"Doesn't that mean we're trapped?" Jespar asked. "If Kawu can't end the hypnosis, and the dreameater keeps Oonai asleep?"

Lysia opened her mouth. Closed it. "Bloody hell, you're right. Unless we get Oonai to wake up."

They were quiet for a while, processing the realization. Then Jespar stood. "We can't leave him here like this," he said. "Let's carry him."

They each slid an arm under one of Kawu's shoulders and lifted him. His skin was still warm—it would stay this way for about half a day, then his body would grow stiff and heavy as cadaveric rigid-ity set in, then-

Stop. Why are you thinking this? Stop.

"Ready?" Lysia asked.

Jespar left it at a nod.

The ziggurat had changed since their last visit. The red vines that had sprouted from the pyramid's base were now thick veins that covered half the façade and culminated at Oonai's statue at the apex, where they slung around his legs as though to stop him from fleeing. Insects, some as big as wolves, swarmed the stairs and the arcades, scurrying off whenever Jespar and Lysia came near. They were on their way to the physician's room, hoping to find Oonai there when a cold prickle spread in Jespar's forehead.

He stopped dead.

"Jes?"

A light rain set in. Jespar moved his mouth while the sensation spread further, sending shivers down his spine; then it dawned on him.

"Jes? Jes, what's the matter?"

Slowly, he faced Lysia. "The dreameater. I ... I think it just ... hatched."

A figure emerged on a colonnade to their right, a man with a noose around his snapped neck. He looked at them dully, then continued down the walkway.

"But ... you're still here."

"Yeah." Jespar tightened his grip on Kawu. He had gotten colder. With the time distortion, would he still be warm in the waking world? Had Agaam even noticed he'd died yet?

Stop. Stop thinking about that.

"Maybe Kawu's shift is still protecting me," he said. "Or maybe it can't pull me anywhere while I'm still in somebody else's dream. I have no idea."

Lysia exhaled softly. "And now what?"

"I don't know. Let's just keep—" The prickle cut him off, stronger than before, like a hundred tiny eels twitching under his skin. *Longing*, he thought. *Search*—

"Wait," Jespar said. "I have an idea."

"What?"

"I can't say for sure, but think I can feel it, I don't know, *pulling* me somewhere. Maybe it feels drawn to its mother?"

"You mean to Oonai's dreameater."

"Yes. We could use it as a compass of sorts."

Lysia chewed on her lip. Then she nodded once. "Sounds like our best plan. Give it a try then."

Jespar let his eyes drift over his surroundings: up the stairs, where he saw the faceless girl in the pale-yellow dress again, sitting on the steps and hugging her stomach; up to the tier with the Ma'saa's orchard, where a millipede as big as a horse slithered over the façade; down to the forecourt, where blood-soaked toddlers were now playing with the woman-headed alapu, their high-pitched wheezing shrieks and laughs ringing through the humid air. Upon reaching a pathway that snaked around the ziggurat, the prickle returned three times as strong.

"There," Jespar said. "That's the way."

They went down the stairs and followed the path. Leading through a withered hedge maze and a skeletal garden whose dead trees and shrubbery were covered in giant spiderwebs, the trail ended at a small lake from which rose an islet with a pyramid upon it. A plank provided a bridge over the water. The prickle now reached from Jespar's hairline down to the bridge of his nose; the rain was pouring down, stirring up a miasma of decay. They crossed the lake, Jespar's arms growing heavier and heavier under Kawu's dead weight.

In waking life, the islet pyramid was probably made of lapis-lazuli and gold; in the nightmare, it was ashen gray and mustard. A chaotic mess of red vines covered the façade.

"The Ma'saa's chapel," Lysia said.

Jespar gave her a questioning glance.

"This place, it must be the chapel where the Ma'saa fell asleep and had her 'vision', the one where she saw you. Remember?"

The memory seemed to come from a different life. He nodded. "Right."

"And you're sure Oonai's here?" she asked.

It didn't feel like a real question. Despite that torpid anger that had kept Lysia going since the riot, despite her promise to "make Oonai see," Jespar sensed that a part of her wanted to stall this confrontation as much as he did. Why? Because, irrational as it was, it was sometimes easier to give up before you even tried, since trying meant a possibility of failure. What was this undertaking, if not mad? Their attempt to trick Vel'Nyx had been ambitious enough; now here they were, intending to talk a man off a cliff he had already jumped from.

What were the odds?

It doesn't matter. Because Kawu died for this.

"I'm sure he's here," Jespar said. "Right behind that door."

Lysia let out a long breath and gazed up the chapel. An amber glow shone through the slit windows, and a large portion of the roof was broken.

"All right then," she said. "After you."

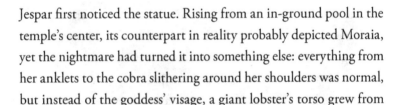

Jespar first noticed the statue. Rising from an in-ground pool in the temple's center, its counterpart in reality probably depicted Moraia, yet the nightmare had turned it into something else: everything from her anklets to the cobra slithering around her shoulders was normal, but instead of the goddess' visage, a giant lobster's torso grew from her neck, its grotesquely large claws spread toward the ceiling.

A figure cowered at her feet, bathed in the glow of a hundred floating candles.

On Jespar's first visit to the nightmare, Jaaros Oonai's simulacrum had been one step from a corpse; the man in the chapel had long crossed that threshold. His clothes were in tatters, and pus-filled blisters covered his gaunt face. White glowing slime oozed from his orifices, trailing down his cheeks like tears. It was a portrait right out of hell, and the parasite that grew from Oonai's skull completed it: almost a stride long now, the dreameater resembled a giant centipede that had wrapped itself twice around Oonai's neck and was now resting its head on his right shoulder.

Gruesome as the sight was, it was something else that made Jespar stop dead at the sight: *familiarity.* For some odd reason, seeing

Oonai like this filled Jespar with a bizarre sense of *knowing* and even empathy which he had not felt on his last visit. *Why?* What was it about this broken man, whose life could not have been more different to Jespar's, that felt so bloody familiar?

"... okay?" Lysia was saying something. "Are you okay?"

Jespar turned his head. "I'm fine. Let's put Kawu down."

They carried Kawu to the outermost ring of the prayer cushions that encircled the pool and eased him onto the ground, propping his head upon a pillow. His body was cold by now, and his skin had taken on a yellowish hue. Watching him, the fury and the grief made a brief reappearance, but the numbness smothered them within an instant. Rising back to his feet, Jespar was not surprised when he realized there were corpses all around them. Kneeling on the cushions, they all gazed at Jespar, their palms folded across their chests with their fingers touching the brass rings around their upper arms, as if in prayer.

They were the same as in the swamp court: the villagers, the man with the breadbasket, the Girl and her father. His own sister, whom he tried so hard to forget. His brothers were also there, as was his fencing teacher Meyser Faris, their governess Meydame Dorta, and the Dal'Varek manor's six servants, all of whom the Revenants had killed and marked with a blood lotus cut into their foreheads. The Corpse himself sat near the pool, wearing his telltale sorrowful rictus, his hands burning soundlessly.

"Tō 'ō āpa ku ānū e ni'ē e 'atete ku, hīo ū," a voice both familiar and alien said. Jespar looked down. A rotten Kawu had replaced the real one, and the creature was clasping Jespar's ankle. Insects swarmed from his ears and mouth, bits of bone showed through the spots where they'd eaten the skin. "Tō ,ō āpa ku ānū e ni'ē e ,atete ku."

Show me the Sunset Trees.

"Jes? What's wrong?" Lysia stood by the Corpse, one leg passing through his body as if it were a mirage.

"Tō 'ō āpa ku ānū e ni'ē e 'atete ku," Kawu's corpse whispered.

"You can't see it?" Jespar asked softly.

"See what? What do you mean?"

"I ... I'm hallucinating." He stepped away from Kawu. There was a bit of resistance as his phantom hand held on to Jespar's ankle, but it let go. "My dreameater must have connected with its mother or something."

"Connected?"

"Yeah, and they're sending me hallucinations. At least that's what I think."

"... Will you be okay?"

Good question. Would he? Looking for comfort, Jespar guided his thoughts back to the night in the cockleshell alcove, but the emptiness he'd been feeling ever since Kawu died shrouded all of his feelings. Instead, he found reassurance when he looked at Oonai, and that odd sense of familiarity overcame him once more.

There is a way.

There was a way through the labyrinth of this man's mind, and at its center lay the key to waking him up.

They could find it. The only question was how.

"I'll be okay," he said. "You remember the plan?"

Lysia's gaze lingered on the human-lobster statue, her thumb trailing up and down her scar. She dropped her hand and looked Oonai straight in the eye.

"Yes. Let's end this."

CHAPTER THIRTY-FOUR
FISH BOY

DAY SEVEN

1ST MOON OF RAINY SEASON, 1226 A.L.

All the corpses were watching him. The moon filtered through the shattered ceiling and limned the chapel in violet light. Oonai was looking at Jespar and Lysia as they crossed to the temple pool, but his eyes seemed to pass right through them, like a dying nomad staring at a fata morgana. The parasite, on the other hand, did see. Its head fixed in their direction, its three feelers circled round and round and round.

A thought: *This could be you.*

An image: Jespar's corpse in the swamp court, dead locusts around him, about to be resurrected. A dreameater growing from his head like a living tumor.

Time and again, the pair flashed through his mind as Jespar approached Oonai, yet like everything else that had happened since Kawu's death, they made Jespar feel nothing. The fog swallowed it all.

They stopped at the basin. Light rain trickled through the cracked ceiling above, the drops pattering onto the water in a mesmerizing rhythm. Jaaros Oonai looked even worse up close: Tiny insects crawled through his beard and hair, and a layer of grime covered his ravaged skin. The glowing slime had caked around his eyelids.

"Ready?" Jespar asked.

Lysia nodded and closed her eyes. Opened them. "Just what I expected." The emptiness and the sorrow were gone from her voice. Resolve and anger had replaced them.

Oonai did not react.

"Is that really how you wanna do this?" Lysia asked. "After all you did, you're just gonna sit there pretending I'm not here?"

Nothing. Oonai continued to look through them. *React,* Jespar thought, fists clenching. *Bloody react.*

"Tell me something, Jaaros," Lysia went on, "do you ever think about her? Our daughter?"

Oonai slowly lifted his gaze. "You don't know that, hio."

Hio. It was working. As Agaam had predicted, Oonai thought Lysia was Yamin.

Lysia hesitated. "I don't know what?"

"That it was a girl," Oonai said, his ragged voice matching his appearance. A ruin. "You don't know it was a girl."

Lysia's lips pressed together, a vein pulsing along her neck. It was so convincing Jespar briefly forgot she was acting. "Yes, Jaaros, I do. Mothers know."

Oonai withstood her gaze a second longer. Then he began to cry. The dreameater's feelers perked up, and it set into motion, slithering up his neck and across his face, as its body swelled and shrunk, swelled and shrunk, until a new segment emerged from the hole in Oonai's head.

It was feeding.

When Oonai's tears ceased, the dreameater stopped contracting and rested its head back on its host's shoulder, white slime and blood dripping from the new segment. A baby materialized in Oonai's cradled arms. It looked healthy at first glance, but there was something unnatural about its stiffness and the waxen sheen of its skin. Noticing the toddler, Oonai croaked before softly pressing it to his chest. "Look, hio! Look, she's still alive!"

Lysia's mouth twitched. "You know that's a lie, Jaaros. She's dead, just like me."

"*No!* No, you're *wrong!*" He pressed the child tighter against his chest, stroking its wispy hair to soothing, hushing sounds. "Just look at her, look at how fine she looks, look at–"

The baby's head snapped off. For a tick, Oonai held the little round thing and stared. Then he dropped it with a scream, sending it tumbling over his knees into the prayer pool, where it spawned a blossom of blood. Jespar was still processing what he had just seen when Oonai screamed again: the baby was now falling apart in his arms, first the hands, then the arms, then the feet and the legs, all rolling over Oonai's cradled arms into the water until only a bloody torso was left.

"Gods, what d'ye want from me?" Oonai wailed. "I'm suffering, I've paid, so what why can't ye *just leave me alone?*"

Lysia glanced at Jespar. His cue.

Act, he thought.

But he couldn't. He was rooted to the spot, his lips refusing to move.

Fucking act.

He snapped out of it. "What do you think we want?"

Oonai seemed to notice him for the first time. "Who-who are you?"

"A friend of mine," Lysia said. "He was out of the country all year and had no idea what had happened to me."

"I'm sorry," Oonai whispered. "I'm so sorry."

"I don't want an apology, I want an answer," Jespar said, hoping his words sounded more convincing than they felt. "Why do you think we're here?"

Oonai stared at him. Then his eyes wandered back to his lap, where the baby's torso had become a pulsating red clump. "My sins," he said, so quietly Jespar barely heard. "You're more punishment for my sins."

It was precisely the kind of answer they'd been hoping for: to avoid an immersion break, they had to understand the dream's structure, the story Oonai and the parasite's minds had spun around this place. Did Oonai's simulacrum believe it was still alive? Did it know it was trapped in a nightmare? Or did the dream make him think something else altogether?

They needed more.

"Your sins," Lysia echoed. "So you think we're, what, ghosts come to haunt you?"

"Of course you are."

When Oonai said nothing else, Lysia shot Jespar a pleading glance.

He followed a hunch. "So you still think the entire world revolves around you. Gods, you're really as rotten as Yamin said."

Oonai's gaze flicked up. It seemed like he would cry again, but then a dreamy expression took over, and his eyes wandered skywards, into the rain. "No," he said. "I used to be like that, but I've changed. I ended it, and now I'm here, in hell, paying for my transgressions."

So that was the dream's narrative: Oonai thought he had killed himself and was now suffering in the Light-Born's Netherworld, the place Tyr sent the souls he decided were not worthy of the Gods' different Beyonds.

Lysia scoffed. "And you think that changes anything? You slap yourself in the face a couple of times, and everything's forgiven?"

Smiling wanly, Oonai shook his head. "You don't understand, hio. This was never about forgiveness, I'm long beyond that. This is about suffering for my crimes. It's about justice." He regarded his hands. Only the baby's tiny heart was left now, swimming in a puddle of blood. "And I do suffer, hio, day and night, more than you could possibly imagine. But it's all right because I've made my peace with it. I'm a monster, just like you told me back then, and this is exactly what I deserve."

Lightning lit up the chapel, echoed by thunder. The rain slowed to a drizzle. Lysia gave Jespar a sideways glance. He nodded, his balled fists clammy and shaking.

They had mapped the territory. Now came the foray.

"What if I told you that you can still set things right?" Jespar asked.

Oonai met his eyes. "Didn't you listen? I can't. I ended it all, and I'm in hell."

"A hell, yes, but not the one that comes after death. There's still a way out of this one."

The parasite's feelers perked up. Jespar tensed, his pulse picking up the pace. Had he gone too far? Had they broken the immersion?

The world stayed in place.

"No," Oonai said slowly. "No, you're wrong. There is no way out."

"That's what you're telling yourself because it's what you want to believe," Jespar said. "The truth is that you still have a chance to set things right. If not for Yamin and not for any of the people whose lives you destroyed, then for the one person you love. Your wife will die if you stay down here, Oonai."

The dreameater began feeding again, but there was something different about the way it moved now. *Wary.*

Oonai's voice was barely a whisper. "Is ... is something wrong with Nama?"

"Someone hurt her badly," Lysia said. "Her and Enkshi both. In fact, your entire country is falling to pieces as we speak. That plan you and Vel'Nyx made, it spiraled out of control."

"You ... how do you know?"

No explanations, Jespar thought. *No details.*

"That doesn't matter," she said. "What matters is that there's a massive, bloodthirsty mob in front of your ziggurat as we speak and that you, as the last living magnate, are the only one who can turn it around. And *that's* why we're here, Jaaros. To tell you to stop this foolishness, to get back out there and negotiate a truce to save your country, your wife, and thousands of innocents from certain death."

"But I told you, hio, there *is* no going back. I'm in hell!"

His doubtful tone encouraged Jespar for the last push. "And we told you, you are not. You can get out of this place anytime you want, Oonai ... you only need to want it enough."

It was the last leg of their strategy: First, feed Oonai's guilt about Yamin's death and his unborn child to make him malleable. Second, appeal to his love for the Ma'saa, the person he treasured most in the world. Third, tell him that he was the only one who could still save her—because that was the truth.

The drizzle ceased.

A woman's head materialized in Oonai's hands. Though it was made of black stone, Jespar immediately recognized the resemblance to Agaam.

"No," Oonai said.

The rain picked up again, twice as hard as before. "You simply don't get it, hio, you don't understand a *bloody* thing. Don't you think I've tried, hm? Don't you think I've tried to put things right, to *help* for a change? I did. I wanted to be better, but it was pointless!"

The head—it was charcoal—was falling apart under the downpour, crumbling in Oonai's hands. "Before I came to this place, I tried to revoke that cursed decree that I'd drafted to at least stop the riot, but do you know what the magnates did? They showed me a law saying they could kick me out of the Coalition if I ever acted against their interests again. And the worst joke of it all? I wrote that law. Godsdammit, the bloody irony, I fucking wrote that thing!"

Sobbing, he clutched Yamin's head, liquid coal oozing through his fingers. The dreameater was feeding again, expanding and contracting like a wineskin. "I am the problem, hio, that's what it comes down to. I'm the architect of the arena, I'm a disease that corrupts everything it touches, I'm the father of monsters, and I'm never going to save anyone because *I am what's wrong!*"

Lightning flashed. Rain and wind raged through the chapel, killing the candles, whipping at the stone. "You know, I went to a priest after you jumped," Oonai said. "And when I told him what I'd done, he said that every sin leaves a mark on our soul and that these marks fester if we don't atone. Now, tell me, when in my bloody life did I ever atone? I sinned and sinned and sinned, but when did I *ever* atone? Never, hio, never. And you know what that means? It means that if I ever had a soul to begin with, there's nothing left of it by now but a godsdamned tumor."

For a few moments, the crashing rain and the roaring wind were the only sounds in the chapel. Lysia was the first to recover her words, her lips quivering as she spoke. "So you're gonna let her die? Is that it? You're gonna let your wife and everyone else die just because you *think* you can't help?"

Oonai's smile was hollow. "Even if I could, and we survived, it wouldn't be long until I'd start hurting people again. I know who I am by now, hio. This is what I deserve, and this is where I belong."

He sunk back against the statue and gazed into the pool. The coal head was gone save for the smears on Oonai's hands, and the dreame-ater had ceased to feed. The pool was overflowing from the rain, water snakes slithering toward the corpses seated on the prayer cushions.

We can't do it.

We just can't convince him.

Jespar sought Lysia's eyes, looking for encouragement, for an idea, for *anything* to turn this mess around. She just stared at the shell of that man who was supposed to save them.

Numbly, Jespar glanced over his shoulder. The corpses were still there, deathbed smiles on their faces—a loving family watching their prodigal son return from his pointless escapade. Beaten, bleeding, dying. The inevitable consequences of his foolishness.

"Come home," they seemed to say. "Come home, where you belong."

And, just like that, something in Jespar's mind moved.

Like water currents shifting under the surface of a deep lake, the nature of this epiphany at first eluded him—and yet he knew exactly what he had to do.

"Like hell you tried."

Oonai looked up.

"You heard me." A strange heat seized Jespar, filled him with anger. "Come on, sauntering into the Coalition and ordering the hyenas *you* placed in those seats to give up the bone *you* tossed them? Did you honestly expect that to work?"

Oonai's face darkened, and the rain took up again. With a chunk of skin missing under his right cheek, Jespar could see his jawbone moving; it should have scared him, terrified him, but it didn't.

"How about Yamin's mother, hm?" Jespar went on. "Her grand-father? Did you ever reach out to them, did you ever own up to what you did, did you do *anything* at all to help them cope with their grief?"

Oonai balled his fists. "You know nothing. You don't know a godsdamned thing."

"I know more than you can fucking fathom, and I know a liar when I see him. Let's be honest for a second: all that 'trying' you did, was it about making amends or about finding a way to wash the blood from your hands because it felt so godsdamned sticky? Let me tell you a thing about 'trying', Jaaros Oonai." Jespar stepped forward into the pool. The rain was lashing down upon him, mixing with hail. "Trying is working your hands bloody in the nuvium mines, knowing your lungs will give out before you're thirty. Trying is going to sleep hungry for the third night in a row. Trying is raising three kids all on your own, trying is stomaching the shame of telling your son you can't afford a physician for that wound that's started to fester, trying is dragging yourself out of bed every single bloody morning knowing *nothing* is ever gonna change for the better! *That's* trying, not some half-assed attempt at easing your conscience, then bailing out when you realize it's actually hard to better yourself!" He stopped a stride from Oonai. "So why don't we just drop the pretense, shall we? You never gave a shit for the people who suffered from your actions, not even about Yamin and your unborn kid—what got to you so badly was realizing that you aren't the hard-working visionary you took yourself for but just another selfish asshole."

Wind was howling through the chapel now, the hail raining down like shrapnel, only that it wasn't hail anymore but chips of bone. The dreameater resumed feeding.

"You have no idea who I am." Oonai rose to his feet. "You have no *fucking* idea what I've been through."

Standing upon the statue's plinth, Oonai loomed over Jespar like a wrathful god, but Jespar held his glare. "That's right, and I don't bloody care! Dammit, do you think you're the only one out there who has a sob story to justify the shit they do? In the end, all that matters is that you left the world a worse place than it was, and for what? Only so that you could be even richer than you already were! Gods, Oonai, that was your child she carried, your own fucking child, and even now, all you talk about is yourself! You're not some kind of martyr, Oonai, and you're not some villain who had a change of heart. You're just another cowa–"

"*I suffer!*" A gust slammed into the gate, bone chips big as eyeballs raged from a sky that had turned into a purple-black maelstrom. The dreameater gorged, twitching and squirming, its carapace bulging under as if about to burst. "*You have no idea how much I suffer!*"

He could kill you, a voice cried out somewhere in the back of Jespar's mind. This is his dream, and he's a god here, and he could kill you with the snap of a finger.

But Jespar didn't care. A mad, cathartic heat had taken him over, filling him like burning blood. "So what? Bloody hell, Oonai, all you did was run! The world doesn't care what you feel, it cares about what you *do*! You could spend eternity down here and get tortured by your nightmares, but to all those people out there, you might as well be fucking *dead*!"

A lightning bolt hit the ceiling and broke off a chunk of stone; it crashed into the statue's head, snapping it at the torso. The dreameater was tossing around now, its whipping feelers brushing Jespar's forehead and cheeks; Oonai's eyes were a mirror of the maelstrom above, flickering between hatred and fear and grief and fury and-

Cracking.

The tempest ceased, and the maelstrom closed. The parasite froze.

Lips shaking, Oonai put a hand on Jespar's shoulder. "I'm better than him." There was no more rage in his eyes. Only frailty and hurt. The eyes of a broken boy. "I'm better than Popa."

The heat vanished in a blink.

Petrified, Jespar grew aware of the pain in his skull, of the blood trailing down his cheeks and temples. The bone chips and hail had left a dozen lacerations on his scalp and skin.

Say something.

But he couldn't—not for the lump this time. It was as if the heat had hollowed him out and left his mind in ashes.

Say something!

"Then prove it." It was Lysia.

Oonai's gaze met hers. "I will."

He gripped the parasite and tore it from his head. A jet of blood and slime erupted from the fist-sized hole in his skull. The dreame-ater twitched and squirmed, soundless, its head craning back toward Oonai, glowing slime spraying from its rear. Then it went slack— and Oonai with it.

When Jespar turned around, the corpses were gone. Only Kawu's remained, as still and lifeless as this dying dream.

The world collapsed.

CHAPTER THIRTY-FIVE
RESURRECTION

"Varek?"

Agaam's face floated above him, shadows dancing across the ceiling. "Ma'sao? Are you all right?"

Jespar grunted. He attempted to sit, but his arms gave in under his weight, and he dropped back onto the floor. His head throbbed, and his muscles were stiff and bunched.

Agaam helped him up. "Are you all right?"

"... Yeah. Yeah, I'm—"

Kawu.

He lay motionless on the stretcher, curled up as if to ward off the cold. But— *Gods.* He was still moving. Kawu's chest was still moving. And of course it was; in reality, that fatal drain attack had happened mere minutes ago, and—

"I'm sorry." Lysia was kneeling beside Kawu, her eyes dull. "His brain gave up. He's gone."

Jespar was about to tell her she was wrong, that Kawu was still breathing. Then he realized that what his brain had misread as movements of Kawu's chest had only been illusions caused by the flickering flame of the torch behind the stretcher.

Jespar wanted to scream. Then the fog closed over him.

"I know it isn't much solace," Agaam said. "But it seems like whatever you did in Oonai's dream worked. He started convulsing during the dreamwalk, so we carried him and the Ma'saa into another alcove, but I was just there, and the physician says Oonai is waking up. You did it, ma'sae—thanks to Ma'sao Nakāni and you, we finally stand a chance of making it through this alive."

Jespar should have probably felt triumph, but nothing came. He was still looking at Kawu, wondering how he could have allowed this to happen, wondering why he still wasn't crying.

"What about you?" Lysia asked. "Your parasite, I mean? Are you-I don't know, feeling anything?"

I don't care anymore. Jespar touched his forehead. It was clammy and hot. He felt no sign of a Pull, but he didn't feel particularly clear either. If anything, there was mild dizziness, as though he'd spent a whole day getting cooked by the tropical sun.

"I'm not su–" Jespar broke off when he realized Agaam and Lysia were staring at him. Before he could ask what was wrong, a dull pain grew in his forehead, a pulsating pressure, as though something was pushing against the inside of his skull. Warm liquid trickled down his cheek.

He touched it. Blood and slime. "What the—"

Pain exploded. Jespar screamed, dropped back onto the floor, hands pressed to his temples; a storm raged in his skull, getting worse by the second and casting a red-white veil over his vision; the next thing he knew, Lysia was before him, gripping his wrist with one hand and pulling up his lid with the other. The pain swelled and swelled and swelled, and-

Stopped.

Something fell from his eye onto the floor. It lay twitching on its back, then flipped around and darted off toward the tunnel. It was almost to the alcove opening when Agaam stomped upon it with a heavy boot. A sickening crunch. Agaam stomped again, then again. When he lifted his boot at last, a black smear on the floor was all that remained of the creature that had almost taken Jespar's life.

"Let me look at that wound," Lysia said. "Come on."

Now that the shock had worn off, his right eye hurt like it was on fire. Lysia covered it with her cupped hand, and her gaze went glassy the way it always did when she performed a shift. The air crackled and shimmered, and a soothing warmth spread over the right half of Jespar's face. When she drew back, the pain was a mere throb, and the red veil obscuring his vision was gone.

"There you go." She took a cloth from her belt and dabbed the blood from his cheeks. "Give it a few weeks, and it'll be good as new."

Jespar began to thank her, but then a scream came from the hallway, followed by a burst of voices.

"Maybe Oonai has woken up," Agaam said. "Come. We'll take the lad with us."

Carrying him between them, they entered the tunnel. Jespar had expected the grief to hit once he would make physical contact with Kawu, but instead, all he could think of was how cold Kawu was.

The second alcove was almost as big as a small cave. All the evacuees were gathered within, crowded around the Oonais' stretchers. Spotting Agaam, the throng parted to let them through. Oonai sat upright on his litter, and Ma'sao Ulanees was applying a bandage to his right eye. The left one was riveted on the crone beside him. Nayima Oonai.

"Stars burn me," Lysia muttered. "Look."

A slimy heap lay beside Sergeant Maadira's feet. Jespar's dreameater had been the size of a thumbnail—this one must have been at least as big as a walnut; pieces of carapace, feelers, and legs lay in the foggy blue-white slime, some of them still twitching.

Jespar's gaze wandered back to Oonai, who was now looking at him. Visually, his real self couldn't have been more different from the ghoulish man they had faced in his nightmare, but the expression in his eyes seemed taken right from his simulacrum: broken and hurt.

How odd it felt. There he was, the man whom Jespar supposedly had been destined to save, the living god who had devised a scheme so terrifying it would go down in history, the father who had driven his lover and their unborn child off a cliff. The man without whom Kawu would still be alive.

On some level, Jespar had expected this moment to be cathartic; yet all there was, was the odd familiarity that had also been there in Oonai's kuluhika. No anger, no hatred, no pity. They exchanged a single nod, and that was it.

"Ma'sae!" Maadira was approaching them. "You're back, you—" Noticing Kawu, she fell silent. "Oh, Moraia. I'm ... I'm sorry."

Agaam adjusted his eyepatch. Then he addressed Oonai. "May we speak in private, ma'sao? Just the outlanders, you, and I?"

There were murmurs from the evacuees. Oonai waved his hand toward the tunnel.

"But I'm not done treating you," Ma'sao Ulanees protested. "I—"

"Ma'saa Varroy will take care of it," Agaam said. "You too, Sergeant. Please."

Maadira seemed taken aback—offended, even—but then she sighed, ushered out the crowd, and left with them. Jespar and Agaam carefully laid Kawu upon the floor as Lysia set about treating Oonai's wound. Considering what a bloody mess the eye was, he should have been screaming in pain. *Etheryme*, Jespar guessed. Ulanees must have given Oonai a whole vial. With rough, mechanical motions, Lysia removed the bandage, cleaned out the wound, then performed a shift, and re-applied the dressing. Oonai stared at his wife the entire time.

"The parasite did some serious damage to the optical nerve when it came out," she said when she was done. "I doubt you'll ever regain vision in that eye, and if you do, it'll be severely impaired."

It was as if Oonai hadn't heard. "What happened to her?" he asked hoarsely. "Who-who did this?"

"We were just about to tell you, ma'sao," Agaam said. "If I may."

"Tell me."

Agaam recounted the events, this time the full truth except for his kinship to Yamin. He spoke calmly and concisely, like a servant reading a message to his master: there was no trace of anger when he explained how they had learned about the Overgrowth Plan, no tinge of sorrow when he told Oonai what had happened to Enkshi and the Ma'saa. Even when he mentioned Yamin's suicide—he kept how he had found out about the affair vague—nothing in his voice suggested she'd been his granddaughter.

When Agaam was done, Oonai's gaze remained on the floor for a long time. "Zagash is dead."

"Yes, ma'sao. A spear through the throat."

He made a soft, pensive noise. "I understand."

Lysia crossed her arms. "So? Can you fix this mess or not? Unless we negotiate a truce, we're done for."

Oonai exhaled wearily. "I don't know. I need time to think."

Lysia opened her mouth, but Agaam beat her to an answer. "I'm afraid we cannot afford more than a few minutes. The rioters could break through the gate any minute."

"I understand." Oonai hesitated. "I need privacy, though."

Lysia shot Agaam an incredulous glance. Agaam's face was a mask. "Then I suggest you take a walk down the tunnel and come back here once you have a plan. Please don't go far, ma'sao."

"Don't worry." Oonai lightly squeezed his wife's hand. "I won't."

"Wait a godsdamned minute," Lysia said. "You're not going any—"

Agaam quieted her with a hard look. Jespar, his thoughts still foggy, watched numbly as Oonai left, his steps slow, as if he struggled to remember the motions. In the mouth of the alcove, Oonai stopped.

"Agaam?"

"Yes, ma'sao?"

"When you found out what I did, why didn't you just kill me?"

For a second, something in Agaam's eye changed—like a mirror cracking and revealing a dark corridor just beyond. "Because you're the only one who can still save us, ma'sao."

Oonai's mouth twitched. Shame? Anger? Hurt? Probably all three.

"I see." He disappeared into the tunnel.

"You're insane," Lysia said when Oonai's footfalls had faded. "You're absolutely insane. He's just gonna run off."

"There's nowhere to run but the bay," Agaam said.

"And how do you know he's not gonna take that chance?"

Agaam nodded at the Ma'saa's stretcher. "Because of her."

Lysia opened her mouth, then closed it. She exhaled through gritted teeth and sank down to the cave floor. Unsure what else there was to be said, Jespar did the same, sitting half a stride from Kawu, or the hull that was left of him. It was as close as he could bear.

"Tell me one thing, Jes," Lysia said. "How did you know?"

"Know what?"

"What to tell Oonai so he would see sense. It was like, I don't know, like you hit straight through a wall with what you said."

Good question. How did *you know?* A lot of it had been intuition, a lot had been despair. But that third part, the epiphany he'd had after seeing the corpses smile, was still a wisp of smoke: it dissolved whenever he reached for it and grew fainter with every passing moment.

"I have no idea. I just knew."

Lysia left it at that, and Jespar was grateful for it. *Oblivion.* He just wanted oblivion, to step into the endless fog that had flooded his mind and let it swallow him whole, forever forgotten. Had it been only him in these tunnels, he would have just closed his eyes and waited until the Scythes found and killed him or exhaustion and hunger did the job for them. Either way: good riddance.

But he couldn't. Not just yet.

He closed his eyes and started counting his breaths.

Ten.

Sixty.

A hundred.

How different those of the others sounded. Lysia's, short but deep. The Ma'saa's, long and ragged. Agaam's, barely audible. Oonai, in contrast-

What?

He looked. It was still just the four of them. Agaam had sat down on Oonai's stretcher, Lysia still cowered in her corner, staring at her clasped, soot-stained hands. And, yet there it was, faint but clearly audible—the sound of a fifth person drawing air.

But-

Jespar leaped over to Kawu and put his ear to his mouth.

There they were. Soft, shallow breaths.

"Lysia," he whispered. "He's alive."

Lysia blinked twice, then hurried over and felt Kawu's chest. "Stars burn me. What the hell?"

"He's alive," Jespar repeated. A wheezing laugh escaped his mouth. "Gods, he's alive!"

Lysia felt Kawu's pulse, his heartbeat, and his forehead, her baffled expression intensifying with each touch. At last, she sat back on her heels. "That doesn't make any sense. He was dead when we woke up."

Agaam came up beside them. "Those 'anchorings' he did," he said. "Could they have been channelings, and he just didn't know it?"

Channelings—shifts maintained over an extended time, the supreme discipline of dimensionism.

"Right," Lysia said. "That would explain why his drain flared up when they entered the tunnel."

"Why?" Jespar asked. "What do you mean?"

Lysia leaned back on her heels. "If Kawu's anchorings were channelings, that means he's been shifting on you continuously ever since that first night—and every time the parasite tried to pull you under, he must have strengthened the channeling to match the parasite's increase in strength."

Jespar's heart sank. "You mean that—"

"Kawu has been shifting *constantly* for almost three days, probably without knowing it," Lysia said. "And what's more, he must have even upheld the channeling when he was already unconscious. That's why he had another drain stroke when the dreameater tried to pull you under in the menagerie—because the link was still there. Bloody hell, I can't even begin to imagine the strain that must've put on his mind, I couldn't have maintained a channeling like that for a single hour. A Sight like this, that's a once-in-a-generation thing."

"A Far-Sight," Agaam said. "Almost certainly."

Jespar groped for words, his brain trying to reconcile his numbness with this new hope. "But how does that explain ... I mean, you said he was dead."

"He was," Lysia said. "My only explanation is that his brain still had a spark of life in it, but the strain of the channeling suppressed that spark. When the parasite died, the link finally broke and brought back that spark before it was completely smothered."

Agaam nodded.

"Is there anything we can do to make him better?" Jespar asked.

"I don't think so, no," Lysia said, studying Kawu. His breaths seemed to be growing in strength, but his complexion was still corpse-like. "I mean, the shift should be over for good now that the dreameater is dead, so that's something, but no matter what, his drain is still severe."

"How about your biomancy? Could you strike a shift to lessen it?"

"If biomancy could cure shifting drain, dimensionists would rule the world by now because there'd be no limit to their power. I can give him some gruntroot and the last of my mandrake powder, but apart from that, all we can do is let him rest and hope the damage isn't too bad when he wakes up."

"Brain damage?"

"Yes," Agaam said. "A shifting drain stroke of that magnitude always takes a toll on the brain, even if the dimensionist wakes up again. If Ma'sao Nakāni survives, he might be lame, mute, or dull-minded for the rest of his life. I fear we'll simply have to hope for the best."

Jespar took Kawu's hand and squeezed it. "He'll make it," he muttered. "He'll pull through."

Lysia and Agaam weren't listening anymore. A man stood in the mouth of the alcove.

"Ma'sao Oonai," Agaam said. "Have you ...?"

"Yes. I know what to do."

Chapter Thirty-Six
Redemption

Day Seven

1st Moon of Rainy Season, 1226 A.L.

ilence reigned in the atrium. It was of a surreal sort, for it should have already yielded to fighting, screams, and the roaring of flames.

The riot was over.

Upon returning to the ziggurat, Oonai had reassumed command with the ease of a master swordsman picking up his weapon after a hiatus. His order had been simple: Maadira would raise a white flag on the battlements and offer to lay down arms, on the grounds of a parley between the Pale Brother and Oonai himself. She had done as he asked, and the Pale Brother had agreed. Ten minutes ago, the guards had opened the gates.

The atrium was a careful arrangement: Jespar, Lysia, and the unconscious Kawu were with the servants, in the shelter of the colossal statue of Moraia, the remainder of the Blue Guard filled the entire back half in formation, Maadira in the front row. Oonai stood on the high dais beneath the goddess' likeness, with Agaam backdropping him like a shadow, and a protective crescent of Jade Snakes halfway up the steps. Flickering braziers lined the blue carpet and evoked the feeling of a temple; the chandeliers and wall sconces were out, cloaking the rest of the hall in darkness.

Impressive as all these elements were, they were just background for the real motif: Oonai.

Having issued his orders, he had retired to his chambers to wash and change. The notion had struck Jespar as bizarre—when your life was at stake, surely there were more important things than a shave. Now he understood. The man standing on the dais was a far cry from the sickly creature Jespar and Lysia had pulled out of its nightmare two hours ago. A gold-and-indigo coat and sable trousers had replaced his sleeping robe, and atop a mane of combed black hair sat the Magnate's Crown, seven spikes of hard, cold gold. Powder hid the pallor of his skin and the dark circles under his eyes; rings adorned his beard and fingers. From a distance, the only discrepancy between him and his statue was Agaam's black eye patch, which he wore to cover his injury; it gave him a mysterious air of severity.

Visionary, First Magnate of the Coalition, and richest man in the Illumined World—for the first time, Jaaros Oonai looked the part.

The gate swung open.

One impression burned itself into Jespar's mind. Not the Pale Brother's bloodied skin and his animal scowl, not how the torchlight reflected in the rebels' spears, pitchforks, and scimitars, not how massive the mob was, stretching on far beyond the atrium portal. It was the sky. A crimson glow spanned the heavens as if prophesying the wrath of the Gods—the shine of the thousands of fires raging in the Alabaster City that night.

Jeers and shouts erupted at Oonai's sight; the mob rushed into the hall, but the Scythes in the front rows held them back. The guards raised their shields and locked their spears on top. Oonai observed the commotion without batting an eyelash, standing tall on his dais with his hands clasped behind his back. The struggle went on for a bit before the mob quieted and fell into restless shuffling and glares. Jespar shot an uneasy glance at Agaam. He was deep in concentration, the air shimmering around him.

Our lifeline, Jespar thought. Yes, the Pale Brother had agreed to a parley, but chances were it was only Agaam's mass channeling shift that prevented the mob from inciting a bloodbath. He had compared it to light rain drizzling on a wildfire: even the best psychomancer in the Illumined World couldn't truly control the minds of more than a dozen people at once, especially for an extended time. The best Agaam could do was to hamper the aggression and make them more susceptible to suggestion—at least for a while.

A bout of nausea crept into Jespar's stomach, and sweat broke out all over his skin—the protests of his crushing exhaustion, innate fear of large crowds, and the knowledge that this might well be the last few minutes of his life.

He can do it, Jespar told himself. *That guy is the best negotiator in the world.*

It'll be fine.

"Step forth," Oonai said.

The mob launched murmurs and insults. Of course they did: those weren't the words they had expected. Where was the groveling, where was the pleading? Scowling, the Pale Brother quelled the babble with a flick of his hand.

"Well, well," he told Oonai. "So ye still think yer callin' the shots, huh?" The mockery that had tinged his voice during the negotiations with Enkshi was gone, leaving only a seething hatred that made the hair on Jespar's arms stand on end. "After killin' me sister?"

Oonai didn't move a muscle, hands clasped behind his upright back. "I asked you to step forth so that we can parley, as you agreed to do. And you should, considering I'm the only one who can still save your lives."

Stunned silence. Then, laughter and shouting.

"Just kill the leech!" someone screamed. "String him across a bloody pond!"

"Cut him open!"

"Shut his fuckin' mouth!"

Jespar put his hand on his longsword—for all the good that would do him against ten thousand bloodthirsty commoners gone ballistic. They really were dancing on a razor's edge—one wrong word, and the mob's bottled-up energy would explode. Whether it was Oonai's performance, Agaam's shift, or pure luck, the outburst had not yet come.

The Pale Brother let the clamoring continue for a bit before he hushed the crowd and started into the atrium, the mob at his heels. It was a chilling thing to witness: this unending procession of hatred pouring through the gate, lit by a thousand torches that rivaled the sun. Five strides from the line of Blue Guards, the Pale Brother came to a stop.

"Say yer piece, then. After that, we're gonna string ye up over a swamp and have the insects eat ye."

Deafening cheers.

"I will—" Pain shot over his face, and he staggered backward, right into Agaam. Whether it was from the outrageous amount of etheryme in his system or the weakness from his coma, Jespar could not say. Alarmed glances passed through the line of guards.

Oonai caught himself. The tumult died down.

"I will say my piece. Trust me."

As if there were no reason to hurry, he let his eye roam the crowd, stopping at a point somewhere at the far end of the room—an old orator's trick that made each member of a crowd feel like the speaker was looking at them. "First, let it be clear what I'm about to say concerns *you* and your loved ones above all others. You, the people whom this man pretends to represent."

Jeering from the crowd. The Pale Brother chortled. "What, that's yer grand plan? Yer really gonna try to turn them against—"

He broke off. A jolt went through his body, and his arms dropped to his sides; his jaw fell open, tongue lolling out of his mouth.

A commotion broke out. Two Scythes hurried to the Pale Brother's side and tried to steady him. They spoke to him, but he gave no reaction, frozen to the spot, only his eyes moving as they frantically darted about the room.

Jespar glanced at Lysia. Her gaze bore into the Pale Brother, a vein pulsing at her temple. Jespar tugged at his scarf. While the entire plan was a tightrope act, silencing the Pale Brother was the biggest gamble. Oonai had deemed it crucial: not only did he expect the Pale Brother to be highly emotional due to his sister's death, but he also predicted that he would quickly put an end to the show once he figured out where Oonai was headed. Someone had to take him out of the equation, at least for a while—and that someone was Lysia. Hoping that no one would notice Lysia was responsible for the shift— they stood in the shadow of the statue, relatively shielded from sight but not invisible—Jespar turned his attention back to the scene.

"He's only immobilized!" Oonai's voice boomed over the din. "All I want is a chance to tell you the truth! Give it to me, and we will let him go!"

Shouting, insults, jeers. A couple of rioters pushed toward the front of the line, trying to jostle their way through. The guards tightened their grip on their spears, a hundred viper fangs poised at the crowd.

"A chance for the truth! You deserve it!"

Not in a million years had Jespar expected this to work, yet it did. One by one, the voices ebbed away until all that was left was an angry murmur. It went on for a bit, then a hulking man stepped forward from the first row of Scythes. Even though a cowl covered the lower half of his face, the nest of scars on his cheeks and forehead was enough to put a butcher's chopping board to shame.

"All right," Scarman said. "Speak."

"Good." Oonai's mien was calm, but Jespar saw his hands, which were clasped behind his back, relax. "Let us start with your leader, Vyrias Zaevathal, better known as 'The Pale Brother.' He and his sister both work for me."

Murmurs rose from both the mob and the guard. Maadira gave Oonai a confused glance.

Scarman scoffed. "Bullshit."

"Of course you would say that. Because anything else would require you to admit you've been played." Oonai addressed the crowd. "But a truth remains a truth no matter how hard you try to deny it. This entire riot and what led to it during the last moons were part of a scheme originated by Third Magnate Makiima Vel'Nyx and myself. We *wanted* you to torch this city; we *wanted* you to kill the five other magnates; we *wanted* you to bring down the Coalition. All this was part of a plan to make me and the Third Magnate the two rulers of Kilay."

Incredulous laughs rose from the crowd, followed by insults. Oonai raised his voice. "Vel'Nyx and I drafted the Golden Soil Decree fully aware of the damage it would do to you, and then we hired the Twins to channel your anger so they could guide it to kill the other magnates and the dissenting voices in the Coalition." Scarman opened his mouth, but Oonai continued. "And, no, of course it was not supposed to end like this. General Daato and the

Blue Guard should have stopped you on the meadow by the water-fall, and they would have done so if your leaders hadn't betrayed us."

Some people cheered, but the majority of the rebels seemed con-fused. It made sense: whatever they had pictured would happen in the atrium, the Master Leech confessing to a crime far worse than what they accused him of had not been part of it. Of course, the bewilderment in Jespar's half of the atrium was growing as well—Oonai had instructed the Guard to stay calm and hold formation no matter what he said, but, like the mob, this wasn't what they had expected. Not for the first time in these past weeks, Jespar wished he were a theist. Had there ever been a time for prayers to Erodan, the god of Good Luck, this was it.

They'll think it's part of the strategy, Jespar told himself. They have to. Or did they?

The Pale Brother let out a growl, his shoulders twitching. Lysia balled her fists, the air around her warping like over a bonfire.

"I know, I know," Oonai went on. "You think they did it for you, don't you? You think they double-crossed Vel'Nyx and me because they are secretly on your side, the side of the poor, struggling com-moner. Well, let me assure you, they are not."

He tossed the Pale Brother a grim look. The Aetäerna's eyes bore into Oonai's, seeping hatred that made Jespar's throat close up. "This man and his sister are the vilest scum that ever crawled out of the Kilayan underworld. They betrayed me for a reason far worse than whatever you could imagine."

"All right, this is gettin' ridiculous," Scarman said. "D'ye hon-estly expect us to believe that?"

"Not from me. But perhaps you will believe it when you hear it from him."

Agaam stepped up beside Oonai. Aside from the veins showing along his wrinkled neck and the subtle distortion of air hovering around his body, nothing about Agaam suggested he was channeling a complex shift. Jespar tried to imagine the non-dimensionist equivalent of this feat—possibly balancing a boulder on one's head while giving a speech. "My name is Agaam," he said. "I'm Master Oonai's bodyguard and former captain of the Jade Snakes."

Boos and jeers. Agaam spoke louder: "The reason I lost my position thirteen years ago is that I refused to carry out an order. I'm sure you all remember a certain accident that took place back then, in the Pit on Hapana. The 'rockslide'."

The boos gave way to outrage, then settled on low murmurs.

"That's right. You already know most of the story—the Miner's Movement that spread across the entire Archipelago and their demands for rights, and how that didn't sit well with the Coalition. I'll be brief: the rumor that the rockslide was no accident is true. First Magnate Vel'Tani suggested this solution—'Operation Green Dawn,' as they called it. Only the magnates were in on it." Agaam paused. "It was as simple a mission as I'd ever been given. A handful of Jade Snake operatives disguised as miners were to sneak into the Pit at night, plant tyenite barrels in the shafts, and ignite them come daybreak. I refused the order—and that's why the magnates axed me."

The murmurs quieted to whispers. The aggression was still there, but it felt aimless now, as if they couldn't decide how to feel about this old man's story. Jespar shot Lysia a sidelong glance. Her exertion was starting to show, her hands trembling, and her lips pressed tight. *Just a little longer. Just a little longer.*

"How sad," Scarman said. "And? Even if ye ain't lyin', what's yer point?"

The crowd voiced its agreement. Agaam remained calm. "My point is, I was secretly hoping the Snakes would follow my example and would, therefore, discourage the magnates from going through with the plan. And, who knows, maybe it would have worked—if it hadn't been for two of my highest-ranking officers, who pounced at this opportunity to prove themselves." Agaam looked at the Pale Brother. "Frankly, I never liked them. Terrific soldiers, for sure, but something about those two always felt ... how to put it? 'Off' to me."

The hall was almost silent now, all the attention focused on Agaam. Though most rebels probably still didn't believe him, they wanted to hear where this was going.

"As you may have guessed, the two officers in question were Cara and Vyrias Zaevathal. They took over and carried out Operation Green Dawn, and when the reports of the casualties came in, their first reaction was to dismiss one of their operatives for botching the placement of a charge. No pity, no remorse. Quite the opposite, in fact—they seemed to take pleasure in envisioning this bloodbath. Four-hundred seventy-nine innocent men and women ... torn to pieces by the tyenite or buried by the rockslide."

Lysia inhaled sharply. The shimmer around her and the Pale Brother vanished, and both of them buckled over. Jespar steadied Lysia; the Scythes steadied the Brother. A commotion broke out in the mob.

"Shut up!" the Pale Brother shouted. "Everyone, shut up!"

Pointless. The din of disbelief, confusion, and anger—most of it aimed at Oonai and Agaam, but some at the Brother as well—only grew louder.

"Shut the hell up, or I'll cut yer fuckin' heads off!"

The clamoring stopped. The Pale Brother spun around to Agaam. "Bloody fool, ye really think anyone's buyin' this bullshit? Yer a liar, and I've had it!"

The Aetäerna's border hysteria was the exact reaction Oonai had gambled on. The fire-spitter killing Cara Zaevathal had been a massive fluke, without which Oonai's plan would have failed for sure. Whereas the Sister had been as cryptic and calm as a foggy lake, the

Brother's savage temper was dangerous but predictable. *Calculated anger is terrifying,* Oonai had said. *Tantrums and hysteria are pathetic.*

Agaam stepped back. His shifting drain must have been crushing by now, but his expression remained stoic.

Oonai once again addressed the crowd: "You know it's true because you've seen it as well. Come on, don't tell me you didn't notice that strange look in their faces, that emptiness in their eyes. This man and his sister, they aren't like us. They aren't right in the head, and that's precisely why Vel'Nyx and I chose them. Because we knew that, with them on board, things would get bloody."

The Pale Brother glared at Oonai, nostrils flared, a predator craving the kill. Jespar was sure he'd snap. Instead, he made a sound that was probably intended as a chuckle but came out as two croaks. He faced the mob. "All right, I've heard enough. Let's kill them leeches."

But the mob didn't obey. Weapons were drawn, and there was shuffling and shouting, but they stayed in their half of the hall, eyes flicking back and forth from Oonai and Agaam to the Pale Brother.

Oonai stepped forward on his dais. "In the end, whether you believe us or not doesn't matter. Even if the Twins weren't the imposters they are, the undeniable truth is that they will knowingly lead you to your deaths—in fact, they already have. Two weeks ago, the Light-Born themselves decreed to send a division of five hundred Holy Keepers to the Archipelago to put an end to your rebellion. And they will be here within the week."

The shock was palpable. Jespar couldn't blame them: while he had grown up in a country under the authority of the Order, everything these people knew about keepers came from sermons, legends, and fairy tales; to them, they weren't just the elite soldiers of the Order but fabled warriors of the Gods who had devoted their lives to carrying out their divine will over the world. With many of them being dimensionists—mages, as Uninitiated would call them—they were not only considered the closest a human could get to being invincible but also the epitome of all that was good, virtuous, and holy.

What did that make their enemies?

"Bullshit," the Pale Brother said. "Each country governs itself, that's the third amendment of the Treaty. The Order of Light ain't gonna do nothin'."

Tentative approval. Scarman nodded.

"*Unless* something happens that threatens the very foundation of the Illumined World," Oonai said. "The Order does not meddle in politics if it can be avoided, you're right about that. But a coup carried out through mass murder? The Gods cannot and will not let this stand, even if that were what they wanted. Take it from someone who's met them."

A wave of bewilderment rippled through the mob. Just like the size of that division of keepers headed for Kilay was half as many as Oonai claimed, him personally knowing the Light-Born was an embellished truth. Yes, the Illumined World would not allow the Scythe to take over the Archipelago, but if anyone ordered an intervention, it would be the Order of Light and not the Gods themselves, for they hadn't spoken to a soul since the Silence. Each rioter knew this and had surely found his or her place on the spectrum of faith. Yet was the idea that a man as powerful and godlike as Jaaros Ismirael Oonai had knowledge about the Gods that the commoners hadn't really so absurd? Perhaps the Gods *were* still alive as the Order of Light claimed. Maybe Tyr, in this very moment, was watching from high up in Inodân, taking note of their sins for the afterlife.

"Ye haven't met the Gods 'cause they're dead!" the Pale Brother retorted. "And even if yer right, if the Order doesn't accept our revolution, we're just gonna make short work of 'em!"

A roar went up in the crowd, but the Pale Brother was the target of their indignation. For all their hatred of the Coalition, the idea of murdering a keeper was outrageous, even to nontheists or atheists. An attack on the Order of Light was an attack on the Illumined World itself.

Steering the narrative, Jespar thought.

That's what Oonai was doing. Until an hour ago, this riot had been the archetypal story of the oppressed overthrowing the oppressors—had Oonai pleaded for mercy or attempted to appease the mobsters with money and treasure, they would not have thought twice about ending him. After all, what could possibly be a more glorious and fitting end to the story than the pawn striking the killing blow to a groveling master? Oonai had taken the tale in a new direction, and it had started the moment the angry crowd had set foot into the atrium. Every word was insinuation, every visual symbolic: Oonai was no longer the greedy, dying Master Leech. He was a god-king openly confessing his sins and crimes, a turn no one had expected. Yes, he was still the villain of the story, but the Pale Brother? Liar, monster, blasphemer. Word by word, Oonai had pushed the mob toward the realization that their leader was not the liberator they had believed him to be, not a hero and not a protagonist. And if they had followed a man who blew up mines and openly spoke out against the Gods, then what did that make *them*?

Chills crept up Jespar's fingertips. Agaam had not exaggerated: Oonai *was* a brilliant negotiator.

The Pale Brother whirled to face the crowd. "Bloody hell, it ain't gonna come to that! Don't you idiots see he's trying to play us off each other?" Jespar wasn't even surprised to hear the Pale Brother forgetting his working-class dialect. Like his impassioned speeches about injustice, it had been an act. "If the Gods have any sense of justice left in them, they'll be on our side! They'll negotiate and—"

"And what, set a precedent?" Oonai looked into the crowd. "This man is lying to you, ma'sae, and you know it. If the Order of Light were to agree to negotiations with you, insurgents all across Vyn would try to follow your example. Don't fool yourselves—there is only one way this will end, and that will be a war of you against the rest of the Illumined World. How do you think this is going to play out? Sure, you're thousands, and you're powerful, so maybe you can hold Uunili for a couple of weeks, but eventually, you will fall, and there will be a bloodbath. You'll lose everything: your homes, your livelihoods, your loved ones, and even ten years from now, the wounds of this war will still burn in your flesh and in the flesh of this country. Face it: the Illumined World would rather go down in flames than accept your rule. You made sure of that when you laid waste to this city."

"Which was your idea!"

A hush fell.

Bullseye.

Oonai smiled. "So you admit you worked for us?"

Even though Lysia's shift no longer held him, the Pale Brother stood as still as a sculpture, his lips pressed shut. Oonai descended the dais, his guards clearing a lane. The chills had reached Jespar's wrists.

"It's all true, isn't it? For you and your sister, this was never about justice or ideals. It was about money and entertainment, just like when you blew up the Pit all those years ago. You knew from the start that a true revolution is a pipe dream, just like you knew you were leading these people to their certain deaths—and yet you did it because you just enjoy killing so damn bloody much."

He passed Maadira, who stood in the front row, and stopped a few strides from the Pale Brother. They must have been roughly the same height, but the Magnate's Crown and Oonai's boots made him appear a head taller. "You are a freak, Zaevathal. A monster who enjoys chopping peoples' heads off, and you lust for that pleasure just like your freak necromancer sister did. Let me tell you something, Vyrias: in whatever hell she is burning now, I pray to Tyr that she suffers."

The Pale Brother stared. Then he scoffed and headed back toward the mob.

At least that was how it seemed. A few steps in, the Aetäerna spun around and lunged at Oonai, yanking his saber up. Oonai had anticipated an attack, yet he only dodged the slash by a hair's breadth; he reeled backward into a guard. Maadira and two Snakes were by Oonai's side at once. She covered him with her shield while the soldiers thrust their spears at the Pale Brother. He dodged the first stab, but the second hit him in the shoulder. Crying out, he dropped his saber; the next stab pierced straight through his throat.

Gasps. Jespar held his breath.

Eyes wide open, the Pale Brother croaked and clutched the spear; briefly, it seemed as though he would simply tear it back out and resume fighting; then, he collapsed. For a few moments, his mouth twitched, red spilling from his lips like the bloody pantomime of a dead fish. Then he went still.

Before Jespar had even processed the events, Agaam groaned on the dais and staggered backward, stumbling into the massive plinth of Moraia's statue. The air distortion around him had faded, indicating the shift was over—he had reached his limits.

Shit.

It wasn't supposed to happen like this. The Snakes should have knocked the Pale Brother unconscious, and Agaam's shift should have lasted at least another ten minutes, enough for Oonai to make his offer. Without it, and with the Pale Brother killed by the guards, the mob would snap. Jespar's muscles bunched, his clammy hand clutching the pommel of his longsword.

Nothing happened.

No screams. No rebels charging from the crowd. The mob just stood there and stared at the Brother's corpse, a blossom of blood growing beneath him. It might have still ended in a bloodbath had Scarman not decided to seize command. He stepped forward and pulled down his cowl, revealing a clean-shaven jaw sharp as flintstone.

"If all that ye said is true," he began, "then why in the world would we let ye live?"

Oonai was quiet for a long moment. Then he waved Maadira— she was still covering him—away and stepped back in front.

"I told you already," he said, loud and clear. "Because I am your only chance of making it out of this alive."

Hesitating, Scarman glanced back at the mob as if looking for guidance. All eyes rested on him. At last, he gave the smallest of nods. "All right, then. Make yer offer."

A pause. "Very well. I will start by saying you're right."

"About what?"

"Me. Everything you say about me, it's true." Fixing his uninjured eye on that spot just above the crowd, he yanked a ring off his thumb and let it fall to the floor. "I made my fortune by tricking a rival into poisoning his plantation, buying it for a steal, then building it anew." Forefinger and middle finger followed. "I made people slave away until their bodies gave out, then put them on the streets, well aware it meant death in poverty. I built nuvium mines near townships, knowing the fog was poison for the miners' lungs." Ring finger. "I issued the Golden Soil Decree anticipating it would ruin you and drive people into suicide, I plotted this riot and hired the Twins to get rid of my rivals. I picked my greed over your lives every single time I had the choice."

The last ring came off. "And all of that is just the tip of the iceberg. You are right about everything you said about me: I am a leech, I am a tyrant, I am a murderer. And no matter how this night ends, I know that there can be no forgiveness for the things I've done."

When Oonai had told Jespar, Lysia, and Agaam he would say something in that vein, Jespar had had his doubts, worried it would come across as dishonest or theatrical; hearing him say it, he was fascinated instead. Oonai managed to make every word sound like it came from the bottom of his heart, without ever slipping into pathos or losing his air of eminence. Was it acted or authentic? Jespar couldn't tell. Either way, the mob seemed to be equally impressed: there were no insults and no shouts, only mumbling and solitary whispers.

"How very movin'," Scarman said. "But I asked for yer offer, not for self-pity."

"This is not about self-pity, it's about making it clear that I have no illusions. I do not deserve forgiveness for my crimes, and I am aware of that." His unscathed eye wandered through the mob. "For you, however, and for the soul of our country, there might still be hope. And I want you to keep this in mind when you make your choice. I want you to remember that your decision will not only affect your lives but also the lives of your sons, daughters, and, hopefully, the many generations to follow."

Mutters passed through the hall—some angry, some nervous, all of them restless.

Arms crossed, Scarman shifted his weight from one leg to the other. "Get to the point."

Oonai nodded. "Once this conversation is over, you will have two choices." He lifted a finger, indicating the statue of Moraia. "One, you butcher my servants and me under the face of our goddess and seize control of the Blue Islands. As I have told you, the keepers will arrive within the week, and you'll be in for a long and terrible war that will inevitably end in your defeat. The Order will restore the Coalition, and the surviving officials from Maitepo will return to the Jade Hall, fill the chairs your riot emptied with their cousins and friends, and elect seven new magnates. Within a couple of years, everything will be back to the way it was, except that our boneyards will be ten thousand graves richer."

He raised his other forefinger. "Two, you let my guards, my servants, and my wife leave this palace unscathed, and you keep me hostage. When the keepers reach Kilay, I will arrange a parley with their commanding archkeeper, in which I will tell them that you were misled by the Twins and that we came to an understanding." He paused. "Then, we, together, will create a new Kilay."

This time, the whispers and mutters came from both mob and guards alike. "What the hell is that s'posed to mean?" Scarman asked. "'New Kilay'?"

"It means we will build a new country from the ruins of this one." Oonai made an all-encompassing gesture. "Just look around—what was tonight, if not proof that our system is broken? As I told you before, if the keepers take Kilay by force, things will only go back to the way they were, and we cannot let that happen. What we need is to turn the page and rebuild Kilay on values both old *and* new ... values that allow us to be a land of Great Dreamers but which also ensure that the fate-stricken or ailing don't get left in the roadside ditches."

Perfect, Jespar thought. Emotional but not theatrical, firm but not arrogant. Like a prophet proclaiming a vision that had yet to be realized but inevitably would be. Jespar glanced at Lysia. Her lips curled downward, yet her attention was riveted on Oonai, like that of the mob.

"And just how are ye plannin' to do that?" Scarman asked. "Words are cheap."

"We rewrite the rules. Don't forget that I am still the First Magnate—and with five of the other seven dead and Vel'Nyx out of the country, I possess the power to change the laws as I see fit."

A female Scythe stepped from the crowd and joined Scarman, delicate features showing above her mouth cloth. She could have been no older than Kawu. "That's a lie. The officials who's still alive would need to agree as well."

"Under normal circumstances, it would be so," Oonai said. "But the country is in a state of crisis, so all power goes to the magnates. By law, the officials are powerless right now, as is the Order of Light, at least as long as I'm still alive. If we establish our new world through righteous means, and respect the Treaty of the Illumined World, we have full sovereignty."

We.

How quickly and naturally the word felt when he used it now. From enemy to ally. From villain to savior. "Our very first step will be the redistribution of power: there will still be a Blue Islands Coalition and seven magnates, but it will share control with another assembly, one made up of representatives from each pillar of our society. Miners, farmers, craftsmen, merchants, you name it. The only way for a new law to come into effect, or any major resolutions to be made, will be for the Coalition and this new 'Council of Guilds' to approve it." He stepped forward. "Step two, while we rebuild our city, the Coalition and the Council of Guilds will draft a new constitution—only this time, it will be one representing *all* our interests, not just those of the upper class. There will be food banks for the hungry, laws against exploitation, and sick houses for those who cannot afford treatment. And that will only be the beginning. By the time we're done, our country will not only be better, but it will also be a flagship of what humanity can be if we work *together*. If we fight the true enemies out there instead of each other."

His words echoed through the hall and left a hush in their wake. Whispers were traded, looks exchanged, muscles tensed.

"Even if ye keep that promise," the young Scythe said, "who's gonna punish ye for what ye did? The Justiciars are dead."

"The Order of Light's war tribunal. Once the treaties for our New Kilay have been signed, I will confess to everything I've done, from the first plantation I poisoned to the scheme Vel'Nyx and I came up with."

The pause that followed seemed like an eternity.

"No," Scarman said. "No, I ain't buyin' it. Yer just gonna play along till yer safe, and then tell the keepers to kill us."

Agreement from the crowd, but it was tentative and nervous.

They want to believe him, Jespar realized. *They* want *to accept his offer.*

"Even if I had the authority to order a keeper to do anything," Oonai said, "who would I have them kill? The two of you? Yes, maybe I could memorize what you look like, and the Order could track you down. But let's be realistic—there are just too many of you. Whatever crimes you committed tonight, chances are no one is left alive to report them, so they will go unpunished. But trust me on this one: your souls will bear the mark of those sins for the rest of your lives. I know." His good eye wandered toward the sky spanning beyond the parted snake-and-sabers gate. The clouds there were still tinged crimson, but a pale blue line showed on the horizon. "Sometimes, the best one can do is try to be better. It's not much, but it's something."

It was the ensuing silence that told Jespar he'd been right. Yes— the mob wanted to believe Oonai. Through rhetoric and strategy alone, he had done the impossible and doused the inferno.

When the Scythe girl spoke again, contempt still tinged her voice, but something else overshadowed it. Perhaps it was fear. Perhaps it was hope. Perhaps it was "Ilonūka e untu", the "Dark Respect" Kawu had spoken of.

"So yer tellin' us to trust *ye* of all people to save us. Is that it?"

"No," Oonai said. "I'm asking you to understand that I'm the only one who still can."

CHAPTER THIRTY-SEVEN
THE ARBITRARY

DAY EIGHT
1ST MOON OF RAINY SEASON, 1226 A.L.

The riot was over, but the violence wasn't.

That was what Maadira's scouts reported after the dazed survivors had stepped into a hazy morning at the end of the escape tunnel, accompanied by Scarman, who ordered the ambushers in the bay to lay down their arms. There were outbursts of violence across South Uunili, the report went, from the murdering of guards and uppers to infighting between rebels to vandalism and looting. Jespar wasn't surprised. Yes, the Scythe had agreed to Oonai's deal, but small fires continue to burn even when one tames the inferno.

While Scarman and his Scythes returned to the capital, Maadira took the evacuees and the Ma'saa to a military seaside outpost where they would board a ferry to Maitepo. Agaam, Jespar, and Lysia went to Southport to sail to what Agaam had called a "special hideout", taking the unconscious Kawu with them. It had been Oonai's last request to Agaam before surrendering himself into Scythe captivity.

A few hours later, on the morning after the bloodiest night in Kilayan history, a little cutter left Southport, the very same harbor where Jespar's journey had begun eight days ago.

The sea was as silent as Jespar's sleep.

A tiny atoll made of white sand, palms, and a lagoon with a coral reef, Nayima Island lay far south of Uunili and had been Oonai's wedding gift to his wife. Reaching it in the late afternoon hours, Agaam anchored the boat in a bucolic fishing village on the islet's northern tip; they had just finished mooring the cutter when the troubled village mayor came hurrying to the docks. Introductions were made, explanations given. When the mayor asked Agaam about the red glow that had spanned across the southern sky all night, Agaam told her it was complicated and took her for a walk.

"I need something to eat," Lysia said after she and Jespar had hoisted Kawu's stretcher onto the pier. "Should I get you something?"

"I'm good. Thanks."

Lysia nodded and headed off. Jespar regarded Kawu for a bit. Still fast asleep, he was ghastly pale even in the westering sunlight; his hair stuck to his forehead in matted strands; a droplet of sweat beaded on the faint little scar below his chin.

You're cured. He'll live.

The thought made him feel nothing. No relief, no hope, no joy. The fog still shrouded it all.

Jespar pulled the stretcher into the shade of a nearby pavilion, sat upon a mooring post, and looked off to the beach. The waves sloshed gently over the seaside rocks and the ivory sand, all bathed in a magnificent sunset.

You're cured, he thought again. *He'll live.*

What only yesterday had seemed impossible might now become a reality: he would wait for Kawu to recover, then, after they had taken care of his family, the two of them would board a ship to some land with four seasons so he could show Kawu autumn. And if the drain stroke had damaged Kawu's brain? What if he'd never walk or speak again? Then they'd figure something out. Either way, Jespar would stay—not just because he had promised, not just because he owed Kawu his life, and not just because he desperately wanted to protect him, as horribly as he'd messed up that part before. Jespar would stay because he *wanted* to. Because this was real.

Then why did he still feel so numb?

When Agaam, Lysia, and the mayor reappeared a bit later, they brought with them men carrying two palanquins. Jespar helped lift Kawu into one, then joined Lysia in the other-Agaam insisted on walking. The palanquin set into motion, and before long, the rocking eased Jespar into a dreamless slumber.

When Lysia woke him, they had arrived at a white pyramid-style manor. Nestled in a sprawling garden on a seaside hill, it was the antithesis of the simple adobe houses and palmwood huts of the fishing village they had just passed through. His muscles aching, Jespar stepped out of the palanquin, the sun an amber sliver over the horizon. An old Makehu servant led them into the cool, spacious lobby, where an imperial staircase rose to a mezzanine. At its center was the statue of a woman whose benevolent smile was so vivid Jespar wondered if the sculpture would spring to life. Young Nayima Oonai. The Makehu showed Jespar and Lysia their quarters—Kawu was given a room beside Jespar's—then the two met Agaam at the gate.

"It will be a while until the situation in Uunili stabilizes, so you should lay low here until then," Agaam said. "I will procure your pay in the meantime."

A breeze drew up. Jespar pulled his scarf a little tighter. "How long are we talking?"

"A week or two, maybe three. I suggest you use the time to recover. The servants will tend to your every need."

"Three weeks?" Lysia asked. "But I need to get back to the clinic! Juusew, he's still—" She broke off. "I *need* to get back."

"I understand, ma'saa, but it's just too risky at this point. The island is in anarchy, and there's already talk of the 'two outlanders' who helped Oonai 'weasel his way out.'"

"But they agreed to the truce!"

"The *Scythe* agreed, not every one of their supporters. Look, I will bury your assistant, if you permit, and I'll let you know where I've laid him to rest. But I simply can't allow you to risk your life after you've made it this far."

Lysia began to protest, but then a deep exhaustion washed away her agitation, an emptiness that had become all too familiar on her face since the clinic. "All right. Whatever you say."

"Someone needs to tell Kawu's family what happened too," Jespar said. "At least that he's alive and will return to them as soon as he wakes up."

"I'll see to it and give them some money to help them pull through," Agaam said. "Now go rest. You've earned it."

A beautiful prospect: two weeks in a luxury manor on a picturesque island. Two weeks he would use to lick his wounds and care for Kawu.

If only Jespar could feel a thing.

His first night's rest was corpselike: he just collapsed onto the luxurious bed and plunged into oblivion, dreamlessly sleeping well into
the afternoon of the following day. He washed, shaved, and combed
his hair for the first time in what felt like weeks, then went to see
Kawu. With the curtained room shrouded in twilight and a flower
wreath on the nightstand, the bed reminded Jespar of a bier in a
crypt. He pulled up a stool, sat, and took Kawu's hand.

Tō ,ō āpa ku ānū e ni'ē e ,atete ku, kito nū'i kei kuio e li.

Show me the Sunset Trees when all this is over.

No emotion. *Why?* Dammit, it just didn't make any sense. He
should have been relieved, grateful, happy. But no matter how hard
he tried, he felt nothing.

It'll pass, he told himself. *You're still in shock. It'll all pass.*

He sat there for another minute, waiting for something to happen,
then gave up and joined Lysia in the dinner hall, where they shared
a late luncheon and made noncommittal conversation. They spent
the rest of the afternoon separately, Lysia shopping for herbs in the
village, Jespar exploring the property. At dinner that evening, they
spoke of the past week for the first time.

"I still can't believe the rebels agreed to the deal," Lysia said,
absently trailing her food-sticks over the remains of a rice pudding.

They sat at a table under the portico, the mounted torches around
them shaping an island of light in the nightly panorama.

"It was either that or war against the rest of the Illumined World,"
Jespar said. "Oonai was right about that."

"Still. I would have expected them to, I don't know, fight for what
they believed in."

Jespar dabbed his mouth with a napkin. "Can I be honest?"

The corner of Lysia's mouth lifted a fraction, but the dull look in
her eyes remained. "No, please lie."

"If you ask me, most of the rebels didn't actually believe in the cause of the revolution. They just wanted food for their families and figured the Scythe was their best way of getting it."

"You mean they were pragmatists?"

"Pretty much."

"Hm." Lysia speared a slice of mango and lifted it to her lips, but then ended up putting it back on her plate. "Didn't feel like that to me when they screamed 'The dream is a lie!' and butchered everyone."

"Yeah, because in those moments, they *believed* that they believed."

"What does that mean?"

"It means that they convinced themselves that they shared the ideals of the Scythe because it was the only way they could still see themselves as the good guys. Think about it: if you were torching houses and slaughtering children just because they wear clothes made of silk, what would you rather tell yourself? That you're carrying out righteous retribution by setting fire to the boot that's been kicking you your entire life, or that you're really just fucking angry and hopeless and hungry and want to stop hurting? They *had* to believe they were fighting for a higher cause because they had to protect their self-image. The integrity of their souls, if you're feeling poetic." He took a snakefruit from a bowl on a side table and peeled it. "That's also why Oonai's speech worked, by the way. He didn't just make the mob realize they were marching to their certain deaths, he also showed them that they had fallen victim to two crazy imposters. And that, even though Oonai *was* still a villain, they had *also* allowed themselves to become villains in the process." He ate the fruit, bitterness flooding his mouth. "The second that sunk in, their self-image cracked, and their minds opened up to a new narrative. It all—"

"—boils down to perspective. Full circle, huh?"

"I guess."

"Wouldn't that mean nothing we do is our choice, though?"

Chewing, Jespar gave it some thought. "Honestly, I don't know. I just think we rarely do anything that conflicts with our physical or spiritual survival."

Lysia grunted, her gaze drifting to one of the torches. Katakos circled it, repelled by the citronella coating of the wicks. The servants came out and cleared the table.

"If you're right," Lysia said when they had left, "that means Oonai is gonna weasel out of it. There'll be no 'New Kilay', and he won't pay for his crimes." Her right hand clutched her chair's armrest, a stark contrast to the flatness in her voice. "He'll just use his power to save his golden arse like he did his entire life."

"I'm not sure about that."

"Jes, you just said people never do something that goes against their survival."

"No, I said 'rarely', and 'physical *and* spiritual survival.' Yes, we want to stay alive, but protecting our self-image is as vital. If you ask me, that's also the only reason people truly change ... because something happens that compromises their self-image to such a degree that the mind can't go on the way it used to."

"I didn't know you were a scholar of the soul."

"It's just how I see it." Jespar fished for another snakefruit, then, realizing it was the last one, offered it to Lysia. She shook her head. "Think about it: why did you leave your monastery when you did? Because that lightning strike showed you that life could end any minute, and you realized you didn't want to spend it as a priestess behind walls."

"That maybe set it off, but, in the end, I left because I wanted to."

"Yeah, but would you have ever *wanted* to leave if that lightning hadn't hit you?"

"Maybe later, but yes, I would have. Living in the monastery just made me feel trapped."

"Same thing then. Had your parents put you into a less restrictive monastery, you might still be a priestess today. Either way, it wasn't your choice."

"Well, okay, maybe *feeling* that way wasn't. But taking the plunge and deciding to leave bloody well was."

"Do you really think so? From what I can tell, you have quite the, I don't know, decisive temperament, so what if you had been born with a more timid personality? Or if the sum of your experiences from childhood to adolescence had taught you to be wary of snap decisions? Look, we could go on like this forever. All I'm saying is that literally every person in the world only does what they feel is 'the right thing to do,' and our brains decide what that right thing to do is before we even know it." He rubbed the eye from which the dreameater had exited. It still itched and his vision blurred at night, but otherwise, the wound had closed completely. "What I'm getting at is that we don't *choose* to change our beliefs. It's all just a combination of subconscious processes and sheer chance that makes these kinds of decisions long before we even know it. We just tell ourselves otherwise to not go mad."

Lysia met Jespar's eyes, combative, as if about to challenge his point. Then the same thing as during yesterday's conversation with Agaam happened: the energy evaporated and gave way to weariness. "If that's true," she said, "then existence is arbitrary, and we're just slaves to our minds. Is that really what you believe, Jespar?"

The question made him pause. He had not come up with all this on the spot—his view was the result of long musings during the past eight years of his life, of books he'd read and conversations he'd had. This, however, was the first time he had truly *felt* the words—as if his many ruminations had built a house in his mind, and recent events had finally shoved him inside and locked the door. *Was* it what he believed? He didn't want to, that was for sure. It terrified him.

If only he had much reason to think otherwise.

"I don't know, and I hope I'm wrong," he said. "As far as Oonai is concerned, though, I *do* think he has changed. I guess we'll just have to wait and see."

Silence stretched out between them. Then an empty smile settled on Lysia's lips. "And here I thought you were a pessimist."

They spent the rest of the evening drinking and discussing various matters: Jespar inquired about Kawu's health and Lysia's prognosis, but even though he felt relief when she told him she was optimistic he'd make a full recovery and wake from his coma soon, it was in no way as powerful as he'd expected it to be. Yes, of course he wanted Kawu to live, yes, of course he still wanted to be with him; but, for some reason, all these thoughts felt like dry intellectual exercises now, something that had no relevance for his emotional life whatsoever.

Jespar Dal'Varek, he thought. *Coward, failure, plague.*

Might as well add "cold asshole" to that list.

Refusing to accept his feelings, he went to see Kawu again after dinner: since his condition was stable, he was only being checked on three times a day, once by Lysia and twice by a caretaker from the village who bathed him, fed him liquid food, and changed the beddings. Jespar had offered to help, but the caretaker had politely declined.

We made it, Kawu, he thought as he sat there, holding his hand and noticing how haggard his shape looked in the sheets. *We survived.*

Numbness. Fog.

He repeated his mental mantra from yesterday, that his feelings would come back if we just gave it time, that he was still exhausted and under shock. Who wouldn't be? Then he returned to his room.

Where yesterday's sleep had been leaden, tonight's was restless. Jespar rolled from side to side, his mind replaying the memories of the past week over and over, like a pendulum in perpetual motion. Not until dawn did he finally drop into a shallow, dreamless slumber.

The next night, the swamp nightmare returned with a vengeance.

Not only was it more vivid than it had ever been when the Corpse carried out Jespar's punishment for refusing to *see*, the dream didn't stop. It went on and on, the noose breaking Jespar's neck over and over again, locusts swarming from his mouth in a green-black cloud.

See.

Lysia was shaking him. He screamed and tried to throw her off, but she'd pinned him down.

See!

"It's all right! You're awake!"

See!

A few terrible seconds passed as Jespar's mind hung between dream and reality, swamp and manor.

Awake, he told himself. *I'm awake.*

He stopped struggling. Lysia released him and handed him a glass of water. "What happened?"

Blearily, Jespar sat up in his bed. "Just bad dreams."

"What was it about? Do you want to talk about it?"

The lump, sealing his throat. "Can't remember."

Lysia pressed her lips into a line. "Okay."

She left. Watching the door fall shut, a maddening longing for her company—*any* company—welled up inside him. He wanted to run after her, beg her to come back, beg her to just be with him so he wouldn't be alone. But he couldn't. Just like the lump prevented him from speaking, his muscles refused to carry out his will.

"Relapse," he whispered to himself, staring into the dark room. *Just a temporary relapse.* An echo of the dreameater, a reaction to the stress, his brain processing the strain of that fucked-up week. There was only so much a mind could take. He gave up trying to sleep by the time the morning sun flooded his chamber.

Following a strange hunch, he did not go see Kawu the next day, opting to spend most of his time trying to distract himself from his exhaustion, the fear of the coming night, and his bad conscience. In the evening, he asked a servant for a bottle of rice wine and a pipe and killed both alone on the beach. The swamp dream returned, just as it returned the night after and the night after that, and while the booze and petals didn't fend off the dreams entirely, they did dull them, so he smoked and drank harder.

On the fifth evening—he hadn't visited Kawu once, still following that nervous hunch—Jespar sat on the terrace steps and watched the constellations through the rings of purple smoke. It was his third pipe that day, and with a bottle and a half of rice wine in his stomach, his lungs were in good company. Lysia joined him, told him she was worried. Too exhausted to even try defying the lump, he hid behind evasive answers until Lysia gave up and left.

"Cut back on the drinking," she said. "Unless you want the tale of Jespar Dal'Varek to end with a case of alcohol poisoning or liver rot."

Oddly moved by her concern—what had he ever done to deserve it?—Jespar had nothing else that evening and went to bed semi-sober. The nightmare reached a new height of terror, and minutes after waking up, Jespar could still feel the locusts in his mouth and hear the Corpse's words in his ears.

See. See. See.

Jespar drank until he passed out and crashed into a dreamless slumber of utter exhaustion.

The following morning, he joined Lysia for breakfast in the shadow of the portico. Thanks to the booze, it was the first time he'd gotten more than four hours of sleep, and though calling him refreshed would have been a crass exaggeration, he at least didn't feel like a human shipwreck anymore. Nibbling on a fried plantain chip without appetite, he noticed Lysia was looking better too. Her spark still wasn't back—and probably never would be—but the bags under her eyes had faded and, every now and then, the emptiness in her eyes filled with a glimpse of life. When they were done eating, Jespar gazed at the ocean, deep navy under an azure sky. Birds sang alongside cicadas, wind rustled the fronds—a true Beyond. If only the mess that was Jespar's mind had allowed him to enjoy even a second of it.

"... gotten grayer."

"Hm?" Jespar said, turning back.

Lysia pointed to her temples. "I said, I think your hair's gotten grayer."

"Really?"

"Yeah, your beard too."

Jespar smiled wanly. "Well, here's hoping it adds to my rugged charm."

A corner of Lysia's mouth twitched. "I think he's getting better, by the way."

"Who?"

"Kawu, of course. I checked on him just now, and his eyes were moving under his lids, meaning he's dreaming again. Knock on wood, but I think it won't be much longer until he wakes up."

His guts curled at the idea, briefly followed by a stab of guilt for feeling this way. "Oh. That's good."

"When was the last time you checked on him?"

Yes, Jespar, great question: when was the last time you checked on the man who saved your life? To whom you promised you'd stay and show autumn? You're a useless, ungrateful piece of shit.

He had told himself this often over the past few days, but it hadn't mattered—he just couldn't bring himself to walk these few steps and see him. The more the fog had cleared, the more the idea of even just looking at Kawu made his insides turn, a venomous blend of guilt, fear, and that strange hunch Jespar couldn't describe.

Jespar splayed his hands, pretending to study the freckles on their backs. "It's been a while. I've been so damn tired."

"His room is right beside yours."

"Yes, I know. I'll go see him today, I promise."

Lysia studied him. Then she finished her drink and stood. "Yeah, you should."

"Where are you going?"

"To the coral reef in the lagoon. Ma'sao Umō said it's safe to dive now that okepi spawning season is over."

"O-what?"

"Okepi. Nasty underwater beasts that look like a stingray and a shark had a baby." She took her belt from a nearby chair and girdled it. "I'll be back for dinner."

No invitation to tag along. "Okay. Be careful."

"Don't worry."

Jespar watched her leave, then, pipe in mouth, took to sharpening, cleaning, and polishing his longsword and dagger. When he was done, he went for a long walk, then for a swim. It was late afternoon by the time he finally ran out of excuses and went to see Kawu. With the servants on break, the house was silent save for the clicking of the travertine under his boots.

Piece of shit. Piece of shit. Piece of shit.

Selfish, ungrateful, useless piece of shit.

"Shut up," he muttered. He'd gotten no more than twelve hours of sleep in the past four days, and he'd spent the better part of those twelve hours being choked to death by a noose and eaten from the inside by locusts. Who could blame him for slacking on his responsibilities a little?

A responsibility? Is that what Kawu is to you now?

All right, that was a bad word. Oh, for fuck's sake, he didn't know what to think or do anymore, he was just so *godsdamned* tired.

Jespar circled the mezzanine at a snail's pace, hand dragging along the cold railing. At Kawu's door, he stopped and considered going back to his room. The hunch was back, stronger than ever before, a shapeless terror worming through his veins.

Summoning all his courage, he went in.

Staring at the floor, Jespar crossed the dank room and sat upon the bedside stool. He studied the marble floor for a time, memorizing the veins and patterns. Gods, he *wanted* this. He wanted to keep his promise, wanted to show Kawu autumn, wanted to find out where this thing would lead. So why in the world was everything just ... gone?

Why was it so fucking hard to find peace?

He lifted his eyes and looked at Kawu.

In an instant, the hunch became the phantom noose and yanked tight.

He stormed out of the room.

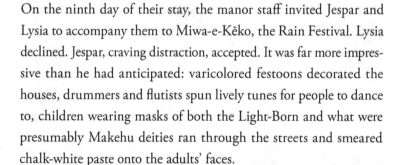

On the ninth day of their stay, the manor staff invited Jespar and Lysia to accompany them to Miwa-e-Kēko, the Rain Festival. Lysia declined. Jespar, craving distraction, accepted. It was far more impressive than he had anticipated: varicolored festoons decorated the houses, drummers and flutists spun lively tunes for people to dance to, children wearing masks of both the Light-Born and what were presumably Makehu deities ran through the streets and smeared chalk-white paste onto the adults' faces.

Not a care in the world, Jespar thought, observing them.

Whatever the islanders thought about the destruction of Uunili, they had created their own sheltered reality for tonight. Jespar drank, danced, and played cards and dice with the locals until well after midnight, his sun-bleached hair making him the attraction of the festival; two women approached him during the night, but Jespar politely turned them down. He forgot about Kawu and the nightmare for a while, but his diversion remained only that—a diversion. After the umpteenth pitcher of rice wine, his mind went blurry. The next thing he knew, he woke in a pile of hay in some back alley, hungover as hell, and his throat burned from the nightmare locusts. He didn't get up. He just lay there and stared at the dawning sky.

Yes, Lysia. I believe it.

Existence is arbitrary, free will is an illusion, and choice doesn't exist. We're slaves to our minds who mastered the art of ignoring their shackles.

That was the truth, no matter how much you wanted it to be wrong. No matter how fucking much.

The next few days passed like fog crawling over a barren landscape. High as Inôdan and hammered as Erodan's anvil, Jespar's psyche was a marriage of drugged apathy, crushing exhaustion, and anxiety over the coming night; paradoxically, getting out of bed became harder and harder, to the point where, sometimes, he didn't leave his room until late in the afternoon.

Not once did he visit Kawu.

The pattern broke on the thirteenth day when a servant burst into the terrace at luncheon and said there was news from the mainland: the keepers had arrived in Uunili a few days ago and had met with the Scythe to parley. Since yesterday, heralds had been sailing across the Archipelago, and one would come to Nayima Island this evening. The staff left for the village in an excited buzz. Lysia joined them; Jespar, too tired to even care, stayed behind in the manor.

Grateful for the silence on the property, Jespar seized the chance to stock up on wine from the kitchen, downed half a bottle, then went to the garden and slumped in the shade of a palm tree to read a book. One of the manor alapus, a black puppy, waddled out of a thicket and eyed him quizzically. Jespar first wanted to shoo it away, then he lifted the book from his thighs, making space. The alapu hopped onto his lap with a squeak and snuggled his head against Jespar's stomach.

Petting it, he turned his attention back to his book—a treatise on the untapped potentials of dimensionism by a Qyranian scholar named Fatana Nay'Darim.

... shifting drain remains the biggest obstacle in exploring the vast potential of dimensionism. A common analogy is having a fortune of a million sêr but being unable to use more than one coin at the same time. One can only fathom what ...

His lids grew heavy.

Don't. Don't sleep.

He made to stand, but the alapu grunted in protest, pressing his snout against Jespar's wrist. Sighing, he sank back down and returned his attention to the book. *It'll be all right.* As long as he stayed awake, everything would be fine. He realized he had skipped a few pages but didn't bother going back to where he'd left off. It wasn't like he'd been paying attention anyway.

... among the most fascinating of these rumored Sights is undoubtedly the ability to shift one's self into parallel realities, most recently coined "planeomancy" by ...

THE SWAMP FOREVER

SOMEDAY
SOMETIME

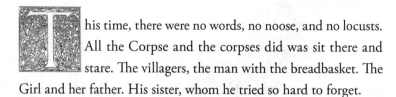

T his time, there were no words, no noose, and no locusts. All the Corpse and the corpses did was sit there and stare. The villagers, the man with the breadbasket. The Girl and her father. His sister, whom he tried so hard to forget.

We will never leave, their dead eyes said. *We'll be with you forever.* Hopelessness swallowed him like a black maelstrom.

CHAPTER THIRTY-EIGHT
IT'LL GET BETTER

DAY TWENTY-ONE
1ST MOON OF RAINY SEASON, 1226 A.L.

espar awoke to a deluge. All around him, water crashed from the sky, wind tore at the trees, lightning flashed behind clouds so dense and black that they blotted out the sun. Jespar leaped to his feet—swaying from the booze in his blood—and rushed for the terrace, but halfway there, he realized he'd forgotten his wine and his pipe. He was just about to bolt back when two sentences echoed through his mind—and he stopped dead.

We will never leave.

We'll be with you forever.

And there, in the downpour of a storm, something inside Jespar Mitumial Dal'Varek turned: one lever among many in a complicated machine his mind built over the last sixteen years, a lever that had always been there but whose existence Jespar only now truly accepted. Slowly, his eyes wandered to the path snaking down the hill to the ocean.

The phantom noose loosened, and the fog disappeared.

Of course there was a way to beat his mind. Of course there was a way to find peace.

He'd just never had the courage.

"You can't hurt me," he whispered. "You can't hurt me."

Jespar ran for the sea.

Wind and rain whipped at his face, and pebbles cut into the soles of his feet, but he kept running, running toward that beautiful roiling ocean, carried by that lightness growing inside him, free of worries in a way he hadn't been since that day he and his sister had snuck out to the forest lake to go stargazing. Halfway to the beach, Ma'sao Umō came hurrying up the hill, shielding his head with a basket; he froze in his tracks.

"Ma'sao! Ma'sao, what are ye doin'?"

Jespar kept running.

"Ma'sao, it's dangerous!"

"It's fine!" Jespar shouted back. "I'm fine!"

And it was true. The lightness had taken hold of his entire body, made him feel like he was running on clouds; he went faster, the roar of the rain and the screams of the wind drowning Umō's voice behind him; he reached the beach, a white crescent before a raging body of water, and sprinted to the banks, a wave slammed into his legs, sent him staggering backward; he waded further in, and when the next wave came, he threw himself into it back first, like he had done so often on Goldenforst beach with his sister.

Adila.

Her name was Adila. Why did he never say it? Why did he try so hard to forget her? Why did he pretend she was dead?

Saltwater sloshed over him, flooded his mouth. He coughed it out and swam in further; another wave came rolling, loomed over him like a colossus.

Her name is Adila.

The wave crashed down upon him and took him under. And as the world turned dark, an image formed in his mind.

Night, the Dal'Varek estate.

Headed for the privy, little Jespar tiptoes over the floorboards, trying hard not to make them creak. Halfway there, he hears talking from downstairs. Curiosity gets the better of him, and he sneaks down to the lobby. Jespar steals up to the library door where the voices come from, peeking around the jamb. Father and his friend, the one with the bushy red beard, sit in front of the hearth.

"He always makes a scene," Father says. "When he lost to that Dal'Kaban boy, he cried the whole day."

"Damean, he's ten years old."

"The twins are eight and aren't like that."

Long pause.

"Some souls are softer than others," Redbeard says. "He'll make a good heir, Damean, I know it. I mean, just look how much he cares for his sister, he's—"

Father's gaze ices over. Redbeard falls silent.

Father asks, "Did you bring the trial notes?"

Jespar broke through the surface, gasped for air. Lightning flashed down the horizon like radiant veins, water whipped at his skin. He *was* the lightness now, a feather riding on the wind, soaring higher. He swam out farther, skipping the waves until another blue beast shoved him under.

Adi, on her bed in Redbeard's villa. She doesn't move and doesn't speak, just stares at the ceiling. Like she's dreaming a nightmare but with open eyes.

Jespar sits down beside her. "Hey. Hey, Adi."

Nothing.

"Adi, are you ... are you okay?"

A stupid question, but it works. Slowly, Adi turns her head.

"He was still alive, Jespar." It sounds so odd, hearing her use his full name. So old. "I saw it. Rorik and Alvric, they weren't breathing anymore, but Father, he was still alive." She sobs. "And ... and he was looking at me that way again, like whenever he spoke about Mother, and I ... I just ..."

Now the tears come, heavy, fitful sobs, like she's drowning, gasping for air. And she had drowned, Jespar would understand much later. She had drowned the day they had found Father and Rorik and Alvric hanging from the walls dead and with the blood flowers carved into their foreheads. It had taken Adi's mind seven years to realize it and draw the conclusion.

"Hey, it's okay." He slides closer, squeezing her hand. "It's okay, Adi, everything's okay now."

"He hated me," she sobs. "Even at that moment, he hated me. It's just not fair, Jes, it's just not fair."

Jespar reached the surface again, saltwater stinging in his eyes, his muscles burning. The lightness was still there, but it was consuming him now, a white sun bursting inside him, its brilliant light devouring his soul. "You can't hurt me!" he screamed, sobbing. "You can't—"

Water, darkness.

"He didn't hate you," Jespar wants to tell her, but a lump has formed in his throat, and his lips won't move. Of course Father hated her. He hated them both, Jespar because he was soft and cowardly and a failure who'd never be the heir the Dal'Varek family deserved, Adi because she killed Mother. And now Father is dead, everyone is dead except for them because they snuck out to the cobalt lake to stargaze.

Jespar looks at her, tugging at the blue scarf that Adi had weaved him for his last birthday.

And anger grips him.

She's right. It's not fair.

He wants to stop the thought, but it grows like fleshrot. Yes, Father hated them both, but it had always been Jespar who got the worst of it, Jespar who got the scoldings, the lectures, the beatings, while all Adi had to deal with was the occasional frown.

So why does he *always have to comfort* her?

Why does he *always have to be the strong one?*

But he doesn't say it. He shouldn't, he can't, he has no right to. He must be there for her like he always has been, must say something to stop her from hurting.

"You want to know a secret?"

Her sobs fade, and her eyes meet his. Slowly they move, fragile little windows turning on rusted hinges.

"It'll get better. It always does." *He sticks out his pinkie.* "I promise."

It's that thing they've always done, that sibling thing. For a few moments, Adi just looks at his finger like it's some curious object from those fantastic worlds she draws.

She locks her pinkie around his. Her sobs grow softer, and her breathing evens. And while Jespar smiles, the thought keeps coming.

It's not fair.

It's not fair.

It's not fair.

The very second this last memory dissolved, Jespar's survival instincts kicked in.

No. No, what the hell have you done?

He struggled to the surface and gasped for air, choked, gagged, coughed. The wind roared, rain crashed down upon him, lightning illuminated the sky. The lightness was gone, and panic had replaced it.

Idiot, idiot, idiot, what have you done, what have you-

A wave from behind pushed him back underwater. He gasped, sucking water into his windpipe. He frantically tried to swim back up, but his arms were too weak and the current too strong, and it pulled him down, down, down, Gods what had he done, he didn't want to die, he just wanted to stop hurting, he-

THE SWAMP
EMISSARY

SOMEDAY
SOMETIME

The seats were empty.

Moonlight illumined the swamp, tinting the mud and the leafless willows a cadaverous blue. Jespar lay on the ground, hands folded across his chest and encircled by a ring of dead locusts.

"You sadden me," the Corpse said. "I wish you would have just seen. But perhaps it's better this way."

He was kneeling beside Jespar, gently stroking his hair, water pouring from his mouth and nose and ears. His hands were not burning anymore, and, unlike the rest of him, they weren't putrefied. They were smooth and unscathed, the skin dotted from the sun.

"Seen what?" Jespar sobbed. "What do you want me to see?"

At least that was what he tried to say, for even here, in the realm of the dead, the lump kept him silent.

The Corpse seemed to have heard nonetheless. His lips curled in his mournful deathbed smile, his eyes warm and gentle. "It's so simple. It's so simple."

You can't hurt me. You can't hurt me. You can't hurt me.

"Oh, my child," the Corpse said. "I never meant to. I was only the emissary."

CHAPTER THIRTY-NINE
BLOOD MONEY

DAY TWENTY-ONE
1ST MOON OF RAINY SEASON, 1226 A.L.

 ook at him," the voice says. "Isn't he perfect?"

Arms cradle him, gently sway him from side to side. The air is cold, but it's all right because the arms keep him warm.

"Come, honey. Hold him."

Cold, but just for a heartbeat. Then he is in other arms, different arms, harder arms, but just as warm. They are tense at first, then they grow softer. A face hovers above him. Familiar. Smiling. Loved.

"He's perfect."

⁂

A warm dot on his forehead.

Blearily, Jespar opened his eyes. Sunlight blinded him; he closed them again. Groggily, he sat up, shut the curtains over his bed, then slumped back down.

Bed? Where the hell are you?

He jerked up.

A spacious room, fancy furniture, draped in twilight except for the outline of sunlight around the curtains. Head swimming, Jespar drew his conclusions. He was alive. Someone had saved him.

"Bloody hell," Jespar said—and his lungs burst into flames. He croaked, groped for the glass of water on his nightstand, and gulped it down. The burning grew worse, liquid fire racing down his throat and leaving a series of combustions in his chest, but then it fell to a throb. Panting, he dropped back into bed.

His memories returned. The storm. The lightness. The waves.

"Idiot," he whispered. "You bloody idiot."

What the hell had he been thinking, running off into the ocean like that? Why in the world had he done this? He tried to be angry at himself, but all that came was a hollow feeling in the pit of his stomach.

You know exactly why you did it.

He lay still for another minute, then dragged his legs over the side of the bed and stood. His stomach felt like someone had punched a hole in it, filled it with acid, then roughly sewed it back up; his shoulder wound throbbed, and his right eye stung. He wore white linen trousers and a sleeveless blue shirt, his own clothes lying in a folded pile on a nearby chair.

"Fucking coward," he said. "You fucking coward."

The words scorched his lungs, but he savored the pain.

He limped downstairs and onto the terrace. The sky was a perfect blue, cotton tuft clouds lazily drifting across the horizon; a breeze went, and puddles gathered in the flagstone's rills and indentations.

Under the portico, he ran into Lysia, her belt and physician's para-phernalia spread upon a table. Her loose hair hung in tousled waves, grass stains dotted her white shirt, and mud caked her trousers. He turned away, but Lysia had already noticed him. Relief turned into anger, then ended on the tired emptiness that had now become her trademark expression.

"You're awake."

"... Yeah." Jespar approached. "How—" He cleared his throat. "How long was I out?"

"A day, give or take." Lysia nodded at the chair across her. "How are you feeling?"

Jespar sat, wincing as pain flared up in his ribs and shoulder. "Not too bad. My chest hurts a bit, and my stomach feels like I spent a whole night throwing up."

"Yeah, swallowing a gallon of saltwater does that to you."

When Jespar—already trying to think of an excuse to leave—didn't reply, Lysia shook her head and resumed cleaning her tools. The black alapu pup came hopping up the terrace stairs and tossed Jespar a probing glance. Jespar patted his thigh, and the pup scurried over and jumped onto his lap.

"I have no idea, you know?" Lysia said.

"Sorry?"

"I said, I have no idea." Lysia was polishing a spatula, her gaze fixed on the steel. "No idea what I should say, no idea what I shouldn't say, no idea what I should do. I mean, it's not as though you're gonna tell me what's going on in that head of yours anyway, is it?"

I want to. I want to, but I can't. "Tell me if you find out."

Lysia scoffed. "You're unbelievable, Jes. You're fucking unbeliev-able."

His lips were already forming another quip, but he caught himself. "Look, I know what I did was stupid, but—"

"Stupid?" She slammed down the spatula. "Stars *fucking* burn me, Jespar, you ran naked into the ocean in the middle of a fucking *storm*! If it weren't for Umō, you'd be dead! Or, who knows, maybe that's what you want?"

Unable to bear her glare, Jespar resumed petting the alapu, inspecting the grey dots in its fur. "Umō?"

"The old servant," Lysia said. "He went in after you and pulled you out."

"Oh. Okay."

Lysia let out a strained sigh. "Jes, please ... just talk to me, for once. I *really* want to help you, but I can't if you don't let me."

Her genuine concern brought back the deep affection he felt for her, and, for a second, he wanted nothing more than to speak: about Adi, about the Village, about the Girl. About the phantom noose, how he didn't even understand himself anymore, how he had run into the ocean because at least that would have stopped the nightmares and the shame of being such a selfish, useless failure who couldn't even care for the man who had saved his life.

But he just couldn't. Before he knew it, the walls were back up, the lump paralyzed his throat, and the mere idea of speaking made his insides curl. Also, who was he to waste Lysia's time with his stupid sob stories, Lysia, a woman who had just lost everything? There were millions of people more deserving of her empathy than him.

"I had clothes on."

"What?"

"You said I ran in naked." His smile probably looked as pathetic as it felt. "I had clothes on."

Lysia looked about to scream. Then her face iced over. "Okay. Okay, don't say I didn't try." She thrust the spatula back into its sheath, then took a scalpel and scrubbed it harshly. "Whatever you do, at least have the bloody decency to thank Ma'sao Umō. He could have died in—"

"I'm sorry."

Lysia's hands went still.

"I'm sorry you have to put up with me." It was only a few words, yet they cost him the utmost effort to get out. Every part of his mind revolted, his mouth filled with liquid steel. "I know I'm a fucking mess. I didn't think it was that bad before I came here, but now I know it is."

Lysia's frown softened. "Then let me help you."

The alapu grunted, as though in agreement. Mechanically, Jespar scratched it behind the ears. "It's not that simple."

Lysia waited for him to go on. When he didn't, she went on scrubbing the scalpel. "Well, just make sure to thank Umō. He could have died out there."

Bad shit happens wherever we go.

"Yeah, I will." He was about to get up when a thought crossed his mind, one that had been lurking around ever since he'd woken up. "By the way, what did that herald say?"

Lysia froze. "Right. How would you know?"

"What happened? Did Oonai stick to his word?"

Lysia put down the scalpel, then pulled up a chair and sat. "The Order of Light agreed to Oonai's proposition."

"... Really?"

"Yeah. I mean, Oonai was right, they had no choice, considering he was still the rightful ruler of the Archipelago. Kilay will be rebuilt with a new constitution that shares the power between the Coalition and the 'Council of Guilds'. The Order of Light will form an interim government of sorts until all the details are sorted out and representatives for both parties have been appointed."

"Huh. And what about the rebels? They agreed to all that too?"

"Well, they didn't have much of a choice, either. Once the keepers showed up, most of the rioters in the ziggurat made a run for it. You got that part right, it seems. People only believe in something until it gets ugly."

"What will happen to the ones who did stay behind?"

"They'll be tried once the new government has been installed. Until then, they'll be handled as war criminals. There was a small skirmish when the Order announced there'd be no unconditional pardons, but the keepers settled that in a flash."

"... I see." Deciding his head had been sufficiently petted, the alapu rolled onto its back, paws in the air. Jespar moved on to the belly. "And Oonai?"

"He's dead."

A curious feeling spread in Jespar. Surprise, mostly, but a skewed kind of sadness as well. *Why?* Oonai had had it coming. Hell, if his speech in the ziggurat were to be believed, he had even accepted this fate himself. "Really?"

"Yeah, really. The keepers strung him up over a swamp in Uunuma only a day after he confessed to the Overgrowth Plan, before a crowd of hundreds. Death by honey. With the injuries and the aftereffects of the coma, he didn't last three days."

"No trial, then."

"Oh, there was a trial. But considering he was found guilty of both mass murder and high treason against the Illumined World, the verdict was unanimous."

A picture rose in Jespar's mind: Oonai walking up to the edge of a pond, accompanied by two keepers and the jeers of the crowd. Oonai, standing straight as the executioners tie him to the pole. Oonai, a hundred insects crawling over his skin, his last impression of the world the hateful faces of the people he had once ruled over.

Jaaros Ismirael Oonai.

Fish Boy, Magnate, Greatest Dreamer of the Archipelago.

Died a mad tyrant.

"So he did see," Jespar said.

"Hm?"

"Oonai did see what he had done, just like you wanted him to. His wife, Enkshi's corpse, and the ruins of the city."

Lysia studied the scalpel. "Yeah. I guess."

"How do you feel about that?"

Her eyes turned glassy, and she looked into the garden. "Honestly? I don't feel anything."

A cool breeze blew over the terrace. Two chattering servants emerged from the orchard and walked up the terrace steps, casting Jespar a wary glance. Probably they had heard about his little trip into the ocean.

"For what it's worth," Jespar said when they were out of earshot, "I'm sorry this happened to you. All of it."

Lysia's smile lacked all emotion. "Likewise." With a look suggesting she didn't want to talk about it anymore, she picked up a vial of pellets and emptied them into her hand. "You woke up at the right time, by the way. Agaam is gonna meet us tonight regarding our pay."

"He's back on the island?"

"Yeah, apparently he arrived today. Ma'sao Umō said we're to meet him in the village come nightfall."

"Pay". There was something surreal about the idea: the two of them and Agaam in the village inn, exchanging coin pouches over a glass of rice wine. It felt dirty. Final.

They were silent for a bit. At last, Lysia stood and girdled her belt. "The gate by sunset. Get some rest."

She left.

Jespar stayed for a few more minutes, then went looking for Ma'sao Umō, whom he found sawing branches off a storm-felled tree in the garden. Somewhat awkwardly, Jespar thanked him and offered a handful of coins, which Umō politely refused. Then Jespar went to see Kawu and spent ten minutes staring at the floor.

The noose was cutting into his neck as though trying to break it. His mad trip into the ocean had changed nothing.

Music and chatter greeted them in the marketplace. The colorful pavilion tents from Miwā-e-Kēku were still up, and the villagers were gathered beneath them, eating and laughing. When Jespar asked a man handing out free rice pudding and fried plantains what they were celebrating, he looked at Jespar as though his question had been the most foolish one ever asked.

"New Kilay."

Jespar muttered thanks and caught up to Lysia. They found Agaam by the dock. Clad in civilian clothing, he stood at the pier gazing into the moonlit water. When he turned and hinted at a bow, Jespar realized he had already forgotten what Agaam's face looked like.

"Ma'sae, may you prosper. I trust you've been well?"

"Yes," Lysia said. "How about you?"

"I'm well, thank you. I assume you've been told I'm here concerning your payment. Despite the unfortunate developments, you've succeeded in your mission, and before his passing, Ma'sao Oonai explicitly wished for you to be compensated for your services in full."

"That's good," Jespar said, taken aback by the formality. "How is the Ma'saa? Do you know?"

"According to Sergeant Maadira, quite weak. She has had periods of wakefulness, but she isn't quite lucid yet."

A bizarre thought crossed Jespar's mind: *who will take care of her pets now?* "Does she know the Ma'sao has ... passed? Or what happened in general?"

"I don't believe so. Now, please follow me. We're expected."

Agaam guided them out of the village, down a rocky path along the beach. Katydids sang, lizards zipped past their feet, waves lapped on the shore. They had been going for a while when Agaam spoke up.

"I suppose I still owe you an answer."

Jespar looked up from the road. "What do you mean?"

Agaam continued to gaze straight ahead. "Back when I found you in the cellar, I told you I kept Oonai's secret to myself because I wanted to be certain first. As I said back then, that was only one of my reasons. If you wish, I can tell you the other one now."

"Mind if I guess?" Lysia asked.

"Go ahead, ma'saa."

"You wanted to see him suffer," she said. "You knew Oonai's coma would cause chaos, but at the same time, you just liked the idea of him burning in a literal hell for what he did."

The path snaked around the shore. A bit farther down, a derelict blue building sat on a small promontory jutting into the ocean.

"Actually, no, I took no pleasure in that idea. It didn't matter how much Ma'sao Oonai suffered because I knew it wouldn't bring back Yamin."

Jespar, who had assumed Lysia was right, cocked up a brow. "Then what was the reason?"

"You may not remember, but on our way back from the Kaiawaika Massif, I told you I went into Oonai's service so I could limit the damage he could do. I still believe that was a deciding factor, but if I'm perfectly honest with myself, something else played a role too. Vanity. Think about it: who was I after the Snakes let me go? A disgraced general forbidden to speak about why he was dismissed. No reputable organization dared take me into their service out of fear of offending the magnates, and if Oonai had not thrown me that lifeline, I probably would have spent the rest of my days in poverty or working for some mercenary corps."

"You didn't want to lose your purpose," Jespar said.

"That makes it sound a lot nobler than it was. I was afraid of becoming insignificant."

They reached the building on the promontory. With a courtyard full of crates and weathered barrels, it had the air of an old trading post; a couple of pigs and their offspring gathered under an old pavilion, which they had seemingly made their home. Agaam stopped and faced Jespar. "I didn't realize all this until after the conversation we had on the way back from Kaiawaika Manor, but now I believe I held on to the truth about Oonai for a similar reason. As long as I was the only one in possession of that secret, I was in power." He grimaced. "Gods, it sounds so pathetic when you say it out loud, but that's what it boils down to. An old man wanted to feel important, so he allowed an entire country to fall into chaos."

Jespar wished he knew how to reply, but everything that came to mind sounded trite. In the end, Agaam was right, wasn't he? If he hadn't been so secretive, many people would probably still be alive. On the other hand, had the riot never happened, would there have been this chance for a New Kilay?

"Did you tell him before they executed him?" Lysia asked. "I mean, that Yamin was your ..."

"No."

"Why?"

"The same reason I didn't tell him before all this. Because doing so wouldn't have brought her back." He studied the ground for a bit, a gleam in his good eye. Then he shook his head. "Anyway, there is your answer. Now, come, we got somewhere to be."

But where? Jespar thought, studying the derelict building.

Lysia wavered. "Um, where exactly are we? I thought this was about our reward."

"It is. You'll see."

When they still didn't move, the corners of Agaam's mouth twitched. "You think I would harm you?"

"No, we just ... " Jespar trailed off.

Agaam snorted. "Well, I suppose I brought that on myself. But trust me, I would *never* hurt you. I swear on Yamin's name."

After a small pause, Lysia nodded. "All right. Lead the way."

They headed for a stair leading down to a cellar entrance, the piglets fleeing to the shelter of their mother's belly as Agaam approached. With weeds covering the steps and yellow fungi sprouting from the cracks in the wall, the polished metal door looked at odds with its surroundings. Agaam pulled a key from his coat and unlocked it; it opened without a creak. Inside, dank air greeted them, the scent of the coastal breeze retreating as mold and dust took its place. When the door clicked shut behind them, the darkness was complete. Jespar heard clothes rustle and the sound of metal scraping against the floor. A second later, light poured from a lantern in Agaam's hand.

"Just this way," Agaam said.

He led them down a decrepit hallway, past moldy, toppled furniture and cobwebs. After several turns, they came to a stop in front of another pristine metal door, light shining through the crack. Agaam knocked twice, waited for a beat, then knocked again three times. A lock turned, and the door swung open.

Like Agaam, Maadira was clad in civilian clothes. Her hair was cut to the length of a thumbnail, and she looked as though she hadn't slept in days. "Ma'sao Dal'Varek, Ma'saa Varroy," she said. "May ye prosper. Please, come in."

She stepped to the side. Even though shadows draped the room, Jespar immediately recognized the figure on the stretcher. The Ma'saa. She was still a crone, but with her hair combed and dressed in a simple but elegant white robe, she did look better, noble, even. In suffering, she more than ever reminded Jespar of the first impression he'd had of her, a saint from the devotional paintings in his mother's memorial shrine. A man, presumably a physician, sat on a stool before her and inspected the new arrivals. Cropped gray hair contrasted his dark skin, and a dense beard shadow covered the lower half of his chiseled face. Merely a squint in his right eye marred the symmetry.

Jespar's heart skipped a beat when he understood.

"... Oonai?" Lysia's voice was thin as a spider's thread.

"Yes," the man said. He rose and extended his hand. "Varroy, Dal'Varek. It's good to see you again."

Dumbstruck, Jespar shook, once more feeling that odd, uneasy sense of familiarity as they touched. Perhaps sensing it too, Oonai quickly broke the handshake and turned his attention to Lysia. With only his healthy eye moving and the other one—it was glass—staying in place, the effect was jarring. "Lysia Varroy."

Lysia ignored his hand.

He dropped it. "Sergeant Maadira, please wait upstairs."

When the door shut behind her, Oonai turned back to them. "I believe I owe you–"

Lysia hit him. It was just a slap with the back of her hand, yet it sent Oonai staggering backward.

"It should've been *you*," Lysia said through gritted teeth. "You should be the one lying on that stretcher."

Oonai felt for his jaw, his expression a mixture of surprise and anger. Then what looked like resignation washed it away. "You're right, Varroy. It should be me."

Lysia glared at him. Then she shook her head and went to a corner by the door. "So it was all just another lie? There was no execution?"

"There was." Oonai returned to his stool and signaled Jespar to sit on another one nearby. "It just wasn't me they executed."

Jespar sat. "Who was it, then?"

"Raajas Daavun, a blacksmith imprisoned for murdering a Coalition official. He thought the man had raped his daughter, but it turned out he'd gotten the wrong one, so he was sentenced to death."

"So what," Lysia said, "they just dressed him to look like you and no one noticed?"

"Well, we looked quite alike to start with, and with a wig and a fake beard, we might have been twins. Agaam did the rest."

"Mind control," Jespar said, shooting Agaam a glance. The old servant stood by the door, gaze fixed on a point on the opposite wall.

"More of a suggestion, like he did in the ziggurat. Also, macabre as it may sound, Daavun was covered by insects from head to toe, so it was hard to tell." He raised a hand as if to get ahead of a protest. "Before you ask, he agreed to it. I gave his wife and children a lifetime pension in return."

Lysia's mouth hardened. "And the keepers were in on this?"

"Only the commanding archkeeper and a few others. We came to an agreement."

Lysia regarded Oonai for another second. Then she scoffed and stared at the ground.

"Will you at least allow me to explain?" Oonai asked.

She said nothing. Jespar nodded.

"Thank you." Oonai brought his fingers to his chin, as if to stroke his beard. Realizing it was gone, he dropped them. "First, I want you to know that I meant everything I said back in the atrium. I've made terrible mistakes, and there's no making up for them, not in this life or in the next. It's just ... I lost my way. I don't know when and how it happened, but it did, and thousands of people paid the price for that." His good eye strayed off while the other remained fixed on Jespar. At first, Jespar thought he was looking at his wife, but then he noticed an ornamented vase standing on a nearby shelf. *No. Not a vase.* It was an urn.

"Enkshi?" Jespar asked.

"Zagash, yes. I never—" Oonai faltered. He let out a breath. "When his fiancé drowned in a tempest, Zagash often talked about how he wanted his ashes to be spread in the sea instead of buried in a boneyard, as is the custom. I intend to fulfill his last wish." He regarded the urn for a bit longer, then turned back. "Either way, what I'm trying to say is that I know I deserve punishment for what I've done. And if you believe in an eye for an eye, then, yes, it should have been me strung up over that bog pool. But do you remember what you told me in the nightmare, Dal'Varek?"

Jespar shifted in his chair. "What in particular?"

"That, at the end of the day, it's actions that matter, and not sentiments. You've said it yourself, I could have spent a lifetime being tortured by that bug in my mind—to the rest of the world, I might as well have been dead." He paused. "The Order has seized all my wealth and will put it toward the foundation of New Kilay, but that doesn't include the many investments I hold across the Illumined World: property, shares, businesses, and most importantly, secret stashes for situations like this. Sure, it's a far cry from what I used to own, but it's more than enough for a fresh start." He leaned forward, elbows on knees. "Now, think about it: if I were to die, all that potential to do good would vanish into thin air. It would be just like when I infected myself with the dreameater. I cannot let that happen."

Jespar saw where he was headed. "So you want to build another empire and use your power for a higher cause this time? Is that what you're getting at?"

"Is that such an absurd idea? You've said it yourself, results matter. If I do it right, I could change thousands of lives for the better."

"Or you could just hand 'all that potential' to someone who's not a mass murderer and let them do the world-saving for you," Lysia said. "Better bloody credentials, if you ask me."

"What, and kill myself afterward? It doesn't work that way, Varroy. Unjust as it may be, there's a reason people like me run the world, and not kind wayfarers and noble souls." Studying his lap, Oonai slowly shook his head. "No ... this game needs a master, someone who understands and knows the other players, like it or not. And even though it's foolish to believe a single person can change the rules all by himself, I *know* I can make a difference." His eye lifted to Jespar's. "And I won't waste any time. Tomorrow night, my wife and I will sail to Nehrim and assume new identities there. Then I'll do what I should have done a long time ago: build instead of destroy."

It was strange. Here Oonai sat, a man stripped of his title, his home, and the lion's share of his wealth; even visually, shaved and with dyed hair, he was a far cry from the god-king whose statues had adorned the Alabaster City not long ago. But despite all that, he still had it: the aura of a visionary, the aura of an emperor. The aura that made Jespar believe him.

Then again, who could tell?

Even if Oonai was honest right now, who knew whether he'd feel the same a year from now? Or four?

"So, that's it?" Lysia said. "Your new self gets to go down in history as a saint, while all those people you've killed get to rot below the ground? No, I won't accept that, *I fucking won't*!" She reached for her clawblade, but her fingers froze before they reached the hilt.

"Please, ma'saa," Agaam said, the air around him shimmering. "Don't."

He ended the shift. Lysia stared at him, then exhaled sharply and withdrew her hand from her belt.

"Your assistant, Varroy," Oonai said quietly. "His name was Juusew, wasn't it? Juusew Seel?"

"Don't you dare say his name," Lysia said. "Don't you bloody *dare*."

Oonai went on. "There are millions of orphans across the world, and most die of cold or starvation before their twelfth birthday. Juusew was one of the lucky ones, thanks to your kindness. One of the first things I will do once I reach Ostian is build an orphanage—the city is still in ruins from the war, and there are hundreds of children living on the streets, maybe thousands. Tell me, what do you think they would prefer? Me rotting in some coffin, or a warm bed, food, and a chance at life?"

Lysia didn't answer.

"I *will* build that orphanage, Varroy, and once I have recovered the means, I will build a dozen more. I swear on Nayima's life." He paused. "That said, if you think death is the only way I can pay for my crimes or you simply don't believe me, go ahead and do it. Take that dagger of yours and finish the job."

"Lysia—" Jespar began.

"Let her. If this is how it ends, then so be it."

Lysia's lips quivered. Then she lunged at Oonai, neck-locked him, and pressed her clawblade to his throat. Oonai struggled, but only for an instant. He dropped his hands.

"Do it," he said hoarsely. "Just get it ... get it over with."

Lysia pressed the blade closer to Oonai's neck. Tears trailed down her cheeks, blood down her blade. "Everything," she sobbed. "You destroyed *everything*!"

His answer was hardly a whisper. "I know."

She let go.

Oonai buckled forward with a gasp, grabbing his throat. Lysia dropped the clawblade. It clattered onto the flagstone.

"Fine." Her tears were still coming. "Fine, have it your way." She turned to Agaam. "I have only one question. Do you think this is just?"

A long, long pause.

"Sometimes," Agaam said, "what's right and what's just are two different things."

Lysia stared at him. Then her mouth creased in the ruin of a smile, and she headed for the door.

"Wait!" Oonai called. "Your pay."

Lysia stopped and looked over her shoulder. "Keep your blood money."

She slammed the door shut behind her.

A moment ticked by. Then Oonai sighed and looked at his sleeping wife. "To be frank with you," he said, "she's the other reason I can't go yet. What that woman did to her, it's ... I still can't ..." He broke off, pressing the heel of a palm to his eye.

"You don't want to abandon her," Jespar said. "I understand."

"No, it's more than that. I want to heal her."

"You mean ... undo that shift? Is that even possible?"

Agaam joined the conversation. "Not by conventional means, no. But there are rumors about a hermit in Ostian who has cured people of the fleshrot. The Ma'sao is hoping it's some new, unknown expression of biomancy."

Oonai nodded. "It's a shot in the dark, but it's better than nothing. Frankly, that's why we're going to Nehrim, of all places. If that hermit exists, I will find him." Oonai brushed a lock of hair from the Ma'saa's forehead. "You hear that, Nama? We're going to heal you. I swear it."

She answered with silence.

"Will you tell her?" Jespar asked. "What you did, I mean?"

When Oonai looked up, the torchlight reflected in his eye. Jespar recognized the look: it was the same one he had worn in that last minute of the nightmare. The face of a scared little boy. "Once she's well enough, I will, yes," he said. "If she decides to stay with me, then we're going to build these orphanages together. If not ... well, I'll accept it. The Gods know I never deserved her."

But she won't leave you, and you know it.

No, Nayima Oonai had not known about the Overgrowth Plan or Yamin, but she *had* been aware of her husband's transgressions or at least suspected them. What were her words "he has allowed the Corruption into his heart," if not an admission of this? And yet she had stayed. In the end, it was probably all about the impregnable bond the Oonais shared. Jespar no longer doubted its strength, not because of anything either of them had said or done, but because of the look he had seen in both their eyes whenever they had spoken of each other. It was one Jespar remembered from the rare occasions when Father had spoken of Mother and warmth had melted the ice in his expression for a few fleeting moments until he had remembered she was gone. Losing his soulmate had broken Damean Dal'Varek— the Ma'saa had probably feared the same.

Jespar watched her. Her eyes moved slowly under their lids, indicating that she was dreaming. Probably about a time before the Pale Sister had stolen thirty years of her life.

So this is what love looks like, he thought. *Or dependency.*

"I see," Jespar said. "I hope you find that hermit."

A look of silent resolve hardened Oonai's face. "I will. If it's the last thing I do in this world." He took a satchel from a nearby table and tossed it to Jespar. Coins clinked as he caught it. "One hundred thousand sêr in gold coins. Sixty thousand as my wife promised you, and approximately another forty on top. See it as a token of thanks."

As was his habit, Jespar took a coin from the satchel and studied it.

Oonai snorted. "They're real, Dal'Varek. Feel free to take a bite. What about Varroy's share? Do you want it?"

Jespar dropped the coin into the satchel and shook his head. "Use it to pay off her loan shark if he's still alive. Otherwise, give it to someone in need. It's what she'd want, I think."

"All right, I'll see to it. And Nakāni, the dreamwalker? I was told he's still recovering from the shifts?"

At the mere mention of Kawu's name, the phantom noose inched a smidge tighter. "Lysia says he's on the mend. I can bring him his share if you'd like."

Oonai took another satchel from his coat and tossed it over. "Thirty thousand sêr and the skystone. Altogether, that makes around one hundred eighty thousand, enough for the boy to buy himself into high society if that's what he wants. I hope he'll put it to good use."

"You can count on that. Without him, neither of us would be here." Though it was nothing but the truth, it felt dishonest to say it. Like someone praising the qualities of his partner after abandoning them.

You haven't abandoned him. You haven't abandoned him, and you won't, because whatever this bullshit is that you're feeling, it will pass, and things will go back to normal.

The thought brought no reassurance.

"Right, you were infected too," Oonai said. "Agaam mentioned that."

There was a questioning undertone as if inviting Jespar to share. One more time, the familiarity between them returned, like two estranged childhood friends who are visiting each other after spending decades apart.

Jespar looked sideways. "Yeah, but I'm good now."

Taking the hint, Oonai nodded, stood, and offered his hand. "Well, I guess that settles it. I'd like to thank all three of you, but since you are the only one present, you'll have to do. Thank you for everything, Jespar Dal'Varek—I still don't believe in premonitions and divine trials, but I'm glad my wife put her trust in you. I never liked the saying, but considering your father saved her and you saved me, it really does seem that the apple sometimes doesn't fall far from the tree."

Jespar suppressed a snort. *If only you knew.* They shook. "Glad I could help."

And it wasn't a lie, was it? From an entirely objective perspective, had it really ended that badly? Had Jespar, Lysia, and Kawu not taken on the job, Agaam would have probably held on to his secret forever, the Scythe would have gone through with the riot, and there would have been no truce. The Illumined World would have had no choice but to reconquer the Archipelago and restore order, which would have meant a long and devastating war. *No,* Jespar thought. The first spark of this inferno had been struck long before he had even set foot on the Archipelago, on the day Oonai and Vel'Nyx had begun their work on the Overgrowth Plan. This mission had never been about saving the world. Just about limiting the damage.

That's not true. New Kilay will be a better place for everyone.

But would it? Lysia might call him a pessimist, but Oonai had been right when he had said it was foolish to believe a single person could change the rules all by themselves. The new constitution would lay the foundation for a better future, yes, but in the end, it was up to all of the people, from the worker to the wealthy upper, to ensure the vision would become reality.

"Don't go back on your word, Oonai," Jespar said. "Please."

Something flickered across Oonai's face, gone too fast for Jespar to read it. "Never." He sat beside his wife and cupped her hand. "Thank you again, Dal'Varek. Ma'sao Agaam will show you out."

Jespar nodded and headed for the door.

"Actually, there's one more thing," Oonai said, stopping him.

"Yes?"

"Do you think I'm a monster?"

Jespar took a long time to answer. Was he? Judging by the blood in his footprints, the answer was undoubtedly "yes." But judging by the man he was now and his future deeds?

"I think you're the only one who can answer that question," Jespar said. "And you should ask it every single day."

Oonai held his gaze, his expression blank. Then he smiled wanly and nodded once. "Agaam, please talk to the mayor once you've taken Ma'sao Dal'Varek back to the manor. I—"

"No," Agaam said.

"What?"

"You heard me. Walking out this door will be the last you ever see of me."

"... I don't understand."

Agaam took a step toward him. "Do you want me to explain? I can, ma'sao. I can explain everything."

Oonai moved his lips, but no words came out.

"Come, Dal'Varek," Agaam said. "It's time."

They left the former First Magnate to his withered wife and the ashes of his best friend.

CHAPTER FORTY
DUSK

DAY TWENTY-ONE
1ST MOON OF RAINY SEASON, 1226 A.L.

ergeant Maadira slouched on a barrel in the backyard, smoking a pipe. When Agaam told her that he wouldn't be joining her and the four Snakes who would accompany the Ma'sao and the Ma'saa to Nehrim, she asked why but didn't push him when he gave a vague answer. After these past weeks, who could be surprised at anything anymore?

"Goodbye, Dal'Varek." *Gud-baie.* She didn't even bother to conceal her accent. "Thank ye for everythin'."

"You too."

He and Agaam walked in silence on their way back to the village, the old servant always a few steps ahead. Reaching the docks, he headed straight for a little cutter in line with the other fishing boats. When they reached the gangplank, Agaam turned around.

He seemed a different person. All the stony strength had sagged from his posture, and his wrinkled features appeared tired and worn, snakeskin weathered from decades of wind and rain. For the first time, Jespar felt like he truly *saw* the old man's face. Because that's what Agaam was: one of the deadliest psychomancers in the Archipelago, and a broken old man.

"I suppose this is where we part ways, ma'sao."

"I suppose. Where will you go?"

Agaam studied the water, which was almost still in the windless night. "Frankly, I don't know. Maybe Arktwend ... an old friend of mine is with the pioneers there."

"There are pioneers in Arktwend? I thought that place is a deadland."

"It is, but archaeologists found a massive Pyrayan ruin far inland. They suspect it used to be the center of their empire, so an Arazalean nobleman financed a pioneering mission some six years ago. From what I've heard, they found a fertile patch of land on the west coast and built a settlement there. It'll be rough living, but maybe I can lend a hand. As long as this old body allows it, that is." He snorted softly. "Cowardly, isn't it? My country is on the cusp of a new era, yet here I am, running to the edge of the world. But I don't know, it's just ... I'm too tired. Too bloody tired."

"I can relate."

Agaam nodded once. "Either way, my first stop will be the capital. I still have some business to take care of with Natana, Yamin's mother."

"Is she okay?"

"Yes, she is. She and Yamin lived in a tiny house in a Jade District back alley, and the rioters never reached it. It's ironic when you think about it ... Natana always complained about 'being stuck in that rat hole,' and now that rat hole saved her life."

"Life's a joke, and we're the punchline," Jespar said.

Agaam cocked up a brow.

"Just something a friend of mine used to say. Are you going to tell her about Yamin and Oonai?"

"Yes, I will. I'm almost certain it'll be the end of our relationship if we ever had one, but still, she has to know."

"You think she's going to blame you?"

"I do. Natana never liked me to begin with, but after my son died, it became even worse. She always accused me of 'sabotaging' Yamin because I didn't use my position to springboard her career. It was foolish, really ... We only have one family, but so often we don't appreciate it until it's gone."

"Hm. Can I ask you something, ma'sao?"

"Of course."

"That hermit, the miracle healer Oonai mentioned. Do you really think he can cure the Ma'saa?"

A peculiar expression settled on Agaam's mouth, something between a smile and a frown. "There is no hermit."

"You mean he's just a rumor?"

"No, I mean that there is no Nehrimese miracle healer, just like it's impossible to reverse a necromantic shift. I invented him."

"What? Why?"

"Because this way, Oonai will have something to fight for. Then again, the man's entire life is a rebuttal to the word 'impossible', so maybe he will manage to overcome even this obstacle. Gods know the Ma'saa shouldn't suffer for Oonai's flaws, and Yamin shouldn't have either." His good eye twitched at the mention of her name, and he gazed into the distance again. "I wish she could be here."

They were just six words, yet Jespar's heart stung at the weight they carried. Yes, Yamin should be here. That young woman Jespar would never know, with her incorrigible pride, hair draughts, and big plans to study alchemy in Al-Rashim. That young woman whose Great Dream had turned into a nightmare. Jespar had no answer, but Agaam didn't seem to expect one. For a minute, they stood there, watching the orange glow over the village roofs and listening to the laughter and chatter of a people dreaming of a better world.

At last, Agaam turned to face him. "You're a good man, Ma'sao Dal'Varek. Whatever those demons you're wrestling with are, make sure they don't get the better of you again."

"What do you mean?"

"You know what I mean. This is what they want, to convince us all those lies our mind keeps telling us are true, that it never gets better, and that giving up is the only way to stop hurting. Yamin listened to them. Make sure you don't."

A protest was on Jespar's lips, but then he looked at his feet instead. Ink-black waves lapped against the dock posts, dark silhouettes zipping through the depths. "Does it, though?"

"Hm?"

"Get better. Does it always get better."

Agaam studied Jespar as if pondering the question. "The Makehu have a saying for that, you know?"

"They do?"

"Yes. Tae ite nū'iwilo, tae hūnā 'o. 'You won't find out if you give up.' Because that is what it comes down to with melancholia and despair: just as other people lie when they tell you things always get better, your mind lies when it tells you that it doesn't. The only way to know is to stay and find out ... as hard as it might be."

Jespar regarded Agaam. He bit his lip and averted his eyes.

"Either way," Agaam said, "I should leave. Take care of the lad, will you? He will need a shoulder to lean on after everything that's happened."

A brush at his neck. *I want to. I want to, so much.* "I will."

"Good. I could use some help with the cutter. Would you mind, ma'sao?"

Jespar and Agaam unmoored the cutter and prepared the sail, then Jespar hopped back on the dock, and Agaam rowed the boat toward the open water.

"One more thing," Jespar said.

Agaam looked up, his white hair bright against the night sky.

"If we should meet again, call me Jespar."

Agaam's mouth curled in a smile. Far from beaming, far from carefree, and yet a smile. "Very well. I'm Xeelo."

Soon, the boat was a shrinking dot on the horizon.

Since Jespar couldn't find Lysia at the marketplace and had no idea where else to look, he returned to the manor. He could have hitched a carriage ride, but he chose to walk. A ride meant conversation, and he didn't feel like talking; he wanted to think. After all that had happened, could anyone blame him?

Liar.

He walked because he was stalling. He walked because it meant more time until he had to see Kawu, more time before the self-loathing for being such an ungrateful piece of shit returned, more time until the nightmare would pounce on his mind the second he couldn't keep himself awake any longer.

By the time he reached the palm tree avenue, it must have been around midnight. "We got a letter an hour ago," the guard told him as he lifted the gate. "From the Sergeant."

"Yeah?" Jespar replied without interest. "What did it say?"

"That yer welcome to stay here as long as ye like and that Oonai *bikeethed* the place to Ma'sao Umō." Judging from the jealousy in the man's words, he had probably meant to say "bequeathed".

"Okay. Thanks."

Inside, with all the servants out celebrating and no wind going, an eerie silence clung to the manor's many hallways. Jespar looked for Lysia, but when he couldn't find her and his knock on her door remained unanswered, he figured she had gone to sleep. Back in his own room, a note lay on his pillow.

"Ferry to Uunili leaving tomorrow noon," it read. Below it, hastily scribbled like an afterthought: "Waiting in the town inn to say goodbye."

Ignoring the sting the word "goodbye" left in his chest, Jespar reread the note, then tucked it into his shirt's breast pocket. He glanced at the wall to his right, toward Kawu's room.

When all this is over, do you think I could come with you? I'd love to see what autumn looks like.

With a single sob, Jespar shut his eyes and pressed his hands against his temples. Then he snapped them open, hastily swept up his backpack, stuffed his belongings inside, and stormed out of the room. Halfway down the lobby stairs, he abruptly plunked down on the steps and buried his head in his hands.

Why?

It just didn't make any fucking sense. The promise he had made Kawu in the cockleshell alcove, he had meant it. He *wanted* to stay, wanted to nurse him back to health, *wanted* to show him what autumn looked like. Why couldn't he? Why did this bloody nightmare and this bloody noose have to mess everything up?

What did the Corpse insist he had to *see*?

Panic welled up inside him. Jespar swung his haversack to his feet, grabbed a bottle, and drank. The liquor—some brandy—burned like a bitch, but he forced it down and took another belt, then another. His throat felt like fire, but the noose loosened the slightest bit.

"Piece of shit," he muttered. "Useless, selfish piece of shit."

Why was he so bloody *destructive*?

And suddenly, Jespar saw.

He was petrified. Brandy trailed from the corner of his mouth. His blood seethed, his heart hammered into his chest. His stomach was a hard, cold knot.

Then a perfect calm took hold.

Jespar stoppered the bottle, put it down beside him, and went to see Kawu.

All of the curtains were shut. Jespar waited as his vision adjusted to the gloom; black turned into silhouettes, silhouettes into shapes. The bed. The nightstand with a bowl of herbs and a sheet of paper on top. Kawu, wrapped in sheets.

The phantom noose was slack.

Jespar crossed to the bedside table and picked up the parchment. A letter in Lysia's handwriting. Most of it was her thanking Kawu for what he had done. She apologized for leaving him here and told him about the meeting with Oonai. *It's like this entire island has his taint,* she wrote. *I just can't stay here.* The letter mentioned Jespar toward the end when Lysia wrote that she counted on him to bring Kawu his pay. She ended by wishing him a swift recovery and saying she hoped they would meet again, even if it wasn't likely. Jespar replaced the letter and sank to his haunches by the bedside.

I am only the emissary.

This was what the Corpse had said in the nightmare after Jespar had run into the ocean. Now, almost a moon since Jespar had visited the swamp for the first time, he finally understood.

He saw.

Yes, it had been Kawu's choice not to tell him about the anchorings. No, Jespar had not meant to get infected and cause Kawu to get hurt. Neither had he meant for Adila to slit her wrists or the villagers to die or the Girl to be defiled because of his stupidity. But when intention and result always ended up on opposite ends of the spectrum, who wouldn't start asking questions?

Bad shit happens wherever you go.

Foolish thoughts, surely. Just guilt and melancholia telling him things that weren't true.

They weren't.

And yet they were.

If this past week had proven anything, it was that humans had far less control over their minds than they believed. The brain made decisions before one even knew it, and free will was a lie. In the end, one was just a puppet reacting to whatever grew from the seeds life randomly tossed into the soil of the mind.

And even though Jespar despised self-pity, there was no question the seeds he'd been thrown hadn't sprouted daffodils. Mother's death, Father's contempt, the murder of his family, Adila's attempted suicide—they had only been the first of the many rotten seeds life had merrily chucked Jespar's way—and the thicket they had sprouted would not be winning any gardening contests.

A swamp.

Jespar cupped Kawu's hand. His skin was warm and dry, just like it had been the dozens of times he had anchored him, each time sacrificing a portion of his own life. Jespar's eyes burned, but no tears came. No, he still didn't believe Naka's foolish notion that his soul was some kind of bad luck charm. It was as childish an idea as it got, based on the assumption that the individual was the center of the universe when, in truth, a human's consciousness was barely a speck of dust. But then why *did* knowing Jespar never change anyone's life for the better?

Simple.

Because the mess that was his mind made him fuck up whatever he touched. Because he *was* the swamp, and the swamp was him. *That's* what the Corpse had wanted him to see. Even before coming to Kilay, the purpose of the nightmares and the noose had never been to torment him but to remind him he was broken. In a way, he had been like a wisp beckoning people into the moor, stubbornly believing the bog wouldn't swallow them just because the wisp didn't mean any harm. Had he meant for them to get hurt? No, of course not. Should he have known better? Yes. The sheer scope of his self-deception would have been funny had the punchline not been a suicide attempt by his sister, a razed village and a defiled girl, and a foolish young man misled into thinking Jespar's sorry, useless ass was somehow worth saving.

He was the swamp. He was broken. And he always would be.

It was a bitter epiphany, but somehow all Jespar felt was an immeasurable relief, like a fleshrot patient accepting he'd never beat his disease.

Jespar let go of Kawu's hand and rose.

Deep down, his affection for Kawu had never diminished, he felt that now, and a part of him still desperately wanted to stay. But wasn't the definition of insanity trying the same thing over and over, expecting a different outcome each time? Adi, driven into suicide. The villagers, butchered. Kawu, almost killed. Even if there were a slim chance that this time would be different, that Jespar's swamp mind wouldn't cause him to make some stupid decision that would end in Kawu getting hurt again, what could be more selfish than taking that risk? Just so he didn't miss out on his shot at romance? He was a loose cannon; that was the long and short of it. The reason life during his drifting years had been "all right" was that he had been where he should be: far away from anyone he could hurt, far from anyone he loved. Yes, he wanted to stay. Yes, he wanted to show Kawu what autumn looked like.

He couldn't.

Jespar went to the desk and quietly searched the drawers for charcoal and parchment. He found both. *I'm so sorry*, he began. *I wanted to stay, but-*

Stop. It will only make him come after you.

He crumpled the paper and started over. The new letter suffered the same fate as its predecessor, as did the one after that. Six tries later, he had settled on two lines:

Good luck with everything.

— Jespar.

It sounded horrible, but an irrational fear that Kawu would wake any moment now had wormed its way into his stomach, making his palms so clammy the charcoal almost slipped from his fingers. He went to Kawu's bed and put the note next to Lysia's letter, together with the pouch containing the skystone and the gold. Then he left without looking back.

Back in the village, Jespar found himself feeling better than he had in days. The celebrations were ongoing, music and chatter filling the air, people dancing.

"Oi, wakemō!" someone called out as Jespar went past a colorful pavilion. A Makehu man was gesturing toward him from a packed table, a drunken grin revealing gleaming white teeth. "Is them balls of yers as pale as yer face?"

Chortles from his friends.

Only a few hours ago, Jespar would have just kept walking. Now he found himself returning the grin. "Why don't you ask your wife?"

The table exploded into laughter. The Makehu looked sour for a second, but then he joined in, offering Jespar a seat. He declined, wished them a good night, and went on.

Lysia was in the second of the two village inns, a modest cobalt building by the docks. A poorly drawn stingray-shark creature— presumably an "okepi"—arched over a sign so weathered the lettering had turned illegible. Lysia sat at a table in the corner, studying a steaming mug she held in her hands. A deck of Akati playing cards was laid out before her.

Jespar joined her. "Fancy a round?"

Lysia gave such a hard start that she almost knocked over her mug. "*Bloody* hell ... Jespar?"

"That's my name," Jespar said, plunking upon the stool across from her.

Lysia peeked over his shoulder. "You on your own?"

"Yeah."

"You could have come tomorrow, you know? The ship doesn't leave—"

"Before noon, I know. Actually, I'm—" He broke off as the innkeeper came over to take their orders. Jespar considered the wine, then went with warm milk instead. His burning need to drink had disappeared, at least for the time being.

Perhaps the nightmare has too.

"Milk?" Lysia asked when the innkeeper had disappeared into the kitchen. "You?"

Jespar unshouldered his haversack. "Variety is the spice of life." He nodded at the cards. "Are you playing again?"

Biting her lip, Lysia averted her gaze. "Oh. No, just this once. A couple of fishermen invited me to join them, but they left when I won three rounds straight." She squared her elbows on the table as if to cover the cards. "Anyway, you were gonna tell me something?"

"Yeah, right." Jespar laced his fingers. "I'll leave the island with you."

"What? What about Kawu?"

"I left him his pay and a letter. He'll be fine."

Lysia's lips parted, then closed again. The innkeeper returned with the milk. Jespar paid and thanked him.

"Look, it's for the best," he said as soon as the man turned away. "I've been thinking, and I realized I'm no—"

"It's all right," Lysia said. "I left too, so I'm hardly one to judge."

"No, it's for his own–"

"Jes, it doesn't matter. Kawu saved our arses, and we're not even waiting for him to wake up. Whatever our reasons are, in my book, that makes us pricks." Lysia sipped from her wine. "I just hope he'll be fine. Ma'sao Umō promised to take care of him and get in touch with his family, but for all we know, he'll never walk or talk again."

"You said he was getting better, though, didn't you?"

"I said it seems like he'll come out of the coma, but even that's not a given with a shifting drain seizure of that severity. There's absolutely no saying what it did to his brain."

"He'll be fine, Lysia. I know it."

"Well, in that case, what could go wrong?" She leaned back and studied the cards nearest to her, trailing her forefinger across the paper: three full moons and the Red Star. Jespar hadn't played since his first night in Southport, but he still remembered a hand like this was a surefire win. "You know, I've been thinking a lot. About that conversation we had just after we came here."

Jespar relaxed his hands around his mug. "Which one?"

"The one about freedom of will and the arbitrary."

"Right. And, any new insights?"

"Yeah. You are both absolutely right and utterly wrong."

"... You're gonna have to explain that."

"I'll try." Lysia took a card, a sun, and bent it between forefinger and thumb. "You're right in that I probably made it too easy for myself. In a way, I always knew not all the uppers are bad guys and *choose* not to give a shite about anything. Thing is, you lose the nerve to remind yourself of that fact when your twelfth patient dies from some simple disease because they can't afford treatment." She smoothly moved the card onto the tip of her extended middle finger and flicked her other hand's forefinger against it so that the card spun. "Even so, in the end, it wasn't the evil uppers who destroyed my clinic and hurt Juusew but a bunch of angry commoners. That's just how it is. I mean, we saw what happened that night, right? Those people razing the city weren't cutthroats, they were normal folk like the ones I used to treat every day. It was as if someone had poured poison into their brains and ... I don't know how to put it."

"Turned them rabid?"

"Yeah, maybe. Had it 'only' been the clinic, I would have probably told myself that those people had been a few rotten fruits, but they were just *so* fucking many." She stopped the card and flicked it back onto the pile. "So, yeah, maybe it's like you say: people don't choose to be good or evil, and it's all just a mixture of chance and predisposition. Stars burn me, who knows? Maybe *no* choice we make is truly our own, and we really are puppets reacting to events that we have zero control over."

Hearing Lysia say this, a weight settled on Jespar's shoulders. He wanted her to argue, wanted her to convince him he was wrong. "Some philosophers believe that, actually."

"I'm not surprised." She tossed the card back to the others. "Here comes the part where I think you're wrong, though. Even if choice *doesn't* exist, we need to tell ourselves that it does."

"Why?"

"Three reasons. One, living by that idea might become a determining factor itself."

"As in, if you believe you can't change, you won't even bother trying?"

"Yeah. Think about it: if you're just some kind of, I don't know, an actor playing a role that's all written out for you, why bother trying to be a better person at all? It's not like it's in your control anyway."

It isn't. "Hmm. What are the other reasons?"

Lysia picked up the cards and sorted them back into a stack. "The second one's simple: that kind of mindset completely erases the idea of responsibility. In a society believing there's no free will, no one could be held accountable for anything."

The death of responsibility. Jespar knew the conundrum, both from the scholars he'd read and from his own musings. "Maybe not morally, but legally for sure—actions matter, not intentions. Justice shouldn't be about morality anyway, but about protecting people."

"I suppose. The third reason is the most important, though. If we can't tell the difference between a real choice and one that's been made for us—why not just believe it's ours?"

Jespar took a sip of milk. "That's a paradox. If choice doesn't exist, how can you *choose* to believe it does?"

"Honestly, I don't know. But maybe that little bit of self-deception is the closest thing to freedom we'll ever get."

Jespar pondered her words. She was right, in a way. If you really thought about it, what had Jespar done these past days that had truly been his choice? Even his decision to accept his fate and leave Kawu had been more of an inevitability, just the result of a long chain of cause and effect, of disposition reacting to circumstance. But wasn't it better to believe it had been his call? That, for once in his life, he had *consciously* done the right thing?

He raised his mug to Lysia. "Here's to freedom through self-deception, then."

Smiling wanly, Lysia toasted. "To freedom through self-deception."

———⟡———

They slept in separate rooms. Still dreading the nightmare, Jespar stayed awake almost until dawn, reading and smoking. His last thought when his lids grew too heavy to keep them open was of Kawu. Reading that letter would hurt him. It would hurt him a lot.

Yeah. As does cutting out a tumor.

His sleeping mind took him back to the swamp, but there was no noose and no locusts, and the corpses just sat there and stared. What else were they supposed to do? He had accepted his fate. He had *seen.*

———⟡———

Only a handful of other passengers shared the ferry with them the following day. Lysia spent most of the voyage alone, gazing out at the windless sea, while Jespar busied himself with the dimensionism treatise he'd been reading before the storm. By the time he finished it, Uunili was already on the horizon.

Under the red night sky of the riot, there had been something surreal about the destruction. In daylight, it was as bright and clear as blood on glass. While the Jade District had, without a doubt, been hit the hardest, the damage covered all of the Alabaster City. Charred homes. Skeletal palm trees. Crumbled walls. If there was a silver lining, it was that the repairs had already begun: scaffolding and ladders leaned against the ruined façades, donkeys and horses pulled carts stacked with mud brick and lumber, and Blue Guards patrolled the pier, here and there joined by a keeper in shining armor and red cape. It felt bizarre to see them here, those fabled warriors from Jespar's homeland, transplanted from one world into another.

When the sailors had moored the ferry and lowered the gangplank, Jespar was among the first to step off the boat. Relishing the ground under his feet, he stretched his legs as he observed the other passengers disembark, the rigidity of shock, consternation, and numbness marking their expressions. The Alabaster City, the heart of Kilay, the wealthiest metropolis in the Illumined World, was ruined.

"What a mess," Lysia said as she came up beside him. "What a bloody mess."

Bloody indeed. And only the years to come would decide whether it had been pointless as well. "Yeah. What are you gonna do now?"

"Probably go to the clinic and see if any of my stashes survived the fire. After that, I'll visit Juusew's grave. Agaam said he didn't put him into one of the corpse pits, but it's still going to be a lot of tombs, so it might take a while to find it," she said tonelessly as if laying out plans for a perfectly normal day.

"I can help you search if you want."

Lysia squinted toward the city, shielding herself from the sun. "Thanks, but I need to do this alone. If you want, we can meet for dinner later tonight."

"I'd like that."

She gave him the description of a nearby inn, and they agreed to meet at sunset.

Jespar spent the rest of the day wandering through the city. It was both fascinating and unsettling to walk those ruined streets. So many people had lost their lives and livelihoods, and the echoes of the suf-

657

fering and destruction still clung to the air like ravens cawing over a silent battlefield. And yet something else sprouted amid all this bleakness, showing up in the little things: a merchant reassembling his trashed stall. A couple mending their ruined home with rubble from the streets. Two giggling boys kicking a forlorn helmet back and forth, neither of them old enough to wonder who it had belonged to.

It was the sense of a new beginning.

As day bled into dusk, Jespar found his way back to the harbor and the inn where he and Lysia had agreed to meet, a lime-green building nestled in an alley that had been spared from the riot. She wasn't there yet, so Jespar lit a pipe and waited. When the day grew dark, and there was still no trace of Lysia, he went inside. A lively babble filled the cold cellar room, tapestries mounted between the crosshatched ceiling beams. Jespar asked the innkeeper if he'd seen a woman fitting Lysia's description, but she shook her head, so he ordered fish soup and tea and ate at a table near the entrance.

Lysia didn't appear until an hour later. Her hair was tousled by the sea breeze, and she had a bulging haversack on her back, metal clanking inside it as she descended the stairs.

"Sorry," she said. "I had to run some errands."

"... No worries." Jespar cleared his throat. "You hungry?"

She sat in the chair across. "I already ate, thanks."

"What do you want, then? Drinks are on me."

Lysia regarded him pensively, as if he had just posed a complicated riddle. "What I want," she said, "is to get hammered."

And so they did.

Killing the first pitcher of rice wine, Lysia told Jespar about how her clinic had been burnt to the ground, and how she had caught a woman trying to dig up Juusew's secluded grave. At knifepoint, the woman started crying and confessed she'd been searching corpses for valuables because her little tailor's shop had been pillaged and her husband killed. By the second pitcher, a tipsy stupor had dried the tears on Lysia's cheeks, and they mused about New Kilay and whether it would all work out. By the third, they were howling with laughter as Lysia recounted the day she had to extract a buttered pastry brush from betwixt the buttocks of a baker who ardently claimed he had slipped and fallen on it. An hour later or so—the inn was still packed—Jespar found Lysia staring into her mug with a dull expression when he returned from the privy.

"You all right?" Jespar asked, sitting.

"What? Oh, yeah. Sure." She turned her mug on the spot, studying the clay as if looking for imperfections. "So, I'm guessing you aren't staying? In Uunili, I mean?"

"Probably not, no."

"Any idea where you're heading next?"

Good question. Where are *you headed?* He recalled his last conversation with Agaam. "I don't know. Maybe Arktwend."

"Arktwend? What in the world would you want in that hellhole?"

"See something new, I guess. Agaam said there was a pioneering mission a few years ago, and I'm sure they have use for guards or day laborers. How about you? Are you gonna rebuild your clinic? I'm in no rush, so I could lend you a hand."

Lysia scoffed. "I won't rebuild shite."

The answer surprised him. Maybe it shouldn't have. "Why, because of the money? I asked Oonai to pay off your loan—"

"It's got nothing to do with that. I just need to get away from this mess. As far as I bloody can."

Too drunk to think of a meaningful reply, Jespar left it at a grunt. Lysia poured herself another mug, then offered the pitcher to Jespar. He shook his head.

"You could come with me, you know?" he said. "I'm sure those settlers would be grateful for a talented physician like you."

Lysia gave him her lopsided grin, and while it wasn't as bleak as it had been a week ago, something about it had changed. "I told you, Jes, no need for the flattery. We already shagged."

"No, I mean it. You're a damn good healer, and I'm sure there's plenty of demand in that colony. It's–"

"I'll think about it, thanks." She downed her wine in a single gulp. "Back to the fun bit. Did I tell you Ma'sao Pastry Brush came back the moon after?"

The inn was almost empty by the time a drunk Jespar walked a drunk Lysia to her room. It took her two attempts to hit the keyhole of the shabby door, and when she did and unlocked, the door swung open and sent her staggering forward. Jespar caught and steadied her. When they broke from each other, the ripples of a dreamy smile played around Lysia's eyes, and she kept her lips close to him.

Suddenly, it was all back.

That night in the boat to Hapana. Her lopsided grin through the nightflower smoke, her naked skin on his. Their talk after that first hallucination, the way she'd listened, how her presence had always calmed him. Trust.

"Thanks," she whispered, leaning in toward him.

Jespar kissed her.

He didn't know why he did it, after all that had happened. The booze played a role, for sure. The loneliness he'd been feeling ever since leaving Kawu, despite knowing it was the right choice. Or the knowledge that, whatever the reasons for Lysia's newfound affection for him were, she knew he was damaged goods and would seek nothing deeper.

She shoved him.

There was hardly strength behind the push, yet it came so unexpectedly, she sent him reeling back into the corridor; Jespar groped at a wall tapestry to catch himself, nearly taking it down.

"What the ...?"

Seeing her scowl and the tears pooling on her lids, it struck him how utterly he had misread her. There had been no affection in that dreamy smile, let alone desire; her leaning in hadn't been an invitation but simply her swaying from the alcohol.

"You're such an arse, Jespar, you're such a bloody *arse*. How can you be like that, how?"

"Wait, that was a mistake, I–"

"I was late because I went to the harbormaster and bought passage for a ship," she said. "Don't ask which one and don't follow me. I mean, if staying with me is what you really want this time, who the hell knows? It's not as if you ever let anyone in on what's happening in that *fucking* head of yours."

"Lysia, I–"

"Save it, Jespar. I don't fucking care."

She went into her room and slammed the door.

Jespar stared, his head swimming from the combined punch of booze, surprise, and hurt.

He knocked.

No answer.

"Lysia?"

Nothing.

He slammed his palm against the wood. "Godsdammit, Lysia, what the hell? This is unfair!"

More silence.

"Fucking hell. *Fucking* hell!"

Heart racing and hands trembling, Jespar went down the corridor. Halfway to the stairs, he heard the door open behind him. "Go on, Jespar." Lysia stood with one arm propped against the doorjamb, a deep line etched between her brows. "Lecture me on fairness."

Jespar turned back around, but the sudden movement caused a rush of vertigo. Cursing, he grabbed hold of another tapestry, almost tearing that one down as well. When his head had stopped spinning and he looked up, Lysia was still there, glaring at him like a boxer ready to fight.

He snorted. "Yeah. You think you have it all figured out, don't you?"

"Do I?"

"Yes, you do. You think I'm just a lying drunkard who doesn't give a shit about anyone. Jespar Dal'Varek, the selfish, cynical asshole who abandons the man who saved his life."

Lysia said nothing. His heart beat faster. "Well, guess what, you don't understand the first *fucking* thing about me. You, you think you're all high and holy with your judgmental bullshit morality, but the truth is, you know nothing about how people work. You're a child, Lysia! A bloody child who still thinks the Moon Kobold will one day show up on your windowsill if only you wish for it hard enough. The world isn't black and white, it's gray, and it's messy, and—"

"You're destructive," Lysia said. "You don't care, and you're bad for the people around you. *That's* what I think."

Her words quelled his anger like an avalanche. He fell silent.

"I mean, honestly, Jes, you're a bloody mystery. All that wisdom you have to share about the human condition, all those smart things you told Oonai to get him out of his self-flagellating fantasy, and *yet* you somehow manage to go through life without ever pausing to think what the fuck you're doing. Stars burn me, you're not the only one who's been through some shite, and when you broke that promise to me, it bloody hurt. Did you ever think of that?"

"You told me it was okay," Jespar said hoarsely. Suddenly, he felt very, very small.

"Well, what else should I have done? Thrown a tantrum and risked the mission over some stupid drama? But, yeah, I guess it was okay. I mean, it was just a stupid promise and a stupid kiss, and we're all grown-ups who are way above *that*, aren't we?" She scoffed, touched her scar. "That shite you pulled on Kawu, though? *I* feel like an arse for leaving him, but that lad almost killed himself for you because he's in love, and this is how you thank him? Gods, Jespar, you either *are* not aware of what you're doing, or you choose not to be, and I genuinely don't know which is more pathetic."

Unable to bear another second of her glare, Jespar stared at his feet. "You didn't let me explain."

"Yeah, as if, this one time, you would have given me a straight answer. I just don't care anymore, that's the long and short of it. I think you're selfish, I think your promises don't mean shite, and I think you're destructive, and even though I'm sure there's some tragic story to explain it all, I'm just too bloody exhausted to deal with you anymore. Stars burn me, I can't even deal with myself right now."

Whatever went on in Jespar's expression, his hurt must have shown. Lysia sighed, and her features softened. "Listen, Jes ... I know there's a good man under all that rubble, trust me, I do. But whatever you're trying to exorcise those demons, it's not working. You're–"

"Stop."

Lysia fell silent.

"Message received," Jespar said. "Spare me the fucking sermon."

Cheeks burning, he stalked down the hallway, but just a few steps in, he stumbled over a bump in the carpet and fell. Pain shot up his wrists as he came down hard on the ground; the booze in his head erupted into a cloud of fire.

"*Fuck!*" he screamed and slammed his fist into the floor; His wrists exploded, bile shot into his throat. He punched again, then again, and again. "Fuck, fuck, fuck, *fuck!*"

Groaning, he rolled onto his back, a firework of stars blasting across his vision. His eyes burnt as if someone had dipped them in acid, but the tears still didn't come. He drew a ragged breath, then another, then another. When he looked up, Lysia was still in the corridor, but her expression had changed.

Pity.

"Don't you dare," Jespar said. "Don't you dare look at me like that."

"I'm just—"

"Don't you fucking dare!"

The concern vanished. Lysia stepped back and reached for her clawblade.

And something in Jespar cracked.

Lysia was afraid of him.

She thinks you'd hurt her?

A strange sound escaped his throat—and took the lump right with it.

"You know what?" Jespar said. "You're right."

Lysia took another step back.

She really does. She thinks you'd hurt her.

The sound came again, now almost a chuckle. Was this the kind of man he had become?

"When I was twelve years old, my father sentenced the son of an underworld kingpin to death, fully aware the man would pay him back in blood. Two moons later, three Revenants show up at our manor, butcher my father, my brothers, and the entire staff, and set the place on fire. The only reason my little sister, Adi, and I survived is that we snuck out that night to go stargazing."

Lysia relaxed her grip on the clawblade. She closed her mouth.

"Thing is," Jespar went on, "a part of Adi *did* die that night. And after seven years of crippling melancholia, it finally got the better of her. She tidied up her room and made her bed, put all her drawings onto a neat little stack, then laid down and sliced open her wrists with a kitchen knife." He started to laugh, but a sob got the better of him. "She even dusted off the godsdamned furniture. I mean, can you imagine? She dusted off the fucking *furniture*."

"Jes, I'm so—"

"I was the one who found her." The words gushed out now, black swamp water rushing through the cracks of a dam he'd ignored for so many years. "And you know what was the first thing she told me when she woke up? 'It doesn't get better, Jes. It just doesn't.' Because that's what I kept telling her, that 'time heals all wounds,' that 'it always gets better,' to 'hang in there and stay strong,' the usual bullshit we tell melancholic people when we really just want them to shut up and put a smile on. Because that's what it comes down to, you know? I said that shit because dealing with her had gotten so fucking tiring. It wasn't fair, that's what I told myself, it wasn't fair that I always had to be the strong one." He snorted. "Bullshit, Jes. You just couldn't be bothered putting up with that endless sadness anymore, because, damn, didn't that remind you how little *you* actually cared father and Rodrik and Alvric, and everyone else was dead, and how that proved what a heartless, selfish piece of shit you really were. Bloody hell, Lysia ... I stood by and watched my sister run toward suicide because I preferred to go out and enjoy myself to being there for her when she needed me most. I might as well have slit her godsdamned wrists myself."

Lysia sat beside him and reached for his shoulder.

He backed away, edging toward the wall. "Four years later, I join this mercenary corps in Nehrim that's supposed to help civilians, thinking I'll do some good for a change, and guess how it ends? Correct, my unit butchers an entire village because I'm a bloody idiot who can't tell a breadbasket from a tyenite barrel! Great help I was, huh? So, yeah, Lysia, you're damn right, I'm destructive. I'm a useless mess, and I fuck up everything I touch, and all this shit, it was just more of the same. Kawu almost died because I was dumb enough to get myself infected, and I'd be a rotten idiot to believe I wouldn't find some other way of messing things up if I stayed because that's just *what I do.*"

The last word came out shrill and hysterical. The light from the wall torches hurt his eyes, the rancid smell of the carpet made him nauseous, the floorboard splinters were red-hot nails in his shaking hands. "It's just so godsdamned ironic, you know? All that shit, it's exactly what my father's corpse has been trying to tell me for years, and I ignored it like a champion and told myself life was all right. It never even *occurred* to me that all he was trying to do was make me see just how messed up I am and that *nothing* is all right with me. I mean, who knows how much more damage I would have done to you if you hadn't turned into the Corpse that night and to Kawu if the nightmares hadn't gotten so bad when we reached the island. Those bloody demons ... they were never here to torment me. Only to keep me from hurting others."

The swamp water stopped coming. Exhaling, Jespar sank back against the wall and buried his head in his hands.

Away.

He just wanted to get away, away from Lysia, away from this island, away from the endless thought spirals and endless hurt. He just wanted the ground to swallow up him and this fucking thing that was his soul.

Oblivion.

When he looked up again, Lysia was still by his side. She had taken her hand from his shoulder and studied him.

More pity.

"I'm sorry," Jespar muttered. "I'm not ... I shouldn't have ..."

"What do you mean, 'I turned into the Corpse?'"

"... What?"

"You said, 'I turned into the Corpse that night.' Or, I think that's what you said. What did you mean?"

Jespar waved his hand. "Ah, some messed-up hallucination I had back when we went to that manor. I had this nightmare, and when I woke up, you had turned into the Corpse from my dreams, into my father. That's why I ran off into the jungle."

"A hallucination," Lysia said slowly. "From the dreameater?"

"Yes. I mean, I know it wasn't real, but still, it just ... it *broke* something. Everything I felt for you was gone, just like it was with Kawu." He heaved a breath. "But I told you. It was for the best."

Silence followed.

"The Corpse isn't real, Jes," Lysia said. "And neither are your nightmares."

Jespar scoffed faintly. "I know that."

"That's what you say, but, deep down, I don't think that's what you believe. Gods, you don't only talk as though they were real, you let them completely dictate your actions. No one blames you for getting infected, and it's not your fault Kawu didn't tell you the anchorings were killing him. But abandoning him afterward? That was your choice."

Jespar weakly shook his head. "Did you even listen? I didn't want to leave, I *had* to. I would have hurt him again."

"Jes, that's *exactly* what the Corpse wants you to believe!"

A pause.

"No," Jespar said hoarsely. "No, you don't understand. The nightmare and the noose, they just killed everything there was. If I–" He faltered. "If I hadn't listened, they would have killed me too."

Lysia looked at him, looked at him with those eyes that had been so different a mere moon ago. "Don't you think Oonai told himself the same thing the day he decided to infect himself?"

Seconds ticked by.

Then the image of the swamp court appeared in Jespar's mind— but it was different: the perspective had shifted. Instead of kneeling at its center, Jespar saw himself standing several strides away; the corpses were still looking at him, but something about them seemed strange.

The image vanished.

It took Jespar all his courage to lift his gaze.

"Don't leave," he whispered. "Please stay."

There was a flicker of hesitation. It stayed just that—a flicker.

"I can't, Jespar. I just can't anymore. I'm sorry."

She stood, went into her room, and turned the lock. Jespar sat there for another minute. Then he staggered out of the tavern and into the humid night.

CHAPTER FORTY-ONE
NIGHT

DAY TWENTY-THREE
1ST MOON OF RAINY SEASON, 1226 A.L.

he days blurred into a drunken stupor. When he dreamed, he wanted to wake. When he was awake, he wanted to dream. He drank to smother the thoughts. The nightmare of the swamp court was brutal, but the booze and the fatigue made it as hazy and distorted as reality, and it slipped from Jespar's mind the second he woke. At some blurry point in time, Jespar was lying curled up on the floorboards of some dank tavern room, a voice whispered into his ear.

The Corpse isn't real, Jes.

Was he dreaming?

Was he awake?

The Corpse isn't real.

He was back in the swamp court. One moment, he watched from a distance; the next, he was in the center, choking on locusts bursting from his mouth.

It isn't real.

The days slogged by, and every time Jespar visited the swamp court, he stayed in the distance a little longer. What was it about the corpses that looked so odd? And why did it even matter? He knew they weren't real. He always had. It didn't change the truth of their message: that he'd always be a swamp.

When he woke one day, crippling guilt filled him, paired with smothering loneliness. He downed a full bottle of rice wine, but that only made it worse.

Kawu. That's who he needed. That's who he had *always* needed.

What have you done, Jespar?

What have you fucking done?

He went to the marina and asked for a boat to Nayima Island.

The next ferry didn't leave until a week later, so Jespar paid a fisher-woman to take him instead.

"Ye should sleep," she said as the boat glided out the busy harbor. Clouds spanned the sky, foreshadowing rain. "We ain't gonna be there 'fore nightfall."

Jespar heeded her advice, curled up on the side bench, and shut his eyes. His first sober sleep in days, the swamp nightmare was vivid and terrifying, but just when the noose pulled tight and the locusts stirred in his guts, his perspective shifted again, and he found himself outside the court.

He finally saw why the corpses looked so strange.

They were translucent.

The manor gate was shut, and Jespar's ringing of the bell remained unanswered, so he climbed the fence and sneaked up to the entrance.

He rapped the door knocker.

No one came.

"Hello?" he called.

Nothing. Two katakos fluttered up to him and circled him, looking for an opening. Jespar shooed them away, dizziness flooding him, his body's reward for a week's worth of abuse. He waited for the vertigo to subside, then rounded the terrace and tried the back door. Locked.

Just wait. Wait and come back in the morning.

You can't.

He fished a nail from his belt pouch and slid it into the keyhole. Five minutes later, he was in. Draped in darkness and silence, the lobby gave off that feeling so often innate to lavish places like this one. Decadent, not luxurious; intimidating, not impressive. Vast, not spacious. The way Redbeard's manor had so often felt on those bleak winter days when all the servants were gone, and Adi wouldn't get out of bed all day. Quietly, Jespar found his way to Kawu's room, closed his fingers around the handle, blood rushing in his ears.

He went in.

The bed was empty and made. The nightstand had been cleared and tidied up, the surface dusted and polished to a gleam.

A terrible picture formed in his mind.

No. No, don't you dare think that.

But he couldn't help it. Like a haruspex vision from a pool of blood and bone, the image became clearer and clearer, opening a black hole in Jespar's heart. Sweat broke from his forehead, and the noose inched tighter, though something about it felt different now. He grasped at the doorjamb for support.

A shadow moved behind him.

Jespar's hand shot to his sword, but he was too slow: something hit him square between the shoulders and sent him lurching forward. He fell and cried out as pain exploded in his bruised wrists. Rolling onto his back, he saw a silhouette looming over him, raising what looked like a tree stump over his head.

"Wait!"

The figure froze.

"It's ... it's me. I–" Jespar broke off, groaning.

"... Ma'sao Dal'Varek?"

With its strong Makehu accent, the voice was familiar, but Jespar was too dazed to place it. The figure stepped out of the doorway, into the cone of moonlight filtering through the window. Two dark eyes studied him from within wrinkled, umakoed sockets. "Ma'sao Dal'Varek? That ye?"

It was Ma'sao Umō, the old Makehu who had fished him out of the ocean. Holding a bust of Oonai before his wrinkled, scarred chest, he made for an odd sight, a tribal warrior in his twilight years forced out of retirement.

"Toli," Jespar sighed. "It's me."

Umō lowered the bust. "Ūkonō, I'm so sorry. Ye all right?"

"Yeah, I'm okay." He made to stand. Umō came to his aid, pulling him up with surprising strength.

"What ye doin' here? I thought yer in Uunili."

Jespar rubbed his left wrist with his right. It still hurt, but the pain was already letting off. He hadn't broken it. "I was. It's just ... I'm looking for my friend, Kawu."

Umō peeked over Jespar's shoulder. "Litō 'o pi'a 'ī?" *The boy isn't here?*

"No. Did he wake up?"

"Toli, he do," Umō said, putting the bust on a table. "Five days ago."

"And he's all right? I mean, he can walk, talk ...?"

"Mm-hm. He is a bit groggy for a day, but that's it. Actually, he said he go leave the day after tomorrow, so yer lucky ye didn't come any later."

"Okay, but where is he now? Do you know?"

"Outside, I guess. Since he wake up, he always go on them long walks to 'clear his mind,' as he said it. He was a bit ... ūkonō, what is the word ... 'kā e uwaika'?"

"'Cloud eyes'? You mean distant?"

"Toli, that. Can't say I blame him after all that's happened." Umō glanced out the window. "I'm sure he's fine, though. How about ye wait here 'til he comes back? Or ye just get some sleep and talk in the morrow. Ye look as if ye need it if ye don't mind me sayin'."

Jespar wavered. "I think I'll go look for him. Do you know which direction he went?"

Umō's forehead creased. Then he shrugged. "Sure, I can show ye. Come."

They went to the beach, took off their shoes, and followed the shoreline. Waves broke and withdrew lazily around their ankles, washing away their tracks right after their feet printed them into the sand. Struggling to keep his thoughts and that lurking anxiety in check, Jespar listened as Umō recounted the events of the past week: most of the manor staff had left the atoll along with two dozen islanders, headed for Uunili; despite the tragedy, a pioneer spirit had seized young people across the Archipelago, prompting many to start a new life in the Alabaster City. The Great Dream, Ma'sao Umō said, had survived what many people hadn't.

At the Makehu's last sentence, the terrible, empty picture Jespar had seen when he stepped into Kawu's empty room returned. The noose tightened.

"Bullshit," Jespar said. "He's fine."

"What?"

"Nothing. Sorry."

It must have been about half an hour later when they stopped at a rock formation jutting out into the ocean, and Umō made a contemplative noise. Jespar felt for his scarf. "Something wrong?"

"No, it's just ... this is where the pi'a go yesterday, so I reckoned he'd be here." He shrugged. "But as I said, don't worry. Okepi spawning season is over, and we hardly got snake or panther here, so it ain't dangerous. I'm guessin' he just wanted some time to hisself, 'kano leie īpene i awō i upi kū.' Sometimes—"

"... 'You gotta let a good breeze clear your head,'" Jespar finished the sentence. Naka had used the saying a lot, replacing "wind" with a variety of liquors or words for a woman's privates. Umō was right. Jespar had been away for over a week, so what difference would a night make? He was tired, and he was overreacting. Everything was going to be okay.

Except that sometimes, it wasn't.

"No, I have to find him," he said. "I'll keep looking."

"Huh. Well, all right, yer choice. Just don't go too far into the water, there's riptides. I'm gonna leave the door open for if ye come back alone."

Jespar muttered his thanks, then briskly continued down the shore. With Umō gone and no conversation to distract him, the noose tightened with every step, to the point where it was hard to breathe. He knew why it felt so different now: until today, there had been something unreal about it and the anxiety it brought, a phantom that vanished in daylight, like the wingback chair in Jespar's childhood room that always looked like a hunchbacked monster in the dark.

Now it felt like the monster would be there if he lit the candle.

"Idiot," he said, walking faster. "That's bullshit."

But it was pointless. The noose pulled tighter and tighter until he could feel the phantom fibers cutting into his skin, tighter and tighter, spawning more of those haruspex pictures that clung to his mind like mud to a bog mummy.

A tidy room, sun rays falling on the polished tables.

He walked faster.

Sparkhooves on the nightstand turned away from the bed.

He broke into a jog.

Blue lips and wine stains on the sheets.

He was running now, water splashing up at his feet, his heart pounding into his ribcage; his eyes shot across the beach, but it was just sand and palms and rocks and driftwood as far as he could see. The katydid screeches rose from the jungle, the stones and shells cut into his feet, the humid air weighed heavy in his lungs. He had no idea how far he had run when he finally noticed a shape in the sand, curled up with its back facing Jespar.

"No," Jespar said. "No."

He sprinted to Kawu and sunk to his knees beside him.

Kawu wasn't moving.

With a sob, Jespar sat back on his heels. The noose was cutting into his windpipe, his breaths short and ragged, every heartbeat a hammer's blow. Something screamed inside him, urged him to flee, to speak, to *do something*, but, just like when he had found Adi on that summer day, he couldn't. He sat there and stared.

It must have been minutes until he was able to move again. Hands shaking, he reached for Kawu's shoulder and rolled him onto his back, revealing a pale face and the bloody cuts on his arms.

"You wanna know a secret?"

You killed him.

"It'll get better."

You killed him.

"It always does."

You killed him.

There was no blood.

There was no blood, and there were no cuts, and the pallor of Kawu's face wasn't the pallor of death. He was pale and gaunt, but his chest rose and fell under his barkcloth shirt.

Kawu's lids opened.

To call it awaking would be wrong. Being a dreamwalker, his gaze showed no confusion, no disorientation. He was just there as if he had been waiting with closed eyes all this time.

How odd it was. Jespar had envisioned this moment many times since the fight with Lysia, always unsure what kind of expression Kawu would greet him with. He had imagined surprise, anger, hurt, even indifference—but there was none of that. Kawu was looking at him the way he'd look at a stranger.

"... Hey," Jespar said.

The look disappeared, and Kawu was back. "Jespar?"

Bit by bit, Jespar's hands stopped shaking. The noose loosened, and a tingle spread in his belly. Why in the world had he left? He tried to recreate the thought spiral that had led to his leaving that note that dumb, pathetic, stupid fucking note, but the emotions and the justifications now seemed utterly alien.

What did you do? What the hell were you thinking?

"Jespar? Are you okay?"

He snapped out of his stupor. "Yeah. It's ... I'm fine."

"But you left. I don't understand why ... why are you here?" He spoke slowly, pronouncing everything as if it were a foreign word.

"Can we talk, Kawu?"

Kawu hesitated, then nodded and propped himself up. Jespar unshouldered his haversack and sat beside him, knees tucked up and leaning back on his palms. For a time, he studied the sky. When he finally found the courage to look at Kawu, Kawu was regarding him. How different he seemed—no trace of shyness, no trace of the shame he so often showed for his resonance. Just these two algae-green eyes, studying him like some curious museum exhibit.

"I'm sorry," Jespar said.

"For what?"

It wasn't the answer he had expected. "Well, for leaving. You saved my life, and I promised you I'd stay, and then I ..." Jespar sighed. "Look, I messed up, that's what I'm trying to say. I have no idea what I was thinking, but I messed up, and I'm so sorry."

Kawu stretched out his legs and looked down the beach. "All right. I accept your apology."

"You're not angry?"

"Angry?" Kawu paused as if pondering the meaning of the word. "No, I don't think so. Frankly, I should have never expected you to stay."

"Kawu, I wasn't lying back then. That promise I made, I meant it."

"Yes, maybe you did. But I'm a dreamwalker ... People have felt uncomfortable around me for as long as I can remember, even if they *want* to like me, like my father or my siblings. It was only logical you'd leave sooner or later."

"No, that's not true. It has nothing to do with your resonance, I told you, I don't even feel it."

"And yet you left."

"Yes, but ..." Jespar pressed a hand against his temple as if trying to calm the whirlwind in his head. "It's the Corpse, Kawu. It was always that fucking Corpse."

"The Corpse? You mean from the dreameater?"

The lump returned, locking up Jespar's throat.

No. No, you won't.

"Yes," he said slowly. "The corpse of my father."

And he started talking. At first, every word was a struggle, but he refused to back down even when the lump and the crippling anxiety prevailed—and because he didn't give up, each sentence came easier than the previous one.

He told Kawu of the swamp nightmare and how overpowering it had become after they'd reached Nayima Island. He told him of his mad run into the ocean during the storm. He told him how he thought he had finally "seen," realized how his fucked-up mind made him hurt everyone close to him, and how that had led to him abandoning Kawu and leaving that letter. When he reached his fight with Lysia and the part about returning to Nayima Island, he delved far back into the past and told him of the death of his family, of Adi's melancholia and her suicide attempt, of the tragedy in the Village, and his escape into the wilderness.

He told him about his insomnia, about the noose, and about the flashbacks. He told him how he had spent three years sleepwalking through life, convincing himself things were all right, when, in truth, all he had done was lock away the corpses until they'd risen and dragged him to court.

When he finally finished speaking, the rustling of the palm fronds and the rush of the ocean were the only sounds on the beach.

The warmth he felt for Kawu was still there, but a deep unease overshadowed it now; he felt naked, exposed, as if, by defying the lump, he had disassembled the core of his being and laid out the pieces for this man to judge; this man he had met not even a moon ago but felt so strongly for.

"Hm," was all Kawu said. He shifted into a cross-legged sitting position and began to draw a circle into the sand using his forefinger. "I see."

Tense, Jespar waited for him to say more. He didn't.

"So?" he asked when he couldn't stand the quiet any longer. "What do you think?"

"About what in particular?"

"Well, about what Lysia said. That I'm, I don't know, letting the Corpses dictate my actions."

"It sounds plausible. Then again, I think the only one who can truly answer that question is you." Kawu faced him. "May I ask you something now, Jespar?"

"... Sure."

"Why did you come back?"

His scarf itched on his skin. He pulled it looser. "I told you. Because I made a mistake."

"That's all, then? You're only here to apologize?"

His first instinct was to backpedal—then he caught himself. What was the point? He had told Kawu more about what truly went on inside him than he had ever told Naka. He had defied the lump and the noose. What did he have left to lose?

"No," he said. "I came back because I miss you."

"But you said the Corpse killed all your feelings."

"Yeah, that's what I thought, but it only shrouded them. Lysia was right about everything, I mistook my fears for the truth. Those feelings I have for you, they're still there, and they're even stronger than before."

Kawu nodded slightly but didn't respond. Just when the silence was about to get uncomfortable again, his eyes lifted to Jespar's. "Are you talking about love?"

A three-letter word formed in Jespar's tongue, but before he could voice it, the warmth in his belly died. Two dirty-snow eyes materialized in his mind, staring at him from a rotted face. *Love?* No. These eyes knew no love, only disappointment, shame, and contempt, hidden under a fake deathbed smile. And even now that Damean

Dal'Varek was long, long dead, Jespar could still feel his stare as though he were sitting right beside him, a burning hand on Jespar's shoulder, his graveyard breath cold on his neck. And wasn't he right? What had Jespar ever done to deserve love? How could he even consider putting Kawu at risk again? If his life had proved anything, it was that no good ever came from his affection.

That's precisely what the Corpse wants you to believe, he heard Lysia say. *Don't you think Oonai told himself the same thing?*

"Yes," Jespar said. "I think I am. If you still want it."

Kawu scooped up a fistful of sand and slowly poured it into the center of the ring he had drawn.

He'll say no. He'll say no because I abandoned him. Because-

Kawu kissed him. It was so sudden that Jespar barely reacted. Kawu withdrew, a curious look about him. Sadness?

"Is this okay?"

"Yeah," Jespar said. "Yeah, it is."

He leaned in and kissed back.

How good it felt.

Kawu's warmth, his smell, his taste. The tingle in Jespar's stomach traveled all the way up into his cheeks, spreading like the wonderful heat of a campfire on frosty skin. *Trust.* Jespar let out a breath when they parted, slid his fingers around the back of Kawu's neck, and pressed his forehead against his. They stayed this way for a while, motionless but for the rise and fall of their chests.

"Thank you," Jespar said. "I just ... I never ..."

Kawu's lips found his.

If sex was a language, this night at the beach taught Jespar a new way of using it. Yes, there was pleasure, and plenty of it; Kawu's soft gasps as Jespar's kisses trailed down the side of his neck. The tingle when Kawu slipped his hand under the waistband of Jespar's trousers. The rush when Jespar lifted Kawu's feet onto his shoulders and began to move.

Yes, there was pleasure.

But it was only the surface of a river running deep, the expression of a bond that went beyond whatever sensations their bodies alone could conjure.

Jespar felt found.

CHAPTER FORTY-TWO
DAWN

DAY THIRTY
1ST MOON OF RAINY SEASON, 1226 A.L.

Jespar awoke to a sunrise. Pink clouds hung on the horizon like flamingo feathers, a note of salt clung to the air, and the upper firmament glowed in the indigo of early dawn. How strange the ground felt, Jespar thought as he came awake blearily. Soft. Cool. Wet.

Water.

Jespar leaped up. The water beneath his feet slightly gave way under his weight yet remained perfectly solid like a tautly pulled sheet. He looked around—and his heart skipped a beat.

He stood on a broken ocean.

At least that was the first word that came to his mind. To either side of him and up ahead, the water stretched on with no land in sight, but behind him, some hundred strides away, it broke off and gave way to a black expanse. If that was the right term for it—*expanse* implied space, and somehow Jespar doubted this concept existed there. Not only was the black the purest Jespar had ever seen, but it also seemed to consume everything it touched; instead of pouring into the abyss like a waterfall, the ocean simply *ended* at the edge, and the rays from the sunrise that shone into it didn't fade but vanish. Even the sounds coming from its direction were muffled.

This wasn't the Imūma. So what the hell was it?

His head swam as he went over what he could remember. After the sex, they had gone for a swim, then cozied up on the beach and spoken quietly until Jespar had drifted off.

"A dream," he said. It had to be. Then why was he lucid? Also, he couldn't say why, but this world didn't feel like his own creation.

"You're safe."

Kawu stood behind him—he hadn't been there seconds ago. Back-dropped by the sunrise and cloaked in shadows, something about him looked different, though Jespar couldn't pinpoint what it was. He wore a brown barkcloth skirt and his bone necklace.

"Are you ...?"

"Real? Yes. As I said, don't worry, you're safe."

"... Okay? What happened, Kawu? Where are we?"

"Don't you remember?"

Jespar was about to say he didn't, but then a memory returned: the night he and Kawu had spent on the finger-shaped rock.

What do your dreams look like today?

They're just an ocean I can walk on now. Only water as far as the eye can see.

"We're inside your dream?"

"We are," Kawu said, approaching him. "I took you here after we went to your kuluhika."

When he stopped a stride from Jespar, Jespar understood why he looked so strange. His eyes. Umako framed them, fine lines snaking away from his sockets like jellyfish tendrils.

"You have ..." Jespar said, pointing to his face.

"Umako, yes. I finally found my kikiete."

A memory stirred somewhere. Naka, telling Jespar about Makehu customs. "You have to wait until the idea 'comes to you,' right?"

Kawu nodded. "I never understood what that was supposed to mean, but I do now. When I recovered from the shifting seizure, I knew that this was the design I wanted."

"I see." Jespar shifted his weight from one leg to the other. "Why are we here? I don't understand."

Kawu's mouth twitched. Then he gazed skyward. "You will never see those corpses again, Jespar. Not your father, not your sister, not that girl from Nehrim, nor any from that swamp court. I dealt with them."

Jespar blinked. "You ... how?"

"A shift, but the details don't matter. Just keep in mind this only eases the symptoms ... you have finally started to confront your demons, but until you've tamed them all, they'll always come back in another shape or form. See it as a helping hand if you will. A reprieve from the struggling." Kawu clasped his hands behind his back and regarded him pensively; it was yet another gesture that seemed so unlike him.

"Are you angry with me?" Kawu asked. "Mother always said the only time one should enter someone's dream without their permission is if their life is at stake."

"What? No, of course I'm not angry. I'm just ... confused, I guess. Why didn't you tell me?"

"Because it's my goodbye present."

Kawu's answer was so unexpected Jespar's mind went blank. No thoughts, no emotion.

He doesn't mean it. This is some stupid joke.

When had Kawu ever joked?

"You'll be alone when you wake up," he went on. "In fact, I'm in the Okepi Inn right now, and I'm using your scarf as a Compass. The only reason I'm telling you where I am is so that you know where to pick it up once you wake—my ferry to Hapana leaves in an hour, and I do not want you to come after me or even try to contact me. There's no—" Something flickered across his face—something that looked like the old Kawu—and he faltered. It disappeared like a stone in a pond. "This is goodbye, Jespar. I'm sorry."

The blankness lasted for another second.

"No," Jespar said. "That doesn't make sense. I mean, we just ..."

Kawu sighed. "Haven't you noticed anything about me?"

Yes, I did. I just didn't want to see it. "No, I didn't. Kawu, what are you talking about? You're not thinking straight, you—"

"I'm not who I used to be. Something happened to me while I slept."

"... The drain stroke."

"Yes. I had dreams." Kawu's umakoed eyes wandered to some point over Jespar's shoulder, some point in that black void that cut off the ocean. "Real dreams, like the ones normal people get every night. It was incredible, Jespar, simply incredible. Everything just ... *happened*, and my mind accepted it. I can't remember the last time I've felt such relief." Despite his words—*incredible, relief*—he spoke flatly, almost a monotone. *He didn't sound like that last night.* Or had he, and Jespar simply hadn't wanted to hear it? "I don't remember much of these dreams," Kawu went on, "but there's one memory that stuck: the black void you see here. It—"

"What does any of that have to do with *us*?"

"Let me finish." He spoke calmly, but Jespar broke off at once. "This void was in every single dream I had, and even when I recovered, and my dreams were lucid again, I couldn't make it go away. This has never happened to me before." He touched his bone necklace and trailed his fingers up and down its chips. It was odd how he did it, slowly and consciously—like a shapeshifter's imitation of a pensive gesture. "Do you remember what I told you about the Pale Twins? About how they are tawahe?"

He did remember, but he didn't want to, didn't want to think, didn't want to listen, didn't want to hear any of this. He just wanted to wake up on the beach, Kawu in his arms, the way it had been when Jespar had fallen asleep.

"A tawahe's dream is all blackness," Kawu said. "And I believe that's what this void is."

Jespar forced himself to speak. "You're saying you've become like the Twins?"

"Yes, but not completely. I don't feel the emotions I used to feel, but I don't have any desire for violence either. I won't lie, it was terrifying at first. But the more time went by, the more I began to feel ... how to put it? Liberated, I suppose. So many things that once confused or agitated me in the past make perfect sense now. It's as though I used to hear the world through this mind-numbing din, and now that din has become perfectly quiet." Kawu looked into the blackness. "And it has made me realize a few things."

That you want to leave me? "What?" Jespar asked hoarsely.

"That you cannot cure a tree when the roots are rotten," Kawu said. "This game we all play, it was broken from the very start. Think about it, what is this 'Great Dream' we're willing to kill for truly about? It's about wealth, power, and attention. All the rest, justice, truth, compassion, ethics, they're secondary at best and expendable at worst, and then we gasp in surprise when we realize this world is broken. It's not only pathetic, it's also so ... I don't know, so asinine. As though a thousand years of history have taught us absolutely nothing."

A bleak smile formed on his lips. "You cannot cure a tree when the roots are rotten, Jespar. And that's why I won't use Oonai's money and the skystone to become a 'Great Dreamer' but to buy a small island and set up a community there, a commune of sorts. It'll be part of Kilay, but it will have its own rules and laws, and most importantly, it will be based on new ideals, the best from Makehu culture, and the best from the Illumined World. It will be ..."

Jespar wasn't listening anymore. *No*, was all he could think. *No*. It just didn't make any sense. He had opened up to Kawu; he had told him everything. For the first time, he had shown someone the core of his being rather than just the charming veneer, and Kawu had accepted him. It just didn't make any *fucking* sense!

"Kawu." He despised how he sounded, fragile, weak, and soft. *He always makes a scene*, his father's words rang through his mind. "I don't understand. What does any of this have to do with us?"

Kawu faced him. How dull his eyes were, how empty.

He thought: *Tawahe*.

He thought: *Soul-dead*.

"There's just nothing left, Jespar. I'm sorry."

His words struck like a blow. Jespar's throat felt hot and tight, the skin crawling. "But the beach," he said. "We ... I mean, that was ..."

"It was a try, that's what it was, and it didn't work. I simply don't feel anything for you anymore. No love, no friendship, not even familiarity. I—" Sighing, Kawu looked at his feet. "For what it's worth, you and my family were the few people who didn't feel like complete strangers to me right after I woke up. That's also why I didn't tell you at once because I kept hoping that this bond we had would come back if only I tried hard enough. That kiss, though, and the sex ... it only confirmed what I already knew. That it's really all gone, and that I was chasing a mirage." Something in Kawu's face changed as he said this. A fragment of his old self: buried and hidden, but unmistakably, undeniably there.

"It'll come back," Jespar said hoarsely. "We just need to give it time."

When Kawu lifted his gaze, Jespar realized his mind had played a trick on him again—as it did so often. There was no old Kawu, not even a fragment. Like Kawu when he had tried to resurrect this bond, Jespar had fallen victim to a mirage.

"It won't."

"You don't know that."

"Yes, I do. And, frankly, it's probably better this way. Let's be realistic, even if I stayed with you, you'd only start feeling restless again and leave like you did before."

"What? No, Kawu, I've told you, I've changed!"

"If that's true," Kawu said, "then you know you have to leave. For your sister."

A pause.

"What the hell are you talking about?"

"You know. You're not responsible for what she did to herself, but you went to Nehrim without even telling her. I mean, did you ever write to her, did you ever let her know you're still alive? You're the only family she has left, and you know it."

Jespar said nothing. He felt as though he stood far away, watching two strangers talk through a dusty window.

"I told you, Jespar, you're far from done dealing with those corpses, and you won't be until you've faced every last one of them." Kawu reached for his hand. It was cold and smooth. "I can't tell you what to do about your friend and the village, but I know your way to closure starts with your sister. Go find her and tell her why you left. That's the first step."

When Jespar spoke, it was barely more than a whisper. "Kawu, please. I was going to show you autumn."

Kawu answered with silence.

Jespar tore away his hand. "Wake me up. Now."

"Wait, I—"

"Wake me up!"

Kawu did.

Not here. This was Jespar's first thought when he awoke on the beach. Kawu was gone. Then: his skin was on fire.

A bright lobster red, he was sunburnt all the way from the waistband of his breeches up to his forehead. The sun hammered down from above, a white-hot disk between scattered clouds. Jespar sat up blearily, groaning as his skin sent waves of pain across his body. Sand stuck to his back and the undersides of his arms, chafing the spots that hadn't been scorched. It must have rained because his hair was damp, and his throat itched.

Godsdammit. Godsfuckingdammit.

He dressed and made his way back to the manor, the sun continuing to batter the back of his neck, his mind a wheel that wouldn't stop turning. He silenced every thought about Kawu.

"Idiot," he told himself. "You're an idiot."

He had survived the war in Nehrim, a blizzard in the Cahbaet Mountains, hundreds of fights; he had beaten a brain parasite, convinced a man who'd killed himself to return from the dead, and helped prevent a civil war. After all that, what kind of whiny sissy was he to be upset about *this,* some stupid infatuation with a heartless freak?

Don't call him that. It's not fair.

Well, fuck fairness. There were more important things to take care of, more important things to do, things actually worth brooding over. He'd just do what he should have done long ago: man up, learn from his mistakes, and turn them into strength. Frost poured into his stomach, filling up that new, daunting, comforting warmth he'd felt last night. Maybe the purpose of the noose and the Corpse wasn't just to make him see and keep others safe, but to keep *him* safe as well. Had he never met Kawu or Lysia, had he never agreed to this mission, he would have been spared all this nonsense. Had he just burned that fucking letter from the Ma'saa, he'd still be out there wandering the roads of Northern Nehrim, with a book in his haversack and a pipe in his mouth and alone—not the life that he had been dreaming of but a life that was all right.

Protests sparked up in his mind, his better self telling him that that was not true, begging him to not sully the memories, even if nothing about this had ended how he had hoped it would, even if the only person he'd ever opened up to this way had rejected him, but he killed those protests one by one, slit their throats and ripped their tongues out like a maniac butcher.

When they were all dead, he stopped still and looked at the ocean. A perfect and effortless blue, it seemed a mockery of the mess he was. Jespar balled his fists. "Idiot," he said again. "You idiot."

A silly loss of perspective, that was all. Nothing worth wasting his breath on.

Then why did it hurt so fucking much?

Ma'sao Umō was carving a wood sculpture on the terrace, some weird gigantic bird with a human face in its chest. Jespar tried to sneak past, but the old Makehu noticed him and raised his chisel in greeting. Jespar gave a halfhearted wave in return.

"The pi'a come here earlier this mornin'," Umō called to him. "He sayed he's gonna wait for ye in the Okepi."

He won't. Seemed like lying was another skill Kawu had picked up from Jespar's many virtues. "Yeah, I'm on my way there. Thanks."

"... Is there anythin' I can do for ye, waikā? Ye don't, um, look so well."

"Just sunburn," Jespar said, glancing at the gate. "I'm okay."

"No, I mean—" Umō pointed at his chin, but then dropped his hand. "Ah, never mind. Ye stayin' for lunch? I get some fresh fish from the market this mornin'."

"No, I should be going. Thanks for the help, though. And ... goodbye."

Umō studied him for another second. Then he nodded. "May ye prosper, ma'sao."

"You too." *May you fucking prosper.*

Only when Jespar was past the manor gate did he feel a salty droplet on his lower lip. He felt for his cheeks. They were hot and moist, and the tears were still coming.

Jespar wanted to scream.

He wiped his face and kept walking.

<hr />

The ferry to Uunili only left once a day, so Jespar spent the night in the Okepi tavern. The innkeeper, a half-Makehu woman, recognized him as soon as he entered and asked if he was "the pi'a's friend."

Jespar grunted.

"He left somethin' for ye," she said and tossed him his scarf from under the counter.

Jespar caught it. "You got rooms?"

The innkeeper scoffed. "Half the people are off the island. I'm lucky to get two guests a week."

With his pay from the mission, Jespar could have probably bought the entire inn twice, but he asked for the smallest and darkest room instead. She led him to a stuffy room in the attic. As she left him, he locked the door, plunked down on the edge of the bed, and downed the last of his rice wine. Then he slept.

THE SWAMP DELIVERANCE

SOMEDAY
SOMETIME

A dream.

He was in the swamp, but there were no seats, no dais, and no corpses. Kawu had told the truth after all.

Jespar lay in the mud, naked except for his breeches. The air was neither warm nor cold and was perfectly still, the branches of the dead weeping willows hanging limp like curtains weaved from veins. Through a cloud of nightflower smoke above him, Jespar saw strange, bright apparitions flicker across the starless night sky, bathing the landscape in a pale mauve and green light.

Kawu and Lysia were walking toward him, both naked. Wordlessly, they sunk to their knees beside him and began caressing and kissing him, from his face to his chest, from his chest to his navel. The noose appeared around his neck, and his stomach curled while blood flowed into his groin. He wanted to struggle, wanted to speak, but his body did not respond. Like a marionette in the attic of a dead puppeteer.

The kisses ceased.

Moving in unison, Kawu and Lysia sat straight up and stared at him, the apparitions' paradox light shrouding them in a surreal glow. Then both turned their faces up and inhaled deeply; the night-flower cloud above them rushed into their mouths. When they had sucked it all in, they closed their mouths and once more focused on Jespar, tufts of smoke licking from the sides of their skeletal grins. The noose was so tight that every breath was torture, but the morbid excitement in his groin had only grown.

"We are punishment," said Lysia.

"We are emissaries," said Kawu.

"We are guardians," said both.

They forced open his mouth, pressed their lips onto his, and exhaled; as the smoke left their lips, it turned into locusts that greedily ate their way down Jespar's throat and into his guts. He tried to struggle, tried to scream, but his puppet body remained powerless as it always was, powerless before his broken mind, powerless while the insects flooded his body and the noose tightened, and that twisted pleasure swelled, until both Lysia and Kawu let go, corpses now, and leaned in to whisper in his ear: "We are deliverance."

The noose snapped his neck.

CHAPTER FORTY-THREE
SCORCHED EARTH

espar sat on a bunk bed on the lowest deck of the *Crimson Toki*, a Kilayan trading ship bound for the pioneer's town on Arktwend, Tyr's Cradle. Though the voyage would take over three moons and Jespar could have easily afforded a single cabin, he didn't like the idea of being on his own for too long and had decided to sleep with the commoners and fortune seekers in the cargo area instead—just like he had nine years ago when he had left for Nehrim. Tired to the bone from two sleepless nights, Jespar unbelted his longsword and put it down on the wall-facing side of the cot, then stowed his dagger and his purse under the pillow. Sixty thousand sêr. If anyone found out he carried that much money, they would probably murder him in his sleep.

Good riddance.

Jespar closed his eyes.

Sleep did not come.

He rolled onto the other side, then onto his stomach, then onto his back—the choreography of the insomniac. Nothing helped. At last, he sat up, fixed himself a pipe, and dragged himself up to the main deck. It was deserted except for the helmsman and two sailors at the stern. Pulling his scarf tighter to shield himself from the breeze, he walked to the railing and looked out over the sea.

It was beautiful.

Unlike its twin in the psychic dimension, no humans passed through this ocean's depths in search of their dreams. Just fish and whales and cephalopods and other wondrous creatures, growing more foreign and mystical the deeper one went—another world, unblemished by the terrors that haunted the surface.

Dark. Vast. Silent.

Inviting.

The noose was back, but this time, he savored the way it hurt.

Sometimes, it didn't get better.

Wasn't that what it came down to?

Even if there were a way to grow the swamp into a pasture, at what cost? More Kawus, more Adilas, more Villages, more people whom Jespar would inevitably hurt on his desperate quest for improvement, and all just so one selfish man could have a tiny shot at happiness. Frankly, what were the odds? People were so quick to point at all those inspiring stories of catharsis, completely ignoring the fact that the vast majority of the broken never beat their demons, that the drunkard's son stayed with the bottle, the war widow never conquered her loneliness, and the defiled child never wiped that imagined black stain from their soul. Because in a world that worshipped the victorious, who the hell wanted to hear about the defeated? *No.* It was far more likely that Jespar would never triumph over the corpses, that he'd just keep being himself, a useless, weary mess of a man whose swamp mind caused him to hurt anyone foolish enough to get close.

He edged up to the railing, toward that beautiful black depth.

Go back and help Adi? Him? Better jokes had been told. Whatever he could bring to his sister's life would inevitably hurt her again, because that was the nature of the plague: it didn't choose to kill, it just did. And if "swamp to pasture" wasn't an option, what did that mean for him?

Simple: he'd have to go back to drifting, to staying away from people and pretending that life was all right, which it wasn't, no matter what his stubborn self insisted. On and on he'd go, a solitary piece of driftwood floating along the stream of time until he was old and feeble, and the rest of his hair had gone gray, and he would die the way he'd lived: alone.

The noose was cutting into his flesh now, and a shiver crept up his ankles, terrifying, thrilling, liberating.

He'd never find peace. That was the long and short of it.

And he was tired of trying.

Clutching the wood, he glanced over his shoulder. This time, no one would pull him out of the water. Perhaps the two sailors at the stern might hear the splash, but by the time they'd moved closer to get a better look, they wouldn't even see ripples. An empty smile creased his lips when it occurred to him just how right Kawu had been. Even with the corpses banished from his nightmares, Jespar was still as powerless as ever. It was precisely as his undead father had told him in the maze of taxidermic animals.

"I am not real. But my judgment is."

A picture rose to his mind: the Corpse on the dais, smiling.

Smiling because he knew he had won.

Something inside Jespar shattered.

No.

A tremor shook the swamp, borne from deep beneath the crusted earth.

No.

The air stirred, heat rose. Grass wilted, shrubs curled, the willows trembled.

I won't let you.

A pillar of fire erupted from the ground.

It was a devastating blaze, an inferno crashing through the soil like a fiery geyser, the wrath of a lifetime of shattered hopes and dreams, and as the flames connected with the air, they exploded in a wave that burned it all down, the swamp, the guilt, the hurt, the noose, a cataclysm that raged through the deadland and obliterated everything until nothing was left but a plain of smoldering black earth, so vast and terrifying and empty that all Jespar wanted was to scream until his lungs tore and cry until eyes bled, and *vanish*, vanish into the cold dark place from which existence began.

But he didn't. Instead, he touched his scarf and whispered, "You can't hurt me."

Who was he speaking to? The corpses, his past, or himself? Had there ever been a difference?

"You can't hurt me."

He tore the pipe from his mouth and tossed it into the ocean, ripped the nightflower satchel off his belt and did the same, the tyenite, the firetwigs, the dagger, the brandy. He hesitated. Then he yanked the scarf from his neck and threw it too. Briefly, the little blue cloth seemed to float on the water, as if refusing to sink. Then it soaked up, turned the color of the sea, and slipped into its depths.

A heartbeat went by. Two. Three.

Jespar closed his eyes.

Gray was the color of his past.

How clear it was all of a sudden.

Yes, he bore a part of the blame in the tragedies that had happened. But had they been his doing? The answer was no. True, he should have been there for Adi, and he should not have left without so much as a letter, but the choice to put a knife to her wrists had been hers and hers alone. He also shouldn't have thrown that knife at the man with the breadbasket, shouldn't have abandoned the Girl, but it wasn't his fault the Wayfarers had raided the Village and Naka had done what he did. And Kawu? He should have never broken his promise by abandoning him. But it wasn't his fault that Kawu had kept the anchorings a secret and driven himself to the brink of death.

He'd had all these thoughts before, many, many times. But it was one thing for the mind to know something, and another for the heart to believe it.

Jespar opened his eyes.

Gray.

Yes, maybe, in another life or a parallel world, it would have all ended differently. Perhaps he'd have never betrayed Lysia's trust, perhaps he would have never gotten himself infected with the dreameater, and Kawu would have never had the drain stroke that had so drastically altered his soul. Perhaps Jespar would have never broken his promise to stay, and they would now be on a ship together, headed toward somewhere where there was autumn.

But it wasn't this life. And that was all right.

Jespar breathed in deeply.

The black plain was still there, filling the space that had once been the swamp, and it was still every bit as intimidating as when the inferno had ceased. Even now, Jespar knew the burns it had left behind would continue to hurt, maybe forever—but he also knew that with time, care, and the right new seeds, even scorched earth could grow something new.

A voice pulled him from his thoughts. "Shame about the pipe."

Startled, Jespar turned. At first, he thought he was imagining things. But when the hooded figure standing a little farther down the railing lifted the corner of her mouth, he knew he wasn't.

"... Lysia?"

"Yes."

For a few moments, they just stood there: Jespar too stunned and relieved to speak, and Lysia studying him, questions pooling in those dark eyes of hers, hidden beneath an armor of wariness. And after all that had happened, who could blame her?

The lump balled up in Jespar's throat, but he withstood Lysia's gaze, ready to defy the corpses. Ready to share, as he should have done so long ago.

But no questions came. For whatever reason, Lysia's guardedness disappeared, and she nodded. "It's me."

Slowly, Jespar recovered his composure. "But I thought ... I mean ... I had no idea you were on the ship."

"Probably because I have a cabin on the upper deck. And, to be honest, I've been avoiding you since I realized we had the same idea." She turned back to the sea. "So, Arktwend, huh? A fresh start?"

Moment melted into moment.

"Actually," Jespar said. "There's somewhere else I need to go first."

EPILOGUE
WINTER

Day One
8th of Moneth I, 1227 A.L.

ee you tonight, then? At the … what's it called?"

"The Dancing Nomad," Jespar said. "I might be a while, though."

Lysia nodded, sending snowflakes dancing from the fringe of hair that hung over her forehead. Even after three days in Ark, it felt unreal to see her in these surroundings, a page torn from one book and glued into another.

"Just take your time, okay? And … you know."

"Yes?"

A breeze blew over the courtyard. Lysia smiled and shook her head as if contemplating a joke or a pleasant memory only she remembered. "Nothing," she said and squeezed his shoulder. "You'll be fine."

She left.

Jespar watched her walk away until the path leading down the bluff snaked into the evergreen forest, and she disappeared from sight. He let out a white-clouded breath and faced the Dal'Tarbak manor— his foster home and the place where Adila had tried to take her life.

Perhaps because it was what one always read in the stories, Jespar had expected the property to look just how it had the day he'd left for Nehrim. It didn't. Nine years ago, the ivy had only covered one half of the house; today, the leafless climbers concealed most of the façade. Nine years ago, the Malphas statue that graced the courtyard fountain had been a testament to Endralean craftsmanship; today, a mossy tint marred the white stone. Nine years ago, two perfect lines of slim oaks had framed the avenue to the entrance; today, three of them were missing, leaving behind a barren, asymmetrical formation of skeletal fingers. Backdropped by the fiery sunset that seemed paradoxical over the desolate winter landscape, the house had an almost haunted air to it.

A twinge of remorse overcame Jespar as he thought of his foster parents. Childless and grief-stricken, they had done everything in their power to make this place feel like home to the two young Dal'Varek orphans, but in retrospect, it had probably been a hopeless endeavor from the start.

How had they felt finding Jespar's room empty, a mere week after Adila had tried to take her life? Had they blamed themselves? Had they tried to find him?

For just a flicker, the guilt was so bad that Jespar considered turning tail again, an urge he'd fought all too often since their ship had arrived in Ark. The feeling was always the strongest in the mornings, after awaking from another of his nightmares, which his somnolent mind still conjured with regularity, epiphany notwithstanding. That was one of Jespar's first lessons since the night he had burned down the swamp: change isn't a flash but a long and rocky road.

Looking for strength, he turned inward. The memory his mind proffered was not at all the one he had expected: the look in Jaaros Oonai's eyes when he had torn the dreameater from his head, and thereby chosen fight over surrender.

Jespar said: "You can't hurt me."

Eight heartbeats later, the ring of a bell sailed through the Endralean winter.

Afterword

If you're like me, you'll skip over this section, but having finished this beast, I know it has to be here. First and foremost, I'd like to thank my family and friends. It may seem tangential to this novel and even a bit clichéd, but I've been to some dark places in my life, and who knows if I'd have ever gotten out of them without your help. Mum, thank you for showing me that it's possible not only to talk about ideals but to actually live by them. Dad, thank you for being the living example that—let's just disregard determinism for a second—any dream can be realized if you work hard enough. Jannis, thank you for never ceasing to challenge my views. Daniel, what can I say? I simply wouldn't be the same person without your long friendship, our long midnight walks, and our adventures, be it hitchhiking through Germany and crashing in allotment sheds or trekking through jungles in Southeast Asia. Johanna, thank you for being the best and most patient flatmate there is, one of the funniest people I know, and a damn good friend. Pale, you'll always have a special place in my heart, and I hope things are looking up by the time you're reading this; keep in mind, we have many years of friendship to look forward to, and the world has yet to see the fantastic stories you write. Jonas, it has been a roller coaster, but I wouldn't want to miss a thing. Lastly, thank you to my friends at Munich Write Night. I've never been much of a tribalist, but with you guys, I just feel like I belong. I could go on for many pages, but to the rest of you, you know who you are. Your support and friendship make my work possible.

On the professional end, I'd like to thank my editor, Kim Catanzarite, for her terrific work and fantastic feedback. One of the biggest ironies of being an indie author is how hard it is to come by frank criticism—somewhat understandably, people will tell you your photo-bashed cover looks amazing and that your prose kicks ass, worried they'll otherwise lose you as a customer. You made this book a lot better than it would have been otherwise. Miro, thank you for your unrelenting patience and your terrific proofreading and copyediting help. You went through this manuscript, what, four times? God knows I wouldn't have had the patience. Julia, thank you for proofing 709 pages in two weeks. You're incredible, and it's safe to say that you made this book a whole lot better. David, I can't thank you enough for your work on the Makehu language and your linguistic counsel. Not sure what I was thinking, merrily slapping vowels and consonants together and thinking that would make for a proper language in the web edition, so let's just forget that ever happened. Matt and Caro, your beta feedback was eye-opening, and I shall compensate you in butter jars. Fabian, I don't know how a single person can be so knowledgeable on so many subjects, but I sure as hell won't complain. Thank you for those fantastic maps and for helping me make this world feel just a little more real. Dominik, I'm a novice at art, but as far as I can tell, you're a genius. I hope you'll illustrate the cover of every single book I write. Thank you for putting up with my nitpicks and my perfectionism.

A heartfelt thanks also to the Enderal Discord crew and your continuous support and priceless feedback—Vani, Emily, and Joyce, in particular. Another, naturally, to the Enderal development team. This novel wouldn't be possible if a certain someone wouldn't have asked me to join SureAI one fall day way back in 2011, and I genuinely don't know where I'd be without it. I know working with me wasn't always easy—it still isn't, I guess—so thank you for putting up with me. A special shout-out goes to my patrons who helped me shoulder this project financially. A painful lesson I had to learn is that "indie" doesn't necessarily mean "affordable," especially if you want to do it right. I've said it before, and I'll say it again: you rock. Lastly, a gargantuan thanks to the whole Enderal community who played and loved the game. I'm not exaggerating when I say that your fan art, songs, fanfiction, and emails kept me going whenever I felt like burning this book and scattering the ashes in some catacomb where no one would ever find them. Putting out any kind of authentic creative work is always an emotional striptease, and your love for Enderal made me glad I shed the covers. Okay, that's a weird metaphor, but you get the idea.

In the unlikely scenario that you're still reading, let's end this on a more serious note about one of the book's central themes: mental illness. Needless to say, if you're affected, your first step should *always* be to get professional help—no novel or nugget of wisdom can cure mental illness singlehandedly, and whoever tells you so is a liar. That being said, I've been to some dark places myself, and Agaam's quote, "You won't find out if you give up," is the most helpful advice I've ever received. Because of that, I'd like to elaborate a little. In my experience, once you reach a certain mental state, survival often becomes a matter of defying destructive emotions and urges. You have no interest in the future, and you can't take joy in anything because all you want is that crippling anxiety—the fog, to stick with the metaphor—to go. In a desperate attempt to stop the pain, your mind tells you that the only way to achieve that is to stop existence altogether.

The thing is: you don't know.

Just like your well-meaning friends and parents don't know when they tell you that things will surely get better, neither does your mind when it tells you it won't. You have absolutely no way of knowing what direction life will take—for all you know, the next month will be when you finally start an effective therapy (I'm no psychiatrist, but I'm looking forward to the day microbiome therapy becomes a standard auxiliary treatment for mental health disorders—it certainly helped me) or something drastic happens in your life that gradually turns things around. The only way to *ensure* it will never get better is to give up. I personally found it helpful—and again, this is just my own experience—to see these urges and emotions as a part detached from myself—my "soul", if you want to get poetic. If your brain, whose evolutionary purpose is to keep you safe, tells you all kinds of irrational bullshit and urges you to end it, I think it's safe to say you're dealing with a conman.

In that sense: *Tae ite nǔ'iwilo, tae hūnā 'o.*

You won't find out if you give up.

Nicolas Lietzau
Munich, 10/23/2020

ABOUT ME

I'm a German author best known for my writing for the indie video game *Enderal: Forgotten Stories*, which grew from an insider tip to a sleeper hit. Growing up in both the heart of Munich and a bucolic Bavarian farmhouse, my love for stories began by reading German fairy tales in the attic (and getting traumatized by those of Struwwelpeter) and was nurtured by copious amounts of fantasy, horror, and historical fiction.

Many things have shaped my own writing: a turbulent childhood, living in five different countries, and numerous encounters I've been fortunate enough to have with fascinating people from all walks of life. I feel drawn to all things off the beaten path and do my best to make my work reflect that.When I'm not writing or reading, I make music, travel, longboard, study languages, and try to see and experience as much of the world as I can. I'm currently working on the second Enderal novel.If you'd like to stay informed about my current projects, you're welcome to follow me on my social media, listed below. Finally, if you enjoyed the novel, I'm deeply grateful for every honest review or rating on Goodreads and Amazon. There's a stigma around indie publishing, and it's incredibly hard to get recognition and visibility without a big publishing house to back you up. Even a two-word review is a huge help.

Thank you in advance!

INSTAGRAM.COM/NISEAM_STORIES

GOODREADS.COM/NICOLASLIETZAU

FACEBOOK.COM/NICOLASLIETZAU

PATREON.COM/NISEAM

DISCORD.COM/INVITE/ZDJYUHV

("The Enderal Novels" Section)

NISEAMSTORIES.TUMBLR.COM

REDDIT.COM/R/ENDERAL

PATRONS

"Passionate Pragmatist" tier or a lifetime contribution of $10 or more, sorted by total contribution in descending order. A giant "thank you" for your support—this novel wouldn't exist without you.

Nicolas Barcacci · Dr. Uwe Schreiber · Alkiviadis Chatzivasileiou

MissLizzyLP · Xenia Kostenko · Shen Zhou

GeneralJade · Emily Rose Daniels · Markus Hauck

Jannis Lietzau · Jhara Ivez · Tetiana Hrynko

Yanran Li · Tom Walters · Hans-Georg Rauh

Mark Müller · Robert Kirkpatrick · Morsalisk

Kris Choi · Caleb Maher · zombie

Koroleva Olga · André Ehgartner · OverDev

Kriatyrr · JaxonNola · Ellis Delira

Mae · Wiebke Stamerjohanns · Melanie Godehardt

Tschoo · Anne · Julia Rateike

Anastazja Pospieszynska · Michael Vietz · Benjamin Van Oers

Grey_vi_Ory · Genessa Zucker · David Weker

Max Poley · louka breault · Dragon's Barb

Brian Litchfield · Samuel Waldstein · Matthew Lathrop

T'Shenak · Kathrine Novitskaya · orgadevi

Taaj · Maximilian Högner · JackOfSpades

Mark Howie · Pierre Kleindl · ScientistOtter

Lola Lohne · Chelsea & Emily Davis · Dagný Ósk

Tori Cuori · Carys Hughes · Moravia300

I.Holvan · Jan Heidler · Yael van Dok

Ekaterina Sukhova · Joonas Kuitunen · Aderian

UmaikiGames · Katrin Ha · mystie-eyes

Jaki Teo · TullaDoVenen · Damien Doninger

Carolyn Tix · Warden · Bifbof

Fehnu · James Bonner · teefox

Kevin Rothe · Marina Dmitryukova · Rifmaz

Zero Period · Jeremias Siebenwirth · Patrycja Zawiślak

tanact · Tanya M · Caro Tuts

Amalia · Wayne Naylor · Jerome

Madison Kalo · Josef Probst · Ruslan

Irish · Eric He · Cortney A Berg

PMong · Dolph Busche · Branting

Jarno Vierros · Jan Hübner · Lucaria32

Kevin · The Morbid Curiosity Podcast · aiko493

Sinitar Gaming · Antti Rannanjärvi · Jackson Wajer

Francisc · Rebecca Davies · Babbel

Till Appolt · Kate · Fryxl

Katja Köhler · Endhorizon · bayleaf

Bec Hochhausen · distcreation

CPSIA information can be obtained
at www.ICGtesting.com
Printed in the USA
BVHW072204080221
599695BV00008B/91